THE REI
of
VENUS

THE REBIRTH
of
VENUS

LINDA PROUD

GODSTOW PRESS

First published 2008 by
Godstow Press
60 Godstow Road, Oxford OX2 8NY
www.godstowpress.co.uk

Typeset in Aldine 401 by Jean Desebrock of Alacrity
Cover design by David Smith
based on original design by Joanna Turner

Printed by SRP Exeter

To my beloved husband.

*Also in memory of the many friends recently
departed, particularly Cynthia and Michael
Macmillan, Thérèse FitzGerald and John Allit:
a splendour of souls in divine company.*

And though I have the gift of prophecy, and understand
all mysteries, and all knowledge; and though I have all
faith, so that I could remove mountains, and have not
charity, I am nothing.

I Corinthians 13, 2

But how are you to see into a virtuous Soul and know its
loveliness? Withdraw into yourself and look. And if you
do not find yourself beautiful yet, act as does the creator
of a statue that is to be made beautiful: he cuts away here,
he smooths there, he makes this line lighter, this other
purer, until a lovely face has grown upon his work. So do
you also: cut away all that is excessive, straighten all that
is crooked, bring light to all that is overcast, labour to
make all one glow of beauty and never cease chiselling
your statue.

Plotinus, *'On Beauty'*

CONTENTS

The book consists of a journal, written 1505-1507,
enclosing a chronicle of 1482-1499.
The journal is listed in italics.

England

This spindle-legged boy has no interest in the ancient poets or philosophers, no interest in the knowledge of things; he is oblivious to beauty, impervious to fine thought. Poxed by adolescence, his beard preceded by pimples, he looks on my books with over-boiled eyes.

De Greye studies because his father commands it; and his father commands it to please the king and impress his peers. The English nobility prefer to hunt and to hawk rather than to read, but the new king would have his courtiers follow Italian fashion and acquire at least a modicum of learning. *Basta!* I closed the Greek grammar, written in Egyptian hieroglyphs so far as he is concerned. 'It is enough. Let us spend the rest of the morning reading Latin.'

I drew forward my copy of Plato's Dialogues, written out by me so many years ago, when I lived in my own country with my own kind. When I was a member of the Platonic Academy. When the Platonic Academy existed. When Ficino lived.

'We shall read from Plato's *Symposium* in Latin translation.'

The words of Plato in my finest script: blue ink on vellum, titled in ultramarine obtained from Botticelli – without Botticelli's knowledge – and gilded roman capitals that catch the light, as near perfection as I have ever achieved. The young boar regarded it in scathing silence. No gasp of admiration from my swine at this pearl. Nothing. Chin sunk in his hands, he was determined not to be impressed.

1

'Let us start here, with the speech of Socrates. I will read the Greek and you the Latin.'

He sniffed, turned his head and gazed out of the window where, through the leaded panes, he could see a hawk poised in the sky.

'Come on, boy. Just because the words are in a book and not an inch high on slate does not make them any different.'

He went to speak but was choked by phlegm, that humour so often excessive in the English. He snorted into his sleeve.

'By Apollo! That is disgusting!' I handed him my piece of linen. A thousand years ago the Roman Empire was overrun by barbarians. Here their blood is still strong. Ficino told me, 'Take Plato north, to England, and cultivate men as a gardener.' But this boy is beyond cultivation: he needs to be pulled up by the root and composted.

So there I was, standing over a fourteen-year-old, pale-skinned heir to a quantity of acres near Greenwich, his father a courtier of King Henry VII, teaching him the languages of civilisation – and failing. He looked up at me with the naked cruelty of youth, then his face tightened and his brows knitted together.

'What is the matter?' I asked, thinking he was in some sudden agony.

'Nothing,' he said, relaxing. 'I just wondered what it was like to wear your face.'

I am an Italian. For all my stoic philosophy, when my temper breaks I cannot hold it. Although I remembered what Colet says about loving your pupils, it was no use. My temper exploded, as sudden as a storm in the Appenines – a rolling black cloud coming out of nowhere, emitting tremendous noise and flashes of lightning. I thundered at him, this pustuled son of England who thinks he is a noble.

'Read the book!'

He just grew more sullen. 'What's the point?'

'The point, you ape, is that this is a book about Love.'

He laughed, then, and turned back to watching the hawk.

I tried to swallow my bile. After all, if a boy resists knowledge, but the father still pays, what is it to me? But as I brought the book, my book, my treasure, back under his nose, he snatched it up and flung it at the window, with such force that the latch on the casement gave way and the book flew out. Then my rage burst any bound and, as the boy had snatched my book, so did I snatch him. He whirled and flailed in my grasp, but I was stronger. I had him by that curly red hair so that the more he struggled the more it hurt him.

'You jumped-up scribbler!' he shouted. 'You droning, spleeny oil-drinker! Basta – pasta. Get your hands off me! How dare you touch me?'

I flung him against the desk and ripped his hose down in one movement – truly, I was Hercules, I was Achilles, I was Hector all in one.

Now the birch rod, to my mind, should be an impotent symbol of office, but this morning I snatched it up and used it. I pushed the boy over the desk and thrashed his buttocks. His buttocks – as pale as his face if not paler, with blue veins visible in the white skin, skin now rising with both goosebumps and red weals, skin that was trembling. Skin that was innocent. I stood back, my breath juddering, and for a moment saw just arse and legs, thin, pathetic legs. Of course he was soon round and facing me, and the demon staring out of him, but for that moment I had seen him as he truly was: just a poor little body being beaten, and not for the first time. It was enough to douse my rage.

'You – are – *finished* – here,' he said through his teeth.

'Indeed I am, but not before you have restored my property. Go now and find my book.'

'I do no servant's bidding!' he shouted as he struggled out, drawing up and tripping over his hose as he went. 'Go back to Italy, inky fingers, you son of a peasant!'

A *peasant*? I am a Maffei, one of a family who has served the papacy for generations! Illegitimate, yes, I admit that. A love child. A lust child. Son of a fine man who could not resist the daughter of the house steward. But not a peasant. I found the book in the garden below the window, lying in mud amongst dormant lavender bushes. Its spine is broken but all its pages are intact, and the mud will brush off once it's dry. I suppose I am fortunate not to have been pursued by de Greye's servants and given a similar beating myself, but no doubt a letter of dismissal is on its way.

So now here I am, back in the City of London, enjoying the peace of the deanery of St Paul's, a recipient once more of the generous hospitality of John Colet.

Ah, I wish I were a chameleon and took on the colours of my surroundings. Instead, I do the reverse and stand out in stark contrast. Here in this serene and holy place I rage in Tuscan. What Italian would be proud of his lack of knowledge of the humanities, of Greek and Latin languages? But here in England the nobles consider literature a matter for classes of men lower than themselves. The king champions the New Learning; therefore all his lords and knights must follow suit, but they want the skills I can teach as mere plumes in their fashionable caps, at any expense but no effort on their part. Thus I railed about philistines today, my voice bouncing off the Dean's panelled walls. Colet, who has enough of my language to know what I was saying, smiled fondly. 'Whenever you break into your own vernacular, I can feel the hot sun on my skin and can taste olive oil. It quite takes me back,' he said, remembering his journey through Italy ten years ago. 'All that vocal passion. Is there another race on earth as capable of expressing itself in voice? Whether you are singing or prophesying, wooing or quarrelling, you Italians are better at it than anybody. Come along, Tommaso, food is on the table.'

If Colet himself is a quiet man, it is because he has made himself so. Everything about him says repose, restraint, and it all comes from self-discipline. Not himself from the stock of boar-hunting barons, but from what they call here the 'yeomanry', Colet enjoyed a good education from boyhood and here is its

4

consequence: a gentleman. I would rather have supper at his table, no matter how simple it might be, than any manorial banquet.

'Ah, John,' I said, calming down and taking my place at the table. 'I am unemployed again and need your help.' Shakily at first, and then more boldly, I told him all that had happened and confessed to him that I had used the rod on my pupil. 'And I know how you feel about schoolmasters who beat children.'

'No doubt he deserved it,' he said generously. 'You may stay here as long as you wish. It costs me nothing to accommodate you.'

I sighed. 'If I do not earn my living, my sense of dignity will rub me like a hair shirt.'

'Scratch away if you must or else stay here and share my good fortune. The choice is yours. Of course, the boy was right,' he added, stabbing at a pickled walnut. 'You know nothing about love.'

I stared at him. 'That's not quite what he said.'

'But it is what he meant.'

'I know a great deal about love. Who is it who has the *Symposium* by heart? Can I not discourse for hours on the seven steps by which the soul may return to its source by way of love? My master was Marsilio Ficino, the chief priest of the Higher Venus. I can sing his hymns to Venus – indeed, I believe I can even invoke her. Fetch me a lute and, with the grace of the goddess, I shall attain a divine frenzy and speak in her own words.'

John laughed. 'Oh, you pagan.'

'And if some brat snatched the Bible from your hands and flung it out of the window, how would you feel?'

'The hurt would be considerable – and an error on my part. Does Plato not say that we make a mistake if we consider beauty to reside in an object? I would make the same mistake if I were to think that a mere book was God. What is more important, a book about love, or love itself?' He placed his hand on my chest. 'Here is where love is. If you believe in love as you say you do, you would not beat a child, even if he is your enemy. Love is not a philosophy, my friend, it is a living substance and a practical reality. If you love Love, then practise it.'

5

London, November 7th, 1505

We celebrated Plato's birthday yesterday with a symposium in the private chamber of the Dean of St Paul's. Where it does not seem strange to us that John Colet, Master of Arts, should have been elected to one of the highest positions in the Church, it is most gossip-worthy amongst Londoners. Discounting his lately (and hastily) awarded degree in divinity, they say he has been advanced by favouritism, being the son of an ex-mayor. They have no concept of merit. They want what they are used to: a doctor of divinity swathed in scarlet and holding banquets, not this slender upstart not yet forty, who goes about the churchyard tacking up notices that say, 'This is holy ground – urinate elsewhere!'

What is exercising Londoners in general, and the cathedral clergy in particular, is that this new dean stands in the pulpit of St Paul's and tells them how to live the Christian life, in terms so simple that they cannot help but understand. Some fidget and blush during his sermons, others scowl. As for the clergy, he encourages them to practise what they preach. If they knew he was a cabalist and a Platonist, they would have the reason they seek to depose him. So we meet in secret; that is, when we have dinner, it is a simple meal the dean is sharing with friends. None of the servants need know it is Plato's birthday.

As usual there were eight of us, and as usual we set out nine oak chairs. It is four years since Erasmus vanished from our lives. The last we saw of him was at an inn on the Dover road, just beyond Southwark. There we embraced him, bade him godspeed and watched him leave with a party of travellers bound for the coast and France. Each of us had given him money: he would not want on his journey.

We've never heard from him again.

Each time we gather together, this fledgling Platonic Academy in London, we put out his chair and, at the beginning of the evening, say a prayer for his soul. Year on year it gets no easier. Death at least brings grief; vanishing has no resolution. I have persuaded myself that his dear bones lie somewhere in a French ditch while our money is easing the lives of bandits, but Will Lily is convinced he is still alive.

'Alive or dead,' said John, 'he has a soul, and we pray for that.'

I was invited to read a passage of my choice from the *Symposium*; I chose the speech of Socrates on love and recited it from memory. Grocyn followed by reading it out in Greek. I closed my eyes to imagine myself in the agora of ancient Athens, but where my imagination took me was to Florence twenty years ago, and I was listening neither to Grocyn nor to Socrates but to Marsilio Ficino. These words, these Greek words on love, have eternity in their core.

One by one the circle read a speech – More did an excellent Alcibiades – but when it came to Colet, he left the book aside to give his own discourse on love.

'I have been thinking much about schoolmasters,' he began, surprising us all. 'It is commonly thought that, in order to learn, children must be beaten, tenderised by the rod and made receptive.' I blanched and kept my head down. 'It is not necessary to beat a child. If a man loves his learning and loves his pupils, he can communicate by love,' he said. 'Higher love, love of God, does not mean spending hours on your knees in a chapel. It means loving all creatures, as if they were God.' Colet's voice rose, became oratorical as if he were addressing his congregation; in his small, panelled chamber in the deanery, the effect was magnified. Satisfied that he was not criticising me, but using my experience as a guide, I dared at last to look up and found him smiling at me.

'Love,' he said, 'is a practical matter, not a theory. Do you agree, Tommaso?'

'Of course.'

He looked me gravely and over-long in the eye. To my relief, Thomas Linacre stood up and invited us all to raise our glasses to Dean Colet, Plato and God.

'And missing friends,' Colet added, raising his own glass to the empty chair.

London, November 9th, 1505

In the mirror I see a face that is mine and not mine – a sitter for a portrait in the manner of Flemish painters. The last time I studied my own features was nearly thirty years ago, when Sandro Botticelli made a picture of me. It was the time when I was grieving over my brother's death and Sandro caught the image of a reflective youth in a brown jacket and red cap. Now that grief is etched in lines, lines beneath the eyes, lines running from nose to mouth. And my pupil was right, there is indeed a frown puckering the forehead, a frown so habitual that it's nigh impossible to relax those muscles. Here is the portrait of an angry man, a failed philosopher. The healthy brown complexion of a Florentine has become sallow, almost grey, and a black English cap covers hair as dull as a dry conker. It never really recovered from the shaving. I want to step back, out of the mirror, for all I can think is, 'That is not me!' But I must confront the image if I would know myself. I can hear Ficino laughing, saying, 'A man who would know himself does not look in mirrors!' But I must, for there is something to be seen here. There is a film over the man in the mirror, perhaps the effect of candle smoke, but this ghostly image of anger stares back at me. Anger is the flame; melancholy is the smoke. This is a portrait of misery.

And worse. This is the portrait of a man who looks for love in books; a man who beats a young boy for not being interested in learning; a man who teaches that which he himself has forgotten.

The man in the mirror is a hypocrite.

Though I have read the Dialogues of Plato and know several by heart; though I have read all the Enneads of Plotinus; though I can elucidate Porphyry's text on the Cave of the Nymphs and can interpret Iamblichus; though I know the plays of Aeschylus, of Euripides and Sophocles, and have played Orestes more than once; without love, I am nothing. Where is Erasmus?

London, November 12ᵗʰ, 1505

He lies in no French ditch, his bones whitened by crows, but is alive in Holland! I received a letter today, sent care of St Paul's. The dean himself brought it to me, his slender hand trembling with excitement. 'I know this crabbed handwriting! And this doodle-portrait on the back – who else could it be?'

'Oh, John, John – he's alive?' I tore the letter open and read it out loud.

Dearest Tommaso, have you ever felt shame? It has taken me four years to summon courage to write this letter, and even now I cannot write to Colet direct but must go through that friend who, above all others, may understand how I feel. Have you ever felt shame? Yes, I believe you have. I think you know what it is like to live with a sense of failure. There, I have insulted you. It was not my intention.

Let me start again, this time at the beginning. Those funds you all donated so generously to pay for my journey to Italy were stolen. I never reached further than Holland, where I have been hiding for the past four years, too ashamed to tell you all what had happened. For a man who loses what his friends have given him is no friend. He is a failure and, with his cowl up at all times, hides amongst monks.

But Tommaso, you understand the whims of fortune better than most. I charge you to tell our friends my story and then judge if they would welcome me back. When I left London it was with a purse full of gold coin but at Dover I was intercepted by officers of His Majesty's customs. The king had revived an old law which states that no precious metal may be taken out of England. Your gold was confiscated by His Majesty's Exchequer! What kind of law is that? Not one of God's, to be sure.

I was put on the boat for France not as a happy pilgrim but as a beggar being deported. I made my way as far as Paris and there I stayed, sick in body and soul, making what living I could by tutoring. Once I had sufficiently recovered my spirits, I came to Holland, not daring to contact my English friends to say what had happened. What did I fear? Not your wrath – you are too generous for that. No, you would have railed against the king and found me blameless. What I feared, and still fear, is your further generosity when I have cost you all too much already. But worse than that, I fear appearing weak in your eyes. Better you think me dead and keep your good opinion of me. There, it is said. Is shame not shameful? But four years is a long time to live with a falsehood, and it is working its way out of me like a thorn. I am now about to leave for Paris, wanting to put everything right, for a man at odds with his friends is at odds with himself. I wish to return to England, to be with Colet, More, Grocyn, Linacre and Lily again, to grow in their company.

Although it remains my ambition to visit your Italy, I will not try again unless God wills it. I hope that you have spent these past years anticipating this moment and writing out the rest of your history. If not, if my disappearance silenced your muse, then cut your quill at once. You have told me very little of Pico della Mirandola and I would know more about Savonarola. Many believe him to have been a true prophet of God but whenever we discussed him in Oxford, you fell quiet and would not speak, as if you dared not voice an opinion contrary to that of others. Tell me the truth, Tommaso, since you were in Florence at the time and knew these figures who, in death, have become legends.

Meanwhile tell me if the weather is set fair for my return to London, or if I will be met with that penetrating damp that is English disdain.

Il tuo Desiderio Erasmo.

I looked up at John to find he had tears in his eyes. 'Only an innocent man,' he began, but had to clear his throat. 'Only an innocent man would let his soul be stained by the sins of another. Blessed are the meek… Reply at once and tell him the weather is heavenly.'

Have I kept up my writing? No, I have not! Whether it is the lack of my reader, or the want of energy, I do not know. The story is unresolved. It is a chronicle of death with no resurrection. I must sharpen my wits as well as my quill.

London, November 13th, 1505

Thomas More bounced in this morning and thrust a roll of papers at me tied up with ribbon. 'My translation of *The Life of Giovanni Pico della Mirandola*,' he announced. 'I would be grateful if you would read it and give your opinion. You'll notice I made a few cuts – don't get on your high horse! – I had to. I thought, pared to its essence, it would make a perfect spiritual handbook for nuns.'

He left me stunned. What could there be in the life of my friend, Pico, that would inspire nuns? I opened the roll of papers, weighted them down on the desk and began to read, not a little regretful that I had not read the original before I gave it to Thomas. As he has not returned it, I have nothing with which to compare this 'translation' and cannot determine what are the lies of the author and what the distortions of the translator. It begins with three letters which Pico wrote to his nephew, Gianfrancesco, praising him copiously. They, obviously, are Gianfrancesco's own forgeries. The rest of the book is hagiography, for Gianfrancesco would have us believe that his uncle was a saint. Forlornly I read the section entitled *Twelve Rules Directing a Man in Spiritual Battle*. There is nothing cut here – it is all addition. A pithy original statement by Pico has been elaborated in rhyme royal into a sermon about sorrow, adversity, grief and pain. This has the sound of More in his breast-beating humour. After all, he would be a Carthusian monk by now if Colet had not intervened and encouraged him to marry. Perhaps he is enjoying the marriage bed too much and wants to put his hair shirt back on, if only in his choice of literary work.

This adulteration of words, the cuts and additions of editors and translators for their own purpose, it is a kind of rape. Who could know Pico della Mirandola from this book? Worse, those who read it will think they *do* know him. They will read about the saint of the nephew's imagination in the pious translation of More and consider themselves informed. Worse still, they will believe that Pico della Mirandola *was* a saint! These earnest men of religion – have they no respect for simple honesty?

When More called in later to see if I had read it, I listened to myself telling him how fine a work it is and what a blessed service he has done for nuns. What else could I say, that would not have crushed him? I have obviously picked up the English habit of not telling a man to his face what you think. But now, by the virtue of Erasmus and the vice of More, I am driven to set down the truth about Pico, in so far as I know what the truth is.

THE CHRONICLE OF TOMMASO DE'
MAFFEI FROM THE BIRTH OF
VENUS TO THE DEATH OF THE
ANTICHRIST, 1482-1498
FOR DESIDERIUS
ERASMUS

1 THE HEART IN A PRESS
1482

'TELL ME,' I SAID TO MARSILIO FICINO, 'ABOUT THE HIGHER and lower Venus. Are we talking about one Venus or two?'

'The higher Venus was born of Uranus, the sky, and the lower one of Jupiter and Juno.'

'Two, then.'

'Will you never understand?' Ficino was plucking at thyme, rosemary and lavender, tearing leaves from the shrubs and sprinkling them over me where I lay on my back in a bed of camomile. 'Keep inhaling and concentrate on the sky.'

I gazed up into the blue empyrean. Happiness groaned in its chains. 'Stop this!' I said, coming to my feet. 'Stop showering me with pungent weeds!' I went back inside his house to my desk in a gloomy corner.

After the murder of Giuliano, the hanging of the conspirators, the resulting war with Rome; after the death of my wife, I was living like a recluse in Ficino's villa at Careggi. His usually potent cures for melancholy were failing to work. I found interest in nothing. It was as if only my body were alive, as if my spirit were not so much melancholy as dead. I had achieved all I had ever wanted: I'd had a house, work that fed my soul as well as my body and a wife who completed me. Losing her, I had lost everything; all thoughts in my mind had dissolved into the sound of one long, continuous scream. I woke to it every morning and lived with it through each day, as if all sounds had been reduced to this single, horrible screech of discord. It was the soul's response to a mind which said, 'I have had everything I have ever wanted, and I have lost it. What do I want now? To repeat it, only to lose it again? No. Therefore I want nothing.' It was the mortal scream of dying ambition. I was an automaton. Only my body was alive.

'Let go of the past and live in the present,' Ficino had often counselled me, but one may as well tell a man not to put his tongue in the warm and bloody cavity where his tooth has been. He tried to restore my spirit by invoking the planetary influence of Jupiter, but his fine wines and golden honey, his heliotropes and sweet, Jovial music – none of these things could remove the weight of Saturn from my soul.

He followed me in, bearing rose-oil in a little dish which he placed on my desk. 'Rub this over your heart,' he said.

Obediently I unlaced my shirt and rubbed in the warm oil. Its scent, reminding me of Elena, nearly made my heart crack. 'This is no good,' I said. 'Nothing works, nothing will work.'

'Not while your will is opposed to recovery.'

'It is not my will, it is fate. This terrible fate which brings death to anyone I love.'

'Do not be shackled by such illusions. That belief is of your lower nature. You must rise and transcend the stars.'

'But how?'

'By willing it.' He returned to his own desk and left me to my work, which was a fair transcription of his book *The Platonic Theology – concerning the immortality of the soul*. Work was my only relief. I concentrated on rendering fine words in fine letters, listening to my nib telling the page what to say. To calm my troubled spirits I applied my attention to constructing a particularly fine capital letter at the head of a chapter. Two hours later, Ficino smacked me on the back of the head and told me off for wasting time. 'This is only for the printer! All that is required of you is legibility!'

In no mood to sacrifice my art and dismayed that he should embrace the new invention so readily, I let fly. 'How can you of all men, the high priest of Beauty, ask me, Tommaso de' Maffei, to cripple my art in the cause of haste? Truth is in Beauty and God is in Truth – is that not what you teach us? But now you want me to dash off a manuscript so that you can take it to a printer who will, with all his might, turn it into a book as ugly as the *befana*. How could you? How could *you* betray Beauty?'

'Surely by now you understand Plato's *Symposium*?'

'Of course I do. I've written it out twice. I've even written out your commentary on it.'

'Yet you know nothing. What are beautiful letters if you do not connect with their meaning?'

Ficino could always identify a man's blind spot. I said nothing and sat there with an expression of petulance unbecoming to a member of the Platonic Academy.

'On the seven steps of Love, what is the second step?' he asked.

'To appreciate the beauty of fair ideas.'

'And the first step?'

'Fair forms.'

'So you are still on the first step. The beauty of Plato is the beauty of fair ideas. My book is devoted to those fair ideas. Why should it be adorned with flowery margins and little cupids? It is the ideas that are beautiful, and the printing press, that marvellous invention, allows us to reproduce that beauty and broadcast it across the world.'

He was right, of course. Beauty of ideas does not require beauty of form, or else Socrates would have been a good-looking man. But I had trained for years to become a scribe, striving always for the elusive beauty, and I could not give it up, not at once.

'Allow me this much at least,' I said. 'Allow me to find for you a printer who has some idea of harmony and proportion in letters.'

To my relief, Ficino agreed.

To many the Platonic Academy was a meeting of *eruditi* interested in discussing matters of philosophy, theology and literature. It could take place anywhere, sometimes at Santa Maria degli Angeli in Florence, sometimes at the Badia on Fiesole, sometimes at San Marco monastery; but it was because it often took place in villas of the Medici that many wished to attend, affecting an interest in

17

philosophy so as to keep company with Lorenzo, to be seen with him, to be one of his intimate circle. That was the attraction for many.

For some, the attraction was intellectual. The ideas and insights that abounded at such meetings excited them and they gathered up the seeds of knowledge like eager sparrows, chirping and squabbling amongst themselves. These men were impressive in discussion, citing ancient authors and myths in dazzling profusion. Others, musicians, painters and poets, found our Platonic evenings plucked the strings of their souls and inspired them with fine words and mysterious images. Ficino fed everyone, casting out handfuls of seeds, nuts and bread to suit every need and taste.

But for a few there was another, inner academy of men who sought to make the teachings of Plato a living reality, thereby to transform their lives and make the ascent of the soul. For them, to sing an Orphic hymn was not to entertain others but was for the soul alone and a daily ritual; they were unlikely to hold a debate, challenging all-comers with logical arguments, but they could recite long passages of Plato, memorised by heart. That I was not one of these was an aggravation and a puzzle. Was I not ready to shun the world of the body? Grief, Ficino said, had opened the doors for me, so why had I not been invited in? I wanted nothing now from this mortal life. The liberation of my soul was my only desire. Or so I persuaded myself, as a drowning man with lead weights tied to his feet thinks, I will rise, I will rise.

Among the printers in Florence, I chose Antonio Miscomini to publish *The Platonic Theology*. He had printed the edition of Homer and was a man sensitive to our intentions. He also, I discovered, used a type fount somewhat similar to my own script. It had been less than a decade since the first printer set up shop in Florence, yet already there was a street of them, close to the Palazzo del Podestà. I would rather have traversed Dante's Inferno than walk that street, yet sometimes duty called me to it, as on one hot day as the city was beginning to empty for the summer, when I took Ficino to see Miscomini.

I had always supposed printing to be a noisy affair as loud as a forge with the great presses stamping out books. In fact it is an almost silent occupation with each man in the shop intent on his work, the only sounds that of the tamping of the ink dabbers, the tapping of hammers on formes, the screw of the press as it is turned. I looked around me in disdain. Compositors arranged letters on a 'stick' while others were engaged in cutting new type, setting pages, making up galleys or inking at the press. Ficino looked on it all as a wonder of the world and a gift from God.

'It takes us less than a day to do a page,' said Miscomini proudly.

'Pah! It takes me only an hour or two,' I said.

'And if you had to copy that page again, how long would that take?'

'An hour or two …' I said, fully aware of the trap I had entered so stupidly.

'I can give you a hundred copies of that page in two days, two hundred in three days.'

'Wonderful!' said Ficino. 'Quite wonderful!'

I despaired. 'So how long before we receive the book?'

'November.'

'November? Why not next week?'

'Each page has to be set up, don't forget. Has to be set up, printed and taken apart again, since we need to use the same letters for the next page. That's what takes the time. Five hundred copies of a book with this many pages will take us several months. How long would it take you?'

I smiled wryly despite myself. Even Hercules would have been defeated by such a labour.

'Wonderful,' Ficino repeated as we left.

'Diabolical,' said I.

We had timed our visit to the city to coincide with a visit to the workshop of Sandro Botticelli, where a new picture was to be unveiled to a small and very select group of men. Ficino, who came less and less often to the city these days, looked about him keenly as we rode through the city, and I saw through his eyes the division of men into rich and poor. It was easy to distinguish them: the rich wore colour and the poor wore undyed wool. Nor did they mingle overmuch. The crimsons and purples, yellows and blues, the silks, the velvets, the high cap-feathers, all kept each other's protective company in a city mostly comprising the undyed. The republican ideals that had inspired the government during Ficino's boyhood were now quite vanished; no one even made a pretence of them any more, except that Florence was ruled by a prince who pretended to be a citizen. Lorenzo, popularly referred to as *Il Magnifico*, was everywhere, visible and invisible. He was visible in the wealth paraded by those families affiliated to his. He was invisible in the favours granted that bound men to him; the arguments resolved with a gift; the marriages brokered; the benefices gained and bestowed.

The Medici bank was failing through mismanagement and Lorenzo wanted little to do with it. Because the war with Rome had been his war, he had more or less paid for it. When his own resources had run dry, he helped himself to the enormous fortune he was supposed to be protecting for his wards, his Pierfranceschi cousins, until they came of age. Similarly he helped himself to the fund for dowerless girls. He brought in new taxes which crippled the priesthood and the poor but left the rich untouched. When I say 'he', I mean of course the government, but the government *was* Lorenzo, invisibly. By secret ways the Medici had long been in control of those who chose the names for the ballot of each *signoria*, two months in duration.

Looking through Ficino's eyes, hard hit as he was himself by the new taxation on priests, I saw a city built on corruption and greed. Looking through my own eyes and myopically, I saw Florence as a city of beauty. But then I was a beneficiary of Lorenzo's generosity. He had given me a house in return for saving his life on that dread day when the rival Pazzi family had sought to assassinate him in the Duomo. He had also permitted me to wed Elena de' Pazzi at the very time when he was arranging for the government to pass a new law that no daughter of the Pazzi family may marry or bear children. Why had he done this? Yes, he was grateful to me; but it was more than that. Lorenzo liked to give to others what he could not have himself. What he gave to me was a marriage based on love.

'She will have no dowry,' he had told me grimly.

'She is my wealth,' I replied.

And tears had come into his eyes, in that time when he cried easily and for good reason. In the death of Giuliano, he had lost not only the brother he had loved, but also a young and prudent counsellor he had never listened to. Lorenzo was alone. He needed friends. He gave us gifts of that which we held most precious and we were bound to him, as flies in the honeyed dew of certain plants.

I wanted Ficino to speak his thoughts out loud, but he kept quiet, looking to the left and right of him as we passed through the streets. The deprivations and ills we had suffered during the dark days of the war, the hopelessness and despair, had been swept away like the stinking silt after the flood of '79. The city was alive and at work restoring itself. It was growing in beauty, with new palazzi being built on ancient principles. There was a new order. The city militia was more evident than it ever had been, and there were police. The bankers at their green baize tables in the Old Market exchanged money as the Medici had done four generations ago – out in the open and according to custom, if not in strict adherence to the spirit of the law forbidding usury. Lorenzo no longer dealt in money. These days he dealt in benefices. He kept the best for his second son, seven-year-old Giovanni, and gave the rest as gifts. And who did not want a benefice? I would have liked one myself, to free me from the burden of earning a living by the skill of my hands, allowing me to copy books of my own choice and at a calm pace. Few recipients bothered with the requirement to be in holy orders, let alone follow the rules of those orders. What we all wanted, Ficino included, was a life of leisure to pursue what we desired. The only difference between men was what they desired: Ficino wanted a simple life devoted to what he called 'the hunt for truth', whereas some, such as Bartolommeo Scala, once again the Chancellor of Florence, wanted fabulous wealth and to live like a prince. But it was all on the back of benefices, one way or another.

I speak with hindsight. At the time we could barely see the foundation on which we built our lives. It was the invisible part, the secret ways. It was normal. That men were divided between those who earned a living and were poor, and those who derived a living and were rich – that was normal. The poor went to church and prayed there. The rich went and gave generously, funding chapels that were to bear their names, having their own images painted on sacred walls. I did not have a benefice, but I lived by the hospitality and generosity of those who did.

On this day as we went to Ognissanti, I saw the hearts of men. There were those who greeted us affably in passing. They were the men who were part of the Medici system. Then there were those who turned their backs or just stared with cold eyes. They were the ones who hated Lorenzo, as I myself had hated him once. With some it was resentment and envy; with others it was with just cause. I knew their bitterness intimately, could understand but not condone. And then there were those who took no notice of us one way or another, being too busy laying out their stalls, skinning their meat, stirring their vats, planing their wood. The ones who live amongst dust and stench, converting the earth into a living. To them we were as we were, two men on horseback, of no relevance to their lives.

'What is this painting, Father?'

'Be patient. You will see it soon enough.'

'But it is shrouded in secrecy. Why?'

'Privacy, not secrecy. My young Lorenzino is a very private man. Only I have been invited to this unveiling, and Poliziano, of course, since we both designed the picture with Sandro. Lorenzino wants us to see it at the same time he does. Always considerate.'

The Lorenzo he spoke of was not il Magnifico but his cousin, Lorenzo di Pierfrancesco de' Medici. The painting we were going to see had been commissioned to celebrate his recent marriage to Semiramide d'Appiano. He was only nineteen, but il Magnifico, having found the perfect match for him, had seen no reason to wait.

There was much talk in the city of a rift in the Medici family, caused by the guardian spending the patrimony of his wards on the war. 'Will il Magnifico be there, do you think?' I asked.

'No, it is just the select few who will be there, at the most propitious moment for this celestial image to be uncovered.'

'Celestial?'

'Be patient, Tommaso.'

2 VENUS IN A SEASHELL
1482

ENTERING THE WORKSHOP IN OGNISSANTI I REVIVED, AS a vegetable gone limp plumps up in water. It was a temporary revival but enough to remind me what being alive felt like. Filippino Lippi said I walked in like a ghost and took on all the colours of what was around me. Colours. Pinks and duck-egg blues, dark greens and coral reds: Sandro's palette was a natural one and not overwhelmed by ultramarine and gold. The workshop was busy and many panels were in the process of completion but the large canvas in the centre of the room was shrouded in linen. All around were charcoal studies tacked up roughly: nymphs and goddesses dancing in flowing, diaphanous gowns, flowers of the meadow done in realistic detail, studies of trees, of feet and hands. Such movement, such vivacity! While other painters of Florence continued in the long tradition of holy scenes, Sandro Botticelli had returned to Arcadia.

Far from a select few, many men were crowding into the small space. Having heard about the event, Lorenzo de' Medici had arrived, along with his usual entourage of companions numbering at least ten, including two of his sons. And they were not the only young ones. Other men had brought their sons and, to add to Botticelli's distress, a four-year-old neighbour who had taken possession of him and called in daily to pose – unwittingly – for devils and demons was pushing roughly through the crowd towards the painter with a very determined look on his face. I remember the boy's name: Ridolfo Spini. Unable to pronounce it, he called himself Doffo.

'Tommaso! Are you here too?' Sandro seemed bemused as to what my connection to the patron could be.

'I'm with Ficino.'

'Well, make yourself useful and help Filippino clear the place of juveniles.'

'Even Lorenzo's sons?'

Sandro sighed heavily. 'Do what you can.'

I took Doffo Spini by the ear and led him spitting and snarling from the workshop. Outside Filippino Lippi was bribing other boys not to re-enter, but they were mobbing him, taking his money and not moving off.

'They've heard our Venus is naked,' Filippino told me, exasperated. He had his own workshop by this time, but was still found frequently at Botticelli's, convinced as he was that his erstwhile master could not function without him. Particularly at viewings. 'Where did Doffo go?' he asked, barring the way to a young Vespucci.

'O Dio …' I went back inside and found my charge sitting in front of the covered panel, facing the audience as if he were the one all had come to see. With his pointed ears and spaced teeth, he did indeed look like an imp from the inferno. Before I could reach the child, however, the babble of voices suddenly quietened. I turned to see the Pierfranceschi at the door, Lorenzino with his hooded eyes and mop of unruly hair and Giovanni with his broad brow and startling innocence. Several years younger than his brother, Giovanni was taller and as eye-catching as an angel. One always had to make an effort to draw the gaze away from him to his brother. If Lorenzo di Pierfrancesco was surprised or upset by the heaving mass of visitors, he did not show it. The prize pupil of Marsilio Ficino, he was a very polished courtier and in his sweetly modulated voice he expressed delight that so many had come. As he glanced at his guardian, however, he blinked once or twice before walking towards him, his arms open for an embrace from the one he had always called 'father.'

'You forgot to invite me!' said il Magnifico, playfully pulling his young cousin's cap down over his eyes.

Lorenzo di Pierfrancesco straightened his cap with a smile. 'This was intended to be a preview. I was going to invite you when it is formally hung in my house.'

'Well, I could not wait for that.'

Lorenzino had a fine and noble bearing that left no one in any doubt that here was a scion of the Medici family, descended from the same forefather as il Magnifico himself. Their grandfathers had been partners, but Lorenzino's father, Pierfrancesco, had been bought out from the banking enterprise and had retired with a considerable fortune. Twenty years younger than il Magnifico, Lorenzino was closer in age to Lorenzo's eldest son, but he and Piero had never played together as children, and Lorenzino always took his place close to il Magnifico, to stand with the same posture of superiority no matter how old he was. Years notwithstanding, he was il Magnifico's equal, at least in his own eyes.

Sandro nudged me. 'Get rid of the children,' he hissed.

I crossed to where Piero de' Medici, abandoned and neglected, sat alone on a table staring at his cousins with smouldering hatred. Too young to understand the subtleties and undercurrents of relations between grown men, Piero took things at face value and considered himself usurped. 'Your father wants you to wait for him outside,' I said.

'No he doesn't!' he said, brushing me off like a fly. Vanquished as ever by the imperiousness of this boy, I went looking for his brother, but little Giovanni had squeezed in between his father and Lorenzo di Pierfrancesco and was standing on his father's feet, hanging on his belt and staring up at him with piggy eyes full of adoration.

'Come, Sandro, off with those covers,' said il Magnifico, swinging his pudgy son to and fro. 'The day is hot and our curiosity is scalding us.'

'Not everyone is here yet,' said Sandro nervously, waiting for the instruction of his patron rather than his patron's guardian.

'Who is missing?'

'Angelo Poliziano.'

'He's here,' said several voices.

Just inside the door, Poliziano stood sweating and breathless. 'Forgive me,' he panted. 'I know we need to catch the moment, so I ran.'

'The moment?' Il Magnifico glanced around and, noticing the hour glass for the first time, looked abashed, realising that Ficino had timed the unveiling to coincide with the movement of the planets.

Lorenzo di Pierfrancesco invited Poliziano to come forward and greeted him affectionately. 'You're not too late,' he assured him. There was still some sand trickling through the hour glass.

Little Giovanni, who had been pushed gently away when his weight had begun to trouble his father's feet, was now lifting the linen to peak at what was behind. Doffo Spini, considering himself in charge of this event, poked him spitefully and told him to stop. Giovanni ignored him. The new tonsure on his pate, strange as it was on such a young head, was not enough to remind Filippino Lippi that the child, whose hand he now smacked, was not only a priest but an abbot.

Giovanni dropped the fabric and, laughing at his own naughtiness, went off to torment his brother. He tried to climb the table to join Piero but so lacked agility and grace that finally Piero had to haul him up to save the family any further embarrassment.

'Magnifico,' said Botticelli in desperation. 'It is too hot and stuffy for your little ones.'

'And it'll be even hotter in a moment,' said Filippino to me.

But all eyes were now on the hour glass and the final stream of grains. Ficino raised up his hands and began to sing a hymn, an Orphic hymn to Venus. As the last note of the hymn resonated in our expectant silence, Sandro Botticelli nodded to Filippino who, with a simple flick of his wrist, disrobed the painting. From the men came one sound: a deep, intestinal grunt; from the boys, yelps and titters. Doffo Spini gave a penetrating whistle that seemed incredible for a boy his age. For what we were looking at was a naked woman, life-size, gazing at us with such benign innocence that our lust was simultaneously both aroused and doused. Fat little Giovanni clapped his hands to his mouth. Too young to have much awareness of being an abbot, he looked from the painting to his brother, his face a shining mixture of fascination and horror, while Piero himself stood on the bench, his eyes popping. This was clearly what Botticelli had feared, not that his painting would corrupt the young but that the young would corrupt his painting, its proper reception and understanding. But the initial grunts that had come from the adults were now converting into sighs of aesthetic pleasure, and he had to be content with that.

She was as pale as marble, with long, golden hair flowing about her. One hand partly obscured her breasts from our hungry eyes, the other, grasping the end of her long tresses, covered her pudenda. That she was standing in a scallop shell the size of a coracle and attended on her right by zephyrs and on her left by a nymph waiting to cover her with a robe, were details that only impressed themselves later. The Cyprian sea, the coastline in the background and the roses raining in the air barely reached the eye that fastened on female nudity.

Botticelli himself gazed at us. Always nervous in anticipation, once the covers were off a work he enjoyed himself. He was growing somewhat stout with age, and his fair, wavy hair did not seem to have had too much attention of late. His delphic eyes, where light danced as on water, rested on the face of Lorenzino. The young man seemed to be two-in-one, half of him falling in love with this goddess in the basest manner and the other, more noble part, appreciating the literary references he could read in the painting. His approval was obvious, and that was the important thing.

Lorenzo de' Medici had recently given his cousin a painting by Botticelli originally intended as a gift for Giuliano, a gesture of reparation he needed to make for spending the Pierfranceschi wealth. The painting, the wonderful, enigmatic *Realm of Venus*, a Platonic picture of the transformation of the soul through love, had been presented this very year, on the occasion of Lorenzino's marriage. Immediately Lorenzino had commissioned a new work. Here it was: *Venus Anadyomene* – the new-born Venus rising from the sea and wafting to shore on a shell.

Lorenzino called on Ficino and Poliziano to explain the painting to everyone present, Ficino to discourse on Love and Poliziano to recite the passages from Lucian, Ovid and Apuleius that had provided Sandro with the imagery for the painting. But in a booming voice, Bartolommeo Scala interrupted to give us his own philosophical interpretation of the myth, so tediously allegorical that I turned away. I noticed that, among Lorenzo's companions, Girolamo Benivieni was crying. His brother, Antonio, tried to comfort him but Girolamo shrugged him off and hurried from the workshop. Il Magnifico looked askance at Antonio Benivieni, who gave one word as an explanation for his brother's behaviour: *Giuliano*. Lorenzo nodded gravely and sympathetically and turned back to Scala.

Since the death of Giuliano de' Medici, Girolamo Benivieni had worn a mask of melancholy and carried a fear of death that was palpable. The shock of the assassination had created such a depression in the young poet that he woke each morning believing the day to be his last. For reasons that were not lost on me, the painting had reminded him of Giuliano. It was an image Giuliano would have understood at once and have loved. He might even have commissioned it himself, had he lived. My own eyes curiously dry, I stood gazing around the workshop.

'Look at the picture,' said Ficino softly. 'Look on the goddess.'

I could see it was full of significance; I could consider its symbolic meaning; what I could not do was *feel* it. It was like having a cold: the senses of the soul were blocked. When Scala had finally stopped speaking, Ficino began to explain the myth and I heard his voice as if through a seashell held to my ear, muffled and distant. 'And the sea is the soul and thus fertilized by Uranus it creates Beauty within itself. This conversion into Beauty and its birth from the soul is called Venus.'

Memories. Images. Understanding. Sandro's paintings, like Poliziano's great but unfinished epic on Giuliano's Joust, telling the same story: the ascent of the soul through Love to God. And Love is Beauty. Beauty...

'I notice,' said Angelo Poliziano, 'that Sandro modestly avoids showing the castration of Uranus and the actual birth of the goddess from his foamy semen.'

'Boys!' said il Magnifico to his sons. 'Go and play outside.'

'Unless,' Poliziano said thoughtfully, 'that is what the spume-flecked waves signify.'

Botticelli, staring at his picture, said nothing but smiled.

'It is an important part of the myth,' Poliziano continued, 'but I've never understood it. Marsilio, will you elucidate it for us?'

'Plato forbids it,' said Ficino. 'You do not need to dwell on it to enjoy the picture. It is often said that there are two Venuses, but in fact there is only one, in two aspects. One governs human, reproductive love, the other, the love of the Divine. The lower is represented as clothed, the higher as naked. Here we see the higher Venus being wafted to the shores of earthly life by the gentle west wind, and waiting for her is an Hour, representing time and temporality. She will clothe the goddess in a mantle. Thus, what Sandro shows so admirably is both aspects in one. What we are to understand is that human love is divine love, cloaked. That is to

29

say, any man who loves is capable of loving God – he just has to remove the covers on his soul.'

Whatever its neoplatonic themes, this was a painting with a specific purpose, I thought, a painting to soften a bride and warm her frigidity, a painting to unlock a girl and free the woman. I gazed at Lorenzo di Pierfrancesco, just married, and envied him so fiercely that my throat filled with bile. I followed Girolamo Benivieni outside, but there was no sign of him in the street, although Lorenzo's sons were playing knucklebones close by, Giovanni asking Piero what 'castration' meant and being told he was too young to know.

'It means having your cock cut off,' said Giovanni di Pierfrancesco, standing over them, his arms folded. Seeing me, this fair-haired youth as beautiful as a girl smiled disarmingly and walked back into the workshop. Piero de' Medici pulled a face at the retreating figure, which Abbot Giovanni imitated.

'He stinks!' said Piero.

'He really stinks!' said Giovanni.

I turned away to look on the daily life of Ognissanti, the bright cloth of the dyers stretched along the streets to dry: crimson, damson, saffron. Everywhere in the city there was a fever of building and the stone dust that hung in the air like a cloud settled on the new cloth. Men leading mules back from market, laden with supplies for their households, stopped whenever they met a friend, to stand awhile, cough and complain. The building of the Strozzi palace alone was causing much resentment, and men moaned about their taxes and the price of staple foods. That Lorenzo had saved Florence from becoming a papal state kept him high in people's esteem, and it was other rich families that took the brunt of popular displeasure. Inside the workshop the few, discussing philosophy, outside the many, discussing the trials of life. Who here among the artisans and grocers knew anything about the higher Venus? Not one. They went to church regularly to petition God for good health, for wealth, for acts of revenge against those who had done them harm. And sometimes they wondered if He was deaf. But love God? – that was the preserve of a few old crones who had lost everything else in life and had nothing left to love but the Virgin and the baby Jesus.

Filippino Lippi joined me. Since receiving the commission to complete the frescoes of Masaccio in the Brancacci Chapel at Santa Maria del Carmine, he had grown in confidence and stature. After saying something about the noise and dust of palace building, he asked how I was and I replied with a sigh.

He leant against the wall of the workshop contentedly. 'God be praised for Lorenzino.'

'Why so?'

'He commissions us where il Magnifico does not.'

'Lorenzo cannot afford it.'

'How come? Has he not stolen a million florins from his cousins?'

'You exaggerate! It is a large amount but not that large, and it was used to pay the debts incurred by the war. He has given them his villa at Cafaggiolo to compensate.'

'Chicken feed!'

The thought of that large fortress and great estate being called chicken feed made me smile. 'Even with the loss of half their wealth, they are still richer than Lorenzo by far, rich enough to commission a painting. Francesco Sassetti said that the total amount spent by Lorenzo in Naples to buy our freedom was so vast that he could not bring himself to write it down.'

'Think of how many commissions that could have been.'

'Do you ever think of anything else?'

Filippino's wide mouth curved in a lascivious smile. 'Of course.'

I struck out at him. 'Ficino is wrong: there are three Venuses. The higher, who governs divine love, the middle, who governs human love, and then that voluptuous siren who inspires lust.'

'My goddess. Have you seen Lorenzino's wife?' Filippino made a thrusting gesture to show in his alleycat way what he thought of Semiramide. 'Did you know she is the niece of Simonetta

Vespucci? She has the same beauty: that Venus in there is her portrait. And poor Giovanni di Pierfrancesco – betrothed to il Magnifico's Luigia, only four years old and with the figure of a spindle. It's a long time to wait until she's nubile.'

'He's hardly nubile himself yet.'

'Don't you believe it. Can men be nubile? Well, if so, that one can and already is. Like Ganymede he's being seduced by every woman and every man with a taste for boys, all of them intent on either keeping him straight or bending him. Who would not be the prize in such a contest? It's hardly surprising if he's not very keen on being betrothed to whey-faced Luigia.'

'It's a matter of duty, not taste. Lorenzo wants to heal the rift in the family. The betrothal is his masterstroke to make the two one.'

'It will get rid of a daughter without payment of a dowry.'

'Cynic!'

'Realist. You philosophers, you are so busy looking for the causes that you don't notice the effects.'

'What are you talking about?'

'Don't ask me!' Filippino laughed in that infectious way of his that dissolved all disagreements. And then he sobered, in the quick and changeable weather that was Filippino Lippi. 'It is good to see you smiling, Tommaso.'

'You have been avoiding me.'

'It is true. Forgive me. I haven't known what to say since it happened. You know how I struggle with words. Forgive me if I seem to have avoided you. Wait – I have something that will speak for me.' So saying, he went back inside the workshop.

I could hear Angelo Poliziano within, quoting the lines from his poem on Giuliano's Joust which had informed the painter.

You would call the foam real, the sea real,
real the shell and real the blowing wind;
you would see the lightning in the goddess's eyes,
the sky and the elements laughing about her.'

When Filippino returned he handed me a piece of folded parchment, inside of which was a loose sheet with a drawing of Elena that he had made from memory. He had captured her likeness perfectly and I gazed on the lovely face of my wife, her eyes lowered, her hair falling softly over her shoulders.

'I wish I could have drawn her smile, but it was beyond me.'

Tears welled.

'You know, you should marry again.'

'And suffer loss again? I could not bear it. No, I shall never marry.'

'When you fall off your horse, get straight back on it, that's what I say.'

It was an unfortunate analogy and, realising it, Filippino coloured.

'Oh God... I'm sorry... I wasn't thinking. Elena... horse...'

'You are right, Pippo, your pictures are more eloquent.'

Filippino stared at the ground, his mouth open and slack. I squeezed his shoulder, thanked him for the picture and told him to keep practising with words.

'Meet me for chess sometime,' he said. 'I have a new piece. A bishop by Ghirlandaio.'

Somehow Filippino was persuading every major artist of the time to carve a chess piece for him. Perhaps it was the air of competition, following the knight Leonardo had carved for him as a gift, that made all comply with his odd wish. I agreed to meet for a game, and he went off muttering that he had to go and see Piero di Cosimo about carving a queen.

When I was alone again, I felt as Orpheus must have felt when he saw Eurydice in Hades. How greedy his eyes. How unobtainable their object. I kept opening and closing the fold of parchment, feeding on its contents, until at last I put it inside my jacket, next to my heart.

3 THE WRONG LOVE
1482

RETURNING TO THE PALAZZO DE' MEDICI, LORENZO IL
Magnifico walked at the head of the long train that was his family
and companions. The Pierfranceschi brothers went arm-in-arm
behind him, Lorenzino staring straight ahead while his silky-haired
brother smiled at the people doffing their caps, drawing the gazes
of the lascivious and the envious.

A friar coming out of San Lorenzo halted to let the party pass,
which it did, oblivious to him. I stopped to let him go on his way
and his look of indignation softened as he thanked me. I caught up
with Angelo Poliziano and Ficino.

'Wasn't that the Dominican who has been driving people from
the church?' Angelo asked. 'What is his name? I can't remember
but I hear that San Lorenzo is lucky to draw two score these days,
and most of those women and children. It's not surprising: he has
the face of Nemesis. Marsilio,' he said, turning to the philosopher,
'while I have you to myself, tell me about the castration of Uranus
because I do not understand its meaning, other than literal. If all
myth has deeper significance, if the stories of the gods are for our
self-understanding...'

'More than that, my Angelo. They convey the deepest
mysteries.'

'And often one can discover them for oneself with reflection,
experience and a flash of insight. But this one... I need your
guidance.'

'It is a violent myth about the divorce of heaven and earth. We
could understand the earth to represent our physical body, and
heaven our divine essence. Once upon a time men lived in heaven
here on earth. As Hesiod tells us, every night Uranus covered Gaia.
So men hunted by day but at night they rested under the starry sky
and remembered themselves. Re-membered themselves. These

34

roofs, these houses,' Ficino pointed to the jutting cornices above us, 'what are they but the sickle blade, cutting off heaven? In protecting ourselves against the sun and the elements, we become divorced from them, forget who we are and mourn for the golden age. But from the genitals of his father that Saturn cast into the sea Venus was born. She provides our route of return to our true source; love is the way in which we may become whole. Because that is what Man is, potentially: the union of heaven and earth.'

His words made me curl up over my wound and I fell out of step with my friends. Love. She might have been born from castration, but castration may also be born from Love. I had dared to surrender utterly to Aphrodite and I had been left a cripple with a wound that would not heal. While the rest of the party turned into the Palazzo de' Medici, I veered away, unable suddenly to bear their cheerfulness. In the courtyard, Angelo's voice lifted in a song and other voices joined in chorus, making the fine vaulted arcade and galleries of the courtyard echo with their harmonies. The notes of the hymn fluttered like the rose petals that were raining on the gentle sea in Botticelli's painting.

Roses... I remembered a rose falling from a window in the Palazzo de' Pazzi, the sign from a young girl that she loved me – and suddenly the roses were all thorns raining on me like daggers. Gouts of pain were coming now, pounding in my heart as memories of a lost wife became as tangible as the massive wall of the palazzo I was leaning against. I let the darkness wash over me. It seemed then that nothing could reach me, nothing could pull me back to this world, but that I must journey on to the depths of Hades as I had done so often since Elena died. I let the images come, of her brown hair waving across the pillows on the night we were married; of her rounded belly filling with our child; of her frequent laughter at my foolishness; of her wisdom as she explained the mysteries of womankind to me. I see the stillborn boy covered in afterbirth, and Elena drained and exhausted by the trials she had suffered. I see Lorenzo's infant son, born at the same time, suckling at her full breasts.

I used to spend many hours in copying Plato. It was my leisure, my meditation, my income. Each copy was my attempt at perfection, perfection not only of handwriting and page design, but of myself. It was my via sacra. I would sit at my desk by the window and, each time I needed to sit back and stretch, my gaze would fall on my wife, her head bowed over her needlework, her lustrous hair tucked behind her ears – for at home I forbade the netting, the snood, the linen veil of the married woman, as I forbade all cosmetics and jewellery. I would sit back and gaze on the untainted beauty, the perfection of my wife. And then I was content. Sometimes she accused me of neglecting her. Once she said that if she were to fall out of the window the same time as my Plato, she would stand small chance of being saved. That stung and for a week I gave up my copying. Then she asked me to return to it, saying that she preferred being neglected to living with an irritable bear with fleas in its fur.

My breath is short now and I am panting, unable to face any more memories. Tears course down my face.

'My son?'

I opened my eyes to the young Dominican friar, his chin blue with stubble, his eyes black under the cowl, his face overshadowed by a great hooked nose. Girolamo Savonarola, that was his name. I remembered now. His mission to speak bluntly of holy things in the church patronised by the Medici, where the very stone had been polished to a high sheen by the cadences of the most eloquent preachers of our time, had been a disaster. Men of highly-wrought sensibility had been offended by his tearful exhortations to study scripture and complained that his voice grated on their cultured ears. Lorenzo, who had said that the friar's inelegant sermons were causing great distress to the corpse of his grandfather, which was trying to rest under the floor before the altar, was negotiating with the prior of San Marco to have the young man transferred elsewhere.

'What ails you?' Fra Girolamo asked, laying his hands gently on my tense shoulders. His piercing eyes were the colour of gun metal. 'The pain of the world is insignificant compared to the suffering of Christ.'

'I know, *frate*.'

He brought his powerful face close to mine. His breath smelt stale, as it does after a fast. 'The love you love,' he said, 'is the wrong love.'

That was what he said before he turned and went north up the street towards the monastery of San Marco. Dominicans are the learned friars; it is the Franciscans who speak of love. I gazed after him, wondering how he had known the content of my heart, and what his words had meant.

4 THE NIGHT THE SKY CAUGHT FIRE 1482

LATE ONE EVENING AFTER A DAY'S LABOUR AT THE DESK IN Ficino's villa, I went for a long walk up the hill above Careggi and into the wilder parts, but the smell of the woods, of pine and chestnuts, conjured up the image of Giuliano the hunter so vividly that the pain of his loss made me veer away and take a track down to where the Villa Medici lay below. Almost abandoned since Lorenzo's mother had died in March of that year, it stood in a pool of sadness. Lorenzo visited it occasionally but only briefly. It was getting dark, the villa was deserted and there was no one to be seen in the fields. At the place where my wife had fallen from her horse in wild flight from our enemies I laid face down with my arms outstretched as if to embrace her. And then I began to cry and as I cried I felt my tears run into the soil and I prayed that they might nourish her spirit in Hades. You see, even in grief the Christian in me was contradicted. I had read too much literature of the ancients and was ready to feed the earth with my blood if it would give the spirit of my wife some substance. But none of this gave comfort, only deepened the sense of loss.

When I returned to the villa, a crescent Moon had appeared in the west, attended by bright Venus. I found Ficino on the terrace staring up at the sky through a sextant. 'Make a note, Tommaso. The Moon is newborn, has just entered Taurus, and is eighteen degrees below Venus.'

I went indoors to fetch my notebook. I had become adept at writing by starlight and had the eyes of an owl.

'And bring your figure,' he called after me. 'This is a most propitious time for the operation.'

We had been making it for a month, a cross cast in silver and bearing Ficino's design of the sign and symbols of Venus which I had engraved myself. A talisman to restore me to gaiety and health, neither of which, at that moment, I particularly wanted. He placed it in a flowerbed and directed it towards Venus, cupped as she was by the Moon, to be impregnated by her influence.

Was it the countering, negative influence within me that made the horizon bloom red? I thought so at the time. Waves of red light suddenly arose where the sun had set an hour or more earlier. As we both stood there, silent and transfixed, flames began to belch into the sky as if the sun itself were being consumed and would never rise again. We Italians are short in stature but Marsilio Ficino was shorter than most, almost dwarfish. He had fair hair falling in waves and a face wrinkled with many lines and furrows, and yet he was a handsome man, his features open and his eyes frank. He had a way of staring into the air as if communing with subtle spirits. He stood there now, facing west, his arms upraised to the sky as if to receive the cosmos and its message. I dared say nothing to disturb him and had to restrain any expression of the terror I felt. At last, coming back to himself, he turned to face me, the side of his face illuminated by the red light in the sky.

'Tommaso,' he said, weakly, almost gasping. 'This is a sign of the antichrist. This is where the end begins.' Possessed by the god, he was predicting the future as soundly as blind Tiresias.

'What do you mean?'

'It is to end in fire.'

'What is?'

'Our work. Our truth. Our philosophy. Our age. It will burn to ash. But you, you will take the seeds of our work north and plant them in new ground.' He picked up the silver talisman. 'Destroy it. You do not want the influences that have gone into this metal.'

It had cost me too much to throw it away. I stored it until the next time I went into the city and could visit the silversmith and have it melted down. But of course I forgot, and having worked its way to the bottom of my clothes chest, it stayed there for the next twelve years. By the time I came across it again, Ficino's prophecy was in the dawn of its fulfilment. Then I remembered that night, and knew that it had all begun in 1482, the year when *The Platonic Theology* was published, the year that Sandro unveiled his Venus, the year when Savonarola first came to Florence and preached to an empty church at San Lorenzo, the year the sky caught fire.

London, November 23rd, 1505

He has the face of a friendly, trusting rat, if there is such a thing. How fine to hold those sharp cheekbones in my hands again, and stare into those small, bright eyes, to push my soft, Italian nose against that pointed Dutch one. Of course, Thomas More possesses him. It is good to see them walking together again, arm-in-arm along Bucklersbury. Am I envious? A little. I would have Erasmus for my own, as would Colet and every other man in the circle. He has a facet for each of us. But for More – watching those two together, I see again Angelo Poliziano and Giovanni Pico della Mirandola: two men whose love for one another transcends common friendship and strays nowhere near that other common relationship between men. Platonic. The only word for it: Platonic love. The ecstasy of good company.

More, more – so often on Erasmus's lips. 'Tommaso, have you kept up your writing? I want more of it.'

No, I have not kept it up, and now that my reader is back, I am dashing it off in a frenzy.

'I want to hear more about Poliziano.'

'More wants to hear more about Pico della Mirandola; Colet is only interested in Marsilio Ficino and Savonarola. It will be a long book, and one ending in multiple deaths.'

'A tragedy, then.'

'It is not in me, I think, to write a divine comedy.'

Erasmus looked at me askance. 'Why not? Tragedy is only unresolved comedy. Has it occurred to you that your story did not stop in 1499?'

5 PLATO RESTORED
1483

AFTER THE PUBLICATION OF *THE PLATONIC THEOLOGY* MY task had been to go through a copy of the book and correct every mistake the printers had made.

'Printers?' Ficino had cried in despair when he saw what a pottage of error Miscomini had made of his book. 'Mis-printers, more like! It is your fault, Tommaso. You are to blame for this. You should never have made the choice on appearance alone. The print may be beautiful as print goes, but it is useless if it is not accurate!'

The correction of this book, in preparation for another printing, delayed completion of Ficino's translation of all Plato's writings from Greek into Latin. With his faith in Florentine printers destroyed, when the great work, his life's work, was finished, he decided it should be published in Venice, but he could not allow his work to make such a journey without some safeguard. 'Tommaso,' he told me, 'I need you to make a copy.'

The complete works of Plato and all Ficino's commentaries.

'What else have you got to do?' he asked, to which there was no answer, and I went to the city to buy fresh stocks of parchment and quills. This served me in two ways. Firstly, it gave the opportunity to spend an hour with my old friend and master, the bookseller Vespasiano da Bisticci, and listen to him growl and grumble about the decline of civilisation with the invention of printing. Secondly, it gave me another taste of city life, a taste so disgusting that when I returned to Careggi it was with a new sense of gratitude for the task ahead of me. If work was to be my therapy, with such a weight of it there was some hope of a cure. What I did not do, could not do, was to look further, beyond the work. Nor, I think, could Ficino. He had, after all, dedicated his life to the task; who could blame him for delaying its end? The future after Plato was a black void.

Whenever I could, I asked my philosopher questions, a few of them profound but many of them stemming from mere curiosity, such as the one about the history of the Platonic Academy. Rumours were abounding of it being a secret society of great antiquity.

'I have heard the story,' he said, 'that after Plato's Academy was closed by the Emperor Justinian its members went to Persia, were there at the birth of Islam, were behind the Greek learning of the Arabs and the rise of the universities; that many generations later they returned to Greece, to Mistra, and counted Michael Psellus amongst their number and, later, in our own time, George Gemistos Plethon. I have heard that Cardinal Bessarion himself was a member, that the order was put under the protection of Cosimo de' Medici and that I am its current leader.'

'Is it true?' I asked breathlessly.

In his customary way, he answered with a question. 'Why do you want it to be true?'

Why indeed. Because it thrilled me to be a part of a line of souls, quite possibly transmigrating souls, that spanned history; I wished to be authenticated by the past, made real and purposeful. I wanted to know that my forebears had been there in Egypt, in Athens, in Arabia, in Mistra.

'You were there,' said Ficino, reading my mind.

'So the soul does transmigrate?'

'That is not my meaning. There are two ways, Tommaso, the way of the sun and the way of the moon. Women see clearly by the light of the moon, men do not – that is why Theseus could only enter the labyrinth with the aid and foresight of Ariadne. The way of the moon is dark and mysterious, full of ciphers and symbols, secrets and initiations. It leads through twisting tunnels and what do you get at the end? A minotaur!'

'To be slain.'

'Indeed. It is a valid way, but long and arduous and littered with the bones of seekers. Or at least, the bones of their wits.' He chuckled. 'The way of the sun, of Apollo and not Dionysus, is not so appealing, often arid and harsh, full of discipline and austerity. On this path you do not accumulate knowledge but surrender what you know. It is a hard route but a quicker one. I am telling you this, Tommaso, to warn you not to go wandering off down tempting byways such as enquiring after the history of the Platonic Academy. *In the heavens he hath set a tabernacle for the sun.*'

'I am that tabernacle.'

'No. This is the point: you are that sun. That's the very crux of it. When you become one with God, who then is Pythagoras, Hermes or Plato? Merely embodiments of yourself. If the soul transmigrates it is because it is still lost, still does not realise who it is in truth. The way of the sun is to know yourself through reason, through self-examination, by discriminating between the true and the false within yourself.' He stared at me, expectantly.

'What is it?' I asked.

'That was it.'

'What?'

'I have told you the heart of the mystery. That was your initiation.'

'What, no rites or ceremonies of which I may not speak?'

'You will hold your own; when the time comes that you understand my words as a living reality, you will fall to your knees in the light of your own Sun.'

In the spring there was an eclipse of the full moon, which Ficino and I watched from the terrace of his villa. The following day Angelo Poliziano arrived and told us of many strange things that had happened in the city, including a few sudden and unaccountable deaths. He did not himself believe there was any connection between them and the eclipse but he enjoyed a good story, and even more he enjoyed teasing Ficino with curiosities, for

Ficino took such things very seriously. Divine Providence, said the philosopher, shows itself by natural signs. Poliziano grunted. Since having become a professor he had grown sceptical of our mystery religion. I had lived with him long enough to know the cause, and it was in language. When the philosophers spoke in abstractions about things without form, the brilliant scholar simply did not understand. His brain lost the structure of understanding and floundered. He thought – and wrote – in images, and when there were no images he struggled as if in mud.

I sat between the two of them, believing with Ficino or scoffing with Poliziano, depending on which of them I faced at any time. I have to record, however, that for a month after the eclipse it rained steadily and did not stop raining until the Florentines brought the miracle-working statue of Our Lady from Imprunetta to the city. Then the rain stopped. And the King of France died and was succeeded by Charles, eighth of that name.

Around the same time, Angelo's brother also died and Angelo brought his widowed sister-in-law and two nephews to live with him in Florence. He did not intend for the cruel custom of *tornata*, according to which Cammilla should have abandoned her sons and returned to her own family, to make orphans of his nephews, so he took the family into his house on the Via de' Fossi. But it is never easy to fly in the face of custom, and as the rumours began to spread of the scholar's bordello and the infamous practices he indulged not only with his sister-in-law but with his nephews, Angelo fled to Fiesole and the villa that Lorenzo had given him, taking his sister Maria for company.

'What will you do when you have finished the Plato?' he asked me one day at Careggi.

'Will I ever finish? I am like Sisyphus – every time I reach the summit of the mountain with my boulder, I lose hold of it and it rolls to the foot again. I sometimes think,' I confided in him, 'that Ficino hesitates to finish his life's work lest his life ends with it.'

Angelo looked at my copy. 'What a labour of love.'

44

'Especially when you know it's going to end on the fire. Once the printers have torn out its pages and spattered them with ink, the fire is its certain fate. But it is the ideas which are important.'

'Should the day ever dawn when you get your boulder to the top of the mountain, I'd like you to come and live with me in my villa. It is nothing grand – very small in fact, as small as this place of Ficino's – but it is my own home and you are welcome to share it. My duties in the university are ever-increasing and there is too much work for me to concentrate on my own studies. When Ficino has no further need of you, I could do with your help and I can afford to employ you. Speed up.'

To my surprise, the offer was appealing. I don't think at that time I confessed even to myself the nature of the attraction, and I shrink from confessing it now. Put it this way – apart from Ficino's mother and nieces, who lived in his town house, I had not spoken to a woman in a year. It was not that I wished for a new wife or anything of that kind; just that, in the seat of my soul, I needed female company. It was not Angelo I wished to live with, it was Maria.

Throughout Elena's travail, Maria had been there; she had helped me bury my stillborn son; she had stood by me as I buried my wife. Maria was as much my sister as Angelo's, and in her company there was some cure against becoming a ghost myself. Maria did not philosophise about bereavement. In those grey times when I was being sucked down into despair, she put her arms around me and warmed my soul back into life by mere touch.

All things do come to an end, even if it is in a petering fashion. With each passing day there were fewer pages of the Plato to copy than the day before. In late summer I passed the middle of the book and thereafter there was more weight on the left of it than on the right. The work drew to its close with the year and by the Feast of the Nativity I had completed my copy. But as I put down my quill with a great inward cry of thanks to God, Ficino told me to read the copy through from the beginning to check for mistakes. He was becoming a Penelope, each night unravelling what she had woven during the day so as to delay her suitors.

The publication of the Plato was being paid for by a young merchant of patrician family called Filippo Valori; during Epiphany he arranged for the printing to be done by Lorenzo Francisco de Alopa in Venice and had a contract drawn up.

'What kind of type fount does he use?' I asked.

'I am not sure,' said Valori. 'Does it matter? The important thing is that Francisco is known for his accuracy.'

'That is an oxymoron, a contradiction in terms. There is no such thing as an accurate printer,' I said.

Valori smiled. 'How can there be? Is printing not the devil's invention? The work is bound to be attended by imps.'

I liked Valori. As the new year of 1484 opened up into spring, I think he began to despair himself of ever seeing the Plato completed. He took Ficino away to his own estate at Maiano to make the final revision 'in peace', by which I think he meant, 'where I can keep an eye on you.'

'I set you free,' Ficino told me with a smile as he set off with his burden for Maiano.

6 THE VILLA BRUSCOLI
1483

I TOOK THE ROAD FROM CAREGGI TO FIESOLE, CROSSING the valley between the hills and going up to the Badia, where Angelo was waiting for me. Together we rode up a lane, so small and hidden I had never noticed it before, ascending Fiesole on its darkest side.

'There are witches here,' Angelo told me. 'They live upstream a little, in the shadows among the rocks, but on my property.'

Now all men love their villas, but where most extol their vineyards and olive groves, he boasted about his 'nest' of witches.

I looked to see if he were smiling, but he was not; he was quite serious. The villa was small and on that cold, windy, forested side of Fiesole where few live. Under the previous tenant the estate had fallen into ruin and the terraces had disappeared under scrub, yet Angelo loved the place, relishing all its quirks and peculiarities, for it was home and, to one born when the sun was in Cancer, one who had been orphaned young, home meant more than heaven.

Apart from the witches, the Villa Bruscoli had another attraction. Behind the house and down the hill a few paces was a natural grotto. A spring issued from the rock to run through crevices filled with hound's tooth fern and trefoil, pouring in a little waterfall into a stone basin. A statue of the Virgin had been placed at the spring's head, which Angelo explained as 'a Christian conversion of an element of nature'. This site, he said, had once been dedicated to the Muses and was becoming for him a constant source of inspiration.

'It is called Fontelucente. I come here often, to compose a piece of prose or verse in my mind before I cut my quills.' In his own estimation, since moving to the villa he had written his best work yet. It was small wonder that Poliziano was happy to have witches and Helicon's fount where other men only have statues and fishponds.

Just approaching his villa made me feel better. Though so close, Fiesole is very different in nature from Careggi and her open meadows on bare rock. The hill of Fiesole, surely Dante's model for Purgatory, is a conical mound carved with terraces where the ascending paths wind under the retaining walls of villa gardens. Between the stones of those walls lie miniature landscapes, little caves at eye-level in which grow ferns, harebells and mosses. It was raining as we arrived and I did not care. The beauty of the place deepened in the mist, while the dripping water gathered into little streams that shared our path.

The first time I had met Maria had been during the great flood of Florence, when Poliziano was away and I was charged with looking after his house. I had rowed in a boat with Botticelli and Filippino to check on its welfare and had seen what appeared to be the ghost of Angelo at an upper window. Unbeknownst to Angelo, his little sister had run away from Montepulciano and was now squatting in his house along with his cousin. When I mounted the stairs and met her face to face, she had stared at me with an expression of surprise. The shock of familiarity. I suffered it, too, but then I had good cause, for she was the image of her brother. But who did I remind her of? She never said.

When I arrived at the Villa Bruscoli, she wore the same kind of look, even though she was expecting me. She gazed at me, her mouth slightly open, her eyes moist seemingly with wonder, and then she grew flustered as if embarrassed. I cut through any awkwardness by embracing her fondly as my sister. She returned my embrace, grateful and relieved. Her hair had been washed in rosemary and lavender. It smelt of woman. I inhaled.

I had lived with Poliziano as his scribe and companion when he himself had lived with the Medici. I had lived with Maria before, having taken her in to my own house during Angelo's exile from Florence. I had never lived with them both together and under their own roof. It was quite different. In each other's company they regressed in years and reverted to childhood. They took me inside as if into their secret den, glowing with pleasure as they showed me, their first guest, my room. Maria, whose worldly duty was housekeeping for her brother, had put there a vase of sprawling flowers she had picked from the kitchen garden.

'She's becoming a witch herself,' Angelo remarked affectionately. 'How often I find her bent double in the herb patch, muttering to her plants.'

Assiduous in her studies, Maria was fast becoming a learned lady, able now to read and write in Greek as well as she could in Latin. But she bore the air of the Cumean Sibyl and seemed able to see things obscure to the rest of us. Under her brother's protection and with his encouragement she lived a life denied to most women outside of a convent's walls, a life of study and contemplation. Though she was obedient to Angelo, she was completely free. This most rare quality in a woman made her both attractive and remote. My heart had stirred at seeing her as it may stir at seeing one's native home after a long journey in foreign lands. Her black hair burnt brown by the sun, her round eyes, deeply lidded, her aquiline nose, her large, strong teeth: these were not the classical elements of beauty, and yet they were the features best suited to her nature, which was open, friendly and generous. Maria listened; Maria laughed; Maria was *simpatica*.

Friendship between man and woman is so rare that even the ancient writers do not to my knowledge discuss it, except in elevated terms such as the story of Socrates's instruction in love by Diotima. Certainly I have not met any contemporary of mine who has experienced it, but such friendship is as capable of profundity as that between man and man, perhaps more so. Even brothers and sisters do not, so far as I know, experience the same level of love and honesty that Maria and I achieved. Therefore let it be said here that a man may love a woman who is neither his wife nor his sister but simply his friend, and turn to her, talk to her, be pleased to come home to her, without ever desiring her in his bed, since such a desire would dishonour her. *Convert the object of beauty into an idea of beauty*, Ficino had taught me. *Reflect that the body in which beauty shines is not the source from which it springs. In your appreciation of beauty, restrict yourself to the sense of sight and of hearing. These two faculties are servants of reason, unlike touch and taste. This way you may feed your soul with beauty without being prey to the miseries that attend sensual love.* I had loved once as a man loves a woman, desiring to beget children, and the misery of loss will haunt me forever. I had no intention of repeating that step on the ladder of ascent. So with Maria I learnt to love the qualities of nature, to appreciate her beauty through the mind and the faculty of reason.

One evening in May we dined outside in the garden for the first time in the year. Little moths sizzled in the flames of lanterns, the shadows were fragrant with herbs, and the crickets made a carpet of sound over the Arno valley. I became aware of Maria staring at me, but she was not looking at me so much as into me.

'What is it?' I asked.

She blinked and now regarded me in the usual way that one human being looks at another. 'I see children all about you, many children.'

My wife had died without issue other than a stillborn. As I had no intention of remarrying, I greeted her words cynically. 'What are you saying?'

She studied me with that penetrating stare again. 'You will have many children, who you will raise in truth and they will found a new nation.'

I looked to Angelo for help. He was grinning at his sister. 'O Sibyl of treeless Avernus: your meaning is obscure. Repeat your prophecy.'

'Do not mock me, brother,' said Maria tartly. 'You think you are learned because you have read all the books in the world. But you see nothing and know less!'

I was impressed. I had never heard anyone speak to Poliziano that way; and I had never heard a woman speak thus to any man.

At the university, Poliziano was introducing his students to the ancient poetry of Greece. Sometimes, after a long day, he did not return at night. Maria said nothing about it except that 'he will be staying at the city house'. I wanted to ask her about Cammilla but did not wish to offend with mere curiosity. Besides, there was no need. Within the walls of this home, the truth was both obvious and unsurprising. Angelo's mind was so fully occupied with ancient Greece and Rome that ancient morals had become more natural to him than Judaeo-Christian ones, such as the Levitican law which states that a man may not marry his dead brother's wife. If some of the rumours were true and Angelo was in love with Cammilla, the only thing preventing him making a legal match would be Christian custom, that and his being a priest. But where he could buy himself out of the priesthood, he could not buy himself out from custom, not this time. So we lived our lives under the protection of Lorenzo and the common law. In Angelo's frequent absence, I looked after Maria.

While we men fretted over right and wrong, in Maria the disparate worlds of pagan and Christian met in harmony. Each day she would go to the spring's head at Fontelucente with a prayer for the Virgin and flowers for the Muses. She also went down in to the valley with gifts for the witches. Angelo firmly prohibited this, but she went when he was absent from the house, and begged forgiveness of God for the disobedience which came to her as naturally as obedience.

'Angelo quotes Plutarch,' she told me, 'and says that witches have artificial eyes which they can put in and take out at their pleasure, just as old people do with their spectacles and false teeth. He says they put their eyes in when they go to the city, and take them out at home.'

'It is a metaphor for busybodies,' I explained, 'people who only have eyes for other people's business and are senseless with regard to their own.'

'He says a witch has the eyes of an owl or a spy and can find out a grain of sand, and bury herself in the smallest cranny. But as soon as she gets home, she takes out her eyes and puts them in her pocket. Then she sits there spinning yarn and humming a little song to herself.'

'He's just trying to frighten you.'

Maria loved her brother's stories, culled from the ancient poets and not from the lives of saints, told to her of a summer evening in the olive grove, or of a winter's night by the fireside, as if she were five years old. This brother and sister, who had been parted by fate and custom for fifteen years, had since their reunion been enjoying a belated childhood together. At home the Professor of Latin and Greek was as likely to be chasing his squealing sister round the house as making ready a lecture on Homer. When it was cool in the evening and we gathered at the hearth, Angelo dismissed the servants and sat on a low stool, possessive of the log basket and his function as fuel-provider, grudgingly allowing Maria to feed the fire with kindling and pine cones. They treated fire-feeding as ritual and not as labour, and between them always got a roaring blaze going. Then, after an invocation to Hestia, the stories would begin.

'I think what Angelo is trying to tell you,' I said to her, 'is that the women in the valley are busybodies and gossips, and that you should not be too familiar with them.'

'The trouble with men is that you sit in towers and theorise,' she said. 'You have lost touch with the world.'

London, November 27th, 1505

Gathered in St Paul's this evening was a large and mixed congregation, a motley throng of lawyers, guildsmen of the city companies, merchants, artisans, canons of the cathedral and divines. Most were there, of course, out of curiosity. The word has spread through London that the son of the old mayor, Sir Henry Colet, has returned from Oxford to take up one of the highest clerical posts in the land. John Colet is a literary man, a Master of Arts who studied grammar and rhetoric at Oxford. How does he have the audacity to stand in the pulpit of London's cathedral and preach? So they came to hear what he has to say, and found themselves pinned by the ears. Colet is using all his literary skills to understand and expound the Gospels, stripping them of centuries of accumulated idea and opinion. He stood erect in the pulpit and, in a ringing voice that has been trained on the precepts of Cicero, addressed the Londoners as if they were the Corinthians and he St Paul himself.

He accused them of being divided and factional, of being carnal and not spiritual, of praying to martyrs and saints and not to Christ. 'Look at this Church,' he cried, 'festooned with the tawdry baubles of superstition.' He threw out his arm to indicate the chapels, the carved wooden screens, the tapers, the images. From the ceiling hang standards, some richly hued, others torn and colourless with age; in the little chantry chapels are a host of images of saints, each of them venerated by candles; everywhere tombs of dead crusaders with their trophies and arms hanging above. You cannot move in St Paul's without stumbling on such memorials and a hundred little sanctuaries to private saints made in the patron's memory. The cathedral is like the city, a barnacle heap of one thing on top of another, a very encrustation of life which, as it grows, becomes harder and more fixed. Colet has already cleared the place of the vendors and money-lenders, but these more superstitious and sentimental fixtures are harder to sweep out.

'As the Church, so the hearts of men,' Colet cried. 'Our hearts and minds are stuffed with half-understood opinions of half-learned men, and we shuffle from one holy day to the next, as if following the Calendar year is all it takes to be a Christian. It does not. It takes more. And before we begin we must strip out all this stuff and cleanse the inner sanctum. We are not Christians until we are practising Christians, and by practising Christians I do not mean the practice of ritual observance. I would have you be the kind of men who love their neighbours, and if you would be that kind of men, then listen now to the words of St Paul.

'In this work, we work with God. You are like a house being built to his plan. I, like a master-builder who knows his job, by the grace God has given me, lay the foundation; someone else builds upon it. I only say this, let the builder be careful how he builds! The foundation is laid already, and no one can lay another, for it is Jesus Christ himself. But any man who builds on the foundation using as his material gold, silver, precious stones, wood, hay or straw, must know that each man's work will one day be shown for what it is. The day will show it plainly enough, for the day will arise in a blaze of fire…'

Suddenly there was a sense of blockage in my ears and that sudden high ringing sound which is troubling me more and more these days. I closed my nose and snorted to clear the passages, but the ringing persisted. I missed the rest of the sermon until suddenly Colet's voice was very clear indeed: *'Don't you realise that you yourselves are the temple of God, and that God's Spirit lives in you?'*

Feeling less like a temple of God than His bell tower, I thought about what John was saying. What Ficino had said to me – 'You are that Sun' – John also knew: the essential innermost unity of Man and God. But Colet could hardly declare that truth from the pulpit, especially in the presence of the bishop, who is such an enthusiastic hunter after heretics.

The sermon continued for over an hour, with Colet expounding the virtues of the true Christian life, a life which seems to others to be folly – what St Paul calls 'the folly of the Cross'. No one is in any doubt as to Colet's intention: he and the Apostle together are going to clear this Church of its accumulations of sin and false doctrine. All the musty tomes of learned opinion shall be dust before his broom; centuries of superstition and corruption shall be scrubbed off the good, bare wood that is Christ's church. I swear the very cobwebs in the cathedral shrank back, knowing their end is nigh.

And now everyone knows it, that if the new dean has studied theology privately and not in the Schools, it is so that he may keep clear of theologians. Colet is a literary man, and he has come to know God through the Word. Naturally this enflames those who have spent their lives in the formal study of scripture, and who are advancing their careers in the usual, elbow-bruising fashion. They resent this upstart who has gained his benefice by the preferment of the king.

My skin began to prickle and I glanced about. Sometimes you know you are being stared at without seeing the eyes. The cowled head of a blackfriar was turned in my direction; his face deep in shadow, I was being watched by an empty space. A Dominican – Domini-cane, hound of the Lord – is on my scent.

When Colet descended from the pulpit we, his companions, gathered protectively about him, needing to shield him from both well-wishers and critics; but we were too few to form a tight circle and, besides, we had to step back when the bishop approached.

'I congratulate you, Dean, on an interesting sermon, yes, most interesting and illuminating; but I have to say that I am in awe of your temerity, that you should find within yourself the authority to speak directly from the Gospels. That is not usually done for the laity.'

'Authority comes from God,' said Colet, hoarse after his sermon. 'The disciples had only Jesus as a master, and I would be a disciple of the Lord himself, not of his interpreters.'

The bishop's feigned affability vanished, revealing fury. Here was the face of a Church that does not wish its ways to be disturbed.

'What gives you –' he began, but Erasmus intervened bodily and hustled the dean out of the church.

I kept close to the group. When I glanced back at the cathedral, the blackfriar was still watching me but now he had his cowl thrown back. He is not an English Dominican but an Italian one, I am sure of it.

7 THE SECRET OF GOOD GOVERNMENT 1484

LORENZO DE' MEDICI LOOKED AT ME WITH A DOCTOR'S EYES, detached and yet compassionate. He sat comfortably in his chair, father of his city, father of us all, and let me speak without limit of time. And I spoke in a rambling fashion, now choking on grief, now taking command of myself, answering my own questions, prescribing my own therapies.

'According to St Paul,' he said, cutting across my fumbling speech, 'if you are bound to a wife, do not seek to be loosened. But if you are loosened, do not seek to be bound.'

'I thought you had called me here to say you had found a new wife for me.'

'For any other man, that would be my solution, but not for you. What do you want, Tommaso, apart from the impossible?'

'I want work, but not of the kind I'm having to do now that the Plato's finished, bits of this and that in exchange for accommodation. I want steady craft, my craft. I want to wake each morning with a sense of purpose; I want to finish each day with a sense of completion. I want to copy books. Not the romances and histories that most men want, but books I may learn from, although preferably not Plato. Not for a while.'

He nodded, understanding. 'Tommaso, you know I cannot afford such luxuries now, not at the moment. My wealth was exhausted by the war.'

I was disappointed and it showed. 'Then why did you send for me, Magnifico?'

He leant forward and gazed into my eyes. 'Angelo tells me you cry in the night. Tommaso, what can I say? You must learn to transmute grief into joy.'

'Have you succeeded in that alchemy?'

57

'Ficino once said that Giuliano and I were one soul in two bodies. Now we share one body. There is no need to grieve. If this philosophy of Plato is true, if our Christian faith is true, there is no need to grieve.'

'It would help if I had something to concentrate on.'

'Go and see my cousin, Lorenzino. He is commissioning manuscripts.'

In the summer months, Lorenzo di Pierfrancesco de' Medici lived in a newly built villa called Castello, about ten miles north of the city, beyond Careggi. There this young man, barely twenty at the time, often held symposia and I went to one with Botticelli. I knew everyone there – all familiar faces from the Platonic Academy, including Ficino himself.

The topic of discussion was good government. The company was in agreement that tyranny – benign or otherwise – is not good; that good government depends on a council of the wise. But how do you find wise men? And, having found them, how do you get the people to recognise them as such? And obey them? Lorenzino was of the opinion that they needed to be well-born and well-educated but Ficino disagreed, saying that children of the city should be selected for their merits and then trained up for the task of government.

On the wall of the chamber was the *Venus*. I gazed at the goddess and she gazed back at me with that quiet smile that offered so much and gave nothing. Now sixteen, Giovanni di Pierfrancesco, with his high, clear brow and large eyes, did more of the talking than his elder brother, was animated while the more reflective Lorenzino remained quiet. These two seemed to be a re-cast of Lorenzo and Giuliano, with everyone captivated by the younger one and deferential to the elder.

'Are we boring you, Tommaso?' Giovanni asked, snatching my attention from naked Love. 'What do you consider to be the secret of good government?'

Caught dreaming, I grasped the first idea that came to mind.

'The secret of good government begins with the individual. Men must learn self-discipline before they put themselves forward to govern others, learn to curb their appetites, to develop reason, to act for the greater good and not their own self-interest. Therefore, the secret of good government is education in virtue. It is our duty, as educators, to raise the governors of tomorrow.'

'Bravo!' Ficino exclaimed, smiling on me with approval, he, my own educator. There was general appreciation for what I had said, but Giovanni stared at me with no smile on his lovely face. A watchful seraph; a recording angel.

'I see you do not just copy out Plato's words but read them with understanding,' said Lorenzino.

'I have several of the dialogues by heart,' I replied, looking into his light-dark eyes.

'And do you yourself have this virtue you would teach others?' Giovanni asked, at which the company dissolved in laughter, each man vying with another to list my faults. It was true enough: I am not patient and do not practise forbearance. They did agree I have fortitude, but only when it comes to copying Plato for years on end. At this even Ficino laughed.

A week later came a commission for a fine copy of the works of Hermes Trismegistus in Latin. The request was flattering: 'Only a patient man could produce work of the quality you achieve. Only a man who has a beautiful soul could produce such fair forms. I would have you make a copy of the *Corpus Hermeticum* for me,' Lorenzino wrote, and then went on for a further two pages as to which copy I was to use as an original, which vellum, which inks and their colours, what illumination was required. 'The border of the frontispiece should include my emblem, the orobulos.'

The orobulos, the circular symbol of the serpent biting its own tail, is described by Iamblichus as the symbol of eternity and bore, therefore, the same significance as il Magnifico's motto, *Semper*, 'Always'. But the younger Lorenzo had found an image for the word which not only made the symbol more resonant but showed, to those who knew, that he was familiar with the Neoplatonists. To him 'eternity' meant the immortality of the soul. The commission, for one of my best-loved books, from a young man sensitive to philosophy and to symbol: it was almost enough to make a man happy again.

London, December 1st, 1505

As we left the cathedral this evening, the air was filled with the usual London odours: dead fish and urine, horse dung and the sweet stink of breweries. How I hate English ale: the smell of hops makes me gag, especially when mixed with the reek of the Thames. London is tinged with grey-green light as if the air reflects the sea, even this far up the estuary. As the night drew in, grey-green turned grey-blue.

There was no blackfriar haunting me this evening, but my skin is now beginning to prickle whenever I am out of my lodgings. All the time I am expecting a thin hand to grasp my shoulder from behind and an Italian voice to say, *Tommaso de' Maffei?*

'These canons and theologians,' said Erasmus, 'are like mangy bats – the kind that get caught squeaking in your hair when you have been brave enough to walk in the dark.'

'I see them as crows,' said young Thomas More, who hangs on to the arm of his Dutch friend as if he dare not let him go. 'They peck up the good seed only to shit it out.'

'Thomas!' said John Colet, leading the way across the yard to the deanery, 'this is sacred ground. Reserve such language for the inns of court.'

Thomas and Erasmus exchanged amused glances. 'Tut!' said the Dutchman, slapping his young friend across the back of the head. 'The eloquence and rhetorical skills of barristers, eh? You lawyers have mouths full of mud.'

I smiled at them both fondly, aware of how dirty Erasmus's own mouth could be when not in earshot of his revered friend and mentor, Colet. Thomas hesitated at the threshold. 'I thank you for the invitation to supper, Dean, but I must go home.'

'Come now, was the admonition that severe?'

'I have a difficult brief to study before appearing in court tomorrow.'

'Brief?' said Erasmus. 'I thought her name was Jane. There's nothing quite like marriage to draw a man away from his friends.'

'I love my new wife dearly, but I can wait another hour before I see her. It is work that draws me away, believe me.'

'No,' said Erasmus. 'In the face of truth, let us be honest – it is the thought of one of Colet's suppers that sends you flying. And you, no stranger to austerity!'

As this banter continued, a servant of the king rode up to us and, having apologised for the interruption, insisted that the physician, Thomas Linacre, go with him to Westminster to attend his master. Linacre promised to return as soon as he could.

'See that you do,' Colet urged him. 'I have things to discuss of great import that will affect you. And Master More, though I appreciate your need to be ready for the law courts, tonight it is the Heavenly Court that requires your attendance.'

Colet has a way of speaking that brooks no argument. More bit his lip and followed the dean indoors. William Lily hesitated on the threshold. 'Dean? Do you include me also in this invitation?' His voice was so soft it was barely audible.

'Of course, come along.'

Although Lily has been to Jerusalem, although he has studied Greek in Italy with Poliziano, he always assumes he is the least of men and not fit to keep the company in which he finds himself. His uncertainty inspired my own. 'And do you include me, Dean?' I asked.

'Maffei, you Florentine, though you are a pagan and a foreigner you are not only welcome at my table but I insist on it. What is the matter with you all tonight?'

The matter with all of us is that we have dined with Colet before, many times; without exception one leaves his table with an empty stomach and an intellect so brimming with inspiration and aspiration that it is impossible to sleep that night. Such evenings with John always turn out to be the best one has enjoyed since the last such occasion, but oddly each time begins with this same reluctance and a massive desire to be doing something else.

Erasmus laughed out loud and said, 'John, although I have longed for so many years to be with you again, still your hospitality has all the attraction of a cold bath.'

Colet was not offended. 'It is my duty to live by scripture and to avoid, as best I may, being a hypocrite. My predecessor as Dean of St Paul's was renowned for his banquets, but who has ever said anything about his spiritual fare?'

The deanery is constructed of the same stone as the church, with slender pillars and turrets and many mullioned windows. On the ground floor is a hall with panelled walls and high ceiling, but Colet never dines there. We went upstairs to the small chamber where the air is full of the smell of beeswax polish and the oaken floor glows. The ceiling, panelled in the same wood, is so low that it seems to press down on your head. In my several years in England, I have never got used to the ceilings and the sense of breathlessness they inspire. This is a raw, rude country which, though it may have heard of the beauty of Italian architecture, has yet to build anything in the style. The English cling to tradition and do not like change.

Around the walls are niches which Colet has emptied of their mediocre statuary and woodcarvings. There remains only a crucifix and a sweet figure of Our Lady. There are marks on the walls where rich tapestries once hung before they too were stripped out and sold, the proceeds going to the poor of the parish. A generous fire burned in the hearth and the table had been laid out by the servants for precisely the number of guests the dean would have once Linacre returned to us. The food that was on the table could not go cold since it was cold already.

'What I like most about England as the winter draws on,' said Erasmus, his thin lips down-turned at the sight of fruit and cheese on pewter dishes, 'is hot chestnuts, with those lovely brown shells blackened by the fire, and that wonderful smell. Chestnuts, John, cannot be an obstacle to the spiritual life, surely?'

We took the seats assigned to us, with William Grocyn, as usual, given the place of honour, since he is the eldest of us, the pioneer of Greek studies in England and Colet's own fount of inspiration. Grocyn is so weak-sighted that, to save what eyesight he has, he never writes anything but teaches the Word by the word, that is, through speech. Because he sees so little, he lacks the ready smile of a man meeting a friend and stares at you in a way that is easy to misinterpret if you do not know the cause. His hair is sparse and white, his cheeks sunken over gums missing many teeth, and spittle collects at the corners of his mouth. But his spirit is as lively as that of any youth and to see Grocyn is to understand the Platonic notion of the body as a prison of the soul.

Will Lily – or, as More calls him, 'Willy Nilly' – gets lost in general conversation and never contributes anything other than an amiable smile and the occasional nod of agreement, muffled as he is by the belief that his intellect, like his body and his name, is diminutive. He sits like a child, his knees together, his legs splayed apart and his feet inturned. In the presence of this company, which includes not only the Dean of St Paul's but also Will's revered godfather, Grocyn, he is silent, lost in muteness, until the conversation turns to the topic of language, when he shoots out of his shell, his gigantic claw of intellect ready to grasp the subject and devour it. At such times he wonders – as we all do – who the other William Lily is, but once the topic changes, so does the man, and he retreats back behind a bemused smile.

As we took our places at the table, Colet enquired about More's happiness since he abandoned monkish austerity for a wife. More declared himself to be very content to have joined Lily in the happy state of being a householder. 'I would recommend it to you all, as it was recommended to me. Choose a girl as pliant as a willow sapling, whom you may educate as you would a child, and raise her as a helpmeet for your work.'

'Marriage is not for me, alas,' said Erasmus, crunching on celery.

'Since you are a canon of the order of St Augustine, that goes without saying.'

'It is not my vows that keep me celibate,' Erasmus complained. 'It is the lack of opportunity to break them. What girl in Christendom would have an ugly stick like me?'

We are used to such self-deprecation from our Dutchman, and I sometimes wonder if he has a distorting mirror. I told him – and perhaps I sounded trite – that beauty, according to Plato and Plotinus, does not rest in the object but is self-existent and may be seen in anything. 'The cognition of beauty depends upon the seer.'

He looked at me with those bright, dark eyes as if with great amusement. I was not sure what he was seeing and began to grow troubled. Whenever I speak these days, and it is happening with increasing frequency, I hear myself rattle out truisms of the Platonic theology, and they seem more and more like – just words. Good words, fine words, but losing their efficacy with time and repetition. I coughed to hide my sudden sense of embarrassment and fell into silence.

For the sake of Erasmus and myself, the group avoids any temptation to lapse into vernacular English but converses in Latin throughout. Erasmus speaks the ancient tongue with a Dutch accent, a very sibilant and juicy sound with quizzical inflections. To hear that sound again – it calls to the soul like the trill of a blackbird in winter. How I have missed him! To have him with us again is to complete a circle that has been, if not broken by his absence, then imperfect. The difference between a polygon and a circle – worth reflecting on. Together we constitute what Colet calls the 'true community of scholars in London', given that we are the only men versed in both Latin and Greek. If this sounds few, Colet thinks our number is greater than even may be found in Italy these days, and he could be right.

Such Latin has not been heard before in London. In this company the rude church Latin, with its mangled grammar and rough phrases, is never spoken. In this company men speak the polished, euphonious – sometimes scatological – language of the ancient authors; here in the deanery it is as if Cicero, Ovid and Virgil live once more. Each man delights in the linguistic accomplishments of the others, and each uses the noble tongue as if it were his own *volgare*, so that even lewd jokes and witticisms spill out of us fluently – but never in Colet's presence if we can help it.

After moving from Oxford to London, More shared lodgings with Lily near Charterhouse, that great Carthusian monastery outside the city wall. Together they polished their Latin on the translation of epigrams and, as with all young men, had a disposition for the delights of the flesh. They would spend as many hours in exchanging jokes and comparing experiences as they did in sober study. But as Lily's youthful lust began to convert naturally into the love of a particular woman called Agnes, whom he made his wife, More's converted into a sense of sin. He went frequently into Charterhouse to live a part-time life of a penitent, while the rest of the time he studied law, growing ever more ascetic, sleeping on the floor and wearing a hair shirt, until Colet intervened.

While himself celibate, Colet stands with St Paul that it is better to marry than to burn, and he interpreted More's pallor as the consumption of spirit by the inward fire of lust. He instructed him, with the full authority of St Paul resounding in his voice, to get himself married. More went to his father at his estate at North Mimms, and old John More told him to visit the Coles at Roydon in Essex, 'who have a good crop of girls'. More chose the eldest, though she was not the prettiest, and returned to London with a sixteen-year old who was to become his experiment in education. This young girl, who had not even heard of Cicero, was soon reading out loud from his works.

Sometimes Jane More throws her book at her husband and, jumping up in tears, cries out loud for her mother, but as the months pass she is growing used to her tormentor, and with More being as attentive to her well-being in bed as he is out of it, she is growing patient with his strange whims and even begins to enjoy his instruction. More is convinced that girls can thrive as well as boys on education – as Plato has shown in the guardians of his ideal Republic – and More's wife, though started late, is proving him right.

After much opinion had been expressed on this topic, I spoke up as one who has had experience of it, since in Italy learned women are more common than here in England. 'I would like to agree that women should be educated, if they wish to be, since I know – or have known – so many splendid examples of literate ladies. However, education can ruin a girl, since society will treat her as a miracle at best, at worst as a freak of nature, but never as a scholar in her own right. Take Poliziano's sister, Maria, for instance. She had to live as a recluse in his house, and all manner of rumours ensued.'

Lily and Grocyn concurred, having met Maria themselves when they were in Florence, students of Poliziano and living in his house. 'Alas, society does not allow for learned ladies,' said Grocyn.

'Then society must change!' said More. 'And it is up to us to change it. I have many plans...' And thus the conversation shifted to More's favourite topic, which is good government. The group is divided between those who think a nation should be governed by monarchs born to the duty, those who think it should be by men polished in the art of statecraft, and those who think that it should be run by holy men. The majority prefer the latter, saying that the other systems are too prone to corruption. I have lived under all three of these systems and was about to speak up for my own preference when we were interrupted by the return of Linacre. Ushered in by a servant, he entered with a draught of cold air clinging to the black cloak and the scarlet robe he bought when he was in Italy. Tall and lanky, he somehow manages to convey, without saying as much, that here is one with an Italian doctorate, a graduate of the University of Padua with a degree in medicine. It is one thing to be a student of the humanities; quite another to have obtained a degree in one of the traditional subjects most noble and most difficult. But to have obtained that degree in Italy – that makes Linacre a giant in the eyes of his friends. While we have looked into Homer and can identify Greek metre, Linacre has peered into corpses and can name a man's inner organs. But both in Florence and at Oxford, Linacre has studied literature, and when he is with us the mighty doctor transforms into a poet-philosopher.

'Ah, good, as I had hoped – pears and dried figs!' Alone of all of us, Linacre approves of Colet's choice of diet and says that, if all men ate so frugally, he would be struggling to make a living. As it is, he is called out daily to attend victims of gout and gallstones, especially at court, and is becoming very rich indeed. 'Are you still drinking that vinegar, Tommaso? I tell you, if you want an English complexion, you must drink English ale.'

I grimaced, as much from the taste of my imported wine as from the thought of ale. It is true that my heavy red wine from Siena has turned to vinegar while at sea. John called a servant to fetch 'the signor a thimble of mead.'

'If you are going to buy imported wine,' More told me, 'let it be from Bordeaux.'

'Nothing wrong with English wine,' said Eramus, raising his glass.

'It's white,' I muttered.

'And it's good for you,' said Linacre, draining his own glass and holding it out for a refill.

In his presence, our talk turned to the king and, as so often these days, quickly became critical. King Henry Tudor, while being in so many respects our benefactor and protector, is becoming more miserly with age and his increasingly tyrannical acts are giving weight to the arguments of those who favour republics. Lily wanted to know how someone so avaricious can be so thin.

'Misers are always thin,' Erasmus replied. 'It is themselves they consume, not their wealth.'

'I hear His Majesty is trying to exact an even greater subsidy from the public purse than he is allowed by law,' said Thomas. 'If I could but have him in the dock, I would ask him a few questions about justice and the duty of a monarch in respect to the people.'

'Hush,' said Erasmus warningly, glancing at Linacre.

'I am confident,' said More, 'that in this company even courtiers will not be spies.'

'My loyalty is to learning,' said the good doctor, 'and being frequently in the presence of the king does not turn my head. Besides, he is not the incorrigible tyrant men think he is. Only this evening he spoke to me of his intention to build a new hospital.'

'Does he want you to be its director?'

'He wants me to help with the plans. He has heard from Francesco Portinari about the hospital of Santa Maria Nuova in Florence and is fired to build one just like it here in London, on the site of the old palace of John of Gaunt at Savoy in the Strand.'

Everyone looked at me. I nodded. I know Portinari and I know the hospital which was founded by his illustrious ancestor. 'It is the finest in the world.'

They guffawed and accused me of Florentine pride.

'No, he is right,' said Linacre. 'It *is* the finest in the world, a place where a man is healed as much in the spirit as in the body. Tommaso, do you know anyone in Florence who could draw its plan for us?'

'No. No one.'

So far as I know, Botticelli and Michelangelo still live, but one is too aged and the other too exalted to draw plans. No, I know no one. No one alive. Better to leave the past where it is. Better that it exists only in my dreams.

'There must be someone. Will you at least make enquiries?'

I agreed to do so.

My conversation with Linacre was drowned out by that of More and Erasmus, who were enjoying a contest of insults. Colet looked on with a tolerant smile and an expression which said, if the spirit that loves life and humanity must burst out with jibes worthy of fish porters, so be it. No doubt the apostles were the same when they gathered together to eat. He raised a slender, graceful hand for silence and said, 'If you want to create heaven here on earth, it must be done with love – there is no other way. A selfish society, comprising selfish individuals, must be penned in by legislation of increasing complexity as governments struggle to maintain order. But a society based on love and service needs few laws.'

'How could such a society be established?'

'Ah, I am coming to that. First I have a question to put to you all. As you know, my beloved father recently left this life, and as his only surviving child I stand to inherit a considerable fortune, and I have no one to pass it on to. I want your advice. What should I do with it that is for the good of all?'

'Banquets,' Erasmus said at once. 'Simple ones, of course, and nutritious, but with plenty of roasted chestnuts.'

'Oh, it goes without saying – you should found a college at Oxford,' said Linacre.

'This is a wonderful act of Providence,' said Grocyn. 'Without doubt I say you should found a library for the great works of antiquity, a library to rival that of the Medici, containing a copy of every book available. You could hire an army of scribes to do the copying work – you already have in us the scholars to do translations.'

My heart leapt at the thought and I agreed vigorously. London could become as Florence in the 1430s, when Cosimo de' Medici had agents scouring the world for precious and rare manuscripts. Yes! A thousand times yes! It was that work of Cosimo that had brought about the great flowering of arts and learning in my city for which Erasmus uses that lovely French word *renascence*. 'Yes, Dean! A library!'

Everyone was in agreement. Books – learning – these are the elements for the rebirth of a culture.

'But we are not talking of culture,' said Colet quietly. 'Young Thomas wants a just society and for that we need to establish the Kingdom of Heaven here on earth, where men live according to the commandments, loving God and their neighbours, where the wealth of the land is available to all and not just the few.'

I shivered. I had heard such words before. Colet had been in Florence in the heyday of Savonarola: surely he was not about to repeat that dreadful experiment of the 'New Jerusalem' here? I considered him guardedly, for I am never quite sure if I fully know John Colet. He contains within himself so many people I have known: in his interest in Cabala I see Pico della Mirandola; in his love of Plato, I find Marsilio Ficino; but in his strict piety, yes, I see Savonarola. So many personalities in one man, personalities who, in life, were at odds.

Thomas More, after some consideration, spoke up. 'I think you should furbish your father's estate as a villa of the kind described by Petrarch, to which we may retire whenever we may, to live and study in seclusion. The estate should be run on the model of Plato's Republic as an experiment in right living and good government. It will be the acorn from which will grow the mighty oak.'

'All these ideas' said Colet, 'are selfish.'

'How so?' exclaimed More, stung.

'You are all thinking of your own pleasure – however noble and exalted that pleasure may be, it is still pleasure.'

'Heaven and earth!' Erasmus exclaimed. 'I suspected as much! He intends to open a public bath with cold pools for the health of society.'

'What I have been thinking of,' Colet replied sedately, 'is founding a school, a school for children of the citizens of London.'

A school!

'What?' cried Erasmus, 'an institution for the flogging of children?'

I flinched and looked away. While the others laughed at Erasmus's remark, I felt unclean. I can no longer rant about ignorant schoolmasters who are vindictive and cruel, not now that I have used the rod on a boy.

'Not a private school,' said Colet, 'such as London has aplenty, schools that teach the barbarous tongue that passes for Latin, that use textbooks which may be called Blotterature rather than Literature. Away with it all! No, we shall found a public school for children, where they will be raised in the New Learning, fed on Latin and Greek grammar, reading the poets in the light of the

Christian doctrine. If we can harmonise intellect and devotion, then we can fashion men who are true Christians and not lip-servants to a faith they do not understand. Children who are born innocent and pure are being raised up by beatings, and grow into sour and selfish men, just like their fathers. Let us try instead to raise them up by love, and then perhaps you may have your new society. It is a great project requiring great men, and that is why I have invited you here tonight. You are to be my schoolmasters.'

Maria's prophecy fulfilled! I wrote about it just a few days ago, and now it is coming to pass. I shall be surrounded by children who will found a new nation. The strangeness of that distracted me awhile. I came back to the discussion when Grocyn made a protest.

'Are we not already too busy to fulfil all our duties? And now we are to become schoolmasters? Giving our time and intelligence to teach children? It would mean spending all day every day on rudimentaries. One may as well yoke arab stallions to ox carts!'

'You have all learnt and studied enough,' Colet said. 'It is time to give of your knowledge for the benefit of the world.'

Every man present was sitting with his mouth agape like a Galilean fisherman commanded to put down his nets. Before we could recover from the shock, Colet delivered a fresh one. 'After much consideration on the matter, I shall require all my schoolmasters to be married.'

Married! Then Maria's prophecy could not come true.

'Why so, John?'

'In married men I find the least corruption.'

'Then I am free of this onerous duty,' Erasmus exclaimed. 'Since I cannot be married I cannot be a schoolmaster!'

I waited keenly for Colet's reply but he only said that, with Erasmus he was prepared to make an exception. I wondered if he would he make an exception of me, too, if he were to know the truth. But I would have to confess it first, and I cannot. The secret has lived so long in me now that it's like a rusted nail.

'I do not intend to establish my school, which shall be here at St Paul's, for five years. In that time, you must prepare yourselves for the task ahead and make provision for what will be required. Thomas More, I want you to find out the best curricula and teaching methods.'

'Where shall I find them?'

'Search the world, if needs be. Doctor Thomas,' he addressed Linacre. 'From you I desire a Latin grammar suitable for a child's understanding.'

'You wish me to write for children? Impossible! My intellectual powers have been honed to a fine and subtle point. Simplicity is a virtue I no longer possess.'

'Then you must find it again, for we must be as little children if we would enter the Kingdom of Heaven.' Colet turned to Erasmus. 'My dear friend, I need you fighting on another front. You have studied theology in Paris. If you would take your degree and become doctor of divinity, you will gain the authority for your ideas that men respond to, for they will not listen to truth unless its speaker has the right qualifications. If we live in a world that is swayed more by a man's certificates than by his character or intelligence, then we must gain those certificates.'

Erasmus quibbled, not wishing to take a degree, but finally he said that he would, provided he be allowed to take it in Italy and not in France. 'If I gain it in Bologna, how my status will be improved in the eyes of men! I shall even be above Linacre, who only received a degree in medicine and at Padua.'

At the end of their bargaining, Erasmus looked very pleased with himself, for he had just won his excuse to try again to make the journey to Italy he still longs to make. But then Colet followed on with the instruction that he write a textbook on virtue for use in his school.

'But I am busy! I have my Adages to be revised and my translations of Euripides to complete...'

'You have five years, you reprobate, to get this love of literature out of your system and replace it with a love of God. Master Grocyn, to you it is charged to produce a Greek grammar for English boys.'

'My eyes! I cannot read Roman letters one foot high let alone write little Greek ones!'

'Lily shall help you. And William,' Colet added, turning to Lily, 'I want you to raise your own sons in the manner you will wish to employ on the sons of others.'

'Me? You shall want me for a master?'

'You are to be the High Master.'

Leaving Lily blinking with astonishment, Colet turned to me. 'Well, Tommaso de' Maffei. What of you? Will you marry again?'

'I cannot, Dean. I am celibate.'

'By which he means, Dean,' said Erasmus sweetly, picking fig pips out of his teeth, 'that he is impotent.'

I protested, flushing with embarrassment.

'It is true!' Erasmus insisted. 'Ask Saggy Annie. She says the only thing that stiffens in him is his joints.'

Colet tried to hide his laughter while his philosophers crowed, wanting to know how Erasmus knew the prostitute of Paternoster Row. 'All men and women are my brothers and sisters in Christ,' he said amiably. Erasmus will talk to anyone without judgement, even if it is only to get a story or folktale out of them.

'Is there something you want to tell us, Tommaso?' Colet asked.

'I've never heard of Saggy Annie.'

'Believe me, we know a Dutch joke when we hear one. Is there something else you wish to say?' His eyes were bright, challenging me to honesty.

'About marriage?' I asked, blanching.

'About being a schoolmaster.'

It was time to confess publicly, at least some of the truth. 'Dean, my brothers in Plato, I have something to tell you. I am a hypocrite.'

Erasmus sat back and grinned. 'Why do men think they keep secret that which is so transparent to others?'

'Please – this is difficult enough for me. A few weeks ago I beat my pupil with the birch rod. That is why I am no longer tutor to Giles de Greye. My heart swells with your idea, Dean, but my mind warns me to know myself. I cannot love. I am a stranger to love.'

'You who have the *Symposium* by heart.'

'Precisely. I know the theory and not the practice. I am a hypocrite.'

John Colet leaned towards me, held me with his eyes. 'Maffei, you are to go back to Italy and find what you have lost.'

I stared at him. 'It was the express instruction of Marsilio Ficino that I come to England, bringing the seed fire of the Platonic Wisdom to a new hearth.'

Colet's face is soft and gentle even when his voice is most steely. 'My friend,' he said. 'Your fire is out. Go home and find what it is you have lost. You have five years.'

London, December 5ᵗʰ, 1505

Ash. All the past is ash. Memories float like smuts over a blackened land. Thoughts of Italy should bring sunshine and Etruscan smiles, images of olive groves and gem-like seas, but I dreamt fitfully of home last night and saw everyone garbed in penitent robes, shuffling and fearful, with their hands clasped in front of them. And then, suddenly, fire. Flames behind the figures. Lightning forking in heaven to jab fizzling at the earth and catch a whole culture in choking, dense smoke and roaring flames. Flames to roast people in. The smell of charred flesh. Human flesh. A bit like pork.

The memory of the evening with Colet is tender and my mind goes to it cautiously, as to a wound. To dream of home and find it is a nightmare: it was only to be expected.

My window overhangs the cobbled streets of London where ravens watch from the thatched roofs of timber houses that know no right angles. The air is clouded by the smoke of domestic fires and the sound of a hundred bells tolling in the towers and spires of a hundred churches. They say that London is the most pious city in the world, but a man who measures piety by the number of churches is a fool.

The shock of England when I first arrived took a long time to dispel. Generations of wars, which ended at the Battle of Bosworth Field and the extinction of the Plantagenet line of kings, have retarded the country. Stepping off the boat in 1499 I went back a hundred years. Art here is crude, unrealistic. The English script is like its architecture: squint at it and you see a page full of mullioned windows, all strength in the uprights, none in the horizontals. For several years I despised it and everything English until I once chanced into the Divinity School in Oxford and became amazed by fan vaulting. Being ignorant of architectural principles of stress, yet wishing to build soaring cathedrals, they keep buildings standing with flying buttresses. But fan vaulting goes beyond mere expediency. Fan vaulting is art.

London is so crowded and dense that only when crossing the Thames on a wherry can you see the distant hills; otherwise there is no sense of horizon here as there is in Florence, no rural context for urban life. This is a squalid city reeking of human excrement, where pigs roam as freely as the pimps, the procurers and the scabby child beggars.

Colet has given me a mission, but I already have one, given to me by Marsilio: to bring philosophy to a new home. By 'philosophy' he meant the teaching that has been passed to us from ancient Egypt by poets and philosophers such as Orpheus, Hermes Trismegistus, Pythagoras, Plato, Plotinus, and – in our own day – by Ficino himself. 'Take this teaching north,' he instructed me, 'carry it like seed fire from our hearth to whichever place will have it. But carry it, most of all, to Colet, destined by God to light the torch in England.'

I have done as bidden. I have brought what I know and teach Greek to whoever will hire me. In the evenings, with my friends, I reveal the 'hidden wisdom' as St Paul calls it, the Platonic wisdom. Behind closed doors of oak I tell them what I know of Cabala and natural magic. I have done what I was asked to do. And yet somehow, I know, I have failed in my duty. And all-seeing Colet knows it.

I understand his plan to open a school for children. He wants this wisdom to be available to all and to spread its light throughout society. Yet inside I roll up at the thought of it and refuse to participate. Why? Because it will require me to love, and I dare not. That's the nub of my hypocrisy: I teach what I do not practise. Colet is not sending me on some quest, he is expelling me from his circle. Get thee gone, thou hypocrite. But to return home? That is impossible. I hear the sirens' song but I must resist.

In my memory I can hear the whirring of cicadas and feel the heat of the sun on my skin. As I gaze over wet London streets now, my mind drifts away to those almond blossom times when we sang songs of love, enamoured as we were of the Creator and His creation, those Orphic times of hymns of praise to ineffable Beauty. Those Aphrodite days. I see her rising out of the foamy Cyprian sea as Botticelli painted her, the naked, innocent soul wafted ashore by zephyrs in a breeze of rose petals to be clothed with a mortal embodiment.

And then I see her image bubbling in the flames lit by Savonarola to cleanse Florence of sin. Love has been incinerated and I have nothing in my heart now but scar tissue.

8 THE PLATONIC ACADEMY 1484

IT WAS IN MAY THAT I HEARD THAT FICINO HAD FINISHED THE Plato at Valori's villa. There was to be a banquet to celebrate but I did not expect to be invited, nor was I. It was for Ficino's most intimate friends and those who had given him financial support over the years that he had spent on his great work. I did not mind missing the banquet, but I was upset that the book should go off to Venice without me bidding it farewell. After all, I had lived with it for several years. I also heard that Valori was commissioning hand-written copies of it for presentation – real, old-fashioned, proper copies with vines and peacocks framing the pages. And then I was very upset. Half of me dreaded the commission, for as much as I love Plato I could not bear to think of writing that book out again, no matter how beautifully; the other half, of course, absolutely ached for it. When the commission went elsewhere, I was very sour indeed.

'There is a message from Ficino,' Angelo told me the day after the banquet. 'You are to meet him at Careggi tonight.'

'Why?'

'He did not say.'

And thus I returned to my place of purgatory, to find Ficino alone with two books of Plato. One was his translation, awaiting collection by a courier; the other was the original manuscript. When I expressed surprise that the book had not yet gone to Venice, he said he had thought it more appropriate that it should leave from here, the place of its birth. 'I have consulted the heavens and the most propitious moment for its despatch is at dawn tomorrow. I do not wish to spend this night alone in case I die.' He laughed suddenly. 'Or am I being superstitious? But when you finish your life's work what else can you expect?'

We kept vigil all night, fasting and in prayer, with the original Greek manuscript sitting in the centre of the room like a god in a temple of ancient Egypt. Ficino's memories were stirred. 'I was born,' he told me, 'in the year Plato came to Florence.' He touched his treasured book reverentially, the book he had lived with since Cosimo had presented it to him, the only complete copy of Plato's *Dialogues* extant in western Europe. Its binding had lost its colour with age, and the leather on the spine was turning to dust. It smelt of a thousand years in the desert amongst camel herders and was an object to attract no eye, yet Ficino referred to it often when he lectured on beauty, using it as an example of subtle beauty, the beauty of ideas. 'This is the object of greatest beauty I possess,' he would say. 'While men set store by agate vases, precious gems and cameos, this is my treasure. Its beauty is not to be known through the senses, but through reason alone. When I read in this book, my soul is in joy. Now, any man who would seek to keep such beauty to himself would be considered a fool, would he not? Yet men hoard their worldly treasures and are not considered fools. Often we say they are wise.'

The book sat immutable on its rest. Its presence in the room was palpable; everything revolved around it. I have heard that Egyptian priests attended their gods at dawn, washing and dressing them as if they were alive. The Plato sat like a god on a pedestal and, yes, it was alive, infused with divine spirit.

There are two versions of history, one exoteric, one esoteric. Exoteric history is the true story of dust and bone, of fading documents mostly legal and administrative. It is the history of time, of dates running backwards to that age before time when there were no dates. Exoteric history written down by scribes and historians becomes itself a document and in time, along with the historians, dust and bone. Esoteric history, however, is oral, passed on from one generation to the next as a story, a myth or a teaching.

'No book holds the truth,' Ficino told me. 'What I know, what I pass on to you is not derived from books.' And then he confirmed the secret history of the Platonic Academy. Having survived nine hundred years since its inception, the original academy had been closed by the Emperor Justinian. The philosophers emigrated to Arabia and Persia; wherever they went, civilisation began to flourish. They taught caliphs and sheiks. Wherever they went, universities sprang up. The Arabs became the wisest of men, numerate, inventive and deeply philosophical.

'Arabia was the repository of knowledge, while here in the west, after the barbarian invasions, we sank into superstition and ignorance. In time philosophy returned to her home in Greece, but not Athens. She came to rest in a corner of the Peleponnese called Mistra. And from Mistra in the 1430s came the last of the academicians to seek out the man who had obtained this book. George Gemistos Plethon found Cosimo de' Medici, and to him imparted the teaching which I impart to you. To say we have refounded the Platonic Academy here in Florence is no empty rhetoric. *We have refounded the Platonic Academy.*

'I remember the moment vividly. There was old Cosimo, Pater Patriae, the father of his country, but not as I had ever seen him before. We were in his own chambers and his usual look of stern resourcefulness, of grimness, was absent. We had discovered in each other a shared love of truth, for that was where his questioning had led – into the heart of me. Despite the years that separated us, we found in each other the same thing. Can you understand? I had grown up in a large family utterly alone, with no one to whom I could confess my innermost feelings, my desperation at the world and its ways, the shortcomings of our faith, the *need* for some principle by which to live. My reading had given me a thirst for Roman stoicism, but here was Cosimo telling me there was something better, something more ancient.

'He told me that the original Stoics, who inspired the Romans, were great men, but their works were lost in the burning of the library at Alexandria. There was a greater man, however, whose works – though for centuries lost to us in Christendom – had survived in Arabia. "I have them here," said Cosimo.

'Unlocking a painted chest of the kind that usually holds golden treasure, he lifted out this very manuscript, heavy and dull with age. "The man I speak of was called Socrates," he said. "His wisdom is enshrined in the *Dialogues* of Plato. I have been initiated into that wisdom by George Gemisthos Plethon, and what he has taught me will live with me. I need to read this book, Marsilio, but it is in ancient Greek and there is no one who can translate it."

'As I touched it, it was as if waking up from the delusion of time. There were no eighteen hundred years since the founding of the original academy. Wisdom has this exquisite property of being of the present moment and therefore it has no history. It is now and only now. Here in this book was the ancient, eternal flame passed on by generations of philosophers. Plato himself said he had received it from the school of Pythagoras, Pythagoras from Orpheus, Orpheus from Zoroaster, Zoroaster from Hermes Trismegistus in ancient Egypt. We do not know its ultimate origins, but I believe it has always been here in the world – a thread of gold in the dross of life.

'Cosimo said that the work would take a lifetime. He looked at me with such far-seeing eyes. Would I grasp the torch? I made the decision without struggle, telling him I wanted for nothing else.

'He said, "Our work is to wed the holy philosophy with our faith. Philosophy is not an alternative to religion. By this wisdom, Christianity will be enriched, will find its roots again. What do you say, young man?"

'"Father," I said, for in this hour he had become the father of my soul as Diotifeci Ficino was the father of my body. "Father, I surrender my life to you and to this work." After that, I was taken from my family to be brought up by the Medici and educated by the finest Greek scholars. When I had mastered the language, Cosimo held a ceremony in which he presented me with all the Greek texts, not only those of Plato but also those of Plotinus. Then, a little while after I had begun, there came to Florence the book of Hermes Trismegistus and Cosimo told me to put the Plato aside and translate Hermes first. I did not return to the great work on Plato until 1463, when I was thirty, and Cosimo only survived a year after that, but he heard Hermes in Latin, and the first dialogues I had completed. At Cosimo's deathbed, the Florentine Academy of Plato met for the first time.'

Ficino fell quiet and reflective.

'Father,' I said to him quietly. 'Your work on Plato is now done.'

He did not answer.

'What will you do next? Plotinus?'

'Cosimo never asked me to translate Plotinus. Perhaps he did not wish to burden me, I do not know. All I know is that I must await further instruction.'

'From whom?'

'From the father of my soul.'

Cosimo had been dead for twenty years.

'Do you not understand what I have said, Tommaso? There is no death in Wisdom. It is eternal. It is now.'

'There must be a thousand projects in mind that you wish to turn to.'

'Of course, but I have always tried to avoid following my own will. I am at the end of the road that was laid out for me. I could wilfully plunge off in another direction, or I could just wait to see what Providence wants of me.'

'You truly think you are going to die?'

'It would be very neat and timely. I have enjoyed a life where there has been no question about how I should spend it. Only a monk could be happier. But now I am like an ox turning in a gin that has run out of corn. I have no desire to amble at leisure in the fields. I need something else to grind.'

'Well, I am sure someone will commission something from you.'

Ficino shook his head irritably. 'You do not understand. I am not looking for something to do, or some money for doing it. I want to know what it is that my master desires!'

★

The courier arrived an hour before dawn and loaded our bag and its precious contents on to his saddle.

'Take very great care of it,' Ficino said.

'I take very great care of all my mail.'

'Especial care. Always take the safe road. I do not mind if it adds weeks to your journey.'

The man agreed he would do so.

'Mercury is in a very good aspect to Venus,' said Ficino. 'You have the blessings of heaven upon you.'

'I'll be off then.'

Ficino had not let go of the saddlebag. Gently I prised his hands away. 'Let it go, Father.'

'Oh, Tommaso! I'm convinced I've forgotten something. What if I have? In a few months there will be a thousand copies of this book. What if I have made a blunder?'

'You haven't. We've checked it. Angelo has checked it. There are no blunders.'

I smacked the rump of the courier's horse and sent the Plato off.

Ficino stood watching the road long after the courier had disappeared. Finally he came back into the house and sat at his empty desk.

'What will you do?' I asked, concerned about him.

'Oh, write some letters.'

'And then?'

'Only have concern for the day, Tommaso, not for the morrow. Go now and leave me to my work.'

I bowed and left.

As I went down the road into the city, I met a party of some young prince or ambassador, bright in flowered brocades and mounted on white horses, which I presumed to be making for the Villa Medici. As they passed, I glanced at the tall young man at its head but only recognised him once he had gone by. I stopped and turned in my saddle to watch Giovanni Pico della Mirandola ride past the Villa Medici and take the lane up to Ficino's house.

9 PICO DELLA MIRANDOLA ARRIVES WITHOUT SAYING HELLO 1484

WHAT HAPPENED NEXT BECAME FOLKLORE WITHIN THE WEEK, with many variations embellishing the tale. Giovanni Pico, it was said, had had a vision in his sleep in which Cosimo de' Medici appeared, after which he hastened to Florence to see Ficino. Or, Ficino had been raising angels and Giovanni Pico suddenly appeared. Or, just as Ficino was putting the finishing touches to the Plato, Pico appeared and compelled him to start work on the translation of Plotinus. This last version was near enough the true one. Ficino interpreted Pico's sudden, unannounced visit as the message from Cosimo he had been awaiting.

Inspired by reading *The Platonic Theology*, Pico had decided to become Ficino's disciple. Always impetuous, no sooner was the desire seeded than Pico was on the road. When he arrived at Ficino's and discovered that the Plato had just left for the printer's, he told Ficino that he must turn to Plotinus immediately, with such force and authority, Ficino said, it was difficult to believe Pico was only twenty years old.

'I was born,' Ficino told him, 'the year that Plato came to Florence. You were born the year I began the work of translation.' Ficino did not believe in mere coincidence. 'You were born with Saturn in Aquarius. So was I, thirty years earlier.'

Pico shone with the light of opals, a self-conscious light acknowledging his own part in this cosmic event as being natural and only to be expected. 'It is obvious that somehow, in the divine scheme of things, we are connected. Wonderful! I have no doubt that it is the desire of Cosimo de' Medici that you begin work at once on Plotinus.'

Ficino was about to agree when he found himself being forcefully guided towards his desk by this smiling angel.

'At once!' said Pico. 'Now! Do not waste a moment.' He went

to the books on the study shelf, leaving Ficino to begin his new work, but not a minute had passed before he was asking questions and commanding the philosopher's attention. Ficino looked up, wondering – and it would not be for the last time – if his young guest were slightly mad, but whenever he looked into that seraphic, unblinking gaze, he remembered God and forgot his objections. Frenzy, after all, is a natural condition of the God-lover.

That Pico wore rings on his thumbs and had threaded a strand of his long, wavy hair with pearls seemed somehow unremarkable in such a youth. He was the kind of man who chooses what to wear according to the planets and not to whim; that is to say, his choice of apparel and adornment were significant, but only to himself. It was not difficult for him to capture attention; neither was it difficult for any of us to become enslaved.

And thus it was that Marsilio Ficino, without even a short space in which to be challenged by having nothing to do, finished Plato and began Plotinus. In the year when Saturn was conjunct with Jupiter, when Pope Sixtus the Fourth died and went to hell, when a statue of the Virgin at Prato wept tears, when Charles VIII came to the throne of France, when Lorenzo de' Medici began his work of cleansing the Church by ordering that all wax tapers and banners be removed from the baptistery; in that year Pico della Mirandola came to Florence like a magus following the star and impelled Marsilio Ficino to the next part of his life's work.

Angelo had met Pico for the first time at Lorenzo's villa on Fiesole five years before; they had met again in Mantua, during the long months of Angelo's exile. Since that time, whenever Pico's name arose in Angelo's conversation – which was often – it was always accompanied by an air of loss and longing. I confess I was somewhat irritated by this, as if my company, or that of any man, was dull in comparison. Whenever a letter arrived from Pico, Angelo would leave it to last, like the tastiest morsel, and then go away to read it alone. Afterwards he would be cheerful for several hours. When he heard that Pico was in Florence, Angelo got up from his desk so quickly that his stool fell over with a crash.

To describe Pico physically would be to mould him in clay when it was not his features that attracted, but that which animated them, his spirit. In brief, his hair was longer than the fashion, his complexion paler than a man's, his eyes the colour of rain. There, I have done. I shall not mention his height, his robust figure, the bewitching power of his smile. Pico seemed to me to be a creature from a previous age, as if he had been sculpted for a niche in a French cathedral but had stepped down to join the living. He stood like a son beside Ficino but beside Angelo as a brother. Pico and Poliziano: where one was tall and fair, the other was short and dark, where one was mystical, the other was pragmatic, where one was deeply Christian, the other had a pagan heart. They were twins from complementary signs of the zodiac – Pisces and Cancer – and between them they covered all knowledge and all learning. Each found in the other what he considered himself to lack and that, according to Plato's definition, is love.

When he spoke, Pico's youth seemed to be an illusion. His studies had vested him with such authority that we listened to him as to a master. He said repeatedly that he wished to study with Ficino, to 'drink wisdom from the fount of Plato', but he seemed less a disciple than an heir to the estate. Called to dine in the garden of Lorenzo's villa, the Platonic Academy listened in fascination to a conversation between Ficino and the young man devoted to comparing the teachings of obscure philosophers. It was like watching two expert swordsmen at play, neither of them intent on killing the other, only in proving his skill. As they parried and thrust, I began to suspect that it was the first time that Ficino had met any intellectual resistance of a strength to try him. His ideas, too long unchallenged, were now being exercised by this animated youth.

Pico changed swords frequently, using now the blade of Aquinas, now the point of Alexander of Aphrodisias, now the edge of William of Ockham. Ficino had only one sword, forged in heaven and inscribed with the name *Platone*. For unlike Pico he was not an independent thinker deriving his ideas from many sources but was the disciple of one master. The swords rang. The younger man's made a pleasing sound against the clang of the elder, but suddenly, and for no reason apparent to us lesser mortals, Pico suddenly put up his weapon.

'I have come to learn from Plato, not destroy him,' he said, and apologised to Ficino for his hubristic display of learning. 'I have to *know*,' he explained. 'I have to know *everything*. It is not enough to take anything on faith. Any proposition I must attack, for only that which survives is true.'

'Poor Truth!' said Ficino with feeling, but he gazed on Pico fondly, as if to say, 'This is my son, in whom I am well pleased.'

It was on that night that I realised for the first time that Ficino was not antipathetical to Aristotle. I had always believed that, in the fight between the Aristotelians and the Platonists, Ficino was unquestionably of the latter camp, but in this conversation he revealed himself much more sympathetic to Aristotle than I had supposed. Pico, in his years at the universities of Paris and Padua, had absorbed the traditional philosophy, which was Aristotelian as interpreted by Saint Thomas Aquinas; now he wished to absorb Plato, to compare one with the other, and, if he could, to harmonise them. Not for nothing was he the Count of Concordia.

Angelo was growing restless. He had had enough philosophy and wanted music. He sent an attendant to fetch Ficino's 'Orphic lyre', reconstructed by an instrument-maker from an image on an ancient engraved gem. As the sun sank in the west and the fireflies danced in the glow of lamps, Ficino plucked at the strings in the Aeolian mode and chanted a hymn to Apollo. The notes dissolved in the air like salt in water, purifying it, making it clearer. For a moment there was no such thing as time; I could have been one of the first men, listening to Apollo himself. Such hymns have been sung since time began, and to hear one now was to inhabit all time. Ficino's enunciation of the Orphic hymn was so precise and sweet that it seemed to me that I fully understood Greek and knew the meaning of all words. For a moment the world was the right way up and I understood that knowledge is the true condition while ignorance is mere enchantment; it was as if I had spent all my adult life struggling with a language I already knew. There were no flames in the sky on this night, just streamers of vivid colour in the west. Little moths danced in the air and in my state of enhanced vision I saw the air to be full of spirits, and that they too were dancing in this blessed company that included Lorenzo de' Medici, Marsilio Ficino, Angelo Poliziano and Pico della Mirandola.

I saw all this and in the seeing knew myself to be separate, kept apart from the union of the company and the moment by grief, a blackness in my soul which was a hatred of God. I abjured goodness and kept apart. These men were happy, but I was not happy, could never be happy again, without Elena. Like leprosy, my loss was a disease without cure. I had to learn to live without my limbs, to drag myself crippled through the realm of love, forever condemned. All I could hope for was the power to accept my lot with good grace, to envy no one his wholeness and to limp through life the best I might.

Ficino once had healed me of grief in an earlier time, when my brother was killed, but it was a different grief, one that was open to his philosophic balm. I remembered it well enough to wonder now that I felt no angel standing behind me, his hands resting on my head, warm and full of love. I wrested myself from the moment and looked away to the distant hills, outlined by the last light of the day. I was – I am – an exile from heaven, and must be content.

10 DOING THE WASHING
1484

WHEN ANGELO WAS BUSY, I WAS OFTEN DEPUTED TO VISIT his sister-in-law, Cammilla, at the house on the Via de' Fossi. She was easy to look after, being a fully domesticated woman. She knew how to greet me, having her sons bow politely and her servants present me with refreshment and cakes. We would discuss arrangements in the house, what shopping she required, what bills to be paid. She spoke of her brother-in-law with gratitude; her affection she reserved for her sons. If Angelo was bedding her, she showed no sign of it.

Out of town, on the hill, was Maria; if she was domesticated it was only on her own terms. We had servants, whom she was supposed to command, but she was more likely to join them in their work, housekeeping a game she enjoyed but never won. After a session of preserving, she would leave the kitchen looking like an alchemist's study after an explosion. Far from demure, she was always talking, and to anything in sight: the broom, the floor, the cat, the wild birds, the trees. She attacked her work with an energy so great that it was expended before the task was complete, so that the more she went about clearing up, the more mess was created. 'Non finito,' she replied when Angelo remonstrated with her, reminding him of the theory of poetry which Lorenzo upheld, that inspired work should be left unfinished. 'As you are at your desk, so am I in the house.' Her affection was confined to none but showered on all, including me. And the witches.

She told me of a prediction they had made, of great, momentous changes to our world, of a coming apocalypse. Having been left in charge while Angelo was in town for a few days, it seemed to be my role to bring sense and reason to the young woman.

'Maria, I keep telling you, there are no such things as witches, except in your brother's stories.'

'What do you know, you who gather knowledge only from dead books? Come with me to the next *bucato.*'

'Plato counsels us to withdraw from the world, and we have servants to do the washing.'

'Either Plato is wrong, or your understanding is faulty. And why should servants get all the best work? Come with me tomorrow!'

Accordingly the next day I put aside my copying and went with her to the stream, helping the servants to carry the baskets of linen. The shallow ford was as busy as any market. A cheerful group of women, their skirts hitched up around their thighs, was standing out in the stream, engaged in merry banter, gossip and laundry. They lathered, rinsed and slapped their washing on to large stones in the stream, all the time talking as if they had not seen each other for years. Maria hitched up her own skirts and waded out to join them, greeting them all by name, asking after family and children, telling the news of our own home lightly, that one of our chickens had laid a black egg and that the housecat had had a litter of kittens.

'Come on, Tommaso!' she called, beckoning me in.

'I'll get wet!'

'Take your hose off!'

I hesitated, feeling as shy and modest as she should have been. But if Maria could do it, then so could I. Accordingly I unlaced my hose, pulled them off and waded out after her. The stream was cold and made me cry out, whether in pleasure or pain it was hard to tell. The women laughed and made much of me, judging my legs like those of a horse at a race and finding me worth a bet. At first I was outraged, then discomfited, and finally enchanted and blushing like a boy. And of course I judged their legs, too, standing like Paris before a display of goddesses. To my surprise, Maria won the contest – she had good legs, not over-shapely but straight and strong, inducing admiration more than desire, but then I was not a fool like Paris. No, I gave Minerva the prize of a fish I had caught, tossing it at Maria. She squealed and ducked.

Handing me the olive soap, she showed me how to lather the washing. Then I became as a child, with my feet among the fishes and my hands slithering over the linen. Even the rinsing was no chore, with the running stream doing all the work. The wringing and tugging of sheets that we did between us ended in Maria falling backwards into the water.

'You did that on purpose!'

I shrugged. 'You should have seen it coming.'

The day was hot. She soon dried, sitting on the warm stones amongst the linens we had spread out. The company rested, eating bread and drinking wine, treating us without deference and making no comment on our relationship. That Maria was a spinster living with her bachelor brother and his friend was not something that was remarkable in the country.

At last the women departed, to go home to tell their husbands what a hard day they had had.

'So much for the witches!' I said to Maria as we returned to the villa.

'Oh, they were not the witches. The witches were not there.'

'Of course not, too busy eating naughty children.'

Maria rounded on me. 'There are witches,' she insisted. 'Not ones from books or from your imagination, but real ones, ones that heal with plants, ones that read the heavens. Your Ficino would be called a witch if only he were a woman. There are witches, Tommaso, but they were not there today. I have seen them, I have spoken to them: they live further up the valley and are women of much wisdom. Of course they don't take their eyes out! That's just a scholar's funny story made up to scare us. They are like you and me. And according to them, right now the planets are spelling out the doom of Florence.'

I scoffed and told her she was speaking nonsense.

11 THE WITCHES
1484

DECIDING TO LIVE IN FLORENCE AWHILE, GIOVANNI PICO della Mirandola rented rooms close to Ficino's house in the city. The day he first came to the Villa Bruscoli, Angelo was absent, but Pico said he needed to borrow a book urgently and he was certain Angelo would not mind. Maria looked stiff and constrained as the Count of Concordia bowed before her.

'You had hair like a boy's the last time we met,' he said. 'You were fresh out of the convent.'

In the intervening five years she had become a woman and her waist-length hair was tied up. Where other young women indulged in a multitude of plaits or, more demurely, covered their heads with a light veil, Maria had devised a way of tying her hair in a simple knot that was very quick and practical. In her view, time spent on one's appearance was time ill-spent. When the Count mentioned her hair, however, she began to pat and feel the knot on her head as if concerned for once with how she looked. Our Maria of the firm and unorthodox opinion was, in the presence of Pico della Mirandola, uncertain, unsteady and undone. As was I. Captivated, we were heliotropes to his light, tracking his every movement.

He told us that Angelo had invited him to come and see the villa, but this had been his first opportunity. 'I hear there is a nest of witches close by.'

I laughed. 'Angelo compensates for our poor position on the hill by converting our humble neighbours into characters from folktales. There are some washerwomen who use the stream; I have never seen any witches.'

'They do exist, my lord,' Maria told him earnestly. 'Women of much wisdom, conversant with the gods of old. They can heal with herbs as well as Ficino can.'

Pico gazed on her, bright with interest.

'Please my lord, it is the truth.'

'I do not doubt it.'

'What they say does not contradict our Faith – just precedes it.'

'Ha!' Pico seemed intrigued by Maria's odd remark. 'Precedes it. Yes, quite.'

I asked him to explain.

'The truth is eternal, yes?'

'Of course.'

'Christ is the Truth?'

'Without question.'

'Christ was born fifteen hundred years ago. As a syllogism, there is a fault here. If Christ is Truth, then he too must be eternal, and not temporal. He precedes himself.'

Maria nodded in emphatic agreement. The next thing I knew, she was putting on her cloak and inviting Pico della Mirandola to visit the witches in the valley.

'Maria,' I said sternly. 'This is most improper.'

'There is nothing improper in my intention, or in the Count's. Therefore it is not improper in itself, only in the imagination of petty minds.'

Pico and I exchanged a bemused smile. Neither of us had met a woman quite like this before. 'I shall look after her,' he assured me.

'It takes two,' I said, putting on my own mantle.

As we made our way, Pico told us of his studies, of how since a boy he had devoted himself to the cultivation of the soul and the acquisition of the knowledge of the liberal arts. 'I have Latin and Greek and am now studying Plato with Marsilio Ficino. I mean to harmonise Plato and Aristotle – a task that has defeated all before now.' His words tripped over each other, spilling from him in a torrent, and his gait was buoyant with enthusiasm. 'I can learn anything, anything I set my mind to.'

Maria stared up at him. 'You ride knowledge as Bellerophon rode Pegasus.'

I was about to remark that Bellerophon's ride ended in a fall when Maria made us stop. We had come to Fontelucente and the spring with its statue of the Virgin. 'Hail Mary, full of grace,' Maria said as if greeting a friend, and dipping her hand in the basin of spring water, she crossed herself.

'This is Angelo's Helicon,' she told Pico.

In wonder at these learned references that seemed to come so naturally from this strange young woman, Pico glanced at me over her head.

'She is her brother's sister,' I explained.

We went down through the woods, the way strewn with pine needles that made a clear and fragrant path. Under the trees it was dead, no vegetation able to survive the close canopy of the umbrella pines. The darkness of the wood made me fearful but Maria seemed to enjoy it.

'There is a place in the soul that is dark,' she said. 'It is the womb from which everything comes, all impulses that are creative, all good ideas. The dark woods remind me of it.'

'Beasts and demons also dwell in the dark,' said Pico.

'That is a different kind of dark, a godless place.'

The path led down to a tributary of the stream in the valley. On its bank were growing some lovely white irises, the flower that is the emblem of Florence, the city of flowers; the emblem, too, of our florin. Pico stooped to pick some. They were magnificent, with three petals forming the shape of a flame and two petals curving downwards.

'Such beautiful lilies,' sighed Maria.

'They are irises.'

'But we call them lilies.'

'They were called *flos iridis* by the Latins.'

I agreed. 'They are sacred to Juno, since Iris the rainbow was her attendant.'

'But these are white, not many-coloured, and to the Christians they symbolise the dove descending, and also the Trinity, and therefore the iris is the lily of the Madonna,' said Maria.

'The artists show the Madonna with the white waxy flower we also call "lily",' I said.

'Then they are wrong,' Maria insisted. 'According to legend, the Virgin gave Clovis, King of the Franks, a lily at his baptism, and I am sure it was an iris.'

Along the river a few paces was a hovel of the kind dwelt in by woodcutters and charcoal burners. Smoke was rising from its roof and a great pile of pine logs was neatly stacked under a shelter. A tethered goat watched our approach with slitted yellow eyes. So devilish was its gaze that I stood fixed to the spot, staring back at it.

'Go on without me,' I told the others, 'for I have no desire to meet a witch.'

Maria, demure and ladylike with Pico, jumped towards me with the face of a teasing cherub. 'You have listened too well to your nurse's stories – and those of my brother. Come along...' She took me by the arm and pulled me forward. A glance at Pico and I could see that, in him, too, curiosity was at war with fear.

'Who cuts the wood?' he asked, his voice a little higher than usual.

'They do it themselves.'

'Women cutting wood? How unseemly.'

At the open door Maria called, 'Monna Angelica?'

A young woman came out, blinking in the light after the gloom within.

'Carmina, is your mother home? I have brought my brother's friends to meet you both.'

The young woman, dressed in a fustian shift the colour of the forest floor, welcomed us in unsmilingly. The place was full of smoke and the unholy stink of tallow candles. Besides the large hearth, in which hung a cauldron stewing who-knows-what mess of ingredients, was a basket of pine cones to be used to add some fragrance to the acrid smell of the place. The earthen floor was strewn with musty rushes; an ill-shaped table and two chairs were the only furniture. Such poverty! My fear was overcome by compassion.

A rickety ladder was propped against a hole in the ceiling which led to a loft where presumably the two women slept, and down this ladder, gathering her foul skirts in one hand, came Monna Angelica. Her dark hair was streaked with silver and she wore it loose, a strange thing for an old woman to do and most fearful. My compassion evaporated. Her face was hard, her nose high and arched, her cheeks drawn in, her eyebrows heavy. Every inch a witch. My knees began to tremble.

Maria greeted her with an embrace. 'This is Giovanni Pico, Count of Concordia, and this my adopted brother, Tommaso.'

The crone nodded to me briefly but concentrated her attention on Pico, and his flowers.

'Why have you snatched these living beauties from my river bank?'

'I would have them adorn my table, Madonna.'

'And now they will die.'

'They would die anyway.'

She looked at him keenly. 'But not so young, and as nature wills it, not by the hand of man.'

I began to discern a softness behind her severity, or else it was the effect of the Count upon her.

'Where was the sun at the time of your birth?' she asked him.

'In Pisces. I was born in March.'

'When the chill winds of spring do blow, and a late frost kills the fruit in its bud.'

Pico blanched. 'They say you are a witch, and I would know what that means.'

'It means I am a widow who has not remarried and that I have knowledge of herbs, that is all.' Her coarse laughter revealed teeth that had once been large and handsome but were now grown old, separated and blackened. If I squinted at her, I could just see the kind of woman she once was, and how striking a beauty she would have been, like her daughter. 'It means people are suspicious of me because I succeed in living without a man and because I grind up iris bulbs for orrisroot.' She spoke in the Tuscan dialect and was born of generations of this region.

'There are no holy images in this house,' Pico observed.

'I have the Christ in my heart and I live in the church that He made and which He adorns Himself. The pine tops are the roof and the trunks the pillars of the many aisles. I have no need to go to your stone church and kneel down with hypocrites.'

Maria's eyes shone with amusement as she watched Pico conversing with her friend.

I looked around. It was true that there were no holy images, but neither were there any demonic ones, no toads pinned live to the walls, no crows hanging upside down from the rafters, just a bunch of dried grasses in an earthenware pot.

'Are you an astrologer?' Pico persisted. 'Do you have the prophetic gifts?'

'I am a widow, that is all. If I can see into people's hearts, there is nothing supernatural in that.' Here she turned her dark eyes on me. Her gaze was both haughty and terrifying, as if she were physically stripping the clothes from me. Then, as soon as I was naked, she went on to strip the veils from my soul. The sweat stood out on my forehead.

She winced, as if she saw the condition of my heart. 'If you continue to bury your misery, it will fester within you like a splinter or a thorn. Pull it out, whatever it takes.'

The sweat began to run and my mouth was too dry for me to reply. So I croaked like a frog. Pico glanced at me with the expression Odysseus must have worn when his sailors were turned into pigs by Circe. I smiled nervously at him, to reassure him I was not a frog.

Monna Angelica's gaze had returned to the white irises, which were already beginning to droop in Pico's warm hand.

'It will happen in the time of the lilies,' she said.

'What will?'

'Everything you fear – for all of you – in the time of the lilies. All will die – a long and agonising death by the hand of man.'

We glanced at each other, each of us silently willing the others not to be gullible or superstitious. She was just an old woman who spent too much time alone.

She offered to make us a meal of the food Maria had brought in a basket but we declined, saying that she and her daughter should make full use of it themselves.

When we went outside, our eyes adjusting to the light, we saw the daughter near the river, turning slowly in a circle, her head down and her hair covering her face. She began to move quicker, dancing to the music of the river and the wind. The dance grew more frantic and she threw her head back but her hair whipping from side to side continued to hide her face. One caught glimpses of chin, throat, closed eyes. This was no dance of the noble palazzo nor even of a peasant festa, but wild and ancient, a dance of Maenads in a bacchic frenzy, though eerily soundless. Her limbs obeyed no laws but bent and twisted in abandon, unpredictably. There was no pattern here, only chthonic rhythm. And as she danced she grew even more beautiful; my eyes fastened on her, lawless and insatiable. I was Actaeon to her Artemis. Reason was dethroned. The same frenzy was in my blood and beginning to arouse me. I snapped away, breaking her enchantment by turning my back. Her dance slowed – I could feel her coming up behind me, could hear her dress rustling, her arms reaching out to me.

'Touch me not, woman!'

Her arms encircled my waist and her mouth was against my ear. 'Your philosophy has no seed.'

When she touched my right arm, my hand tingled as if stung by nettles.

'So what have we learned?' Pico asked cheerfully as we made our way back through the woods. 'Nothing, except to fear the month of May.'

'Why May?'

'The time of the lilies.'

'Oh, I see.'

'Soothsayers of their kind are dangerous. A few ambiguous pronouncements made darkly by someone with bad breath and we are all a-shiver with mortal dread. They pretend to know the future, and their victims are those who would know the future, but the future is best left to God. For what would we do if we knew the future but strive to change it?'

'Is it then inexorable?'

'Ah ...' he said, and as we made our way slowly back up the hill, Pico della Mirandola expounded on his ideas about free will and predestination. Maria absorbed every word.

12 PLATO IS PUBLISHED
1484

A TRAIN OF WAGONS ARRIVING FROM VENICE LOADED WITH merchandise made its way through the city to the Palazzo de' Valori. Several of us were there, not for the fabrics, the crystal cups or the spices imported from the East, but for several large wooden crates which held five hundred copies of the Plato *Opera*. We were like children, each of us eager to take a copy of the book, but we held back so that Ficino should be the first. On instruction from Valori, a servant prised open one of the crates. So many books and all identical! But they were not as we had expected, handsomely bound in Moroccan leather. For cheapness and expediency it had been decided to have the books bound in Florence, so what we received were the unbound quires loosely sewn together. Ficino stood with a copy in his hands.

'Open it,' said Bartolommeo Scala, as if in charge of the event.

But such was his anxiety of what he would find within that Ficino stood with it clutched tightly under his arm. Giovanni di Pierfrancesco stepped forward and took another copy out of the crate. We all gathered about him as he held the book open and towards us as if he were a lectern. My heart sank at the sight of the title page. With a slightly unsteady hand, Valori reached forward and turned the page and then we saw the text for the first time.

The type was Germanic black letter. What an abomination! Oh, dear God! A hundred years of Italian advance in calligraphic beauty undone in the hour! Lines of letters stabbed down like daggers on the lines below, and the capitals had so many strokes they were unreadable. Oh, the shades of Poggio Bracciolini, of Niccolò Niccoli, of all our most worthy scribes rose up in horror, and that of Cosimo de' Medici ran shrieking away.

I am not sure what I said out loud, but Filippo Valori said I was giving fine rhetorical expression to everyone's silent thoughts while Bartolommeo Scala accused me of over-reacting.

'It is the ideas which matter!' said Ficino forcefully, opening his copy at last. Scala read the page over his shoulder and then pointed a long, tapering finger to a particular line.

'There's a mistake,' he said.

At that, Ficino trembled and had to put the book down. But Giovanni di Pierfrancesco, back at the crate, was handing out copies. As we all glanced through the book, we found many more mistakes, each of them made by the careless, inadequate printer. After a few minutes, Filippo Valori said that the mistakes on their own would have filled a crate.

Later, when he had recovered, Ficino told us that when a man is let out of prison he is bound to be filthy and emaciated. 'But Plato is now free,' he said. 'Let Phoebus, the Sun, shine on him.'

13 PREDICTIONS AND PROPHECIES 1484

CRISTOFORO LANDINO, THE HEAD OF THE FACULTY OF poetry at the university, had studied the recent conjunction of Saturn and Jupiter marking the completion of an astrological Great Year and said that a great religious reform would commence on the 25th day of November. As I rode with Poliziano from the city to Fiesole on the evening of the 26th, we spoke of portents and prophecies, speculating on Landino's strange astrological prediction. Had the reform taken place, Poliziano wondered? What was it? Where was it?

'Clearly it refers to the publication of Plato,' I said. 'Once the Platonic teachings are disseminated, and men understand the imminence of the divine and the immortality of the soul, they will take much greater care in how they live life. Then everything will be renewed.'

'That is a subtle renewal which will take years to come about. We need something more drastic. With the nature of the modern papacy and the corruption of the curia, I find it increasingly difficult to be a Christian at all. Some say the Book of Revelation is about to be fulfilled, that the Apocalypse is nigh. Sometimes, when I see the degradation of men's souls, I hope it is true and that I live to see this city of ours quite flattened by Divine Wrath.'

'You do not mean it!'

'Only sometimes. Other times I love Florence as my mother.'

Over the following year nothing appeared to happen to renew Christianity. The death of Sixtus IV had merely brought us Innocent VIII. As popes go, he was better than most, but not one to inspire men to the spiritual life. Lorenzo, however, found he was someone he could do business with, and not just the business of the Medici bank. So far as Lorenzo was concerned, no renewal of the Church could take place until the Medici were in the Vatican. Thus he began to negotiate for a cardinal's hat for his son Giovanni. He wanted him to become a cardinal as soon as possible. Age notwithstanding. By the time the boy was ten, he had been an abbot for four years, a priest for three and a canon of the Cathedral for two.

There were many other predictions coming from astrologers. Ficino refuted them, saying that the astrology which looks for causes in the stars is false: the stars are guides, not causes. But even he, studying his ephemerides, became apprehensive. The patterns of the skies told of great changes ahead, cataclysmic changes. The sidereal message was that our world was about to be destroyed.

14 PICO LEAVES WITHOUT SAYING GOODBYE 1485

IT WAS A PEACEFUL SUMMER SPENT AT THE VILLA BRUSCOLI. Into the copy of Hermes for Lorenzino I poured all my art and talent, rendering beautiful ideas in a beautiful form, so beautiful, I hoped, that men would be inspired to ignore the printing press.

Maria was content under her brother's protection, spending each idyllic day either in study and composition or in transmogrifying the kitchen and so tidying the house – throwing anything left lying about into the nearest chest – that nothing could ever be found again.

Pico had been studying with Ficino about a year when we met in the city by chance one day in July and he told me that he was departing for Paris on the next. I was shocked and wanted to know the reason. He would not say, although I heard later that he had had a disagreement with Ficino on the subject of Love. 'Pico,' my informant told me, 'thinks that Marsilio does not understand Plato properly.' What hubris! I could only imagine the heated exchange.

'Does Angelo know that you are leaving? Or Maria?' I asked him.

'No. Nor shall I tell them. I'll be back soon enough.' His was a free spirit demanding of his friends that they love him utterly without any claim. 'Love me and let me go,' should have been his motto.

I took the news of his departure to the Villa Bruscoli.

'*Gone?*' Angelo stared at me, looking like a man who had been robbed of his soul. Maria left us abruptly to go to her room. Later, as I passed her door, I heard her pen scratching: the sound of a woman writing poetry. What kind of poetry does a woman write? Like that of Sappho? If so, verses of love and grief were being written by candlelight in the room of our housekeeper. Since the arrival of Pico, I had watched her fight against his attraction and lose. He was her Charybdis, drawing her down in the whirlpool of his self-absorption. Whatever she was doing, Pico would want to be involved. He would as readily discuss her studies with her as techniques of pickling. He had a way of making it seem that she was the lodestone and he the helpless piece of iron, when in fact it was the other way around. It was cruel of him to give her so much attention, always complimenting her intelligence and caressing her with his adoring eyes. But it was the way a child looks at his mother. He sometimes sought her out when she was alone at the villa because, he said, he enjoyed her company above that of any other woman, and then he would talk energetically about divine love and celibacy. The philosophical journey, the ascent of the soul to God, he said, required a man to be pure, and Maria was an aid rather than an obstacle in that.

'Women are fickle, vain and pleasure-loving,' he once told her. 'I have never seen the point of engaging any of them in conversation. But you, you are so different. *La mia unica Maria.* Earthly love between man and woman always tends towards coitus,

103

an unseemly act. Divine love occurs between man and man since such love does not involve coitus. Can there be divine love between man and woman? I thought it was impossible until I met you, my wise woman, my Diotima.'

'What form does divine love take between man and man?' she asked.

'The closest one may come physically to the beloved is the kiss.'

'Have you ever...' she blushed and cleared her throat. 'You and my brother?'

Pico nodded. 'In the kiss, souls meet in union, so perfectly joined together that they are at the same two souls, and one. The most perfect and intimate union which the lover can have with the heavenly beloved is represented by the union of a kiss.'

'Is it, you know, a long, passionate kiss or a peck of affection?'

Pico looked at her, hesitated, then overcoming any restraint he might have had, pulled her to him and kissed her on the mouth until she went limp in his arms. This is how he treated a young woman barely out of the convent! A young woman who, as she passed marrying age, was working so hard to convince herself that she wanted no husband.

'I hope you did not mind me doing that. Example is always the best way to teach.'

Maria was unable to reply.

'I love you as I love your brother, Maria,' Pico said. He meant it as the highest compliment, but it destroyed Maria's equilibrium.

She told me about it in confidence, after swearing me to secrecy, but as soon as I heard the story I felt as tense as a drawn bow and wanted to go and have the matter out with Pico, this man who, under the aegis of philosophy, had violated my sister. That was how it felt – a violation – but Maria laughed and said, had she been violated, she was perfectly capable of defending herself. She brought her arms up as if holding an imaginary sword with both hands and, saying *swissshhh*, swiped it through the air to remove his imaginary head. She was overly fond, I thought, of the story of Judith and Holofernes.

'You do not understand him. He is not of this earth, Tommaso. The laws do not apply to him. Kissing Pico is as lustful as kissing Saint Thomas Aquinas.'

Yet when Pico left Florence, she translated her grief into poetry and mourned like a nightingale.

Angelo, however, once he had recovered himself, grew angry. He went out to chop wood in such a mood that I pitied the logs splintering under his blows. Naturally we had servants to do such work, which, besides, is the work of autumn, not high summer, but log-chopping had become Poliziano's regular exercise, especially when he needed to free his brains from his emotions.

15 THE CASA VECCHIA
1485

WHEN THE MEDICI FIRST CAME DOWN FROM THE HILLS to live and thrive in the city, they built a house on the Via Larga which still stands, beside the new palazzo built by Cosimo. The old house was given to the Pierfranceschi. While they were young, the sons of Pierfrancesco were much a part of the main household, the house of their guardian, present at meals, at lessons and other family events, but now that they had grown, and Lorenzino had come of age, they kept to the Casa Vecchia, establishing in that house of only two storeys a home to rival that of il Magnifico.

After I had completed the *Hermes* and had had it delivered, I was invited to visit. Crossing its threshold for the first time, I walked into an aesthetic haven of good taste. From the very entry of the building, up its staircase, through its sala to an antechamber decorated with scenes from the life of Bacchus, the house shone with the attention of a man of exquisite sensibility. Where il Magnifico, inhriting a house of three generations, had merely added to its contents, Lorenzino had swept out his forefathers and brought in the upholsterers, the fabric merchants, the furniture-builders and wall-decorators to create an harmonious whole. I did not turn my head from side to side like the vulgar curious, but even with my gaze downcast I could take in the blue leather, the marble, the wood intarsia, and the merest glance showed the perfection of placing, whether it was the bust of a father on the cabinet, the chair beside the hearth, the candelabra. Sconces on the wall either side of a tondo of the Madonna and Child were a hymn to symmetry.

In the chamber where I met him, however, my attention was divided between my host and the large painting above the *lettuccio*, that painting done by Botticelli of Venus, the Graces and Mercury.

'Beautiful, no?' said Lorenzino, following my gaze.

'Yes,' I agreed, 'beautiful.' I said nothing about having been locked up with it in the cellar at the Medici palace while the mob in the street was howling for those who had murdered Giuliano. Nothing about having been carried into the angelic realm by the song of this octave of figures. 'Very beautiful.'

Lorenzino was dressed simply in doublet and hose, a man as much at home in himself as in his house. He apologized for his appearance. 'Some recommend that a man should wear his Sunday best when he studies, but I approach my books as an artisan, not an ambassador, and I like to be comfortable while I work.' On a table was a pile of open books: I had interrupted him in his study of Plato in the original Greek. In the centre of the room on a lectern was my *Hermes*, open for reading, the light falling on its gilded capitals and making them shine.

'I had to thank you in person,' Lorenzino said, smiling. 'It is even better than I had hoped and asked for. With all due respect – I'm sure you will understand what I say – I could have commissioned a scribe with a finer hand...'

I swallowed my outrage and returned his smile.

'... but when a scribe understands his text, when he is at one with his text, the beauty he achieves is sublime and far deeper than mere outward appearance. Not that,' he added hurriedly, 'it is not outwardly beautiful. It is. Most will recognise it as a work of outstanding beauty, particularly in its proportions, but I am afflicted with senses more acute than those of most men, and I can see the shaky descender on this p, or the untrue angle of that o…'

'Tommaso,' said Giovanni di Pierfrancesco, walking in, 'take no notice of him. He would find a pimple on the Virgin's cheek. This,' he said, joining us in front of the book, 'is *bellissima*, and if my brother finds he cannot live with its imperceptible faults then I shall have it.'

'Forgive me,' said Lorenzino. 'Have I hurt you, being truthful and forthright?'

'Not at all,' I lied pleasantly.

'Only I judge you to be a man who values Truth, worships her, indeed.'

'I would like to be considered so, and I would be the first to criticise my own achievements.' First and *only*, preferably.

'I have upset you,' said Lorenzino. I assured him he had not but knew it was hopeless. No one could feign anything before those penetrating, hooded eyes. He took my right hand in both of his, caressed it, raised it to his lips and kissed it. 'There – that is what I wanted to do when I saw my book. Let my actions sound louder than my words.' Releasing my hand, he returned to the book, turning its pages reverentially. 'Beauty,' he said, 'opens the heart. When I read here, the words of Hermes go straight into my soul.' He read from the book: *This is life, my beloved; this is beauty, this is the Supreme Good, this is God.*

I would have liked to concentrate on the words being spoken in his melodious voice, but I was being stared at by Giovanni, who had thrown himself into a chair and had one leg dangling over its arm. I believe he was pitting himself against Hermes Trismegistus to see who would get my attention. When I glanced at him and his boyish face, so sweet and disingenuous, I felt badly about having such a thought, but as I turned back to the book, he interrupted.

'Is it true about Poliziano?'

'What?'

'That he's buggering his nephews.'

'Of course not!'

Lorenzino looked pained. 'Giovanino, this is my study – a holy place.'

'Sorry. I was just curious. But you live with him and his sister,' he persisted. 'What's the arrangement in the house? Sorry, sorry! Just curious. I'll go.'

Bringing his legs back together again, he sprang out of the chair and went whistling away into the adjoining chamber. Watching him go, I noticed another Botticelli painting, this one showing Pallas Athene with a centaur, hanging above the door to the antechamber. Lorenzino was a man who knew how to spend his wealth.

'I apologise for my brother,' he said. 'He's very young. Sit, talk to me awhile. I, too, am curious, though not about rumours. You are a Volterrano, correct? And yet you are very close to my cousin, even saved his life when he was attacked. How is that? Have you no feeling for your patria?'

Lorenzino was easy to talk to. I told him how much I had hated Lorenzo after he had brought about my city's downfall – Lorenzino nodding all the while, understanding and sympathetic – and how I could not learn to love Lorenzo even when I eventually came to live in his household. 'It was during the attack by the Pazzi. When I turned to see my brother's dagger raised to stab Lorenzo, I acted without thinking. Hatred, Ficino once told me, is merely a corruption of love. You cannot hate without having first loved. With that involuntary action of mine, the hatred dissolved. Lorenzo has been very good to me ever since.'

'In what way?'

I listed all the things Lorenzo had done for me.

'Forgive me, but do you not see he is buying you? Through you he is absolving his sins, in the eyes of himself if not of heaven. Be wary of my cousin, Tommaso. Once he feels sufficiently absolved, he will forget you.'

I shifted uncomfortably, remembering the interview with Lorenzo when I had asked for a commission and been refused. Was il Magnifico as poor as he claimed, or merely tiring of me?

Lorenzino's gaze had turned to his desk. Suddenly he rose from his chair decisively. The meeting was over. 'Thank you for coming,' he said, grasping both my hands. 'I have enjoyed our conversation. My bursar will give you something on the way out, for I think your fee for this work was too low. If ever I can help you in any way, Tommaso, you will come to me, won't you? Promise?'

I promised.

The bursar, waiting for me in the sala with a purse of five gold florins, was Amerigo Vespucci, yes, that same Amerigo Vespucci whose recent exploration of the lands discovered by Columbus have convinced him that they are not Asia but a new continent: the man who has changed the map.

On the way out through the serene Casa Vecchia, down the Via Larga, all the way to the Cathedral, I floated on a sense of well-being. Then I saw Lorenzo il Magnifico riding by with his entourage, and he called out in greeting to me, '*Salve*, Tommaso!' Suddenly I knew, deep in the soul, that in the Casa Vecchia I had been deliberately seeded with suspicion. Here was the man I could trust without doubt.

'*Salve*, Lorenzo!' I called back, as if to a fellow student or close friend.

16 AT THE HEARTH
1485

LORENZO HAD DIVIDED THE UNIVERSITY OF FLORENCE into two parts. The older, nobler parts of the curriculum – theology and law – he transferred to Pisa. Ostensibly he had given the university to the port town in our dominions, but in reserving for Florence the faculty of poetry, Lorenzo had elevated that subject by isolating it. No longer were the professors of poetry overshadowed by lofty theologians sweeping through halls and cloisters. Now they had the place to themselves. The head of the faculty, Cristoforo Landino, was the author of the tremendous commentary on Dante, and the lecturers and professors included the best poets of our time and place. This was the heart of Lorenzo's work, to educate Florentines in ancient literature and to raise the vulgar tongue, to make Tuscan as good as the ancient languages in the expression of truth and beauty. For Lorenzo saw Italian literature as an education in *virtù* and a powerful force for the advancement of mankind.

These were inspiring ideals, but the daily reality was of facing dull students having trouble with their Latin and Greek. They filled Angelo's town house, either visiting for tutorials or staying in the house, as was the custom. Instead of writing poetry or reading the ancients, the poet was compelled to read a growing stack of mediocre essays.

To quell gossip, whenever we were resident at the house on the Via de' Fossi, Angelo's sister-in-law and nephews lived in the villa. But in December of 1485, the wind suddenly turned hot. Animals came out of hibernation and we walked abroad without our coats on. Indeed, it was so hot that the walls of the house began to sweat. Angelo told the servants to pack. 'If it is going to be this hot,' he said, 'we may as well return to the villa.' Florence had become for him a torment of distractions. He could not walk down the street without being stopped by men wanting his opinion on their poetry, or wanting him to compose love letters or mottoes for them. If fame is honey then people are bears. 'I am tired of the city,' Angelo said. 'We shall winter in the country.' We would spend Advent on Fiesole, just the three of us, while Cammilla and the boys returned to Florence.

As soon as we were back at the villa, my dear friend stopped sighing and found peace. His Muse had begun to speak again, and though the hot wind was soon displaced by an icy one, which whistled along the valley and rattled our doors, we had found such bliss in our rustic life that we decided to continue with it.

Maria spent her time searching Roman and Greek authors for mention of household gods – lares and penates – and became increasingly convinced that our villa was populated by benign, domestic spirits. She wanted to know the correct procedure for libation and sacrifice to such gods. Angelo said they were too lowly and needed no sacrifice or libation: one simply has to acknowledge their presence and live with them. Maria was not satisfied.

One evening as she and her brother fed and stoked the fire, each of us lost to private reflections, and Maria's lips working on a silent hymn, she suddenly picked up Angelo's glass and flung its contents on the fire. 'To Hestia!' she said, and the flames roared up, sizzling, to grasp the sacrifice.

Angelo was outraged. It was his best wine. He was so angry he chastised Maria, telling her that what she had done was wrong. It was impulsive. It was womanly and wasteful. Sacrifices require planning and careful ritual. They should be taken seriously.

'Oh, you are just upset about the loss of your wine,' she said cheerfully. She turned to me. 'He always justifies his personal will with grand principles of universal law.'

This set off a storm of ill temper in Angelo which even Maria could not ride. She struggled, listing badly, to the safe harbour of her own room.

I have nothing of Maria's poetry but only this, on a piece of yellowing parchment, cracked where it has been folded and tucked into my journal.

How to kindle a fire
by Maria Poliziana

1. *Find dry twigs that snap easily. Break them in quick short snaps to attract the fiery demons. Place them in the hearth end up so that they form a kind of pyre.*
2. *Take a poem, your favourite, the one you have just completed, crumple*

111

it and place it in the middle of the structure. *The fragrance of this sacrifice will attract the gods.*

3. *Strike a spark from the tinder box to catch the kindling. Once alight, add more twigs and small logs.*

4. *To please the gods, once the fire is ablaze throw in pine cones and resinous branches of pine or yew, apple or olive.*

5. *When all is as you would wish it, take your brother's glass of wine and throw its contents on the fire as an oblation to Hestia, the goddess of the hearth.*

6. *More poems may be added, but take care they are not your brother's, for his mood will already be grim at the loss of his wine.*

Left alone by the fire, and the storm now passed, Angelo confessed to me that he had received a proposal of marriage for his sister from the Bardi family.

'The Bardi?' I gasped, suddenly choking on an olive. 'A good family!'

'But a poor branch of it. I sent the fellow away.'

The olive came free in my throat.

'Was it remiss of me to make my own mind up without consulting her? Perhaps I was just being selfish. Do you think she may want to marry, no matter how much she protests to the contrary?'

'I think she does not. She is happy here.'

'Tommaso, do you think she is in love with Giovanni Pico?'

'Who is not? More to the point, is he in love with her?'

'He has a fine taste in women,' Angelo said, 'and finds them a pleasant distraction. But Maria, I believe, he looks upon as his own sister. As for marriage, he has no intention of it. To lead the kind of life he wants to live, he needs to be free. Free to wander...' Angelo sighed and poked at the fire.

'I want to apologise about the wine,' Maria said softly behind us.

Angelo swung round. 'How long have you been standing there?'

'You need not be concerned: I would have refused marriage to a Bardi, whatever his fortune.' She gave Angelo the list of instructions she had just written on how to kindle a fire. He read it, groaned with remorse and handed it to me.

'Maria, I do everything out of love for you. Am I growing selfish? You have a right to your own happiness.'

Maria declared that she enjoyed more happiness than anyone had a right to, and that she did not wish to try for that which fate had put beyond her reach. She settled herself by the fire again, and we stayed up long into the night, telling stories. While Maria enjoyed the myths her brother recounted, what she loved were stories about women, women of strength which our times were beginning to throw up in profusion. There was Anne of Brittany who, since the accession of her little brother, Charles, to the throne, had become regent of France. There was Isabella d'Este, who often seemed more the Marquis of Mantua than her husband; and her sister, Beatrice, powerful wife of Ludovico Sforza of Milan. And then there was Sforza's niece, Caterina, a young woman of Maria's own age. Caterina combined everything that Maria declared to be 'the ideal woman' – she was beautiful, slender, well-spoken, and extremely well-educated. Since her marriage to Girolamo Riario, she had borne him a child each year.

Angelo did not want to discuss anything related to Riario, the nephew of Pope Sixtus and prime instigator in the plot to murder the Medici in 1478.

'The man is a monster,' Maria agreed. 'But that is what is special about Caterina. She is so loyal to him. The people of Imola love her absolutely. She is their queen.'

'I met her once,' I said.

Maria yelped. I might have said I had met the Queen of Sheba.

I regretted saying it, for I did not want to talk about that time when I was called to present myself to Girolamo Riario, and his haughty young wife sitting there beside him, the time when I was examined to see if I were fit to join the conspiracy that was to lead to the death of Giuliano. By the grace of God I had failed the test; nonetheless I still felt tainted by my closeness to the conspiracy.

'So what is she like in the flesh?' Maria asked.

'I saw her at a distance and did not speak to her. But, yes, she is beautiful.'

Just the name 'Imola' and 'Riario' brought both Angelo and me out in a sweat, for the whole conspiracy had blown up from the desire of Pope Sixtus to buy that fortress town for his nephew, but Maria continued to chirrup about this object of her fascination, Riario's wife. While we were still celebrating the death of Sixtus in the previous year, here was Maria feeling sorry for Caterina Sforza who, no longer the recipient of papal monies, was now dependent on her own resourcefulness.

'Her own. That stupid husband of hers is incapable of anything but losing money in the gaming house.'

'That and a little bit of killing,' said Angelo sourly.

Such was Caterina's resourcefulness that she had inspired the Riario family to take up arms in the fight to get their candidate elected as the next pope.

'All the Riario menfolk are inept,' said Maria. 'It was Caterina who belted on a curved sword and rode to take over the Castel Sant' Angelo.'

'She is quite inept herself. The coup failed.'

Indeed it had, and the new pope, Innocent VIII, was a friend of the Medici and not of the Riario. Girolamo and his wife had retreated to their castles in the Romagna, sometimes at Imola, sometimes at Forlì, and were living on the only resources available to despots: taxation raised on the people of those unfortunate towns.

'She is no Saint Joan, I grant you,' said Maria. 'But her strength of character is impressive, you must agree.'

Angelo said that powerful women are aberrations of nature and that the image of a woman brandishing a sword was going to give him nightmares. For that reason he made us stay up late and by midnight we had fallen to confessing to what we loved and wanted for ourselves. For Angelo it was a woman of his own imagination, a Venus who threw all mortal women into the shade, but a Minerva also, for his ideal woman had to have a knowledge of Latin and Greek as sweet as the curve of her breasts. For me it was Elena, my Eurydice. 'I wish the impossible, long for it with a longing that hurts, strain for it, challenge God for it, shouting at him: *Give her back to me!* I cannot understand why God gives only to take away again. What I want is Elena, more than my life's breath.'

'She is closer than you think, Tommaso,' said Maria.

'What do you mean?'

'Everything we seek is closer than we think. There is no time and space in love.'

'And you,' Angelo asked her gently. 'Tell us, do you long for Giovanni Pico?'

'Of course, but not, as you think, to become my husband.'

'Lover, then?'

'Of a kind.'

'What kind is that?'

'The noblest,' she said simply. 'Platonic lover.' Her words made us both abashed, but she had more to teach us, this young woman. 'What we have spoken of,' she said, 'is desire for the impossible: neither your Venus-Minerva nor your Elena are attainable.' She turned her gaze on me, a lingering, mellow-eyed look that was both love and compassion, and something else. 'What unites all three of us is this frustration of our desires. That is the fire in which we burn, and it will turn us into gold.'

London, January 4th, 1506

Erasmus is ecstatic, having received a papal dispensation which more or less declares him legitimate. We did not know he was illegitimate, born of parents who loved each other but were not married. He has lived well enough with his illegitimacy, as have I, but he needs ecclesiastical benefices. Now with this dispensation he may gain them and make his life as a scholar secure.

'Was it that easy?' I asked. 'You wrote to the pope and he granted your request?'

'I had many influential men write on my behalf but, yes, it was easier than I supposed, but then Julius the Second is a good pope.'

Now there's an oxymoron: a good pope.

Pope Julius is a della Rovere, another nephew of Sixtus IV. Inspired by his kinswoman, Caterina Sforza, he tried to oust the previous pope by the sword but failed and had to wait for him to die in God's good time. A man of more than sixty, Julius is trying to free my homeland from the monster that is Cesare Borgia. That is a good thing. It is also good that he plans to rebuild St Peter's basilica. But the news that reaches us, of Julius outlawing the practices of simony and nepotism, well, that is the usual hypocrisy. He is just a man who, having reached the roof, draws up the ladder so that none may follow.

Erasmus is lodging at More's house and they spend their evenings reading Lucian in the Greek. When I took the book to Erasmus and More, it was to show them the beauty of printed Greek as done by Aldus Manutius of Venice, but they were too struck by the text itself to notice the beauty of its letters. Captivated by the mordant wit of Lucian, they took it from me and began at once to translate it into Latin. The winter is now being warmed and spiced with

Lucianic jokes, and often one walks down Bucklersbury to hear the laughter of the two friends ringing from an upper window in the Old Barge.

Colet objects. He tells them that they should be spending their time on Holy Scripture, or translating the works of the Fathers, but Erasmus argues that, to do so, he must perfect his Greek, and how better than by keeping company with one of its most eloquent writers?

It is increasingly difficult to remember that Erasmus is a monk raised by the Brethren of the Common Life. He often stays at Greenwich with Lord Mountjoy and is learning to ride and hunt.

'Practising for my journey!' he declares. '*Our* journey,' he corrects himself and throws his arms about me and kisses me on both cheeks in the fashion of the English, something we Dutch and Italians find akin to being tickled.

I resist his assumption that I am going with him as I resist Colet's command. It is not possible for me to return home. Ficino set me a task here which I have yet to fulfil. Besides which, to go home would be folly. What no one understands here, since I have not told them, is that I am on the run, an outlaw. I saw that friar again, yesterday… Perhaps I should move on. Perhaps it is time for me to make a pilgrimage to Jerusalem, but to do that I would have to go through Italy… I am too ill for all this. I have hardly slept since John gave me that command. Just as sleep comes, my breathing seems to stop and I wake up in panic. And the chilblains are making furnaces of my toes. I must go and see Linacre.

17 INVOKING ANGELS
1486

WHEN PICO RETURNED FROM PARIS, THERE WAS AN EXOTIC crowd of scholars riding in his train: bearded Byzantines, handsome Arabs and some heavy-eyed Spanish Jews. One Italian wearing a bizarre costume emblazoned with the Greek letter, Tau, had a face looking as if it had been clawed by the devil. Behind this procession followed a mule train laden with book chests. Pico's hair, crimped in the latest French style, hung in tight ringlets down to the middle of his back and he wore an apple green hat with a long and severe point. Arriving at the Palazzo de' Medici, he called Lorenzo out of a meeting and had him send for Ficino and Poliziano at once.

Angelo, about to deliver a lecture, was torn. He affected anger. 'For the Count of Concordia, things are either urgent or of no interest. There's nothing in between. Tell him,' he said, prodding the Medici servant, 'that I am unable to attend him.' The servant nodded and was about to depart when Angelo stopped him. 'Tell him instead to attend me, at my villa this evening. There...' he brushed his hands of the matter. 'Counts! Nobles! They come, they go, they give orders.' He went to the window and looked out. 'I wonder what's so urgent?'

'Angelo,' I said, 'concentrate on your lecture.'

In the evening Pico rode up to Fiesole with his motley band of scholars. At the villa he leapt from his horse and threw his arms round Poliziano, saying how much he had missed him. Before Angelo could complain about Pico having gone off without saying goodbye, Pico was saying that it is a mark of true friendship that you don't have to be in sight of one another to be close. 'When two souls are joined, no amount of miles can sunder them.

Distance makes no difference. That is true friendship, when one is free to come and go without explanation, with no demands being made.' He turned to embrace Maria. 'And when the beloved is in dual form, male and female both, how blessed can a lover be?'

One of the Jewish doctors watched this scene with stark disapproval and took Pico aside for a whispered conversation. Pico beckoned to Maria and introduced her to the Jew. 'She is my sister, Mithridates. She is my soul. I want her to hear what we have to say.'

Mithridates exchanged glances with another of the Jewish doctors, then nodded sourly. 'It is not for the guest to say who shall be present.'

Once we were all settled in the villa's loggia, Pico told us what he had imparted to Lorenzo and Ficino earlier, that he had discovered a system of knowledge in the Jewish tradition called Cabala, a source of wisdom that would one day unite all men in devotion of God – Jews, Christians, Muslims alike. 'In essence,' Pico said, unfolding some charts covered with Hebrew signs, 'the system is a code enabling one to unlock the hidden mysteries of scripture. It shows us that everything in the history of creation, from Genesis onwards, prefigures the Son of God; that the name of the Messiah is Iesu.'

'We know that,' said Angelo.

'We do, but the Jews don't. My friends here are converts, and wish all their fellows to convert. If we were to unlock the whole Bible with this key, we could change the course of human history.'

I felt the hairs on my neck rising, and said so.

'Tsssh,' said Pico, 'a fine literary conceit. Your hair lies as usual. But yes, you feel the prickle of terror, as I did once. And you feel the same wonder. Mithridates here has taught me the system of letter manipulation, which I shall now show to you.' He unrolled a scroll showing a diagram, in shape a kind of kite with circles at its angles numbering ten in all, each with a name and called the *Sephiroth*. He spoke rapidly and with many Hebrew terms that were mystifying, but at the end of the demonstration he had drawn an eleventh circle and written within it the name *Iesu*. With that he sat back, his eyes huge and expectant, as if he had not only discovered the secret of the universe but proved it. 'Cabala, the secret wisdom of Moses, predicts Christ. What Cabala shows us is that there is one Law, one Truth, and it informs everything: all forms, all institutions, all religions. All creation, in its infinite variety, springs from one source.'

Angelo, struggling to remain sceptical in the face of this vivid demonstration, stared at Pico as Peter the fisherman must have looked at Christ. 'I cannot believe the truth can be so simple.'

'Why should it be complicated, if it is true?'

Pico invited Mithridates, an expert in Oriental languages and a speaker of many tongues, to explain to us how, by manipulation of letters and the incantation of names, one may mount the heavens to the angelic realm and, beyond that, to God. This was a journey, Pico said, so blissful, so transcendent of the body, that it may only be made under the guidance of a magus, and its goal is the *mors osculi,* the death of the kiss. 'According to our wise teachers, many of the ancient fathers died in a rapture of the intellect called *binsica*, which in Hebrew means death from kissing. They say that this is what happened to Abraham, Isaac, Jacob, Moses and Mary. This is what Solomon refers to in his song when he says, "Kiss me with the kisses of thy mouth". This is the kind of kissing Plato refers to when he speaks of the kisses of his Agathon, and not the kind that many believe of him.'

Maria gazed at him, her mouth slightly open.

'The question is,' said Pico, 'whether they are speaking of physical death, or a symbolic one.'

'It is physical,' said Mithridates, in a tone which invited no argument. 'Of course it is physical. Why should a man who has found union with the Divine wish to continue living in mortal bondage? It is a physical death. You see God, you die. The end of it.'

Elia del Medigo, a professor of philosophy at Padua, disagreed, saying that the mystic death was but the death of the false self, the selfish person with whom we identify, usurper of the throne of the intellect.

We Florentines listened agog to such occult, Jewish speculations.

Maria sat staring out into the night and the winking fireflies. 'We should not speak of death so lightly,' she said. 'To welcome death is to misunderstand the nature of life.'

'Go on,' said Pico, encouraging her to speak her thoughts.

'Life is God,' she said. 'Life is eternal. Our bodies die, and we should not mourn them; but we should not shun life.'

Mithridates looked down his long nose at her. 'My lord,' he appealed to Pico, 'it is not acceptable to have a woman arguing with us.'

Maria apologised and said she had not meant to argue, only to offer her point of view.

'She speaks as she finds,' Pico said, 'and, when she does, it is worth listening to her.'

The man with the scarred face, an Italian called Mercurio, put out his hand and rested it on Maria's head. 'She has the sight,' he said, speaking out of one side of his mouth, for the other was frozen by the scarring.

'A woman? It is not possible,' said Mithridates. He rose in agitation and began pacing the loggia.

Pico looked up at the stars. 'Pray, continue your discourse about the heavens.'

Mithridates looked at Maria is if she were polluting the purity of the intellect but then he sighed and acquiesced. He stepped outside the loggia, threw up his arms to the sky and called on us to look on the spheres of the planets. We could identify those of Mercury, Mars and Venus, but Jupiter and Saturn were not visible. 'And yet we know that they are there,' said Mithridates. 'Likewise we go beyond the senses to proceed on this journey. We go beyond the planets, to the spheres of the angels – thrones, cherubim and seraphim. This is beyond the senses, but still part of the intelligible world. But beyond the nine spheres is the tenth, which is motionless and beyond human knowledge.' He spoke in symbols and allusions, of the seraphic fire of love, the cherubic fire of knowledge, and by such words we were drawn far from the world of the body and its carnal concerns, our souls travelling by Jewish maps, sphere by sphere, through the circles of the planets to the outer limits of the cosmos and the tenth sphere, where nothing moves but all is still: absolute peace.

'So if it is beyond knowledge,' said Angelo, 'how do we know about it?'

'By becoming it,' said Elia del Megido. 'When all movement ceases, mental and physical, when you find that stillness within yourself, then you know not by the mind but by the being, by experience.'

'This is the truth of Hermes,' said Mercurio.

'It is the truth of the Cabala,' said Mithridates.

'It is the truth of Plato,' said I.

Pico told us it was the truth of all wisdom. 'This is where all the divergent faiths and systems of the world meet in harmony: at the source.'

Although Angelo threw his hands up and muttered about angels and fairies, saying we would all be burnt for heresy just listening to such things, he allowed Pico to use his house as a cabalistic academy on Fiesole. Lorenzo de' Medici came frequently, and his Pierfranceschi cousins. Men came from much farther off, from places such as England, Portugal and Germany, ostensibly students of Poliziano, but the best of them, such as the mature Grocyn and the young Linacre, were drawn into our academy. I was a keen student, for I believed in this Jewish system of understanding the cosmos and shared Pico's desire to introduce it into Christianity. Although Angelo disapproved, saying it would 'excite her brain', Maria joined me each day to study and practise Hebrew letters. With her heavy, black hair tied in its knot, in which were often stuck a couple of spare quills, she was a distracting fellow student and sometimes I sat back from my studies to gaze at this woman bent over her books and breathing through her mouth. If she had been a man, I would have worked in silence, keeping my knowledge to myself until such times that I could devastate him with a display of brilliance. Instead I found myself asking for her help when I needed it, and she always gave it in a way that did not diminish me in my own eyes. I called her my sister, but even sisters can be competitive, and she was not. Every now and then we took a line from the Bible and translated its letters into their numerical equivalents to find the deeper, hidden message. Each time we were startled by what we found.

When Pico came to the villa, attended by his oriental companions, he often kept us up late into the night discussing his multitudinous and often obscure ideas, filling us with awe and wonder as if we were children listening to the tales of a spiritual adventurer. He was twenty-three and at his boldest, lavishing his wealth on books and scholars who could translate cabalistic texts for him. He was inflamed with the idea that, now that we had brought back from obscurity the works of the ancient Romans and Greeks, the next step was to become familiar with the wisdom of the East, of the Hebrews, the Persians and the Indians.

On one particular evening celebrated in the Jewish calendar, at the Palazzo de' Medici Mithridates performed a rite, intoning certain chants and swinging a censer to fill the room with dense clouds of fragrant smoke in which we might see angels. What angel did we raise that night? I saw nothing myself, although others claimed to have seen shapes or figures of light in the billowing smoke of frankincense and storax. I grew frightened – what if we raised a demon and not an angel? I reminded myself that, according to the Neoplatonists, daemons are agents of the Divine, and may probably be equated with angels. Even so, some more primitive fear took hold of me and I dreaded seeing anything in the smoke. Therefore I was not sorry when I saw nothing, and later, riding home with Angelo, agreed with him that it had been an interesting experiment producing no results. But as I write this, I begin to think that our ill-fortune began on that night, was coalesced, made strong and focussed. Not a man there who wasn't touched by it in some way, the Angel – or demon – of Death.

Am I saying that Mithridates purposely summoned that dark angel? No, I am not. But such magic may only be performed by the pure. What I am saying is that Mithridates was not pure.

London, January 9th, 1506

'Hmmm,' said Linacre, taking my pulse in five places. 'Ha.' Sitting on a low stool in front of me, he went down between the sharp angle of his knees to look at the blue bruises on my toes. 'Oh, dear.'

'What is it?'

'Sssh. Be quiet. I am having a conversation with your body. Hmmm. Not been looking after ourselves too well, have we?'

'Are you expecting a reply from me or my feet?'

'Too much vinegar. Wine should be drunk where it is grown, you know.'

'You want me to drink that horse pee from English vineyards?'

He sat up and tapped his fingers together under his nose, many times and quickly. The draught lifted his fringe. 'It is good. Good wine,' he said, rising from the stool. 'How are your joints?'

'Supple! I am only forty-eight.'

'And your *pene*?'

'Pendulous.'

'How come?'

I was surprised by the question. 'By my will, of course.'

Linacre laughed. 'Who do you think you are? A saint? Perhaps Saggy Annie was right.' He went to the bench to make a note in his patients book. While I put my hose and shoes back on, he stood tapping his quill against his lips.

'I came to see you because I'm short of breath,' I grumbled.

'Hmmm?' He dipped his nib and wrote more notes. 'Ah, well, you rarely find a cause in the area of the symptoms.' Inhaling loudly, he turned and leaned against the bench with his arms folded.

'Melancholia,' he pronounced, with that joy of a man to whom knowledge has dawned in all its glory.

If this annoyed me it was because I could have recognised it myself and not have troubled a busy friend with something so obvious. Melancholia – the excessive influence of the planet Saturn – is a disease so common amongst scholars that Ficino wrote a whole book on it, and I copied it out twice. Why have I not been able to see it for myself? I thanked Linacre and, when he began to prescribe remedies, interrupted to say that I know them off by heart. 'In short I need the influence of Jove and should wear gold, eat honey and drink mead.'

'Far from it. You need the moisture of Venus: peaches, pears, figs, grapes and olives. And coral.' He went to a small drawer in a great chest and took out a handful of red pills made he said, from Sardinian coral, and dropped them into a pouch. 'Take three of these twice a day until they are finished. Of course, the best remedy of all would be the sea; a journey on the sea, even a short one, would do.'

'Such as crossing the English Channel? This is not a remedy, it's a conspiracy. By a not very subtle method you are telling me to obey Colet and go home.'

'Your body is telling you that. Do not take these symptoms lightly. If you continue in this fashion, always working, over-indulging in study, leading a secluded life in damp lodgings, your heart will kill you.'

'Then it is a choice between death and death, for if I am to find what I have lost, then it is to Hades I must go.'

'Florence is not hell, my friend. There are many fine things there still, including that wine you love. Remember how that tastes under a hot sun? Nectar! I do not understand why you do not wish to return home.'

'I am tired of travelling and long to settle.'

'Open your mouth and put out your tongue.' His spare, bony face came close to mine. 'Hoo – too much garlic last night! But it looks alright.'

'What did you expect?'

'Rows of bright red pimples: the tell-tale sign of a liar. No one would choose to live in England in preference to Italy.'

'Here you do not have Cesare Borgia, laying waste to cities.'

'So Cesare Borgia himself chased you out of Italy, did he? Well, you can go back now since Cesare himself has fled to Spain.'

'He has?'

'I heard it last night at court.'

I sighed. 'There is a more practical difficulty: I cannot afford the journey.'

'You could sell me your copy of Plato.'

I looked at him in horror, unable to believe what he had said.

Linacre shrugged. 'Is it not true that, to find God, we have to give up our most cherished possession? Indeed, it would speed your ascent if you were to give it to me rather than sell it.' He grinned suddenly. 'I am only teasing.'

I turned my head this way and that to loosen the muscles that had gone into spasm.

'I have a commission for you. The king is still anxious to obtain plans of Santa Maria Nuova, to build a hospital on its model at Savoy on the Strand. He has learnt considerable detail from the Florentines in his court, and from the Portinari family in Bruges. But what he cannot find is a drawn plan. He was asking me recently what I could remember of the building but I could only say how it is shaped like a church and has courtyards and cloisters. "Oh, for a plan!" the King complained. When I told him you were preparing to go to Italy with Erasmus –'

'– *What?*'

'– he offered to pay your expenses. And there will be a reward on your return. Tommaso, you have drawing skills and are adept in the science of proportion. You must return to Italy, if only to visit this hospital and measure it for me. Pace it out so that we know its distances.'

I told him that I have no intention of making any journey. I am tired. Let me rest. God, let me rest.

London, January 12th, 1506

God has joined the conspiracy. This morning I received a letter from the Prior of Blackfriars demanding to see me. I went there straightaway; better that than dwelling on it. The interview was short. Either I return to the habit and go back into a Dominican house, or I must go to the pope in person to request absolution of my vows. There is to be no more running.

'One more thing, brother,' he said, as I was about to leave. 'I have heard rumour that the Dean of St Paul's is a Platonist and Cabalist. Is it true?'

'I have never met a more authentic, ardent Christian.'

'You were once a servant of Pico della Mirandola, I believe. If I find that it is you who is sowing seeds of heresy in this land, I shall not hesitate to report you. The burnings have not stopped, you know.'

'The Count of Concordia was absolved of heresy.'

'By a Borgia pope for a considerable amount of Medici money. That is not the kind of absolution heaven recognises.'

I wanted to ask if heaven would recognise absolution from my sins by a della Rovere pope but the Prior is not a man to argue with. Hypocrisy – is it any wonder I suffer from it when it is so rife?

18 PICO AIMS TO CURE THE WORLD OF IGNORANCE 1486

THE HUMAN MIND TENDS NATURALLY TO METAPHOR – some would say that life itself is a metaphor, that somehow creation is a semblance of a divine truth. Certainly it seems that we can hardly speak without likening one thing to another. But Pico della Mirandola defies analogy. He was unique. I did not understand him then; I do not understand him now, even with the benefit of hindsight and the wisdom of age. There was and is no one like him. Except perhaps Phaeton, who fell to his death while riding the chariot of the sun.

Some say that Pico was brash and arrogant, but it was his youth and his soaring intellect that upset them. A man of his brilliance of mature years would have been called neither brash nor arrogant, merely 'master'. Who knows by what divine agency he was endowed with superhuman powers of study? Angelo Poliziano had the most prodigious memory of any man I knew until Pico arrived, and then he was outshone. Pico had only to hear a poem once to be able to recite it, not only forwards but backwards also. Ficino said that that was all that Pico's learning amounted to: a prodigious feat of memory. Perhaps.

Pico always got what he wanted, not in the fashion of a spoilt child but as one who cannot see any reason, given that all his work was dedicated to world harmony, why he should be denied. To deny him was surely to act against the Will of God. He was always arriving in the homes of friends, rushing in like the west wind and asking for the loan of a book or manuscript. No matter how precious or rare, no matter that it was at that very moment being studied by its owner, he had to have it. And have it he always did.

'I shall be back in a few days!' he would promise as he left, and not be seen again for at least a month. Men treated him like a favourite puppy who had chewed a shoe, giving him a stroke and a word of praise rather than the slap he deserved.

When he returned from Paris, his ambition if not his powers had been infinitely increased. He was distressed by what he had found at the Sorbonne. All faiths and religions were prone, he said, to dissension amongst their doctors and theologians, but none so much as our own Christianity. At the Sorbonne every scholar was at war with his fellows.

'What is the point of studying,' Pico asked during a meeting of the Platonic Academy, where we had our own fair share of acrimonious debates, 'if it is just to disprove somebody else? The only goal of study should be Truth, but she lies torn and bleeding in our universities. We come from God as an emanation: intellect from God, soul from intellect, body from soul. Likewise our philosophies all arise from one source, as an emanation of wisdom. In unity they agree; in multiplicity they disagree. We need to follow wisdom back to its source. I am working on a system by which that might be achieved.'

A system to reconcile Plato and Aristotle, Averroes and Avicenna, Thomas Aquinas and Duns Scotus: a system to reconcile everything. More, it was to be a system that replaced the doctrines of the scholastics with true philosophy. Through Cabala, Plato would become safe, acceptable, and integral to Christianity. Is it any wonder that no one could resist Pico? He was so fired by his ideas, which had come to fruition in Paris, that he wanted, quite literally, to tell the world. He was compiling a list of theses – propositions that had been controversial for centuries – which he wished to debate, to resolve, in an open arena. In Paris? we asked. Padua? Pisa? Bologna?

'Rome.'

'There is no university at Rome.'

'There is the Vatican. Imagine,' and here he addressed himself to Lorenzo de' Medici in particular, 'imagine a Church actively engaged in the pursuit of truth. I want to lay out my ideas before the Pope and the college of cardinals.'

Lorenzo could imagine nothing more ambitious and less likely to succeed, but if it should... 'O Count of Concordia, how well-named you are.'

19 THE TREE OF KNOWLEDGE 1486

THERE ARE TWO MAIN TRADITIONS OF CABALA, THAT OF the *scientia sephirot,* or knowledge of the centres of energy within a man and within the cosmos; and the tradition of the *scientia semot,* the knowledge of the names of God – employing techniques of gematria, where numerical values are given to letters, hidden messages and ciphers may be discerned in scripture. Pico inclined towards the *scientia sephirot* and by this means was, he claimed, advancing towards true knowledge. He told us that Cabala, which reveals the mysteries of the universe and of Man, is the key to knowing everything.

He expounded to us the four levels of meaning, 'the Tetragrammaton of scriptural study'. He had discovered that the theory of the four levels, often found in Christian writers, originated in the Jewish tradition. First there is the literal level, the level of common understanding; then there is the allegorical level, where one thing signifies another; the symbolic level, where by the use of symbol things may be understood in a revelatory way; and then there is the anagogic level, where the reader and the word become one. 'This is the union of the soul and God, and the Hebrew name for the anagogic level is "Cabala".'

Pico had a favourite story he had found in his oriental books. 'There were some blind men travelling in a group who came upon a horse. One touched its head, the other its ears, one its back, another its flanks, one its mane and another its tail. Asked what a horse was, the blind men, convinced that they knew, said, "It is a warm hide; it is rough hair; it is a like a waxy flower; it is a breathing box." Each man knew only part of it but, believing he knew all of it, he went to war with his fellows. To know the truth we must lose our blindness. This is the pass we have come to: we are trying to understand by use of the mind what is beyond the mind, and it is impossible. Only through Cabala may the blind begin to see.'

I fell in love with the alphabet of God, and devoured any translation as soon as it was made by Pico's Jewish scholars. These were mysterious texts, not revealing very much to the uninitiated. Such was my longing to be an initiate that I even had a dream in which Pico appeared and invited me to a secret chamber. There Mithridates invested me with a parchment jerkin and hat on which were inscribed the names of God in Hebrew characters. After a fast of four days, I went by night to a lake and called out the Name over the water, and I watched to see if a green or a red form appeared in the air. Then I waded into the water and put on the garment and the Name, and was invested with terrible strength and the power to invoke angels. I called the Name. There was a great beating of wings and agitation of air. In terror, I woke up.

What I did not know was that, at this time, Pico himself was not yet initiated. One evening at the Villa Bruscoli he raised the subject, saying that Cabalistic initiation was like baptism – a required stage in the spiritual life. I grew shivery with my imaginings, but Pico discussed it as freely as a trip to market. He said his was to happen on the eve of the Feast of Weeks on the fiftieth day after Passover when, in a rite to be performed by Mithridates, he would be married to Lady Truth. He did not say more or explain what he meant but glanced at Maria with such effulgent eyes that she dipped her head to hide her blushes. Why did she blush? Could she not see his meaning? If Pico equated Poliziano's sister with his divine beloved, it was an allegorical equation, for he retained his doubts that a woman could truly love platonically. Women, he said, unlike men, have no control over their passions.

The initiation was to take place in Rome.

'You are leaving again?' Angelo asked.

Pico ignored the plaintiveness in his friend's voice. 'Will you let me borrow Tommaso?'

'No.'

'There is so much copying to be done; truly I need a whole scriptorium.'

'No! I need him.'

'I shall only be away a month.'

'A month! No. Definitely not.' Poliziano was engaged in a series of lectures and essays proving that poetry was the mother of civilisation; I was helping him find the sources for remembered quotations.

'He is not your slave,' said Pico. 'May he not answer for himself? Tommaso, what do you say? I have more than a lifetime's work to do. Will you lend your skills to the service of my work? However much he pays you, I will double it.'

I looked from Pico to Poliziano and back again, so often that in the end Angelo threw his hands up in resignation. 'Go with him if you like. What do I care?'

Pulled between two such strong forces, one for going and one for staying, I still hesitated.

Maria put her hand on my arm. 'Go,' she said. 'And then come back.'

'One month,' Angelo grumbled. 'No more.'

Hearing of the plan, Ficino called me to see him. He greeted me solemnly and when he bade me sit, the request was formal. This was not my friend or my master: this was my spiritual guide, and he was angry.

'I hear you are throwing everything aside to follow Pico della Mirandola.'

I gasped. 'I am going because he asked me to, and I have nothing to throw aside. It is work, Marsilio, that is all.'

'When one meets a wall, one has to be patient. You have had this experience before. The one you seek to escape is yourself.'

'Who speaks of escape? It is merely a journey.'

'An adventure.' He peered at me when I refused to agree. 'An adventure, yes? You want the oblivion of new impressions.'

'It is an excellent opportunity to visit my family in Rome.'

'*Beh!* Confronted by a wall, you will follow anything that moves, even if it is a will o' the wisp crossing a marsh.'

'Is that your view of Pico?'

Now it was Ficino who refused to answer. 'Stay here. Be patient. Patience is a virtue, let us not forget. Patience is not the restraint of impatience; it is an absolute quality. Let patience fill your heart.'

'What is it that I am waiting for?'

'What is it that you want? Truly, what is your desire?'

It is for that which I cannot have, I thought. 'I do not know. It seems I want nothing, other than to practise my art. Writing notes and letters for Angelo is all very well, but… I want to be copying and improving my skills. I've had no commission since the *Hermes* for Lorenzino. Will he commission me again, do you think, or was he disappointed?'

'Disappointed? Far from it. He often extols you. A commission will come soon, I am sure, from someone if not Lorenzino himself.'

'Call it impatience if you like, but Pico is offering me secretarial work with responsibility and more… more…'

'Adventure?' Ficino leaned forward, his papery face softening. 'Tommaso, do not go. This is not advice, it is an instruction. Stay here and let the universe have charge of your destiny. Adventures court danger and at the end nothing is attained that could not have been found at home.'

This was the philosophy of an old man! Even as he spoke, I made my mind up: I would go with Pico. Pico, I thought, may be impulsive, but at least he had the courage and faith to follow his impulses. He was god-driven, and I wished to follow the god. It seemed to be my chance of living again, of having life throb in my veins. To stay meant getting too comfortable with the Poliziani. I wanted the large horizon of an unknown, unpredictable future. I wanted to transcend the stars, to be a lion and not a sheep.

If I had listened to Ficino and stayed, I would still be a scribe and quite possibly remarried. But I went and, thinking I had nothing to lose, lost everything, including my destiny. Is that possible? How can you lose such a thing? What is fate and destiny? Ficino would have said it is what is in you to be fulfilled; Pico would have said it is what is. Every path forks. I chose to follow the one who believed we may carve our own future, the man of will.

This time the Poliziani insisted on their right to say goodbye. As Angelo embraced his friend, I encouraged Maria to present herself. Nervous in her shyness, she curtsied before Pico and fumbled at her purse.

'Oh dear, oh Mother of God,' she muttered, tugging at the knot in the purse strings. Pico took the purse from her; as he picked at the knot, his head bent forwards and rested lightly against hers. Maria stopped trembling then and became calm.

Pico drew a medal from the purse. 'What is it, Maria?'

'It is a gift,' she said. 'From Angelo and me. We've been looking for an occasion to present it to you.'

Angelo had had the medal struck at the time when he became a professor. On one side of it was his image and, on the other, Maria's. The likenesses, made by the elderly sculptor Bertoldo, were excellent. Pico closed his fist round it, kissed Maria gratefully on the top of her head, rested there a moment, and then turned to throw his arms round Angelo.

'I wish you would come with me,' he said. 'Truly without you I am only half myself.'

Angelo nodded. 'My duties at the university… Tommaso will be our eyes and ears. We shall want letters daily,' he said to me.

20 VENUS LAYS A TRAP
1486

I HAD HAD EVERYTHING I EVER WANTED IN LIFE AND HAD lost it. According to Pico, I was to look on that as a blessing. 'Only a man released from earthly concerns is free to purify his soul, and there is nothing quite like marriage to keep a man earth-bound. Instead of contemplating God, he worries about the future; instead of studying scripture, he works on his ledgers. You have been freed, Tommaso: be grateful.'

His words were thoughtless and hurtful; I said nothing in reply.

'Then should we not enter a monastery?' asked his secretary, Cristoforo.

'Oh, do not be deceived. It is harder, not easier, to be pure when enclosed. No, our work is to be both in the world and yet celibate.'

That is what he said to us as we rode to Arezzo.

Over the years I had been, and continued to be, the object of attention from several ladies of minor families, all of them married. They sent me messages, made themselves obvious at public festivities. I ignored them. My fondness for Maria lay in this, that she was not a sexual woman. She liked to play, to talk, to learn, and was always straight with me, never practising the art of allurement. Such a thing would have struck her as absurd and dishonest.

'Coitus is so repetitive,' Pico said. 'Always the same. Make a dessert of apples from a thousand recipes – all taste of apples.'

There were about twenty-five men in Pico's entourage, half of them on foot, half of them mounted, two of them armed. The footmen had left hours ahead of us and we did not catch them up until we reached our night's lodgings. We were a relatively small party but an impressive one in outlandish head gear: tall Byzantine columns, French peaks, Jewish hoods and Paduan caps. When we reached Arezzo on the following day, the Aretines opened their gates to the Count of Concordia, whom they knew well enough from his previous visits. Accommodation had been arranged with relatives and the learned men of the city gathered to dine with this young man who would know everything. Our host gave a banquet and among the guests was a distant relation of Lorenzo de' Medici accompanied by his new wife. Pico, with his wide-eyed and boyish enthusiasm, and his habit of treating all women as embodiments of Aphrodite, paid court to the bride accordingly.

Why was this woman, called Margarita, different? Yes, she wore a low-cut gown, tightly-laced to make her breasts swell and, as she breathed, the thin covering of fine, hide-nothing lawn – a whore's attempt at modesty – fluttered and trembled. But who of us had not seen that before? It was a common-enough sight, besides which breasts are just swollen mounds of flesh. No one gets excited by udders on a cow. Yet I could not draw my eyes from this breathing flesh that exuded the scent of musk roses. As for Pico, he went pale with desire. He who knew better than anyone how to capture attention was himself held fast. Cupid had shot his dart.

I have often wondered. I think it was because, apart from being beautiful, she had a will to match Pico's own. She had seen him on previous visits, had become inflamed with love for the Count of Concordia and arranged that he should sit beside her. By the end of the evening Pico, having been drawn from the lofty conversation with the man on his right to the very personal details of the lady on his left, was utterly caught in the web of Margarita's lust. She was, she told him, the widow of a wealthy man; her new husband, although a Medici, was a mere tax collector and she was now confined to a small and empty house.

'Love,' Pico told her, 'will furnish the house.'

'I have loved no one, my Lord,' she said so that none but he could hear, 'since my eyes looked on you.'

Pico was used to women falling at his feet like ripe pears. Why could he not step adroitly past this one as he had with most of the others? It is said that demons come in the most beautiful guises and it is the only explanation that fits, that it was not a woman seducing the Count but a devil. Or Venus, in revenge for Pico's preference for Minerva. Pico was drawn into Margarita's desire as a man falls into a fever; one moment he is healthy, the next he is sweating and delirious. In a secret and whispering discourse they devised a plan between them for Margarita to escape her husband and Arezzo.

It has been said since that it had all been pre-arranged on an earlier visit. Not true. Even Pico was not so mad as to plan to hold a great debate and elope with a married woman at the same time. No, it all happened on this one night, the desire, the impulse and the act.

'You are insane!' his secretary, Cristoforo, exploded later when Pico told him what he intended for the morning.

Pico looked at him with those amused eyes that seemed to be in constant wonder at the world and its inhabitants. 'Who was it who said that there is no law for lovers?'

'A fool.'

'Come, Cristoforo, we'll send the footmen off early. No one will miss Margarita until, when? Night time? We can be in Siena by then.'

'*Siena?* I thought we were going to Rome!'

'We only have to cross the river to be under the jurisdiction of Siena and out of that of Arezzo. We shall go on to Rome later. Trust me. Aphrodite and Apollo will attend us.'

I was so familiar with the tales of Ovid in which gods snatch mortal beauties that half of me believed this adventure could be successful, at least for the god. Margarita would of course be turned into a white daisy or a pearl, but so be it. Mithridates and Elia del Megido, however, were so outraged that they left the city with the other scholars and arranged to meet us in Perugia, warning Pico that he was sacrificing his great, ambitious project to mere lust. 'And for a woman!' said Mithridates in a bitter mixture of distaste and disappointment.

Before dawn the footmen set off on the road south. We followed a few hours later, leaving Arezzo at a nonchalant walking pace, telling everyone we were making for Cortona and thence to Rome. It was a fine day and we looked like a travelling party without any cares, talking amongst ourselves as our horses ambled towards the great gates. Beyond the gates, the open road. Beyond the gates, a small church from which the lady Margarita emerged as we passed. In one swift movement, Pico lifted her up and put her behind the saddle of his secretary. For that short while of leaving the city, he had carried us all in his belief that he was beloved of the gods, above the law, that he could take what he wanted from creation. But as soon as he had picked up Margarita, and was seen doing so, reality returned, along with the operation of that divine law that we should covet no man's property. At once the city bell was ringing in alarm and the militia of Arezzo was pouring out of the gates to chase our party down the Chiana valley.

Pico shouted to Cristoforo to abandon the woman. 'Run, men!' he cried. We galloped down the valley and crossed the river at the bridge leading to Monte San Savino. There we caught up with our footmen, whom Pico commanded to scatter, telling them that each man should make his own way to Siena and meet us there.

When the Aretines came to the bridge half of them went off in pursuit of the hapless footmen, the rest came after us. Pico raced on. The scholar who had been raised as a knight in the court of Mirandola could ride at an incredible speed. Cristoforo kept up with him but I began to fall behind. I willed Pico to turn and meet his pursuers in battle, as a true knight of old, but he opted to escape. The last I saw of him as crossbow bolts began to whistle past my ears was a cloud of dust making for the village of Marciano. When a man riding near me reared screaming in his saddle with a bolt piercing his body, I reigned in at once and slid from my horse to give myself up, terrified of losing my life in such a stupid escapade as this, for what fate then would befall my soul? Better to spend my days in an Arezzo gaol and die reconciled to my God. But the pursuers were not interested in any prisoners except one, Pico himself, and they were slaying our men whether they surrendered or not. The last I knew was a broad sword coming down on me, and me raising my arm against it.

They left me for dead, not caring one way or another.

When the pursuit was over, Pico and Cristoforo captured at Marciano, the local people came out to see what was to be done. They made a pile of the dead and set light to it. The injured they helped as best they could. I was taken to a local apothecary who stanched the flow of blood while I thrashed in pain. 'I can't move my fingers,' I cried.

'Only time will heal that, my friend, time and prayer.' The apothecary put a sponge to my nose and, inhaling an infusion of poppy, mandrake and hemlock, I passed from pain and fright into sleep. When I awoke it was in bed in an inn. Gingerly I tried flexing my fingers again but none would respond. I stared at my hand, its brown skin, its fingers blackened by a lifetime's companionship with ink, its nails well-shaped but grimy, its lines and contours. My hand – the hand that had been kissed by Lorenzo di Pierfrancesco – such a devoted yet neglected servant. If it were a horse, it would have had to be put down, for it no longer worked and had outlived its usefulness.

I saw books in my imagination, the most beautiful books with exquisite illumination, borders of ivy, irises and *putti*, great capital letters and a script that in its harmony and clarity served the sacred word; books that I had copied, books that I intended to copy. My left hand, like a second son, youthful, indolent and suddenly promoted through the death of the firstborn, was completely inadequate to the skills required, the skills of the right. They say you can train your left hand but it is like training a mule to run the palio. It cannot compete. As the effects of the soporific sponge wore off, so did the indifference, the curiosity, and any vestige of hope. My life as a scribe, a true scribe, an initiate into the laws of beauty, was finished.

21 HOW TO FORGIVE
1486

MYSTERIOUS ARE THE WAYS OF THE MEDICI. BY THE TIME I arrived home, Lorenzo, far from expressing outrage at what had happened to his relation's wife, had negotiated Pico's freedom. The scholars of Florence considered the affair a huge joke – the young upstart had tripped on a woman! – although Poliziano treated the wound to my arm seriously enough. It was now festering and when he tried to remove the bandage I turned into a wild and cornered animal. In the end he and a servant held me down while Maria, with appalling indifference to my cries, tried to free the stuck bandage so that she could peer into the wound.

'Nasty...' she muttered. 'It stinks.'

'Maria...' I pleaded, but as her eyes met mine, even as she smiled at me, she yanked the bandage off with one deft movement.

When I came round, brother and sister were heads down in conference over my arm. The treatment they decided upon was three parts Galen to two parts the herbal lore of witches, or so I thought until Angelo told me it was all from the *materia medica* of Dioscorides.

'Maria has a way with herbs, that is all, and somehow gets the measure right when the book is silent.'

'I am an *experiment*?' I struggled to sit up.

'You are a beneficiary of the restored knowledge of the ancients,' Angelo replied, pinning me down harder.

And so I was treated with many things, including drops of the juice of comfrey and an infusion of lavender in a hot poultice.

The wound was clean and healing after three days and the fingers of my right hand began to move again but were given to sudden bouts of numbness. Any attempt to hold a quill ended with it falling to the floor. I began to practise writing with my left hand.

'Pico is in Perugia,' Angelo told me, having received a letter. 'He enquires after you and your health. He thanks God for his own survival and that of his secretary, but is stricken with guilt and remorse at the loss of his men. He says Mithridates is translating Hebrew works into Latin at a rate of a thousand pages a month.'

I did a quick mental calculation on the average amount of words to a line and lines to a page and discovered that this was equal to three times the length of Virgil's *Aeneid* – each month!

'I do not trust Mithridates,' Angelo said. 'He says he reads Arabic, but how do we know it is true? He could be writing down all manner of nonsense and none of us would be any the wiser. He says he has the Chaldean Oracles in the original Chaldean. How do we know that for sure? How much is Pico paying him for these books pouring in from the East?' He busied himself at his desk, muttering about forgeries and impostors. 'I presume you have realised,' he said, raising his head again momentarily, 'that Mithridates is in love with Pico and rejected? Are rejected lovers to be trusted?'

I agreed that they are not.

Pico's initiation had taken place at the hour originally planned, but in Umbria rather than in Rome. He stayed in Umbria for five months, and it was in that time that Mithridates performed his astonishing feat of translating six thousand pages of Hebrew, and esoteric Hebrew at that, into Latin. Rumour had it that the Count of Concordia had exhausted his fortune on Cabalistic books and that he was now paying Mithridates by supplying him with boys.

'God save me from magic,' Angelo complained. 'There is knowledge enough in history, and even more in literature, without having to burrow in dung heaps for it. I wish Pico would come home.'

Whenever Pico was discussed, Maria became silent and sullen. She alone had found nothing amusing in the abduction of Margarita. The man she loved, the man who claimed to be on the return path, abjuring sensual love for the divine, had run off with a woman in a frenzy of lust. Her Apollo had revealed himself as Bacchus.

'Pico's scholarly reputation is in shreds,' I said to Angelo. 'He is now considered an impetuous adulterer. I feel as rancorous as Maria does, and yet you seem completely unmoved.'

Angelo looked at me, his brown eyes merry. 'I cannot tell you how delighted I am to have discovered human weakness in our friend. It makes me feel so much better!'

'Well, I am glad of that,' I replied petulantly. 'What am I supposed to do now?'

'You can still write, albeit with the grace of a drunken monkey. I have more than enough work for you to do.'

I should have felt grateful; indeed, I did feel grateful, at least towards Poliziano, but for Pico and for Providence I felt only gall. All those years of training and practice, killed stone dead in a moment's recklessness – and that the recklessness of another. Naturally, indulging myself in this bitterness, I avoided Ficino, who would surely remind me I had only myself to blame; that, given a choice, I had chosen unwisely. It was a matter of pride that I blame Pico.

Angelo looked at me sternly from under his thick eyebrows. 'Pico has asked that you forgive him, and you have not done so.'

'What is the nature of forgiveness? How is it made?'

'You of all people ask me that? You, who forgave Lorenzo his crimes against your native city? You tell me how it is made.'

'Through love,' I said grudgingly.

'Then turn your mind to that, and no more bitterness from you.'

Bitterness on bitterness. Whom did I blame in the end but Almighty God, who had taken away my wife and now the one thing I had left – my art. I felt like a man being dismembered before a crowd curious to see how much he may suffer before he yields up his spirit. But did I hate Pico? Not really. As more and more tales of heroic scholarship came out of Umbria, my admiration of him began to revive. And when I received a letter myself, eloquent in its expression of guilt and remorse and begging me to rejoin him, I decided to accept, though I did not give him the pleasure of knowing my decision for at least two weeks. When Ficino called for me to visit him, I did not go.

22 POETIC THEOLOGY
1486

AFTER YEARS OF DISCUSSION WITH LORENZO, POLIZIANO was now setting down the line of poets beginning with Apollo, son of Zeus. Just as the philosophers have a line of teachers to revere, and the priests a line of learned doctors and Church Fathers, so the poets are the inheritors of inspiration, one from another, over a tremendous span of time. 'Lorenzo,' he told me, 'has been inspired throughout his life by Dante. He talks to Dante – did you know that? Each time he sits down to write poetry, he lights a candle in the memory of Dante. Dante himself had the same relationship with Virgil, Virgil with Homer, and so it goes on back and back.'

The line to the source – whether Apollo or Zeus – passes through names both familiar and obscure, some mythic, some biblical, through prophets and muses, sirens and oracles, touching Orpheus and David on the way to Bacchus, Pan, Prometheus and Apollo. As Angelo, with head tilted back and his eyes closed, recited his litany of names, I heard a sound behind the words, informing the words, a wild and ancient lament, the sound of the poetic soul cast out of Eden.

He was writing a poem he called *Nutricia*. 'Nutricia', a Latin term denoting a fee paid to a wet-nurse. The poem was Poliziano's fee to that which had nursed his education, his culture, his erudition: poetry. In about eight hundred lines he mentioned everyone on his tree of poetic inspiration, and it was to serve as a reading programme for his students in the next academic year: Dante, Petrarch, Boccaccio, Cavalcanti, Propertius, Ovid, Horace, Virgil, Claudian, Homer, Hesiod, Orphic hymns, Psalms of David, the books of Moses.

'And you,' I said. 'Who inspires you?'

If the answer surprised me so much, it was because I had always assumed it was Homer, the loftiest of lofty ancients.

'Boccaccio,' he said, and left me stunned.

But now that he had mentioned the name, it was as if a stopper had come out of him and there was a flood of enthusiasm for his master who, above all men, truly understood poetic theology.

'When I was a boy and living in poverty with my uncle, I needed books. I had been brought up on books and now I was starved. Food I could do without, but books? – I was craving. I used to go to church at Santo Spirito and one day I had a conversation with one of the monks and learnt that the church was the repository of the library of Giovanni Boccaccio. It was kept in a beautiful cabinet and, as soon as they learnt to trust me, they let me have the key so that I could help myself. I read it all. It was sparse, but it did have some of the ancient poets. It also had some autograph manuscripts of Boccaccio's. And so I read his works in his own hand, and his spirit came, embraced mine and led me to the next step – the translation of Homer.'

He gazed at me, assessed my credulity, decided to continue. 'There is in poetry – perhaps in all arts – a sense of immortality. Once you get to the heart, there is no time, no sense of transience. You walk in a living stream. You become part of it. While I was studying late one evening in Santo Spirito, I fell asleep over my book and I dreamed I was rowing a boat on a river in Greece. It was dark; it was night time. There was war in the land and the banks of the river were high – I had to keep rowing. But then I saw a break in the defences and had a view over a vast plain. Two figures were walking towards me. One was Homer, the other was his wife. Madonna Homer! For that element I have no explanation. But they came to welcome me to their province. And as I climbed out of the boat and up the bank to enter their land, I woke up, knowing that I was accepted. I was accepted by the realm of poets. It was then that I began the translation of Homer, with more confidence than a boy of my age could rightfully expect to have.'

Having satisfied himself that his most private, secret story was not making me laugh, but that I believed him, he continued and spoke of Boccaccio's work and aims. I listened in wonder, as if on a hillside listening to the pipes of Pan. 'Theology', literally, the Word of God, has come to mean rational analysis of scripture and doctrine. Here in Arcadia it had cloven feet, shaggy legs and horns. This was the Ancient of Days, the oldest god, prelapsarian and free. Something in me began to quiver; I was a lion drawn by the lyre of Orpheus; I was a stone rolled by the music of Amphion. This was the Word of God spoken direct into the ear. Theologians as we understand them study the Word as revealed to someone else, a saint or an apostle. Poetic theologians hear it for themselves. The difference is that they do not always understand what it is that they have heard.

We were out in the garden, sitting in the area that had a view through the trees of Florence below in the valley. The late summer sun was dappling the orchard and a bird was bathing itself in Maria's bird bath, its fluttering wings sending up sprays of droplets. Maria herself had joined us, sitting on the grass and leaning against my knees. While we listened to Angelo, I idly let down her hair and began to plait a strand of it. She took no notice, captivated as she was by her brother's discourse.

'Will you give us the poem, Angelo?' she asked.

And thus, in the groves of Fiesole, looking down on our city, we heard *Nutricia* for the first time. This was the fourth of four poems he called *Sylvae*, each one written to outline a term's work, each one composed in one of Lorenzo's villas – except this one, which was composed in his own. I continued plaiting Maria's hair while we listened to the Latin hexameters dancing in the air.

The poem began with the story of Prometheus and his discovery of poetry, by which the mind of man may come to understand the thoughts of the gods.

Just placed on earth in the freshness of the world, through God's care, was this new kind of animal which would raise its eyes to the heavens, and with its sharp mind would survey all Nature's handiwork, and would tease out the hidden causes of things, and would grasp the existence of the artificer of eternity...

The afternoon had become evening, with the moon in the sky before the sun had set, when Angelo came to the end. Maria was looking like Medusa with a hundred plaits snaking from her head. The poem had introduced me to all the poets and dramatists of antiquity, along with a survey of history and the tutelary divinities of poetry. Truly I had spent the afternoon in that Arcadia which exists forever in the mind of poets. The poem ended with a description of the works of the last in the line: our own Lorenzo.

– If praise of mine can charm thy cultur'd ear;
For once, the lonely woods and vales among,
A mountain-goddess caught thy soothing song,
As swelled the notes, she pierc'd the winding dell,
And sat beside thee in thy secret cell;
I saw her hands the laurel chaplet twine,
Whilst with attentive ear she drank the sounds divine.
Whether thy nymph to Dian's train allied,
But sure no quiver rattled at her side;

Or from th' Aonian mount, a stranger guest,
She chose awhile in these green woods to rest –
Thro' all thy frame while softer passions breathe,
Around thy brows she bound the laureate wreathe;
– And still – as other themes engaged thy song,
She with unrivall'd sweetness touch'd thy tongue…

Angelo had been trance-like in recitation: now he woke up with a start to see his Gorgon sister staring at him.

'Are you going to recite that at the university?' I asked.

'What, and find myself being tried as a pagan heretic? No, it is for private ears only.'

I went to the inaugural lecture of the new term, filing into the university hall with a stream of men, some of them young students as you would expect, many of them much older. There were men of the guilds, priests, bishops and bankers, the most notable scholars of the day and, of course, the poets.

The Pierfrancesco brothers were there, both in discussion with Amerigo Vespucci and his uncle Giorgio Antonio. There was no more pretence of familial relations between the two branches of the Medici since the Pierfranceschi had resorted to law to get il Magnifico to pay his debt. The case was continuing, with Lorenzo claiming he could not pay, and Bartolommeo Scala running between both parties trying to find an agreement. On this day in the hall, they stood well apart and men were having to choose which group to stand with. The Pierfranceschi had the Vespucci with them, the Greek scholars and Ficino. With Lorenzo il Magnifico were the poets, Naldo Naldi and Cristoforo Landino, Girolamo and Antonio Benivieni, and the young Lorenzo Tornabuoni. I hesitated, aware that Lorenzino was watching me. Then I made my decision and joined neither party but stood alone. Lorenzo's son, Piero, fifteen years old and an able student himself in the faculty of poetry, now stood with his father as the undisputed heir. His rotund brother, Abbot Giovanni, gazed about the company to satisfy himself that there was no one else present who was only ten.

Vespasiano da Bisticci, the bookseller, was sitting in the Chancellor's chair, as if the most honoured guest. There were many others, too many to name, but suffice to say that anyone interested in ancient poetry was there on that day, gathered together in one place. The vaulted hall was soon full and young students were climbing up to the deep window ledges for a good seat and better view. Just as the doors were about to be closed, Sandro Botticelli squeezed in. I caught his eye and he made his way through the crowd to join me, grateful to find a man of his own status in a hall full of people he considered to be superior to himself. He looked around briefly but his gaze lingered on Giovanni di Pierfrancesco. It was not the look of lust, it was the gaze of the artist. Since Giovanni had sat for his portrait a year earlier, he had begun to appear frequently on Botticelli's holy panels as an angel.

When a man is painted, he forms a bond with the painter: subject and object bound by the verb *to observe*. Lorenzo Tornabuoni, looking over his shoulder, smiled affectionately at Botticelli, who lifted his cap to him. 'I must do him full face sometime,' Sandro said to me. 'Those eyes, those oriental eyes, not done justice in profile. What a sweet face.' He sighed, not so much with envy as simple longing. Lorenzo Tornabuoni, eighteen years old, had everything a man could desire: good looks, a lithe figure, an excellent mind, a style of dressing copied by everyone else and now, just this year, a wife from the Albizzi family, so fine in every respect that poets were saying that she had been bestowed on him by Venus. We men could have responded to these bounties of young Tornabuoni with our usual venom if he had not been so pleasant that we all wished to befriend him. He was good at his Greek studies, but the copious praise he received from Poliziano was not only on account of his literary prowess: it was praise for the man. Whenever a philosopher spoke of a man of *virtù*, the image that came to our minds was that of Lorenzo Tornabuoni.

The hall quietened into a hush of expectancy as Poliziano came to the raised lectern and mounted the steps. They were expecting a poem: they received a discourse. In Latin, and careful to offend no one, Angelo outlined the history of poetry and claimed that poetry is the source of civilisation. 'To behold the infinite, a man's soul must be refined, tuned up to an exquisite note. When I speak of poetry,' he said, 'I use the term in its original sense and refer to all literature, not just that set in metric form. Writing – language – the Promethean gifts that make man able to comprehend the heavens: that is my subject.'

He went on to list and describe every poet that students should be familiar with, their works, the mythic realms they dealt with. Suddenly it stopped being a list of names in my ear and became a library of books in my mind's eye. I had seen a volume of everything he mentioned. Whether an ancient manuscript, a modern copy or a printed version: all these books existed, here in Florence. Then I woke up to the significance of this moment. What Angelo was outlining was the potential for any Florentine to make himself familiar with this tremendous heritage, and to be among the first men ever to do so. For fifty years the Medici library had been accumulating, at San Marco, at the Badia on Fiesole, in Lorenzo's own house, thousands of volumes, always with the intention of their being publicly available. The work of three generations had come to fruition. The library had come to maturity. I am sure mine was not the only heart thudding at the prospect opening before us.

When he finished there was tumultuous applause. It seemed to us then on that day that Angelo Poliziano had inaugurated a new age. The work begun by Cosimo de' Medici, the work of a generation of scribes such as myself, Poliziano's own work in collating copies and making definitive editions, had resulted in a library in which one could read Homer and Hesiod, Virgil and Ovid, Horace and Propertius, not to mention Cicero, Quintilian, Plato – every great name in the history of human literature.

The dark ages were over. The Golden Age was here, now.

23 THE SIX FRENZIES
1486

THERE ARE FIVE FRENZIES, NOT FOUR. BESIDES THE FRENZIES of prophecy, love, poetry and madness there is the frenzy of knowing. In Pico's retreat in the hills near Perugia, in a room that had become part library, part scriptorium, there were more scholars than there were desks and some men worked standing up. The books being studied were arcane texts that were arriving from Spain, Persia, Turkey and India. A whole network of agents was finding these books, if books you could call them, for some were scrolls and others great sheets of parchment, containing the most ancient and esoteric lore. Pico's wealth was haemorrhaging with the cost of these rare texts.

Unshaved and unkempt, he was dictating to Cristoforo Casale as I arrived, an essay based on the text from St John, 'I give you my peace, I give you my peace, I leave you peace.' Thoroughly excited by his own words, he was dictating so fast that Cristoforo could not keep up.

'Ah, Tommaso, good, you are here,' Pico said. 'I need a man who can write at speed.'

'I am no longer such a man,' I reminded him.

Pico frowned as if trying to fathom my meaning, then he turned back to Cristoforo – who had been shaking his wrist to relieve it – and continued with the essay on peace that was to be part of the Oration addressing his audience in Rome. The words came like a waterfall and it seemed mad that such a subject be delivered with such urgency. I thought, truly, here is a hypocrite. He should be practising what he preaches. What does he know about peace? Yet when I read that essay later, I found that the words did what they said and brought peace to the soul, the wild horse of the unruly mind tamed by the steady hand of the trainer.

Before retiring, Pico took me by the arm and walked with me in the garden. It was cold and raining but he was not the kind of man to be influenced by the weather. He apologised for appearing rude earlier. 'When the Muse is upon you, it is difficult to remember the gentle courtesies. I read in the Gospels every day and this morning these words about peace leapt out and the Muse was speaking; you know how it is, a moment's interruption breaks the flow and you forget what you heard. There is *so much* to be done, *so much* to be said. Do you think they will understand, Tommaso?'

I was distracted, worrying about my shoes, now squelching. 'You want me to help but I have lost my skills.'

'I have said how sorry I am.'

'I am trying to be practical. What can I do to help?'

'I need you to collate the theses.'

'Seven hundred of them?'

'At the last count it was nine hundred. By next week it could be a thousand but nine hundred is a better number so I mean to limit myself. They need to be copied and checked and arranged under headings. I will write the headings. We need to keep everything simple. If you cannot copy them yourself, find someone who can. I want you to take charge of the work. We are leaving for Rome in two weeks.'

'You want me to finish this work in two weeks?'

'One week, because I need you to go ahead of us and find a printer. I want the whole text printed by the end of Advent and distributed to every university in Italy. Do you not have a brother in the Curia? There must be some system of communication among the universities, as among the churches. We need to use it. I want my theses sent to every university along with an invitation to all scholars to come and debate them in Rome in January. At my expense. All travelling costs will be at my expense.'

'Can you afford it?'

'Tommaso, such questions are for my secretary, Cristoforo. I am not to be distracted in my work, do you understand? Find a printer,' he said. 'No arguments. I am aware of your principles, but I do not have time for them. Find a printer. One that can do Greek and Hebrew letters.'

By any reckoning, nine hundred theses is a vast amount. I found help in the city and oversaw several men labouring day and night to meet the deadline. It is hard to convey the sheer vivacity of both Pico and his scholars. No one wanted to do anything but work. I should tell you about the theses, given that today it is impossible to find a copy of them, thanks to the discrimination of his nephew and editor, Gianfrancesco. I should tell you about them, but forgive me, Erasmo, you might as well ask a worm to describe God. I have not studied at a university, am not a theologian, cannot speak Hebrew and Arabic, do not know what prime matter is, am not concerned with the principles of motion, have only a passing knowledge of metaphysics, astrology and numerology whilst knowing nothing at all about scholastic theology. I did try to understand this compendium of world knowledge but soon gave up. And perhaps that was a blessing for, not distracted by this plethora of mind-numbing detail, I could see the larger picture which, forgive my arrogance, I believe was not understood by the great doctors of the universities and the mighty cardinals of Rome.

So here, for your benefit, I give you the whole picture. You can fill in the details and find all the proofs for yourself.

It all begins with the Word; from the Word, through the alphabet of God, wisdom emanates, unfolding through the ages of Man. The original language was Hebrew: all languages derive and devolve from that, decaying with age, while the pure, original language has magical power even in its letters. The emanation of wisdom, according to Pico, ends with the Arabs. In the Latin West we display nothing of it. Instead we squabble over various interpretations of early fathers and ancient philosophers. The task is to reconnect with the fount of wisdom, to lay aside our hostility to the Jews and our overweening arrogance, to become humble disciples of truth, to become proper philosophers. To this

153

end, Pico devised a 'new philosophy', derived largely from Plato and Aristotle, but one particularly fitted for our own times and understanding. There are a certain number of key propositions:

Multiplicity begins in unity. Therefore all things are related.

Different religions express the same truth in different ways.

Omnia sunt in omnibus modo suo – everything in every reality is reflected in some mode in every other. Thus all nature is joined in various occult friendships and affinities. This great cosmic principle is the key to decoding all sacred texts.

If we would study the Bible, then we must do so in Hebrew and Greek since words in translation are stripped of their primal power.

What was also obvious to me, although Pico seemed peculiarly blind to it, was that to argue such propositions in public with doctors and divines, whose task it is to keep strays within the fold, was foolhardy. How could he hope to succeed? But Pico was shining with an ethereal light, as if in raising angels he had become one. To him, nothing seemed impossible.

What he wanted in place of logical disputation in the universities, where Platonists squabbled with Aristotelians, and the followers of St Thomas Aquinas heaped scorn on those of Duns Scotus, was mystical contemplation. His intention was to dethrone the scholastic theologians. Perhaps there is a sixth frenzy – that of a man with a vision of Truth.

Something else I should tell you: it is usual in debate to defend propositions you agree with, but a great number of Pico's propositions did not reflect his own opinion; they were the opinions of others that he wished to reveal as false. But no one understood that, and they took the whole confusion of propositions to be Pico's own statements of truth. And for that he was condemned.

London, January 23rd, 1506

We dined with Colet this evening and, once again, discussed his plans for a school. Afterwards I walked with More and Erasmus to More's house by Wallbrook. Erasmus has by nature a conviction that he is exempt from the rules that bind any position he happens to be in; it is a simple underlying assumption that, though they are necessary and good, laws of institution and society do not apply to him. Thus he is an Augustinian canon who has not lived in a monastery for years, a Dutchman rarely in Holland, a pious Christian not too often seen at mass. Such constraints that fetter the rest of us he casts aside to roam freely upon the face of the earth. This tendency is something which Colet simultaneously loves and abhors, for it creates in Erasmus an independent scholar of magnitude who will not do as he is told. On the way to Wallbrook, Erasmus was enthusing about the idea of a public school as something we (that is, the rest of us) should devote ourselves to wholeheartedly, with his full support.

'Teaching children?' I said. 'It creates such a state of intellectual exhaustion that your own studies are soon neglected. To teach beginners is a purgatorial punishment: anyone good enough at his subject to attain the level of teacher is thereafter sentenced to repeat elementary rules over and over again, usually to those too young to appreciate them. To earn a living I am condemned to an infinite repetition of the Greek alphabet from alpha to omega when I would rather be at my own books, deepening my own understanding of the finer points of syntax and accidence, striving for ease, so that I may read Homer or Plato fluently.'

'What is important, Tommaso,' More asked, 'if one would promulgate this knowledge? To keep it to ourselves or to give it to others? To teach children is the highest service to mankind.'

'It is casting pearls before swine.'

'Your view of children is harsh, my friend.'

'Were you not a barbarian when a child yourself? I certainly was.'

'And who civilised you?'

It was Antonio degli Agli, Bishop of Volterra. Remembering my kind benefactor, I at once regretted my words and revised my opinion. 'Yes, very well, you speak truly. It is most noble to educate children – but many of them at once? It is that which I find disagreeable. I consider it most ill-advised.'

As we walked along Bucklersbury, one of the swarm of urchins who torment citizens like mosquitoes approached me and tugged on my gown. I brushed the little thief away. Erasmus, however, took a coin from his purse.

'Stop!' I said. 'You know not what you do!'

Sure enough the gift was a honey pot to attract the rest of the swarm. Urchins came from every alley to buzz around us, each one demanding a coin with such increasing and hostile persistence that Erasmus was soon in danger of being robbed. Thomas and I swatted at the children, driving them off.

'Christ enjoins us to give to the poor!' Erasmus complained. 'How can we practise it?'

'These are not the poor,' I said. 'These are beggars trained by thieves.'

'True,' said Thomas. 'We cannot help the individuals. We can only cure the society which, through injustice, creates orphans and beggars in the first place. And that, I think, is what makes Colet's idea magnificent. As Plato said, give me a child before the age of six…'

More and Erasmus are not fitted by nature to be serious overlong and soon a lighter exchange was taking place. When they are together, the very air becomes merry. More has been quite transformed since the return of his friend and now steps along as if in a dance. They are more alike, someone said, than any pair of twins. I am not sure if it was their companionship or their happiness, but sharing their company exacerbated a sense of agitation that had been sown during the evening.

'John Colet has the purest view of love,' Erasmus said. 'But love means different things to different people. For instance, to a young man it means the desire to impress the beloved, so that he cannot meet her before he has shaved off every whisker and put every hair in place, so as to present her with a picture of perfection; but in marriage love is the freedom and trust to have a belching contest with your wife, because such love brooks all imperfections.'

More laughed heartily and said he had not yet attained that altitude of love.

I tried to laugh, but was too disturbed by the joke, since I remembered that Elena never wanted to be seen by me until she had completed her toilet and dressing. I ascribed it to modesty, but Erasmus was suggesting it was lack of love! It could not be possible. He was wrong.

'Such things are true only of peasants and the Dutch,' I said.

Bucklersbury is unusual in London in that it smells sweet, due to the presence of many apothecaries, spice merchants and perfumeries. In the darkness of night, the fragrance was intense. I paused and lifted my nose to the scent of roses. Such beauty in a smell...

During the dinner, Colet had asked each of us what plans we had made to fulfil the mission he has given us. Only Eramus had anything to say.

He had, he said, been tirelessly translating the plays of Euripides and then presenting them to great men in the hope of patronage. He has even rowed across the Thames to Lambeth Palace with Grocyn to visit the Archbishop of Canterbury. I listened avidly, expecting to hear descriptions of the palace and the man, but all Erasmus had to say was that he received three farthings or thereabouts for his *Hecuba*, not enough to send a letter to Italy, let alone a man.

'It is hopeless, John. I am a pauper. And, before any of you offer, no, I am not going to accept gifts from you. Not again.'

157

'Will you accept a gift from God?' Linacre asked. 'Just this day I heard that my fellow physician of the king, Gianbattista Boerio, is making plans for his sons to complete their education back in their native land. He is looking for a tutor. He will pay all travelling and living expenses for two years.'

Erasmus stared at him with his mouth open. Once he had recovered, he begged God's forgiveness. 'How often do I presume I am in control of my life? How often? Too often!'

John Colet had the look of a father swan watching his first cygnet take off in flight. 'Now,' he said, gazing round the table, 'what about the rest of you?'

I left my friends at More's great stone house by the stream, an old manor, a relic from a previous age. The door his servant opened revealed the warmth of domesticity within and Erasmus jumped across the threshold with great happiness, crying to Mistress More, 'Bring me food, Jane, and lots of it! For I have dined with Colet this night and am starving.'

Having said goodbye, I stood there and watched the door close before turning back. I returned to St Paul's going by Cheapside, a wide street lined with shops which by day sell goldware, each small piece the product of the work of up to twenty men who labour in the cramped workshops of Clerkenwell. Here their pieces are sold to the wealthy citizens of London. It is a street that attracts Italian merchants, so I only walk it when the shops are closed, hugging the shadows, avoiding any chance meeting with someone who might recognise me, especially if he be a Dominican. For the same reason I've chosen these lodgings near the cathedral in a dank courtyard tenement which Erasmus calls 'Aphrodite's Alley'. I tell him I live here because it is cheap, as cheap as the drabs who hover at the door of the tavern at its entrance.

'It would be cheaper to lodge in the deanery: it would be free,' he said.

But the Dean of St Paul's is too often visited by officers of the Church and by friars.

'I want my independence,' I tell Erasmus.

And so I come home, walking past the drabs who have given up trying to interest me in their questionable charms. I have never lain with a woman other than my wife, and I do not intend to do so. I have sworn in solemn ceremony to be chaste and although I have broken my vows in every other respect, in that one I remain true.

I shall not marry. I shall not return to Italy. I shall not be a schoolmaster.

But what, then, shall I do? Live out my days until I die.

On my desk is a letter from the Prior of Blackfriars. I dare not open it.

24 A WARNING FROM MY BROTHER 1486

THAT WINTER, PICO DELLA MIRANDOLA HAD ROME TALKING about God. Now, that was a wonder. The great debate, for which men began to arrive from all parts of the Christian world, was scheduled to begin at Epiphany, the day of the Magi. For the first time, the Platonic tradition was to be submitted to public debate so that, in future, it would no longer be considered errant, pagan or strange. Pico was going to cut off the stagnant canals and redirect the water into its original course, the river of wisdom that flows from God.

I heard that, back in Florence, Ficino was expressing dismay. Under the influence of Mithridates, Pico had in various places in his theses insulted Ficino for limiting his study to Plato while ignoring the later platonists. That, of course, hurt Ficino considerably, but what caused his dismay was that his teaching, corrupted, as he saw it, by Pico's own lack of understanding, was to be put on public display in Rome by one who was not yet twenty-four years old. It was bound to fail, to bring further ignominy to Platonism rather than the hoped-for acceptance.

I celebrated the Feast of the Nativity with my brother, Rafaello, at the Palazzo de' Maffei. Afterwards, when we were alone in his chamber, he sat by the fire, head down, studiously pulling his shirt through the gap between lower and upper sleeve, seemingly intent on making a fine puff of linen. I knew that I would not like what he was about to say.

'The Pope is calling for the debate to be postponed until the commission has studied this unheard-of wealth of propositions. Nine hundred! Why, the eldest and wisest amongst the commissioners is famous for his own debate on twenty propositions, a number considered extraordinary at the time. Tell Pico, warn him, to do everything he is told to do with quiet obedience and respect to His Holiness.'

I told Rafaello of Pico's aim to convert the squabbling theologians from disputation to contemplation. He greeted this cynically. Getting up, he went and closed all the doors to the room before coming back to the fire. He drew his chair closer to mine and said softly, 'This Mother Church of ours is as capable of killing her own sons as Medea. Do not suppose that just because Pico is under the protection of Lorenzo de' Medici he will be safe from harm.' My cautious brother – naturally a man so adept in sealing his lips would find someone like Pico alarming.

'Rafaello, do you want to see this debate held?' I asked.

'I do, and I shall work hard to see that it happens, but tell Pico what I have said, and make sure he understands. The Inquisition is governed by Spain. We Italians, we understand human nature; we can elect a fornicator as pope and still remain sincere in our love of God. Spaniards – it is all light and dark for them, with no shades in between. I tell you, no Christian today is advised to do anything to attract the attention of the Grand Inquisitor. Terrible stories are beginning to come out of Spain about the expulsion of Marranos. It is said that they are Christians on the outside but remain Jews within, and if the Inquisition can prove it against anyone, that man is burned at the stake. They say this purifies his soul; I say it purifies Spanish blood. Queen Isabella and King Ferdinand are dedicated to cleansing the country of Moors and Jews and reuniting Spain under a Christian banner. The worst of it is, Torquemada is beginning to look beyond Jews and Moors for his heretics.'

In the short time I had been in Rome, I had often seen the progress of cardinals through the city, passing through the crowds in the splendour of princes, and the most extravagant, least religious of them all was a Spaniard, Rodrigo Borgia.

Rafaello rolled his eyes when I mentioned the name. 'Yes, I agree, Torquemada and Borgia cannot fit together in one sentence and make sense. But there you have it – light and dark. Beware Spain. I fear for that young pudding, Giovanni de' Medici, who, I can tell you, is set to become a cardinal at the next election. How can a mere boy swim in a sea such as this? If Lorenzo loves his son, he should abandon his ambitions. He has influence in many places, but in Rome very little and in Spain none at all.' He sat back and swilled his wine in its glass, looking at the ruby liquid in the firelight. 'I do not have to tell you, I think, that you are not to mention this conversation to anyone other than Pico, nor use my name to endorse your cause.'

'I wish you would come and live in Florence. You would not have to whisper all the time.'

Rafaello smiled. 'What good would I be to you in Florence? Be grateful that you have me here. But Maso, I wish to live a long life, so please, keep your firebrands away from my hay.'

25 CATERINA SFORZA RIDES AGAIN 1487

THERE HAD BEEN AN INSURRECTION AT FORLÌ A YEAR OR so previously, when the people, oppressed by the taxes that Girolamo Riario had laid upon them, rose up and seized the castle. Riario, suffering some ailment, had been with his wife at Imola at the time. With her husband incapacitated, it had been Caterina Sforza who had ridden to Forlì to put the insurrection down. Now there had been a second insurrection there, and I heard about it in a market in Rome. As before, Riario was at Imola and indisposed; as before, it was his wife who took up arms. Only this time... I listened agog to what a baker was telling his customers.

'Have you heard? Caterina Sforza! She who can put down a mob assisted only by one gentleman and two ladies. Caterina, who rode through Rome in full armour to take the Castel Sant'Angelo for the Riario.'

'God be praised, she failed in that,' said a priest handing over the money for his armful of loaves.

'But she succeeds in the Romagna where she failed in Rome. Ha!'

'So she has put down the good folk of Forlì again?'

'Again! Only this time … this time …' the baker could not speak for laughing. His customers laughed with him, in anticipation of what he was going to say.

'Oh dear,' said the baker, wiping his eyes with his apron. 'Forgive me, padre.'

'What for?'

'For what I am about to tell you. Ha! Ha! Oh dear …'

Before the baker could continue, the man selling olives at the next stall pre-empted him. 'She was nine months pregnant!'

'Nine months?' cried a peasant woman. 'Gesumaria!'

The priest dropped his loaves.

'Rode?' continued the contadina. 'On a horse? Nine months pregnant? On a horse? Rode? Holy Madonna Maria!'

'It is true, it is true!' cried the baker. 'Full with child, she galloped from Imola to Forlì, relieved the castle and then galloped back to have the baby. Those good folk of Forlì, eh? How can a man stand up in daylight and say, "I am a man of Forlì"? Ha! Ha! Oh, the shame! Ow, by God I have a stitch! Oh dear, oh dear. Caterina Sforza – an Amazon. What was the name of the Amazon queen? Pen – Penelope? *Olà*, scholar, what was her name?'

'Penthesilea,' I said and turned away laughing, wondering what the truth was behind these exaggerations. I discovered from Rafaello later that, when it comes to Caterina Sforza, no exaggeration can do her justice. It was all true. Later that same year, on the third insurrection, she had more than sixty men executed. That was the last protest of the good folk of Forlì.

26 ANOTHER WARNING
1487

FOR A MONTH WE WAITED WHILE THE COMMISSION deliberated on the debate. Men gathered in Pico's apartments, attracted both by the man and his philosophy. All of them were eccentric, one way or another. Michele Marullus, for instance. He came to us as a Greek scholar studying Plato in Rome, but we soon learnt that not only was he a soldier of fortune but one of the legendary *stratioti*; not an honest refugee of Constantinople as we had supposed, driven west by the Turks, but one who had been condemned by the Greek church as a heretic. The *stratioti* – those mercenaries who create havoc, storming the enemy brandishing scimitars, sweeping off heads with one strike and impaling them on lances. More than once I had been threatened with them as a child when I was naughty. To meet one and find him a charming and erudite man was a novelty for all of us. In conversation with Pico, Marullus revealed secrets of the *stratioti* that none of us knew except Pico himself, who drew Marullus out with careful questioning.

'Men say that the *stratioti* are a survival of the legions of the Roman empire.'

'We have an oral tradition which says that it is so.'

'Most of the legions, I believe, were worshippers of Mithras.'

His eyes heavily lidded, Marullus looked deceptively sleepy, even dull, but we were looking at a hooded falcon.

'Mithras the bull-slayer,' said Pico.

Marullus yawned. 'I don't think the Romans were interested in sacrificing bulls. To be a member of the cult requires, required, a high level of spiritual and moral discipline.'

The two men regarded each other like chess players. Pico had caught the slip in tenses, as he was meant to. 'Is the cult still alive?'

'It is, amongst the *stratioti*.'

'And you?'

Marullus turned his head slowly left and right, then, looking at Pico, lifted his chin – an almost imperceptible assent. 'More properly,' he said in a low tone, 'a Zoroastrian.' If Marullus had calculated this to attract Pico, that avid collector of men of all religions, he succeeded. What interested Pico most, however, was that here was a Greek who was not a Christian. He admired that courageous streak of individuality. So Marullus joined our circle and enjoyed his status as a figure of legend and terror, although to me he was always pleasant, as any man was who wished to gain the favour of Poliziano.

One of the most renowned scholars in Rome at the time, one who was in the city through his own volition and not at the invitation of Pico, was a Venetian friend of Poliziano's called Ermolao Barbaro. In him Pico found someone neither eccentric nor obsequious. Indeed, after a few minutes' conversation, Pico was treating the older man with deference, eager to earn his good opinion. Barbaro was working on a new translation of Aristotle with a group of scholars, some of whom you know, Erasmo, for among them were our own William Grocyn and Thomas Linacre. You will have heard from them of the splendour of this man. If you ever wondered why Linacre the physician is at heart a poet, we have Barbaro to thank. His very speech was lyrical; he, a son of Harmonia, commanded large groups in a soft and gentle, almost lisping voice.

Such was his standing that I did not try to approach him or make myself known. I, the companion of Pico, of Poliziano, the friend of Lorenzo de' Medici, was cowed by the reputation of this philosopher of Aristotle. But one day I had to go to the papal library to collect books for Pico. I noticed two things on entry: one was that Barbaro was present and alone; the other was that there was a guard in the library standing close to the pile of books reserved for Pico. Even before I could hesitate, Barbaro looked up and called me to him by name.

'Ah, Tommaso,' he said, 'thank you for coming. I am having trouble with this passage. How do you read it?'

Bemused, I bent over the Greek volume open on the table.

'Do not pick up those books,' Barbaro said in pure Attic.

'Is it a trap?' I asked in the same language.

The librarian approached. 'Are you the secretary of Pico della Mirandola? I have some books put by for him.'

'This,' said Barbaro, straightening to his full height, 'is the brother of Rafaello de' Maffei. He is working with me. Please, do not disturb us.'

The librarian lifted his chin with a sniff and left us.

'Is it a trap?' I repeated.

'They are keeping a close eye on Pico and are looking for evidence against him. Do not pick up those books: they are Hebrew texts.'

Barbaro was one of those men to whom neatness and good-grooming come naturally so that he looked as if he arose each morning already shaved. His face seemed to be the work of a sculptor with its slender, aristocratic nose and polished jaw. Everything about him said that here was a Venetian, one of the families of the Senate, a republican. Kings wear their wealth in gold and jewels to overawe their subjects; Ermolao Barbaro needed no such trinkets. In this unadorned man, his words were his jewels, unostentatious but rich and glowing.

Poliziano, who had befriended Barbaro during his exile in Venice, truly admired but few men, and this was one of them.

'Go back to Florence,' Barbaro said. 'Pico is inflamed with God to the point of rashness. He is too young to understand the ways of men. They are jealous of him and will destroy him if they can. Everyone thinks he is at best vain, at worst a heretic. We know he is neither.' He gazed at me with his large, sympathetic eyes. 'He thinks he has only to convince Pope Innocent of his ideas and Christendom will be transformed, but those ideas of his are quite crepuscular. That he is running rings around the logicians as to make them giddy will not persuade them to his view. No man lays down his beliefs on the argument of another. What does Pico seek to prove? That logic is a false trail? Well, the logicians will prove him wrong and, if they do not, they will burn him. The wise man walks quietly and draws no attention to himself. Why, last summer, that man called Mercurio arrived in Rome and was promptly arrested for a rite he had performed in public two years previously. Sacrificed a peacock as I heard it.'

'That was a lie. Besides, they set him free.'

'Yes, but only after he had tried to commit suicide by ripping the flesh off his own face. The authorities did not have the heart to kill him after that.'

I had not heard that gruesome detail before.

'Pico's motley, cosmopolitan, heterodox companions, that exotic train of Jews, Arabs, Zoroastrians and Brahmins, Mithridates, Mercurio, Marullus – can you not see the danger of mere association? Tommaso, leave. Go back to Florence and my dear Poliziano. Stars that shoot are dying stars. Return to that heavy planet which is our Angelo. With him you will be safe.'

'Do you not see the value in what Pico is trying to do?'

'Of course I see the value, but such an endeavour is for a mature man. Pico should not attempt this alone. Public disputation!' Barbaro leaned even closer to me. His mantle was fragrant with cleanliness. 'Get him home to Florence. I will come there shortly. The three of us – Pico, Poliziano and myself – will work on Aristotle together to free him of the distortions of his Arab commentators. We shall reveal him in his purity, clear the barnacles off him, sweep away the false interpretations, strip him down to his pure Greek self.'

The image that came to mind as he spoke was that of the Three Graces, the triple aspect of Venus. Pico – Poliziano – Barbaro in the dance of the love of language and of truth.

'I shall see what I can do.'

'Leave the books. Tell Pico that it is too dangerous to collect them.'

27 PICO IS CONDEMNED
1487

PICO APPEARED EVERY DAY AT SITTINGS OF THE EXAMINING council which comprised bishops and theologians well-versed in the methods of scholastic dispute.

'It is not going well,' my brother told me. 'Murmurs of heresy are growing and Pico is not helping himself by being brash and dismissive of the council.'

'Heresy' is a word by which the righteous seek to terrify the unrighteous. I had heard one theologian define 'martyr' as a man who is willing to die for his beliefs and Pico ask breezily if this definition did not also apply to a heretic. The man's eyes had narrowed to slits.

'Seven of the propositions are to be condemned,' Rafaello said. 'They have decided that Pico is "in heresy". This is not the same as being a heretic. Many of us are in heresy, whenever we choose to understand God's mystery in the light of our own reason rather than accept it as a matter of faith. Nevertheless, he courts danger. He must be advised to surrender his intellect to God and make peace with His Vicar. He must not take the step from being in heresy to being a heretic, or it will be the duty of the Curia to hand him over to the Spaniards to purify his soul with fire. Warn him, Tommaso. Convince him. While he believes himself sent by God and immune to all danger, he is in the worst danger of all.'

I attended the court the next day. Pico defended himself vibrantly, his voice steady and clear, his grey eyes steely. Convinced that a man of truth may win any battle against evil, he stood there like a young king or crusader while around him pressed the infidels, eager to see him fail. I watched from the gallery. After weeks of wearying accusation and defence, the men of the Church, lined up on the bench like rooks, made sombre pronouncement:

seven of Pico's nine hundred propositions had been exposed as heretical, and a further six were of doubtful orthodoxy.

I wanted to jump to my feet and demand, 'What of the other eight hundred and eighty seven?' but cowardice prevented it.

Pico stood tall and defiant with only the ghost of surprise showing on his face. He said nothing, made no protest, but after a moment that was silent but for the shuffling and tapping of documents by the whey-faced doctors of the Church, he turned and left the court.

The Pope ordered Pico to do nothing – no debating, no writing – until he had received his decision on the matter. You might as well tell a bee to leave flowers alone. Pico retired to his rooms. During each day he gave every appearance of idleness, but at night... over the next twenty nights he dictated an *Apologia*, explaining the process of debate to His Holiness as if to a simpleton. As each page was finished, I had to read it through, looking for errors. Those precious, blooming days of May were spent asleep while at night we kept company with bats and demons and ruined our eyes working by candlelight. Cristoforo and I presumed that Pico was writing for future publication, but the clandestine nature of the work was only because Pico did not wish to be arrested before he had finished. As soon as the project ended, he told Cristoforo to send it to Pope Innocent.

'My lord, my lord,' said Cristoforo, shaking his head. 'If you will remember, it was His Holiness who banned you from writing anything.'

'I know, but once he has read this even he must see reason. We must trust in God.'

A few days later, Rafaello overruled his own counsel for circumspection and went himself to visit Pico. 'I advise you to leave Rome at once. Incensed by your disobedience, His Holiness is initiating the process to condemn you for heresy. A courier is leaving for Spain and the Grand Inquisitor tonight.'

'I am more ardent in my faith than most men. What is meant by this word "heresy"? In Greek it simply means "choice". What is it I am choosing and why is it a sin?'

'The laws and liturgy of the Holy Roman Church have been established over the centuries by Great Councils, but you are choosing to tread your own path and find your own authorities, many of them pagan – that is the heresy. A son of the Church may do nothing but follow meekly in the way laid down by the Fathers.'

'That would be all well and good if the result was a faith that was followed by its adherents, but all we have in Christianity is varying degrees of hypocrisy, and the closer one gets to the Pope, the greater the degree of it. I speak to you as a friend, Rafaello.'

My brother nodded. 'These things may be spoken of in private between friends, but your challenge to Church authority has been very public indeed.'

'I have no intention of challenging Church authority. The wisdom of the Church is received wisdom, passed down generation after generation by men of varying levels of intelligence and understanding, until what we are left with is a fog of ideas that is supposed to be the basis of our lives. What I challenge is those ideas. They need to be dragged out of the cellar and examined. If anything needs to be put on trial here, it is the assumptions of the average Christian.'

Rafaello's eyes grew keen, and I knew that if only my brother would be true to himself he would confess to being in full agreement with Pico. But his life was sustained by the offices he held within the Curia, and so he listened as a sympathetic yet wholly orthodox cleric.

'For example,' said Pico, not caring how sympathetic Rafaello was or was not, 'take the doctrine that only a Christian is able to receive salvation. Am I right? Is that a doctrine of the Church?'

Rafaello nodded.

'Am I also right in thinking that there is no concept of metempsychosis in the Church, no thought that a soul may survive the body and migrate to another?'

'Absolutely none. As you well know, the teaching of the Church is the resurrection of the body on the Day of Judgement.'

'So, if I understand it right, and we have only one lifetime, and only Christians may hope for salvation, half the world's population lives with no hope of heaven. What kind of God is it then to have created Jews and Muslims?'

'One does not question God. It is one of His Mysteries.'

Pico leaned forward in his chair. 'Rafaello, do you leave your intelligence outside with your horse when you go into church? Surely you do not believe what you just said?'

Rafaello shifted uncomfortably. 'Of course I do not. And yet better men than I have believed it, and I will follow them.'

'Therefore you consider that our religion is a way of devotion and not a way of knowledge? If I am guilty of anything, it is in believing otherwise. I believe we can make the return to God by way of knowledge, and that we should not fear anything we learn. The Church dreads a man who thinks for himself, and that is why I am condemned as a heretic.'

'That is your choice,' said Rafaello, smiling grimly. 'But while you are talking you are losing time. Leave Rome tonight.'

'What truth is it that cannot accommodate discussion and debate? It is a false truth. Truth itself does not threaten men with imprisonment, or put a wire round their throats and twist them into silence, or put them on a bonfire to die choking on the smoke of their own flesh. The truth sets men free, but everywhere this Christian faith has put men in chains. Something has gone badly awry and must needs be discussed.'

'They will have the tongue out of your head first.'

'I will place my trust in God,' said Pico firmly. 'I shall not fly.'

28 THE ACADEMY
UNDERGROUND 1487

THERE WAS ANOTHER POPE IN ROME, A SECRET ONE WHOM everyone spoke of but few met. Pomponio Leto was the head of an academy which had been outlawed a generation earlier and men spoke of him as if he were a fabulous hero of legend. Pico had tried many routes to meet him but all had failed. We knew he lived on the Esquiline but despite all messages sent to his villa, no invitation arrived. Then one evening a boy came from Ermolao Barbaro, telling Pico he was to come with him.

The boy took us out to the Appian Way and far along that old Roman road, making sure we were not followed. The first Christians had had their own secret meetings here, in the catacombs. These places had been forgotten, had become overgrown, but we were led into one of them by the boy who knew his way well. We went down into a tunnel which, at first, was utterly dark, but there was a faint glimmering light in the distance and we followed it, feeling our way along, sometimes our hands falling on bones stored in one of the many niches that ran the length of the wall. As we turned a bend in the tunnel, more light became visible until, at last, we came into a small cave fully illuminated by flaming torches set in sconces. The chamber was filled with men sitting in a circle around the sage, and by the dancing light I recognised many of them, including Michele Marullus and Ermolao Barbaro. And there, in the corner: did my eyes deceive me in the flickering light? But no, when he looked up and met my gaze I recognised my brother, Rafaello. That circumspect, upright member of the Curia was sitting at the feet of Pomponio Leto, a disciple of philosophy.

Pico went forward and grasped the old man's hand. 'I was beginning to believe you were a myth.'

'I would have it so,' said Leto quietly. The group dispersed so that these two could speak in private. From Rafaello I gathered what I could about the one they referred to as 'Pontifex Maximus'. He told me that Leto was the master for everyone who followed the way of the Sun, who sought that inner transformation that would free the soul from its earthliness.

'And that's why you meet in the dark?'

Rafaello smiled.

'Honestly, brother,' I said, 'I cannot tell you how it pleases me to see you here. Why did you never confide in me?'

'I never confide in anyone. It's safest that way.' Taking a torch, Rafaello guided me around the subterranean galleries, showing me graffiti and wall paintings from the earliest times of our faith. 'Christianity must be restored to its original purity,' he said, tracing two arcs of a circle that crossed to form the shape of a fish, a shape known as the *vesica piscis*. It was known to me well enough: you can see it in most cathedrals from barbarian times, but here was its original. My heart pounded in my chest.

'Why does the truth have to be underground?' I asked him. 'What are we hiding from?'

'The force that would snuff the truth out, that wants no one to know it. Often it takes the form of the pope.' Could this be my guarded brother speaking? 'Everything went wrong when Christianity became the religion of the empire. It became a part of the structure of power, and its essence, which is love, was forgotten.'

'Some of the men here are not Christians at all, but followers of Mithras and Zoroaster.'

'That's why we have the sun as our symbol: it unites us. Pontifex Maximus has no interest in any faith that divides. He seeks unity alone.'

'Another Ficino.'

'Indeed, another Ficino. They work together.'

'They have met?'

'Not on this plane, perhaps, but the physical world is not the only one, as you keep telling me.'

It is one thing to have interesting theories, quite another to discover they have a reality. Ficino and Leto, he told me, meet often in the angelic realm. I looked to the old man talking so earnestly with Pico. Every fibre in Pico was quick and alert, as if knowing this one conversation was all he would ever have. Their faces were so close that nothing could be heard of what they were saying: it was like looking at Socrates being interrogated by an impatient disciple. Leto's quiet repose was unruffled by the young man's vivacity. He answered all Pico's questions briefly and in ways, I heard later, that surprised him.

I realised what we had in Florence: a sage of the ancient wisdom who walked abroad in daylight. We had no need for clandestine, secret meetings in subterranean burial grounds. While Lorenzo ruled Florence, the truth walked free. Then I kicked myself for having been unwise: I should have stayed with Ficino as instructed and not followed this self-intoxicated flibbertigibbet, Pico, who, while men so much older and wiser than he met in secret, had chosen open battle with the Church. But my other half, the would-be adventurer, snorted at this. We, after all, were attempting that which no one else had the courage to do: challenging the dogma and authority that shackled us.

When we returned to our lodgings by starlight along the cobbled path of the Appian Way, our step was light and bouncing. I felt as if I had walked this way before, many times over the aeons, and always with the same purpose. Pico said that Leto had told him that what he was doing was risky, but that a man who risked so much was beloved of God.

'He told me to have no fear, that the work I do is divine work, and divinely ordained. He said that the sun clearly shines in my breast and that I am to trust it. I shall be remaining in Rome.'

'Oh, my lord, no!' said Cristoforo.

29 PICO IN FLIGHT
1487

IT TOOK NEARLY A YEAR FOR THE POPE TO MAKE UP HIS MIND on the troublesome subject of Pico della Mirandola, but in August Rafaello told us that a bull of excommunication was being drafted. Pico did nothing but stayed on in Rome. Then, in Advent, it became public and the bull was read out in every church throughout Christendom. What did the average layman make of it? – this long document in Latin that condemned the Count of Concordia for offering to debate certain propositions 'savouring of heresy, derived from occult doctrines, renovating the errors of pagan philosophers, cherishing the deceits of the Jews, and promoting certain arts, disguised as natural philosophy, harmful to the Catholic faith and human kind.'

I had a picture of the good folk of all parishes shifting restlessly through this meaningless and interminable bull, perhaps explaining it to each other afterwards, if the priest had not translated it for them, that the pope was angry, that someone was a heretic and would surely be burned, that Concordia was a tiny state somewhere in Italy.

In Florence, however, cries of horror and outrage went up. In a letter Angelo told me that he had heard it read out in the Duomo in sombre tones by the archbishop. 'I cried out as if pierced by pain; Maria, in the women's section, sank to her knees; Marsilio Ficino, among the canons, had tears coursing down his face. Lorenzo, however, strode to the high altar, ripped the bull from the hands of the archbishop and tore it in half.'

Hearing that he was about to be arrested, Pico, who had stayed so long in Rome that he had rubbed the patience of his secretary raw, suddenly had to leave.

'Where to, my lord?' Cristoforo asked, irritably. 'My joints have rusted up but now you want me to gallop away on a horse. Where to?'

'France.'

'*France?*'

'We're not safe anywhere in Italy. If I can get to the Sorbonne, all will be well.'

'You would be safe in Florence,' I said.

'Ah, but Florence is where they think I will go.'

True enough, no one bothered to pursue us when we finally left Rome. In Siena, however, we were watched, and when we left, we took the road to Florence, deviating later to a route leading to Lucca and the north.

It was noontide when we entered the gates of Lucca a few days later and the streets were almost deserted. We rested by a fountain while a servant went to find accommodation. When the servant returned, I thought he looked nervous.

'The Signoria wish to make you welcome, my lord, and have invited you to the town hall.'

'How come? I told you to reveal my identity to no one.'

I caught the servant by the throat and squeezed. 'Who is with the Signoria? Who did you speak to?'

'The papal nuncio,' he gasped.

'And you were not going to warn us?'

'They threatened to kill me.'

I spat in his face.

Pico was angry with my behaviour – mine, not the servant's – and, having told me to let the poor man go, rubbed his face wearily. 'Is there no escape from this world?'

'Very slowly, without any fuss, let us remount and make our way back to the gate,' I said.

'And what about this fellow?'

'Abandon him,' said Cristoforo.

'Have I taught you *nothing*?' Pico demanded. He told the servant to remount and not to worry, that he was forgiven.

But as we made our way down towards the city wall, the tocsin sounded for the closing of the gates. And then we spurred our horses and raced, bearing down on the bewildered guards like the horsemen of the Apocalypse, charging through them and over them before they could respond. We galloped out of Lucca and, avoiding the road to Pisa, fled into the mountains.

30 A GRAMMARIAN WITH A DREAM 1487

FEELING SAFER ONCE WE WERE ACROSS THE APENNINES and in the Duchy of Ferrara we indulged in a short detour to Carpi. There lived two of Pico's nephews – Alberto and Lionello Pio – whom he loved as sons. Another nephew was also there, Gianfrancesco Pico, who being nineteen was closer in age to his uncle than to his cousins. Pico was cooler with him than with the younger boys since Gianfrancesco was the son of a brother Pico detested; yet Gianfrancesco clearly worshipped his uncle and tried to impress him with tales of his achievements at university.

The tutor of the boys in Greek and Latin was forty-year-old Aldo Manuzio, an enthusiastic – some might say addicted – student of Greek. Having discovered that I was close to Poliziano, he greeted me jovially as if I were an old friend and made sure to sit beside me at dinner, telling me that he thought Poliziano was a Hercules among men, most learned, most fearless of all scholars. 'He has reason where other men only have intuition or opinion.'

'It is true,' Pico agreed. Turning to his young nephews, he told them that Poliziano had read every book in the Medici library. Their eyes popped.

'That,' said Aldo, 'must make him the best-read man in the world.'

'He must know more than anybody,' said Alberto Pio.

'Except me,' said Pico. When the boys hooted and accused him of vanity, Pico explained simply that he, too, had read all the Medici books and many more besides.

'That is not vanity, it is the truth,' Gianfrancesco agreed, staring angrily at the boys. 'Our uncle is the most learned man in all Italy, perhaps the world.'

Aldo told me that his ambition was to become a printer-publisher, specialising in Greek texts. I told him that printing was the invention of the devil designed for the ruination of the world, and that his idea, if successful, would only condemn our beloved authors to the vulgar throng. 'Beautiful ideas,' I told him, 'should be expressed in a beautiful hand, ideally a hand that belongs to a man who knows and loves the Greek language.'

'Books written by hand are books written for the few. Why should men be starved of literature because they cannot afford it? Rich men commission books then lock them away as treasures: they hoard learning. Are all men who are not wealthy to be considered "the vulgar throng"? I am neither wealthy nor vulgar; nor are you. How many books do you possess? Only those you have copied for yourself. I agree that printed books are ugly to any man of taste and sensibility. Have you seen the Plato translated by Ficino and printed in Venice? Full of error: printed by a barbarian in the style of a barbarian. But it does not have to be so. Is it impossible for there to be beautiful books produced by machines?'

'Yes, while the type is cut by goldsmiths. I'll wager there is not a scribe among them; a copyist, perhaps, but not a scribe.'

'What is the difference?'

'The scribe who merely copies the fine hand of another does not even approach beauty. The true scribe, well-trained, knows the secrets of proportion. Aristotle says that beauty lies in the relationship of one thing to another, but that is only partly true.'

'Is it then in the number, the underlying geometry?'

'Harmony is there.'

'Where, then, beauty?'

'It is in the space between. Between the letters and between the lines.'

'Aha!'

'If you want to produce beautiful books by a machine, you will need a man who understands proportion, the relationship of the letters to the lines and the body of the text to the margins.'

He seemed to be charged with light at what I said. 'So, it can be done.'

'Yes,' I agreed, 'it is possible.' We stared at each other for a long moment, then I snapped out of Aldo's dream. 'Nevertheless, the printing press *is* the invention of the devil. It is Poliziano's view that, by its means, error spreads quicker than the plague. What was a fault in one book now becomes a fault in many. Worse, the most stupid ideas can now in a moment be transferred into a thousand volumes and spread abroad.'

'While printing is in the hands of mere artisans it will be so, which is why it is vital for someone such as myself to enter the business.'

I was impressed beyond measure that a man of his age should have such an ambition, not only to change profession but to enter one about which he knew nothing.

'All I need is funding…' Aldo looked expectantly at Pico.

'It will come, I am sure,' said Pico. He turned to his secretary. 'Can I afford it, Cristoforo?'

'You can barely afford a night's lodging.'

Cristoforo explained to Aldo that Pico's fortune was locked up in the books which, loaded into a wagon and in the care of a trusted servant, were now making their way to Savoy. 'What he has not spent on arcane texts, he has spent on paying the travelling expenses and accommodation for the numerous scholars who came to Rome to debate with him.'

'What debate?' Aldo asked, bemused, and then I laughed at him, that anyone could be so wrapped up in his own bookish thoughts as to be unaware of all that had befallen his beloved patron.

'Have you heard nothing, Aldo?' Pico asked.

Aldo shook his head. 'I cannot keep up with you, my lord, you know that. Paris, Florence, Perugia, Rome. I did hear something about a woman in Arezzo…'

Pico interrupted him. 'When a man begins the ascent towards God, every devil in the universe tries to pull him off the ladder.' He spent the rest of the evening recounting his adventures to his nephews and their schoolmaster, the company sitting rapt as if at the feet of a master storyteller spinning tales about fabulous places that do not really exist. Gianfrancesco gazed at his uncle with unfaltering attention, drinking in everything he had to say, consuming the very substance of the man.

Pico was exhausted when he eventually retired. 'My nephew is a leech,' he muttered as Cristoforo helped him undress. 'It was like being touched by the woman with the issue of blood.'

31 THE BURNING OF THE BOOKS 1488

IT WAS THE END OF DECEMBER BY THE TIME WE REACHED Turin and we lodged there for a week or so. Reunited with the pack train that had gone ahead, Pico greeted his wagon-load of books with joy and relief. I had never been so far north before and could feel the chill from the Alps. When we continued on our way in January, the closer we came to the mountains, the deeper was the chill, and as we made our way over the snowy pass it went into my soul. I thought I should never live to see the far side. Travellers often speak of the spectacular views of the Alps which take the mind off any discomfort, but we saw nothing except mist and – dimly – the walls of snow each side of our track, the wall to our right hiding the mountain, the one to the left hiding the precipice. Each step we took was an act of faith and no man in the party spoke throughout the ordeal but each wrapped himself up in his own thoughts and prayers. The only sound was the crunch of hoof and the grind of wheels on snow, the occasional snort of horse, and the collapse of snow walls behind us.

After we had crossed the summit of the pass and begun to wind our way down the mountain, we came out of the cloud and could see again, and what we saw were signs of spring, with little aconites poking out through the melting snow. As we came out of the snow fields, our spirits lifted and, after resting a night in an inn, we went on smartly through Provence.

In the last inn before Lyons we were approached by a young French priest.

'Jean du Pic?' he asked softly, sitting at our table.

Pico conversed with him in French and, hearing what the man had to say, the colour drained from his face.

'They know we are here,' he told us. 'They have known all along. Apparently King Charles has been happy to turn a blind eye, but now the papal nuncios have found out where we are the king can be blind no longer. We shall be arrested tomorrow and tried for heresy.'

He rose from the table, thanked the priest graciously and went outside.

Cristoforo and I were left staring at each other.

'We could run,' I said. Having suffered from one of Pico's escapades before, I did not wish to do so again.

'And leave him to his fate?'

'It is *his* fate.' I was beginning to sound callous even to my own ears.

'The fate of the loyal servant is his lord's.'

'You are a good man, Cristoforo. I wish I were as good. But to be tried as heretics – does your loyalty stretch that far? Let's go and get him and make our escape. Germany, perhaps...' But suddenly and simultaneously there were several shouts of *Fire!*, the smell of burning and the sight of flames through the opaque windows of the inn. We rushed outside, along with the rest of the inn's guests.

181

The Count of Concordia stood looking at a bonfire his servants had made of his books and papers. By the time we arrived, there was no chance of rescuing anything. Within minutes the flames had consumed a library of Cabalistic and other texts worth tens of thousands of florins and many of them irreplaceable.

'*Mammalucco!*' I shouted at Pico, forgetting all courtesy. 'How could you do this?'

'Better the gods have them as a sacrifice than the demons as evidence.'

With that Pico walked back into the inn and went to bed.

Cristoforo shook his head in disbelief. 'Have you ever met a man who lacks the fear of death? It makes him happy and it makes him rash. My lord is like that with regard to money. It has no power over him.'

It certainly had power over me. My bones turned to jelly to see such a fortune curling and melting in the fire. But worse than the loss of fortune was the loss of knowledge.

'Do you think this is enough to save him? To save us?'

'He thinks so. That is enough for me.'

32 THE THRESHOLD OF PURGATORY 1488

WE WERE ARRESTED THE FOLLOWING MORNING AND TAKEN across France chained together in an open wagon, a foul and jolting journey on rutted roads that lasted several days. The fortress of Vincennes has a keep so high that it can be seen from far away, soaring above the tree tops of the royal forest on the edge of Paris. When at last the walls came into view, then we knew how high that keep was, and how disproportionate to its surroundings. A place without proportion is a place without harmony; no wonder it had been abandoned as a royal residence and put to a function more in keeping with its sulphurous-grey stone. It was as surely a prison as if it had been designed as one. Sometimes men of rank and standing are, when incarcerated, given a suite of rooms not unlike their own at home, and I had rather hoped this would be the case for the Count of Concordia, but as soon as I saw the fortress I knew it to be a vain hope.

As we passed through the great gates I looked up in desperation at the sky, at the clouds scudding over the blue empyrean, as if for the last time. Then it was in through the hole to Hades. We were taken across the cobbled courtyard and made to climb the stairs to the top of the keep. 'Heretics,' they told us, 'always go to the top so that the influence of heaven can reach them more easily.' Although the climb threatened to burst my heart and lungs, I was glad I was a heretic and not the kind of sinner who was put underground.

We were pushed into a small chamber that stank of French urine (it's different). The other two crossed at once to the window, to judge how high it was above their heads, while I bent over heaving for breath with a stitch in my side from the climb. When the door closed with a massive thud, when the key grated in the lock and the bolt went home, then my lungs gave out. I inhaled in a gasping wheeze but found no air. As I strained for breath my throat cried like an organ pipe. Pico and Cristoforo turned. They seemed to be unaffected by the suffocating chamber. I fell to my knees, clawed at my shirt, ripping it open at the neck, and implored help from my companions with bulging eyes. Cristoforo drew back in fright, but Pico came and spoke to me as if I were the Gadarene swine.

'Be quiet! Be still!' He laid his hands on my head and the inner juddering gradually ceased. 'You are safe, Tommaso.'

'I have nightmares,' I stuttered, 'of being trapped in a small space. I wake up clawing for breath. When that key turned...' My lungs were squeezed by terror again. Pico's grip on my head grew firmer. 'Trust in God, Tommaso, or if you cannot, then trust me. These are not your last moments.'

He went to the middle of the chamber and calmly looked about him. There was not much to see – not half as much to see as there was to smell – just a couple of benches, a rush-strewn floor and a heavy oak-beamed ceiling.

'How long are we going to be here?' Cristoforo wanted to know. 'Will they try us for heresy? Do they burn heretics in France? Do they kill you first? – oh, God!'

'We have a choice,' said Pico. 'Go mad within the hour, or penetrate the veils of this world. This is purgatory and the choice is to slip into hell or try for paradise.'

Cristoforo slid down the wall and sat heavily on the floor with his head in his arms. 'I am not capable of it.'

'God thinks you are, or you would not be here.'

Hearing the key turning in the lock, I jumped towards the door. It opened and one of the guards coming in held me back with a pike. A man behind them entered bearing a large book. 'Bible,' he said gruffly, 'by order of the King.'

'Take it away,' said Pico at once, proving to our captors that we were indeed heretics, and of the worst kind.

'Oh, my lord…' said Cristoforo in despair.

'I want no books,' Pico insisted, courteously showing the guards out. 'It is time,' he told us, 'time to approach knowledge without reading. Besides, I know the Bible off by heart. What passage would you like to have read?'

'Oh, about St Peter in prison I should think,' I said. Just then the sun reached in through our high window and caught Pico in its beam. He smiled.

'I do believe in angels, as you know, but the freedom I seek is not the miraculous unlocking of physical doors.' Promising to be our Bible whenever we should wish to call on him, he arranged three stools and bade us sit together. He gave us a line to contemplate: *I am the way, the truth and the life.*

I had practised contemplation many times before, with varying degrees of failure. Pico was right: it was easier in prison, for there was no alternative activity to tempt the mind. All three of us went deep on that first occasion and, as day followed day, we went deeper still. Plunging into stillness, into the way, the truth and the life, into the *I am*.

When we were not in contemplation, Pico taught us the mysteries. I had asked him about the 'tenth sphere', the sphere beyond the nine of the Great Chain of Being, saying that I did not understand what it was. He replied: 'Man alone of all beings, whether brutes or gods, has the freedom of choice in his actions and the ability to ascend. In that he is the envy of the gods, who are as fixed in their sphere as the animals and plants in theirs. Man – or the Soul of Man – alone may make the ascent of being. But that man who is happy in the lot of no created thing, who withdraws into the centre of his own unity, his spirit, becomes one with God, in the solitary darkness of God, who is set above all things, and surpasses all. That is the tenth sphere: it is beyond Creation, it contains Creation. It is the source of all.

'Therefore we must disdain earthly things to attain heaven. But if you would attain unity, then you must disdain heavenly things also. By this method, we may hasten to that court which is beyond the world and nearest to the Godhead. There, as the sacred mysteries relate, Seraphim, Cherubim and Thrones hold the first places. If we have willed it, we shall be second to them in nothing. And at last, roused by ineffable love as by a sting, like burning Seraphim rapt from ourselves, full of divine power we shall no longer be ourselves but shall become He Himself who made us.'

'Is this what was meant by the inscription over the gate to the Delphic Oracle, the injunction to "Know Thyself"?' I asked.

'He who knows himself in himself knows all things, as Zoroaster first wrote, and then Plato in his *Alcibiades*. As they say in the East, "That Thou Art". In the Greek tradition, "The Self is the true Apollo". This wisdom has flowed from the East to the Greeks, and from the Greeks to us. It is all in Iamblichus.'

'And is this union the aim of magic?'

'There are two forms of magic and two kinds of magician. One seeks power over nature by the invocation of demons, which is abhorrent. That is the definition of evil: to take things for oneself. The other form of magic is the utter perfection of natural philosophy. The word "magus" in Persian simply means "worshipper of the divine". As the farmer weds his vines to elms, so does the magus marry heaven and earth. Magic is nothing less than high and holy philosophy, and all the great, wise men such as Pythagoras, Socrates and Plato were practitioners.'

We did not spend our months in prison entirely transcendent of all fear. Indeed, Cristoforo and I spent much of the time in agitation, standing on each other's shoulders for a few moments at the window. We could see little of the city of Paris in the distance and nothing at all of the fortress below, but we could hear the sounds of soldiers at practice, for the fortress was a garrison of one of the brigades of the French army. Now this was a wonder that both Cristoforo and I were boyish enough to want to see for ourselves, for we had no idea what a national army could be like. In our own lands, where we knew only mercenary forces, the standing army of the French was as legendary as the sphinx or basilisk. Out of desire and desperation, Cristoforo hoisted himself high by the power of his arms and succeeded in getting his head out of the window – at the risk of losing his ears as he withdrew it again. He told me of a vast infantry in formation below, in such wonder as if he had seen angels. 'They wheel like starlings, the many acting as one. Incredible!'

Pico had no interest in soldiers. Training his mind to rest itself on God, he learnt to disregard all passing thoughts and physical discomforts. Sometimes I had nightmares, my dreams cooked by the flames of imaginary fires, but Pico became more and more quiet and, with the passing of weeks, began to exude a spiritual substance. What do I mean by that? Only that, in his presence, it became increasingly difficult to worry about the future. The peace of his soul bathed the cold stone with subtle warmth and light.

Contemplation is not like carpentry – once taught, ever known. In spiritual disciplines, instruction needs to be regular and constant, and with Pico I had a teacher on hand. I have never found the practice easy and have always preferred the way of action, seeking the Divine in my work. But in prison it was easy. With the body forced into stillness by circumstances, and with the lack of sensory impressions, the mind was starved of the thoughts, dreams and images which are its daily occupations. The slightest fidget or the sound of rats, instead of being a distraction, now acted as a reminder that my attention was drifting. We used various key statements from scripture to contemplate and, after a while, they would disappear, displaced by inward silence; then it was as if resting in a boat on a calm lake. Sometimes the boat would suddenly sink to the bottom and, providing one avoided fright or alarm, there one knew the most profound and limitless peace. Time vanished. All was now and eternity. And the only thought was the fervent hope that this might never end. But then the key would turn in the lock and some stale bread and stewed vegetables be delivered, and the spell which is no spell but a vision of true reality would be broken.

On one occasion, the contemplation went very deep indeed. Peace is not in the mind, it takes it over; it comes from behind, as it were, and engulfs you like a warm wave of the ocean. I was drawn out of myself to become myself, my true self, utterly calm, utterly potent with fine, unexpressed energy, the lord of myself. Know Thyself. This Self. The true identity. All was silent except for the steady, slow breathing of my companions, and then, as if from some infinite distance, I heard a sound which I can only express in Greek: *ei*. The period of contemplation came to an end when each of us simultaneously inhaled deeply, as if life in this world requires more air. It took some time before my eyes would open: in truth, I did not wish to leave where I had been. I asked Pico about the sound I had heard and he said it is the greeting of the Divinity to the one who approaches. '*Ei* – "Thou Art". That is the call into the tenth sphere you wanted to know about,' he said, appreciatively. 'Also known as the Sabbath of the Soul.'

He brought the contemplation to an end with a short prayer. 'Let us wish this peace for our friends, for our century, for the world.'

And then, as if in response to his words, a cock crew. It was many hours before dawn. Pico smiled. 'Ah the cock, the sacred cock, the call to awaken.'

The cock crowed again and its yodelling sounded across the land beyond the fortress. In that moment I knew that all life is a dream.

33 THE DEATH OF RIARIO
1488

SOME ITEMS OF NEWS ARE SUCH THAT YOU HEAR THEM even when in a French prison. One was the very sudden death of Lorenzo de' Medici's daughter, Luigia, shortly before her wedding to Giovanni di Pierfrancesco. Cause of death: 'a fever'. The other was that Girolamo Riario, that name which rolls round the mouth like vomit, Riario, the 'nephew' of Pope Sixtus (in fact, his son), the man who had conceived and executed the plot against the Medici using the Pazzi as his puppets, who had escaped the retribution that fell on the Pazzi, who had married Caterina Sforza and become Lord of Imola, that cowardly turd was dead. *Evviva!* At the news, Cristoforo and I grasped each other by the arms and danced. Pico turned to the guard who had brought us this news. 'How did he die?'

'He got in a fight over gambling debts and was thrown from a window of his own castle.'

Urrah!

'Lorenzo will be pleased,' said Pico.

'Lorenzo pleased?' I said. 'Far from it. He will be annoyed and frustrated.' Lorenzo had been trying for years to have Riario assassinated but without success. Who, after all, had been behind those three insurrections in Forlì? 'The only thing that would quench Lorenzo's lust for Riario's death is to have done it himself, to have pushed his own thumbs into Riario's windpipe and seen his vile, selfish eyes bulge at the realisation of death.'

Now I was frustrated, trapped as I was in prison with only one version of a story to go on. 'Who pushed him from the window?' I asked the guard.

'A hired soldier he owed money to.'

'Are you sure?'

He shrugged. 'It's what they're saying.'

'And what of Caterina Sforza?'

'Ah, now, she ...' Here the guard settled himself on a bench to tell us the interesting part, how the good people of Forlì had risen up yet again and captured her, throwing her into the city's prison. 'They tried to take the castle but failed. Caterina sent a message to the people saying that, if they released her, she would order the castle to surrender. They knew better than to trust her but when she offered to leave her children as hostages, then the people agreed. After all, when a mother pledges her children, she means it, does she not? Back inside the castle, however, Lady Caterina appeared on its battlements and laughed at the people of Forlì, saying they could keep her children. After all, she said, she had one left in Imola and another in her womb.' Here the guard leant back and roared with laughter.

'Beh! She is Medea!' Pico said in distaste. 'That woman is not human.'

'So did the people take the children?'

'No. An army arrived from Milan just in time and rescued them and encouraged the people to pay obeisance to their new ruler, the Countess of Imola and Lady of Forlì.'

Once the guard had gone, taking the stench of the world with him, Pico said we needed to contemplate, to cleanse and purify the soul. 'How fascinating the world is! How it grips us! Leave it now and come with me to the silent place.'

I sat down, closed my eyes and tried but, oh, really, sometimes the temptations of the mind are just too great. I pictured Riario being pushed from the window, and imagined myself doing the deed. I pictured him falling through the air, his arrogant face contorting in terror. I imagined the cracking thud of him hitting the ground. I saw Riaro's broken body spreadeagled, so vividly I could taste his blood. But it was over too quickly, so I went through the sequence again. Then my mind roamed about, thinking up a premeditation of this apparently random manslaughter. I imagined how a man in the pay of the Medici had attained a position in the army of Riario and finally, one April day in 1488 – the tenth anniversary of the murder of our Giuliano, as it happened – contrived to get the bastard thrown out of the window. The imagination is a wonderful thing, and often far closer to the truth than hearsay.

Some time later Pico slapped me on the knee and I awoke with a start. 'A man becomes what he dwells on,' he told us. 'So what is it to be, Tommaso, God – or the corpse of a murderer? Shall we start again?'

34 THE MIDGET MONARCH
1488

A FEW DAYS LATER WE WERE TAKEN DOWN THE WINDING stairs to the great hall. It was empty apart from the guards at attention along the walls. We waited. At last a far door opened and a personal guard in resplendent finery entered but appeared to be attending no one. You would have thought a king would march in behind such a guard. It was only as they came towards us that we noticed the young dwarf at their centre, dressed as a king. His large features were disproportionate to his head, which itself was disproportionate to his body. He was all eyes, nose and mouth, like a frog. Was this a joke at our expense? Were we to be tried by a fool? Thankfully I did not laugh: something in the attitude of the guard told me to take the dwarf seriously, to keep my face as straight as an ambassador's.

'Your Majesty,' said Pico, sweeping low in a bow. Swallowing my surprise, I had a coughing fit.

Charles, King of France, suffered from more than one nervous tic and could not frame a proper sentence in French let alone Latin. Even so, majesty must be honoured and I prostrated myself along with my companions before this misshapen youth. He bade us rise and invited Pico to sit with him. Then he examined Pico in a most informal manner, asking him questions about his religion and philosophy.

'Do not trouble me with the theology of St Thomas Aquinas or Duns Scotus. I cannot understand the language of the universities. Speak to me in my own language and tell me about magic and Cabala.'

So in French and as if speaking to a child or a woman, Pico told the king about his nine hundred theses, their plan and intention, why philosophy unites when religion only divides, and about magic and Cabala. He spoke in the language of the courts, engaging the king with his sincerity and enthusiasm. No one could look in the luminous eyes of Pico della Mirandola and suspect him of anything but what he confessed to: the desire to know God.

'I see no fault in you,' said the king at last. 'It's the pope, not me, wants you in prison. Great men, lots of them, yes, demanding your release. Duke of Milan. Lorenzo de' Medici. My own council, doctors of the Sorbonne, everyone supports you. But the pope, he won't listen. No. Pride, of course. He's denounced you as a heretic so now he has to stick to it. Yes. Have patience, my friend. We shall win. Meanwhile you can stay here, but in my own apartments. Yes.'

'Your Majesty, I thank you, but we have grown to love our accommodation in the tower.'

To my surprise, I found myself nodding in agreement, along with Cristoforo. Accordingly we returned to our eyrie and awaited our fate. Oblivious to what was happening outside, we only discovered later that, such was the support of the king and his council, and of the Sorbonne, that even the papal nuncios were won over. Only the pope remained convinced of Pico's heresy.

Not long afterwards we were again taken down the stairs to the reception hall. This time we were greeted by an emissary of the king who told us we were free on condition that we left the country. He presented Pico with a safe conduct signed by the king's sister, Anne, who was regent of France until Charles came of age. 'His Majesty wishes you well and he wishes you gone,' said the emissary. 'You are to go to Rome and make your peace with His Holiness. Letters precede you.'

A week or so later, when we were in Turin, Pico announced that we were going to go to Germany. During his studies he had become enamoured of the works of Nicholas of Cusa, and to fall in love with the work is to fall in love with the man. He wanted to go and stand on the ground where Nicholas had lived. Patient Cristoforo dissuaded him, saying that the king's safe conduct did not allow us to leave the road south to Rome. Pico said that the only authority who could truly grant safe conduct was God. Even while the two were bickering, a courier arrived from Florence with a letter. Writing on behalf of Lorenzo, Ficino invited Pico to Florence, where he would be safe from prosecution and free to continue his studies.

'Ha!' said Cristoforo and rolled his glad eyes heavenward to that Person with whom he colluded in the protection of his master. Defeated, Pico smiled ruefully and told us to make ready to take the road again. South, to Florence.

Dover, June 4th, 1506

We are to set out on a small caravel bound for France but are waiting for good weather. In June! The day is as grey as February and a chill wind blows up the channel, making fools of us in our summer clothes. The captain assures us that all will be well, that he makes this crossing once a fortnight and has not been sunk yet.

'Always a first time,' Erasmus replies. 'And there will only be a first time.'

Just being in Dover has put him in a ferocious mood, remembering the last time he was here. Our walk across the docks to the waiting ship was made bitter and furtive by his conviction that it was all going to happen again, that he was going to be robbed by Customs officers and was going to end up destitute in Paris as before. Now that we have gained the ship, he finds new fears and goes about looking for rotting timbers and torn sails.

The number of our party is seven. King Henry's physician decided his sons needed two tutors and so we have a man called Clyfton with us, as well as a royal courier who has been commissioned to act as our guide. I am much irritated by this as I need no guide, and especially not an English one with airs above his station. The man wears the royal insignia of a red and white rose as if it were the crown itself. As soon as we were aboard, and out of the jurisdiction of the king's court, Erasmus made it clear to Clyfton that, so far as he is concerned, Clyfton is the teacher while Erasmus is the director of studies. 'I have drawn up a programme of reading for the voyage,' he said. 'Here it is.' Leaving the man speechless, he escaped with me to our cabin.

At sea, June 5th, 1506

The storm that Erasmus dreaded has now whipped up in the straits. The wind howls in the sails and the ship is bucking like a wild horse. This is as much as I can write.

In sight of France, June 7th, 1506

In between bouts of sickness, Erasmus and I talk like boys, mostly about love. He has told me the romantic story of his parents, and about the girls he has adored. Is he an innocent virgin, this monk? He will not say, but I suspect he is not. He evades my questions with little sermons on generalities. I also evade his.

'You say that love between men is purer than love between a man and a woman.'

'Pico said that. I was merely repeating it.'

'So do you believe it?'

'I believe there is the possibility of Platonic love between a man and a woman. I achieved it, I think, with Maria Poliziana.'

'Is that why you did not marry her? To keep the love pure?'

'Marriage is not a corruption of pure love. Far from it.'

'Then why did you not marry her?'

Can I tell him, he, my closest friend? No. I have left it too long. He will laugh so hard the boat will sink. Another time, perhaps, when he is drunk. 'She died. They all died, my friend. I am returning to a land of ghosts.'

Go back to find that which you have lost. When John said that, I thought at once of Maria. There is a double aspect to my Eurydice: Elena-Maria. Both lost, but both irretrievably? I saw

194

Elena buried. I was only told about Maria's death. But even if she does live, she is lost to me. I cast her off with the world. I laid her on Savonarola's altar as my sacrifice. Do I wish I had done differently? Of course.

France

Sick from the sea journey, we stayed at Hammes Castle for a few days before we moved on. Erasmus is still not well and moaned all the way to Paris. Trusting no one locally, he writes to Linacre about his swollen glands, throbbing temples and the ringing in his ears. He says from now on, it is land all the way and he will never go again by sea if he can possibly avoid it. He also says that we shall have to rest in Paris until he is recovered. How convenient, given that he wants to find a French publisher for his writings.

While Clyfton, the courier and the boys amuse themselves with the sights of this fair city, I have time to get ahead, for Erasmus has had all I've written and is now snapping at my heels, impatient to hear about Savonarola.

'Stop scribbling!' he says. 'Just tell me about him. Whenever his name comes up, you become a very Hermes of silence.'

I try, I do try, but the effort to transmute thought into speech makes my eyeballs turn up in my head and my mouth hang open. Every single thing I want to say is tripped and opposed by its contrary. If I think with my quill, at least I can make many crossings out and additions. Perhaps, just perhaps, if I set it all down as it happened, I will discover for myself the truth about the man and be able to state it without getting into an argument and being accused of impiety. But this matter troubles me so much that I find I am reluctant even to write about it. I have to explore my own heart, my faith, my beliefs, and so confront my own agonising doubt. The question is, Was Savonarola the prophet people now say he was, or was he the antichrist?

35 THE FRIAR OF BRESCIA
1488

IT WAS ON THE ROAD THROUGH LOMBARDY THAT WE MET a notary coming from Brescia who told us about a Dominican friar lecturing so passionately on the Book of Revelation that he was causing the people to repent of their sins and turn to God.

While I was scratching my head, wondering where I had heard the name 'Girolamo Savonarola' before, Pico told us, vibrating like a bowstring after an arrow has been shot, that he knew the man well. 'I met him in Reggio, four years ago. It was at a convocation. I had just left university, and he, he had just been expelled from Florence.'

Ah, yes! I remembered the friar I had met outside the Palazzo de' Medici on the day that Venus was unveiled. 'Expelled? He was merely transferred to another city, one where they like their wood rough-hewn and not polished.'

'He told me he was expelled by the Medici for speaking the truth.'

I laughed. 'He was just a buzzing fly that other men were complaining about. Angelo says that any man who would speak in public absolutely must have command of the periodic sentence.'

Now it was Pico who laughed, fond memories of his friend aroused by what I had said. 'Goodness is what counts, not a man's syntax, and Girolamo Savonarola is a good man. In amongst all those sophists at the convocation, he stood apart as a man of simple conviction. So, he has found his voice, has he? Confidence was all he lacked.'

I heard later, within San Marco, that Savonarola's transformation from an inept, barely audible preacher to the great orator he became was due to Pico. Savonarola's treatment in Florence had crushed him but the young man he met in Reggio, who told him repeatedly, 'Speak the truth, whatever the cost, speak the truth,' had given him new vigour.

Pico suddenly announced that we were to turn back and go to Brescia, but Cristoforo grabbed his reins. 'We have the king's safe conduct on the road and Lorenzo's protection when we are in Florence. We must not divert.'

'Cristoforo! You are a slave to fear. Must you always be swayed by caution?'

'If I would keep you alive, yes, I must.'

Frustrated and grumbling, Pico turned his horse back in the right direction. Cristoforo looked at the sky and shrugged. We continued on our way south and as we travelled we met others with news of this fiery preacher. Whether or not it was true that a halo appeared over Savonarola's head while he was in the pulpit, he was certainly making sufficient impression that his reputation was running through the veins of Italy.

On our arrival in Florence, Pico went directly to the Palazzo de' Medici. This time Angelo abandoned his duties to meet him there.

'Angelo!' said Pico at once. 'There is a friar...'

'You are condemned for heresy; you've been in prison; I thought I had lost you forever; why do you want to tell me about a friar? Come, Lorenzo is waiting.'

'Magnifico,' Pico said to Lorenzo, as soon as the niceties of reunion and expressions of gratitude had been performed. 'There is in Brescia a true man of God, preaching the gospel in such a way that his audience is filled with terror and love in equal measure. He is no sophist, no erudite priest or loquacious monk, but a man full of integrity and the power of Truth. His name is Girolamo Savonarola.'

'I know that name. Was he not here at San Marco a few years ago? So graceless and offensive that the Vicar General did not know what to do with him. I told him to send him to Reggio.' Lorenzo gazed on Pico with amusement.

Angelo laughed. Pico scowled.

'Believe me,' he said, 'he has changed, I know not how or why, but he has found his voice, and it is a voice we should listen to. I tell you, this is the man who will put the Church right.'

Lorenzo raised his eyebrows. Then, like an indulgent father who can deny his son nothing, he relented and told Pico to compose a letter, inviting Savonarola back to Florence, which Lorenzo would put his name to.

Who was Pico della Mirandola? He was a changer of destinies. The paper Lorenzo signed and sealed was to prove the ruin of the Medici family.

As we had approached the Palazzo de' Medici, I noticed that the Casa Vecchia was shuttered. There was no mention of the Pierfranceschi in Lorenzo's house, and when I asked Angelo about them, he quite clumsily changed the subject. I was forced to seek out a more fluid source of information.

'The Pierfranceschi?' Filippino said over our next game of chess (the set now including a rook by Signorelli). 'No one's seen them since Luigia died. And it's not because of grief, if you follow what I mean.'

'No, I don't follow,' I said, gazing at the board. Filippino could talk and make strategies at the same time. I could not.

'Work it out for yourself.' The queen carved by Piero di Cosimo kicked one of my bishops – a plain fellow – off the board.

Filippino was not by nature a man able to keep his mouth shut, either physically or metaphorically. I only had to wheedle a little before he was telling me the gossip of the taverns, that Giovanni di Pierfrancesco had broken off his betrothal to Lorenzo's daughter with a phial of poison.

'Do you believe it?'

'That youth with the face of a seraph is capable of anything. Living proof, if ever you needed it, that the idea that a beautiful body houses a beautiful soul is just so much platonic drivel. And yet we all believe it, don't we? That beauty and goodness are inseparable?'

'And so they are. Perhaps we are confusing beauty with attractiveness.' I gazed despondently at my growing pile of vanquished pieces. Leonardo's rearing knight was causing devastation in my ranks.

Filippino's eyes glazed over, as they always did when his mind was presented with abstract concepts. 'I'll tell you this much. Giovanni is having an affair with the wife of Tommaso Parenti. A lustrous woman and very curvaceous,' he said, drawing her figure in the air with his hands. '*Attractive*, you might say, and jealous. It's only a theory, but I'm not the only one to hold it. Luigia was well and then, suddenly, very suddenly, on the eve of her marriage she was dead.'

'Did Giovanni weep?'

'Not one tear. He wore brown for a while – in which, of course, he looked *very* attractive – and led her cortege, but he had no trouble hiding his emotions, for he had none to hide.'

'Do you think Lorenzo suspects him?'

'Of course, but he's not going to let scandal sully the family if he can avoid it. But that's why the Pierfranceschi live in their villas these days.' Leonardo's knight suddenly leapt over my rook in a way that seemed to defy all laws of the game.

'Check!'

The next time I saw Lorenzino was at a meeting of the Platonic Academy at Ficino's house. I went hoping and expecting to have a conversation with him, for I needed some commission. Had he not, after all, promised to help me in any way he could? He would, I thought, be generous enough to find me something to do which would not require fine handwriting. As I approached him, he glanced at my hand.

'I hear fate has cruelly robbed us of your talent,' he said. 'What will you do now, Tommaso?'

'I was wondering if there could be any service I might perform for you.'

He was obviously surprised that I should ask. 'No, nothing,' he said. 'Not that I can think of. I will make enquiries.' He looked as if he had been cornered by a diseased rat. 'What exactly is it that you can do?' he asked tightly.

I shrugged. 'Teach Greek. Secretarial work. Editing. Any of the talents Poliziano has brought out of me.'

'Does he have no work for you himself?'

'Not enough.' To release us both from increasing discomfort, I bowed and turned to leave.

'If I can help in any way...' he said to my retreating back. His brother, Giovanni, who had been talking to Ficino, glanced at me with an expression of sympathy. He looked neither like a bereaved man nor a murderer, just an avid student of Platonic wisdom. Feeling a sudden need to be with men I could trust, I went to join Poliziano and Pico, but they were sitting so close together, and so intent on their own conversation, that I veered away and found a place by myself in a corner. I sat massaging my fingers. I had enough work from Poliziano to keep me occupied. It had been stupid of me to hope for a commission from Lorenzino, stupid. I had embarrassed him and embarrassed myself. I looked around at the men of the Academy. Each had a purpose. I had none. I had sought adventure and suffered the consequences. It was time to settle down now and stop aching for that which I could not have and that which I could never be. One thing, and one thing only, gave solace: with Pico I had learnt how to contemplate, and in that practice I continued.

36 THE TRIUMPH OF THE SEVEN PLANETS 1488

A YEAR LATER, AND AFTER AN EXPECTANT HOUR OF LOW chatter in the sala of the Palazzo de' Medici, there came the distant sound of fanfares followed by the rapping of drums. As the music grew steadily louder everyone gathered at the tall windows to see the Triumph pass below. Disinterested, I leant against the frescoed walls and watched the excited room with a jaundiced eye. Lorenzo himself, leaning on a stick, was making a good show of happiness. He had designed this Triumph himself and was looking forward to seeing how it was received; but as he limped past, he noticed me and I saw in his eyes the mirror of my heart. Although Lorenzo had raised it far above its usual tawdriness, Carnival was still a young man's festival of madness and frivolity, the youth of the city, dressed in fancy costumes or women's gowns, singing, clowning, having fun. We were no longer young. It was Lorenzo's sons who were out in the streets on this morning, as they had been out all night while their father retired to bed at a sensible hour. He paused and pointed his stick at me.

'What are you doing skulking and scowling, Maso?' he asked. 'The procession is on its way. Get out in the streets.'

'If you would pardon me, Magnifico...'

'Twelve years is long enough for grieving, don't you think?' he said, peering at me with his currant eyes. He was both myopic and all-seeing, the physical world a fuzzy blur, the hearts of men transparent.

I kept quiet, said everything in the gaze I returned him. He flinched a little but said, 'Time to find yourself a new wife.'

'At Carnival? What, would you have me marry a wanton?'

'You know better than that. You need to get your blood up.'

'The good philosopher transcends desire.'

'The philosophers in ancient times were married men.'

The previous Carnival that he had designed himself had been the Triumph of Bacchus and Ariadne; it had thumped home the message he was giving me now. This one, however, was the Triumph of the Seven Planets and it had a different intention, a more philosophical one. I was surprised at what he was telling me.

'It is a question of balance,' he said. 'Your excess of Saturn needs tempering. Get out there and look for Venus.'

'Magnifico!' some at the window called. 'The procession is in sight!'

'Get out there, Maso. Let me know how the people greet my Triumph.'

I reached the street just as the Chariot of the Sun was approaching, a golden chariot led by oxen dressed in red and blue trappings. Sun himself, gilded all over and with gold-wrought beams radiating from the crown of his head, threw his arms wide open as if to embrace Lorenzo, who was smiling down on him from the first floor. Musicians preceding the chariot played and sang the Homeric hymn to the Sun. It was an awe-inspiring sight, reminding me of the goal of philosophy, to reach the inner sun. But what did the sun signify to the people dancing by hand-in-hand in garlands, or who stood staring up at the splendid chariots? It meant merely the golden ball in the sky that heats the earth. The earth, their own centre, the geocentric ones. They did not even notice that the order of the planets had been changed with the sun coming first. Jostled by the ignorant and the greedy, the mountebanks and minstrels, tumblers and jugglers, I moved against the flow and went up the Via Larga towards the Medici garden from whence the procession was issuing. I wanted to see the chariots but I did not wish to follow them into the ever-thickening city.

The chariots themselves, made by the city's finest artists, were wrought with scenes in relief showing the stories of the gods in astonishing detail. On the chariot of Mercury the god stood hand on one hip contrapposto, holding his snake-entwined wand up towards heaven, precisely as Sandro Botticelli had depicted him in his *Realm of Venus*.

The Venus of the Triumph, too, had been inspired by Botticelli. In a flowing white chiton, her breasts encircled by bands of laurel leaves, she stood one hand clutching a red mantle artlessly draped about her, the other hand raised as if in benediction. Behind her the Three Graces danced entwined in a circle. 'Look for Venus,' Lorenzo had said. I stared up at her. Her unsmiling gaze met mine, with such intensity that I looked away. She was a very beautiful young girl; the daughter, someone beside me told his neighbour, of the Chancellor, Bartolommeo Scala.

Before the next chariot, that of Mars, arrived, I was kidnapped. A group of boys dressed as nymphs threw a sack over my head and carried me off kicking and struggling to the Duomo. Despite their masks and disguises, I knew them to be boys from the Ognissanti district and, by his pointy ears, recognised their leader as Doffo Spini. Now about ten, he was finding more to interest him in the streets than in Botticelli's workshop, to Sandro's immense relief. There was no sense in being angry with him and his friends: I had played the same tricks at their age and I was not so old that I'd forgotten it. The forfeit I had to pay was that Doffo should ride me like a donkey once round the cathedral. I refused to go on all fours and ran round with the boy on my back, he grasping my hair like reins, kicking me in the ribs and screaming for ever greater speed. I pitched him off once we had returned to the steps. Then I found myself in the very thick of the crowd that had gathered to see an alternative procession arriving from the Piazza della Signoria. Seven carts with the seven planets, but a buffoon's version, built and manned by artisans, running in the usual order of Mercury-Venus-Sun. No beautifully struck poses and lofty, ancient hymns here, but the thumping of naker drums, the wheezy drone of bagpipes and the lusty singing of bawdy songs.

This Venus was pouting at any young man who caught her eye while Cupid, standing behind her throne, was firing off dummy arrows into the crowd. Keeping my eyes lowered, I concentrated on getting through the crush, but then a sprig of laurel hit me on the head. 'Olà, Master Misery!' called one of the Three Graces. 'Cheer up! It's Carnival!' At that, all Three Graces began to sing a hymn to Bacchus. *If you would enjoy your life, do it now. Nobody knows what will happen tomorrow.* It had been composed years before by Lorenzo, who was as skilled in composing popular songs as he was sacred ones.

By the time I got back to the piazza San Marco, the chariot of Saturn was leaving the sculpture garden. The god sat back-bowed,

205

head in hands, apparently oblivious to the crowd. This picture of melancholy suited me well. I could have got up, taken his place and done the job better, for this man seemed to be asleep. Saturn is not sleep: it is a plunging of the spirits into a sucking mire. As I stood staring at the chariot, a masquer crashed into me, already drunk an hour before noon.

'Where's your mask, cowpat?'

'I'm wearing it,' I said. 'Realistic, isn't it? Behind this image of melancholy I'm laughing.'

'Oh, that's clever,' he said, staggering sideways. 'Clever! Ha!' He slapped me on the back and lurched on with the procession.

On the far side of the square Savonarola was giving a sermon to a small, a very small crowd. I admired his faith, that he would try and capture attention on such a day. Seeing the Count of Concordia among the sparse gathering of tailors and carpenters, I crossed the square to join him. Pico wore a simple black gown, no jewels, and his hair was undressed. The change in him was marked, and some said it was because he was a condemned heretic, others that it was the influence of Savonarola. I knew it was the result of our experience in prison. Pico was abjuring Carnival as he had begun to abjure the world.

I had not heard Savonarola since his return to Florence the previous year, but I had heard about him. It was said that he was receiving visions, which he tried to ignore, but that sometimes in the pulpit he was moved to speak, and the speech was invariably terrifying. Given the tendency of men to exaggerate, I had taken no notice.

Savonarola was by now nearly forty, his naturally striking features becoming pronounced with age and asceticism. He had known failure and humiliation but somewhere between his two sojourns in Florence he had been given the power to preach. As he addressed this small congregation, though still rough in voice, there was yet some gentleness to him that made him appealing. His text was the Book of Revelation and he used it to warn us against frivolity and lax morals. The Triumph of the

Seven Planets had been designed by Lorenzo to lift the people up out of daily concerns and make them think about the heavens. But Savonarola saw it as a gaudy parade of untold extravagance and more to do with the Whore of Babylon than anything celestial. I was in as much mood for righteousness as I was for licentiousness and was about to move on when Savonarola's head dipped suddenly to his chest. He was breathing heavily and trembling. His listeners tensed in expectation. When the friar lifted his head again, his aspect had changed, as if he had been infused with divine and terrible power.

'*Florence!*' he cried, and his voice reduced the sound of revelry to a distant tinkling. '*You will be scourged! Hear me. The Church will be renovated. These things will happen soon, in the One and a Half Time, the Millennium. PREPARE YOURSELVES, FLORENTINES, FOR THE SCOURGE WHICH IS TO COME.*'

I was struck by these words and the power of them, foretelling a future that I desired. Pico, beside me, his face lifted to the sky and his eyes closed, was shaking his head from side to side, sending his long hair flying about. It seemed in that moment possible that one man speaking the truth was all that was required to cleanse the Church of its iniquities. The rest of the sermon was given in a calmer tone, but those lines resounded within me like the Vacca bell.

When I returned to the Palazzo de' Medici, I tried to avoid meeting Lorenzo but he saw me come in. 'Well?' he said. 'What do you have to report?'

I told him with the polished glibness of a courtier how the people had been struck by amazement at his Triumph. I said nothing about Savonarola.

Paris, June 15ᵗʰ, 1506

Erasmus is very pleased to have found a publisher-printer, a man called Bade, who has agreed to do his translations of Lucian and Euripides.

'So,' said Clyfton amiably, 'we can continue with the journey.'

'Not until I have recovered,' said Erasmus, holding his head. Meaning, of course, 'not until I've seen the books come off the press.' He also wants Bade to do his *Adages*, a collection of stories he has already published but since enlarged, the number now standing at over eight hundred. We shall be here for months.

37 THE BATTLE BETWEEN TRUTH AND BEAUTY 1490

LORENZO'S GRANDFATHER, COSIMO, HAD RENOVATED SAN Marco monastery and used it as a retreat from his worldly cares, studying in the library that contained his own fabulous collection of books, praying in a cell reserved for him. The cells had each one a scene from the life of Christ painted by the friar they called Angelico, but I had never seen them. In the cloisters, however, where Savonarola often preached, were some frescoed lunettes of saints, powerful in their simplicity, and on the wall opposite the gate there was a large fresco showing St Dominic at the foot of the Cross. The cloister itself was called after Antonino, a saint of Cosimo's time who had been prior of the monastery and spiritual guide to Florence. So that is what San Marco meant to us by association: Cosimo's retreat; his library; his saintly friend; the painter they called 'angelic' – learning, art and spirituality. By the end of Lent, they were beginning to say that Fra Girolamo Savonarola was a new Antonino. Pico's faith in him appeared to be justified.

Angelo Poliziano, oblivious to both Carnival and Lent, had his head down in study. He listened to what Pico told him about Savonarola but the only thing that interested him was Savonarola's refusal to come to the palazzo to meet Lorenzo. It seemed to him simply bad manners and not how a holy man should behave.

'Come and hear him yourself,' Pico suggested, and not for the first time. 'There will be a Vespers sermon tonight.'

Angelo's lips turned down, locked into a *No* that was not to be argued with. God himself could not have had him go to hear Savonarola, not while Savonarola insulted Lorenzo by staying away. 'You've made a mistake, Gianni,' he said. 'That man is no saint.'

'You should hear him before you judge him. You make your mind up on no evidence.'

'Poets do not need evidence. We hear the whispers of the gods.'

'Demons more like,' said Pico. 'Tommaso will come with me, won't you?'

I glanced at Angelo. He shrugged. 'It is Sunday,' he said, 'and you should not be working.'

'Neither should you.'

'Life does not allow me leisure to study during the week and, besides, study is not work. It's up to you whether you go or not. But I do think it is foolish to think that a man who speaks of God all the time is more holy than one who does not. Do you not agree, Gianni?'

Pico rolled his eyes. 'I shall not argue with you.'

I sat down at the desk with a sigh.

Even Poliziano could not resist forever and, if only to appease his curiosity for wonders, at Easter he allowed Pico to take him to San Marco to hear a sermon. While most looked up at the friar in the pulpit with expectant faces, Poliziano listened with a knitted brow, often wincing, sometimes gasping. At every rhetorical error made by Savonarola, he said '*ohibò!*' or '*davvero?*' and spoiled the sermon for everyone standing near him. Later the Count berated Angelo and said that when the Bible addressed itself to 'the one who has ears to hear', it plainly did not refer to him.

'Truth is the sister of Lady Grammatica,' Angelo retorted. 'If Grammar is abused, so is Truth.'

'Meaning lies in the heart, not on the tongue!' the Count said. This was a familiar argument between them, one that had been stalemated for years. It was perverse but, in order to prove that the words of Truth should be naked and unadorned, Pico was often compelled to use the high-flown language of the gifted rhetorician. Every argument ended with Angelo repeating some eloquent thing Pico had just said and laughing heartily at the contradiction. But now, after the sermon, he grudgingly agreed that there was great power in language that is blunt and uncompromising, simple, comprehensible to all levels of society.

Pico took a step backwards. 'So you agree? You think Savonarola is impressive?'

'Impressive, yes. But a true man of God? I am not convinced of that.' He did not say why.

Pico, nonetheless, was now in the ascendancy in their contest. As the champion of eloquence, Angelo did not regain any ground until we received a visit, a month or so later, from Ermolao Barbaro.

Recently appointed by the pope as the new Patriarch of Aquileia – the Venetian equivalent to an archbishop – Barbaro arrived in an entourage. His robes wafted the scent of rosemary and lavender as he entered the sala of the Palazzo de' Medici. Although he was dressed in ecclesiastical finery and attended by many servants, he was still our Ermolao, whom I had last seen in the catacombs in Rome. A member of the Roman academy, a brother, one of us. Pico and Poliziano stood to one side, impatient with the formalities, as Piero de' Medici came forward to greet our honourable guest on behalf of his father. He apologised and explained that Lorenzo was away at the sulphur baths to seek relief from gout. Barbaro was disappointed at not meeting il Magnifico for he was desperate for Lorenzo's help. The Venetian Senate, contesting his appointment, claiming it was theirs for the making and not the pope's, had excluded him from his native territory. Piero assured him that Lorenzo was anxious to help in whatever way he could.

This was Piero's first official engagement and the fifteen-year-old was dragging it out, making it pompous. Ermolao grew impatient with the speeches. When he was told that a banquet had been arranged for the evening, he turned his large, quiet eyes on the young Medici and said he would prefer a private dinner with his friends. He nodded towards Pico and Poliziano.

Piero de' Medici responded as his father would have done, was gracious, changed the plans for the evening and did not insist on attending the small gathering himself. 'I understand,' he said. 'You would like a symposium, of the kind Plato enjoyed. I will see to its arrangement.'

Apart from Pico and Poliziano, only Ficino and Bernardo Rucellai were invited to the private dinner held in Lorenzo's own chamber. An occasion only for the invited, I waited in an antechamber for what seemed to be hours, watching food being taken in and empty dishes brought out. It was a time of frustration and reflection. I tried blaming many things for my poverty of station. It was my birth – but was I not a Maffei, albeit a natural one? It was my upbringing – but I had been educated by a man who was both a bishop and a member of the Platonic Academy. My lack of wealth, then – but I was not unique in that. My lack of scholarly brilliance? Aye, getting close. I was capable enough in both Latin and Greek, could copy with as much ease as my left hand afforded, could correct other men's work, but I had written nothing myself to contribute to knowledge. I fed off other men's learning. I was a parasite. No wonder I never moved either socially or philosophically: the inner sanctum of the academy was closed to me. Elbows on knees and head in hands, I was pulled down to hell by a sense of failure.

The door to the chamber opened. Ermolao Barbaro himself – the Patriarch of Aquileia – looked out. 'Tommaso,' he said, 'we need you to tell us about beauty.'

Pico and Poliziano had dominated the supper by drawing the others into their argument as to whether Truth is best expressed in plain terms or elevated language. Pico had won Rucellai to his side; Poliziano and Barbaro were in delightful and harmonious agreement with each other. Ficino refused to join either party, saying there was merit in both arguments. I had been brought in – at Ermolao's own suggestion – to settle the matter.

After the past hour's miserable reflections, I was in no fit state to speak and could not think of a single philosophical principle, let alone a decisive one. These famous faces stared at me expectantly. Ficino already occupied the arbiter's chair: I had to come down on one side or the other and, either way, risk annoying a friend. I stared back at them, speechless.

'Come, Maso,' said Poliziano. 'Speak the truth beautifully.'

'It will be more truthful if you state it plain,' said Pico.

What truth? I thought desperately.

'When I met Tommaso in Rome,' Ermolao said, 'I was reading Pliny in the Vatican library. That it was a beautifully illuminated edition was beyond my notice. I was interested only in the text. What did you say, Tommaso?'

'Er, I remember identifying the scribe, and naming the hand he used.'

'Accurately. But what did you say when I expressed lack of interest in such things?'

'Oh, yes, I said that, since it has been written so beautifully, it will not die of neglect, as so many books do. All men appreciate beauty, even if they are philistines in respect to learning. They value it, put value on it.' I was on my horse at last. 'Men may be attracted to truth through beauty.'

'Are you saying that we only read the gospels because we have some beautiful editions of them?' Pico asked.

'No, of course not, but I do not need to tell you about the different degrees of beauty. When Christ speaks, it is beautiful. The parables are beautiful, the ideas.' Now I was galloping. 'When a poet goes into the innermost part of himself, as he must, drawn inwards by the voice of inspiration, what he returns with is beautiful: witness Angelo's work. And yours, Count, and yours, Father Marsilio. The truer you are to that innermost voice, the more beautiful your words. Admit it, all of you, your best words are not your own.'

All heads around the table nodded in agreement.

'And so it follows that the Muse, or the god, or whatever divine force it is you listen to, is of itself beautiful. Therefore, it is not a case that truth must be expressed beautifully, more that it cannot be expressed in any other way.' Now I was careering. 'I'll go further: if plain, blunt speech is not beautiful then it is not truthful.'

213

They all sat up like hares. What had I said? Pico jabbed a finger at me. 'You are going too far. Would you say that Savonarola is untruthful?'

I refused to answer until, after some frantic reflection, I said, 'We should not mistake beauty for adornment. Those scripts that I consider to be most beautiful tend to be simple. There are three principles of beauty,' I declared confidently. 'Simplicity – clarity – legibility. That is what I was taught as a scribe, but these principles would, I think, apply to anything. Beauty is not adornment, and simplicity is not plainness. Beauty lies in proportion.'

'Precisely what Aristotle said!' Ermolao brought his hand down hard on the table. 'The argument is won, I believe.'

'Who by?'

'All of us. In some measure, each of us has been speaking the truth. What we need is an academy of language such as your academy of Plato. Perhaps your friar would deign to join it. For what is required is neither empty adornment nor truth used as a sledge hammer. We need appropriate language for the task each of us is engaged in, clearing the world of sin, error and ignorance.' He also proposed that he, Pico and Poliziano begin a new translation of Aristotle. 'As fine as Ficino's is of Plato. When the peripatetic is heard in his purity, the Platonists will not object.'

Ficino nodded in agreement.

Pico quickened. 'It would harmonise the old quarrel and bring peace to the universities.'

Angelo sighed. 'I wish Lorenzo were here.'

It seemed to me a tremendous work to be made by this trinity of great scholars, but Evil is no abstract concept, and it called on Death to thwart the initiative. Pico – Poliziano – Barbaro: all were to die when the work had only just begun.

214

38 THE PAINTED SMILE
1490

IT SHOULD HAVE BEEN A HIGH POINT OF HIS CAREER WHEN
Filippino Lippi was commissioned to decorate the chapel of
Filippo Strozzi in the church of Santa Maria Novella. Straightway,
however, he went to Rome, saying that he could not afford to
live on the miserable fee the Strozzi had given him and needed
to work simultaneously elsewhere. He had a wife and infant
son to support. The truth was, of course, that he could not bear to
work so close to Domenico Ghirlandaio, who at that time was
completing his fresco cycle in the chancel behind the high altar in
the same church. They would, in effect, have been working on
either side of the same wall.

It was not just that Ghirlandaio had become rich by his art, was
courted by the wealthiest patrons and held in such high esteem,
nor that he was always sumptuously dressed and seemed never
to get his hands dirty; no, it was because Domenico Ghirlandaio
could paint a woman smiling. Leonardo could do the same. I could
not see the difficulty, but apparently there was one, and Filippino
rated painters and sculptors according to their ability to capture
a smile. Strangely, capturing the smile seemed to be easier for
sculptors than painters; plenty of our funerary monuments had
cheerful angels, while Desiderio da Settignano and the Rossellini
brothers had done Madonnas and Infants in marble that could melt
your heart. As for Mino da Fiesole – there were two of his angels
bearing candles on the altar of the cathedral of my native city. If
they did not smile, somehow Mino had caught in stone the look
of inner contentment.

The sculptors had gone, all passing away in recent years,
taking with them, it was feared, all knowledge of sculpture. Only
one man remained alive who had studied with Donatello:

Bertoldo. Now in his seventies and seriously ill, he had been ordered by Lorenzo to put off death for a few years yet and return to work. Bertoldo had done as bidden and revived himself as Lorenzo wished to revive the art of sculpture. Many said it was a miracle, a resurrection, but Ficino said that purpose may often keep a man alive better than any medicine. Bertoldo moved into the Palazzo de' Medici and began to teach young men whom Lorenzo was selecting from various painters' workshops.

'If they are going to revive sculpture,' Filippino Lippi told me, 'it is even more imperative that painters learn to render the smile.'

I looked on him affectionately, considering him to be as all dedicated artists seem to be: half mad.

'If no one on our walls smiles, what a lifeless, wooden age this will seem to men of the future. They will ignore our paintings and seek out our sculptures. We cannot let that happen. Some painters say that the smile is not proper to the subject, that holy scenes should be grave and dignified, but they only say that because they can't do it. Take Sandro Botticelli – he says the smile is inappropriate – but you look at some of his pictures and you will find at least one figure grimacing as if constipated. The trick is, I told him, not to show the teeth. No, it should be gentle, like this…' and Filippino, whose own teeth were protuberant, turned and smiled at me with his lips closed and his eyes downcast as if he were a demure and contented maiden. My sudden bellow of laughter disturbed a mass being held in a side chapel. A priest came to tell us off and, like two boys, we stood with our heads down and our hands clasped before us and promised it would not happen again.

I never knew when Filippino was being serious or playing some long, drawn-out and well-planned trick. But in the matter of the smile, I believed him to be serious, for I had seen many of the studies he had made, none of which pleased him and all of which he threw away. Perhaps his fascination with this human attribute had something to do with a painting by his father, Fra Filippo Lippi, of the Madonna and Child which is most lovely. A little angel in the foreground looks over his shoulder at us and smiles. It is a perfect portrait of Filippino at the tender age of three. It is a perfect portrait of any child born to parents who love him. Now, thirty years on, Filippino was struggling to draw smiles, his brow puckered in a frown.

39 A LACK OF SPACE
1490

DURING ONE OF HIS BRIEF VISITS TO FLORENCE, WHEN Filippino was putting his designs on the chapel walls, he invited me to watch. His apprentices had put up pricked cartoons in his absence and had pounced them with charcoal. Now the cartoons were taken down and, with a fluid wrist and a brush loaded with a weak sepia tint, Filippino joined up the dots. He wore his cap low on his brow to keep his hair out of his eyes. Unlike Ghirlandaio, he did not much care how he looked, at least not while he was at work.

'I cannot bear the usual piling up of scenes, one atop another.' He spoke very loudly, but I doubted that the large force of artists concentrating on their work in the chancel could have heard as he intended them to. His brush flew over the wall, revealing crowds of frenzied figures in scenes from the lives of Saints Philip and John, drawn from apocryphal sources. Setting these scenes within the great architecture and triumphal arches of Rome, Filippino was keen to give them a true historical context.

'Not for me sacred events happening in the streets and squares of Florence,' he thundered like Savonarola, his voice bouncing off the vaulting. 'The disciples lived and breathed in the first century after Christ, when Rome was ruled by Nero, and that is what we should show.' No one came from the next chapel to see what he was talking about.

Whilst in Rome he had been tireless in making sketches of monuments of antiquity, but what had excited him most was the discovery of the Golden House of Nero. Built over by successive emperors, the Domus Aurea had become subterranean and forgotten until a young man, walking in the Aventine hills, had fallen into a hole and found himself in a decorated room. Filippino had had himself lowered down on a rope so that he could see the walls for himself.

He came down from the scaffolding, wiped his hands on his jacket and pushed his cap back. He handed me one of his notebooks. 'This is authentic,' he said. 'This is the kind of thing that Peter and Paul would have seen with their own eyes.' I looked through the pages filled with designs of urns and lamps, winged harpies, griffins, heads sprouting leaves, masks, satyrs, lyres and candelabra, sphinxes and sirens, trophies and herms. It was a teeming world of fantasy.

'These things have no meaning,' I complained.

His snorted in annoyance. 'But it is authentic background. This is ancient Rome the way it appeared to ancient Romans. My pictures will show the real place where St Philip preached and died. Here, look – costumes.' He turned to a page brimming with figures in ancient dress.

'How can you know what they wore?'

'From statues and small figurines. That part is easy. But in the Domus Aurea what we are seeing for the first time are the colours…' It was difficult not to get caught up in his enthusiasm, and it was a familiar argument. Poliziano was making it all the time: text needs context. Things must be seen in the light of their own time. Only then may they be properly understood. And so I approved of Filippino's scheme, even if it did mean that space, that precious element that Florentine painters had gone to such lengths to depict, was now to be filled with ornament.

As well as grotesques, his notebook was full of portraits of a little boy. The father's love shone on the page. According to

Filippino, little Tommaso (no, he was not named after me, but after Masaccio and Masolino) was showing precocious ability with a paintbrush at the age of eighteen months. 'He will grow up to make Leonardo da Vinci weep in his old age,' said Filippino, with that determination which some men have in the place of true faith.

40 A PRIVATE VIEW OF THE FRESCOES 1490

FRESCO PAINTERS COVER AN AREA IN PLASTER THAT THEY expect to finish in a day's work, and so the day ends when the work is done. Because of this, and since they often work at night when the plaster does not dry so quickly, one could never predict when the chancel would be quiet, but one Sunday at dawn, an hour before the first mass, I went with Filippino to Santa Maria Novella and found no one there, either in church or chancel.

'At last...' he said, and went behind the high altar. The decoration of the chancel had been commissioned by Lorenzo's uncle, Giovanni Tornabuoni, who was not at all stingy with his fees (Domenico Ghirlandaio received four times the amount Filippino had been given). The chancel was shrouded by murky hangings that were lashed up at night like a tent, but Filippino found a way through and, by the weak light from the windows, we stood and gazed about us. Out of respect for my friend's feelings, I did not shout out the amazement I felt but stood looking critically as Filippino himself did. Very little remained to be completed: the unveiling was just a month or so away. Filippino took the left wall, mounting the ladders and walking along the scaffolding in front of scenes of the Life of the Virgin. I went to the right wall to see the scenes of the Life of John the Baptist. Filippino was never one to hold back his opinion and considered it his duty to let everyone know what he thought of their work, even if they were not present. He owed it, he said, to the goddess of truth and art.

'Those portraits,' he said, pointing across to the first scene on my wall, 'are of mere bystanders, done so vividly that they draw all attention.'

On the first stage of scaffolding, I gazed upon the face of Poliziano, who had been depicted in a small group of scholars which also included Ficino, Landino and Domenico Chalcondylas. 'Pippo, admit it,' I said, 'you are outdone.'

'Outdone in what?'

'Art.'

'*Art?* Ghirlandaio has no art. He just traces from life. Tell me, my friend, what are you looking at?'

'A perfect portrait of Angelo Poliziano and Marsilio Ficino.'

'What are you supposed to be looking at?'

'What do you mean?'

'What is the story of that scene? What is it depicting? What is its underlying theme?'

As Filippino continued to fire his questions, I struggled to identify the scene as that of the Angel appearing to Zacharias, though I had to admit that what I was looking at in reality was a dense crowd of Florentines.

'Art?' Filippino sneered. 'This is mechanical reproduction. Art changes the viewer as alchemy changes substances, and this does nothing of the kind. It is sheer vainglory – a virtuoso display of technique.'

Was it true? Although I could see what he was saying, I longed for him to be wrong.

'This is a monument to man's hubris. These merchants of Florence – they value themselves above the sacred. They seek immortality of the flesh, and Ghirlandaio is just the man to give it to them. But how flat and lifeless are the holy characters.'

'At least Domenico cannot be accused by Savonarola of using barrow boys as models for his saints.'

'True enough, he uses no models at all for them but that

cannot be the solution – everyday life so vivid that the sacred moment is rendered dull by comparison.'

'No, but it's an accurate reflection of how it is, isn't it? The senses beguiling us.' I had moved up and was now looking at a scene depicting the Visitation of Our Lady to Saint Elizabeth. While these figures could not be described as flat and lifeless, it was true that they did not bear the vivacity of the women in their train, lifelike portraits of Tornabuoni ladies, including Giovanna, the lovely wife of Lorenzo Tornabuoni who had died in childbirth only two years after their marriage. Young Tornabuoni, whose own mother had died the same way, was inconsolable. Whenever I saw him, I saw my own face.

Up another level, I came to the Birth of John the Baptist. Set in the palace of the Tornabuoni, in a room I could recognise, St Elizabeth was being visited by Clarice de' Medici and her mother-in-law, Lucrezia Tornabuoni. The scene was a lively one with a very beautiful serving maid in a Greek chiton arriving with a tray of fruits carried on her head. What captured my attention, however, was the figure of a young woman in a pink gown. Domenico was a poet in colour, making juxtapositions that were surprising and inspired, 'alchemical' said some, given that he had devised a way of rendering gold in colour rather than using gold leaf. This rosy pink, set amongst the terracotta and ochre costumes of the other figures, held me spellbound. The face of the young woman – I reached out to touch it – was achingly beautiful. Domenico at his best was as good as any Flemish painter, and he had the same quality: an attention to mundane detail that somehow made the world itself a sacred place. But this woman was dead, was a portrait of Lorenzo Tornabuoni's mother, Francesca; she was certainly attended by the dead, for both Lucrezia and Clarice de' Medici had left this life in recent years. Lucrezia, Clarice, Francesca, Giovanna – these walls were a memorial to dead women. Stupidly I began to study the figures as I would a crowd in a square, to catch a glimpse of my Elena. Perhaps Ghirlandaio, sensitive as he was, had thought to include her portrait among the attendant maids. Could it be? Of course not. Yet hope made my heart beat louder and it was good to feel that prickle of expectation. Almost like being in love. Almost like being alive.

'Oh, look at this. Who are these two tiny people? Dwarves? Children dressed as adults? Ridiculous! What idiot painted these? Granacci, I'll be bound. I had him long enough in my own studio to know how useless he is. Still, Domenico should keep an eye on what his men are doing. It's his name that will be attached to these walls.' The ladders and boards creaked as Filippino mounted higher. 'Ah, there are no portraits up here – just mediocre stuff. This will definitely be Granacci. He's left, now. Did you know? When Ghirlandaio had to give il Magnifico two apprentices to study sculpture, he took the opportunity to get rid of one who was inept and one who was unbearable. Who can blame him? Have you met Michelangelo? Who could work with that precocious puppy telling you all your faults in his piping, treble voice? It's a wonder he hasn't been murdered.' The ladders creaked again but as Filippino achieved the highest stage there came a silence which, for him, was unnatural.

'Pippo?' I asked eventually. 'What are you looking at now?'

'The Massacre of the Innocents.'

'Is it good?'

'Sublime. Come and see it. All these dead babies… Oh, and this mother pulling on the hair of a soldier. God Almighty…' Filippino was as generous in his praise as he was harsh in his criticism – when he found something worth praising.

'In a moment…' I said. I had not yet looked at the face of every female figure on my own wall. As the rising sun began to spill in through the window, the colour became radiant. Our time was running out. Hearing Filippino descend, I came down my ladders, bade Angelo and Marsilio good morning as if they really did stand before me, and crossed the chapel. Filippino had paused on the first stage, standing before the scene of the Birth of the Virgin. I went up to join him. This was much more elaborate than the birth scene I had been looking at and was clearly all Domenico's own work.

222

Filippino was staring at the nurse cradling the infant in her lap, a young woman quietly, happily *smiling* at a baby. On the point of tears, he gulped when I arrived and cleared his throat.

'Terrible lettering,' he said, pointing to the motto on the panelling of the saint's bed in a vain attempt to distract me.

But I stared at her, as I had often seen her, sitting with the infant Giuliano de' Medici on her lap, smiling down on him. Only here the infant was the Virgin Mary, staring up at my wife and reflecting her smile with her own. My head dipped into my hands. When I looked up again, Filippino had put himself between me and the wall and was gazing at me through eyes welling with tears. His grief was not mine; he did not mourn a dead wife; he was crying in frustration.

'That lettering is truly terrible,' he said eventually, wiping his sleeve across his face.

'It truly is,' I agreed, studying the amateurish attempt to render Roman capitals in gold leaf.

'Domenico should have employed you to do it, and not his youngest apprentice. Never mind, I shall employ you. You can do my lettering. I want the names of the virtues as if engraved in stone by the best epigraphist in ancient Rome. It will ensure your immortality, for these walls celebrating mundane life are bound to sink into obscurity. They will be painted over within a few years, but mine – they will endure forever.'

'He can do it, can't he? Ghirlandaio can paint the smile.'

'Yes, well, anyone can who is prepared to make a pact with the devil.'

Many people who had seen the walls were muttering about magic, saying that such art seemed beyond the power of human capability. 'Come on Pippo, admit it. Domenico's ability to capture a likeness is extraordinary – a divine talent.'

'You are right. All talent comes from God – it's just that Domenico lends his to the devil's work: personal vanity. He gives rich men what they want, not what they need. Art must have meaning, or else it is just decoration. These glowing, sumptuous walls – they have no soul. What has this work to do with God and his Church? Nothing. Nothing at all.'

I disagreed. Something was working on me, some subtle thing. Dead babies. Dead mothers. I turned, looking now at this scene, now at another. The chancel was a monument to Tornabuoni grief. And hope. Before I could say as much to Filippino, he was calling down to a youth staring up at us.

'Ah, Michel-diabolo,' said Filippino. 'Good morning to you.'

'You are not allowed…'

'Neither are you. You've left this workshop.'

Although I had heard much about this boy, I had not met him until now. He seemed himself to have been sculpted by a master artist who suffered from impatience: perfectly formed and strikingly handsome in a crudely-hewn, passionate kind of way. But something in his eyes did not allow you to stare at him too long, some piercing, intelligent thing that burrowed into you, questing for your own truth and integrity. It was hard to meet such a stare without flinching and looking away, particularly when your eyes are reddened by tears.

'Is it true,' Filippino asked him, 'that you have taken up sculpture because you'll never be able to paint as well as your master?'

'Painting is an inferior art. Why content yourself with two dimensions when you can work in three?' Michelangelo went to a corner where rolls of paper were stored and began to look amongst them.

'I think it is an excellent thing that sculpture is being revived,' Filippino said. 'I would like to commission a piece.'

Michelangelo swung round. 'Really?'

'It is a tradition amongst our artists that, for love of me, they each carve me a chess piece. How would you like to do a pawn? Perhaps later, when you have more experience…'

Michangelo's glare was like shards of glass.

'So, it's true that you steal your master's drawings.'

'I left something behind. It's mine, although some say it is not possible that I should have done it. Ah, here...' He pulled out a roll. 'So, do you want to see whether I can paint or not?'

Intrigued, we went down the ladder and stood while the boy – about fifteen at that time and no longer with the treble voice that Filippino remembered – unrolled a picture of the Temptation of St Anthony in which the saint was being tortured by a crowd of fantastic and horrible creatures.

'You didn't do that. It's a print by Martin of Holland.'

'It is a copy of the print and the colour, obviously, is my own.'

Filippino took the sheet and turned until the best light fell on it. 'Hmmm,' he said at last. 'Hmmm.' He cleared his throat. 'Where did you find – how did you think – are these colours from your imagination?'

'No, from nature.'

'Where are such monsters found in nature?'

'In the fish market.'

Filippino laughed and complimented him. 'I concede. Your draughtsmanship is steady; your use of colour is excellent. It must be true – you left painting for sculpture because you chose to.'

Michelangelo nodded, satisfied. 'Now show me your work,' he demanded, as if to a junior rather than to a master of the guild, and led the way out of the chancel to the chapel next door.

'Oh, ah,' said Filippino hurrying after him, pushing his cap back down almost over his eyes. 'It is at a very early stage...'

Michelangelo led my hapless friend into the Strozzi chapel to torture him with his own blunt and merciless criticism.

'Gesumaria!' he cried. 'What a shambles!'

41 IN THE SCULPTURE GARDEN 1490

AS I WALKED ALONE THROUGH SAN LORENZO MARKET I was dazzled by the colours of food and fabric: silk, taffeta, brocade, cloth of gold – exotic luxuries sparkling in the sun. There were stalls of Indian spices and African gold, of lapis lazuli from Afghanistan and jet from England. There were jugglers and tumblers, tight-rope walkers and dancers. Despatch runners hurried through the crowd, money-changers offered unique deals, slave traders paraded negroes and Georgians in chains; in curtained booths astrologers drew up horoscopes and predicted apocalyptic futures. Women rustled past in their silks, their faces chalked with powder, eyebrows drawn on, lips reddened and hair bleached; young men lounged at corners, wearing the latest fashions in a broad palette of colours. It was the Market of Desires, where all the goods of the world were available. If you were stupid enough to want them.

I had arranged to meet Angelo at the Palazzo de' Medici, but outside the church Lorenzo's favourite preacher, Fra Mariano, was addressing a crowd on the Word according to St John. Looking up at the palazzo, I could see Lorenzo at the window of his chamber listening to the sermon. Since Angelo was with him, I stayed outside to listen, to appreciate beautiful ideas being conveyed so elegantly by a man who employed the gestures of a polished rhetorician in the antique mould. The Word, the Logos, by which all things come to be. The ideas, rooted in St John, Fra Mariano elaborated with those of Plato and Hermes Trismegistus. He mentioned these by name but did not tell the crowd how much he was drawing from arcane wisdom to heighten his understanding of our Christian faith.

Lorenzo loved Fra Mariano, who so eloquently expressed all that he himself believed. He was having a monastery built near the

Porto San Gallo especially for the preacher, to enable him to instruct the Florentines in a philosophical form of Christianity and make of his city a fountain of wisdom at which the world might drink.

I arrived in the courtyard at the same time as Giovanni Pico, who had also been listening to Fra Mariano. Where once Pico had been distinguished by the particular fineness of his costume and by his entourage, these days he walked alone dressed in black and lost in thought. Some said the changes in him were contrived to gain an acquittal from the charge of heresy, but it was not true. The costume was the man and fitted the mood of austerity that had come upon him when in prison in France. I told him about the paintings at Santa Maria Novella.

'Truly, the figures appear to live. I have just seen several of them shopping in the market,' I told him. The Count said he looked forward to the unveiling of the frescoes. Then I praised the wonderful sermon of Fra Mariano, telling him it had made my soul sing.

'If you were to listen more carefully and more often to Savonarola, you would soon lose your taste for the superficial pleasures of Fra Mariano.'

'The last time I listened to Savonarola carefully he was saying that our kidneys are rotting with excess, that our hands are stained with the blood of the poor, that we are going to be scourged, that he will hand our souls over to the eternal fires. Is this a man of truth?'

'He speaks as he is moved.'

'What, God talks like that?'

'It is divine rhetoric, if you like, meant to impress the crowd. In private he says very different things. Come with me to San Marco.'

Lorenzo and his companions came down the stairs, preceded by Lorenzo's favourite hound bounding down in advance to turn in leaping, excited circles, waiting for his master. Lorenzo's gout caused him to walk slowly these days, and, while his companions moderated their pace to suit his, the hound yapped at his master to hurry. The sight of them, dressed in their finery for a Sunday walk, made me forget about prophets and I fell into step with Angelo. We went towards San Marco, not to hear Savonarola but to visit the garden Lorenzo was turning into a school for sculpture. Lorenzo wanted to see the work of his protégés while they were taking the day off.

'I met Michelangelo earlier at Santa Maria Novella,' I told Angelo.

'What do you think?'

'I agree it would be a good idea to view his work in his absence.'

Lorenzo's sculpture garden stood behind a high wall that fronted the piazza of San Marco. I had been before, several years earlier, when it was an outdoor museum for Lorenzo's collection of antique sculptures – headless gods and armless goddesses, dug from the earth in Rome or Greece – and also one of the meeting places for the Platonic Academy. In those days, Leonardo da Vinci had had his studio there. At the gate in the wall, Pico disengaged himself, saying he was going to the monastery. He glanced at me questioningly.

'Later,' I lied.

The enclosed garden had a loggia running all round inside its walls, except where there was a small house – a casino – interrupting its flow. It was a cloister garden without a church. The lawn was divided by gravel paths; lemons grew in pots; laurel, oleanders and myrtle bordered the avenues with their lush, glossy green; a stand of cypresses pointed to the sky above. The garden rustled and cheeped with life – you could almost feel it breathing. Well-placed both in the loggia and in the avenues, marble statues stood on plinths, their whiteness heightened by the dark hedges. The word 'paradise', Angelo once told me, is Persian for 'garden'. This, then, was a paradise.

The Pazzi conspiracy and the war with Rome had severed Lorenzo from his garden for several years; in reuniting with it, he had given it a new function. Several students were receiving tuition from Bertoldo here, but only one – Pietro Torrigiano – had so far shown any real aptitude. You may have met him here in London, Erasmo – he is the one who has done the head of the King in terracotta, the first portrait in England to resemble its sitter. Or you may know him as the man who broke Michelangelo's nose. Well, someone had to do it.

We looked at a faun Michelangelo had carved, and a relief of the Madonna and Child. Truly, the boy could be forgiven his crusty manners, as all geniuses must be forgiven. Lorenzo smiled – that is, Lorenzo the poet smiled. This was not a wealthy patron who had discovered talent. It was a poet who had discovered someone else who could give expression to his own innermost thoughts and feelings. What Lorenzo recognised in Michelangelo – and it was a mutual recognition – was integrity. It is, I believe, what every father yearns to find in his son, someone *simpatico* with himself. It was most odd that anyone should find Michelangelo agreeable, least of all Lorenzo. But the lad had been beaten as a child for not being agreeable to his own father, for shaming the family with his ambition to be, as his father put it, 'a stone mason'. Now he was like a horse that, having been broken with the whip, was likely to throw its rider at any time: Michelangelo needed to be retrained in the art of being human.

On this day in the garden, Lorenzo told Angelo of his plan to take the boy into his own family. 'I'll offer the father whatever he desires.'

'You mean, you are going to buy Michelangelo?'

'If that is what is required.'

It seemed to us that Lorenzo was rescuing Michelangelo from the fate of being the son of Ludovico Buonarotti (whose price turned out to be very low – he gave away his son in exchange for a job in the customs house). Now, I sometimes wonder if Lorenzo wasn't rescuing himself from being the father of Piero, Giovanni and Giuliano. What he wanted was a son who saw the world the same way he did.

'In Michelangelo,' he said on that morning, 'the art of sculpture will not only be revived, it will be advanced. And God willing, I shall take him into my own house, to give him the company and education of men such as yourselves, and he shall be refined.' He gave the chief task of Michelangelo's education to Angelo.

'He has a passion for the nude figure which is frustrated by holy subjects. Can you find something for him from the ancient authors?'

Angelo, who had recently been reading Lucian, thought at once of the Battle of the Lapiths and the Centaurs.

'Whatever you come up with, I shall commission from him. Just have as many figures as possible – test him, stretch him – ask of him a multitude of naked men in a huge variety of attitudes.'

Angelo promised him that he would. And so, having decided Michelangelo's future in his absence, the patron and his companions continued to walk the grounds, their discussion turning to plans for a building to house Lorenzo's library, a collection now standing at ten thousand books.

42 POETRY IS AN ART OF DIVINATION 1490

THAT IS HOW IT WAS IN 1490, A FRENZY OF REINVENTION. We had new frescoes, new sculpture and, in the university, new learning. At the beginning of the academic year, Poliziano, building on previous lectures, reached the fruition of his thesis. His opening lecture was a list, a list that went on and on and on, a list of all the occupations of men. Not just a list, but a set of categories, three in all. He had little to say about the first category, which was theology, other than, 'As you all know, it is the noblest subject.' The listing of the second category, however, took over an hour, for it contained all the common occupations of men.

Shop keepers, craftsmen, bargees.

It would have been stupefying if it had not been funny.

Rope-dancers, sailors, embalmers.

The students packed into the hall stared at him without comprehension. Yes, he had drawn all these occupations from his reading in all the books of the world, and where he did not know what a particular term in Greek might mean, he said so. But what was the point of all this?

Buskers, carters, bath-house keepers, armpit-hair pluckers, pimps and brothel-keepers.

New learning? Or a poet who loved words above reason?

'And with these I have reached the dregs of society.' He took a deep breath and began his third category, with which, he said, we would not be familiar: rhetoric.

What did he mean? Most of us in the hall had trained in it, many were part of its faculty. In the category of rhetoric, he said, is poetry. No one was surprised at that. But he went on, and his voice became more lyrical and energetic as if some force other than himself was powering his words. Poetry, he said, is an art of divination. And then the hall went very quiet.

'It is the mother of all arts, since everything I have mentioned to you today, every single word, has been culled from poetry. Therefore poetry contains all knowledge.'

Poetry, he said, is a composite art, partaking of both reason and invention. It depends on discovery and observation, but it also depends on contact with other realms. It is semi-divine, half way between heaven and earth. In this category, along with poets, he placed philosophers, seers, prophets and wise women.

Angelo stood at the lectern, his arms raised, the high priest of poetry speaking to his disciples. The young students of the Florentine Studio ignited. Such an idea was both ancient and entirely new. No longer were Homer and Hesiod, Virgil and Ovid, to be considered mere entertainment; they were sources of true knowledge. But one man present at the back of the hall was not inspired and threw back his black cowl so that he could hear better the heresy of this Orphic professor.

43 POETRY IS NOT DIVINE
1490

TWO MONTHS LATER, SAVONAROLA DELIVERED A SERMON in which, speaking as if possessed by the Holy Ghost, he cried out against pagan ideas that were destroying the morals of the city. He had, he said, looked at all the world's learning and had categorised it. It all flows from sacred theology, flows downwards, ever-descending through grades of materialism and depravity, until it comes to rest in 'the stinking shit which is poetry.'

44 POLIZIANO CONFRONTS
SAVONAROLA 1490

THE FRESCOES AT SANTA MARIA NOVELLA WERE UNVEILED just before the Feast of the Nativity. Angelo was standing with the very men who appeared with him on the wall – Ficino and Landino – each of them dressed as Ghirlandaio had depicted them, with crimson gowns and plum-coloured caps. Other men portrayed in the frescoes mingled in the crowd, most of them of the Tornabuoni and Tornaquinci families, while Domenico Ghirlandaio, in a blue tunic swathed in a red mantle, stood with his brothers and assistants in the centre of the chancel, looking sublimely receptive to the praise he was receiving.

Men gathered in hushed groups, pointing out to each other the wonders of the walls. 'A magician,' they whispered, 'an alchemist.'

There were Dominicans about, as was to be expected since Santa Maria Novella is one of their convents. They said nothing but served refreshments to this notable gathering of the leading citizens of Florence. Lorenzo Tornabuoni joined Angelo's group.

'Fra Girolamo is here,' he said, in that soft, lilting voice that made us all listen, no matter what he said.

'May his heart open to the truth of beauty and his mouth be sweet,' Angelo replied.

Ficino, who was very enthusiastic about the friar and his calls for the Church to reform, frowned at him. 'Do not be cynical about our man of God.'

Angelo considered him, plucking at his lip. At home Maria and I had listened to him ranting about this damned friar who had blasphemed against poetry, ranting about Florentines who were sleep-walking into the lair of a wolf. For Poliziano, Savonarola's sermon had made the matter plain: here was an enemy to everything that Lorenzo de' Medici had built. Why could the rest of us not see it? But in public he was more circumspect.

'I want to believe,' he said to Ficino, 'as you and Pico believe, that God has sent a prophet to Florence, that Savonarola has the power to bring about great change, but the rational disposition of my soul does not allow it.' He gazed at his short friend. 'Marsilio, I have read too much history and not enough natural philosophy. I do not share your unfounded optimism. But I will not damn Fra Girolamo by instinct alone, or else I am sharing your error. No, I'll go and investigate.' So saying, he detached himself and went through the crowd to the preacher. 'So, Frate, what do you think of the walls?'

'Colourful,' said Savonarola, smiling. 'Very colourful.'

'Do you consider it unholy that men of our own times be depicted here?'

Savonarola stared piercingly at Poliziano. 'Vanity, vanity, all is vanity,' he replied. 'Any man who believes he may win favour of God by paying for decorations is a fool. God would prefer white walls if it meant pure souls.' His eyes, staring straight into Poliziano's, blazed. Angelo said later that he felt like a dirty grub in that glare of supercelestial perception.

'We disagree on the matter of poetry,' he said, falteringly.

'We do indeed. Any time you wish to come and speak to me about it, I shall be available to you. God awaits you, my son, God awaits you with open arms.'

Angelo came back to us, drained of colour.

On St Stephen's day at the Palazzo de' Medici there was a conversation about Savonarola. Lorenzo said that he was considering recommending him as the next prior of San Marco. Angelo tried to dissuade him. 'There is something not right with that man.' Everyone at the table disagreed, all feeling the refreshment of having in our midst a courageous preacher who spoke the truth, a man who practised what he preached.

'Lorenzo, please...' Angelo implored his patron.

'What is it, Angelo? Say what it is that troubles you in one sentence. Otherwise I'll presume that your objection is based on resentment.'

'Resentment? What do I have to resent?'

'One sentence.'

The high priest of poetry stood with his mouth open, but the sentence did not come.

45 THE ICE STORM
1491

DURING EPIPHANY THERE WAS A STORM, A STINGING HAIL of tiny balls of ice. One moment we were in sunshine, the next we were being stoned by the large cloud that covered Florence. The ice granules lay on the streets, on the crowns of hats, in the folds of hoods, on the backs of horses, piled up in open carts and made the marble pavements treacherous. They filled your shoes and made them flatulent, or sent you down on your arse, all dignity lost for merchant and notary, artisan or scribe.

Thus it was on the first day. On the second the Arno froze, trapping fishing boats and bringing the mill wheels to a halt. Boys skated between the Ponte Santa Trinità and the Ponte Vecchio, bearing icicles like lances. By the third day, when the trees were festooned with crystals and animals were dead in the fields, the owners of estates went out to consult with their contadini. The wise among them pruned their olive trees down to the stock. People looked at the stumps and began to say that God was angry, that this was a sign of the end of the world. Had not Savonarola been preaching the Apocalypse? Well, here it was. People took the ice storm as a sign that we did, indeed, have a prophet amongst us.

'Every tree that bringeth forth not good fruit is hewn down, and cast into the fire,' Savonarola proclaimed in the square outside San Marco, and made it clear that he had in mind the pope and all men in high places who were not devout and sincere.

I told Angelo about it later, but he was as well-versed in the Gospels as the rest of us were not, and knew where the quotation came from and its context. He read from St Matthew: *Beware of false prophets, which come to you in sheep's clothing, but inwardly they are ravening wolves. Ye shall know them by their fruits. Do men gather grapes of thorns, or figs of thistles? Even so every good tree bringeth forth good fruit; but a corrupt tree bringeth forth evil fruit. Every tree that bringeth not forth good fruit is hewn down, and cast into the fire. Wherefore by their fruits shall ye know them.* He stared into his own fire reflectively. 'We would be less easy prey to false prophets if we read the scriptures for ourselves.'

He, the least outwardly Christian of us all, was perhaps inwardly stronger in the faith than most. Where others went to mass regularly and confessed their sins, he read the book on which our faith is based, at a depth and penetration impossible to the average mind.

'As it is,' he continued after further reflection, 'we let others do the work for us and become enslaved to them.'

Pico, who had listened thus far with grudging appreciation, now objected. 'Are you speaking about Savonarola?'

'I am speaking of all preachers. The quantity of them increases daily and the people are becoming trapped in a cycle of sin and repentance.'

It was true that many were preaching in various churches but only one was drawing vast numbers. To Savonarola flocked the poor, the disaffected, the women. 'Preacher of the Despairing' he was called; if the Count of Concordia had not been regularly in the congregation, it might have stayed that way, but Pico's frequent attendance attracted others, if only out of curiosity. Why should the young, intelligent Count be drawn to this preaching friar? Compared to the other preachers, who had voices like volcanoes – deep, loud and ready to pour hot fury over the people – Savonarola often seemed moderate and just. He only thundered in his prophetic frenzies. These he tried always to resist, but the resistance only made them that much more explosive. When not possessed by prophecy (by the Holy Spirit, said some) Savonarola spoke gently.

Maria had been to hear him herself, sometimes in my company, sometimes on her own. No other preacher was addressing himself particularly to women and he found an intelligent audience in Maria Poliziana. In most arguments, she sided with Pico against her brother, whom she accused of being cynical, but on this evening she swopped sides. 'I wish he would not prophesy,' she said. 'I do not like it when he thunders. His true voice is soft, and he speaks much good sense.'

Pico smiled on her with amusement. 'So you are not keen on the voice of God?'

'Voice of God!' spluttered Poliziano. 'Voice of the deceiving demon, more like. Maria is right. There is nothing wrong with this man when he speaks for himself, but when he starts to shiver and shake, his eyes rolling in his head, well, stop your ears.'

'It *is* the voice of God,' Pico insisted.

'Gianni, Gianni, Gianni. I love you above all men, but sometimes I could stick your head in the well until your brain cools.'

Pico ignored him, concentrating on Maria. 'Do you feel drawn, my sister?'

'Drawn to what?' she asked suspiciously.

'To the conventual life.'

'No, she does not!' I snapped, with such vehemence that everyone jumped. Maria stared at me, as if to fathom the cause of my passion, but I did not understand it myself. Not then.

'Leave things as they are. Nothing here must be disturbed,' I muttered in embarrassment and took myself off to bed.

46 FEAR OF THE FUTURE
1491

IN THE FOLLOWING LENT, SAN MARCO COULD NO LONGER hold the numbers wishing to hear Savonarola. He preached in the Duomo, thrilling the Florentines by denouncing the clergy, saying they were 'given up to outer ceremonies of which they make a trade, while neglecting the inner life of the spirit.' It made you want to cheer out loud.

Somewhat unnerved that his recent threat of imminent evil had come to pass with the ice storm, he made no mention of visions but concentrated instead on morality and faith. But then half way through his sermon, his voice began to swell and he grew powerfully animated and cried, as if to God himself, *O Lord, thy word has become like unto a fire within me, consuming the very marrow of my bones. Therefore am I derided and despised by the people, but I cry unto the Lord day and night, and I say unto you: Know that unheard-of times are at hand.*

I shivered as if ice had just run down my spine. It seemed impossible to doubt that what he said was true. The future, in that moment, became a source of fear.

47 WET DREAMS
1491

THERE WAS ONCE A YOUNG MAN OF FERRARA, A POET OF twenty-two, who woke up in moonlight, the silver beams lying across his body, his charged body that tingled with every sensation. He had dreamt of Laura, so vividly he could feel her next to him in the bed, the warmth of her body against his, her rosy lips kissing his shoulder, his neck, his ear. He groaned and stirred. His hand moved under the sheet, down over his body, down into the hair. It was a sin, a sin, but how could he resist? *Oh, God…* he prayed out loud. And simultaneously grasped his *pisanello*.

What happened then is easy to relate: he was drenched in icy water. But how did that feel? One moment you are in a riot of desire and temptation, the next you are waking up so hard and fast, so unable to comprehend what has happened that you may as well have been knocked out cold.

Freezing water. Buckets of it. Was it his father? Had he groaned too loud in his dream and brought father in? Was it the priest?

Who? He was sitting in his bed, drenched, shivering, his manhood limp in his hand. He let himself go, wimpering, and dared at last to look around. No one. There was no one in the room but himself, sitting in a soaking wet bed.

Buckets of icy water from heaven. Somewhere, angels were laughing.

How would he explain this to the family the next morning? How would he spend the rest of the night?

The next thing he knew, he was waking up in sunlight in a dry bed. The icy water had itself been a dream: a dream of waking up. Such dreams are powerful.

That was the story we heard, of the night in his youth when Girolamo Savonarola gave up poetry for God.

48 LORENZO SENDS FIVE MEN TO SAN MARCO 1491

AT A MEETING OF THE ACADEMY, WE HEARD THAT Savonarola was gathering disciples, men who would accept neither gifts nor alms but only their daily bread, who would dress like the poor, who would not seek office nor build houses. These men would have revelations from heaven and much learning – not the learning of philosophers and poets, but that of their own conscience and Holy Scripture.

Angelo's lip curled in distaste. 'Men who will shrivel from famine and go about in smelly old patched robes. I've seen them. They are dropping like flies at San Marco. I know none of you will listen to me, since I am only a poet and not a philosopher, let alone a prophet, but I am telling you to beware of that man.'

Bernardo Rucellai, Lorenzo's brother-in-law, agreed and was concerned by Savonarola's growing criticism of the Medici. 'You cannot allow him to say just what he likes. He owes everything to you, Lorenzo, and he is going round the city calling you a tyrant. He is whipping up a rebellion. I'm afraid you are going to have to deal with it.'

'What, trump up some charge so as to have him banished?'

'If necessary.'

'That's the way of the tyrant which I am accused of being. Angelo, I am still waiting for that one sentence.'

'I have not yet formulated it. Why do you look at me that way, as if the fate of Girolamo Savonarola hangs on my opinion?'

'You have something to say and I would like to know what it is.'

'So would I! But some thoughts are like truffles that hide deep below the surface. You can only smell them. But I know, deep down inside me, I know something is wrong with that man.'

'You dislike him because of his views on poetry, that is all,' said Pico.

'It is more than that,' Angelo insisted. 'I feel possessed of understanding I am unable to communicate to the rest of you. Or to myself.'

'So what am I to do about him?' Lorenzo asked.

'If he could just stop prophesying,' said Bernardo Rucellai, 'we would have no objection.'

'Go and tell him so, but do not say I sent you. Speak on behalf of the city.'

Thus five men of the Platonic Academy, including Rucellai and Francesco Valori, went to San Marco to tell Savonarola – most diplomatically – to change his tone. Savonarola met them in the sacristy of San Marco and made them welcome. But when they began to say what they had to say, he rose from his chair and cut them short – 'Like a sword brought down hard on a cake,' Bernardo Rucellai reported. Savonarola said, 'I realise who has sent you, that these are not your own words you are speaking. Go and tell Lorenzo de' Medici to do penance for his sins, for the Lord is no respecter of persons and spares not the princes of the earth.'

When Valori hinted that Savonarola might be banished to another city, he replied, 'I have no fear of banishment from this earthly city. The new doctrine shall triumph, and the old shall fall.'

Here he glared at them, and Rucellai said he felt himself burning up in that fulmination.

'Though I be a stranger,' Savonarola boomed in a voice that bounced off the vaulted ceiling, 'and Lorenzo the first citizen of Florence, *I shall stay and he will depart!*'

It was a voice that brooked no argument. It was a prophecy. It was a prediction. God had spoken. Valori's innards trembled, his bowels loosened.

The friar's voice lowered but did not soften. Like a man possessed, they said, he told them details of the state of Florence and Italy that they did not know themselves. And as they stood before him, these amazed leading citizens, they grew ashen at his words.

'Great changes are about to befall Italy. I tell you, within twelve months we will see the death of Pope Innocent, King Ferrante of Naples, and of Lorenzo himself.'

When the five men reported back to Lorenzo, they were not the same five that had been sent out. Valori, indeed, could hardly speak and thereafter came infrequently to meetings of the Academy, while he was often seen at San Marco. Savonarola was gathering his disciples.

49 THE WAY OF ART
1491

ONE HOT AFTERNOON IN EARLY SUMMER, WHEN EVERYONE else was resting, I found Angelo at his desk composing an introduction to his forthcoming course on Ovid. These prefaces he wrote in verse, taking more trouble over them, I suspect, than any other professor in the world. Usually he did not wish to be disturbed, but on this day he looked up with a face transfigured, all its usual heaviness gone and in its place lightness and joy.

'A man's craft,' he said, 'is his route to God. To love what you do, and to serve it with all your might and power, knowing that your beloved and your God are One – it is all.' He was clearly speaking from the experience of the moment. 'There is no need for all this mortification of the flesh or purification of the spirit. The way to kill base desire is to replace it with the desire for something finer. The way home is not by guilt but by love. Love is all. Listen to the Franciscans, Tommaso, and not the Dominicans.'

Unable to speak, I went outside, closed the door softly and leant against the wall. What he had said was true. I ached at the beauty of it; I bent double in misery. Once I had known this truth from my own experience, once writing letters on a page had been a play of light as the sun on water. Not always, but sometimes, enough times to know that what I seek is right here. How I envied Angelo! With a deep breath I drew myself up to full height and strode to my room. Enough of this wallowing – it was time to slough it all off. I made ready my desk, prepared a sheet of parchment with pounce, cut a new quill. I chose a short text and clipped it to the reader. It was time to reunite with my art, to transcend my disability – which anyway Thomas Linacre, the student physician who was in those days staying with us, said not to exist. Then let it not exist! I dipped the nib in the ink pot, dabbed off the surplus, put the nib on the paper.

Charity faileth not... The pen dropped from my hand, splashed on to the desk sending a fine spray of ink over the parchment. I had felt nothing as a warning. When men say, 'you are losing your grip', they know not how literal this may be. One moment the pen is between your fingers, then it is not – the only sensation, a fizzing numbness that comes in the manner of an afterthought.

And so – I was sundered from my God forever, and any hope of true happiness. The misery found a new depth. Mind, heart, spirit – all three were pulled down into Hades. Yes, I designed the lettering for Filippino's frescos, the names of virtues that would appear, amongst all the visual trickery and illusions of that chapel, as if carved in stone, but it was another man who painted them on the wall, who felt the brush in contact with the plaster.

50 DIVINATION BY CARDS
1491

THERE WERE THREE ENGLISHMEN STAYING WITH US, studying Greek with the professor. Grocyn, the eldest and like a father to the other two, wanted to learn Greek solely for the purpose of reading scripture. It was young William Lily and Thomas Linacre who thrilled to the ancient lyre of poetry. Poliziano, who also had students from Portugal and Hungary, lavished time and attention on the foreigners, believing that, in his small villa on Fiesole, he could change the world for the better by 'civilizing the barbarians'. For some reason he had most hope in the English, and certainly this influenced my decision when looking for a new land in which to live, although it was Ficino who sent me and Colet who drew me.

When our three *inglesi* departed for home, Angelo and Pico travelled with them as far as Bologna and then went on to Venice. Lorenzo – who, since Savonarola's death prediction, was going about without a walking stick, saying he had never felt so well – had heard of the disovery in Venice of a codex of Archimedes and he sent Poliziano and Pico there to read it. Without doubt they also had a secret mission, which was to repair relations between Ermolao Barbaro and his native city. Lorenzo, as ever, was weaving peace. While the two were away, Maria stayed with her sister-in-law in the city and I remained alone at the Villa Bruscoli.

When Angelo asked me to look after his property and affairs, he said it was 'in case the French come'. It was only half a jest. In those years the French were beginning to replace the Turks in our nightmares of apocalyptic doom. You can read why in the histories which my fellow countrymen are busy writing. Suffice here to say that France had a claim on the Kingdom of Naples, and the young Duke of Milan, more or less usurped by his uncle, had been promised the support of Naples in regaining his dukedom. That's it, in a nutshell. As soon as young Charles VIII was old enough to govern, Ludovico il Moro, the usurper, invited him to assert his right to the throne of Naples. No one, least of all the councillors of the French court, expected Charles to do so, but the Kingdom of Naples covers all of Italy south of Rome and with it comes the title 'King of Jerusalem', and that rather appealed to the dwarfish, misshapen boy-king who, they said, spent all his days in dreams of knightly valour and holy crusades. If the rumours about his nature were true – and nothing I had seen in him myself particularly contradicted them – he was sufficiently misguided to consider the venture. And so the direction of our fear changed, swinging away from the infidel Turks – who had been quiet since the death of Sultan Mehemmed – and towards our Christian neighbours. The French, said the prophets and the astrologers, were on their way.

'And I don't want them in my house,' said Angelo Poliziano.

I did not like the loneliness and, to keep myself busy, I turned to arranging Angelo's papers. It was something he had often asked me to do, should I ever have the time. I had it now and began to sort them into languages: Greek, Latin and Italian. I read as I sorted, in particular his jottings towards a new *Miscellanea*, his second collection of notes on ancient texts which sought to answer questions and right wrongs. For example, he wrote that the name 'Strotocles' in the first book of Cicero's *De Officiis,* was a misreading of 'noster Cocles.' A small wrong put right, perhaps, but one could almost hear the ancients cheering as the accumulated cobwebs of ignorance were swept off their works. His first *Miscellanea*, a collection of a hundred chapters published three years previously, had made him famous throughout Italy.

Just before he left for Venice, Poliziano had received a visit from yet another would-be disciple, that Michele Marullus I had met in Rome. But the young Greek caught him on a bad day and every charming thing he said struck Angelo as mere sycophancy.

'And so,' said Marullus at the end of the uncomfortable interview, 'here are my own poems. I would be very grateful for your opinion.'

'God's blood!' Poliziano exploded. 'Just because I have read every book ever written, does it mean I have to read every book being written? All this mediocre, maundering stuff that lands on my desk, obliterating my own work. Do you think I have nothing better to do? Give my opinion? You can have my opinion. It's almost certain to be clumsy, contrived or mawkish – probably all three.'

Marullus stood there blinking rapidly, his hand tightening on the hilt of his sword. The student of literature, lest we had forgotten, was also a mercenary soldier. He glared at Poliziano, as if weighing up the consequences of killing him on the spot.

'The professor is tired,' I said, stepping between them. 'He's been up half the night, trying to finish something before he leaves for Venice. He did not mean what he said. If you knew what rubbish men present to him, you would understand. He hasn't seen your work, does not know how good it is.'

Mollified, Marullus began to breathe more normally. He bowed as if his neck were in a brace and left.

'Angelo,' I said, alarmed, 'you have made an enemy of one of the *stratioti*.'

'Oh, I suppose he's going to take off my head and carry it around the city on his lance.'

'Metaphorically speaking, yes, he is.'

★

If Angelo Poliziano had not really read every book available to man in Greek and Latin, he had certainly read more than anyone else alive, and by reading his *Miscellanea* you shared the fruits of his studies. So this second collection, which by this time had reached about twenty chapters, held me captive. The author acted as guide to the labyrinths of knowledge, holding up a rush-light to one idea after another, as if they were paintings on a wall in a dark chapel, and I walked with him in confidence as Dante did with Virgil. It was all details, you might say. Questions such as whether crocodile dung was really used for cosmetics in ancient Egypt are hardly vital for the spiritual well-being of Man. But Angelo believed that, by shedding light on the microcosm one might come to know the macrocosm better. He said that, the laws of Creation being universal, you can see them at work in the worm-cast as well as in the stars.

He wanted to equip us for an adventure into the future, our sense of right and wrong, true and false, sharpened to a cutting edge by the application of reason. Savonarola wanted to shut the gates across the path of human progress and restore the Age of Faith. He believed that men, prone as they are to evil and wickedness, must be shepherded by the Church; Poliziano believed that Man could walk alone and make his own decisions, providing he was well-read and well-educated.

I sat on fences and believed in both.

I came upon a set of cards, each one bearing a Hebrew letter, to be used like *tarrochi* cards. Giovanni Pico had introduced Angelo to divination, finding answers to questions by the art of *sortes*, in which the Bible or other work of scripture, or the poetry of Homer and Virgil, are opened at random while the question is held in mind. It is an art which is peculiarly effective. Pico said that by such means angels communicate with us. But he said that the art was not to be used for predicting the future, for the future lies with God; it was for the examination of the soul. When I came across this pack in my tidying, naturally I was tempted to try it. I was after all of Etruscan blood and the son of ancient augurs, but natural superstition and my solitude prevented it. I did not want to summon angels only to be successful and have no one to whom I could run screaming. So I was good – or cowardly – and put the tempting cards aside.

The windows were open, the still air humming with bees and hawkmoths. Drawn out to the garden, I filled Maria's bird bath with water and sat by a rosebush to inhale its scent. The beauty made me melancholy; sitting with my nose in a handful of crushed rose petals I dwelt on Elena. The dormant pain stirred, then roared up from the depths, the yawning depths, and I jumped to my feet. Activity. I must be at work. Must be doing something. I had become a man for whom leisure was torment.

There had been no sudden gust of wind, not so much as a breeze, but when I returned to the study, Angelo's papers were strewn across the floor. Puzzled, I began to collect them up. The second *Miscellenea* was held together in quires, but another work on separate sheets had become scattered. As I put it together, I saw that it was Angelo's *Account of the Conspiracy of the Pazzi*. He had written this directly after the dreadful events of April, 1478, when our beloved Giuliano had been stabbed to death in the Duomo. Just holding the Account made me tremble as if sitting in a chill draught, for it brought my brother Antonio to mind, and my part in his capture and death. So I was not about to read the Account again, but only put it back in order. It was as I picked up the pages that I saw the spilled cards. Whatever strange draught had come, it had thrown the Hebrew pack over the floor. Some were face up, others face down. The up-turned letters were *hay, vav, tsade, aleph, lamed, aleph, vav, resh,* spelling *Hotze la'or,* which I interpreted as 'publish'. Publish? I jumped back in fright. What was the meaning of this? To what did it refer? Terrified of angels, I dashed from the house.

Maria was on the path. I did not see her until I was up against her. Maria, warm, real, here. If I took hold of her, it was relief, it was safety and security. She returned my embrace, flooding me with her life. No shade, but a living woman. I said nothing of what had happened, other than that I had suddenly felt as spooked as a horse.

'You should not stay here alone. If a man is to keep good company, he is ill-advised to keep his own.'

I smiled. 'That's true enough. What brings you here?'

'I have no idea. A whim. A feeling that something was amiss. I woke up with it this morning and could not shake it off.'

We dined together on what food there was in the pantry, some cheese and ham and fresh salad leaves that Maria had picked in the lane on her way. It was the kind of day for honesty. Maria said I was wasting my life, footling about doing odd jobs for her brother and whoever else had a florin to spare. I was rootless and without direction. Then I told her what had happened before she arrived, that I believed I had just been given direction by angels.

'And what direction is that?'

'It's something I have been struggling with for a year or more, the knowledge of what I should be doing opposed by my not wanting to do it. It was there, spelt out in the cards.'

'Publish?'

'I have a dud hand. I can no longer be a scribe of fine works, just a left-handed secretary. But I could be a printer.'

Maria stared at me, her face mirroring my own horror. 'You? A printer?'

'Well, printer's assistant to begin with. I need the training. But then if I could get the money from Lorenzo ...'

'But Tommaso, no one rants against printing as loud as you.'

'I've been struggling for some time and have not dared to talk about it in case it made it real. But here it is now, out in the open and confessed to you, Maria mia. Aldo Manuzio, the tutor of Pico's nephews, is setting up a press in Venice.' I gave her a letter that had arrived from Angelo the day before, in which he enthused about Aldo and his plans to print Greek texts. 'To avoid errors, Aldo intends to employ editors. Now that's something I am qualified for.'

Maria's face changed suddenly.

'What is it?'

'A bit of bone in the ham.' She picked it out of her mouth, wiped her hands on a napkin and cleared her throat. 'So, you are leaving us for Venice?'

'That's the major part of the struggle.'

'There are printers here in Florence. Could you not get your training from them?'

Women! How come they see light while we poor men grope in fog? I picked up her hand and kissed it. I meant nothing by it – it was a simple show of affection – but to my surprise her face was suffused with a blushing smile.

Paris, July 31st, 1506

Erasmus has just come in, spluttering about printers and the mess that is being made of his translations. He wants me to go with him and read the proofs coming off the press. 'I have told Bade that I have with me a companion who has worked with Aldus Manutius. He is cowed, Tommaso, cowed. He dreads you. Come now.'

'Which do you want?' I asked irritably, not wishing to be disturbed. 'The book I am writing for you or my editorial skills?'

'Both. Bring your book with you. There are frequent pauses in the process. Too frequent. Bring your work with you.'

Clyfton intercepted him on the way out, demanding to know when we shall be continuing with our journey.

'That man is a very horsefly!' exclaimed Erasmus, as he strode through the streets to Bade's printing house.

51 SITTING ON FENCES
1491

LORENZO HAD ANOTHER GARDEN ON THE VIA LARGA,
close to the sculpture garden. Dedicated to peace, repose and
horticulture, it had been bought to commemorate Lorenzo's wife,
Monna Clarice. Angelo had rooms in the casino there and enjoyed
living in the city secluded by high walls. I stayed there when
I needed to be in the city and had my days punctuated by the
bells of San Marco. The windows faced the cloisters on the far side
of the road, and whenever I looked out it was on to the magpie
world of the Dominicans, walking piously in their striking black
and white habits, austere and silent. Franciscans are always jolly,
it seems, and greet the world and its creatures with a smile,
their cheeks reddened by their liquors brewed from herbs. But
the Dominicans, close-shaven and fastidious in dress, have an
unearthly pallor and look on the world as something to be suffered.
In the last two generations the friars of San Marco had become
somewhat lax but Savonarola was setting new standards of
austerity and many were following him in his practices of self-
denial and fasting.

The sculpture garden had become a busy school, overseen by
Bertoldo. Early one Sunday I walked through the stables there to
see the chariots being built and decorated for a Roman Triumph
that Lorenzo was organising for St John's Day. Fifteen chariots of
splendid construction being decorated by Granacci filled the
stables. I had no doubt that, were Savonarola to know what was
happening behind the high walls of the sculpture garden, it would
give him a good theme for a sermon: the extravagant waste of
money spent on a spectacle glorifying the men who had crucified
Christ. All of which, of course, would be true – and missing

the point. Lorenzo never thought of a theme without going through all four levels of meaning, and I knew enough to guess that the coming Triumph was designed to stir up the martial blood of the Florentines and strengthen their patriotism and pride. Lorenzo, who had his nose closer to the wind than anyone, could smell war ahead. But on another level he sought to purify the city of its voluptuousness, and the best foil to an excess of Venus is Mars.

I moved around the chariots, enjoying their details. A thousand stories from ancient poets were painted in their panels in monochrome tints to give the illusion of cast bronze. Stories of ancient Rome, its gods and heroes, which needed considerable knowledge to decipher, were here painted with such finesse that you would think they were collector's items intended for close study in a rich man's studiolo – not scenes that could only be glimpsed as the chariots moved past their viewers. In other words, there was no need for such painstaking detail. Instead of the usual tawdry that is the theatrical or processional prop seen close-to, here was art. How typical of Lorenzo that was. And why? For this reason: the evocation of Mars was not a mere theme for a pageant. Lorenzo was doing it: he was evoking Mars. Not the simplistic god of war, but the god of discipline, judgement and control. That was his way to cure his city of its decadence and, with an exquisite sense of timing, he was doing it at the festival of St John, for Florence has two patrons: the Baptist, and the God of War.

On this day, Savonarola was speaking in the church of San Marco on the Apocalypse of John. As I listened to the lines from *Revelation*, I heard them as if for the first time. Indeed, visions such as the seven lamps of fire burning before the throne, which are the seven Spirits of God, must surely, I thought, refer to Cabala. But although he knew about the art from the Count, Savonarola said nothing of Cabala in his exposition.

Suddenly there came that change in his voice which we all longed for and all dreaded. The mild and gentle preacher began to sound like an earthquake or avalanche. Savonarola had moved on to the subject of the four horses and was telling us that the white signified the apostles; the red the martyrs; the black the heretics. But the pale one...

'It signifies the tepid ones, the fence-sitters, the ignorant; those who live life for themselves and not for God. *And I looked, and behold a pale horse: and his name that sat on him is Death.*'

I began to tremble uncontrollably, even more so when the Friar continued: 'Each horse represents an era of the Church. This pale one is our own. But there is another to come...'

And with those words he left off preaching and began to prophesy.

'THE FIFTH STATE, WHICH IS OF THE ANTICHRIST AND OF CONVERSION, IS ABOUT TO BEGIN!'

The time and the half time. The one and a half millennium: the year 1500 Anno Domini.

'I AM THE HAILSTORM THAT SHALL BREAK THE HEARTS OF THOSE WHO DO NOT TAKE SHELTER! HE THAT HATH AN EAR, LET HIM HEAR WHAT THE SPIRIT SAITH UNTO THE CHURCHES!'

My knees went weak. I could not have run had I wanted to. I felt like a mouse being tossed about by a cat and, once he had finished, I was astonished to find myself not only still alive but allowed to escape. I stumbled out into the open air. All around me were others in a similar condition, and many of them were wailing in remorse for their sins. Passers-by stared curiously: what was this stumbling congregation, heads buried in hands, mourning and lamenting like sinners in Dante's *Inferno*? What had happened to them in the church of San Marco?

I could be ambivalent no longer: I must either stand with Angelo and condemn this friar or I must stand with Pico and accept what he was saying as true. And if it were true, then I had nine years left before the one and a half time, before the apocalypse, before the Day of Judgement. But who needs nine years to renounce all his sins? Nine hours would be long enough, if truly meant. Nevertheless, the future seemed capped: there was no point in looking forward in the vague hope of death-bed redemption. Now was the time to find out what was true and false within my own soul, to get off the fence if I would avoid the pale horse.

52 I TRY MY HAND AT SCULPTURE 1491

THE SCULPTURE GARDEN WAS FILLED WITH CHOKING, powdery air. 'Greetings,' I said, holding my sleeve over my nose. Michelangelo, covered in marble dust, looked like a living statue, albeit one with two purpled eyes. He grunted in reply, obviously not wishing to be disturbed in his work. I wanted to talk to him about Savonarola, about how he could wake up the soul with fire and freezing water and make you want to repent of every evil deed, but the youth, despite his own fondness for listening to the sermons of the friar, was in no mood to discuss the advent of the antichrist, not while he was working. So I settled down to watch him and recover from my ordeal. He had the large hands of a stone-cutter, and under the tutelage of Bertoldo, those hands were working with a power and confidence that made them seem old before their years. Michelangelo was sixteen but his hands were about forty. He struck the chisel deftly, sending chips flying, cutting his way into the stone.

'Father Marsilio told me that Plotinus says we are to carve our souls as if they were statues,' he said.

'Yes, I remember that curious line and could not quite understand it.'

'Oh, it's easy. The ancient Greek sculptors did not make models – that is, build up a figure by addition. They cut away to find the figure trapped in the stone. That is what Plotinus means. Cut away the dross of the passions to find your true self. That is the sculpture of the soul. So cutting into marble is more noble an art than casting in bronze.' His enthusiasm was palpable. 'And that is the way I mean to work from now on, inwardly and outwardly.'

Michelangelo's engagement with his work was infectious: I saw and thought nothing other than what was happening under his chisel as it cut effortlessly into the stone. Other artists these days refer to Michelangelo as a god and speak of him with awe, and whenever I hear him mentioned thus, I am transported to that day in the sculpture garden when I sat gathering stone dust in my hair and clothes, feeling the warmth of the sun on my skin and listening to a chisel as to a fine piece of percussion. My soul, which had been chilled by Savonarola, was coaxed back into the sunlight.

For the past six months Michelangelo had been living in the Palazzo de' Medici and we had grown more used to each other and friendly, despite the gap in our ages. He was such a forthright young man, and so devoted to his art, that his being merely sixteen seemed somehow illusory. He had lost any taste for friends of his own age, if he ever had one, and preferred to keep company with men older than himself. With Poliziano he was developing his skills in poetry; he spent hours in conversation with Ficino, discussing philosophy, especially as it relates to art. To me he came for help with his homework in Greek and Latin. Once that was done, he would talk to me about sculpture, and I listened to myself as I was at his age, talking about calligraphy and the arts of the scribe. With passion.

I gazed on Michelangelo at work. Can feelings echo like sounds? It was a fleeting thing, like the memory of the smell of roses in the midst of winter, a tremor in the vitals, an 'Ah, yes!' – and it was gone again.

'Do you mind me watching?'

'No. You are not like other men who watch me looking for faults, or those who fall asleep with their eyes open. You watch properly. It helps.'

A month previously his nose had been smashed in a fight with Pietro Torrigiani. The worst of the dreadful bruising had gone but he was still dark purple and pink round the eyes. Lorenzo, whose wrath had been so towering that Torrigiani had fled into exile, had tried to cheer Michelangelo up by saying that he took it as a compliment that Michelangelo wished to look like him, for they both now had flat noses; indeed, Michelangelo did find some cheer in this as he had become devoted to his patron. But he still wanted his old nose back.

'Tell me,' he said, putting his tools down for a moment. 'Do you hate Pico della Mirandola for what he did to your arm?'

'He did not injure me himself, or even intend it.' I picked up one of the chisels and weighed it in my hand, appreciating its fine balance.

'It is one thing to lose my nose but if someone robbed me of the ability to work, I would have to murder him.'

I laughed. 'You cannot anticipate such things. Everything happens at the right time for the right reason. It is just not always easy to see what the reason is. In my case it was no doubt divine punishment for disobedience.'

'Did I deserve to have my nose broken?'

'Probably,' I said, not really thinking, my mind disengaged and dwelling on a scatter of Cabala cards. *Publish* ...

'The stone will absorb anything – anger, sorrow, frustration. Here, try it.'

He showed me how to hold the tools. When I hit the chisel with the mallet, the stone was surprisingly yielding. I felt childishly pleased with myself, looking at the chisel marks I had made as if at a fine piece of art. Michelangelo smiled. 'Go on,' he said, 'enjoy yourself.' He gave me a spare piece of stone.

So for an hour I was a sculptor, and made a head that any five-year-old would have been proud of. When at last I put down the tools, Michelangelo turned to see what I had done and barked with laughter. I could only join him. My sculpture was abysmal but I felt better for it, and said so.

'How is it,' he asked diffidently, 'that you can hold a mallet but not a pen?'

I stared at my right hand. Was it cured? But no – it held all manner of things without trouble, knife, comb, glass of wine – indeed, any object except a pen. Michelangelo, curious about human anatomy, made me hold a quill while he studied the muscles of my forefinger and thumb under the skin, manipulating them, making me stretch and grip, stretch and grip. I dropped the quill several times in the exercise.

He examined the tendons of my arm. 'I have no explanation,' he said.

'Neither do the physicians. They say the sword must have killed off the small muscles.'

'Che peccato.' He picked up his chisel and mallet and went back to work and, while I watched, he changed hands, first holding the chisel in his right hand, then in his left. It made no difference to the quality of his carving. He looked to see if I had noticed.

'Were you born that way?'

'No, I trained myself.'

'That is the difference between us. I, too, have trained my left hand, but it can only do pedestrian work, nothing beautiful.'

'Che peccato,' he said again, this time with a shrug. He never had much sympathy for the lack of genius in men.

53 FOOLING A PRINTER
1491

I CONSULTED MY OLD MASTER, THE BOOKSELLER VESPASIANO da Bisticci, long since retired, to see if his opinion about printed books had changed. It had not. He said printing is the art of the devil, but that there had been one exception, and he told me to go to Filippo Strozzi and ask to see the Pliny.

I was fortunate to find Strozzi at home, since he was most often to be found at the site of his new palazzo. A familiar face not only from city life but also the Platonic Academy, Strozzi welcomed me in and took me to his studiolo, where he drew out his copy of Pliny's *Natural History* as if his greatest treasure. He had obviously made a mistake, for I had asked to see the *printed* Pliny, but what he showed me was a manuscript of such surpassing beauty that, as I opened it, I recoiled – if recoil is the right verb to describe stepping back from the divine. What does Mary do when confronted by Gabriel? Recoil? No – she steps back. So, I stepped back, eyes wide. The image of the first page impressed itself upon my soul and I can see it now in my mind's eye: a border with colours so rich – deep red, green, lustrous gold – that you felt within yourself a sense of majesty. A legend in Roman capitals – formed close to perfection, in gold leaf on a ground of ultramarine – announced that this was a translation into Italian made by Cristoforo Landino. The capital D of the text was an exquisitely-wrought window on to the study of a scholar, which itself had a window looking out on to a landscape. One could have stepped into that study and looked over Pliny's shoulder to see what he was writing – for now I was no longer stepping back but being drawn into the book, heart and soul. The margins were in correct proportion, wider at the top than at the bottom, the outer margin broader than the inner. And now that I was in tune with the design, seeing as it were the fine body inside the costume, I went to the text and realised for the first time that this book had been printed. The work of Nicholas Jenson of Venice. Strozzi had had the printed book decorated by Monte di Giovanni di Miniato.

'Nearly had you fooled,' he said amiably. 'It nearly fools everyone, except the Duke of Urbino who knew it straight away for what it was. He said his nose tells him the truth where his eye is deceived.'

Mine should have done the same. I stood back and studied the page, went close and studied the letters. 'I thought it was impossible for printing to be beautiful.'

'Usually it is. Jenson was unique.'

'Did he not have apprentices, someone to continue his tradition?'

'A man called Torresani worked for him and bought up Jenson's shop on his death. But whether he was party to the secrets of proportion I do not know.'

When Angelo returned from Venice, he told me that this very Torresani had become the partner of Aldo Manuzio. He fully approved my change of heart and direction.

'I have had my Italian works published in their hundreds. I am content they will survive whereas, if my work remains in manuscript only, there will be small chance of its survival.'

'When a book is beautiful,' I said, 'a lustrous jewel of ink and paint, it survives even dark ages, for men who cannot read value it for its appearance.'

'The dark age is behind us,' said Angelo. 'Ahead is only light.'

'Said the mayfly of the rising moon.'

'Of course, the best thing about printed books is that I may write notes in their margins freely, or draw a hand pointing to an important line, without people like you complaining about vandalism.'

That was true enough.

I went to Antonio Miscomini, who was setting up Ficino's translation of Plotinus. I told him I was willing to turn my hand to anything: editing, compositing, even inking. Miscomini said he could not afford another wage.

'Then I shall work for nothing,' I told him.

'I don't need anyone. I am fully staffed.'

It seemed I was wasting my time. About to leave, I looked round at the many presses. 'You print on single sheets.' Almost everyone did. On the back of page one, they printed page two. But I knew a way of printing up to eight or even sixteen pages on one sheet and, on its reverse, another eight or sixteen. It did not take a great brain to invent the small book, but you did need to know the law of imposition.

'Single sheets are hard enough, even with two pulls,' he said. 'What do you expect me to do? Print on two sheets at once?'

'I can show you how to do two pages at once, or four, or eight. And I can show you how to make a quire of thirty two pages with only four formes.'

The imposition of pages is something I had learnt as a scribe but it seemed not to have occurred to the printers – at least, not to this one. I decided not to show him how easy it was to work out for himself. Instead I wrote out some numbers: 9/16, 8/1, 10/15, 7/2.

'What is this cipher?'

'It's the number law of Cabala,' I lied. 'A secret formula revealed to Pico della Mirandola by an angel which I am prepared to offer you. The rest of the sequence is five over four, twelve over thirteen –'

'Wait! Wait! I am lost.'

'Nine over three and eleven over fourteen. *Ecco!* The outer forme.'

'Well, you'll have to tell me that all over again. And what do you mean the outer forme?'

'And of course every other number has to be upside down, starting with the first. So, eight upside down over one; nine upside down over sixteen.'

'Please ...'

'Then there is the inner forme.' And I fired the second sequence at him. 7/2, 10/15, 11/14, 9/3. 'And don't forget, the first of each pair is always upside down.'

Miscomini looked close to tears.

'You cannot think in numbers? Here, let me show you.' I took a piece of paper and folded it once lengthwise and twice sidewise. I did this with the dexterity of a marketplace trickster, making sure my hands were a blur before his eyes. I opened it out and wrote the two sequences, one on one side, one on the other, and folded it up again. 'Then you give it the slice of the cross,' I said, pulling a knife through the middle fold, lengthwise and sidewise. Eight pages dropped from my hands to the table, with numbers written on them. 'Then you put it all together. Go on, put it together so that the numbers are sequential.' The poor man was all fingers and thumbs and exasperation. I took the pages back and did it for him. 'At the moment you print two pages on two formes. Here you have a quire of sixteen pages in quarto, also done on two formes.'

Miscomini's eyes bulged and he struggled for breath. 'This is magic. What was that formula again?'

'Take me on and I will demonstrate it to you. In time, if you allow me to do the tasks of my choice, I will reveal to you the secret of the octavo book and give you the formula for a quire of thirty-two pages.'

Stupid fool. Had he only folded a sheet of paper once, twice or three times himself, and numbered each page sequentially as usual, once he opened up the sheet he would have seen for himself my 'cabalistic formula'. Still, it won me a place in his printing house – although the rest of the men gave me a wide bearing.

54 AN INVENTION OF THE DEVIL 1491

IN MISCOMINI'S PRINTING HOUSE THE ONLY SOUNDS WERE the squeak of the great wooden screw on each press, the turn of the wheel as the press stone was moved out on its rails for inking, and the rhythmic clicking sound of the otherwise silent compositors. In the depth of concentration familiar to scribes, with the right hand they picked out tiny metal letters from the case and put them into the 'stick' they held in the left. They had to work quickly, more quickly than the brain: their hands knew the case intimately, the position and location of its many compartments, the capital letters in the upper case, the small letters in the lower case, the compartments ordered more or less alphabetically, and the ligatures set apart in their own compartments at the sides. They plucked letters with the tender confidence of a musician. The central part of the case had larger compartments that held the letters used most often in our language, and with these compartments as 'home', the hands of the compositors moved out two to the left or three to the right, so instinctively that it was said that a good compositor could do it blind. Which is all very well, so long as the letters have been put in the right compartments.

After a forme had been printed, it had to be untied and its letters released back into the case, since a dozen or so pages would take anything up to ten thousand sorts. Putting them back into the cases was the work of the compositor's assistant and for a month I chose it to be my job, distributing the letters at first carefully, and then more quickly, and at last without looking or thinking. A disser who puts any letters back in the wrong compartments was liable to be smacked around the ear, no matter what his age or social standing, as I can testify. Such a thing costs the compositor time – since he is paid by the line – but often these mistakes went undetected. So here was the chief imp of printing – the compositor's assistant.

While his right hand picked out the letters, the compositor gazed steadily at the stick in his left hand. Although he could not fill the line without looking, since it was too easy to put the letters in upside down, he soon trained himself to do it without thinking, to translate each line of the original manuscript and load it into the stick back to front. Compositors never read words: they see letters. Click-click-click they go, swaying back and forward like rowers for two hours or more at a time, whereupon they rise groaning from their stools and go outside and wave their limbs around to ease the pain.

Once a stick was filled, it had to be placed in a galley frame, building up line by line into a page in a forme. Between each line were placed leads which, being lower than the letters, do not print.

Leads are the secret of spacing. Even some of the letters in the stick were separated by leads, for a good compositor knows which letters can sit together well and which require extra space. And then each line had to end at the same place on the right hand side – to be 'justified right'. Scribes know how to do this by judging the script as they write it down, stretching letters or using abbreviations as they come to the end of a line; the compositor does the same with leads and ligatures. Once the galley is complete, it is placed into the forme and made tight with wooden blocks in a huge variety of size, wedged with them until it fits tightly into the forme without moving.

'Do you not make a sample printing of the completed page before putting it on the press?' I asked in my innocence.

'Of course,' said Antonio Miscomini. 'We call it a proof.'

'And then? Do you read it?'

'We check for the evenness of the impression and for any movement in the forme. That is why it is so important to tie the forme up tight – mustn't let anything move.'

'But do you read it?'

'Yes, of course we check for errors.'

'So how come you don't find them?'

'We do find them.'

'But many evade your eye.'

'No, none evade my eye. But in between the proof and the printing, the printer's devils get to work, taking out a letter here, adding one in there. There is nothing we can do about it.'

The compositors and assistants sat back from their work to grin at me.

'There are your devils!' I said, pointing to them. 'If I am going to show you the formula for an octavo quire, I want to read your proofs for you, at least for Ficino's translation of Plotinus.'

'Not before you have learnt to compose yourself.'

'I would not be able to do that. My arm is damaged, or else I would still be a scribe. If I tried to pick up letters, I would drop them.' It was true – but I was also keen to avoid the pain suffered by the compositors as they bent over their cases. I had already tried holding a stick and filling it – each sort added to the stick's weight and by the time you had finished a line your muscles were beginning to scream. 'Do you want that formula or not?' I asked Miscomini.

In an adjoining shop, letter punches were engraved by ex-goldsmiths, made into matrices and cast by foundry men, each matrice providing hundreds of sorts, made of an alloy that was constantly being adjusted and experimented with, for the aim was to find a metal that did not wear out after a few printings. We did not make our own paper and getting sufficient supplies of the right quality was a testing job of administration. Ink had to be mixed, and I was taught how to dab the thick, viscous stuff on the forme with a pad in each hand – a most tedious job given to apprentices or men who deserved punishment. I learnt everything I required as quickly as possible, then refused to do it any more, all the time withholding the octavo formula.

I studied alone at night those things that really interested me. The letters were being engraved at apparently random heights: no one in this shop had considered the letter-to-page ratio which is vital to beauty. The same with the leadings between lines. Here all was arbitrary and the laws of proportion, if ever known, were quite forgotten. Miscomini believed beauty was appearance: if something looked right, then it was. He was a master of fiddling, interfering with other men's work to put in an extra lead here and there, shifting letters along and words down until the page 'looks right'. He would leave a space for a capital letter and have a mediocre scribe fill it in on the printed page – a job surely as tedious as ink-dabbing when you have to do a hundred or more identical capital letters at a time. Such jobs I avoided, dangling my formula before Miscomini as a carrot before a donkey. And I gave him no advice about beauty at all, for I had no intention of staying in this shop. I was on my way to Venice, to present myself to Aldo Manuzio as an editor with printing experience.

Such were my dreams. In reality I spent my days bowed over pages of Plotinus, reading proofs and learning humility. After a month I went to Miscomini and apologised for my arrogance. 'You are right. There are such things as printer's devils. I believe.' For no matter how carefully I read, I missed mistakes. Many of them. By some devilish law errors only become apparent when you take the top printed sheet off a stack of hundreds, but even at that stage not all of them are seen. The worst mistakes only dance naked before your eyes once the pages have been trimmed, stitched and bound together. It is only when you open the finished book that you see them, standing out as if printed in a different colour. Publication day in any printing house is, I believe, a day of groaning and lamentation.

We experimented. We used two proof-readers. Although both found an equal amount of mistakes, they were rarely the same mistakes, and both missed more than they found. We tried three proof-readers, with more success and more failure – more mistakes found, just as many missed. I tried reading a page line by line from right to left, to avoid the temptation to read the text – perhaps, like the compositor, it would help to see words as letters rather than meanings. Nothing, I swear to you, worked. Forgive printers, Erasmo. There is something in the human brain – a Great Corrector – who will see things spelt right even when they are not. But even that does not explain why errors, invisible on the proof, become manifest in the edition. Some things are truly beyond our undrstanding.

55 BANISH HIM! 1491

PICO AND POLIZIANO RETURNED TO FLORENCE WITH A wagon-load of books for Lorenzo's library that included Aristotle's *Poetics*. They arrived at the Palazzo de' Medici when Lorenzo was facing a decision and consulting advisers. 'I have here details of the election of Fra Girolamo Savonarola as the new prior of San Marco,' he told his two friends. 'It only awaits my approval. Everyone here thinks I should seal it, except for my son who says I should banish the friar. What do you say?'

'Trust God and put your seal on the parchment,' said Pico immediately.

'Banish him,' said Angelo, glancing with approval at Piero de' Medici, his erstwhile pupil.

'Why? And remember, when you answer I want it in one sentence.'

Angelo went to speak, then stopped, confounded.

Lorenzo looked to his son. 'Piero?'

'Banish him, Father. Flog him naked in the streets for his presumption. Ever since you invited him to Florence he has done nothing but insult you. Banish him.'

Lorenzo drew some papers from his desk. He softened some wax and let it drip on to the parchment. 'Let him stay. If he speaks the truth, I must bear it. If he speaks the untruth, he must bear it. Either way, I leave the matter to God.' He winced from pain as he stamped the wax with his ring.

After his election as prior, Savonarola was invited to visit Lorenzo. It was traditional, he was told, for new priors to visit the Medici, for the health and well-being of San Marco were due to their patronage.

'I am going to my prayers,' replied Savonarola. 'For it was God who elected me, not Lorenzo de' Medici.'

Orléans, August 12th, 1506

Erasmus wanted to remain in Paris until his *Adages* were off the press, but the courier said that, if we do not move on immediately, he will leave without us, for he has letters to deliver in Rome. Clyfton likewise insisted that we continue the journey at once, saying he no longer believes in Erasmus's headaches.

'If you are that sick, take yourself off to hospital and let the rest of us go on without you.'

So now the *Adages* are left to the clumsy ministrations of Bade and we have moved on.

56 BOTTICELLI IN THE ARNO
1491

SANDRO BOTTICELLI, MARRIED TO HIS ART, WAS OBLIVIOUS to his surroundings and lived in squalor. Although the workshop was as you would expect it, full of pigment and paint, jars, sacks of lime, it also had remnants of meals not cleared away, odd shoes under benches, a film of dust on any surface that was not frequently used. In his living quarters above, the floor of his chamber was strewn with clothes that had missed the cassone meant for their storage. The chest sat with its lid open in the hope of something falling into it. Those things that had fallen in lay drooped over its sides as if trying to crawl out again. His bed was never made, the sheets never changed. It was not that he did not have assistance, he just neglected to give the boy any instructions, and the boy did not trouble to ask for them.

Worried about his friend's health, Filippino Lippi asked Angelo Poliziano, who was Sandro's landlord, to contrive a visit to the workshop.

'Have you come to be harsh about the rent?' Sandro asked, through a brush clamped in his mouth.

'No, I've come to be harsh about you. You cannot live like this, not unless you want the company of rats and cockroaches.'

'It's not as bad as it looks. I clear it up occasionally.'

Angelo studied Sandro, trying to ascertain the cause of his delinquency. Finally he diagnosed absence of mind. 'He is living elsewhere,' he told Filippino Lippi later. 'This world is beneath his notice.'

Filippino, however, believed that the fault lay with Domenico Ghirlandaio. 'Since Sandro worked with him at the Vatican he has not done fresco again, not for public view. Does he envy me the commission for the Strozzi Chapel, do you think? If he does, he has made no sign of it. I think he's given up. He does smaller and smaller things, and for private men, not for churches or public places. I think he's avoiding being compared with Ghirlandaio and found lacking. That's my opinion.'

Angelo agreed that it was a fine diagnosis to put Sandro's messy house down to envy and despair. After all, who would not feel the same? While Domenico Ghirlandaio strode abroad in tunics and capes of fine wool, in startling combinations of colour such as rose, plum and mustard, day after day Sandro Botticelli wore the same linen shirt and brown hose until someone complained of the smell. He had his beard shaved only when the stubble grew too rough for comfort, while his hair, now fading to grey, was never combed but hung from his head in matted coils. Thin on the top but falling thickly down round his shoulders, it looked as if it had been worn out on the pate by the wearing of his cap.

His last great work had been the Coronation of the Virgin, tempera on panel, for the altar to the left of the main door of San Marco. Since then it was true that he had done only small, private pieces, such as the decoration of a cassone for the Vespucci. However, I did not believe Sandro was suffering from envy. While he had been doing the Coronation, he had kept company with the Dominicans, heard what they had to say and had been impressed. I called on him one day after work at the printing shop and, sharing some ham, bread and olives with him at his bench, told him about my becoming a printer's apprentice and how humbling it was to go back to the beginning at this stage in life.

'Be thankful,' he said, eating off the blade of his knife. 'All one needs is good work to do and enough money to live on. All the rest is vanity. Seek only the praise of men you admire. Those who long for the crowd to cry "Hosannah!" forget that soon enough that same crowd will be shouting, "Crucify him!"' He concentrated on prising pips out of a pomegranate.

'So, if a big commission came your way…'

'For a fresco? I'd ignore it. I hate fresco – all those broad sweeps with a fat brush. I will always prefer tempera on panel. But right now I want only to be left alone with a stylus and a pen to do my Dante. Of course, I have to live and so I do small things that do not require me to sweat blood. Small things in tempera with the finest of brushstrokes. Eggshell pigments on smooth, smooth gesso – nothing like it. The feel of it, Maso, the chalkiness. Paint on wet plaster? *Meh!* Fresco painters are always exhausted at the end of the day, whereas I am refreshed.'

After we had eaten he showed me what he was working on: a small picture of the Mass of St Jerome. Where was Venus here, and her lascivious tresses? The scene was one of simple Christianity, the mass taking place in a chapel made of humble wattle. I remarked on its simplicity and Sandro said that it was what the commissioner had wanted. That the head of the saint was out of proportion to his body was not, I knew, incompetence on the part of the painter. Sandro was resorting to an earlier tradition where that which is the most sacred is emphasised.

'Filippino thinks I avoid painting architecture because I cannot compete with him.'

'Is it true?'

He smiled wryly. 'It is not the architecture which is important. It is the figures – more, it is the soul of the figures. These painters today, with their lifelike portraits, their vanishing points, their landscapes… Landscapes! Have you seen anything of Leonardo's recent work? Do you know how it's done, those misty landscapes in the background? I'll tell you. He loads a sponge with various tints of green, grey and blue and throws it at the panel. While the paint is wet he works it into sea and hills. Once it's dried, he puts a few trees in. *Ecco! Una bella vista!*'

'This is one of your jokes! I see you've not lost your sense of humour.'

Botticelli snuffled like a bear.

'If that story gets back to Leonardo, he'll be furious.'

'Will he?' Botticelli grinned at the thought. 'It's my job to throw sponges at puffed-up painters who swagger about calling themselves "artificers". Artisans is what we are. All this perspective nonsense, the depiction of space, capturing a likeness – it's all the wrong reality.'

As the shadows gathered into night, he lit candles. Their flames danced in the cool evening air coming in through the open door, their light flickering over his earnest face.

'What do you mean, the wrong reality?'

'Heaven is beyond time and space – there is no vanishing point there. You may as well treat a panel as it is – two dimensional – than try and fool people with a third dimension. Pictures are to remind us about God, not to make us breathless at the achievements of men. The Byzantines knew all about it.'

'You are not proposing we ignore everything we have learned and retreat to the past?'

He shrugged. 'Why not?'

'Another one of your jokes.'

'To serve God you have to work from the heart,' he said, striking himself forcefully on the chest. 'Everything else is vanity.'

His turn of mind, his frequent mentions of God, I put down to the influence of Savonarola and his friars. When I said as much, Sandro laughed scornfully. 'I have my own prophet, thank you. He is called Dante Alighieri.' He took me across to a portfolio that contained hundreds of drawings in various stages of completion. He had spent ten years or more illustrating *The Divine Comedy* in his spare time. It had been inspired by a commission to illustrate Cristoforo Landino's masterly commentary on Dante's great work, but when it was done he had continued the project for himself, intending to illustrate every episode in the *Commedia.* Each sheet was of uniform size and was fine quality parchment made from sheepskin. He took out the first, a scene from *L'Inferno,* for me to look at.

People say of Botticelli that he was a dreamer who painted dreams, that his figures and landscapes had little to do with the

271

world as we see it. They should look into those drawings with a polished lens. Sandro gave me such a lens so that I could magnify the figures that he himself drew with the naked eye. The sheets were large but the figures were tiny, drafted with a stylus and later drawn carefully with a pen. The pages boiled with figures, most of them nudes, and with a fine nib and brown ink, working entirely in outline and in miniature, Sandro Botticelli showed that he knew as much about human anatomy as Michelangelo, and considerably more than Domenico Ghirlandaio. I stared through the lens at these tiny naked figures, at the linear details so extraordinary that they made me dizzy with admiration. Devils and demons – most of them smiling – scampered about like satyrs, waving torches and jumping out of the towers that punctuated our own city walls. The Styx, across which Virgil and the terrified Dante were being rowed by a bat-winged ferryman, was clearly the Arno. Every single detail was its own perfection. This was Dante in pictures, with several episodes in one composition, so that in the one I was studying there were two figures of Virgil in the boat, one fending off Filippo Argenti who, rising from the mire, was trying to board, the other comforting Dante. The devils were familiar: ancient dramatic masks were their model. Sandro, like Filippino, must have made studies in the Golden House of Nero while he was in Rome working on the Vatican walls. But his anatomies – where had he got those? Looking through the lens so intently that it steamed up, I knew for the first time what old women look like without their clothes on. But how did Sandro know? What labour of study had gone into such miniature detail?

I turned through the collection, page by page. Pick any portion and you would find exactitude – the way a cart was harnessed to a griffin, the fruit in an upside-down tree, a soldier's pike, chains. This man Sandro never went out but that he had his eyes open. And as for the figures – hundreds, nay, thousands writhed on these pages, and I never saw one posture repeated. Some sheets were coloured, and with colour came a sense of depth in the pictures, but the exquisite detail of the penwork was lost; preferring the pen drawings, I looked on the calligraphy of images with a scribe's eye and, as I say, felt faint with admiration.

Sandro turned the leaves, advancing us rapidly through the punishment of sodomites, panderers, seducers, flatterers and hypocrites. 'Everyone,' he says, 'finds himself somewhere in these pages. Where are you?'

I simultaneously blanched and grew hot, told him I would have to think about it.

'It should be clear enough. Here, this is where I am...' He pulled out a drawing of Canto XI in *Purgatorio* showing three figures bent under huge boulders. In one part Virgil and Dante were in discussion of these figures, in another Dante was stooping to look under the boulder at the penitent illuminator, Oderisi, crouched under his terrible burden. *'My heart was set on the desire to excel,'* Sandro muttered. *'For such pride we must pay the fee.* Here we are, you and I, amongst the proud.'

'Proud? You? I can believe it in myself, but not you. It is not a proud man who would work on something so small, so fine, so private.'

'This work is the expiation of my sin, my burden. Each morning I awake with a pain gnawing at me, that I am not decorating some great chapel, with apprentices running up and down scaffolding to my direction. When I was in Rome, I worked side-by-side with Domenico Ghirlandaio. After that, I could no longer deceive myself. The man is a genius. It gnaws me, as the eagle pecks all day at the liver of Prometheus. The liver grows back overnight, to be pecked at anew the next day. I am in a very fever of rage and envy.' He said this placidly, almost off-hand.

'But envy is not pride.'

'No, it is not. The thing is, I believe myself to be great, and it surprises me that no one else thinks so, too. The crowds pay court to Ghirlandaio. Me they ignore and I have to scrape for a living. Now is not the desire for recognition, for hosannahs, is that not pride? For behind it is the belief, nay, the conviction, that I am a great artificer. And what do these hosannahs of the mob amount

273

to? Nothing. *Non è il mondan rumore altro ch' un fiato di vento, ch'or vien quinci e or vien quindi, e muta nome perchè muta lato.* "The world's noise is but a breath of wind which comes now this way and now that, changing its name as it changes its quarter." Dante himself is intimately involved in this canto – this is where he sees himself. We have three figures: the man proud of his birth, the man proud of his power and the man proud of his art. Here, with the third figure, Dante stoops…'

Sandro had depicted Dante's words precisely: Dante stooped. But he had illuminated its meaning.

'Oh, I see! Dante stoops – as if he were carrying a boulder.'

'The stoop of a man who will have a rock on his own back for eternity if he is not careful. And who is he talking to? Oderisi of Gubbio, the scribe and illuminator.' Botticelli peered at me to make sure I was getting the point.

'The scribe and illuminator…' I repeated.

'Who has been eclipsed by Franco of Bologna.'

'Eclipsed…' I thought miserably of Bartolommeo Sanvito and the perfection of his hand.

'The scribe tells Dante how the painter Giotto is dimming the reputation of Cimabue.'

'Dimming…'

'That's right. And then he mentions the poets who are about to be superseded by "another" – Dante himself. It's all about professional jealousy. Was Dante being vain? No. See – he stoops. Dante knew his own greatness, but he also knew his own pride, and in this scene he depicted himself, as he would be if he did not take great care. We are all three here in this little section, Maso: you the scribe, me the painter, and Dante the poet. Marvellous…'

I was not so sure. 'It may have been true a few years back, but now… What do I have to be proud of?'

'Ho! You blame your wound for your eclipse, and keep your vanity intact!'

I shrank wincing in the sudden glare of self-illumination.

'That's my Dante! If he can make you feel that uncomfortable, he has done his work.' He took hold of my right hand. 'Why do these fingers go numb? Is it really the result of a physical wound?'

'Of course – what else?'

He looked into my hand like a fortune teller. 'Whose work is it that makes your fingers go dead?'

Bartolommeo Sanvito, I thought, but refused to admit that this was the cause. Ridiculous! It was a sword blade that had done the injury, not envy. But I understood, suddenly and in the anagogic manner, how it must have felt for Botticelli to work side-by-side with Ghirlandaio.

'Read the whole canto to me, please,' said Sandro.

I did so, and afterwards Sandro recited it without referring to the book, word perfect in each line and stanza. Why had it never struck me before? I had discovered the same fact about Filippino long ago, but Sandro? He, so sophisticated that he could hold conversations with Poliziano and Landino as a man of equal learning, he who consulted professors for details about his figures, he who had such a profound way of layering his symbolic references that celebrated scholars took days to unravel them, he was illiterate.

'You know Dante by heart,' I said tentatively, 'and only by heart?'

'Of course not – I can read as well as you. But for a poem to mean anything it must be stored in memory. The wise memorise. Reading is a pastime for the ignorant.'

I looked at the drawings again, how each episode was so carefully included. These sheets were a memory chart of Dante's journey through the afterlife. Sandro had only to look at them and he could recite the verses. Rooted in the heart, it was indeed a way of knowing that was deeper and more fruitful than merely reading the text. I had read *The Divine Comedy* many times but apart from a few dramatic details could never remember much about it. And I had certainly never identified myself amongst the sinners, let

275

alone suffer that blaze of understanding. Sandro was ten times the student of Dante that I was.

Later we went for a walk through Ognissanti, past the palazzi of the Vespucci and the Spini to the river. The night sky was radiant with stars; starlight lit our way along the bank. Ahead the Old Bridge and, beyond that, San Miniato on its hill, all seen in silhouette. There too the city walls and the towers from which torches hung innocently in sconces without a devil in view. The summer night was velvet and serene and we walked in silence under the paradise of stars. Sandro gazed heavenward, identifying figures of the zodiac and pointing out the Milky Way. To gaze with him was to feel infinitesimal and infinite all at once.

The river was smooth and, this side of the weir, quiet. My friend was filthy. Fumes of his odour kept assaulting my nostrils. He was looking for Leo when I pushed him into the Arno, to launder his clothes, bathe his body and wash his hair. I did it in the spirit of Dante. He came thrashing and struggling to the surface.

'*Aiuto! Madonna! Aiutami!*' He gulped, sank, came up again. 'Tommaso, you bastard! I cannot swim!'

'Swimming? It's a pastime for the ignorant. Try walking on water.'

He spluttered, swore and sank again. I jumped into the spangled river to save from drowning the greatest artificer of our age.

'Cleanliness,' I told him as we surfaced, gasping, 'is next to godliness. Surely Dante has taught you that?'

57 LORENZO LONGS FOR EASE
1492

IT WAS THE YEAR WHICH SAW SPAIN RECAPTURE GRANADA from the Moors, the year when Cristoforo Columbo first sailed west to find a new route to India. During Epiphany of that year, Lorenzo de' Medici disappeared from public view. Naturally the city grew agitated, given that Savonarola was now predicting from the pulpit the imminent death of Pope Innocent, the King of Naples and Lorenzo. *Great times are ahead!*

'It is gout, that is all,' the Chancellor of Florence assured us. 'Lorenzo needs to rest.'

Almost everyone who was seeking an appointment with him was turned away. The priors of the government could see him, and the manager of the bank, and his closest companions, but the rest of us seemed to be in a permanent ante-chamber.

Botticelli waited impatiently for Lorenzo's recovery, wanting him to visit his workshop, as he sometimes did, to discuss Dante with him and study his drawings with a pair of lenses clamped to his nose. This was the Lorenzo that few knew, who walked alone in the city at night to call on a painter in a squalid workshop in Ognissanti. 'When they are done,' he had often told Botticelli, 'sell them to no one before you've offered them to me.' Sandro always told him that they were not for sale.

Michelangelo was desperate for Lorenzo's opinion of his marble relief showing the Battle of the Centaurs, too large and heavy to transport into Lorenzo's chamber. He sometimes gained entry himself and took in sketches, but he wanted Lorenzo to feel the marble and its figures in relief, to see them with his eyes.

Pico della Mirandola was anxious to discuss the collection of books Lorenzo was building for him to replace those burnt in Savoy, but he stayed away; not wanting to trouble the sick man, he did not even make a request to see him.

As for me, I was anxious to speak to him about my ideas for a printing shop dedicated to the translations and original writings of Ficino, Pico, Poliziano and others, a shop fumigated daily against printers' devils, where I would sit at a high desk overseeing everything whilst I designed a new alphabet, a type based on the script of Bartolommeo Sanvito, of such surpassing beauty that even the most discerning men would drop their prejudice against printing and strive to obtain my books. I would print in Greek so that men might read the words of Plato and Aristotle – as well as those of the New Testament, of course – in the original language. And Hebrew, I would print in that, too. Perhaps one day a Bible in all its original languages, three columns of text per page ...

But Lorenzo was too ill to see me.

There was no woman of the house. Lorenzo's sisters, Nana and Bianca, tried to fulfil the role, but they had their own households to look after. His youngest daughter, Contessina, betrothed but not yet married, did her best to emulate her mother and grandmother, but she was too young. There was Alfonsina, Piero's imperious young wife of the Orsini family, but Lorenzo contrived always to be in a different house from his daughter-in-law. Despite all the men milling around, concerned for his welfare and wanting to see him, Lorenzo's chamber emanated a weary air of loneliness. With his brother, mother and wife dead before him, he had only his children left.

Angelo neglected other duties to be in attendance as often as he could. Sometimes one heard laughter from the chamber, but mostly it was only Angelo's, Lorenzo too exhausted to do anything more than raise a wan smile. More often one heard song, with Poliziano's voice rising and falling, solo or in duet with Baccio Ugolini; musicians were often brought in, a consort of viols and other instruments, to entertain il Magnifico and distract him from his pain, pain so severe that sometimes you could hear Lorenzo bellowing like the Minotaur. Servants attended him with trepidation, never knowing what his mood would be.

Since his arrival in Florence, Pier Leone had established himself as chief of Lorenzo's physicians. He had been trained at Padua and for a while he had been professor of medicine at Pisa, at which time he had befriended Lorenzo. A handsome man in his mid-fifties, spare of build, intelligent and very energetic, he was a living recommendation of his own doctrine and regimes. Medicine is as prone as any other discipline to a variety of opinions, but Pier Leone held to his own and never wavered. His lack of self-doubt cut a swathe through his rivals and soon all physicians vying to treat Lorenzo had to consult Pier Leone first.

He fussed over Lorenzo's diet, excluding all foods that would aggravate the inflammation of his limbs. The pain fluctuated and some days were better than others. Pier Leone's system, based on his orthodox training and his reading of ancient Greek texts, put into order and harmonised by his own common sense, was strikingly reasonable, apart from his obsession with water. He blamed all our ills on water and insisted on analysing our urine frequently. On those occasions when Lorenzo was fit enough for the journey to the Volterrana, he would go to the sulphur baths and gain for himself a week of relief. Pier Leone went with him so as to test the water of the baths. His remedy for Lorenzo's current ills was that he be kept warm and *dry*. Once Ficino, overhearing me tell a friend that it was a sign of the law of correspondences that Pier Leone's name began with a pee, accused me of being juvenile.

'If my dear friend fears water,' Ficino told me stoutly, 'it is for good reason. All men fear their own death, but it is not granted to many to know what will cause it.'

'Are you predicting his death by water?'

'I have seen it before, the prescience of a soul made manifest by an irrational aversion.'

When I repeated that to Filippino Lippi, he laughed till his jaw ached, and henceforward never missed an opportunity to mention either dropsy or the threat of flooding in the physician's presence. That Pier Leone invariably flinched was a great test for me to keep my face straight. Once Filippino even told him that the cure for water on the brain is a tap on the neck.

'Most amusing,' said Pier Leone without a smile. He weathered our affectionate jibes, which were without malice, and, for certain, we were glad of his water or drought cures when we suffered our own minor ailments.

One evening, when Lorenzo was enjoying a respite from pain, he had supper with Poliziano, Pico and Ficino in his study. I was not present but Angelo told me later how those few blessed hours had been devoted to philosophy and literature and, at the end, how Lorenzo had declared his intention to retire from public life in order to devote his days to study.

'He is going to promote Piero to head of the family.'

'Piero? He is too young!'

'That is what I said, but Lorenzo reminded us that he had been the same age when he took over from his father.'

'But his father was dead: there was no option.'

'It won't happen: no one will allow it. Poor Lorenzo – how he craves to be himself and not *il Magnifico*.'

When the first trees were in blossom and bulbs beginning to flower, Lorenzo had himself carried on a litter to his villa at Poggio a Caiano. The villa, standing out bravely on its hill near Prato, was visible for miles but its walled gardens were private, whispering places, dedicated to Ambra, the nymph beloved of the river Ombrone that embraced the estate. The villa in its architecture, the estate in its agricultural principles, Poggio a Caiano was Lorenzo's vision of the life made good by culture and work. On that day, arriving in a litter, he was overcome by a grief, not his own, but one that runs like a river through the history of man, grief at the apparent transience of virtue, that all heroes must be killed by villains, all great works vanquished if not by vandals then by time, everything good from the past surviving in a state ruinous and fragmented, as if the truth can only be heard hiccoughing in history, as if the only things that are eternal and not transient are human poverty, misery, injustice. Tears ran unchecked down his tired, sallow face. Such an effort to be good, so easy to be evil... Thinking upon Atlas and Hercules and drawing what strength he could, he raised himself up in his litter and called for the gardeners to discuss the planting of trees that would not be fully mature until the middle of the next century.

In order to convey his ideas, he called for paper and a metal point stylus, which were duly brought to him, but when he reached out for the stylus and tried to hold it, his body shook from the effort and his face contorted in agony. His daughter, Contessina, took the pen from him. 'Tell me,' she said, 'what it is you wish to draw.'

Gasping for breath but relaxing, Lorenzo described groves and copses of trees, pathways, planting schemes for box hedges and laurels, creating in wood, leaf, grass and stone a garden for Philosofia.

His body was weak from pain. But not the soul.

58 THE INVESTITURE OF A CARDINAL 1492

GIOVANNI DE' MEDICI WAS AS UNSIGHTLY AS HIS ELDER brother, Piero, was handsome. Corpulent at sixteen, snub-nosed and with weak eyes which, even at that young age, were beginning to be protuberant, he was decidedly lazy. While his brother was at the jumps, he would still be in bed. He seemed to love his bed immoderately, except at night when nothing could draw him to it. While Piero stood up straight and impressed everyone with his skills as a courtier – easy and fluent speech, gracious, musical, athletic and martial – Giovanni shuffled about apparently lost in a daydream. But when he spoke, he was tactful; he never pretended not to know you but always greeted you by name and affably. Piero could make a great show of his learning; in Giovanni, it shone out, if fitfully, as intelligence. He did not seem troubled by an ecclesiastical career that had begun at the age of six; and as for all his benefices, he was neither proud of them nor ashamed. He needed them. They were his living; and no one was in greater need of wealth than a cardinal.

He had been made a cardinal by Pope Innocent three years earlier, but it had been kept secret while Giovanni was still at university at Pisa. After the formal investiture, planned to be held at Fiesole since Lorenzo was too ill to travel to Rome, Giovanni would have to keep himself and his court, perhaps not in the ostentatious splendour of a cardinal such as Rodrigo Borgia, but at least in something worthy of the office. And then, if the integrity which his father advised did not work, he would have to pay for every single favour he required. Gifts from perfumed gloves to antique statues would need to be liberally bestowed on kings, princes and bankers.

Always with him, as close as his shadow, was his cousin Giulio, a boy of about twelve at this time, and powerfully alike to his father, Giuliano. Always together, one rotund, the other slender – Poliziano said meeting them was like being accosted by the number ten.

A man in constant pain is as fierce as a tormented bear. Life in the service of Lorenzo was near intolerable for those pages and attendants close to him. Unable to find relief in any position of his body, Lorenzo could go three or four nights without sleep and then a kind of madness came upon him, a snarling fury that would break out without warning. It was always followed by remorse and apology, but that did not stop everyone doing all they could to avoid upsetting him. And so we tip-toed about, spoke in whispers and drew straws for delivering anything amounting to bad news. Lorenzo's eyesight, never good, was growing very weak: many took advantage and stood just outside his range of vision when having to ask him some question likely to annoy him, such as what he would like to eat at the next meal.

He was attended by physicians from Rome, Naples, Venice and Milan, each state sending their best, desiring that il Magnifico should recover, for the peace of Italy depended on him. By his careful statecraft he held the fate of Italy in his hands. With his work on poetry and language, he was creating a vernacular to unite the country into a single entity. That was the deep work. The outer work, the daily affairs revolving on letters and meetings, kept ambitious states in check. Florence was the hub of Italy; our allies were the wheel.

Despite the finest doctors Italy could send him, however, Lorenzo did not recover. Indeed, something else began to afflict him, something that came on so gradually we did not notice it for nearly two weeks. Slowly, slowly he weakened, his colour changing as it does with fever. Pier Leone analysed Lorenzo's urine and said he did have a fever but not one of the blood. 'It is a fever of the bones and muscles,' he said. No remedy Pier Leone administered had any effect: Lorenzo was beginning to waste away, that fine figure becoming thin, his once strong hair now lying limp on his head.

On the day of Giovanni's investiture, Lorenzo was too ill to attend even at Fiesole and had to be left behind in the palazzo, weeping with frustration. I joined Angelo in the long and elaborate procession to the Badia at Fiesole to attend our young protégé as he stood before the high altar in that church of quiet beauty and had the insignia of cardinal bestowed upon him.

This church of the Badia, with its elegant nave and aisles of smoky stone, was our church, for the Platonic Academy met frequently in an upper loggia of the cloisters. It was a building that bridged worlds, neither physical nor invisible but somewhere in between. Now with the investiture of Giovanni we seemed to stand at a threshold. Oh, how many plans had been laid by Lorenzo to reform the Church from within. Now his second son was at last being given the sapphire ring, the red mantle and the broad-brimmed, tasselled hat of a cardinal of the Church, and in

Giovanni were vested all our hopes. He was one of us, and he would carry our philosophy into the heart of Rome. We were grafting him on to the papal stock in the hope of better fruits, and it was the intention of heaven, we prayed, that he be pope himself one day. Not a man in the church that morning was unaware of the weight of responsibility being placed upon this young man's round shoulders. 'Live with regularity, rise early in the mornings,' his father had written to him. 'Avoid ostentation but collect antiquities and beautiful books. Maintain a learned and well-regulated household rather than a grand one.'

As Giovanni turned from the altar to face us, I could see tears in his eyes, whether from the solemnity of the moment or the absence of his father, I could not tell. Perhaps both. As his father had said, 'this elevation comes not from your merits but from the grace of God'. He was neither proud nor humble. He was just Giovanni in a big red hat. His brother Piero took charge of him and led him from the church to meet the waiting crowd.

There was something in Piero's stance that day as he took on the function of his father, a delight in the role that was disquieting. He played it well but not well enough. He was charming and courteous but only to those men he knew; the rest he ignored. And he had something about him which said, 'Look at me!' – an air never worn by il Magnifico. His wife, Alfonsina, standing tall in gold brocade and large with his child, looked over the heads of the women around her, a group which included Lorenzo di Pierfrancesco's wife, Semiramide, daughter of the Lord of Piombino.

'You must be very proud,' Semiramide said to her.

Alfonsina, as if surprised to be addressed by the wife of a mere cousin, did not deign to reply. Humiliated, Semiramide detached from the group and went to join her husband and whisper to him. Lorenzino put his arm round her and looked darkly, now at Alfonsina, now at Piero.

'We are leaving,' he said, his thin lips down-turned. This caused consternation. The division in the Medici family affected us all and very, very few of us succeeded in belonging to both camps. Lorenzino leaving early had every man weighing up the repercussions in going or staying. For some it was an easy decision, and members of the Vespucci family readied themselves for departure. For others, there was much dithering.

'Please, do not go,' said Cardinal Giovanni to his cousins, his father's advice still sounding loud in his soul. His attempt at diplomacy was supported by Bartolommeo Scala, who waved his arms about crying, 'Now, now,' as if a calming word from him would solve any dispute.

'I will not stay where my wife is insulted,' said Lorenzino.

I looked across to Angelo who had his eyes closed as if in prayer. He was one of the rare men who belonged to both camps, as was Ficino. Both men, looking anxious and distressed, conferred. Ficino was particularly torn since he was a beneficiary of patronage from both the Pierfranceschi and the Vespucci. He decided to go, Angelo to stay.

Alfonsina, the cause of the trouble, looked at the men with cool amusement.

'What a farce!' Lorenzino said to his brother as they made for the horses. 'That porker a cardinal, indeed.' The angel-faced Giovanni di Pierfrancesco looked over his shoulder and smiled mockingly at the boy-cardinal.

After his disastrous interview with Poliziano, Michele Marullus had found a sympathetic and supportive patron in Lorenzino, and had gathered about him other Greek scholars, refugees from Constantinople who, Angelo said, had the arrogance to believe that, just because they were born on the same soil as the ancient Greeks, had a better knowledge of the ancient tongue than an Italian could ever have. Angelo, the first Italian to hold the Chair of Greek, naturally disputed this. He kept his face averted as Marullus, Lascaris and the rest walked past him in the train of Lorenzino.

Wearing the ceremonial half-armour of a man-at-arms, Marullus grasped the hilt of his sword in its scabbard in such a way that it stuck out behind him. As he passed close to Angelo, he turned suddenly as if he had been called from behind and succeeded in grazing Poliziano on the thigh.

He turned back, his eye glinting, obviously expecting to find Angelo drawing his sword; but Angelo carried no sword and Marullus noticed it for the first time.

'Professor!' he said, making much of his authentic Greek accent. 'Have I hurt you? A thousand apologies!'

'I think you will find I am immortal, Marullus.'

'Ah, even Achilles had his heel and Hercules his poisoned tunic.'

'I trust the tip of your sword is not as lethal as your tongue.'

Marullus stared at him through heavy-lidded, insolent eyes and then abruptly moved on.

Pico cut his way hurriedly through the crowd. 'Are you hurt?' he asked Angelo.

'Just a graze.' Angelo was lifting up his robes and inspecting the wound. 'But it might be poisoned.'

Pico laughed merrily. 'Why do you always expect the worst?' He shielded his eyes against the sun. 'What's Lorenzino doing?'

Having reached the horses, Lorenzino had now doubled back to confront Piero and his wife. 'How is it that the city fountains are flowing with wine?' he shouted, 'if not that your father stole our patrimony? And as for you, madam, your supercilious Roman airs do not suit our climate!'

'Now, now!' said Scala, thoroughly agitated.

Older members of the Vespucci family, assisted by Ficino, calmed Lorenzino down and encouraged him to leave with what dignity he had left. Those remaining glanced at each other, and each man's eyes said the same thing: that this would not have happened had Lorenzo been here. Angelo moved swiftly to Piero's side and counselled him in a low voice, after which Piero announced that all would be leaving, to go into the city for a reception at the Palazzo de' Medici. Trounced by this manoeuvre, the Pierfranceschi took another road back to the city and did not attend the banquet at the palazzo.

The cardinal's train was so long that he had almost entered Florence before the end of it had left Fiesole. This mighty and splendid procession, including elephants from Lorenzo's menagerie, made its way to the Palazzo della Signoria through streets thronged with cheering crowds.

The Florentines stayed up all night to celebrate the accession of their first cardinal, dancing to musicians who played in squares by the light of bonfires, lubricated by the wine flowing out of the public fountains. Friars walking amongst the crowds made plain their disapproval. A church run by princely cardinals rich enough to turn water into wine was a church requiring purification and renewal!

In the palazzo, dining alone with just a few companions in his chamber, Lorenzo heard about the events at the Badia and sent an order that the Pierfranceschi brothers and their creatures were not allowed to enter Lorenzo's part of the palazzo – ever. Growling, he pushed his trencher away and said he had no appetite.

59 JANUS TIMES
1492

DURING THIS TIME OF BANQUETS, SAVONAROLA FASTED. It was Lent and he preached daily to a crowd, now said to number fifteen thousand, who looked on his increasingly gaunt frame as that of a new Jeremiah.

Lorenzo, no stranger to self-flagellation of the body, wanted no scourges for the soul; ignoring fiery preachers, he had the musicians and monks of San Lorenzo perform the chants of our forefathers. While most of Florence heard prophecies of tumult in the city and blood in the streets, we, the Mediceans, listened to music most divine, the hymns of our ancestors ringing in the roof of San Lorenzo's nave, resonating in eternity, one pure note after another, the cleansing, purifying teaching of Our Lord sung in human voice at its most sublime.

'*And there will be tumult in the city, tumult outside the city, tumult in the piazza, tumult in the palace, tumult for forty hours, tumult for eleven hours, tumult for twenty-four hours. Evils worse than evil most evil.*' Thus roared the Dominican, Fra Silvestro, at the Duomo.

We heard a new mass by Ockegenheim.

'*Blood will be everywhere. There will be blood in the streets, blood in the river; people will sail boats through blood, lakes of blood, rivers of blood…*' Thus fulminated Fra Domenico at Santa Maria Novella. '*Two million devils are loosed from hell because more evil has been committed in the past eighteen years than in the preceding five thousand.*'

In San Lorenzo we listened to the music of Heinrich Isaacs and felt our hearts melting in that surrender of the soul which is love of God. My eyes would fasten on the paintings, not the new ones venerating Man, but old ones of the Holy Virgin against a sky of burnished gold. I wanted to reach out to the certainties of the past, the piety of the artists, the virtue of the governors, the devotion of the poets. The future – as predicted by the soothsayers – was becoming a source of deep fear. I wanted to remove the clever hands from mechanical clocks; I wanted to take the gnomons from all dials, to snuff out the calendar candles and arrest the sand in hour glasses; I wanted the heavenly spheres to stop in their orbits and for the sun itself to become fixed, because something terrible was coming.

These were queer times, Janus times. Pico had bought and moved into a villa on the slope of Fiesole just above Angelo. This proximity allowed one to run to the other, even in his night clothes, when some interesting fact had been discovered in his reading. Indeed, Pico had a path cut down through the woods so as to enter our villa through the garden and save five minutes on the road. Often they read together, Pico standing at a lectern, Poliziano chin in his hands at a desk. You would think it the ideal of conviviality, but sometimes during the meals they shared they could come close to blows over Savonarola, each shouting at the other to wake up and see the truth. Then they would return to the study and their work on Aristotle.

Angelo was also engaged in translating Greek medical texts with Pier Leone, intent on finding a cure for Lorenzo. Pier Leone's treatment for Lorenzo's gout was simple and wholesome: Lorenzo went regularly to the sulphur baths, but for the rest of the time he kept warm and dry, ate no pears and swallowed no grape pips. The gout was not cured thereby, but the inflammation was reduced; the main cause for concern now was that strange, creeping fever. So he and Poliziano scoured the works of ancient physicians looking for knowledge deeper than the 'necromantic cures and potions' favoured by some of his contemporaries.

'We have restored the ancients in our arts and letters,' Poliziano told Lorenzo. 'Why not medicine? I am bringing the works of Galen and Hippocrates out of Greek. But, as with all these things, knowledge is of no use if it is not practical. Pier Leone has gathered many ideas from these pages. Lorenzo, permit us to try some cures advised by the ancients.'

Lorenzo agreed with the theory but was cautious about being the subject of any experiment. But his son, Piero, lent his weight to Poliziano's arguments: everything must be tried which might effect relief if not a cure. At last Lorenzo relented and agreed.

'Shall I tell Pier Leone, then, to obtain the ingredients?'

'If that is your wish,' Lorenzo sighed, falling back on his pillows. Although he was in great pain, he was not expected to die. According to Pier Leone, gout does not kill and fevers may be cured. Indeed, the thought would not have been in our heads but for those awful words of the Friar, 'Within a year ...' Eight months had elapsed. As Ficino said, it sometimes seems with prophecies that, having been uttered, they must happen. But if that is so, what is the difference between a prophecy and a curse? One would reply, why, it is the intention of the speaker. In which case, Savonarola's prediction was a curse.

Lorenzo, however, ignored it. He said that his illness was a blessing for it had given him the opportunity to spend time with what he loved best: the Tuscan poets and poetry itself. Each evening we took it in turns to read to him and, just as the men around the deathbed of Cosimo had formed the Platonic Academy, here the School of Poetry was being reborn. Angelo Poliziano, Cristoforo Landino, Naldo Naldi, Girolamo Benivieni – these men were the setting for the gem that was the real poet among them: Lorenzo himself.

60 LORENZO IN HIS BATH
1492

ANGELO HAD BEEN DEPUTED TO BE LORENZO'S ATTENDANT poet at bath time, but with Lorenzo wanting a bath with increasing frequency to ease the pain in his joints, one day I was called away from the printing house to substitute for Poliziano. Miscomini was indulgent, as was everyone when it came to Lorenzo.

I found Lorenzo in his chamber, soaking in a steaming three-quarter barrel, only his head and shoulders showing. 'Ah, Tommaso, good,' he said, and nodded towards the reading lectern. I crossed to it and found that the manuscript thereon was the *Four Books of Architecture* by Leon Battista Alberti, written in his own, fine hand. As Lorenzo soaked in his tub, his great head turbaned in silk, I read from the master who had been a friend of Lorenzo's father and whom Lorenzo had known when he was a boy, a man who, in extolling the architecture of the ancients, had inspired our age.

Lorenzo squinted at me, sometimes nodding, sometimes sighing at Alberti's ideas and expressions. Sometimes he asked me to repeat a line, three or four times, so that he could fix it in his memory. I felt like a conduit, a transmitter of ideas from one great mind to another. When I came to the end of the chapter,

Lorenzo said, '*Basta!*', as if Alberti were rich food to be had in moderation. And then he stood up, water falling from him, to be towelled dry by servants and helped to step back into the world of pain.

Although he no longer enjoyed any sport, he retained the physique of an athlete. Only the swollen joints, reddened by the hot water, betrayed his illness. He was an original, black-haired Tuscan. When so many Florentines were fair Lombards, Lorenzo stood naked, brown-skinned, black-haired, original. Etruscan. The Medici, like the olives, had been born of this soil generation after generation stretching back into antiquity, before antiquity. Original. While invaders had swept in, built castles, called themselves lords, the Medici had farmed in the hills of the Mugello. Bright sons had trained in medicine; brighter ones became bankers. They kept to their hills while the so-called nobility fought their battles on the plain. When, at last, they came down from the hills, they outwitted those false rulers, not in battle but in business. Lorenzo il Magnifico was our king, but clever enough not to claim such a title. Natural, original, ordained by God – the Medici.

While he dressed, I studied the marble bust of his father, Piero, that stood on a column in the chamber. Sculpted by Mino da Fiesole, it was the likeness of a pseudo-senator of proud chest and firm jaw, far removed from the bed-ridden invalid Piero had been.

'Not as I remember him,' Lorenzo said, noticing my expression. He joined me, holding out his arm for his servant to lace the sleeve. 'I used to be out doors all the time when I was a boy, hunting, at the lists, wrestling. I used to dread coming home, because my mother always made me visit my father in his chamber. He was nearly always in bed. Wan, drawn, in great pain. I never knew what to say. I pitied him, of course, but with all the condescension of youth, presuming, fit as I was, that such a thing would never happen to me. Now I have to suffer my own son coming in, rich with the smell of sweat, to tell me about the game of football he's just won in the streets.' Lorenzo sighed. His dress complete, he settled in a chair and winced as the servant lifted his feet up on to a stool.

'Come and talk to me awhile,' he said, dismissing the servant with a gentle word of thanks. 'What is this I hear about you working in a printing shop? Why didn't you speak to me about it first? If it's money you need – '

'No, Magnifico. I'm trying to acquire the skills, that is all.' And I told him then of my ambition, to print all the works of the Greeks and in editions without error.

'Would you steal another man's vision? Angelo has told me about Aldo Manuzio.'

'But Aldo is old,' I said, then tried to swallow my words.

'Forty-one. Two years my junior and presumably just as close to death.'

Had I made this mistake with the ruler of any other state in our land, I would have walked from that room into the nearest dungeon. But then I would have been more on my guard with any other man; with Lorenzo it was too easy to relax. After frightening me for a little while with a hard, beady stare, he threw back his head and laughed. 'You are right – it is too ripe an age for a new venture. Carry on.'

I told him more of my ambitious plans.

'How much will this cost?'

I plucked a figure from the air, double what I thought he would consider, half of the real cost involved. Lorenzo snorted. 'It's cheaper to be a cardinal. Have you spoken to Lorenzino? He's the only man I know who could afford that kind of sum.'

I said I had not. Lorenzo nodded, grateful for my loyalty.

'But do you approve of the idea, Magnifico?'

He sat back and studied me. If he was reading my soul, it seemed that the script was not clear to him. 'Let us leave it with God,' he said at last. 'When a man chooses the right path, the way opens before him. Do what you have to do, Tommaso. Whatever it is, you will have my blessing.'

I rose to go.

292

'No, stay a while longer. There is something else I wish to discuss: the matter of a new wife. A man should be married or in orders. Anything else is unnatural.'

My mind worked furiously to anticipate his. It was one of Lorenzo's chief occupations, marriage brokering, linking this one to that with the careful deliberation of a spider making a web. He had joined together half of Florence this way. But of what use could I be in his schemes of kinship?

'You will not always have me, you know.'

'Lorenzo...'

'Think on it. You live at the Villa Bruscoli in some strange, celibate ménage à trois. Under my protection. Without me here to stop the gossips, what will happen to your little nest? It is Maria I am concerned about. What is she now, twenty-seven? Beyond any hope of finding a husband, and not only because of her age. Rumours dash like rats from house to house. I want this arrangement made legal. I've spoken to Angelo and he has agreed: it is my wish that you marry Maria Poliziana.'

The blood rushed to my head, my face, my neck. 'She would not have me.'

'Have you asked her?'

'No, there is no need. She plays Clare to Pico's St Francis. It is he who should marry her. It is he, and only he, she would take as a husband.'

'That is not my will. I will speak to Pico and you will speak to Maria. There, that is the end of the matter.'

With that, I was dismissed.

I stayed in my chair.

'What is it? Speak.'

'Things are so clear-cut for you, Magnifico. Do this, do that. You are a master of decision. It is not so clear for me. I walk in the fog of the underworld, seeing ghosts. When I was a boy in Volterra, I met a Greek gipsy who foretold my future, mine and that of my brother, Antonio. Everything he said has come to pass, including the manner of Antonio's death with all the features cut off his face.

What he said to me was, "Everyone you love will die before you."'
I struggled to continue but could not.

'So you will not marry Maria in case she dies?'

'Why repeat happiness only to suffer a repetition of sorrow? I could not bear it.'

'If this curse is true, whether you marry Maria or not is immaterial. Loving her is enough to endanger her.'

'That is it, you see. I do not love her. Cannot love her. Must not love her. I twist the neck of every emotion I feel in her regard. Do not make me her husband.'

'Tommaso, I speak to you as a dying man. Yes, dying. Embrace your fate and accept the will of God.'

Now the tears were spilling down my cheeks. 'You are not dying. You cannot die. Gout does not kill. Just because one mad friar said –'

Lorenzo reached out and held my face. 'I am dying,' he said, 'but not before I have you all standing on your own feet.'

Bourges, August 16th, 1506

I was on my way to the Cathedral, having heard that it has some smiling statues nearly a century old, when, passing between two gabled, timber houses I saw a figure riding past in the market square ahead. Just a glimpse is all I had, of a man on horseback, an Italian, a Florentine, surely, by the straightness of his spine and the tilt of his head, the flowing, waving hair, the jutting chin and lower lip – that Medici lip. A chance resemblance, that was all, but for a moment my head swam, giddy with irrational hope.

I hastened into the square and searched for the rider but he had vanished, as ghosts do. But, ah, for that moment Giuliano lived again and, by the thudding of my heart, so did I. Gain and loss. Whether living or dead, he had vanished and my heart dropped like a dead bird. Why go back to Italy? The past is not there. It lies only in my imagination.

61 A HAIL OF LIGHT
1492

IT WAS AN HOUR BEFORE MIDNIGHT. FEW WERE ABROAD, but almost everyone within the city heard it: a tremendous searing of the sky like a ripping of silk, immediately followed by an explosion in heaven and a mighty crash in the city. Even before the final reverberations had died, people were out on their rooftops and balconies in their nightshirts. By the flashes of lightning that were rupturing the sky, those in houses around the cathedral could see what had happened. Brunelleschi's great dome had only been completed a few years earlier when Andrea del Verrocchio made the ball to crown its lantern. Now the ball was gone and the lantern split almost in half.

Inside the Duomo they found that the roof and vaulting were broken in five places and jagged fragments pierced the brick floor at the very spot where each morning the multitude gathered to listen to Savonarola. Bricks and debris continued to slide through the holes for the rest of the night, sending up clouds of dust. In the surrounding houses people found themselves walking on rubble that had flown through the air: it was a miracle that no one had been killed. There was not a man in Florence who did not agree that this was the work of no ordinary thunderbolt but of divine agency, particularly as the weather was fine in those days, without a cloud to be seen in the sky. This was on the fifth of April.

Savonarola had been up late, preparing his sermon for the next day, working hard and in vain to develop the story of Lazarus. Suddenly, according to the brethren, just before the thunderbolt struck, his voice had roared through the monastery like that of the Lord Jehovah: *Ecce gladius Domini!* Behold, the sword of the Lord, swift and sure, over the peoples of the earth.

When he was told about what had happened at the cathedral, and that the pulpit was pierced by many jagged fragments of the roof, he asked, 'In what direction did the lantern fall?'

'It points to the Via Larga,' he was told.

In the Via Larga, Lorenzo was asking the same thing. The next day he had himself carried to Careggi. But the following night, over the hill of Careggi, there were red flames flashing and expiring in the sky, dagger-shaped it was said, jabbing spears of fire, each flame vanishing as quickly as it had appeared, a constantly renewing hail of fiery lights.

I heard about it in the morning, when I stopped off at the bakery on my way to the printing house.

'There was wolves,' said a miller who lived out in the hills. 'Lots of folks heard them, up in the forest, wolves. And those that looked out of their windows to see the wolves saw the sky on fire.'

'Sky on fire?' said the baker, kneading dough with arms like hams. 'Again?'

'Not like the last time,' said the miller. 'This was different: a rain of daggers.'

'Yes, that's it,' agreed a tanner. 'Did you see it yourself then? A rain of daggers, they say. Bloody daggers. And what did that friar call out night afore last? *Ecce gladius Domine*. Wasn't that it? Behold the sword of the Lord. So he's done it again. I tell you, he's a prophet.'

'Or in league with the devil. Difficult to say.' The baker swung the dough round so that it lengthened alarmingly before he caught it, twirled it and threw it down on the table to be kneaded again. 'After all, when the lantern fell, everyone started saying that it was pointing at the Medici house and that was significant.'

'Even Lorenzo said that.'

'But why? Think about it. Didn't all the debris strike the very spot where Savonarola makes his sermons? So who was the sign for? Just because the Friar predicts flaming swords doesn't mean they won't be aimed at him.'

'But all this was on Careggi. And there's another thing. There was a woman at mass at Santa Maria Novella yesterday who went mad, running about screaming she was, saying that the church was being torn down by a raging bull with bloodshot eyes and flaming horns, that it was falling round her ears.'

'Well, you don't have to be a soothsayer to interpret that one.' The baker, with his loaves ready, lifted them on to the long-handled shovel and slid them into the oven. 'It's my opinion that, if we have fire raining on our heads, it's all the fault of that ranter at San Marco.'

'It is the will of God!' said the miller. 'What did the Friar prophesy last Advent? That within the year they will all be dead: Lorenzo, the Pope, the King of Naples. It's coming true, I'm telling you. It's coming true.'

62 IN ONE SENTENCE
1492

WHILE LORENZO WAS ILL, POLIZIANO WAS LIVING AT THE Medici villa on Careggi, I moved back into my own house, which was close to Miscomini's, and Maria lived with Cammilla in the town house. After the interview with Lorenzo, I avoided seeing her. Let time sort the matter out – I had work to do.

I was at the printing house, reading the proofs of an edition of Virgil's *Aeneid*, lost somewhere in book six thereof, when a letter came from Angelo saying he needed to see me urgently. Obtaining leave from Miscomini, I went to Careggi. The house was taut and subdued, the air within sickly with too many contending fragrances. It was April but still winter, as if the land itself was holding its breath. Asking for Angelo, I was directed to Lorenzo's chamber. I entered cautiously, not wishing to disturb the sick man, but Lorenzo was hidden by a large gathering of physicians around his bed. A servant told me that Angelo was in the studiolo and I crossed the bed-chamber to the door of that inner sanctum. I knocked gently and Angelo called me in.

The only man allowed to use Lorenzo's private study, Angelo was lying on the day bed, hands behind his head, staring at the ceiling which was painted with a portrait of the heavens as they were at the time of Lorenzo's birth. He sat up as I entered, looking as if he had not slept for a good while.

'How is Lorenzo?'

'He is better today. Some say he is recovering'

'How are you?'

'In need of company.'

On a pedestal was a marble bust of Lucrezia Donati, the woman who had been Lorenzo's lover and his Beatrice; on a shelf a stack of his favourite books: the Bible, Dante, Leon Battista Alberti, Ficino's translation of Plato. A cabinet held a collection of curiosities to remind him of the breathtaking inventiveness of the Creator; there also some of his favourite treasures, a vase made of porphyry, a bronze statuette of Hercules, an exquisitely carved Roman cameo. This was Lorenzo's sacred place where he came to be himself. The door to the chamber was so constructed that from within the studiolo you could hear everything happening in the main chamber, but in the chamber you could hear nothing from the studiolo. Lorenzo's sanctum was a perfect spy-hole.

'I sit here and listen,' Angelo told me. 'Sometimes I go out, but I can never get near him for physicians and family.'

He told me that each day brought a new physician in a long train of assistants and apothecaries. All were housed in empty rooms and admitted into the chamber at the wish of Lorenzo but against the advice of Pier Leone, who protested that a mixture of theories and treatments could only be detrimental to the patient: Lorenzo should stick to one system only. Lorenzo agreed that such a thing was to be desired, but at the same time he could not offend the dukes and princes sending their best physicians.

Of this contradiction of doctors, some wanted the patient to arise at dawn, some said he should only arise when he woke up, others thought that he should not rise at all. Some said he should have only hot food, others said that all food must be raw. Many were not so much doctors as magicians, brewing strange potions and asking Lorenzo to turn three times in his bed before drinking them. Pier Leone rose up against these and asserted himself. He did not care if they had been sent by King Solomon himself, they were not to be allowed near Lorenzo. He arranged that no one could gain entry to Lorenzo's chamber who did not have a degree in medicine gained at Padua. But even the learned and orthodox had some strange remedies.

'The only thing all these men have in common,' Angelo complained, 'is a single-minded belief in themselves and their cures, which turns the ante-chamber into a rookery, with enraged squawks disturbing the peace.'

Throughout it all, Lorenzo displayed gentle magnanimity, agreeing to take whatever remedy was offered so as not to offend the man offering it. But he stayed in bed, too weak now to rise.

'These learned physicians have taken him off all dairy food and increased his consumption of garlic. Some analyse his humours and find him sanguine; others declare him melancholic. Some recommend carrying him in a litter to the sulphur baths; others say such a journey would kill him. Some administer emetics, others study the consequences. They grind up poppy seed, or mandragora, or extract of willow, or comfrey. One man not only boils silk but blue silk, and makes Lorenzo drink the water. Others consult charts of the heavens and, at the appropriate moment, they make a cordial of ingredients with properties corresponding to the planet Mercury. Some are traditional and with their cups and leeches try to bleed the disease out of the man. The best of them pray. And there is nothing I can do but sit and listen to it all.'

His exhausted head, sunk into his hands, raised at a terrible, grinding, lapidary sound. He went wearily to find out what this madness of medics was doing now. Through the open door I could see something of Lorenzo, propped up in his bed, surrounded by doctors, himself asking what that terrible noise was. Angelo went to him, to explain that Lorenzo di Pavia, a physician who had just arrived from Milan, was pounding precious gems in a mortar – emeralds, garnets, pearls and opals.

'Oh, Angelo! Are you here?'

'I've been here all along, Magnifico.'

Lorenzo grasped Poliziano's hand, wanting to speak to him, but Angelo's feelings, pent up in a heart that had been frozen for days, were suddenly released. He rushed blindly back into the studiolo where he fell on to the bed. I closed the door behind him.

'I can't let him see me like this,' he stuttered. 'Oh, God, do not take him from me!'

Like anything that has been imprisoned too long, once freed his grief was loud and violent. I was glad nothing could be heard of it in the chamber. It was nearly an hour before he could venture out again and this time he sat on Lorenzo's bed and calmly conversed with him. Lorenzo wanted to know where Pico was.

'He is at San Marco. He does not wish to intrude.'

'Send for him. If he will come, I would see him.'

And so it was that, in the evening, Poliziano and Pico sat with Lorenzo, talking, even joking, but the air in the room was a melancholy one, the air of leave-taking. Angelo lay on the bed beside Lorenzo so that he could hear him better.

'That one sentence …' Lorenzo said hoarsely.

'What leads us away from God is desire.'

'That is true. Is that your sentence?'

'No, it is my preamble. Savonarola calls on us to long for God, to be quick with eagerness. But if desire leads us away, then even the desire for God will not take us to God. It could even be the greatest obstruction.'

'Is that your sentence?'

'No. It is this: beware the false self that longs for the true one. The greatest vanity of all is spiritual. That is the antichrist.'

'That was three sentences.' Lorenzo laughed, and coughed up blood.

His frightened companions were ousted by anxious doctors. When Angelo returned to the studiolo, I asked him what the remedy of powdered gems had been.

'It was an *epithema*,' he replied.

'What is that?'

'Is your Greek so poor?'

'*Epithema* means "to lay on",' I replied, stung.

'It is a poultice.' Then he lifted his head, as an animal does to the wind.

'What is it?'

'Nothing.'

There came a sound of someone entering the chamber, an entry which caused a hush amongst the servants and attendants. Angelo went and put his ear to the door.

'Magnifico,' said a dread and familiar voice that carried easily into the studiolo.

Angelo turned and stared at me in disbelief. 'Fra Girolamo!'

It was all I could do to refrain from going out to have my eyes confirm what my ears knew, that in the chamber was Savonarola. Angelo stared at the door with his mouth open.

'Magnifico,' Savonarola continued, 'should it be granted by God that you live, you must be firm in the faith and free from crime.'

'And if it is His will that I die?'

'Accept it willingly.'

'I do accept it, Frate. Nothing will be sweeter to me than death, if it be the Will of my Father. But if it is His will that I live, then my life will always be guided by my religion. As it always has been.'

'You have erred.'

'Who does not? But give me your blessing, Fra Girolamo.'

In a gentler voice, Savonarola gave Lorenzo de' Medici his benediction.

I stared at Angelo. 'Was he invited?'

'Pico. Pico must have persuaded him to come!'

It was a fine, sweet resolution to the years of hostility, brought about by the Count of Concordia.

Savonarola's was the last visit. After that Lorenzo began to bleed from mouth and nose and soon was in a coma so deep that we only knew he lived when someone held a mirror to his mouth and we saw the mist form that is the breath of life.

63 THE DEATH OF LORENZO 1492

DURING THE NIGHT, LORENZO REGAINED CONSCIOUSNESS. Piero was with him, alone except for two servants and a priest who was reciting psalms.

Judge me, O God, and plead my cause against an ungodly nation.

Disturbed by Savonarola's visit, Angelo walked in tight circles in the studiolo, having a dialogue with himself, saying that it is the man who understands his own nature who is close to God. 'Reform starts here,' he said, patting himself on the chest.

O send out thy light and thy truth; let them lead me; let them bring me unto thy holy hill, and to thy tabernacles.

'Get this right and then worry about the rest of the world,' Angelo told himself. 'Those who preach – they want the world to change before they do. It is the wrong way round.'

Yea upon the harp will I praise thee, O God my God.

I went into the upper loggia overlooking the garden, which was as beautiful in moonlight as it was by day, and became lost in my own reflections.

Why art thou cast down, O my soul? and why art thou disquieted within me?

A light breeze ruffled the new leaves in the garden. The day before last it had rained on warm earth and I could smell the rush of greenness in the land and in the mild night air. A nightingale in the holly tree sang of exquisite longing in the soft darkness. In the sky Venus seemed even brighter than usual.

Hope in God…

No, it was not Venus. Planets do not fall, as this star fell, in a shower of light. As I stood staring at heaven there came a silence, a silence so profound that it woke me from my reveries, a silence that is not an absence of sound but the presence of the Divine. The cantor had stopped mid-sentence and everything in the house had become still. Silence descended, as before rain in a wood, except for those liquid trills of the nightingale.

Lorenzo was gone…

Then came another sound, as if in duet with the bird. A sound Greek, ancient, oh, of such fathomless antiquity, an Orphic sound, of pure grief finding its voice. In a mythic keening that seemed to tear the very veils of reality, Angelo Poliziano lamented his lost god.

64 WHERE WAS FICINO?
1492

I AM OFTEN ASKED WHY FICINO WAS NOT AT LORENZO'S deathbed. Angelo Poliziano was there, Pico della Mirandola was there, even Savonarola was there, briefly. But Ficino? He was in his villa higher up the hill of Careggi. As Lorenzo died, Ficino was sitting on his terrace, looking down in sorrow at the Villa Medici below. Circumstances had forced him to find a patron in Lorenzino, and 'all the creatures' of the Pierfranceschi had been banished from Lorenzo's presence.

I do not believe Lorenzo included Ficino in his proclamation, made in acute pain, but Ficino was not sufficiently confident to put it to the test. Theirs had been a touchy relationship, Lorenzo often blasting Ficino for telling him the truth, that the real life is one of contemplation. Lorenzo had a city to run; and though he would have preferred to have been a hermit – or so he said – he was conscientious of the needs of others, which is surely a virtue. 'It is my duty!' Lorenzo had raged at his philosopher.

'It is your desire,' the philosopher had returned.

I believe that Lorenzo wanted Ficino more than anyone at his deathbed, to assure him of the afterlife, of the transmigration of souls. But the constant refrain that came from Lorenzo in his last days was that he wished to cause no trouble to anyone. He took all that was offered and asked for nothing.

65 A DEATH BY DROWNING
1492

I WENT TO THE STABLES AT DAWN, HAVING BEEN GIVEN several messages to deliver in the city. There were several horses steaming under their blankets, the head groom was putting a salve on the scratched flanks of one of them, his assistants cleaning mud off the hooves of the rest. These horses had been ridden in the dark. One of them was Piero's. By the time I returned, a few hours later, I had forgotten about it.

Lorenzo's body had been laid out in his chamber, where a sculptor was applying layers of plaster to the face to make a death mask. I stared down at the corpse and knew that, whatever had constituted Lorenzo, it was not here: it had nothing to do with the body, with that white, frozen face. While priests intoned their prayers, I said a silent, Orphic prayer to aid the travelling soul.

Angelo was with Piero de' Medici, helping to arrange the funeral. All the physicians had left. 'Scuttled away,' said Angelo. 'All of them blaming Pier Leone, who cannot be found.'

'Only the guilty run away,' said Piero. Angelo shot a glance at him but said nothing.

Wherever I went there was whispering, in the kitchen and stables, the garden rooms and cellars; and the word that was passed from man to man was *murder*. Lorenzo, they were saying, had been murdered by his chief physician. That Pier Leone had fled only proved it. I tried to counter the gossip with reason, telling them that there was no point in murdering a man who was dying anyway. They said that the poisoning had been going on for weeks.

Then a man rode into the villa and jumped from his horse, calling for Piero. The physician had been found dead in the well of a villa at San Gervasio. 'It seems he took his own life,' the messenger told Piero, who nodded in silence. The story was that a servant going out to the well to draw water at dawn had found the bucket impeded by something. Getting help and some flaming brands from the fire, she had returned to the well and peered in to see the slippered feet of a drowned man.

When I spoke to Angelo about it, he said that obviously Pier Leone had been unable to live with such an overpowering sense of failure.

I looked at him doubtfully. 'Pier Leone? Killed himself by diving head first into a well? Angelo, that is difficult to believe.'

'Suicide,' Angelo repeated, his eyes dilating as if daring me to contradict him.

It was the first time, the only time, I ever heard Poliziano lie.

Then I remembered the sweating horses I'd seen at dawn, and I made my own assumptions. At the time, everything was such a muddle of rumour and report. I could not work out the whole story of Lorenzo's death to my satisfaction – was it murder? A curse fulfilled? Or was it natural? But I was certain that Pier Leone had been murdered by Lorenzo's son, presumably in revenge for his failure.

Now that I am writing the story down, however, I am troubled once again by the manner of Lorenzo's dying, and I am thinking about that epithema of powdered gems. They say that Lorenzo died of gout, but he did not; he clearly died of a haemorrhage. That poultice, I am certain, was administered internally. Through ignorance or design? Whichever it was, it was the remedy not of Pier Leone but of the physician from Milan. Milan. The physician of Ludovico Sforza. Hindsight is a wonderful thing, and I know now what I did not know then, that Sforza was in league with the King of France who wished to assert his right to Naples. This Lorenzo would have opposed, forcefully and successfully. It was in the interests of Milan that Lorenzo be removed. What queers that theory is that Lorenzo was dying anyway. Or was he? There were signs of recovery in those last days. But then that long fever, which the servants believed was poison, that would surely have taken him.

But let us say that Pier Leone was killed because he knew the truth. If that is so, then he was not killed by Piero de' Medici. Let us say that the assumption I made at the time was false. There could have been other reasons why Piero had been out riding in the night. He could have been trying to outrun his emotions. Or perhaps he had been racing to deliver the news to relatives, or to the Signoria. As I remember, the villa at San Gervasio where Pier Leone was murdered belonged to friends of Lorenzo and Giovanni di Pierfrancesco. 'Ah,' you say, 'you have got me believing the murderer was the Duke of Milan. Now you are casting suspicion on the Pierfranceschi. Were they, then, in league with Milan?' Possibly. They were certainly in league with France. And they stood to gain Florence.

The truth is, Erasmo, I do not know. What I am certain of, however, having relived these days, is that someone did murder Lorenzo. But who would kill a dying man? And why?

66 THE FUNERAL OF MAGNIFICENCE 1492

IT WAS AN HOUR AFTER SUNSET AND THE AIR WAS SWEET with the scent of new herbs springing up in the grass. Silent but for their tread on the path came the Company of Zampillo, hooded and robed in white with many torches and tapers, bearing the coffin of Lorenzo the Magnificent. The way from the villa into the city was lined by citizens in black robes come to do Lorenzo honour. The black, the white, the silence, the simplicity, this was the funeral of il Magnifico. The coffin was carried all the way on the shoulders of his spiritual companions to the Church of San Marco, there to rest for the night before the funeral on the morrow at San Lorenzo. And as if God thought we were being too sombre, in the dark sky to the north strange lights began to swell on the horizon, waves of pink, purple, blue and green rising and falling, swaying behind the mountains. Those who believed Savonarola's prophecies hunched into themselves in fear; those who did not gazed at the sky in wonder.

'It's the Aurora Borealis!' said Angelo, familiar with the heavenly phenomenon only from books. 'Here. Now. In Italy! What a miracle! Heaven is weeping light for Lorenzo.'

With the angelic display pulsing in the sky above, the cortege continued its way, each man somewhat diminished in his own esteem by this reminder of the power and splendour of the Cosmos.

As was customary with the Medici, the funeral on the following day took place without much pomp. But what the ceremony lacked in visual splendour, it made up for in music. Plainchant filled the nave and chapels of San Lorenzo as the choir performed a mass by Dufay, interspersed with hymns of Lorenzo's own composition.

The family was led by Piero de' Medici. His pale skin and light brown hair stood out against the black of his costume, making him even more handsome than usual, and magnificent in his solemn dignity. His wife, Alfonsina, was absent, being in confinement. Following Piero was Cardinal Giovanni and their cousin Giulio, along with Lorenzo's youngest son, fourteen-year-old Giuliano, he who had been fed on the milk of my wife. Fourteen years, and it seemed like yesterday. These young men walked with the poise of those who have been trained to dance a pavan. I had known them as boisterous children always ready to play a prank, prone to tantrums, scrapping with each other. But on this day the sons of Lorenzo walked like knights.

The choir began to sing a new piece, a specially-composed elegy. The music began simply with two lines weaving, but then more lines entered and the sound began to billow through the church. I did not notice him at first, that fine tenor within the choir, but then his voice began to rise, to leave the swelling music and follow its own line, standing out against the rest as a bird in a blue sky, floating on the up-draught of grief. As lonely as Orpheus mourning his lost wife, Angelo Poliziano sang his elegy to Lorenzo, set to music by the Flemish master, Heinrich Isaacs. If he had borrowed the strange metrical scheme from the ancients, I know not from what source. I had never heard its like before. I believe, for once, he sang from the heart as moved, unconcerned about antique models, and the song was the song of fountains and waterfalls, of lonely hillside streams trickling over rocks, of rain on city pavements and the sea washing on the shore. It was a song of tears, and Poliziano wept as he sang.

The laurel tree lies struck by lightning. The lyre and voice of Phoebus, which once rang out sweetly, have now grown silent.

The climax of his passion was in that last line: the lyre and voice of Phoebus have now grown silent. In accordance with the Laws of Poetry, his meaning was neither literal, allegorical nor symbolic, but all three together. He referred to Lorenzo, of course, but most of all to the death of poetry itself. And in realizing this, I suffered the anagogic meaning – the highest level of meaning which trembles in your sinews and becomes part of your being. I put my face in my hands and wept. This was too great a death to bear.

Thus Magnificence was buried to a song of ravishing sadness.

67 HOW TO BE A SYCOPHANT
1492

WITHIN THE CITY WE HAD TO ACCUSTOM OURSELVES to referring to a twenty-one-year-old for our authority. The government had hastily declared Piero de' Medici to be one of the Council of Seventy in his father's place and eligible for all offices. Obviously this was arranged by the Medici party, but the other factions – and there were many of them – began to wax in strength, and it would not be true to say that grief at Lorenzo's death was universal. Not then, at that time. Too many saw it as an opportunity for power. Almost at once enemies of the Medici such as the Pazzi were seen walking abroad again, trailing their ambition like fine gowns.

After a few weeks had passed and Piero had settled in, I went to see him about my plans to set up a printing press. In the sala, in Lorenzo's chair, at Lorenzo's table, sat the son who had been born with a look of disdain, the watermark of his mother's family, the Orsini, visible through the weave of his nature.

'What can I do for you, Tommaso?' he asked, not as Lorenzo would have asked, leaning forward, interested and concerned. 'What can I do for you?' he asked, making it clear by his tone that I was interrupting him. My long-rehearsed argument for a reliable printer in Florence died within me, shrivelling to nothing.

'I came to ask, Magnifico,' I said to this man ten years my junior, 'what I can do for you.'

His eyes narrowed as he smiled, gratified by my question. 'What did you do for my father? I always wondered.'

'Oh, anything he needed that I was capable of: carrying messages, reporting…'

'Your wife was my brother Giuliano's wetnurse.'

He said this as if it confirmed my status as a contadino, someone from a village who hung about the palazzo like a fly, forgetting that my Pazzi wife had been called upon at the direst hour when no suitable village woman could be found. I had allowed it because Elena wanted it, distraught as she was at the stillbirth of our son; because Lorenzo had begged it of me. I had allowed it because of my love for them both.

'She was, Magnifico.'

This boy whom I had helped Angelo to raise and educate seemed not to know me but for this one fact: or was he uncomfortable in the presence of one who had watched him grow through a troubled childhood, not always behaving in a way he would like to be remembered?

'I have no need of a wetnurse,' he said. His secretary and page both laughed.

'I have no wife to offer the service.'

'I believe you are unable to write following an injury to your arm.'

'I can write, but not with the beauty of a scribe.'

'So, a crippled widower. I'll let you know if I need anything from you.'

I left the sala to the sound of laughter, vowing I would never serve Piero de' Medici in any capacity whatsoever if I could help it.

I returned to work at Miscomini's. The printing of Ficino's translation of Plotinus was almost complete when Ficino came into the shop with a new version of the preface, revised to include an address to Piero de' Medici which implored him to be a rock-like support to Plato and Plotinus as they came into the light. Did Jesus name the apostle Peter after a rock with a sense of irony? Did Lorenzo name his son from a similar intuition? Piero de' Medici was as rock-like, as trustworthy as quicksand.

Having read Ficino's new preface in his presence, I looked at him with raised eyebrows. He shrugged. That was how it was then, amongst members of the Platonic Academy: raised eyebrows, shrugs, glances exchanged, all in silence. Each man kept his doubts and fears to himself. It was not safe to do otherwise.

The exception was Poliziano, who somehow had persuaded himself that Piero, being the product of his education, was not only a man in whom we could all have faith, but one who was tantamount to being his own son. He attended Piero like a doting father and missed no opportunity to offer him advice, the kind of advice Lorenzo would have given him himself.

Piero rejected his advice in favour of that of friends of his own age. Things would have slipped into decadence had not God intervened. Fra Girolamo Savonarola, he whom Piero had once asked Lorenzo to banish, he who had refused to visit the Palazzo de' Medici, now came frequently to offer Piero the paternal support he lacked. And Piero accepted it. It was a strange sight, the pale young man beside the hook-nosed friar with skin the colour of figs. But it became a familiar sight, and Angelo looked on in horror. This association between the Friar and Piero could not be allowed. Piero was heir to his father, to the work of the Platonic Academy and to the School of Poetry. He must not be swayed from that. Angelo, alone among us, gave voice to his fears. Savonarola, he said, was the antichrist who would destroy everything we had worked for. Since Angelo was deluded in his opinion of Piero, we considered him deluded in this, also. After all, when in August of that year Pope Innocent died, why would anyone listen to a university professor while we had a prophet in our midst? Savonarola had predicted the death of the Pope, the King and Lorenzo himself. Two out of three was enough to prove this man's powers of foreknowledge. That King Ferrante did not die for another two years was a fact we all overlooked, too distracted now by a rising crescendo of prophecies being shouted from the pulpit of San Marco.

68 THE IMMORTAL SOUL PACKS A PUNCH 1492

THERE WAS A MUSICIAN CALLED CARDIERE, A FAVOURITE of Lorenzo who had often entertained him by singing to the lute. One day he came to see Angelo in great agitation.

'I have seen il Magnifico,' he said. 'In a dream I saw his ghost. He was naked but for a ragged black mantle thrown over his body and he ordered me to warn his son that in a short time he will be banished from Florence, never to return.'

Angelo and I glanced at each other. There was something compelling in Cardiere's story, and to see the genuine fright in the man was to believe him.

'You must go to Piero at once,' said Angelo.

But the poor man seemed more scared of the living than the dead. He went away, saying he would do as Angelo had advised, but he did not look as if he had the courage. Sure enough, a few days later Cardiere returned, this time with a bruise on his ashen face the size and colour of a kidney. Had he been in a street fight? Set upon by bandits? He shook his head, his chin trembling.

'At midnight the ghost came to me again. Lorenzo himself, I assure you, though dressed as he was never dressed in life. Naked, but for a ragged mantle. But it was Lorenzo, with that stern, watchful face. And... And... I was not asleep when he entered my chamber.'

'How can you be sure?'

'I put my hand into the candle flame and burned it. Look...' He showed us the red weal.

'How did Lorenzo enter? Did he open the door or pass through it?'

'Opened it. I heard its usual creak. Heard his footsteps on the floor. Lorenzo himself. I felt his breath on my face. As real, as physical, as you. "Cardiere!" he said, "you have failed me. You have not done as I asked!" I was shrinking backwards, trying to escape him, but he caught hold of my night shirt and pulled me from the bed so that I stood before him. Oh …!' Here the poor man, shaking like an aspen, had to be steadied by us and encouraged to continue.

'He shouted at me to do as I'd been told, to go to Piero. And then he struck me. Look! See that bruise? It's from the hand of Lorenzo. His hand, I tell you, hard and stinging. Whack! Round the face. I fell backwards, stunned. When I opened my eyes again, he had gone.'

At this wonder, Angelo explored the man's bruise with his fingers. It was livid and tender and Cardiere winced with the pain. Of all the tales we had heard in our lives, none was as strange as this, that a ghost could strike flesh and bruise it.

'A vision most physical – and not much in keeping with the nature of Lorenzo,' Angelo said, 'and yet I trust you and therefore must believe you. You have to do as you've been instructed. Go to Piero at once. He's at the villa at Careggi.'

Whimpering yet nodding, Cardiere left us to go to Careggi. As it happened, he met Piero on the road, so he stopped the entourage and told his patron as boldly as he could what had occurred. Piero de' Medici looked shocked at first but then broke out in laughter. His derision was taken up by his entourage, who scorned and mocked poor Cardiere. Piero's chancellor, Pietro Dovizi, demanded to know why Lorenzo should appear to a lute player and not to his son himself – a reasonable question, though not the manner of its asking. One thing you could say truly of Lorenzo was that, though he had power, he used it carefully and with respect. Piero was acting like the spoilt scion of any great family. He seemed to have forgotten everything he had been taught from the ancient authors.

69 POETRY AND PHILOSOPHY UNDER THREAT 1492

WE WERE SITTING IN THE SHADE OF THE LOGGIA IN THE walled garden of the Rucellai on a drowsy afternoon. I was watching lizards, not too interested in the discussion Poliziano was having with Ficino while we waited for other members of the Platonic Academy to arrive. Whether *ecphrasis* means a literal description of a picture in words, or a literal interpretation of words in pictures was not something Ficino could answer. He thought perhaps it could be interpreted both ways. Angelo agreed and told him that just as we know about the works of Apelles by full descriptions in certain books, so pictures could be used to illustrate the words of authors and, perhaps one day, be all that is left of them.

My eyelids began to droop. On the threshold of dreams, the tread of feet on the gravel path became the march of approaching soldiers, but then Lorenzino's greyhound laid its paws on my lap and thumped its tail against my legs. I woke up to see the Pierfranceschi arriving through the laurel hedges with several men in their train, recognising the round, pink face of Amerigo Vespucci, the slight figure of Zenobio Acciaiuoli, and the tanned complexion and coarse hair of Michele Marullus. I made room on my bench for my friend Zenobio who had been a fellow student of mine at some of Angelo's classes. He had been in Rome and we had not seen each other for a year or more.

'*Salve,*' he said, settling down beside me and declining a glass of wine from a Rucellai servant. 'Are you well, Tommaso?' he asked, while everyone else was greeting the Pierfranceschi.

'As well as can be expected, given the times.'

'Better times are ahead, believe me,' he said. He exchanged a smile of greeting with Poliziano. 'Angelo seems recovered.'

My friend was not a factional man and, despite being a cousin of the Pierfranceschi and living in the villa of Lorenzino, was quite able to sympathise with anyone bereaved by the loss of il Magnifico, especially if he were a favourite tutor of his.

'Why, what lies ahead?' I asked.

In reply, Zenobio inclined his head slightly towards Lorenzino. 'Rule by the just,' he whispered.

'Come away, Mithras,' said Giovanni di Pierfrancesco, tugging on the collar of the greyhound which now had its head in my lap. 'Sorry,' he said to me, and smiled in a way that made my heart leap even though I have no inclinations of that kind. Twenty-five years old now, he had lost none of his boyish beauty, whereas his brother was beginning to thicken at the waist and neck.

Angelo, relaxed on this day, was greeting everyone affably, even Marullus. Marullus, however, returned the greeting without a smile. He may have been born in Constantinople but he was brought up in Ragusa where, I have heard, revenge is a sacred and ancestral custom. When Poliziano had told him his poetry stank, and did so without having read it, he had seeded a complaint in Marullus that he would pass on to his great-grandsons if needs be. Poliziano had since read his poems and modified his opinion. 'They are technically very competent but without heart,' he said, although not to Marullus.

Ficino took up his lyre and struck a chord in the Dorian mode that shook the drowsiness from me. The notes and his soaring voice, amplified and returned by the gentle vaulting of the loggia, called on the Sun to bring health and harmony to the soul. The slumbering garden came to life. The lizards that had darted away with the arrival of the men now came out again. Sparrows hopped towards the singer and stood there, heads cocked to one side. As Ficino sang, the words seemed even to bring the statues in the arbours to life, and the marble Apollo at the end of the cobbled path glowed in the light of that Sun. All enmity must surely vanish, cleansed away by such sweet and plaintive singing. But not for a Dalmatian who considered himself a Greek.

The topic for the day was to be Plato's Myth of the Cave and Marullus offered to recite it for us in the original tongue. Ficino, knowing nothing of the enmity between him and Poliziano, accepted readily. Marullus stood to his full, tall height and, tucking his mass of hair behind his ears, cleared his throat. He stared down at the ground for a little then raised his head, opened his arms, palms upwards, and from memory gave us Plato's words in Plato's language. We listened to the beautifully crisp, percussive rhythms as if we were sitting in the Agora itself.

'Well,' said Ficino appreciatively when Marullus had finished, 'I believe Plato himself has been with us.'

Marullus glanced at Poliziano, as if challenging him, a mere Italian, to match his achievement. Angelo, outdone, looked away.

It was not a contest between equals. In intellect and scholarship no one would have claimed that Marullus was a match for the great Poliziano, not even Marullus himself. But both had their Achilles' heel. Marullus suffered as all refugees from Greece suffered, feeling foreign in their adopted land and, for a soldier such as he, ashamed to have lost their patria to the Turks. His own family deserved no shame; his father and uncles had fought on for ten years after the fall of Constantinople and had died in the last battle. Nevertheless, he felt as all Greek scholars felt, looked down upon and scorned by the Italians. No Greek can abide being a recipient of charity, especially that of the errant Latin Church. Marullus and his fellow Greeks were querulous, proud, uncomfortable guests in our land.

For his part, Angelo was aware that, while his opponent could trace his ancestry back to Argive kings, he himself came from a line of haberdashers and cobblers. He had not studied at a university – in the eyes of Marullus, the Studio at Florence did not count as a university – and had taught himself Greek. Having inherited the pacifist nature of his father, he carried no weapon, while Marullus was trained to take the head off an enemy with one clean swipe of his sword. In his own eyes, the contest was unequal and, no matter how great his intelligence, he was not and never could be a match for this olive-eyed son of Mycenae who had the blood of kings in his veins. Apart from anything else, Marullus was muscular and handsome, while Poliziano had lost his shape to a sedentary life and the heavy wine of his own vineyard.

Ficino began to expound the Myth of the Cave, saying that life is a delusion, a play of shadows on a wall, and that when men begin to comprehend the truth, they find its light painful and prefer the shadows.

'One cannot even look on the physical sun without being blinded,' said Lorenzino.

'That is because we look with eyes made of earth. To look on the sun we must become the Sun and gaze with solar eyes.'

Lorenzino once said that he was the Lorenzo Lorenzo wanted to be, meaning that he had the life of leisure and study that Lorenzo had so craved. Now he was keen to become the Lorenzo he wanted to be: the true successor to il Magnifico. It was like having Lorenzo in our midst again, appreciating what Ficino had to say and asking intelligent questions, but the afternoon was spoiled by the tension between Poliziano and Marullus. When Ficino finished expounding the myth, Marullus said that Plato's cave was an apt metaphor for 'those Florentines who wish to stay in the dark, under the rule of Piero.' This made Angelo jump as if pricked. The eyes of everyone avoided the embarrassed Poliziano, apart from those of Marullus, who watched him closely. I thought he must have been the kind of boy who dismembered animals out of mere curiosity.

Since the death of Lorenzo, we had taken to meeting here in the Rucellai garden and were finding it increasingly difficult to keep our minds on philosophy. With men such as Bernardo Rucellai, Bernardo del Nero and Lorenzo Tornabuoni gathered together, the temptation to discuss matters of government was often too great. Feeling that the Myth of the Cave had been explained to everyone's satisfaction, Lorenzino asked Bernardo Rucellai how Piero was faring in Rome, where he had gone with his brothers in an extravagant and glorious cavalcade to greet the new pope.

'How does he find Borgia?' he asked.

'Do you mean His Holiness Alexander VI?'

'Yes, Borgia.'

We all laughed. Any man of reason, knowing Borgia's reputation, and the story of how he had swung himself into the papal chair after the death of Innocent, gagged on his official name.

'I fear for Piero, and for Cardinal Giovanni,' said Bernardo del Nero, 'both of them so young.'

Lorenzo Tornabuoni flashed an affectionate smile at this man over seventy.

'You think everyone seems young to me?' asked del Nero. 'Well, perhaps it is true. But those two are unseasonably young. *Too* young for the times, *too* young for the task, which is to keep Florence safe.'

In the narrow glance of Lorenzino you could see that he did not so much fear for his cousin, Piero, as hope for his failure. 'I hear he has upset Ludovico Sforza. It is madness,' he said, his voice rising in irritation, 'utter madness to alienate Milan.'

Sforza had wished all the heads of states to present themselves to the new pope simultaneously, but Florence, supported by Naples, had insisted on individual presentations. It was a small matter of vanity, but to upset Milan was to upset the alliance, not something anyone with a modicum of statecraft would have contemplated. Lorenzino suffered the hot iron of frustration, that he could see so clearly what was to be done and had not the power to do it.

Angelo sat forlornly with his chin in his hands. He had been surprised and alarmed when Piero had left him behind, and not taken him as his counsellor and advisor in the embassy to Rome. Now Piero was falling prey to the very people Angelo would have warned him against: his Orsini relations, allies of Naples.

Every Florentine shared the delusion that a new pope was bound to be an improvement on his predecessor, but a month after the accession of Borgia, who to win the election had indulged in blatant and incredible acts of simony, we were sore pressed to maintain this fantasy. Indeed, we almost grieved the passing of that rogue, Innocent. For all his faults, he had at least been recognisably human. In Rodrigo Borgia we seemed to have been plunged back into the days of the Emperor Nero, if not Caligula. Tales had come from Rome of mules laden with bullion going through the city to buy the votes of cardinals, and even if such tales were not true, we could be certain that this election had not been won by spiritual merit. It troubled us that our young Giovanni's first duty as a cardinal had been to vote for the new pope. He was just a boy tossed in a tempest of scheming. Despite imperative messages from his brother in Florence, Giovanni had given his allegiance to Ascanio Sforza. Then he changed his mind and opted for Piero's choice. Then he changed it again and gave his backing to Rodrigo Borgia. Piero had written to him in anger and despair. Giovanni had replied in wretchedness, saying he wanted to be out of Rome. Now Piero was in Rome with him, doing his best to establish good relations with Pope Alexander and trying to steady his unsettled brother.

Lorenzino, however, considered that Borgia had virtues as well as vices, and that magnanimity was one of them. 'Let us make the best of it,' he said. 'I have heard that he intends to decorate his apartments with scenes of ancient Egyptian wisdom.'

'Is that true?' Ficino, who could only equate such artistic taste with philosophical awareness, was intrigued.

'Obviously he does not share the rigorous orthodoxy of Innocent. As for the Inquisition – well, he is a Spaniard himself and has it under his control. We should apply to him to release Giovanni Pico from the charge of heresy.'

This idea was well received by all of us.

'Angelo?' said Lorenzino. 'Do you agree?'

Poliziano, who was lost in thought, came out of his reverie. 'What? Oh yes, of course. An excellent idea.' As the idea penetrated, he woke up to it fully. 'Really, a most excellent idea. Will you write to His Holiness?'

'Would it not be better coming from Piero? He is, after all, our first citizen.'

Increasingly prone to indwelling, Angelo was oblivious to the test he was undergoing, but passed it anyway. 'No, it would be better coming from you.'

Lorenzino smiled gratefully at this expression of confidence. Angelo lapsed back into private thought, and as the conversation returned to the new pope and the intrigues of Rome, he stared vacantly at the ground.

'Since the death of Lorenzo,' said Bernardo Rucellai, 'the country has become unstable. If the triple alliance should break, if, as it seems, Piero will form a new alliance with Naples and break from Milan... You do not have to be a prophet to see the future.'

'France will move on Naples,' said Lorenzo Tornabuoni, 'unopposed except by us.'

The company murmured in alarm. For several months Savonarola had been prophesying that the King of France was going to come like a new Charlemagne; recently he had given a terrifying sermon in which he had predicted the destruction of Italy, with especially severe punishment for Tuscany. Now it was coming to pass, and we puny fellows discussed ways to avert the terrible force of fate.

'We must not oppose the French,' said Lorenzino simply. 'Why oppose them? Embrace them, make them welcome and send them on their way. This is Naples's war, not ours.'

There was wisdom in this but such an action would require us to overrule, even depose Piero. It seemed that all men of power, both within the city and without, were looking for ways to unseat the new rider of Florence who, having got into the saddle earlier than expected, now seemed to be bouncing about and losing control of the horse. To the Pierfranceschi and those around them, it seemed preferable and right that their Lorenzino and not Piero be in charge of Florence. For the academy, after all, it would be an advantage to have one of our own good men as civic leader and principal citizen. But to maintain goodness and not be hypocrites, we could only hope that Piero fell from his horse by himself and did not require a push. That was the view of most of us, held privately and certainly not expressed out loud in a meeting of the Academy, but it was not that of Angelo, who stayed loyal to Piero.

'I will speak to him on his return,' he said, 'and see if I cannot get him to change his mind. It is of course the Orsini behind all this. Rome is a pit of scorpions.'

Ficino, unhappy at the direction the meeting was taking, compromised and switched the discussion to Plato's *Republic*. The men grew animated in argument as to the best form of government. It was of course generally agreed that Plato's own preference for government by the wise was our own, and it went without saying that we were the wise. But how, in practical terms, that could be applied to Florence occupied us for an hour or more. Government by the people was out of the question, since they never lift their noses from the trough. No, it had to be a council of the wise, but should it defer ultimately to one man? A man, say, such as Lorenzo di Pierfrancesco? This was not openly proposed: it did not have to be.

I gazed at Lorenzino, wondering what he would be like at the helm. That he would be preferable to Piero, I had no doubt, but a man tends to change once vested with power. I could easily imagine his irascible nature translating into tyrannical fury. The skin of his face was folding with time and over-indulgence, his eyes disappearing under heavy lids, but with Giovanni by his side, sweetening his mood and captivating both the people and foreign potentates: it could work. But would Lorenzino consult his council of the wise wisely? Even if its decisions contradicted his own? I doubted it. The best we could hope for in Lorenzino was the Lorenzo he wanted to be: the new Magnifico.

'There is another way, one never open to Plato,' said Ficino gently. He showed us a recent publication of Savonarola, a manifesto for the establishment of a Christian state. It read well, if you read it only in part, which Ficino did.

'A theocracy,' said Lorenzino. 'Plato did cover that.'

'But not a Christian one: that was beyond his imagination.'

'I've read this,' said Angelo, taking the pamphlet. He thumbed through it and, finding the passage he was looking for, he stood to read it out loud, in such a good imitation of Savonarola's rhetorical gracelessness that we were laughing even as we shrank inwardly from the meaning of the words.

'I call upon the leaders of the city to drive the poets away and burn their books!' he cried, thumping the back of his chair and then shaking his finger at us. 'Anyone trained in pagan poetics is damned to perdition. Perdition, I tell you! They will burn in hell for all eternity. For poetry is evil, and the source of its evil is that very beauty which poets adore.'

'That's not in there,' said Zenobio, taking the pamphlet from him. His face paled as he read the words Poliziano was dramatising.

'And what is worse than poetry but philosophy?' Angelo cried, still acting the part of the vehement friar. 'The one among them that is chief of this age, who sings so sweetly of divine love, is guilty of moral abuse and the spread of paganism.' Here Angelo bent down and frowned into the face of Marsilio Ficino. Ficino took the pamphlet from Zenobio and re-read the passage which he had not previously supposed to refer to himself.

'This,' said Angelo, subsiding back into his chair, 'is the friar who has the ear of Piero. We cannot be complacent.'

Ficino swallowed. 'Moral abuse? Does he mean me?'

'A corrupter of boys, O Socrates.'

Ficino read the passage again, breathing heavily. 'The Frate is a good man,' he said at last. 'I have no doubt that all his thoughts are directed towards the good. But there are things he does not understand, poetry and philosophy chief amongst them. If Giovanni Pico is not with us today, it is because he is with Savonarola, trying to correct these very faults. All will be well.'

'So you would appreciate government of the city by such a man?' Lorenzino asked guardedly.

'Of course not! I would appreciate a state governed according to Christian principles, but not by a preacher. A man should keep to his role.' To quieten his own spirits as well as ours, Ficino took up his lyre again and re-tuned it to the Hypolydian mode. As he sang an invocation to Venus, I gazed out at the peaceful garden, its hedges of laurel and myrtle, its rose bushes all humming in the heat of late summer. I gazed on it and listened to the voice of Ficino, our Apollo, singing an Orphic hymn, ancient, pristine, a holy hymn prefiguring Christ. This wide view of Christianity as a faith spanning all history thrilled as it always thrilled, making the heart pulse with glory. Moral abuse! Who could say such a thing of our Ficino? Only a man who did not understand.

Savonarola's views on poetry and poets were circulating widely. People of simple faith, unable or unwilling to think for themselves, gained much strength from them. I had seen Poliziano challenged in the street by a fruit seller who told him his work was godless. 'What do you know of my work?' asked the surprised professor. 'That it is godless!' replied the hard-faced, self-assured man who wore a crucifix over his apron. The beautiful, open mind of the city that had fostered so much talent was closing. There was no argument with these followers of the Friar: they had the holy book as their authority, and that was that.

Angelo was disturbed. He wanted to do battle but, without Lorenzo, felt too vulnerable for the task. Nonetheless he fought back from the podium at the university. In his introduction to the new academic year, he argued on behalf of the philosophers and poets, of whom, he said, he was neither. 'I am merely a grammarian, a philologist, and therefore am not defending myself.' These people, he said, who go about looking into other people's business are like the witches in his grandmother's folk tales, who wear their eyes when they are out and about but when at home remove them. 'They see very well what is wrong with me while being blind to their own faults.'

Philosophy is the wise contemplation of truth, and happy and blessed are the men who practise such contemplation. They behave according to the highest standards and do not pry into the lives of other men. Life is but an empty dream, he said, and all its pleasures transient. All that is immortal of us is our soul, which we must worship since God is our soul. 'God is the mind of man, and mind orders the Universe.'

He told the story of Plato's cave to say that it was natural for those suddenly introduced to the true light beyond the cave to want to rush back into the dark. The course he was introducing was going to be on Aristotle, not the Aristotle of the schools or the Dominicans, the old, mistranslated, misunderstood Aristotle on which so much Christian dogma was founded, but the new Aristotle excavated from the texts by philologists such as Poliziano, Pico and Barbaro.

His introduction was published by us in the Miscomini printing house.

Lyons, August 25ᵗʰ, 1506

We are staying at an inn seemingly full of lively girls, daughters of the inn-keeper. Our young pupils – Boerio's sons – are fascinated by their company and are becoming unruly. While Clyfton averts his head whenever the girls are around, as if by not looking at them he will maintain his vows, Erasmus has assumed the manner of an old uncle and delights in their frivolity. He frequently mentions his age, as if being forty places him beyond desire. 'There, my darling,' he says, 'there, my sweet,' and chucks a pert little chin. The courier stands in the shadows, the light just catching his royal insignia, and watches the girls like a fox.

I go out for a walk in the city of two rivers.

And see the ghost again.

It *was* him, as he was, twenty-four years old, tall, dark, slender. On foot this time, walking alone and dressed in black, he was making his way through the lane of shops over one of the bridges; intent on some business and not distracted by any of the goods on sale, he shouldered his way through the milling Lyonese. I did my best to catch up with him, expecting him to vanish before my eyes, but the closer I came, the more real and tangible he was. My faculty of reason grew hoarse in protest: this could *not* be Giuliano de' Medici. But my soul, believing in miracles, hastened me on until I had only to reach out to touch him. His shoulder was robed in linen, and the flesh beneath it was warm. He stopped, turned. 'You! Tommaso!' His lovely eyes stared at me with that familiar expression. *Simpatico*. Yet I had seen him in a pool of his own blood, rent by twenty-nine thrusts of a dagger. But here he was, whole, resurrected, with no wound at all, and no addition of years.

'Giuliano?' Every fibre in me was shaking.

'Giulio,' he said with a smile. 'His son.'

'Oh! Forgive me. Oh! You have grown into his very image.' The slender one, the prime digit always in company with the big 'O'; one half of the number ten.

He grasped me by the shoulders. 'Tommaso de' Maffei! God has answered our prayers. We thought you were dead. Come, come with me. Come and see Giovanni.'

He took me back to the bishop's palace, where he and his cousin are staying, telling me on the way that Cardinal Giovanni is the papal legate in France and, yes, they had been in Bruges ten days ago. I looked askance at his unostentatious dress. He smiled, reading my thoughts. 'It's better that men do not know who I am.' In the matter of the war between France and Spain, Giulio de' Medici is a spy for Rome.

Cardinal Giovanni, too, has grown into a full adult, but in the image of whom I am not sure. Any family likeness is lost in the fat. He was as surprised as his cousin at what fate has put in their path by our chance encounter. We discussed the many things that have occurred since we last met. I asked about Piero since I had heard nothing of him since his failed attempts to retake Florence. The Cardinal told me that his brother, after a period of dissolution in Rome, had become what he had been born to be: a *condottiere*. 'A soldier, not a banker,' he said. 'He died three years ago, fighting for France, but not in battle. He fell off his horse in a river and drowned.' He appeared unmoved by his brother's early death. In the fourteen years since Lorenzo died, Italy has become a carcass torn apart by contending wolves. While France and Spain battle for her possession, state wars with state, city with city, and even families are riven. The Medici brothers had been fighting on opposite sides.

In the Battle of Ravenna, the Cardinal and Giulio had been captured and imprisoned but had escaped. Loathing the Borgia pope, they had kept away from Rome and spent their time wandering in Germany, but now they are finding in Pope Julius someone more favourable to them and have gained favour; at least,

Cardinal Giovanni has. Giulio seems fated to be his shadow, prevented from office by his illegitimacy. And that is what has made them so excited to have found me.

'Tell me,' Giulio said, 'what you know of my birth. Once my uncle Lorenzo told me that, if it had not been for you, I would have grown up in the foundling hospital. What did he mean?'

Ah, the Mercurial mind, how swiftly it acts. Even before he had finished his question, I had my story in place. Truth? Of course I believe in it. Would I die for it? Obviously not. I could see their intentions and their need. For Giulio to advance in a career of his own, he needs to be legitimised, and he cannot gain it by the good will of Pope Julius alone: he needs proof, witnesses.

So, knowing the truth as I do, the unequivocal truth of his illegitimacy, I bent the facts a little. I told them the story, and it took an hour or more, for I told them the story as fully as I could without taking all night. I went back to that day in Pisa, when we heard that the lady Simonetta was dying, telling them how Giuliano had argued ferociously with Lorenzo, demanding he be allowed to return to Florence, how I had aided his escape by making horses ready, how I had ridden with him through the night. 'And then, when we stopped to rest and water the horses, we lay together under the stars, and your father confessed to me what no one, not even his own brother, knew, which was that he had married in secret and that his wife was expecting a child.'

My breath shortened with this portentous moment as I faced that child, now a man.

'Are you sure?' Giulio asked. 'Giuliano married in secret. Are you certain?'

'In so far as I believed what he told me himself, yes. He had no reason to lie about such a thing.'

'We have enemies in Rome and my illegitimacy is their main weapon against me. It keeps me from gaining any benefice and so I depend always on Giovanni. If you were to tell the Pope what you know, it would change my life and my fortunes. You would be very well rewarded. I promise you, Tommaso, very well rewarded.'

Cardinal Giovanni's protuberant eyes were staring at me. 'We were always told that Giuliano was in love with Simonetta, a romantic story full of tears and sighs.'

'It was a smoke screen. Giulio's mother was of very humble birth and Lorenzo would not have countenanced your father's choice of bride. I am not saying that Giuliano pretended to love Simonetta. He did love her, sincerely, but she of course was married and never meant to be obtainable. She was his lesson in love, arranged by the Platonists to cure him of a cold heart. What they did not know was that he did not have a cold heart. That was the pretence.'

'The truth is better than the story,' said Giulio. 'But how did Lorenzo come to learn of me?'

I told them then of my interview with Lorenzo, the night of the day that Giuliano was murdered, how I delivered this fatal blow to a man already half-dead from grief, that his brother had deceived him and was father of a new-born son. 'There is a son, Lorenzo,' I had said, and Lorenzo had cried out in a grief that was also hope, simultaneously felled and restored by this revelation.

'He took you into the family the next day,' I told Giulio.

'And my mother?'

I shook my head. 'I do not know. I presume her family was paid handsomely to keep the secret, and the secret was kept.'

Giulio sat back in relief and joy, but the Cardinal still leaned towards me.

'Now what of you? How are you here, and in layman's clothes? What became of you after San Marco was sacked?'

Could I tell him, the papal legate? But as I stared at him, unable to speak, I did detect a family likeness. It was in his manner, the sound of his voice. A papal legate, perhaps, but this was the son, the trustworthy son of Lorenzo de' Medici.

'I ran away,' I confessed to him. 'I went to Venice and thence to England, teaching Greek.'

The Cardinal's eyes glowed appreciatively. He remains a disciple of learning. 'But you are still a Dominican?'

I blushed. 'In the eyes of God and the Pope.'

Cardinal Giovanni nodded briefly, rose and went away with his secretary to a private room. When he returned, it was with two letters sealed and impressed with his insignia and addressed to His Holiness Pope Julius the Second. He handed them to me to be delivered in person.

I laughed in fright. 'I cannot go to the Pope!'

'The truth will set you free,' said Cardinal Giovanni. 'For the love you bore my uncle Giuliano, do this for his son, and it will set you free.' He took hold of me. 'You have done our family great service over the years.'

'The library?' I asked, for it is of course the library that binds us more tightly than any other service I have done.

'It is safe, thanks to you.'

'No, to you, my Lord.'

'When Giulio and I are back in Rome, when this business is resolved and Giulio is also a Cardinal, contact us. Whatever you desire that we can give, it will be yours.'

I returned to the inn and found it quiet. Erasmus was sitting reading. 'Where have you been?'

'Out for a walk.'

'What, to Paris and back?'

He did not ask what I had been doing for so many hours, and I did not tell him. I left him to his assumption that I had taken a melancholy and very long stroll with ghosts of the past.

'You missed a wonderful entertainment: the girls sang and danced for us. Why do you avoid them?' he asked.

'They are a distraction and a temptation.'

'Temptation. You? Ha! I believe even Jezebel or Salome would fail to seduce you.' With that, he went back to his book.

70 INTIMIDATION
1493

I DEVISED MANY IMPROVEMENTS IN THE PRINTING PROCESS, all with an eye to beauty, all to be kept to myself until the time was right. Since most of these innovations were in letter spacing, it had been necessary to learn how to compose text. I had everything changed about so that I could work left-handed and then practised hard until my hand could fly from case to stick and back again without my thinking about it, leaving my mind free to concentrate on spelling things correctly backwards, and, sometimes, to dream about how I would do things differently if and when I had my own press.

I was by the door one day, swinging my arms about like a windmill to relieve the muscles, when there was a crash and splinters of wood and shards of alabaster raining down on us. Printers bellowed in shock and pain. My wooden stool lay in pieces beneath a great stone that had been hurled through the window. I ran outside to see who had done this thing but amongst the crowd gathering there was no one who knew, or would say, who the culprit was. When I re-entered the shop I found men stooping over the stone on which was written, *For the heretics.*

'I have had other warnings,' Miscomini confessed. 'I've been told not to publish the Plotinus.'

'Who by?'

He shrugged. 'I don't know. Anonymous letters.' He went among the presses to see if any equipment had been damaged or printing ruined. Apart from some bloodied sheets, and the cuts and wounds on the men that proved superficial, no serious damage had been done. But the men met together and decided between them that the printed sheets of the Plotinus should be destroyed. Miscomini called their bluff, knowing that they could not find jobs elsewhere. But he did announce his intention – and posted up notices to this effect – that, henceforth, should any work of a holy, Christian nature come his way, it would always be put first.

Almost immediately, as if on a signal, tracts began to arrive from the Dominicans – broadsheets announcing Savonarola's next sermon or lecture series, pamphlets on the Holy Life and Prayer. Miscomini interrupted the printing of the Plotinus to turn these small jobs around within the day. Such was his apparent ardour that the Dominicans were soon giving him all their printing work.

Miscomini did his accounts and found that a great upturn in his fortunes had come as a consequence of putting religion before the New Learning. This impressed him and made him thoughtful. Before long he changed his place of worship from the local Badia to the more distant San Marco.

I have no reason to suppose that the stone-thrower had been a friar, but we were not attacked again, even though, in fits and starts, we completed the Plotinus and published it.

Miscomini put more effort into Savonarola's tracts than a man with an easy conscience would have done. With my help, he made them quite handsome, using a good Roman type and including woodcuts either of holy scenes or of the Frate himself in the pulpit. The paper was somewhat coarse as is common with publications intended to be cheap, but the typeface and the woodcuts elevated these pamphlets. Miscomini was not going to undergo a conversion without bestowing on Savonarola some antique grace. The pamphlets therefore, perhaps unintentionally on the part of their author, gave the impression that Savonarola was a hybrid of old religion and new learning.

Whenever I looked over a page I was composing, reading it backwards, I got the impression of an author in an ecstasy of piety, calling upon me to meditate upon the wounds of Christ. Why do those who claim to love God scold others? There is nothing loving in the tone of it. I dismissed the writings of Savonarola as hypocrisy, but Miscomini gave me a tract to proof-read that was on prayer. Now it is just as necessary for the proof-reader to divorce himself from meaning as the compositor. The only men in a print-ing house who may read the meaning of words is the publisher himself and the editor. So I began to read through in an efficient and mechanical manner, but the words got the better of me. This pamphlet was good, so good that I checked with Miscomini that it was indeed by Savonarola and we hadn't mixed up manuscripts.

He who prays must address God as though he were in His presence; inasmuch as the Lord is everywhere, in every place, in every man, and especially in the soul of the just.

That could have been written by Ficino.

Therefore let us not seek God on earth, nor in heaven, nor elsewhere; rather let us seek Him in our own heart, as the prophet says, "I will hearken unto that which the Lord shall say in me." In prayer a man may take heed to his words, and this is a wholly material thing; he may take heed to the sense of his words, and this is rather study than prayer; finally, he may fix his thoughts on God, and this is the only true prayer. We must consider neither the words nor the sentences, but lift our soul above our self, and almost lose self in the thought of God. This state once attained, the believer forgets the world and worldly desires, and has, as it were, a foreshadowing of heavenly bliss.

Had this been written by Pico I would not have been surprised. But this man of the Church? The tract ended, *Wherefore we are come to declare to the world that outward worship must give way to inward, and that ceremonies are naught, save as a means of stirring the spirit.* I had not previously realised how deep Savonarola's understanding was, and I folded up a printed copy of the pamphlet and tucked it in my belt to show it to Ficino later. Could Pico be right after all? Was Savonarola the man we had been waiting for to renovate the Church?

Whether from the example of *il capo* Miscomini, or for some other reason, the bawdy jokes and tall tales with which the men had usually entertained each other during their breaks gave way quite suddenly to more serious conversation. They began to report to each other sermons they had heard from the various preachers. This was not just a feature of our shop: it was happening throughout the city. Everywhere the earthy Tuscan artisan with his sarcastic nature and practical common sense was transforming into a God-fearing and honest labourer. Oh, strange metamorphosis!

71 FICINO FINDS HIMSELF IN AN ENGLISHMAN 1493

WHEN FICINO LECTURED ON PLOTINUS AT THE UNIVERSITY, he concentrated on the language of the philosopher, keen to avoid any implication that he shared Plotinus's beliefs, especially when he spoke of the gods, the gods within us. No, we had to look at Plotinus in the context of his times. We were all building up such defences, unable now to speak out boldly, loud and free. 'I am not a poet,' claimed Poliziano. 'I am not a Platonist,' said Ficino. I never thought to hear such words.

The lecture theatre was full, the questions lively. Men tried to lead Ficino out, coaxing him to say more about what he had found in Plotinus, and less ambiguously, but Ficino resisted, saying only that it was an interesting theory that we have the heavens within us.

'It is a useful metaphor for human passions to say that when we are angry then Mars is dominant, or when we are wise, Jupiter. The astrologers speak in such terms. It does not make us pagans.'

One man, an Englishman by his accent, pressed the point. 'Is it possible to believe in Our Lord Jesus Christ and the pagan gods simultaneously?'

'It is not a question of belief. This is a lecture on language and theology. It is useful for us to give names to the stew of emotions, to separate them out and identify them. It is useful, also, to ascribe these passions to the planets. It frees us from their dominion and gives us the means to detach ourselves. Our fate may be signified by the stars, but it is not caused by them.'

'Have you not recently condemned astrology?' the Englishman asked. Clear-complexioned, with honest eyes and a firm chin, he reminded me of Ermolao Barbaro.

'False astrology, yes, that which binds men in slavery to the stars, which considers the stars all-powerful and, worse, malign. But man has the power to transcend the stars.' Ficino's voice was rising, going up a note, out of the rhetorical and into the poetic mode. He was about to get carried away, about to pronounce the truth lyrically, as dictated by his Muse, in a ringing, sing-song voice. Angelo cleared his throat loudly and Ficino came back to himself, glancing round the hall. Looking for black cowls. 'Plotinus himself condemns this kind of astrology,' he said, as if in conclusion.

More questions came, but Ficino raised his hands and called the assembly to a close with a prayer.

When I came out of the lecture hall and into the piazza San Marco, I found Ficino surrounded by a press of students and Angelo waiting to introduce the Englishman to him. His name? Why, it was our John Colet. On his way to Rome, he had stopped in Florence to meet Poliziano, the tutor of his friends Grocyn and Linacre. As he met my gaze I saw – what did I see? Nothing feigned. A simple, open soul. He was about twenty-five years old with a very English face, solemn and respectful. He was shy with Poliziano and merely conveyed his admiration for his work and his teaching methods; it was a rare accomplishment, he said, for any Englishman to acquire Greek, and he would acquire it for himself if he could. He said he intended to learn from Grocyn on his return to London. With Ficino, however, once he was introduced, he was less on guard and anxious to speak to the man whose lecture, for all its ambivalence, had fired Colet with an interest in Plato and Plotinus.

Aware that Colet was more in tune with Ficino than with himself, but happy to play the host, Poliziano invited them both to dine with him, 'You may ask your questions openly in my house,' he explained to Colet. 'And get frank answers, eh, Marsilio?'

'Thank you for coming to my rescue in there,' said Ficino. 'It is so difficult to be both circumspect and honest. Truth disdains danger.'

'All the martyrs know it to be so.'

'What danger?' Colet asked.

Angelo glanced at the monastery across the square. 'We will discuss it later. But not here. Certainly not here.' He led the way across the piazza to the Via Larga and the casino in the garden of Monna Clarice.

That evening, on which we were also joined by Pico della Mirandola, the conversation flowed without check. We discussed the gods and the angels, the One and the Multiplicity, Ficino trying to answer John's questions as to whether it is possible to be both Christian and Platonist without conflict or contradiction. His devotion to philosophy he communicated to Colet. He spoke of Pythagoras in reverential tones, and of the transmigration of souls. 'Heaven, hell and purgatory – these are true enough, but not the whole story. They describe only what lies between lives. For the soul that fails to return to God must come back to earth.'

Colet's English eyes grew huge. Pico took over the conversation, and confirmed what Ficino said by reference to Jewish wisdom and Cabala. Candlelight reflected in Colet's eyes but was not the source of the radiance that shone from them. Physical light seemed dim in the glory of his quickening spirit.

'I have heard much from my friends Grocyn and Linacre, but it is garbled. All I have really been able to understand is their enthusiasm, but not what it is they are enthusiastic about. They grow exasperated and tell me to read Plato myself, which I intend to do. But first I had to find out why I should.'

'Had you come a year ago, you would probably have heard a garbled account from me,' said Ficino, 'because then I had the luxury of wandering in my thoughts, collecting nectar from many flowers and rarely returning to the hive. But now… Now we live in a city where philosophy is unprotected. When time is limited, our thoughts are more focussed.'

'Why are you cautious about the monastery of San Marco? I heard Fra Girolamo's sermon in the Piazza della Signoria two days ago. The square was full – why, there must have been ten thousand people there! I was most struck by him, what I could understand, since he speaks in Italian and not in Latin. Sincerity transcends language, however, and I could understand the quality of the man.'

'He is returning Florence to the certainties of the past,' said Ficino. 'For fifty years or more we have been moderately free of heaven and hell, have been free to search the ancients for knowledge of an afterlife that is not terrifying in its prospect, and we have found it in the philosophy of the Platonists. But with the advent of Savonarola, our Christianity is being purified and made practical. Who would argue with that? I believe he speaks the truth and has the power that we so desperately need of regenerating the faith.'

'He is the antichrist,' said Poliziano.

'Our Angelo bases his beliefs on instinct,' Pico explained. 'Because Savonarola condemns poetry, he sees no good in him at all. But there is good there, and it is my work to persuade the Friar to a philosophical interpretation of the faith. For faith alone, without reason, is a bird with one wing.'

'And you are succeeding,' said Ficino, 'as you must, for if you do not succeed Savonarola will close the Academy down.'

We each shuddered at that.

'The faith,' said Ficino, 'the faith alone, which calls on men to abandon even their own judgement on what is true and false, has held our civilisation in thrall for hundreds of years. What do we get from it but an evil, greedy, rapacious, self-serving papacy we are not allowed to criticise without threat of excommunication or trial for heresy? We must go forward and cannot allow Savonarola to pitch us back. He needs to understand that philosophy – holy philosophy, not that dry grit of the scholastics – must attend faith, so that reasonable men may love God through reason. At the moment we are divided within ourselves, one part

Christian, the other Platonist. These two must be married and become one. It can be done, I know it can be done, and it is my hope that in Savonarola we have found the man who can do it. But if we have not, then we are lost and the work must continue elsewhere, in other countries – such as your own.'

'This is what I have sought my life long,' said Colet. 'I would have studied theology except that I could see nothing to be gained by rehearsing the sterile arguments of the scholastics. Theo-logy: it should be about the Word of God, not about the contrary opinions of men. So I have studied literature, but all the time feeling at odds with myself, as if my studies are a form of self-indulgence that will count against me on Judgement Day. Please, show me the way to harmony within.'

We remained in conversation until dawn, Ficino speaking to Colet of the secret teachings of the Platonists, Pico of the Cabala, Poliziano of the poets, each imparting to him that which is kept from the common people, things which I may not put down in writing. For in Colet we recognised the true spirit of enquiry. He thrilled to our vision to change what is wrong. But he did not share our confidence.

'I am merely a bachelor of arts,' he said. 'What can I do in the field of philosophy or theology?' He resembled so closely our beloved Ermolao Barbaro, his features neat and beautifully drawn, his mouth determined. Angelo smiled at him. 'You love language, so use language. Give the people the gospels in their own tongue, without learned commentary. Let the truth speak through you.'

Colet, now at ease with Poliziano, gazed at him in gratitude. As dawn came, he rose reluctantly, saying he was to leave for Rome within the hour. Ficino embraced him. Despite the difference in their years, this was not the embrace of tutor and student or master and disciple. Ficino embraced Colet as an equal, as his chosen one. A spark passed between them, the fire transmitted, the torch passed on. *Hotze la'or* – the truth was published.

72 THE ACADEMY OF SAN MARCO 1493

IN THE SUMMER I WAS LAID OFF BY MISCOMINI. WITH THE shop closing for July and August, I was free until the autumn. Poliziano invited me to stay with him and Maria at the Villa Bruscoli but I declined. I had enough money to feed myself for two months and decided to spend the time with what I love most: books.

A slab of sunlight from the cloister window fell into the library of San Marco, burnishing the floor and making the interior and its grey pillared aisles seem dim. Once inside, however, the eyes soon adjusted to the gentler light coming in from high windows. Row upon row of high-backed pews, each adjoined to a long and steeply sloping desk, filled the bays of the aisles. The narrow space between desk and bench penned the scholars in rows and kept their backs straight.

The theology desks were crowded while those dedicated to Greek and Roman authors were all but empty. Everyone seemed to have lost their taste for poetry and philosophy. I walked slowly past the empty rows. It seemed we were entering a new dark age, where the ancient works would be kept by monks who did not read them, where the only attention they received was from worms and beetles. I wanted to sit down at the Homer desk and read the first manuscript of the *Iliad* that had been brought into Florence, but to do so would be to draw attention to myself and raise sanctimonious eyebrows. I went instead to the philosophy section, where a few men at least were reading. Old Landino was there, muttering to himself earnestly, his wits threatened by too much study. Whiskers stood out on his unshaved chin, for there is no time for visits to the barber when you are seventy years old and have not yet read the whole of Aristotle. Choosing a seat at random, I sat and breathed the library in, my soul expanding with the scent of leather and parchment.

Every now and again, a creak of wood as someone shifted, a cough echoing in the vaulted ceiling, a muttering of irritation as the man reading Jerome, wanting to get out to relieve himself, had to disturb those reading Augustine and Clement. A rattle of chains and a thud as a book was taken out from the shelf below and placed on its desk. A sigh, a sneeze – a great *choof!* that blew the dust off a copy of some ancient work of jurisprudence.

I had chosen my seat at random, not bothering to read the list of titles that were inscribed on a board hanging from a hook at the bench-end. Drawing a volume out from the shelf, placing it on the desk and opening its cover, I found it was a copy of Plato, inscribed on the fly-leaf and in his own handwriting 'From Cosimo'. Cosimo, our guiding spirit in death as in life. He had built this monastery and this library not to redeem his sins, as many thought, but out of devotion to God, to learning, to truth.

Knowing Plato off by heart, I put the book back and drew out another. It was a comparatively new work, beautifully bound in a soft leather that made no noise when I placed it on the desk. Opening the cover, I looked into a jewel casket: Marsilio Ficino's translations of Pythagoras and Hermes Trismegistus. Opposite the first page was a design of circles, the one in the centre announcing that here, in the little circles arranged round its circumference, were the titles of what was to be found within, and all the circles brought into one design by exquisite filigree patterns in which little scrolls appeared bearing Lorenzo's motto: SEMPER. Always. On the opposite page, the knotwork in the margins and a delicately coloured and gilded capital framed the most exquisite penmanship I had ever seen. Its perfection pulled my heart open and emptied it of its pride. Even if I had not suffered any injury to my arm, even if I had worked for ten hours each day practising my craft, I could never have achieved this. Bartolommeo Sanvito, I was certain, the scribe who was to me as Leonardo was to Filippino: a very thorn in the soul. Beauty shone out of the book. Such a book would never suffer neglect. It had been designed to last forever – *semper*, always – to be kept as a treasure in times of ignorance until the day

340

when, once more, men could read therein and find a beauty deeper, richer still: the beauty of ideas.

I turned the pages carefully, reverentially, until I came to the *Poimandres* and settled to reading.

'*Davvero!*' said a voice close to my ear. I jumped, startled, and turned expecting to see a severe face beneath a black cowl, but it was only Pico, smiling.

'You frightened me,' I whispered.

'Reading Hermes! Do you want to burn? Come, there is a meeting in the refectory.'

I rose and followed him, going not out of the public door but the one leading into the monastery. 'I want to debate astrology with Fra Girolamo,' Pico told me as he went nimbly down the stairs. I glanced over my shoulder at a large, sweet painting of the Annunciation. 'Come on, you can look at that later. He considers astrology to be superstition and wants to rid the city of augurs, fortune-tellers, crystal-gazers and soothsayers. I agree with him about the charlatans, but there is more to astrology than fortune-telling and we need to understand it before we condemn it. If indeed we do condemn it. Was it not a star that led the Magi to the infant Christ?'

His grey eyes, with a new softness to them since he had been absolved of heresy by Pope Alexander, gazed at me affectionately. Here was a man advanced in the process of cleansing his soul. I am not sure why I found this uncomfortable, since I was in the tentative process of cleansing my own. Perhaps I just preferred Giovanni Pico in his days of daring and adventure, preferred flamboyance to quietness, colour to black.

In the refectory, the invited company was dining at a frugal table. I had heard it called 'the academy of the despairing' but found a group of optimistic men more concerned with power than with self-understanding. It was strange to see men of the Vespucci, Ridolfi and Strozzi families eating hard bread and even harder cheese. But strangest of all was to see Piero de' Medici among them, at one with the academicians and the friars. While everyone appeared to be listening to the Friar's disquisition on sacred music, their senses were trained on the young Medici. He only had to twitch and all heads turned. Piero himself attended to everything Savonarola had to say and asked good questions. Intelligence shone in him, but it was as light shining through inferior alabaster. Piero had inherited the nature of his mother rather than of his father, and so, though he asked good questions, he seemed disdainful, and each man in the group was of the belief that, to survive, he had to ingratiate himself with this prince. I say 'prince' advisedly, for Piero was nothing less. The Medici bank and its business interests he left to others while he enjoyed the life of a young royal. His father's injunction, that he should never forget he was a citizen, had indeed been forgotten.

It was so different from one of Lorenzo's gatherings, in which each man had felt free to speak and to hold his own opinions; here a subtle atmosphere of fear pervaded everything, as if no one in this academy dared do anything but agree. Certainly, since the letter had come from Pope Alexander, permitting the independence of San Marco from the Lombard Congregation, Savonarola had an even greater air of confidence and power. I'd heard that the Pope had been browbeaten into agreeing, worn down by very weariness at the interminable arguments for and against, but you would think here it had been a simple decision and a wise one. Although he was now Vicar General of his own Congregation, Savonarola was vested in the same white habit and rope girdle as his two companions, Fra Domenico and Fra Silvestro. His authority was in himself and not in any robe of office.

Soon after I arrived, the conversation turned to the subject of Angelo Poliziano. Fra Silvestro asked Pico if he had invited him to the academy yet.

'It would be better if you did not,' said Bartolommeo Scala quickly. 'No offence to you, Count, but your friend has become rabid and attacks fellow scholars for no good reason.'

'Oh, I have no doubt they deserve it,' said Savonarola quietly. 'It is dogs that become rabid, not professors. I believe the Greek scholars are jealous. It often seems to me that the closest thing to a battlefield is a university. Indeed, the only difference is that soldiers fight cleanly and according to rules.'

The company laughed.

'Angelo Poliziano is the most learned man in the country,' Savonarola continued, 'and it would serve us to honour him rather than denigrate him, for everything he has done and is doing is on behalf of mankind.'

Scala looked taken aback. 'I am sure you are right, Frate, and may God forgive me for my rash opinion.'

Savonarola was thoughtful, his fingers steepled in front of his mouth. The rest of the company waited on him. He remained quiet, pondering the subject of Angelo Poliziano. 'He is a fine man,' he said at last, 'but his soul is in mortal danger. He believes with Aristotle that God is in all created things, and therefore Poliziano loves only created things and binds himself to the earth.' Slowly his eyes raised up and met mine. 'Well, Tommaso Maffei? What may we do to save the soul of your friend and master?'

Everyone was staring at me. 'I... well... I... is it in danger? He has more virtue than most men I know, and if a man be measured by the company he keeps, Poliziano keeps the very finest. If he cannot love God directly, it's because he cannot see Him, so he loves His reflection in others. Surely God would not be so unjust as to damn him for that?'

'We may not presume to judge on God's behalf,' said Fra Silvestro, a man as stern and humourless as an old Roman senator. 'Poliziano needs to get down on his knees and surrender his pride to the Lord.'

'Poets are corroded by vanity – they cannot help it,' Savonarola agreed. 'They feed on praise – birds of praise...'

The company laughed.

'You see them applaud themselves when their poems are read; they can't restrain themselves, their mouths agape with self-congratulation. I have never seen any man as proud as one fellow I heard reciting a poem on the worthlessness of fame. Such men can hardly be healed since they do not realise that they are sick. But if they are not summoned from within by the Holy Spirit, or seek to rid themselves of pride, then pride will begin to nibble away at them.'

What right had Scala to look so smug at that? He who suffered pride more than most?

'Poliziano does pray, Frate,' said Pico.

'Yes, but to which gods?'

'He has recently written two hymns to the Virgin Mary,' I said.

Savonarola was surprised. '*Vero*? I had no idea. Could we hear them?'

'I do not have them by heart, but they are most lovely.'

'I meant, hear them from him. Why does he spurn us?'

I glanced at Piero de' Medici, since he knew the reason as well as I, but he was feeding a hound under the table and stroking its muzzle.

'I do not know, Frate,' I said.

'Go to your master and tell him that the unity of this city depends on him, on his joining us here along with his dear friend, the Count of Concordia.'

I glanced at Pico. He nodded in agreement. 'Angelo should be here.'

Repelled by the taut air of obsequiousness infecting the academy of San Marco, I left as soon as I decently could, crossed the square to the sculpture garden and sought out Michelangelo, who, as I expected to find, was working late.

'I fear the future, Tommaso,' he told me. 'There is a great wave of disaster heading for us, and we do not need Savonarola to predict it. You can feel it in your blood.'

Ever since the Prior of Santo Spirito had given Michelangelo a room in the church where he could dissect human bodies, his workshop had become littered with sketches of flayed corpses, skin and muscle pulled back to reveal to us the secrets of anatomy. Such was Michelangelo's dedication to his art that he made these dissections and did the drawings even while his stomach rebelled.

He was skinny now for lack of food, but still he drew his corpses. All around him, all around me, was incontrovertible evidence of our mortality. I sighed. 'In the Academy we discuss transmigration of souls. Cardiere tells us that he has met Lorenzo after death. But still I doubt. What are we, in the end, but a pump and bellows in a body of meat?'

Michelangelo found one of his studies and forced me to look at it. It showed the organs inside the ribcage of a young Spaniard. 'He was a beautiful youth,' he said, 'but it was not beauty I found inside him so much as wonder. It is clear to me that the Creator of Man is a God of supreme intelligence. The more I look into dead bodies, the less I fear death, for whoever made them made me, and it is His Will whether I live or die, or what happens next.'

'Tell me, do you find Savonarola a good and true man?'

Michelangelo put down his tools to give me his full attention. 'He is the freezing water we all need to wake up. Whatever his faults and shortcomings – and he has them, of course – his courage, his enthusiasm, are making a difference. We cannot call ourselves Christians if we do not live a Christian life – Fra Girolamo is showing us how.' He sighed and shook the hair out of his eyes, eyes that were less defensive these days and more mellow. 'I wake up every morning and thank God for him.'

73 WHAT HAPPENED TO MARIA?
1493

TRUST YOU TO ASK THAT QUESTION. FOR A MONK WHO, SO far as I know, remains celebate, you have a soft and feminine heart, Erasmo. Am I not allowed to lose my story in a blather of information about governments, monasteries and printing houses? For this, after all, is what I tried to do at the time. Where was Maria?

Still with her brother, although I had not seen her since Lorenzo's funeral, when I grew so hot and tongue-tied that I soon moved away to bury myself in a group of men. And then there was another occasion, at the end of summer the following year.

As I said, I had declined Poliziano's offer to live with him at the Villa Bruscoli, preferring to stay in my own house in the city. Its atmosphere of grief was fitting for the time and did not distress me as previously. I lay in my marriage bed and my loss of Lorenzo mingled with my loss of Elena, became one grief. I groaned in my loneliness and prayed to God that he take me, for too much light had gone out from life. Sucked down by melancholy, I had no hope in this new world dawning. We were under the rule of a boy and Savonarola was promising us a scourging. My dreams became infested with devils, little pointy-toothed, malicious imps who wanted my soul in hell.

Maria? Yes, yes, I'm coming to that.

In September, Angelo called me to the Villa Bruscoli, 'on a matter of unfinished business'. When I arrived I found Maria in the garden, weeping over a dead toad. Such tears had not been caused by the toad, merely released by this tiny tragedy. She cried for all dead things. I put my arms around her instinctively and, to my surprise, she responded, burying herself into me and hugging me as if she hugged life itself. I came so close that I touched her mouth with my breath, and hovered there.

Something stirred within me. No, not that, you reprobate! If it had been that, the way would have been clearer, for nothing hastens us into marriage quicker than desire. No, that which stirred was my heart. And I was frightened. Happiness would only lead to loss. The words of the Greek gipsy tolled liked a bell: *All whom you love will die before you.*

I stepped back from her hastily. Laughed. Apologised. Asked, 'Where is your brother?'

I knew why Angelo wanted to see me. He wanted to fulfil Lorenzo's wishes regarding his sister.

'Was he expecting you?' Looking baffled, she told me that

Angelo was with Pico. 'He will be back soon. I don't know why he went off if he asked you to come.'

I knew.

'I will go to Pico's,' I said, and went along the path through the garden that led up to the estate of Pico della Mirandola on the terrace above. In the chestnut wood I circled back on another path and returned to the city, where I threw myself into the urgent work of publishing Savonarola's tracts.

Italy

Of all the routes into Italy, the one from Lyons to Turin via Mont Cenis is the least dramatic but the most beautiful. I would surrender the awful majesty of the Brenner Pass for this drovers' track any day. In the heights it is still spring. Having left August back in the hot valleys of Provence, the higher we ascend, the further we go back in time until, in the upper meadows, we are riding through swathes of June flowers. If we were to go higher still, so we are told, we might see the wonder of purple and silver anenomes that will not suffer to be picked but must be admired on the spot, but that would be a detour for the curious only. Our route south lies across these upland meadows, where the mist is damp and the moorland bleak.

Today we met a shepherd in passing, the bells of his sheep clonking cheerfully. When he greeted us in the dialect of Piedmont, my eyes filled with tears for, despite all its strangeness, it is a dialect founded on Italian grammar. Erasmus chided me, saying that if this easy tearfulness is an Italian trait then he must turn on his heel and run for Holland. But he was close to tears himself, he whose dream is now on the very threshold of its realisation.

Love begins to throb like the return of life after numbness, love of my country and people, an unrequited love of which its object is oblivious. What makes an Italian Italian and not French? We look different, we speak differently, we feel differently. We are more hot-tempered. I thought it was in the blood, but is it in the air? Why was it that, as we crossed from Savoy into Piedmont, Clyfton began to shout at his pupils? Oh, I know the reason well enough: our flamboyant royal courier began speaking Tuscan as soon as he stepped on Italian soil, and this irritated the tutor who insists Latin must be spoken at all times. Erasmus tried to intervene, and remonstrated with the tutor, who was telling the boys that Italian is a vulgar tongue of many dialects not to be imitated.

'That is not the case!' Erasmus said sternly. 'Tuscan is commonly understood throughout the land. It is the language of Petrarch and Dante, of Lorenzo de' Medici and Angelo Poliziano. It is the language of their fathers, and the boys need to learn it.'

'Not from this heraldic woodcock. He is not Italian. He is a walking Babel Tower.'

At which the offended courier began to push the angry tutor quite roughly.

We each carry a dagger as a protection against thieves but now one of them came out for use within our party. You hear stories of handsome men who suddenly reveal themselves as ugly demons; well, here was one such transformation. The light in Clyfton's eye was quite murderous as he drew his knife and lunged towards the courier. With an energy and speed I seem only to possess when weapons are drawn, I caught his wrist and twisted it hard till he yowled and dropped the blade.

'You pumpkin!' he snarled at me in English.

Erasmus advanced upon us to calm things down.

'As for you, you windbag,' Clyfton shouted, still in English, 'these boys are as much in your care as mine, but all you do is tell them stories. Do you think your relentless erudition is enough to educate them? While you three are taking supper and complaining about inns, I am teaching them grammar. You are all utterly inflated with ideas and theories, blind to what is under your nose. You talk – you preach – about learning, about philosophy, about knowledge, about virtue. But what do you practise?'

The ugly demon had undergone another stark transformation, this time into the vengeful angel of the Lord, for what he said was true. Lashed and abashed, we apologised to each other, and to our charges, and continued our journey. Despite these courteous formalities, however, Erasmus was in a furious mood and rode alone behind the party. Then, as the mist cleared and we looked down on the city of Turin, Erasmus rode up to join us. Tomorrow we begin the slow descent into Italy and the return to high summer.

Turin, August 16ᵗʰ, 1506.

From our hosts we hear the news of a country still recovering from the ravages of Cesare Borgia who, during the years of my absence, gave up the priesthood to become the sword of his father, Pope Alexander. Through siege and conquest he brought the cities of the Romagna back under papal control and created a state in the centre of Italy to rival Naples, Florence, Venice and Milan. Cesare was not only merciless and brutal, he was a Borgia, with a Borgia's disdain for God and His laws. His adventures, however, came to an end with the death of his father and the accession of the new pope. Three years have passed, but the aftershocks are still felt. Since Cesare fled to Spain, the Romagna has been lost to Venice. The rumour is that Pope Julius is planning to retake it.

Erasmus has been advised not to travel any further south but to sit his examination here. 'In Turin? I may as well have done it in Paris.'

'It is still an Italian degree,' I told him. 'You do not have to mention where in Italy you obtained it.'

'True enough.'

He has done all the work in Paris and needs only to sit the examination. He thinks we can move on in two to four weeks.

74 THE VOICE OF GOD
1493

IN ADVENT SAVONAROLA RESUMED HIS SERMONS ON Genesis in the Duomo. Even that vast place could not now contain everyone who wanted to listen to the Frate. The crowd was restless during the mass; the introit, the gloria, the agnus dei – all familiar and not what we had come to hear. But then he rose from his chair in the choir and ascended the pulpit, a pulpit of cast bronze, a masterpiece of new art from a sculptor who had studied the ancients. Savonarola appeared in it like a righteous captain who had boarded a pirate boat. He raised up his hands to greet us. Then he began to relate a vision he had had.

'I have seen swords in the sky, and the voice of God issuing from three faces, saying, People, repent before the coming punishment! I have seen multitudes of angels, angels in white descending from heaven to earth. They carry white mantles with red crosses to offer to men, but only some men accept them. I have seen the sword of God being brandished and the air full with vaporous clouds. I have seen daggers in the sky, hail, thunder, arrows and fire. On the face of the earth – wars, plague, famine, a host of tribulations. But one shall come from beyond the mountains like Cyrus, and God shall be his guide and leader, and no one will be able to resist him, and he will take cities and fortresses with great ease.'

Then a strange collective fever took hold. All around me twenty thousand people moved and swayed, a whipped-up sea that Savonarola commanded from his pulpit-boat. He alone was still, suspended above us, half-way to heaven. 'The mighty hand of God is upon you, Florence! Neither power nor wisdom nor flight can withstand it.' A groan came then from the crowd, a terrible sound of human remorse, as if from one of the ditches of purgatory.

'But the Lord is merciful! He waits for you, to shower you with his love and pity. Convert, Florence, to the Lord your God with all your heart, because He is kind and compassionate. If you do not, He will avert His eyes from you forever.'

Cries went up all around, cries of 'I believe!' and 'Alleluia!' and 'Forgive me, Lord, for I have sinned!'

'Know this, Florence! These are not the words of Holy Scripture!' thundered the Frate. 'These are the words of God Himself, direct from Heaven! I speak as I hear. God is with us, now.'

Then many dropped shivering to their knees like the children of Israel before Moses, and threw up their hands in awe.

75 THE CALUMNY OF APELLES
1493

I WENT TO BOTTICELLI'S WORKSHOP WITH A PILE OF NOTES from Angelo – references to stories, fables, mythological characters to inform a new picture. Sandro was working on a painting of St Augustine, trying to concentrate while his brother, Simone, stood warming his backside at the roaring hearth and arguing with Doffo Spini. Although Doffo had not tired of the streets, the curiosity of his childhood for the painter's workshop close to the family palazzo had returned. These days, in the absence of naked goddesses, he enjoyed provoking Sandro's brother.

'Look at you!' Simone was saying. 'You are a peacock, with a peacock's brain. What you spend at the tailor's in one week would feed a family for a year.'

'You're jealous, old man.' Doffo's voice was deep with new manhood. 'You want this tunic and mantle yourself, but what a fool you'd look with your figure.' He turned to look me up and down. If he found little to appreciate, he found nothing to criticise either. His own hair was thin and though he wore it long, it was not as long as mine, and the pointed tips of his ears stood up on either side of his cap. If my own was long – half way down my back, indeed – it was not, I hasten to add, from vanity or, as Doffo supposed, because I was aping the style of Pico della Mirandola. I had simply neglected to get it cut. Perhaps there was something more to it. Perhaps, like Pico, I was reacting to the shorn heads of the new zealots.

Simone jabbed Doffo in the shoulder. 'Did your father teach you no respect for your elders? You are a cuckoo. You are not Spini's son. What you need, boy, is discipline. Do you go to mass? When did you last go to mass?'

Doffo sighed. 'Here it is – the sermon. Next it'll be what the Friar says.'

'What the Friar says is true: we can have no peace while we are at war with ourselves.'

'I can certainly have no peace with you two around,' muttered Sandro, sitting back and squinting at his picture.

'I'm not at war with myself,' said Doffo to Simone. 'I'm at war with you, you weeper. You are corrupting your brother. Where have all those lovely myths gone, Sandro? You should kick this snivelling old goat out – he's oppressing you.'

'God help me.' Sandro glanced up and with a slight inclination of his head, directed me to a back room. I went there with my notes; Sandro came in and closed the door in the face of Doffo who had followed us. Hidden under a tablecloth were the first sketches of *The Calumny of Apelles*, a work he did not want his brother to see, for Simone had become one of the *piagnoni*, or 'weepers' – the name we had given to the followers of Savonarola, not because they had a particular tendency to cry, but because they believed in their own sin to an extravagant degree. 'Breast-beaters' would have been a better name, but 'weepers' was the one generally used.

I read out Angelo's notes to Sandro and discussed them with him while he sketched images of the characters and scenes. Although Angelo met Botticelli frequently, he had delegated the task to me as it was lengthy and laborious – he wanted only to see the sketches in their final stage. Several books from the Medici library were kept in Sandro's back room for consultation: *De Pictura* by Leon Battista Alberti, Lucian's book on slander, *The Defence of Poetry* by Boccaccio and the *Imagines* of Philostratus. These I referred to often, reading passages out to Sandro sometimes for the seventh or eighth time.

The scene is set in a gilded hall in which a ruler with large, asinine ears sits on a raised dais, extending his hand to Slander, a woman beautiful beyond measure who is being adorned by two other beautiful maids: Treachery and Deceit. Near to the ruler and whispering in his large, shaggy ears are Suspicion and Ignorance. Slander approaches the ruler with a blazing torch in one hand while with the other she drags the naked male figure of Innocence. She is conducted by Envy, a wasted, ragged man. These figures are followed by Repentance, a wretched old woman in rags who is glancing back at the figure behind her, naked Truth.

The work had been commissioned by Poliziano himself, intended as a gift – and a lesson – for Piero de' Medici. *The Calumny of Apelles* had been treated before by modern painters, but in this version there was so much more, layers and layers of symbolic reference. Botticelli even referred freely to previous works of his own. He showed me a sketch of the whole design and I sat back in astonishment, recognising a perverted version of his wondrous *Realm of Venus*. Here was Venus again, only this time representing Truth and standing in the position taken by Mercury in the earlier painting, and, like Mercury, she pointed heavenwards. Then there were the three Graces or, rather, three dis-Graces: Slander, Treachery and Deceit. The very composition itself had the serpentine flow of *The Realm of Venus*.

Sandro chuckled at my expression. 'Well,' he said, 'is it not the same message? My work, like Angelo's, has been slandered and is being dragged by its hair to a judge corrupted by Suspicion and Ignorance.' He rubbed his charcoaled hands off on his apron, 'Oh, I am enjoying myself. Let's continue.'

We worked together for an hour or more. When we went back into the workshop, Simone was saying his prayers out loud, rocking on his knees before a crucifix on the wall.

'Ah well,' Sandro sighed, 'back to St Augustine.'

And that was how it was – philosophers, poets and painters in love with the ancient world were beginning to work in secret, covering their shame with holy images.

76 POLIZIANO AT WAR AND IN LOVE 1493

LORENZO'S DEATH HAD ROBBED POLIZIANO OF NOT ONLY a friend and patron, but also of any power of toleration he might possess. Where once he had at least tried to be gracious to his enemies, now he was savage and tore at them without thought to their feelings. The most vicious of his opponents was Bartolommeo Scala.

The rivalry between them had begun many years earlier when Angelo had corrected a letter written by Scala which had contained a grammatical error serious enough to start a war. Although Lorenzo had favoured the man, he had not been above baiting him. For instance, he once sent Scala an exaggerated testimonial of his worth just to inflate his pride. Then he left it to Angelo to 'prick the pig's bladder with the point of his wit.' This drew a letter out of Scala, addressed to Angelo.

'You will hardly venture to compete with my honours,' he wrote. 'The Florentine people have raised me first to the Priorship, then to the Gonfaloniership, and now to the rank of senator and knight, with such unanimity that many are of the opinion that there has never been a more popular man; besides which I have the brilliant testimony of Lorenzo de' Medici that distinctions were never conferred on one more worthy.'

Lorenzo had laughed until the tears ran. What was odd was that he consistently advanced Scala in wealth and office as if he did, indeed, merit the testimonial. Angelo, in whom laughter had not come so readily, challenged him on the matter. Lorenzo said that when he promoted Scala he was moved by 'considerations other than merit'. So often had Scala been promoted that he now lived in a quite beautiful palazzo in open meadows close to the Porta Pinti. As Chancellor he had made orations before princely visitors. When he was elected Gonfalonier, the *Marzocco*, the statue of the lion of the Republic, wore a gold crown for the occasion and the people cried, 'Viva Messer Bartolommeo!' He was a titular senator of Rome, an apostolical secretary, a Knight of the Golden Spur. Scala, whose name meant 'stairs' and whose arms were an azure ladder transverse on a golden field with the motto 'graditim', was born for advancement. His annual income was eight times greater than Angelo's and he had a villa on the sunny side of Fiesole. So when Poliziano tore into him for his solecisms, I suspect it was not entirely on behalf of Lady Grammatica. He was resentful that Fortuna had smiled on such a vain braggart, a man who had once had the cruelty and temerity to beat a soldier in the Florentine army, for no other reason than that he was a cousin of Poliziano. When he attacked Scala, Poliziano attacked Fortuna herself. And she, tricky goddess, planned her revenge.

Scala did have his merits, or he would not have advanced so far. One of them was geniality – when he wasn't torturing enemies, he was being magnanimous to friends. After all, the good courtier knows it is better to be amiable and civil to one's rivals than to be perceived as jealous. Therefore Scala arranged that Poliziano should tutor one of his daughters in Greek, for among his brood was a prodigy. Alessandra was about seventeen at the time and for Angelo, whose female acquaintances tended to be pug-faced Medici women, she had more virtues than it was possible for a human to bear. I thought he was exaggerating until I met her myself but it was more or less true: here was a girl of both inward and outward beauty, with a gaiety and wit that would charm Pluto himself and bring him back to life. Her beauty, her modesty, her eyes full of laughter – all this Poliziano could perhaps have resisted. What undid him was her intelligence. To find such a facility for Greek in anyone would have been a wonder; in a woman, it was a miracle. He began to look somewhat abstracted in those hours – those long hours and days – when he was not with her. One would think that he only drew breath in her presence, that the rest of the time he was living on borrowed air. He who could never find enough hours in the day began to complain of time dragging, and all those suddenly spare hours he devoted to the composition of amorous little verses.

Angelo Poliziano was in love.

77 WHAT IS LOVE?
1493

SAVONAROLA'S SERMONS WERE BECOMING EVER MORE urgent and forceful. He was preparing us, he said, for the 'coming scourge' which we could only meet safely if we purified our hearts. He never avoided striking at poets and philosophers, and in such a telling way that several were burning their works and taking the habit.

'Scripture must be studied in the light of faith. Further than this you may not go, lest you stumble. Origen,' he said, 'over-stepped the limit when he said predestination depended on our previous lives. Heresy! The Pelagians said it depended on our good deeds in this life. Heresy! It is not true that the grace of God may be obtained by our deeds. It comes by God's will alone. Was not St Peter restored to grace, despite his sins in denying the Lord?'

That had everyone talking in the market places, the loggie, the barber shops: if good deeds will not take us to heaven, then what will? If good deeds are of no use, why do them?

Savonarola answered from the pulpit. We perform charity for the simple sake of those who require it. In that way we imitate the life of Christ. We must bring ourselves into tune with the Divine, and that requires us to be good, to be truthful, to pray. But it is a mistake when we take the goodness in our deeds to be our own: all goodness proceeds from God. 'The voice of God calls us. All we are asked to do is to hear it and obey His will. When Love approaches a soul disposed to grace, that soul is inflamed by charity.'

He gave examples. 'Consider the physician who works from love. Love teaches him everything and is the measure and rule of medicine. He will never tire, he will enquire into everything, will order his remedies and see them prepared, and will never leave the sick man. But if gain is his object, then he will have no care for the sufferer and his skill will fail him. Likewise the mother. Who taught this woman, who had no child before, how to nurse a baby? Love. See what fatigue she endures, night and day, to rear it. What is the cause of this? Love. Love is the true and only doctrine, but in these days the preachers teach nothing but empty subtleties.'

With Savonarola as its Vicar General, the reformation at San Marco was dramatic. All costly vestments and precious plate were being sold to feed the poor. 'In the primitive Church, the chalices were of wood and the prelates of gold. These days we have chalices of gold and prelates of wood.' The lay brothers were being trained in the arts in order to earn a living, and schools of painting, sculpture and architecture were being established within the monastery. Men versed in ancient languages were teaching the friars to read the Bible in the original tongues. A scriptorium had been opened, and young friars were training in the art of copying and illuminating. At San Marco they were reviving my art.

In his academy and in the pulpit, Savonarola gave us his teaching on love, love as a means of redemption. 'Those philosophers care only for their own souls. Love teaches us to care for the souls of others. Love teaches us to serve.' This last had me sleepless. Whom did I serve? Only myself. 'The love you love is the wrong love.' That is what he had said to me all those years before, and now the meaning was becoming clear. The wrong love is directed to one person only, and for selfish reasons. True love... 'This love is a gift from the Lord. It is a fire that kindles all dry things, and whoever is disposed to it will find it descending into his heart, and his heart shall be set aflame.'

78 SNOW
1494

AS I LEFT SAN MARCO ONE DAY IN JANUARY, THE SKY BECAME threateningly dark, so dark that many stood looking up at the great cloud hanging low over the city, a blue-black ominous cloud, from which great flakes of snow began to fall. We had seen snow before, of course, but not like this, with flakes so big that they lay without melting. Some people were frightened and ran indoors; others turned into children and stood with their mouths open to catch the snow on their tongues. I gazed at the flakes falling on my mantle and could see the beauty of their crystalline structure; such wonder did I feel then at the Creator. Was this a seduction of the senses or divine rapture? I wondered if I should continue on my way, unswayed by the weather, or if I should dance with those Florentines who saw nothing in the snow but a source of joy. Only the holy is beautiful? Very well. Snow is holy.

Poliziano was now living in the casino of the garden of Monna Clarice. Having ascertained that Maria was with her sister-in-law, I visited him and ended up staying the night, for the snow was settling. By the following morning it lay in great drifts throughout the city, bringing all work to a halt. I awoke to silence and such a pristine light filling the room that I lay in bed awhile, feeling my heart pump with something that seemed to be happiness. Or, the potential for happiness. A servant came to say that Messer Angelo was calling for me.

'Snow, Angelo,' I said, walking into his chamber. I expected to find him at his desk, oblivious to the conditions of the day, but he was at the window, smiling.

'You sent for me.'

'What? Did I? Oh, yes. Listen. I have more notes for Botticelli. He is being very slow with my painting.'

'It is highly complex and, I fear, threatening his sanity.'

'Well, please go and encourage him.'

'Have you seen the streets? They're impassable.'

'Nonsense. Didn't I see you dancing in the piazza yesterday?'

'Me? No, of course not. A man my age ...'

'Dancing like a boy. I think you will enjoy the walk. I'd come with you, only ...'

'You don't want to ruin your shoes.'

'... I'm busy.'

I went out to make the long and hazardous journey to Ognissanti. The piazza San Marco was blanketed, the church and monastery capped by snow. Although my footprints down the Via Larga were virgin, I was not the only one out. A servant from the Palazzo de' Medici was riding up the street towards the sculpture garden.

'Not the best day for riding out to find a sculptor,' he said in greeting, all the colours of his apparel breathtaking in the lucid, bright light.

'Nor a painter,' said I. We laughed and passed on. At the palazzo I looked into the courtyard and saw Piero de' Medici and his brothers playing with the snow, running about pelting each other, just boys. Cardinal Giovanni was with them, for after the election of Rodrigo Borgia to the papacy he had left Rome and had been travelling throughout Italy ever since. Now he waddled breathlessly round the Medici garden, receiving more snowballs than he succeeded in throwing, his pink face full of effort and misery.

By the time I returned from Ognissanti, where I had found Botticelli still in bed, saying it was too cold to get up, Angelo had arrived at the palazzo himself and was standing in the courtyard, blowing on his hands while staring into the garden and a new statue being built by Michelangelo, a statue of snow with a great round body and a ball for a head which Michelangelo was shaping into the form of a man. The Medici were helping, rolling balls of snow round the garden, gathering larger and larger quantities of material for the sculptor. Laughter rang within the confines of the palazzo walls, even Michelangelo's. That was the only commission Michelangelo ever received from Piero de' Medici: at least it made him laugh.

I told Angelo that his painting was still far from complete.

'If it does not come soon,' he complained, 'Piero will be beyond understanding its message.'

I do not know what happened to *The Calumny of Apelles*. Certainly it was never completed before the great surge of events that washed the Medici out of Florence and Poliziano to his grave. It must still be with Botticelli.

79 CONVERSION
1494

THE POET, GIROLAMO BENIVIENI, HAD BEEN A CLOSE FRIEND of Giuliano de' Medici. Even now, fifteen years since Giuliano's assassination, Benivieni still did not smile. In any company he sat staring at everyone around him as if we were all lost in a delusion of life whilst he alone knew the truth: death awaits us all. As Pico became increasingly sombre himself, Benivieni drew closer to him and they often worked together on Benivieni's philosophical poetry. He was also fond of me, given that he saw etched in my features a reflection of his own. I had battled with my own grief, had learnt to live again and tried to find purpose, but Benivieni had abandoned the attempt. 'Tommaso,' he said to me gravely, 'you would enjoy the Academy of San Marco.'

'Enjoy it, Girolamo? I have been once. It is the *accademia sicofante*. All those high-born men pretending they have found religion.'

'Enjoy was a poor choice of word. You would benefit from it, as I do. You know, when we have found what we wanted in life, and then been stripped of it, then we are free. No longer do we chase after fool's gold.'

'Is human love fool's gold?'

'No, indeed, but it is mortal. Do you not feel as I do, afraid to commit your heart again?'

I cleared my throat but could not reply.

'Only then are you free from the traps and snares that catch men and distract them from loving that which is the source of love itself. Tommaso, we spend our lives ignoring the one who gave us life. But you and I have been blessed with the death of human love. We can put these things behind us and, pilgrims of the heart, begin the journey to God. We are free.'

He told me that the *accademia* was only *sicofante* when Piero was in attendance. 'The regular, weekly meetings are for sincere and steady men.'

'Is it a lay fraternity?'

'Of course. And its members have the privilege of listening to the wisdom of Fra Girolamo and speaking to him privately on any matter. We also have the freedom of the monastery – and we may borrow books from the library.'

'We already have that freedom.'

'It may end soon. There is talk of only holy books being available on loan.'

I started from my chair. 'Is that true?'

'Fra Domenico is persuading Savonarola that, for the welfare of the Florentines, access to the works of the poets should be restricted.'

I was already beginning to worry about the Medici collection in the library. Now Benivieni was confirming my fears. In a sudden change of mind, I accepted the invitation and agreed to go with him to the next meeting.

In the garden of the main cloister, Fra Girolamo welcomed me with an engaging humility and introduced me to the members of his academy, who were not the men I had met on the previous occasion. This was, indeed, the academy of the despairing and I recognised my own despair in every face amongst these widowers and childless men. But they had something else in common apart from sorrow: a lack of bitterness. They blamed no one for their ills, only sought a way to endure them well. The discussion ranged from the art of good government to the role of history. Astrology, theology, art – there was not a subject that Savonarola was not familiar with. But his view of literature remained unsettling. It was his opinion that the only literature fit to be read was the Bible and the works of the Church Fathers.

'Of course one may read the poets, but never look to them for knowledge of the Divine. And one has to be very wary of their beauty of language and expression – it's just a sticky trap for flies. I often hear it said in these streets, especially by the Platonists, that truth is beauty. But what is beauty? Is it a fair face and a fair form? An harmonious arrangement of colour? Truth is beautiful, that I will grant, but is beauty truth? Is a whiskery old woman with a pure heart and generous nature beautiful or not? And a handsome youth with beguiling eyes for whom nothing is of interest but himself. Is he true because he is beautiful? Of course not. I have heard it said by certain learned men that the language of scripture is coarse and uses a debased grammar. Does that make it untrue? No. For something to be truly beautiful, it must be holy. The function of art is to remind people of God. But art today has separated itself from this sacred function, and it celebrates Man instead, Man in all his finery, Man in all his vanity. God did not give us talent in art to paint portraits of rich and powerful men!'

To Savonarola, modern painters had irredeemably strayed from the path. 'Leonardo, Filippino Lippi, Ghirlandaio – these men believe their talents are their own and they strive, they burst veins, to outdo each other and gain the attention of patrons.' He pointed to a large lunette in the cloister, the most elaborate painting of the crucifixion I had seen, done in gentle but true perspective. Savonarola raised his hand to it. 'Fra Angelico, for whom painting was prayer in colour. This is the function of art, to remind us of God.'

The scene was complex: Christ crucified, flanked by the two thieves and with about twenty figures at the foot of the three crosses. The movement, gestures and emotions were very affecting. Among the saints were Cosmas and Damian, the patrons of the Medici.

'And yet even this,' said Savonarola, 'is a frivolity. What would St Dominic say if he saw the walls of this monastery so colourfully decorated with paintings paid for by a rich man with a bad conscience?'

Frivolity? I was not the only one to gasp at this.

'The Pope told Cosimo de' Medici that, to save his soul, he had to spend ten thousand florins on restoring San Marco. He spent much more than that. The Pope sent a bull granting Cosimo indulgence for his sins. Did it help? No. I tell you, Cosimo is burning in hell. What pope has the power to affect God's judgement?' He frowned at the Fra Angelico. 'Only in the Eastern Church do they know how to use art in the service of God.'

Savonarola spoke to a friar who went away and returned bearing an icon wrapped in velvet. This he uncovered, slowly and reverentially. As the wrappers came off, my expectation was very high and I thought I was about to see God in paint, but the icon, which showed the Virgin and Child, was so dark and ugly that I turned away, repulsed.

'Look again, Tommaso Maffei,' said Fra Girolamo.

'Oh, that is horrible!' I protested. 'It is dirty, it is chipped, and the figures – well, the man who did this simply had no talent at

365

all.' The eyes of the Virgin were huge, the nose slender, the mouth a little rosebud. Flesh had been painted brown and contoured with darker brown lines. The thing was a travesty of reality.

'Look again, Tommaso Maffei,' said Fra Girolamo. 'Let the image enter your heart and mind, let it rest there. To do so is to welcome in the Lord and his Mother. Do not allow aesthetic judgement to be a barrier between you and God. Let it go. Become one with Him.'

As I gazed upon the image, Savonarola explained that the painter had not aimed at the life-like and failed. He had aimed at the heaven-like. 'There is no perspective in heaven. No time, no space. To paint divine scenes you must look through the eyes of God, not man. You must look into hearts and not linger on pretty forms.'

Surely this was Plato's own view? In the icon I saw my own vanity, in considering to be holy that which I perceived through the senses. I looked and what I saw was not form but intention. Suddenly the small painting seemed to be a window on heaven.

'Do you understand?' Fra Girolamo asked gently.

'Yes, I believe I do.'

'Only the holy is beautiful. This icon is beautiful, truly beautiful. What you call beauty is mere superficial attractiveness, a seduction of sight.'

I quickened at these words, at the truth and simplicity of them. How often had I read, how often had I copied Plato's *Symposium*? I knew the theory of beauty only in my head. It took a black-cowled friar to get my heart to begin to understand.

Savonarola always preferred the open air no matter how cold, but a drizzle of rain sent us into the shelter of the cloisters, and when it became a heavy downpour, we retreated to the library. Savonarola led the way to the dormitory floor of the monastery. At the top of the stair was the fresco of the Annunciation by Fra Angelico, the angelic brother. Frivolity? It was a painting to bring you to your knees. To be in its presence was to be in the very presence of the Virgin Mary and the angel Gabriel. The scene had been set in a loggia that opened on to a garden. Coming up the stairs you could be walking into a Medici villa, or the Badia of Fiesole. This was a contemporary setting, but the scene it contained was eternal, timeless, now. How could Savonarola denounce this?

'He is testing us,' Girolamo Benivieni said in my ear, 'as he is testing himself.'

'What do you mean?'

'He speaks, he always speaks, the truth, but he finds it as hard as the rest of us to follow it in all its purity. Yes, the work of Fra Angelico is frivolous, but you try taking this off the walls in Savonarola's presence. He loves it as we do.'

'And the books, the poets?'

Benivieni nodded. 'The same. The books are safe in his care, Tommaso.'

I looked askance at him, then realised that this man of God had tricked me into coming. But I felt grateful for it. It takes a trick to catch a trickster.

The cells of the friars were being aired and had their doors open. As Savonarola led the way to the library, several of us strayed, looking into each little cell and its single angelic fresco. One that I visited had the Presentation in the Temple. With the background the same colour as the plaster of the cell, it made the figures seem to hang in the air. The grace of Mary, the purity of Joseph, the devotion of the attendant saints, all focussed the attention on the Christ Child. I gazed in awe, rejecting Savonarola's criticism of Italian art. Suddenly it was as if I saw what the painter had seen, and the tears that Fra Angelico wept as he worked began to prick my own eyes, only mine were tears of remorse. I tried to hold them back but could not. Silently they began to well up, spill over and flow down my cheeks. I felt as if I were dissolving in grief. To have lived so long in such error! Overcome by the weight of my sin, my body crumpled to the floor. Still the tears poured. In the rush of water, as in a flood, old possessions floated past – ambitions, attachments, loves. I saw my grandfather raising his arms to the sky like a priest of ancient Etruria; I saw my brother

Antonio flying his falcon in the Volterrana, and, then again, riding bare-back and bare-skinned; I saw my city of Volterra raped by the armies of Florence; I saw the face of Giuliano de' Medici, fresh back from a hunt; I saw a rose, flung from a window, its petals floating on the air; I saw a painting of Venus at dawn with her attendant Graces and Mercury; I saw Giuliano face down in a pool of blood; I saw Lorenzo de' Medici crying. All these things brought forth more welling tears. The warm, salty waters rushed over me and through me, but still I kept my eyes averted from that one image that could kill me. But she came. First as a child, a little girl in a procession, and then as a woman, the wife in my bed. Elena. I cried out then, a great cry of pain that bounded echoing through the monastery.

Fra Girolamo was kneeling beside me, touching my face.

I writhed in the anguish of loss, wondering if this happened to everyone, if this was why his supporters were called the weepers. But this was not weeping – this was the death of the immortal soul. He said prayers over me and, in time, the heaving grief subsided, leaving me spent. He and I were alone – the rest had gone to the library. I lay there staring at the simple, single vault of the ceiling. I needed to confess, everything and at once.

'I will hear your confession,' he said, and, helping me to my feet, guided me to his own cell. A double cell with a desk in the first part and a bed in the other, it was a dark place, undecorated, and smelt like a stable. There I told him everything as best I could, including the worst part, that as predicted in my boyhood by a gipsy of Constantinople, I bore the curse of death, affecting all my loved ones but never me.

Savonarola told me not to persecute myself with such thoughts, that all men have their own fate, that if I am an instrument of divine will, then I should rejoice. He instructed me to pray for the souls of my loved ones, to surrender them to God, to beg God for forgiveness of my errors.

'We have in these corridors two main cells,' he said. 'This one of mine and, at the other end, the one once used by Cosimo de' Medici. I want you to spend time alone in both, and to choose. Today, this day, is your hour of choice. By the time we have finished our meeting in the library, you will have got off your fence, Tommaso.'

How did he know about my fence? I followed him along the corridor, turned left and went towards the library. Pausing at its entrance, he directed me to the double cell at the far end. Here it was as lucid as Savonarola's had been dim. I knelt to pray before a fresco of the Adoration of the Magi, but my gaze went to the image of wise men from the East, painted with great delicacy. I felt as if I followed in their train of wisdom, that stretched back into furthest antiquity. I tried to pray but found it difficult, so I sat and practised the form of contemplation which Pico had taught me, and I found light and sweetness.

I then went back Savonarola's cell, to the bare, vaulted room containing a desk and a crucifix. The air was soft, velvety, the odour earthy. Sunlight – air – faith. So simple. Pure. Here there was a power working greater than my own. I found myself kneeling before the crucifix, my mind focussed on prayer at last. Certainty. That was the way of Savonarola. The faith needs no philosophy; it is enough in itself. Innocence is the source of strength. I could leave Tommaso de' Maffei, shed him with his clothes, take on the habit and have no more of him. It was that easy. The tears came again, but this time they were the tears of relief.

Turin, August 22ⁿᵈ, 1506

Erasmus is on my heels and asking for my latest chapter. I plied him with drink, telling him he needs solace after the gruelling examination for his degree, but he resisted the wine I was about to pour him.

'Then you will have to be sober when I tell you what I have to say, because I do not wish you to read the truth about me before you have heard it from my own lips.'

'What truth?'

'Desiderio, my Augustinian friend, I am not as you have known me these few years, a travelling, rootless teacher. In 1493 I took the vows and entered the Order of the Preaching Friars. I am a Dominican.'

Erasmus slapped both his ears as if to clear them. *'What?'*

'I am a Dominican friar.'

I am home. I am in Italy. If I must meet my fate – and what is the fate of a runaway friar? – then I will meet it honestly. 'I'm sure I'm not the only one. There must be many of us who fled the monastery of San Marco when it was sacked.'

'Sacked?'

'I should have acted more bravely, I realise that now, and gone to Pope Alexander. He would have absolved me from my vows, perhaps even without payment, but instead I fled the country. I have been trying to divorce myself from the past; now I am walking into its jaws. Pope Julius is not as amenable to coin as Alexander was.'

'There is nothing in your book about this. No indication at all.'

'Not yet, but if there is to be any more story, then, well – I had to tell you this part in person.'

'Yes,' he snapped. 'It is well for the man of truth to be honest. You have deceived us. All these years, and you could not tell us, your friends? Then you are no friend, to keep such a secret!'

With that he walked out and has not spoken to me since. What do I do now? The rumours of war coming up from the south are growing ever stronger. I can only go east, to Venice, but I will not leave before I have made my peace with Erasmus. I sent him a note, to which I received a terse reply, that I am to make my peace with God before I try making it with any man.

80 THE COMPANY OF THE LIBRARY 1494

AND NOW I HAVE ANOTHER CONFESSION FOR YOU, ERASMO, should you ever read this. Whether it will make you think better of me or worse, I do not know, but my experience in Savonarola's cell was not that of conversion, and I did not become a Dominican as a matter of faith. In the middle of my prayers in that cell came a vision, a vision of a book – that book of Hermes which had belonged to Lorenzo. What was it doing at San Marco? Now that I thought about it, the Medici collection of books stored at the monastery seemed to have swelled, not diminished, in recent times. I joined the others in the library but had only half an ear to the discussion while I looked about curiously. Yes, there was a discrimination against the poets, but their books were still dusted and cared for. And the more I looked, the more my suspicion was confirmed: there were volumes here that Lorenzo had once kept for his private use. Someone was using the library as a depository for Medici treasures.

As soon as the meeting was over, and I had evaded Savonarola and his enquiry about my decision, I went to the Palazzo de' Medici and sought out Lascaris, who looked after the house library.

'I have been commissioned to make a copy of the *Poimandres* of Hermes. Poliziano tells me that the best edition is that made for Lorenzo. May I borrow it?'

The librarian looked at me guardedly then told me to wait. After a few minutes he returned with Cardinal Giovanni, who wanted to know who the commission was for, and why I would not be satisfied with any of the plentiful copies of the book easily available. I kept spinning lies, trapping myself in a web of my own making.

Finally he interrupted me. 'Why are you lying, Tommaso?'

'I saw the Hermes at San Marco and wondered why it was there.'

'A donation, made at Lorenzo's own request. Many of his books went there.'

'I have heard that there is going to be a restriction on the borrowing of pagan books from San Marco.'

'I have heard it, too. I trust it will not happen.'

'But what if it does? Are you not anxious to retrieve the Medici collection?'

He considered me awhile, chewing his lip. His eyes might have been bulbous, but there was great intelligence in them. He exchanged a glance with Lascaris, who gave a barely imperceptible nod of his head. The Cardinal turned back to me.

'In times such as these, we all have to lie. Lorenzo's books were put in the monastery by me.' The body of a buffoon enclosed a sharp wit that could see the future as clearly as any prophet. 'If the French come, if they take Florence, they will loot the palazzo and take the Medici library. It seemed to me that the safest place to keep the books was in San Marco. I arranged it with Savonarola: our library is a separate collection, merely being stored there.'

'And do you still think it is the safest place?'

'I trust the Friar.'

'Savonarola's intentions may be pure but I do not trust those closest to him. How long will it be before disapproval of reading the ancient authors becomes a ban? How long before those books are put away, only to disappear? Each one is worth a fortune, and the brethren are committed to relief of the poor. This is the library, the great library, which Lorenzo assembled for the benefit of mankind. Will we see it turned into bread?'

The Cardinal inhaled. 'I think God may have sent you to me.'

I twitched. I thought I had escaped God.

The Cardinal turned to Lascaris for his opinion. Lascaris nodded again. 'Invite him in.'

'Into what?' I asked.

'I am forming a company, a band of loyal men. Loyal to the Medici, yes, but loyal most of all to books and to learning, to the freedom of mind and to study. It is their sworn and secret duty to protect the Medici library in whatever befalls us.'

What is love? It is that which makes you act contrary to all sense and reason, that which makes you risk loss, even the loss of life. It is that devotion to something which makes you quite naturally virtuous. And my love is for books. For learning. For the great renewal of men by the wisdom of antiquity.

'I would do whatever you ask of me.'

'Would you? Would you truly?'

'I would, even without knowing what it is that you have in mind.'

Cardinal Giovanni looked at me compassionately. 'We've been looking for someone who is able and willing to give up everything.'

I swallowed.

'If you were to take this duty on, Tommaso, it would serve us best if you were in the monastery. Go to Savonarola, throw yourself at his feet and ask to be accepted into the brotherhood. Savonarola is very disposed to giving his friars work to which they are naturally suited, so it will not be difficult to get yourself placed in the library. I believe it was my father's wish that you marry Maria Poliziana. This you must sacrifice, for the greater good. I realise that it is no small thing I ask of you. At the same time, I do not think I am asking you to do something wholly distasteful. And yet, this conversation must never be repeated to anyone. As far as even your closest friends will know, even Ficino, Pico and Poliziano, you have chosen this path after an experience of conversion.'

One way, perhaps the only sure way, of coming off the fence is to be pushed.

With my head held down by Fra Silvestro's bony hands, I watched my curls floating to the floor to make a heap of vanity. As they fell, they died, the light going out of them, and became sordid matter to be swept up and burned.

'Will you not send them to the wigmaker?' I asked, half hoping I could buy them back and wear them again some day. 'They would fetch a good price.' Fra Silvestro sniffed and kept clicking the shears.

My past lay on the floor, my youth, my time as a man of the Medici, in a pile of hair. A young novice swept it into a wooden bucket and took it away.

81 FALLING STARS
1494

FORTUNA IS POPULAR IN ANY AGE WHEN MEN ARE superstitious about their fate and ascribe everything to the starry heavens. She, the goddess who gives and who takes away, is depicted with a wheel to show her cyclical nature. In our enlightened age, we have deposed her. We study the ancients and argue that the events that befall Man are the result of natural law and not the arbitrary fate meted out by an inconstant goddess of the Roman pantheon. Both Ficino and Pico differentiated between true astrology and superstition. Understanding now that, though the stars may be signs, they are not causes, we begin to look at them with fresh eyes, wondering indeed what in fact they are.

The ages of mankind do not begin and end on certain days. There is overlap, a long period when peoples of vastly different beliefs and outlooks dwell together in our cities. Such is our age. As wisdom pours out of ancient texts, awakening our scholars to a reasonable universe, so the mass of people continue in the old barbarous ways. And not only the people. Some gods and goddesses, finding themselves outmoded, have not gone lightly into retirement. Fortuna in particular. Whether we believed in her or not was immaterial: she gathered her strength for a mighty turn of her wheel, creaking and heavy, to pitch our men of reason to their – predicted – ruin.

Within the enclosure of the monastery, we heard all the news of the city and abroad, often sooner than anyone else. We were not cut off from the world in any respect. One day in the library Fra Domenico told me of the death of the Patriarch of Aquileia and I had to keep my face calm, to nod indifferently and say, 'Oh?'

'He was a heretic,' he told me solemnly.

Ermolao Barbaro was dead. The knowledge seeped through my veins. 'Oh? In what way a heretic?'

'One of these pagan scholars parading about in church robes. A wolf in sheep's clothing.'

'But what was his heresy?'

'He was translating Aristotle.'

'That is hardly heresy. Theology has been based on Aristotle since St Thomas Aquinas.'

'But his translations differed from those of the Angelic Doctor...' Fra Domenico went on to explain about the sin of philosophy and accurate translation whilst inside I was folding up and weeping.

'Did they try him for this?' I asked.

'They were going to, but he was murdered.'

'*Murdered?*'

'Poisoned.'

'Who by?'

Fra Domenico shrugged. 'Does it matter? God's Will is done. His ways are mysterious – and most wonderful. It is a message from heaven to all scholars to return to sacred scripture. I trust they will hear it. Eh?'

Pico came in later, his eyes red and swollen, and told me the full story. Ermolao's death had not been instant. A message had come to Poliziano from Ermolao's servant, Didymus, and Angelo and Pico had swiftly bought and sent an expensive antidote, but it had not arrived in time. Barbaro had died, they heard; more, he had been denied the last rites and was buried in unconsecrated ground.

Pico brought his head close to mine. 'Listen, I approve of what you have done, and wish I could do it myself, but how can I? How have you given yourself to a Church that asks you to surrender reason? To accept things on faith? To dispense with what you know because the authorities are scared of Truth? How have you done that? For my part it would be too great a sacrifice.'

I nodded. 'It was God's will – that is all I can say. But who would poison dear, sweet Barbaro?'

'Envy, Spite, Malice, Ignorance – there are all manner of contenders. I do not know. He is dead.' Fresh tears swelled in Pico's eyes.

'The friars here think it was the wrath of God and that all scholars must take heed.'

Pico's lip curled. 'A bright star in the firmament of literature is snuffed out. God can only weep.'

'How is Angelo?'

'Inconsolable. There is some evil force attacking our friend, stirring up and agitating his emotions to such a degree that his brain is afflicted. He does not study now but spends his time writing verses – doggerel – to Alessandra Scala. He says she replies in fine, Attic Greek, but it is not the lady who is writing, it is her tutors. The Greeks are using her as bait to lure our Angelo into a trap. They mean to humilitate him, not merely embarrass him, but humiliate him to such an extent that his reputation will be ruined and he will not be seen in public again. I keep warning him but he will not listen. He wants that bait so much. It is unbearable.'

'You think he has no chance of winning the lady, then?'

'None whatsoever. She is already betrothed to Michele Marullus. Did you know that? It is Marullus behind it all, of course. Wherever there are Greeks gathered, you hear jokes about Poliziano, and cruel laughter. His past sins are coming to haunt him, and there is no Lorenzo to shield him from the mob. Every insult he has ever delivered is being returned four-fold. It is like watching a bear being made to dance and then brought to its knees amidst howls of derision.'

'And Maria? What of her?'

'She continues to live with him, her brother's housekeeper, but complaints are being made by neighbours, even those at Fiesole. There has even been an accusation put in the *tamburazione* that it is an incestuous relationship, and that Angelo Poliziano is abusing his nephews. Written in bad Italian. The hand of a Greek, I have no doubt. They are destroying him, Tommaso. I want him to come here to San Marco – it is the only refuge these days.'

'What, you would have him do what you cannot and surrender his own reason? Give up his professorship and become a friar?' I laughed.

'For him it is a simple choice between sanity and madness.'

'Between sanity and Maria. Who would look after her? You?' My voice was catching but it was time to speak plainly. 'You do know she is in love with you, don't you?'

'Of course, and that love is returned, but it is Platonic. I cannot be encumbered by a wife. Apart from anything else, my time is short. A daughter of the Rucellai family, a very sibyl by all accounts, has told Savonarola, in a voice much like his own, that I will be dead in the time of the lilies. Have I not heard that before?'

'So, in the month of May. But every year has a month of May.'

'It has nothing to do with the month of May. The lily is the standard of the French, remember.'

Merchants arriving in Florence from the north were bringing news of the King of France mustering his troops. The French were preparing their invasion.

God, Savonarola had cried recently from the pulpit, his eyes starting in prophetic vision, *God will take the King by the bridle and lead him into Italy! The sword of the Lord is upon us! Only those among you who are just may rejoice – for the rest, you vile and worthless slaves, for now you may continue to besmirch yourselves. Fill your bellies with wine that your kidneys rot with the excess, stain your hands with the blood of the poor, for this is your portion and your lot. But know that your bodies and your souls are in my hands, and soon your bodies will be exhausted by scourges, and your souls I shall condemn to eternal fire!*

'When they cross the Alps,' Pico said, 'they will bring my death. The time of the lilies is coming.'

Having allied Florence to Naples, Piero had destroyed Lorenzo's hard-won balance of power. Now, heaping error on error, Piero was determined that Florence should resist the French. He sent Lorenzo and Giovanni di Pierfrancesco to negotiate with the King. They returned, professing failure.

When the people rioted and tried to expel Piero, we closed the gates of the monastery and went to our prayers. It was about that time that we heard that King Ferrante of Naples had died. Savonarola's first prophecy, about the death of Lorenzo, the Pope and the King, had now been fulfilled, and the second prophecy, of the invasion of the French, was upon us.

82 THE COMING SCOURGE
1494

IT WAS DURING A MEETING OF THE SAN MARCO ACADEMY, which the Pierfranceschi had begun to attend, that officers of the Signoria came, accompanied by armed men, and arrested the brothers on a charge of treason, saying that it had been discovered that they were conspiring with the French. The brothers jumped to their feet but were quickly overwhelmed. My friend Zenobio was arrested with them, guilty, it seemed, of nothing more than being their cousin.

All three were condemned to death.

Their supporters took flight, including Michele Marullus. What else could he do? The cause was simple enough: he was implicated in the plot and therefore joined the French. Poliziano, however, seemed to believe that Marullus had only ever courted Alessandra Scala to spite him, and that now, so shortly after their betrothal, he had abandoned her.

Not only the friends of the Pierfranceschi were flying to France; so, too, were the enemies of Borgia. It seemed each day there was news of fresh desertions from Rome, including Cardinal Giuliano della Rovere, he who is now our Pope Julius.

In Italy we had perfected the art of war. Using mercenary forces, it was rare for men to be killed in battles. Oh, yes, there were some sieges for the sake of appearance, and certainly the people suffered in times of war. But bloody battlefields were a thing of the past. The French, however, had a standing army of forty thousand men trained to kill. They also had a new weapon: horse-drawn guns which fired iron shot. And they were on the move. All diplomatic activity to persuade King Charles against an invasion was in vain. Every morning we woke up with our thoughts solely upon the creeping lava flow that was the French.

Poliziano never visited San Marco, not even the library, but from the casino of Lorenzo's garden he sent regularly for books. Whenever I could, I arranged to deliver them myself, trying to repair our friendship. Since I had become a Dominican, he had been off-hand with me, even cold, but on the day the Pierfranceschi were released, he was more voluble.

'I will never get used to you looking like a magpie,' he said with distaste when, in answer to his request, I took him what we had on Africa. He felt the cloth of my habit between finger and thumb. 'Does it itch?'

'It is supposed to itch, to remind me that the body is my slave and not my master. It helps me turn my mind to God.'

He stared at me, those puddle-dark eyes penetrating through to the innermost part of me where the truth lay.

His desk in the loggia of the casino looked out into lush shrubberies that twittered with birds. The city was shut out by walls, cypresses hid the view of towers and domes: we could have been in the country. This idyllic accommodation had been given to him freely by Piero de' Medici.

'Have you heard?' Angelo asked. 'I'm not sure how much you hear in that enclosure.'

'We hear everything, believe me.'

'About the Pierfranceschi being released?'

Indeed I had. Early that morning Piero had gone to the Bargello himself to accompany his cousins into freedom, a freedom that he himself had arranged, 'in his magnanimity,' said Poliziano.

'What freedom is it,' I enquired, 'if they are confined to their villa? It sounds like house arrest to me.'

'It would be a fool who would let them loose. But they are out of prison. The whole city is cheering Piero. Have you ever known a more prudent, magnificent, moderate, humane or friendlier man?'

Now it was my turn to stare at him, uncomprehending.

'Consider his mind, how vigorous it is, shrewd, perspicacious, prudent, grave, strong…'

'Feeble and misguided in my opinion, if he thinks Florence can resist the French.'

'You don't know him. He is utterly determined to maintain our liberty.'

'When a big wave comes, it is better to let it wash over you.'

Poliziano rubbed his face, tired of trying to convince himself, let alone others, of Piero's virtues. 'I am growing old. All I want is a quiet life in which to pursue my studies and to write. Piero can give me that.'

'Old? – you are usually the first to deny it.'

'In one month I shall be forty. Lorenzo was dead at forty-two.'

'But he did not die of old age.'

There was a flicker on Angelo's face as I said this.

'You are hiding something,' I accused him. 'What is it?'

'Tommaso, I promise you, if I were to be open and speak the truth I would be dead before I was forty.'

What truth? 'We are alone, Angelo. Speak.'

'And burden you with knowledge? Be blissful in your ignorance, Tommaso.'

'It was Piero, wasn't it?' I whispered.

Angelo flinched, alarmed, then recovered. 'What, kill his father?' He laughed then.

'Patricide. It is not without precedent.'

'You idiot! You could not be further from the truth. Listen!' he shouted, suddenly thumping the desk with his fist. 'The French are on their way to the Alps. Do you understand? Forty thousand men-at-arms with a weapon that can do in hours what takes our bombards weeks. Great slaughter is on its way. Do you know what this young King of France does? When he comes to a small town close to a city he sacks it with such malevolence that the city itself surrenders without a struggle. They know how to fight wars in the north.

'For all our talk in religion and philosophy, there is only one belief I hold, which is that I am going to die; that there will come a moment when I shall cease to be. It fills me with more terror than any thought of a tyrant, real or imaginary. What am I doing? I shall tell you.' His voice was booming. He was telling everyone in the city. 'I am trying to survive! I am trying to protect my family! Have you no idea of how precarious the times are?' He gazed scornfully at my expression of offence for a moment then subsided. 'Listen, I agree that Piero is a cracked pot. The crack did not show while the pot was empty but now, now that he is filled with power, it is becoming all too visible. The trouble is, it is a pot of my own making.'

'And a very beautiful pot it would have been,' I replied, 'had you not used inferior clay.'

'Even so, he is mine and I cannot abandon him.'

And then I understood. Poliziano was being, as ever, loyal, even when his own reason began to object. Born under the sign of the Crab, Angelo Poliziano held faster in loyalty than any man I have known. I trust God rewards such virtue.

'How is Maria?' I asked, the moment seeming right.

'I cannot tell you, Tommaso, how disappointed I am in you. When I heard about your decision, it came as a double slap, one, that you had made such a decision, the other that you had not told me about it yourself, or even discussed it. Maria? She won't hear your name mentioned. She says you're a hypocrite who has deceived us all.'

I swallowed hard, longing to tell him the truth. 'I trust that, by the grace of God, she will forgive me one day. So, where is she staying?'

'With Cammilla and the boys, who I'm sending back to Montepulciano. I haven't yet made arrangements for Maria.'

'What arrangements?'

'She cannot stay with me any more. The thirst for law and righteousness that now afflicts this city will not allow it. No, she must either return home to Montepulciano or go into a convent, but I cannot decide which.'

Images rose up, of Maria happy in her brother's house, in her garden, in whatever company she found herself, whether it be witches or scholars. I realised then that I had killed her.

'Perhaps Pico...' I began hoarsely.

'Is that not your bell calling you to prayer? Time to lope back to your kennel, you hound of God.'

The rough wool of my habit itched as it had never itched before.

'We need those books back in a month,' I said feebly.

'Phfff,' said Angelo Poliziano.

83 POETRY COMES FROM GOD
1494

IN THE MONASTERY WE HEARD THE NEWS ON THE SEVENTH, that the French had crossed the Alps. But it was on the eighth day of September, 1494, that all the bells of Florence began to toll, calling people to the churches to hear the news. In San Marco we hurried to our places in the choir stalls, ready to receive the frightened people pouring in through the doors, to still their hearts and minds with our prayers.

A week later, even as the hordes of Charles VIII set up camp near Milan, we heard of the death of its duke, Gian Galeazzo. Rumour tried to persuade us that he had died of an excess of coitus; many in Italy may have believed that; we in Florence did not. What convenient timing for the death of the nephew who stood between Ludovico Sforza and his ambitions! As soon as he had assumed the title of Duke of Milan, Sforza began to encourage the French either to move on or to go home. He had, it seemed, fulfilled his intention of having invited them in the first place. After some hesitation, the French moved on.

As the great army approached the Appenines, Piero de' Medici rode out to arrange the defences of the fortresses on our Tuscan borders, and Lorenzo and Giovanni di Pierfrancesco escaped from house arrest and went to join the King.

My own response to the coming tide of invasion was to think only of the library. I was out in the city, visiting everyone who had books on loan, trying to get them back. I went to Lorenzo's garden to retrieve from Angelo the books on Africa, now two months overdue. Outside, by the gate, I came across what I took to be a pile of rubbish but then I saw a claw-like hand protruding from the carapace of oily rags: a beggar on his knees, his forehead on the ground. The palm was held upwards in a silent plea – plea or demand – for alms. I stooped and lifted the rags and found it to be a woman. She looked up at me with a radiant smile on her battered face. A clump of whiskers sprouting from her chin curled upwards in a beard.

'Give,' she said. 'Give.'

'Come, mother, let me take you to the hospice where we can find food.'

'I don't want food. I want you.' And then she laughed and ran her hand up my leg. I jumped back and kicked out simultaneously, sending the heap of rags rolling.

Being a Christian is the most difficult thing I have ever attempted. I was not in a good mood when I went to see Poliziano.

'We need our books back.'

'Tomorrow.'

'Today. Now.'

'What is the matter with you?'

'Perhaps you have not heard it here in your hermitage but the French army is on its way across the mountains.'

'Yes, of course I have heard that.' Urged on by Piero de' Medici, Angelo had spent the summer collecting and collating his letters. He was now tapping the papers into a neat stack held between boards and tying it with ribbon. 'Would you have time, amidst all your sacred duties, to read through these and check for any mistakes?'

'No, I would not.'

He peered at me. 'Why is it that the more ardent a man grows in his religion, the frostier he becomes with his friends?'

I shuddered suddenly, reached inside my habit and scratched my back.

'It is itchy, isn't it?'

'Only when I am with you.'

'Tommaso, sit down. I need to speak to you. No more sparring.'

I brought a chair and sat beside him at his desk, fixed to which was a neat page of his writing with a wide margin he had left to make it easy to write additions or corrections later. This was a page going straight to the printer – no scribe required as an intermediary. It was headed 'On Recognising and Defeating the Antichrist'.

'If Savonarola is to be believed,' he said, 'Death is pounding towards us. I am trying to get everything finished before she arrives. I have a favour to ask of you. I wish you to be my literary executor.'

'Of course, I'd be honoured, provided I do not die with you.' The pressure of the French on the mind was making any thought of the future seem vain.

'I need these books a few days longer, until I've completed what I'm writing on pygmies.'

'*Pygmies*? Angelo, these may be our final hours. If you must write, write about God, not pygmies. Or better still, come with me to San Marco.'

'Should God spare my life I mean to devote myself entirely to philosophy.'

'How many times have you said that?'

'As soon as I've completed my new *Miscellanea* – and I only have forty-four chapters to go –'

'Do it now. Then you could have at least forty-four chapters with something interesting to say.'

'Pygmies are interesting. Can you imagine what they are like, those diminutive men living in African forests? Even as we speak, there they are, a world away, sharpening their arrows, ignorant of theology, and certainly not worried about where the French are. Isn't that interesting? According to Ovid, they were made dwarfish by Juno, angry that they prayed to other goddesses. Now that is interesting.'

'It is trivial!'

'If you were less on your knees and more often at your philosophical studies, you would know by now that God is in all things.'

'Of course I know that.'

'Only in theory. I know it in pygmies.'

He told me that he had invited friends to dine with him that evening and asked me to join them. I said I would be retiring early to my hard bed.

'Do you not want to come?'

'Of course I do, you evil tempter.'

'Then ask permission of the Frate. Tell him, tell him the Platonic Academy is meeting here and you have been invited. I'll wager he'll allow you to come.'

And so it was. 'You may go,' said my spiritual father. 'Tell me everything that is discussed.' He stipulated one thing, that I be accompanied by another friar, and the one he chose was Fra Roberto.

Angelo's guests that evening included Pico della Mirandola, Bernardo Dovizi, Michelangelo, Amerigo Vespucci, Girolamo Benivieni and other poets. We dined outside. It was a honeyed September night and a table had been set in the loggia. Moths with wings like dead leaves clung to the back wall and soporific hornets fell into lamps. Out in the garden, where an owl hooted in a tall chestnut, a lone firefly winked amongst the shrubs in forlorn hope of finding love. It was a night to breathe in and hold in the heart; a night when it was impossible to believe in imminent destruction.

One guest, arriving late, plunged us into an embarrassed silence. Zenobio Acciaiuoli limped in on a crutch, trying to be inconspicuous, trying to put his old life back together, seamlessly. On the release of the Pierfranceschi, he had been left behind in prison. He winced as he sat down and rubbed his knee.

'*Salve,* Tommaso,' he said, sitting beside me.

'Oh, Zenobio, what did they do to you?'

Angelo, staunch supporter of Piero de' Medici, looked on Zenobio with eyes that commanded his silence. Bernardo Dovizi, who was Cardinal Giovanni's secretary, shifted in his chair. To change the subject, Angelo asked Zenobio if he had written any poetry in prison.

Zenobio stared at him as if he were mad. 'No, I did not.'

'I have written a hymn,' said Girolamo Benivieni quickly.

'Then sing it for us if you would.'

Benivieni complied, came to his feet and sang his hymn. Savonarola was encouraging poets to use their talent in service to God, and it was resulting in a fine crop of new hymns for the laity. I thought this was a good example, but Angelo listened with a deepening grimace. 'Is it true that you have burnt your earlier work?' he asked once Benivieni had finished.

'That which is unworthy.'

'All those lovely lyrics?'

'As I watched them turn to ash, a burden lifted from my soul.' Benivieni looked at Poliziano uncertainly, knowing full well what that expression on the professor's face meant.

'What kind of burden?'

'The burden of pride, of competitiveness,' Benivieni replied, borrowing words from Savonarola and trying to draw strength from them. 'Have I ever written a poem and not wondered what it would bring me by way of recognition? Surrender of worldly ambition, Maestro, is the greatest relief to the soul.'

Zenobio followed the discussion closely. 'Do you have no regrets?' he asked.

'About burning them? No, none,' said Benivieni.

'Well, I regret it,' said Angelo. 'A strange thing happens when a man burns his work: he loses his talent.'

A frisson of shock went through the company and all eyes turned to Benivieni. Pico leapt to his defence but Poliziano weathered the storm he had created and continued to gaze at Benivieni. 'Don't sit there sucking lemons, man,' he said. 'Get angry.'

'I have transcended the passions,' said Benivieni.

'Oh, have you? Then you have transcended humanity. Poetry,' said Poliziano, addressing us all, 'comes from a man's soul: we call it the Muse, though it is no external power but an inward one. To hear the Muse you must still the mind, and when she speaks you write down her words faithfully, even if it is as hard as recalling a dream. Everyone here knows what I am talking about. When you give that up with some lofty intention to write in praise of God, what happens? The Muse is silent. Why? Because you are forbidding her to speak.'

'The rational part of the mind does sit in judgement over the imagination,' agreed Pico.

'Precisely. And what takes the place of the voice of the soul? The words of the mind. These hymns are the product not of inspiration but of thought. That is why they sound dead.'

'Ridiculous!' Girolamo Benivieni protested. 'Dead? They are full of my love of God.'

'Sentiment, Girolamo, mere sentiment dressed up as devotion.'

'Savonarola says it is the poet's duty to write holy things.'

'I say it is our duty to write as inspired. It is not the function of the poet to be a priest. He must stay true to his Muse and no other.'

'The Muse is a bawd,' Benivieni retorted. 'A wanton. She encourages men in licentiousness.'

'Sometimes that is true. But it is the function of poetry to civilise men, and a civilised man is one who may discipline his own mind and measure his own passions. He is a free man. Poetry is the mother, theology the father: they have different roles. The mother is not so fierce: she allows for passion, she allows her child to err, but always under her watchful gaze. It is for the father to lay down the rules.'

'Dionysus and Apollo,' said Pico, 'the two gods who men see as opposed to one another, the god of wine and the god of reason. In fact there is good evidence to show that these are two names for one god, that Dionysus and Apollo were the same: the complete man.' Pico was championing Angelo's point of view, and Angelo gazed on him fondly. Although Pico went so often to San Marco, and had tempered his life accordingly, his intellect was still his own.

'Savonarola says...' Benivieni began.

'I had a private audience with the Frate myself yesterday,' Angelo interjected.

I glanced up at him, surprised.

'I tried with all my wit and all my skill to temper his opinion with regard to poetry. I tried everything. I have never argued so well.'

'Did it work?' Pico asked, the rising moon shining in his face and silvering his hair.

'He listened to me patiently and, at the end, he smiled and said, "Angelo Poliziano, take the habit. We need you in San Marco."' Angelo sat back and laughed uproariously. 'Can you imagine me dressed like a magpie? No offence, Fra Tommaso, Fra Roberto.'

As the night advanced, the company grew more animated. Wit and eloquence danced with the spindly, fragile craneflies. Bernardo Dovizi was an intellectual jester; our laughter at his obscene jokes, fuelled by the new wine he had brought from the Medici estate at Careggi, was so loud I wondered if it could be heard at San Marco.

Fra Roberto leant over and put his mouth to my ear. 'We should go back.'

Michelangelo had just been invited to recite some of his poetry. I shook my head. 'You go. I will follow shortly.'

'Brother…'

'Shortly, Fra Roberto, I promise.'

I watched him leave, wanting to follow him in his simplicity and single-mindedness, but I did not know how long it would be before once again I could enjoy this kind of company. I settled back to listen to Michelangelo. He was a centaur, half stonemason, half poet, and his verses rang with that sound of the Muse that Angelo had been speaking of. Were they better than Benivieni's hymns? Yes, incomparably so, and I was in full agreement with Poliziano, but I wished he had not humiliated Benivieni who did not deserve it. It was – it is – a mystery, that secular verses can be more divine than holy ones. I sat with my chin in my hands, reflecting on it.

'Tommaso?' Angelo asked. 'What are you puzzling over?'

'Why are holy hymns sentimental at best, dead at worst?'

'Poetry comes from God, yes?'

'So you say.'

'Believe me, it is true. The best poets are those that interfere least with the song of the soul. Every creative act springs from the Creator. It has to. But those who write or sing in devotion have an image in mind that they are devoted to, and it is not their own creative source. Therefore their words are, as it were, man-made.'

'Man-made,' Pico reiterated, 'and stemming from the idea of unworthiness. Hymns are the poetry of men who believe themselves to be worms.'

Girolamo Benivieni flinched at this. '*All* hymns?'

390

'No, there are some mighty exceptions, the hymns of God singing to Himself, but I have not heard any in Florence – apart from yours, my friend. It all comes down to this: who do we believe we are, in essence? A ray of the Divine or a miserable sinner?'

The company murmured in approval.

'I know the answer when I look on you,' said Angelo.

'I am your mirror,' said Pico. 'You are looking on yourself.'

Not since the death of Lorenzo had I seen Angelo this content. The moment was suspended in time, all thoughts of the French put aside. With his arm thrown across Pico's shoulders, he announced his intention to tell us about pygmies.

'From the sublime to the ridiculous!' said Bernardo Dovizi.

'On the contrary. If what Pico says is true, it applies to pygmies as much as to us.' He told us at length about the little men of Africa, striving to instil in us his own wonder at the great, overwhelmingly great, diversity of God's creation. He questioned Amerigo Vespucci about the discoveries of his friend, Cristoforo Columbo, and we heard about the islands far to the west and the naked people dressed only in paint who wear pieces of gold implanted in the nose. Angelo took notes, planning further chapters in his second *Miscellanea*. Although he was a fund of knowledge and, it seemed, could answer anything we asked of him, he himself was only too aware of his ignorance when every day new stories came in from ever more remote places. I stayed to the end, refreshed and stimulated by the evening. Finally, with my way illuminated by the harvest moon, high and huge over Florence, I departed for the monastery, unaware that this was the last time I was to see Angelo Poliziano.

Zenobio walked with me, limping painfully as he made his way on his crutch.

'I hear they tried to get you to accuse the Pierfranceschi of conspiring in the downfall of Piero but you said nothing.'

Zenobio blew through his teeth. 'I had nothing to say. I knew nothing of any conspiracy.'

'Still, a lesser man would have said whatever they wanted him to say.'

'I would not betray my own cousins.'

My heart expanded at his words. His was the voice of the old republic, virtuous and uncompromising.

'So how did you feel,' I asked, 'when the Pierfranceschi went to join the French?'

'Betrayed,' he said grimly. He looked up at the monastery gates. 'I admire your decision, Tommaso, and wish I could make it myself. But is it right to join an Order just because you have lost your faith in men?'

'Go and speak to the Cardinal,' I told him. 'Tell him I sent you.'

Two months later, Zenobio took the habit and joined me in San Marco as a *librarista*.

84 FEBRIS 1494

RAIN THAT HAD BEGUN IN THE NIGHT WAS BY MORNING teeming from a leaden sky, cascading down tiled roofs, crashing out of wooden gutters. I woke to the sound of the Matins bell, my head thudding with the effects of the deceptive, Medici wine of the night before. As I groped my way into the chapel, Pico ran in, dripping.

'Angelo's sick – taken ill during the night. A fever. We need the physician.'

Under the stern gaze of Fra Domenico, who was at the altar and staring at us disapprovingly, I told Pico where to find Antonio Benivieni, the house physician at San Marco. I had no concentration on my prayers that morning.

When I asked permission later to visit Poliziano, I was told he had been put under quarantine, besides which I was confined to the monastery for two weeks for my sin of staying out late.

'Is it plague?'

'We do not know yet.'

Over the following days, each time I asked permission it was refused. Brothers were visiting him, I was told, men more senior than I, more able to save a soul. Stories circulated, brought back by these visiting brothers, of how the great man held conversations out loud all night long, mostly with the dead. They listened avidly to his wanderings and decided he was locked in mortal combat with his conscience. I paced my cell in frustration.

I heard that when Piero de' Medici visited his sickbed, Poliziano was muttering restlessly in his sleep but, when Piero woke him, he started in terror, drew his sheets over his head and whimpered. 'He mistook Piero for the devil,' I was told. But when Pico della Mirandola was with him, Poliziano's eyes melted in wonder as he looked upon St Peter. Those were the stories we heard in the cloisters of San Marco. It was not plague, they said, it was fever of the brain. Nothing contagious.

For sure, poison is not contagious.

'Poison?' you ask. 'First you would have me believe that Lorenzo was murdered; now Poliziano?'

Aye, and Barbaro. And in that month of September, the Medici chaplain, Matteo Franco, the musician, Baccio Ugolini and the painter, Domenico Ghirlandaio. The scythe of death came in advance of the French.

Savonarola had been giving a series of sermons on Genesis during Lent and Advent of each year, not the mystical scripture as expounded by Pico, but a terrifying one – the book in which God renovated the earth by destroying most of its creatures in a flood. Each sermon followed and built on the last: Savonarola was creating a mystical Ark for the Florentines, a raft of salvation. Lent – Advent – Lent – Advent: year by year the Florentines had been worked to a pitch of terror as Savonarola revealed Genesis not as a story of the past but a prediction of tomorrow. In September,

1494, neither Lent nor Advent, he gave a sermon on Genesis to announce imminent destruction at the very time when the French surrounded us. I stood in the Duomo on that day, chilled and terrified by the voice of God. *For behold, I do bring a flood of waters upon the earth, to destroy all flesh, wherein is the breath of life; and every thing that is in the earth shall die.*

'*Italy!*' Savonarola thundered, his voice carrying the length and height of the Duomo, echoing in chapels and cupolas: Italy – Italy – Italy.

People stared up at the cupola, scared that the dome would fall on them, its innovative, uncertain structure shattered by so much noise and the wrath of God.

'*Italy!*' Savonarola cried again. Italy – Italy – Italy. '*These adversities have come to you because of your sins, O Florence, these adversities have come to you because of your sins, O clergy, this tempest has arisen on your account. You will be destroyed, Italy. Rome will be destroyed. O nobles, O wise men, O humble folk, the mighty hand of God is upon you!*'

These sermons had the power of the surgeon's knife: by the greater pain one forgets the lesser. That is to say, when threatened with eternal damnation and the direst tortures of hell, the French seemed less frightening. It was perfectly clear that Savonarola welcomed the invasion. As the outward show of divine justice? I think not. I believe he saw a saviour in Charles VIII of a wholly political kind. The antichrist he warned us of was the pope, Rodrigo Borgia. Savonarola was encouraging King Charles to call a Grand Council to depose him.

These were the concerns of the Florentines as Poliziano lay dying. I prowled the walls of the monastery like a caged beast. Where was Maria? Who could I ask, who would tell me the truth and not some story for my edification? I sent out a note to Michelangelo, to ask him what was really happening, and to find out where Maria Poliziana was. In his reply he told me that Poliziano was bed-ridden, that he was incapable of performing any bodily function without help, that day and night he talked with ghosts, mostly Lorenzo. Maria was in constant attendance at his bedside and did for her brother what he could not do for himself.

I remembered what Pico said, about Angelo being humiliated to death. Whoever poisoned him during that supper with friends had chosen a tincture that worked slowly and ate away the dignity of a man. Who did it? I suspected Dovizi, at the behest of Piero de' Medici. For what reason? Angelo had appointed himself as Piero's counsellor, was counselling him with the good, sound sense of his father to make peace with the French, and Piero did not want anyone around reminding him of Lorenzo. Is that plausible? Not really. Who, then? The answer, the real answer, is too terrible for me to put into writing. Draw your own conclusions and tremble at them.

85 MARIA'S REQUEST
1494

THEY BROUGHT POLIZIANO INTO THE MONASTERY AND PUT him in a private room in the infirmary. I was still not allowed to see him.

'He cannot be disturbed while he is making his peace with God,' Fra Domenico told me. 'Fra Girolamo is with him, preparing him to be received into our Order.' He painted a picture of a man lying quietly in bed reflecting on his soul, and I knew it wasn't true. If Angelo was quiet it was because he was unconscious.

Pico met me in the cloisters, ashen and distraught. 'Any news?'

'Not that I have heard.'

'It can only be days if not hours. He was barely alive when they took him.'

'Sometimes I think I will go and break down that door and knock out any friar who stands in my way. In truth, I am scared of what I will find. But I should be with him.'

'He never found your company easy since you took the habit.'

I should have told Angelo why I had done it, but Cardinal Giovanni had sworn me to absolute secrecy: 'Tell no one, not even Poliziano, why you are joining the Order.' But I should have broken that. This was an unclean parting, tainted with guilt and separation. 'He was so good to me,' I began, haltingly. 'But all I ever did was repay him with lack of loyalty. And he so loyal himself...'

'Don't lose your own dignity,' Pico said sharply, handing me a parcel. 'Maria asked me to give you this and said you were to let no one see you open it.'

'What is it?'

'You will see soon enough, and understand.'

'How is she?'

Here Pico stared at me as at one who had abrogated his duty. 'Why did you come in here?'

'Surely you, above all men, would approve of my decision.'

'How little you know.'

I went to my cell and opened the parcel to discover within Angelo's finest suit of clothes, an apple-green jacket, blue hose, a fine linen shirt embroidered by Maria herself, a woollen over-gown in the dark red of a scholar. Burying my face in them, I heard the crackle of a letter.

Tommaso mio, believe nothing you are told. They have taken him not against his will because he has no will left, but had he been conscious he would have refused. Angelo has expressed no desire to take the habit in his final hours, nor to be buried in San Marco monastery. I was not strong enough alone to resist them. Tommaso, if you can, dress his body to make him fit to meet his King as he would wish. God alone knows the purity of his heart. How often did Angelo say a white habit will not get you to heaven? If they will use his death to propagate the faith, so be it, there is nothing that can be done, but dress him as he would be dressed. Your Maria.

Even as I was reading the letter, the chapel bell began to toll and I fell, crumpled to my knees, hugging the clothes of the one who had gone. In the refectory we were told how Angelo Poliziano, *Fra* Angelo Poliziano, had been received into the Order at his

396

request in his final hour, having confessed his sins and renounced poetry, so that he might die as he should have lived, at one with God. *If they will use his death to propagate the faith, so be it, there is nothing that can be done, but dress him as he would be dressed.*

That night, I crept from my cell to the mortuary. The coffin was due to be interred in the wall of the secular cloister on the morrow but its lid had not yet been nailed down. As I lifted it, I tried to steel my nerves by thinking of what Michaelangelo did at nights, not only unshrouding the dead, but cutting them open. My work was easy in comparison. I was able to remove the shroud and the habit, even though the body was heavy and unco-operative. This was an intimacy I wished with no one alive, let alone dead! But for the sake of Maria and of Angelo I did the work and dressed him in his finest clothes, and laid him back in the coffin. Then I reached in and kissed him. 'May God take and keep you, and if He loves you half as much as I do, you are destined for the highest heaven.' I laid his hands one on top of the other on his chest and replaced the crucifix. Looking down for the last time on the Professor of Greek and Latin, dressed in his best, I recovered him with the shroud and slid the lid of the coffin back into place.

In the morning, the coffin was interred. In the afternoon, I threw a parcel containing a Dominican habit on a bonfire that had been lit in the kitchen garden.

'What is that?' the brother in charge asked.

'A vanity,' I said.

86 SAVING THE BOOKS
1494

IN ITALY WE STAGED WARS LIKE PAGEANTS. SMALL ARMIES in resplendent colours under private captains, hired by cities and states, would move out to present themselves to each other. Sometimes there was fighting, of course. It was theatre, after all, and not unusual for people to go and watch these spectacles from surrounding hillsides. Now we heard that the French – forty thousand men under one commander – had taken Fivizzano; 'taken' not in the usual way of paying gatekeepers to open the gates; no, 'taken' by smashing down the walls of that stronghold with their cannon and slaughtering the entire garrison. They were worse than the Turks!

Piero de' Medici was riding from fortress to fortress in a defence of the borders seen as heroic by some, vain by others. The days passed and the oppressive, stifling fear of the French created a deadly inertia. News of atrocities reached us in advance of the army and with each new tale of massacre, rape and burnings, we became more rabbit-like, frozen and incapable of action. But there was movement of a kind in the city. Underground snakings of the currents of power. Shiftings. Realignments. New deals made behind closed doors, favours granted, promises made. Savonarola might be saying that it was God bringing this scourge, but most blamed Piero and his stupid alliance with Naples. To be rid of the French, we needed to be rid of the Medici.

Pico had stopped visiting the monastery. In desperation I sent letters to Maria. Each was returned with the message that the recipient could not be located. There was a rumour that she was living alone in her brother's villa on Fiesole; another that she had become the concubine of Pico della Mirandola. Letters to both addresses failed to be delivered. Since the massive army of the French was now at our borders, everyone was distracted and it was impossible to know whether the couriers could be trusted or were merely sitting on the letters for a few days before giving them back and keeping the fee.

I went to Fra Girolamo and told him that there were thirty books out on loan to Poliziano which had not been returned at his death and that they were at the villa on Fiesole. Would he permit me to go there and retrieve them? Permission was granted, although Savonarola looked as if he were not quite sure if he could trust me. He instructed me firmly to be back in the monastery by Vespers.

The villa slumbered like a cat curled up in a patch of autumn sunlight. The lemon trees bore green fruit and from the woods came the call of hunters out to catch the wild boar. Wood smoke curled in the still air. As I unlocked the door, it seemed possible that I should find Angelo and his sister within, reading at their desks, but the place was empty, the acrid hearth cold.

Angelo's desk was as he had left it, clear and tidy. He never owned many books but always borrowed them and several piled on the shelves were from the private library of Lorenzo. I packed them in chests, uncertain whether to send everything to the Palazzo de' Medici or to San Marco. I needed instruction from Cardinal Giovanni before I did anything. What I was clear about was my own possessions which filled a small chest: my copy of Plato's *Dialogues*, my journals, two bronze medals – one of Giuliano de' Medici, the other of Poliziano and his sister – Elena's betrothal ring, her Book of Hours, a comb, a drawing of her made by Filippino Lippi, some lacework of Maria. At the bottom of the chest I found a piece of blackened silver, the talisman I had forged under a malignant sky. Would history have been different had I destroyed it, as Ficino told me to? I thought not. At the same time, I knew that my melancholy was somehow locked into this ore of disobedience. Resolving this time to have it melted down, and to give the proceeds to the poor, I took the chest and strapped it to my saddle. I arranged with Matteo, the chief contadino of the estate, for it to be delivered to the city when he received my advice. I asked him if he had seen anything of Maria, and he shook his head miserably.

'My wife says that she's been seen in the village, but it's just a rumour. The Poliziani have gone.' Now tears came into his eyes. 'And the French are coming…' He looked down the terraces, restored in the last few years, the vines recently picked and pruned, the regenerated olives bearing fruit. His tears spilled, tears for his lost master, tears for his wasted efforts. 'The master's sister,' he gulped. 'I don't know where she is.'

I went up to Pico's villa but found it closed. A servant told me that Pico was in his city house. And Maria Poliziana? The servant shrugged, as if he had never heard of her. I went about Fiesole asking my question and heard that Maria was dead, that she had gone into a convent, that she lived wild in the woods, but no one had seen her. I had spent too long making my enquiries and had to hurry back to the city. As I came to the monastery, the Vespers bell began to sound. I would collect the books and papers from the casino another day – it was so close that I could slip out any time. Meanwhile I must contact the Cardinal.

The following morning news arrived that Piero had abandoned his attempt to defend Florence, had gone to the French camp and thrown himself at the feet of the King.

'We've surrendered!' went the cry round the city. Those of us old enough to remember how Lorenzo had saved Florence by surrendering to the King of Naples realised that, in desperation, Piero was copying his father, but it was a botched attempt. He had given up all our fortresses, our seaport of Pisa, and a considerable fortune in gold coin. But what exercised everyone was that Piero was only a citizen, one of many, and had acted without the authority of the Signoria. Hastily the government sent out an official deputation to parley with the King, this one including Savonarola.

'Tommaso!' I heard my name hissed from the shadows of the cloisters. Michelangelo was concealed in a doorway. 'Come here.'

'Have you heard the news?' I asked him.

'If you were deaf, dumb and blind you would have heard the news today. It isn't true, what they are saying about Piero. Yes, he abased himself and lost his dignity, lying prone in front of that midget king and being mocked by the French, but he has bought the peace of Florence. We're saved!'

'But a second deputation has gone out. Savonarola has just left.'

'For what reason? It's not necessary. We're saved and Piero is returning in triumph.'

'He's returning to his doom. The city will lynch him. Michelangelo, I need to speak to the Cardinal urgently. We need to get Angelo's books from the villa, and from the casino.'

'That's what I came to tell you. The casino's been looted.'

My knees went weak and I had to lean against the cloister wall. 'What is missing?'

'Everything of value – all books and papers.'

My knees gave way and I had to sit down. It was as if Angelo had just died again. Poliziano, the greatest scholar of our age, had just been erased from history. 'Who did it?'

Michelangelo shrugged. 'Could have been anybody. The city's in such a flux. By tonight, the Medici will be gone. I'm leaving for Bologna. Come with me.'

'How can I?' I wailed. 'I'm not leaving now. This is the hour of my duty!'

I went back to the library. Trembling, I looked at the books, the Medici books, and was dismayed. I cared not who ruled Florence, so long as the books were safe. I had failed Angelo – the thought made me want to vomit – but I must not fail the Medici. I arranged for a train of mules to go at once to Fiesole and bring the chests back to San Marco. Having done so, I sat at my desk with my head in my hands, trying to recall everything that had been at the casino: the letters in manuscript, the second Miscellanea, piles of notebooks, his revised account of the Pazzi conspiracy. *Hotze la'or* – I realised now what that mysterious spill of cards had been telling me: not that I should become a printer, but that the works on Angelo's desk that day, works that had fallen to the floor with the cards, should be published. And then I sat up as if jerked by strings, knowing who the culprits were. Yes, it could have been simple thieves, or even literary opportunists, but I felt certain that the Pazzi family wanted that document which condemned them for posterity. But there were copies. I began to make lists, lists of works, lists of friends, of Poliziano's students and correspondents, anyone who might have a copy of anything. Orpheus had been dismembered: I would put him back together again. *Hotze la'or*. It was the least I could do.

What had been irreplaceably lost were the thirty books on loan from San Marco. What kind of librarian was I? If, instead of being duplicitous with Savonarola, I had gone to retrieve the books the previous day, I'd have gone to the casino, not to Fiesole, and retrieved everything. I went to the chapel to find a confessor and somehow make my peace with God. And Angelo.

In the refectory that evening, an evening filled with the sound of tolling bells, we were told that, when Savonarola had entered the King's tent, Charles VIII had fallen to his knees before this man of God and promised, as Savonarola requested, to enter the city and then pass on without doing any damage. About the same time we heard the fanfares of Piero's return, his procession from the Porto San Gallo along the Via Larga to his house.

The following morning I was in the library and making my lists with the help of Zenobio when there came a very fat Franciscan friar. We gazed uncomprehending at this apparition, who was whispering urgently about the danger of the hour. He pulled his cowl back sufficiently for us to see his bulbous eyes

I gasped with relief and told the Cardinal that the Medici books I had found at Angelo's villa were on their way to the monastery. 'You were right not to send them to the palazzo,' he assured me. 'My brother is not being received well in the city. They are barring his entry to the Palazzo della Signoria. It is time to act. There are about a hundred books in the palazzo. We need to get them out and bring them here.' The Company of the Library was being called to action.

He reassured us that he had Savonarola's permission and blessing: he was only in disguise because of the job to be done. When we went down the Via Larga with a small mule train, there were few people about, for everyone was gathering in the centre of the city, forming into a mob to jeer at Piero. We gained entry into the palazzo easily, loaded the mules with chests and took them back to San Marco. Three times we made this journey, but matters were developing around the Palazzo della Signoria and the people were arming themselves. By the time we made the fourth journey, the Via Larga was filling with a hostile mob shouting for the Medici to go. We reached the palazzo through various secret doors and corridors in adjoining houses.

On our fifth and last trip, we found that Piero had returned and was arming himself. 'What are you doing?' he shouted at his brother.

'Saving the books.'

'Try saving yourself! God help us. Books? Get yourself into armour, Giovanni.'

Zenobio and I left by secret doors, sick at heart at what we were leaving behind. Zenobio returned to the monastery but I remained in the Via Larga to do my Dominican duty and call on the people to be peaceful. Someone punched me in the face and I fell back into a doorway on the far side of the street. The mob battered on the gates, screaming for the Medici to come out. At last the gates opened to an impressively martial party – all the young men of the family in full armour and mounted. While the crowd drew back, cowed, the Cardinal rode out waving his sword and rode hard towards the cathedral, shouting *palle! palle!* – the old familiar cry to rally the people. But no one responded other than to pelt him and scream abuse.

Piero and the rest followed him out, but they turned left and galloped up the Via Larga towards the Porto San Gallo, towards Bologna and exile. I remained where I was and watched. I saw the mob burst in, saw through upper windows how they ran through the house, watched them come out, staggering under the weight of statues, heavy tables, tapestries. I saw one man holding aloft a trophy: an agate vase inscribed LAUR.MED. I saw others waving books in the air. The guard of the Signoria soon arrived and enforced order: after that, the State confiscated all Medici property. The following day, Cardinal Giovanni escaped the city and followed his brother into exile.

87 THE DEATH OF THE KISS
1494

THERE WERE A LOT OF BOOKS IN THOSE MEDICI CHESTS, all needing to be inventoried, a task which took me about six weeks. In those weeks the French surged into the city, teeming in our streets and filling our squares. I was in urgent communication with all friends, students and correspondents of Angelo, feverishly trying to put dismembered Orpheus back together again. Books began to arrive, lecture notes, copies of letters. Pico, who I knew would have a great quantity of material, did not reply to my messages. I sent to Matteo to have the chests delivered from Angelo's villa but they never arrived.

I asked to return to Fiesole, saying that the villa had to be protected against French looters. Permission was again granted. In the monastery the 'invasion' of the French made no impact, but it was different in the streets. Florence was having to accommodate forty thousand men. Most were in camp outside the walls, but they spent their days in our taverns and brothels. The King had taken up residence in the Palazzo de' Medici and was stripping it of anything the State had left behind for his comfort. His soldiers, meanwhile, helped themselves to anything they fancied in the city. Out in the piazza San Marco, I stood blinking at what seemed to be a swarming square in Paris. French, not Tuscan, was the language of Florence now, and the Florentines practised saying *Oui!* and *Merci!* to the occupiers, and receiving a blow to the head for their troubles.

I went hastily to the Porto San Gallo – the Medici gate which Lorenzo and his forefathers had developed and protected against the day when the family had to leave quickly. That day had now passed. I'd heard that Piero was now in Venice.

I was half way up the hill of Fiesole when I saw the smoke coiling up from the Medici villa and, behind it, on the left shoulder of the hill and within trees, another, smaller plume of smoke. I did not go too close to the Villa Bruscoli but took on the guise of a Dominican passing by on his way to Fontalucente, a curious Dominican who stopped to stare for a moment. Our home was ablaze, and the men silhouetted in the fire's light were not French. They were Italian. Nor were they contadini enjoying the destruction of the master's property. Although I could not recognise them, I could see that they were young men of good families, firing the villa for what reason I could not tell, whether anger or mere entertainment. Angelo's books – had they stolen them or merely destroyed them? Was it my fate to be so ineffectual in the face of Poliziano's annihilation?

From Fontalucente I went up the lane to Pico's villa. I had not seen Pico for weeks. He came very rarely these days to San Marco, and then only to have private conversation with Savonarola. At the gate I was told that the master was at home but very sick and seeing no one.

'Savonarola has sent me to comfort him,' I lied.

The servant admitted me, muttering something about a stream of friars. Sure enough, within Pico's chamber I found several of my brethren saying prayers. I suppose they must have glanced at me, surprised, but I did not care. I would take the consequences later. For what concerned me now was the man in the bed and the woman at the bedside.

'Tommaso,' Maria grasped my hand. 'Thank God you have come.'

Candles flickered in the chill draughts. Pico lay on his pillows, his eyes moving behind closed lids, his face pallid and damp, tendrils of his hair stuck to his brow.

'What ails him?'

'A fever,' said Maria cautiously. 'The same kind that took Angelo.'

I glanced around the room to see who it was she did not trust. Apart from the friars, Pico's secretary was there, his nephew, Alberto Pio, and two physicians from the court of King Charles.

405

Seeing my surprise, Maria explained that His Majesty had sent them as soon as he had heard of Pico's distress. 'He values him very highly as a man of wisdom.'

Pico's eyes opened and slowly filled with a conscious light, a calm radiance as if he looked on that which he had sought his life long, as if what he had intended to seek as a pilgrim he now found right here at home. We held our breath, not wanting to disturb this silent communion, but he became aware of us, turned his gaze on us, now on Maria, now on me, and the light in his eye did not change. I felt then as if I were dying too, as if everything in me gross and material was falling away: held in that deep gaze, I knew my own divinity, the essence of God within all men.

The moment was broken by a new rush of delirium in him. Maria wiped away runnels of sweat, whispering words of comfort, but as she moved, she glanced at me, and I knew that she too had been momentarily elevated from this world of shadows to divine reality. She smiled, acknowledging our mutual understanding. How quickly the mundane sweeps back in. A blink of an eye, a swift smile exchanged and then we returned to anxiety, to ineptitude, to vomit and sweat. Pico cried out in agony.

'Hush, hush, my lord,' said Maria.

When he was quiet again and sleeping we went outside to look down on the smoke still rising from the Villa Bruscoli. Maria began to sob. I took her in my arms and held her tightly.

'It is not the French,' I said. 'They are Florentines. Looting or just destroying. I left Angelo's books there in chests. Maria – the casino was looted. Everything of his has gone.' I sank to my knees, overcome by failure.

'We have them here,' she said, 'the chests. The family came last week and took away anything moveable. I got there before them. I wasn't going to let those philistines have his books. But our home ... Oh, Tommaso!' A welter of grief took her and I came to my feet quickly to embrace her again. Together we stood looking down through our tears on the valley of the Arno filled with the tents and pavilions, the fluttering French pennants bearing the fleur-de-lis.

'It's the time of the lilies,' she whispered.

'Who has poisoned Pico?' I asked.

Maria did not know. 'He drank the first pressing of the olives and went straight into spasm,' she said. 'Someone wants them all dead, all Lorenzo's friends. The light is being snuffed out.'

She showed me something Pico had given her, a medal. On one side it had his emblem of the Three Graces; on the obverse, a portrait of Maria herself, the same sweet profile that was on Poliziano's own medal. Pico had made a trinity of himself and the Poliziani. Her hand trembled as she held it.

'When did he have this made? How long has he had it?'

'He says years, that he has always kept it close to his heart.'

Stung by jealousy for a dying man, I could hardly look at it.

'Where have you been staying?' I asked her.

'What do you care?'

'Maria, please, believe me, my love for you is more than an image in bronze.'

'Yes, you can say that now, can't you, now that you are in *that*.' She jabbed at my habit. 'You deserted us, Tommaso. I cannot forgive you.'

'Where have you been?' I asked again.

'With my friends in the woods.'

'The *witches*?'

She smiled then. 'As you said yourself, there is no such thing as witches. Where else could I go? Home to Montepulciano? To live life sewing shirts for my brother-in-law? With no one to speak to on any subject other than the trivial, the mundane, the gossip of small lives? I would rather be a vagrant.'

'This cannot continue, Maria. You must enter the convent of San Marco. Be Clare to my Francis, if you would.'

Maria laughed.

'I am serious,' I said irritably. 'What other choice is there? It is not as you think within the Order. Each of us is put to a task in accord with his nature. Fra Girolamo has founded a scriptorium, where the scribes are at work; there are artists painting, sculptors

407

sculpting. In San Marco he is building an ark to protect civilisation until the flood of barbarism subsides.'

'Your brain has been addled by prayers.'

'Even the nuns are put to the work for which they are best fitted.'

'So, I would be allowed to study Greek and write poetry?'

'Your medical knowledge and skill would be of great use in the pharmacy or the infirmary.'

'You may be able to live a double, hypocritical life. I cannot.'

'Maria, let's not argue.'

She subsided, looked up at me with soft, affectionate eyes, squeezed my arm and apologised.

'I am trying to put everything back together again,' I told her. 'Most of Angelo's work exists in copies. I believe I can find it, and then we'll have it published. I'll take it to Aldo in Venice, I promise you.'

'I don't know who looted the casino or why –' she said.

'The Pazzi family, I'm sure of it.'

'– but they wouldn't have found much. When they took Angelo away, the friars, they took his books and papers, some of them, saying they would be safe in San Marco.'

'*What?* Nothing came into the library!'

Before she could answer, a servant hurried out to us. The master was gasping for breath and seemed to be fast declining. We rushed back to the chamber, where Maria fell on her knees at the bedside and grasped Pico's pale, trembling hands. One of the friars took me aside. 'What are you doing here, Fra Tommaso?'

'Fra Girolamo sent me to collect books on loan. What are *you* doing here, Fra Roberto?'

'Saying prayers for the Count's soul and waiting for him to recover enough to be moved. He has expressed a wish to join the Order.'

'*He has not!*' Maria jumped to her feet. 'I have been here nearly two weeks and he has expressed no such thing. Tommaso! Listen to me! Don't let them take him. Don't let it happen again. Do something. For once in your life, *act*, and in accordance with your heart.'

That was not fair. I had not spent my life in dithering inaction. Far from it. Who was it who had once saved Lorenzo de' Medici, at the cost of his own brother's life? And that an act of the heart.

Pico drew an agonising breath.

'My lord,' said Maria urgently, shaking him. 'Is it your wish to be received into the Dominican Order?'

'Madonna!' he gasped. He, too, was having visions, as Angelo had done. His lips worked in a silent conversation with the Holy Mother, then he lapsed back into unconciousness, without having answered the question.

'God has displayed his will,' said Fra Roberto, satisfied.

To convince the brethren of the purpose of my visit, I went through Pico's library, removing those books which belonged to San Marco and, with them, anything of Poliziano's, including one or two manuscripts that I knew that no one else would have had. Another manuscript I came across was Lorenzo de' Medici's commentary upon four of his sonnets, written in his own hand, and I caressed it as a survivor. I turned its pages, reading what Lorenzo had written on the mystic death, and came across a paragraph I had forgotten, a personal, poignant note of the author:

'My persecutors were very powerful men, of great authority and ingenuity, and firmly resolved upon my total ruin and desolation, as to try every possible way to harm me. I was a private young man and without any counsel or help other than that divine goodness and clemency which was shown to me. I was reduced in the soul by excommunication, in property by theft, in the State by diverse conspiracies, in the family and children by plots and distractions, in the life by frequently hidden persecutions, so that death would have been no small grace and a lot less unappetising than all these other things.'

Such were the sufferings – most of which I had witnessed first hand – of il Magnifico. But the rest of the work outlined his philosophy, that the soul may ascend to God through excellence in the field of human activity; that poetry above all things has the power to humanise, civilise, inspire. He believed, he said, that it is the duty of every man to work always for the benefit of mankind. For Lorenzo, the contemplation of beauty through poetry was the way back to God. This was his *vita nuova*, the new life.

I sighed and put the book in the chest I was filling.

I browsed Pico's arcane volumes, full of diagrams and ciphers. Mystic and mystery derive from the Greek word *musticos*, meaning to close the eyes or lips. Secret, esoteric knowledge: this was Pico's route of return. In his Commentary on Genesis I read a quotation from St John, saying, 'No man comes to me unless my Father has drawn him.' Then my eye fell on Pico's words close by:

… in whom you always had life, even before you were made. For he knows us not in ourselves but in himself. Likewise we shall know him in himself and not in ourselves. This is the eternal life. This is the wisdom which wise men of this world do not know, that from every imperfection of multiplicity we are brought back to unity by an indissoluble bond with him who is himself the One.

I carried the book to the bed to read the words to their author, who was now awake again. Though in great pain, Pico struggled to attend and fastened his grey eyes on me with desperation. I read the passage twice.

'Can you hear, Giovanni? Do you understand?'

'I hear and I believe,' he whispered. 'Thank you.'

'Giovanni – all Angelo's papers and books are lost.'

He looked at me in horror. 'That is worse than death!'

'I'm gathering copies of everything I can. May I…'

'Take everything you can find here. Do it quickly, while I live, or else they will go to my heir.'

I thanked God then that I had already put everything I'd found into the chest.

His cheeks sunken, his lips drawn, he spoke Maria's name. 'Come close.'

She bent over him.

'*Mors osculi*,' he whispered. 'I used to argue with Ficino... who said that one could die the mystic death and yet remain alive, but I see no reason to continue living... once full knowledge of the divine has been had and understood.' He drew a shuddering breath and then continued, anxious to impart this knowledge to us. 'At the heart... of all mystery is the uncreated Light. It is where we come from... and that to which we return... It is what we truly are... earth to earth... water to water... fire to fire... air to air... all elements return to themselves... but not the soul. The destiny of the soul depends... on the life... The purified soul returns to her maker. But the impure?'

He looked at Maria in sudden anxiety.

'Do not be afraid. God will forgive the impurities.'

'But do you forgive me?'

'Love forgives everything. Fear nothing, my dear, dear brother. What is death? The end of all ignorance, of bondage in this imprisoning body. It is freedom.'

Fra Roberto intervened in agitation. 'My lord, are you fit to travel?'

'Indeed I am,' said Pico, 'but be so kind as to leave me for a few moments.'

Fra Roberto withdrew reluctantly with the other friars to the far side of the chamber.

'Is it your wish to be received into the Order of the Dominicans?' Maria asked Pico.

'It is not. One must dress well to meet the King,' Pico whispered. 'Do you understand?'

'I understand,' Maria reassured him.

'Now, it is time,' Pico said. 'Do what you have...' His head jerked, fell back on his pillow and was still. The stillness, the absence of life which is death. Even as I stared at him, at the mystery, Maria bent forward, closed his eyes and placed her lips on his open mouth. Suddenly his ribcage swelled and there came the sound of a sigh. The last breath of Pico della Mirandola was received into the mouth of Maria Poliziana.

411

88 THE FATE OF PICO'S SOUL
1494

THE STORIES WERE CIRCULATING EVEN BEFORE PICO WAS buried, that he had died of a slow fever brought on by excessive study; that he had been poisoned by an adherent of the Medici, to bring an end to so prominent a supporter of Savonarola. Then there was the account of Fra Roberto, the man who claimed to have witnessed the deathbed renunciation of Poliziano. Now he was saying he had witnessed Pico's death also, and had seen with his own eyes Savonarola receive Pico's last vows and bestow on him the habit of the Dominican Order. These two reports of Fra Roberto are considered to be most trustworthy and accurate, coming as they did from San Marco.

There was no grand funeral for Pico, as there had been none for Poliziano, but they did accord him one honour: a holy procession led by Dominicans and those weeping disciples of Savonarola, the Piagnoni. Bartolommeo Scala, the Gonfalonier and erstwhile disciplinarian of the Florentine armies, led this lachrymose procession, walking at its head with his wet eyes rolled heavenward. The procession to bury Pico at San Marco keened in an unnatural, disturbing way, the throats of the women vibrating in that sound called 'ululation', a sound so terrible that I could have cried myself, and helplessly. *Virtù* alone kept me dry-eyed that morning. For the sake of the souls of my two friends, I kept my head high and my mind steady. Although the Maenad song made my lip quiver, I held to my intention as a man falling from a cliff clings to a tree root. This emotion swaying the people was not divine, I was sure of it. This was neither repentance nor remorse that I was beholding, but the slavery of the crowd to an idea. These people in black were chained to one another in the belief that they were sinners and doomed to judgement. For the sake of all humanity, I rejected this notion within myself and remained dry-eyed.

The black line wove its way through idle bands of jeering French infantry who were resting on their pikes and crossbows, enjoying this spectacle of Florentines in morbid repentance. The coffin was taken into the church of San Marco and rested there while Savonarola addressed us from the pulpit. I looked over to the female section and saw Maria standing in a group of peasant women from Fiesole.

I felt responsible for her and intended to write to the family at Montepulciano but had not yet done so, haunted by her repulsion at the idea of returning home. What could I do but watch her from afar, and worry for her? The women were groaning and pulling their hair, but Maria stood quietly and unmoved. Both of us, having witnessed Pico's passing, were in remembrance of that moment and the faith that had come with it, that the soul is immortal. There was no cause for tears: Maria was not about to faint or collapse weeping. I knew that she was praying as I was praying, commending the soul of our friend to God. Neither of us had any doubt that Pico's soul, whatever its imperfections, was now merged with the infinite. I stood in the church alone amongst my brethren, believing something slightly different from the rest. Not for me ideas of rising from the grave on Judgement Day to be assigned a place for eternity in heaven or in hell; my Hermetic soul had different ideas of the afterlife. If Maria and I sorrowed at Pico's funeral, it was for ourselves, not for him.

Savonarola had been giving the usual homilies, those platitudes of faith it is so easy not to listen to, but suddenly his voice changed, became energetic and at the same time conversational.

'I want to reveal a secret to you,' he told us, leaning from the pulpit, 'which I have not wanted to tell you before this, because I was not as certain of it as I have been for the past ten hours. Each of you, I believe, knew Giovanni Pico of Mirandola. I tell you that his soul, because of the good works which he performed in his life, and through the prayers of the brethren, is in purgatory.'

In the general exclamation of joy, Maria's shocked response went unheard. She looked across at me, visibly trembling, her eyes haunted. 'Purgatory?' she mouthed. I shook my head dismissively and held up both hands – ten fingers to represent the tenth sphere. The empyrean. The heaven beyond heaven. She understood.

Savonarola's voice was rising. 'He was almost too late in coming to the true religion in his lifetime.'

My mouth fell open. This was the man I believed in, the guide, I thought, of my renewal in the Christian life, and he was standing in the pulpit telling lies.

Suddenly there was screaming. Maria screaming. One woman's pent-up rage given vent in a sound to make men's bones crumble. Several friars hurried towards her, I among them. 'Take her into the convent,' I ordered them.

Yes, it was me. On the authority of Fra Tommaso, librarian of San Marco, Maria Poliziana was enclosed. Where else was there for her to go that was safe? As she was dragged struggling away, she glared at me with mad, Medusa eyes, at me, the man of the black and the white, the good and the bad, the man of two parts. I picked up a parcel she had dropped, a parcel with my name on it.

Once again in the middle of the night I undressed a corpse, removing the Dominican habit and replacing it with an exquisite tunic of brocade of gold and red, the colours of the cherubim and seraphim. I re-covered Pico with the shroud and took another parcel to another bonfire. Another vanity. In the morning they sealed the coffin and placed it with due ceremony in the same wall tomb that housed Poliziano, in the secular wall, the wall of shame, the limbo place for those too good to go to hell, but not good enough to go to heaven. The wall of purgatory. At least they were together.

As soon as I was back in the library, I began to search for Angelo's missing papers that Maria had said 'a friar' had taken from the garden house. I knew every cupboard and every chest, had the keys to every lock. They were not there. What was there was a tower of book chests containing over a thousand volumes of the library of Pico della Mirandola, all to be inventoried. I felt faint at the prospect. The destination of this prodigious wealth of books, I was told by Cristoforo Casale who delivered them, awaited the reading of Pico's will. Cristoforo looked heartbroken to leave them with me, as if in parting with the books he was saying his final farewell to his patron and lifelong friend. All the heart-stopping adventures were forgotten: he missed the Pico of the quiet times, the kind, generous soul who never stood on ceremony, the count who treated him as an equal, the master who had been his friend.

'What will happen to his papers?' Cristoforo asked.

'They will be kept safe until we receive instruction from his heir. Who is his heir, by the way?'

'We won't know until the will is read. I have put the papers into order without changing anything, but they could do with a close edit. And publication, of course. They must be published.'

'We must wait on the heir. Cristoforo, as soon as we know who it is, I shall recommend you for the work.'

He looked content then, as if his grief could be assuaged by further service to the Count of Concordia. After he had gone, I went through the chests looking for anything written by Poliziano that I had missed when taking things from Pico's villa. What I found, I copied.

In the city everyone was busy decking themselves out in new colours. Lorenzo and Giovanni di Pierfrancesco had returned in triumph as part of the entourage of Charles VIII, Michele Marullus and many of the Pazzi family with them. Now what had been cloudy became clear: the charge of treason against the Pierfranceschi had been justified. They had been working on behalf of France for years, for one end only: to take power in Florence. Repossessing the Casa Vecchia, they had the Medici escutcheons removed from its walls and let it be known by proclamation that their name was now not Medici but 'Popolano'. Men of the people. Their new arms were the insignia of Florence and the arms of the people, a red cross on a white ground.

Turin, August 29th, 1506

News has arrived, shivering up the spine of Italy. Pope Julius, having left Rome with a force of five hundred men and twenty-four cardinals, has marched on Perugia. The despot of Perugia, that bloody and violent man who decorates the city walls with spiked heads, came out to meet the Pope. Did he run him through, decapitate him, put up a head wearing the triple tiara at Perugia's main gate? No. He fell on his knees and paid homage. Erasmus, who speaks when our company dines together, but never to me, says it is impossible for any man to be completely wicked. Perhaps so, but I share the general astonishment at the despot's show of humility. Pope Julius – a figure of such *terribilità* that tyrants fall to their knees! I feel nauseous just thinking of my letters and my task.

I have to speak to Erasmus through Clyfton. There is nothing I want to say, other than goodbye. The route south is too perilous with Rome on the march; besides, I cannot be so close to Venice and not visit her. I shall leave as soon as I have finished my book, a work which I have done for Erasmus, in which I speak to Erasmus, which I shall dedicate to Erasmus, and leave behind for him. As I am not completely wicked, so he is not completely cold.

89 THE NEW JERUSALEM
1494

HAVE YOU EVER SEEN A RIVER OR POOL IN DROUGHT AND all the creatures of water left flapping in the mud? So it was in Florence after the French departed. For the King was true to the promise he had made to Savonarola and did not stay even as long as a week before moving on to terrorise Rome and, in time, take the Kingdom of Naples. In Florence we were left without government and, although we were under the dominion of the King, we had no local leadership. I heard that Lorenzo di Pierfrancesco was beside himself with rage, not to have been elevated to what he considered to be his natural place. And the angrier he became, the more the King was convinced that he should invite Piero de' Medici to return!

The time was ripe for reform, and what statesmen we had made long speeches on their proposals for a new republic. In truth, sixty years of Medici rule had robbed us of potential leaders. Those who could speak could not act. Those who could act did not know what to do. Popular sentiment called for power to be put in the hands of the people, but the people are never that wonderful body of innocent beings dedicated to justice and the common good. As one man said, 'Power to the people is just tyranny multiplied.' We had lived for sixty years on bread and circuses and what happened when the French left was that a population of slaves was set free and told to govern themselves.

A Council of Twenty was elected with the elderly and well-respected Bernardo del Nero as Gonfalonier of Justice. They met at San Marco as often as they met in the council chamber of the Palazzo della Signoria. All new laws and statutes echoed what Savonarola was saying from the pulpit, and church and state began to walk hand-in-hand. By the end of Advent it was clear that there was to be no return to the old ways, no government led by powerful families, but by a Great Council to which all citizens above the age of twenty-nine were eligible. In one stroke all my peers were part of the government of the city, had a vote and a voice. Heady days. Savonarola preached to the Florentines to change their ways, to stop acting from self-interest and to begin to look after each other. Reform, he said, starts with the individual. Good states are born of good men. And the weary, frightened, hungry heads of the Florentines lifted up to listen.

'Purify the spirit, give thought to the common good, forget private interests, and if you reform the city to this intent, it will have greater glory than in all past times.' We would, he said, set an example for the rest of the world to follow.

Who would not hearken to such a voice in the wilderness?

Cosimo had once said that states cannot be governed by Paternosters. Savonarola refuted it, saying those were the words of a tyrant. Henceforth, the spirit would rule the body and all temporal good would be subordinate to moral and religious good. The only true ruler of a city was God himself.

It was a strange and exhilarating sight, to see a humble friar governing a city from the pulpit; but this was no ordinary friar: this was the man who had prophesied all that had befallen us. Whatever he proposed was put into effect at once. It seemed little less than a miracle that within the space of a month Florence was transformed from a squabbling commune into a unified city: it seemed that everyone was involved in sudden and vital regeneration.

It is said that the greatest good any man desires is to be part of his city's government. I can think of greater goods, but it is true that in that time I was frustrated to be a friar and longed to be out in the squares, present at councils, a part of this rebirth, this phoenix-arising of the good out of corruption. In fact, the library of San Marco was the heart of the new state, for there learned men were searching books of history and philosophy to find ancient systems to fit current needs. Great tomes were brought in from the State Archives so that we could discover how Florence had been governed in the past, before the Medici. I have to say, looking into these books, I could see that the Medici had ruled by confusion and that the laws of Florence had become an incomprehensible, unworkable jumble. Lawyers amongst us set themselves to untangle them and reveal justice, and daily digests were given to the Frate for his consideration.

I had entered the monastery in an act of deceit, planted there by the Medici. While I stayed true to my duty in protecting the library, a subtle transformation began inside me. One cannot stand in a vat of dye without taking on its colours. Each morning I awoke in my cell to a sense of freedom: there was nothing in there to trouble me; I had no possession to claim my attention other than the small chest of personal treasures I had secreted in the library; nothing in the cell but bare walls and a painting of the Crucifixion by Fra Angelico which I rarely saw, given that I woke in the dark and retired in the dark. I attended all the offices I was required to do, and felt the freedom of anonymity. With a daily shave and a monthly shearing, there was nothing to distinguish me from the rest of the brethren. I need look competitively at no man, nor had I to be concerned about what I was wearing. *Rejoice in the present*, Ficino had encouraged us; *avoid busyness*. Such things were easy here. The past and any thought of it were so painful that I did indeed rejoice in the present, and had no heed to the future. I would not have entered the monastery of my own volition, but now I thanked God that He had seen fit to send me. Relieved of having to earn a living, of paying taxes, of the constant anxiety of sudden political change – all that had gone. I lived a simple life surrounded by the books I loved and each morning I thanked God for it.

My work recovering Poliziano was meeting success. Aided by Angelo's student, Pietro Crinito, and a fervent admirer from Bologna called Alessandro Sarzi, I had now amassed most of his works. All that I missed was the material from the casino: his collected letters, the Account of the Pazzi Conspiracy, and the

419

second *Miscellanea*. If they had been stolen by one of the friars and destroyed, I presumed it had not been with the knowledge of Savonarola.

The city was changing, the monastery was changing, I was changing. It seemed that my work as a Medici spy was done: all that I had left was to become a real Christian. Did I stop being a Platonist? No. In my view, and that of Ficino, one does not have to choose between the two. Of course, Savonarola thought differently, but I was good at keeping quiet. *Musticos* – my lips were sealed in secrecy. When alone in study, I sought to continue Pico's work to harmonise Christianity and Platonism, seeing if I could match terms and make them synonymous. But one day, looking at a beam of light pouring in through an upper window in the library, it suddenly occurred to me in that blinding way of the obvious that there was no need for this work. The two *are* in harmony. There are small matters of difference – well, perhaps quite large ones when it comes to transmigration of the soul or resurrection of the body – but in essence, there is harmony. I am living testament to the fact that one may be both. Or am I a walking hypocrite? Do I keep my contraries in separate compartments, never to meet or engage with each other? Perhaps. But I would find it a very torture of the spirit to have to choose between faith and reason and settle for one without the other. As I stared into that beam of light, I saw that it is not harmony that is required, but marriage, a full union of the two. But how? The answer flashed past my eyes like a kingfisher; dismissing it, I returned to my reading of the Early Fathers, wondering if it were possible for such a study to be made, to interpret Plato according to Christ, and Christ according to Plato, but as I reached out to turn a page I was overcome by nausea and lassitude. I could not focus on the words and any attempt to read only increased the nausea. It was as if a presence beside me were willing me to stop. Shall I give it a name? Yes, very well, it was Pico. And then the answer returned and I did not dismiss it. *Within yourself.* It was a cipher I understood and knew how to unlock. If I practised truth and goodness, and did not worry my head with any theological or philosophical debate; if I simply lived my life according to the Will of God, then any label such as 'Platonist' or 'Christian' was redundant. To be precise: any unity worth having is the unity of the soul with its Creator. From that moment on, I stopped studying like a scholar and read like a friar, taking words of truth not into my head but into my heart. Then the conflict stopped, and any sense of being duplicitous vanished. I was a Dominican who loved Plato – simple as that.

Whenever Fra Domenico was in the library, I no longer hid my books of philosophy or my work on Poliziano. I no longer felt shifty in the presence of Savonarola, and he warmed to me more than previously. I also warmed to him. I understood now what he was trying to teach us: make it practical, make it *practical*. And so I looked on the changes coming about in the city with wonder. Yes, there was protest in some quarters, mostly from young men who are as fond of talking about goodness as chewing on gristle. They had absolutely no taste for sermons about chastity or public service and preferred instead to test the mettle (and the creed) of friars, roughing them up, pushing them around, pelting them with stones and horse dung. It was to be expected: the young, like the poor, are always with us. If it had not been like that in my youth it was because then we were only Christians on high days and holy days. Now it was to be each day of the week and every hour of each day. Naturally the young rebelled.

The rest of the citizens, however, or at least a great majority of the people, threw themselves into Savonarola's experiment. To signify the victory of the city over tyranny, the statue of Judith beheading Holofernes by Donatello was taken from the Palazzo de' Medici and set up outside the Palazzo della Signoria, that towering monument to the Florentine Republic where those elected into the Great Council – now standing at a thousand men – frequently gathered in solemnity.

Almost at once the teeth of dragons were sown amongst us, most artfully. In the old days, the all-powerful Council of Eight had been able to condemn a man to death with no right of appeal.

Many murders had been committed under this legality. Now Savonarola proposed we introduce that right of appeal and that it should be heard not by the Great Council but by a limited body of men well-versed in the law. But the people now had a thirst for power and demanded that appeals be heard by the Council. And that, as the sowers of dragons' teeth know, would be a ripe bed for the dissension and tumult requisite for yet another change in government. Thus those who privately sought a return to the old ways of rule by a powerful family agitated for this to be accepted, and it came to pass. We all know what grows from dragons' teeth: strife.

90 GIANFRANCESCO 1495

THE COMPANY OF THE LIBRARY HAD NOT DISBANDED AND its work continued. The city had seized those books in the Medici library we had been unable to save. Now, staggering under debts to the French, the Signoria sought a vast loan, and offered the books as security. One day a man approached Savonarola on behalf of the Commune to make an offer. The agreement was that, should the loan not be repaid, the books would become our property. All we needed to do was to raise two thousand florins. 'Ridiculous!' Savonarola replied. Then we librarians moved in as part of a pincer action. The monastery owned vast tracts of land. The State would never repay the loan, we persuaded him, and with the sale of the land we would gain the books at a fraction of their value. Zenobio and I left it to Giorgio Antonio Vespucci to make the argument, for this elderly dignitary was much respected by Savonarola. I was surprised by how small a struggle Savonarola put up; he seemed easily convinced that it was better to own books than land. I detected a weakness in him and realised with a start that he loved books as much as we did. To the horror of some of the friars, he capitulated and made the deal with the Commune.

The books came in; my days were filled with yet more inventories and catalogues; a year after the expulsion of the Medici, their library was put back together, with the exception of those books which had been stolen from the palazzo by the looters and by the French. I toured the shelves, stroking the books, enjoying a sense of fulfilment rare in anybody's life. I wrote to Cardinal Giovanni to tell him the work was done. But when I told Zenobio this, he raised his eyebrows.

'You think the books are safe now? What dream are you in, Tommaso?'

My reply caught in my throat. He needed to say no more. I had been a fool to suppose Savonarola wanted a library. 'He's going to destroy them.'

'The ultimate sacrifice.'

'No, Zenobio, no, I don't believe it.'

'It may not be true, but then again it may. We cannot afford to relax our vigilance.'

Cardinal Giovanni obviously agreed with him. In his congratulatory reply he said he looked forward to repossessing his family's property in due course but trusted I would continue in my work as guardian. 'You will be well rewarded when that glad day comes that the Medici return.'

Many scholars were at work in the monastery. One day I was told that the nephew of Pico had moved into one of the cells off the main cloister and wanted his uncle's papers to be delivered to him there. I went with two novices carrying the chest, expecting to find Alberto Pio, he who had been present at his uncle's death and funeral. When I opened the door to usher in the chest, however, I found a gaunt man about my own age whom I vaguely recognised but could not place. Although he wore the white habit, he was a layman and not a friar. Busy arranging a desk for himself, he did not look up when he said where the chest should go.

'May I ask why you require these papers?'

'Who is it who is asking?' he said, looking at me from under lowered brow.

'Fra Tommaso, the librarian. And you?'

'Gianfrancesco Pico della Mirandola,' he said. 'Nephew of the Count of Concordia.'

Then I remembered having met him, the eldest nephew, in Carpi all those years before, when we were on the run to France. When I reminded him of this, a muscle in his cheek flinched. 'Ah yes, one of his secretaries. I remember. Had a certain antipathy to printing.'

'I've grown older and wiser and have worked several years in a printing house.'

This caught his interest, for his purpose, he said, was to put his uncle's works into order for publication. I told him that I was doing the same for Poliziano.

'Your uncle's secretary, Cristoforo Casale, will be keen to help you in any way he can. He knows these papers better than anyone.'

Gianfrancesco looked inside the chest. 'I have no need of his help. Look, everything here is in a heap!'

I did not find myself able to admit that that was my fault – the result of my rummaging.

'Naturally my uncle had not expected to die so young. Thirty-two! Who would expect that? His studies were astonishing, and he had conceptions beyond the usual capacity of the human mind, but he was not the neatest or most orderly of men, as you can see. Neither was his secretary. To be frank, Fra Tommaso, what we have here are the scattered leaves of the Cumean Sibyl which I shall endeavour to collate and make readable. Presumably your own work on the papers of Poliziano is easier?'

'In that respect, yes, he was very neat. But there is much that is missing. I've had the temerity to remove from this collection any letters between Pico and Poliziano for copying. I'll return them in due course.'

When I went back with the letters a few days later, I found Gianfrancesco labouring over his uncle's refutation of astrology.

'It is only in note form: the fruit of his many conversations with Fra Girolamo. The Frate is helping me to expand it into a full text.'

'Then it will be Savonarola's refutation of astrology?'

'No, no, he insists, in his magnanimity, that it bears my uncle's name as author. This work is vital in freeing the Florentines from the grip of superstition, and it will stand as a lasting memorial to Giovanni Pico della Mirandola.'

'And everyone will hate him for it,' I thought, miserably. What could I do? Shout at our guest? Challenge our Vicar General? I resolved to discuss the matter with Cristoforo as soon as I could.

'There is so much to be done to bring Pico's work to completion but I am content to devote my time to that purpose,' said Gianfrancesco. 'He was, after all, my beloved uncle and a very great man, and there is no one else in the family with the wit to understand his writings and intentions.'

Was there a man alive with such a wit? If there was, it certainly wasn't Gianfrancesco. In my own work on Poliziano I was merely gathering and putting into order. Poliziano had spent his life railing against those who made additions to texts, or removed lines they did not agree with, leaving a butchered version for posterity. I was hardly going to do it to him, and I'd rather that no one did it to Pico.

I thought, as Gianfrancesco led me to think, that he had inherited his uncle's papers, but that was not the case. When Cristoforo Casale was next in the library, and I told him what was happening, he paled. 'Who gave him permission to do this work?'

'I presume it was Savonarola.'

'But it is not his to give! The will has been read and the books and papers have been bequeathed to Pico's brother, Antonmaria. You know these Mirandolans, Tommaso: the family is at war with itself, and Gianfrancesco is from the enemy ranks.'

'He says he was Pico's favourite nephew and the only member of the family with any intellectual parity.'

425

'Oh, that is ridiculous! Intellectual parity? Pico considered him a skink. Which cell is he in?'

'Cristoforo, it would not be wise...'

But Cristoforo had already left. A few moments later there was an unholy din in the main cloister, the voice of Gianfrancesco echoing, calling for help, saying he was being attacked. I rushed down to find the two scholars at each other's throat like dogs. Other friars gathering stood back, frightened to intervene in such ferocity. It took Savonarola himself to save Gianfrancesco and pull Cristoforo off him. Wildly accusing us all of tampering with Pico's works to suit our own ends – 'Theft! Forgery!' – Cristoforo left the monastery vowing never to return 'to this den of iniquity!'

'Choose your friends more wisely, Fra Tommaso,' Savonarola said as we dispersed.

'But he does have cause for concern,' I protested.

'He has none.' He gazed at me full in the eyes. 'You lack trust, brother. For all your reading, your understanding is small. I think perhaps you spend too much time with books and it would do you good to meet your fellow men, in all their want and need.'

If this was a threat to send me out on pastoral work, he must have forgotten about it, for I continued the library, seemingly beyond anybody's notice. I avoided Gianfrancesco. Whenever he requested books, I had someone else deliver them.

91 THE SOURCE OF PROPHECY
1495

SAN MARCO BECAME LIKE A SMALL, ENCLOSED TOWN, A CITY in miniature, with one whole cloister dedicated to painters and sculptors. Here one saw icons being painted, crucifixes carved, or the firing of reliefs in glazed terracotta by Luca della Robbia, who had recently joined the Order. The difference between here and the streets outside was that these artisans prayed for two hours or more before beginning work; and when the work was underway, it was not for their own profit. This was the heart of the New Jerusalem. Here was the nursery for a new civilisation.

Savonarola toured the cloisters each day, encouraging the brethren and taking an interest in what they were doing. With him always like a pair of wings were Fra Domenico and Fra Silvestro. Fra Domenico wore a perpetual smile and walked with his hands clasped gladly at his breast, while Fra Silvestro, grey and spectral, looked on the world with sorrow. We scholars called them Democritus and Heraclitus, the laugher and the weeper.

Fra Silvestro was a sleep-walker. Many had met him in the cloisters at night, wafting like a ghost with his eyes rolled up in his head, but I only knew him as a tall man of noble bearing. Around midwinter time, however, I went to Savonarola's cell with some documents for his signature and walked in to find the Frate on his knees with Silvestro's hands outstretched on his bare head. Silvestro, his face upturned and his eyes closed, was juddering as if possessed by some strong force, and he was speaking of wind and sinking ships. I was no jelly-boned novice, but I was shaken and backed quietly out of the cell. This was something I should not have seen.

92 THE BURNING OF BEAUTY
1497

NEITHER THE MEDICI NOR THE FRENCH HAD GONE QUIETLY: central Italy had been left in turmoil. Florentine forces were besieging Pisa, desperate to regain the seaport which Piero had so foolishly surrendered to Charles. The Venetians and Milanese sought to cut us off from our only remaining seaport, Livorno, and bring Florentine trade and commerce to a standstill. Then the harvest failed, leaving us without grain. Those Florentines abroad in foreign lands worked to save us, especially those merchants who were in France. We heard that they had acquired a fleet of ships and filled them with corn and wheat, that the fleet was leaving Marseilles to arrive at Livorno within the week. It was vital that we keep the road open.

Under Fra Girolamo's direction we prayed to God that the soldiers defending the road to Livorno would hold out, but then we heard that the fleet had been lost in a storm. Fra Girolamo ordered the holy image of the Virgin, kept in the village of L'Impruneta, to be brought into the city. This statue, which had performed many miracles, was only called for in the direst times. Going to meet it, all friars walked in the train of Fra Girolamo, going slowly through the streets, our heads lowered, singing lauds, beautiful lauds newly composed with fine words. Every now and then I peeked from under my cowl and saw a city degraded by poverty and famine. With everyone who could walk joining the ever-lengthening procession, the streets were empty except for the starving and homeless huddled exhausted in alleys.

'Look on them,' said the friar beside me. 'Look on them and weep, you who spent what wealth we had on books!'

I was used to such hostility from those thin, dim friars who had as the eleventh commandment, Thou shalt not study. How often they chastised me for my part in buying the Medici books from the state. I changed my place so that I walked with someone else. A gang of bravos on the balcony of the Palazzo Spini jeered at us. 'He doesn't cure our troubles,' one shouted, jabbing a finger at Savonarola. 'He causes them!' A stream of piss arched in the air and hit the friar who had scolded me; God forgive me, I was gratified, but hid my smile beneath my cowl.

As we reached the river, we could see in the distance the incoming procession crossing the Ponte Vecchio, led by the holy image held high on a litter. At that very moment we also saw a messenger galloping over the Ponte Santa Trinità, waving an olive branch. The procession halted. A cry of exaltation came from the front and within seconds we at the back had heard: not all the ships from Marseilles had been lost. The *libeccio*, the south-east wind, had blown some of them to Livorno, so fast that the enemy did not see them coming. Grain was on its way.

Fra Girolamo threw up his hands to heaven and thanked God in a voice all could hear. He told the procession from L'Impruneta to return home: we were saved. And then Florence fell to its knees and believed in God. This was the power of Savonarola: through divine agency, he made things happen. Who could not believe in him?

We were surrounded by enemies and Florence was isolated, in fact as well as in spirit. Our city then seemed to be a single flame of goodness in an ocean of dark. People were beginning to call the Frate a saint; certainly he was a man courageous enough to stand up publicly for the good, to denounce the evil practices both of princes and the Church. If men truly desired good government, now was the time.

But we had enemies also within the city, the Bigi, who called for the return of the Medici, and the Arrabbiati, who wanted the Republic to be governed by the old families. Great names belonged to the latter – Ridolfi, Alberti, Tornabuoni, Rucellai, Spini – and their promise of old certainties might have been attractive but for the spawn of these noble families. Dressed in audacious hose and tight-waisted jackets, the Compagnacci, or 'layabouts', went about in bands, pushing aside anyone in their way, leaving behind them the scent of musk and ambergris. Their leader was Botticelli's young neighbour, Doffo Spini, and his gappy teeth and pointed ears made him a figure of terror in the city. It was harmless enough, at first, when they did little more than amuse themselves by tripping a friar in passing or throwing stones at the faithful and calling them sheep. But then they suddenly grew more threatening and vicious. Some said it was because Savonarola had banned Carnival, and the rich youth had no outlet for their exuberance and energy. Friars were kidnapped and held on ransom; services were disrupted by the release of caged rats; slogans were daubed on the walls of San Marco. But it was obvious that the fierce quarrels in the streets and the many stabbings were part of a campaign being organised by others: the Compagnacci were being used by their fathers to destroy the New Republic. Happily the rules on age kept them out of the Grand Council themselves but the behaviour of these young men disturbed Savonarola. In the refectory that night he preached privately to the brethren from Isaiah: *And I will give children to be their princes, and babes shall rule over them. The child shall behave himself proudly against the ancient, and the base against the honourable. Jerusalem is ruined, and Judah is fallen, because their tongue and their doings are against the Lord. Children are the oppressors, and women rule over them. What mean ye that ye beat my people to pieces, and grind the faces of the poor? saith the Lord God of hosts. Because the daughters of Zion are haughty, and walk with stretched forth necks and wanton eyes, walking and mincing as they go and making a tinkling with their feet, therefore the Lord will smite with a scab the crown of the head of the daughers of Zion. He will take away the bravery of their tinkling ornaments, and their cauls, and their round tires like the moon, the chains, and the bracelets, and the mufflers, the bonnets, and the ornaments of the legs, and the headbands, and the tablets, and the earrings, the rings and nose jewels, the changeable suits of apparel, and the mantles, and the wimples, and the crisping pins, the glasses, and the fine linen, and the hoods, and the veils. And it shall come to pass, that instead of sweet smell there shall be stink; and instead of a girdle a rent; and instead of well set hair baldness, and instead of a stomacher a girding of sackcloth, and burning instead of beauty.*

Even after two years in the monastery, I was still accustomed to understand biblical texts metaphorically, but something in Savonarola's tone and enthusiasm made my jaw fall open. Almost at once Fra Domenico was on his feet, arms raised, crying out that he had had a message from the Lord, that he was to convert the children.

The Piagnoni brought their young ones to Fra Domenico's classes and, before very long, the children of very many citizens were attending. In what became known as 'The Children's Cloister', natural high spirits were quickly calmed and disciplined. They went in noisy and came out quiet. Filippino Lippi sent both his son and his daughter to classes and on the day when Fra Domenico led a great procession through the city, I stood with my friend to watch his children pass by. Garbed in white, wearing garlands of laurel and olive and singing pretty hymns, they looked like little angels. Filippino was not the only parent with tears in his eyes as he looked on this wondrous transformation. The little ones carried baskets and the youngest and sweetest went to the crowds of onlookers to collect money for the poor. Dabbing at his eyes, Filippino said that he wished he'd been brought up so well. My guffaw, arrested by the memory that I was a pious Dominican, exploded as a snort.

'What? Why are you laughing?'

My shoulders shook as I remembered how Filippino had resisted discipline.

'Stop laughing!' he said angrily, then turned to wave to his son who was now walking past, staggering under the weight of a giant candlestick.

It was announced that the Carnival of that year was to be a blazing sacrifice of vanities and a great bonfire of seven tiers was constructed in the Piazza della Signoria. The week before Lent, the children processed with their baskets again, but this time they were not asking for money. What they demanded of the grown-ups was that they surrender the chains, the mufflers, the bonnets and the tinkling ornaments. Amused, people gave up some old clothes and carnival masks. This was not enough. The children were sent out to knock on doors and confront people face to face, telling them to surrender their sin or face the wrath of the Lord. Now the baskets began to fill with more precious things, furs and jewels, wigs and cosmetics. It was still not enough. Convinced that people were hiding what they most valued, Fra Domenico told the children to report anything they saw or heard at home. Their duty and responsibility, he told them, was to the Lord, not to their parents. Now people had friars knocking on their doors, being very specific about what was to be surrendered. One evening Filippino Lippi received such a visit and was told to give up his chess set.

He came to the monastery and demanded to see me. 'I want my chess set back!' he shouted.

'Filippino, I cannot help you.'

'I want my children back! I want them to be naughty. I want them scampering like imps, their faces caked with filth and dried snot. Do you hear me? I want my children as they were!'

'You cannot be serious.'

'Serious? I am gravity itself. I don't want any son of mine taught to betray his kin! You're telling us that we're oppressed by our women and our children. I'm telling you that nothing is quite so oppressive as a po-faced man in a white habit who thinks he knows best. What has happened to you? I want my friend back! I want everything back, as it was, in the old days. God take you all and give us back the Medici!' He left abruptly, slamming the door behind him. The peace of the monastery swallowed his noise and a moment later it was as if it had never been.

The following day I had such a 'visit' myself. Fra Domenico came to the library to tell me cheerfully that all copies of Ovid and Boccaccio were to be added to the pyre, 'by order of the Frate, God be praised!'

Horrified, I went to confront Savonarola. He listened calmly to what I had to say and assured me that he had given no such order.

My heart and breathing returned to normal. 'I am sorry to have disturbed you, Frate. May I then refuse Fra Domenico's request?'

Savonarola shook his head. 'No, no, let us not upset our good brother.' He asked me whether we had any duplicate printed versions of these books, and I said that we had, as well as some manuscript copies of inferior hand and full of errors.

'Put them on the fire,' said the Frate. 'As for the rest, take them off the shelves and store them. Enthusiasm is a wonderful thing, but it does need to be curbed.'

432

When the procession from San Marco to the Piazza della Signoria started out behind the holy banner of the Crucifixion, I followed with a mule laden with a chest of books containing some corrupt and duplicate editions of *Decameron* and *Amores*. Just a few. The rest were obscure works of theology and superstitious hagiography which, in my view, do more to corrupt the minds of men than the pornography of the ancients. I waited until the flames had caught the pyre that rose high in seven tiers before, to gasps of astonishment and admiration from the crowd, I threw on the books. I stood back to watch the mighty heap of treasure burn. Much of it was vain fripperies, the sad stuff of women who think beauty can be applied; some of it was the tools of vice, the die, the cards, the cups of gambling, the boards – a chessboard with exquisitely carved individual pieces. There were paintings of an obscene kind and marble statues being reduced to lime. And then I saw something that made my heart stop, that made me want to spring into the flames and pluck it out, a painting of Venus, riding the waves on a scallop shell, her long, yellow hair flowing over her nakedness.

No!

I looked about wildly and saw Sandro Botticelli walking back into the crowd, having thrown on his offering. Reason spoke to me then, softly, comfortingly, telling me that the *Venus* was safe on the walls of Lorenzo di Pierfrancesco, that this was either a copy or a discarded, early version. Maybe. Perhaps so. But it was the symbol rather than the material object that was exploding in my soul. It was the symbol that was on fire, the image of beauty bubbling in the heat, the wood blackening, the image disappearing. I stood gazing at her, her fatal heat burning my face, and knew horror of a kind my spiritual father would neither understand nor approve.

My gaze roamed round the crowd until I saw the face I was suddenly searching for: Marsilio Ficino was looking not at the fire but at me. And what did he see? A hypocrite, no doubt. An erstwhile member of the Platonic Academy burning books.

93 THE DECEIVING DEMON
1497

IN THESE YEARS, WHEN HE WAS A CANON OF THE CATHEDRAL, Ficino resided in his town house, a tall, narrow building close to the Casa Vecchia. He was in his mid-sixties and, despite his lifelong infirmities, was surviving all his friends. His once golden hair had turned silver and his face was as creased as a screwed-up poem but although his eyes were growing a little cloudy, they still had the power to read souls.

Seeing me passing in the street below on the day after the bonfire, he called me in. 'I presume those were not works of any great value I saw you throwing on the fire?'

I assured him that they were not. He shook his head. 'I don't know why I should be pleased to find you have become such an adept dissembler, but I am. Did the Medici put you in the monastery to be their eyes and ears?'

'I've been sworn to secrecy.'

'So they did. Was it Piero?'

I shook my head.

'Cardinal Giovanni, then. Ah, I see. You are looking after the books.' Ficino leaned forward and gazed at me, into my soul. 'How good a Dominican are you? Can I trust you?'

'Speak, Father. I am your Tommaso.'

'Tell me everything you know about Savonarola. How do you find him at close-quarters? Is he a sincere man?'

I drew out a pamphlet in manuscript that I was taking to be printed by Miscomini. 'Here is something he has written recently: *The Triumph of the Cross*. I think it will answer your questions.'

While Ficino was reading, I sat back and looked around. His desk, placed by a window, was like a shrine, an altar to wisdom. His books, his writing equipment, the magnifying lenses he wedged on his nose as he studied, everything had to it the purity of unwavering intention. Marsilio Ficino had never been thrown off course by chance. I looked at my old friend and master, bent over the words of Savonarola, pulling on his lower lip as he read. There was a scent in the room, a fragrance beyond the various pungent herbs he had been grinding in the mortar. They say that saints give off a divine aroma. So did Ficino. It was a scent that acted like a hand on your back, relaxing all the muscles, removing the cares, removing the world itself. To sit and breathe in Ficino's study was enough: one wanted nothing else. The scent of roses, of jasmine, of heaven.

At last he raised his head. 'Everything he says here is true. I have never seen the Christian faith so clearly set out, free of all dogma and intelligible to everyone.'

'Quite. There is not a philosopher amongst us who is also a Christian who could find fault in this man.'

Ficino rubbed his face wearily. 'Yet there is something wrong. This city which he calls the New Jerusalem has become a dangerous place, full of violent factions. Every night there is a murder and no one dares to go abroad alone. Now I hear that the Frate is proposing that prostitutes, gamblers and sodomites be tried and put to death. Is that the way of Jesus? There is failure in trade, failure in harvest, famine and contagion.' He rocked gently back and forth, his brow creased by thought. 'To judge by our senses, to judge by this pamphlet, we are being governed by a good man, and yet something is wrong. I do not understand.'

I told him about my continuing attempt to be both a Christian and a Platonist at once, without contradiction.

He smiled, knowing himself, as a canon of the cathedral, how difficult that was. 'Do you succeed?'

'Only when I am in the present moment.'

'How often is that?'

'Not very often,' I admitted sheepishly.

He leant forwards and patted me on the hand. 'At least it is sometimes – better than never. I always had hope in you, Tommaso.'

'I have to keep quiet about my beliefs, of course.'

'As one must. Strange, isn't it, that we have to be circumspect only amongst the religious? No philosopher would condemn a man for being a Christian, or a Jew or a Muslim for that matter. That tells me that these men of religion are not true.'

'Someone told me of a saint who surrendered every thought to God, every thought, including his own judgement as to what is right or wrong.'

Ficino shuddered. 'The way of devotion is hard.' He laughed suddenly. 'But who wants to be a saint?'

'Almost everyone in San Marco.'

'Not least its Vicar General.'

'Some of the friars are, well, strange and fanatical. It's Fra Domenico who is converting the children and burning the books. And then there is Fra Silvestro.' I told Ficino what I had seen when I had gone into Savonarola's cell.

'How do you interpret that event?'

'I have heard rumours, whispers around the cloisters, that it is Silvestro who receives the visions which Savonarola delivers as his own from the pulpit. And now I have seen it with my own eyes. But does that matter? If it is the voice of God?'

'That is the crux of it. Is it the voice of God? How can we tell? Demons pose as angels: it is their chief trick. There is even one deceiving demon who speaks as if it were the Holy Ghost, and only a wise man will know the difference. It would be easy to say that, through the power of demons, Savonarola is deceiving us.'

'No, Father. I do not believe that. He is genuine.'

'Ah, perhaps he is not knowingly deceiving us. Perhaps the deception begins with himself. Of course he is a true and sincere man – that's what makes him so powerful – but it is the self-deception which makes him terrible.' Suddenly Ficino's eyes widened and he began to tremble. 'Do you realise, as I now realise, who we are speaking about?'

I shook my head.

'Poliziano, God rest his soul, was right. He was the only one of us to see Savonarola for what he is: the antichrist.'

'But how can that be?' I cried. 'He has no mark of the beast on him. He keeps the commandments like no other.'

'Do not expect to see the antichrist with ten horns and two heads, or the number six-six-six blazoned on his brow. Remember the words of St Matthew: we can only know him by his fruits. Look at this city: it is dying. The work of Cosimo and Lorenzo: destroyed. The Platonic Academy: meeting in secret. These children robed in white informing on their parents; mothers and fathers living in dread of their offspring. He is burning books. Burning books!'

'Nothing of value –'

'Well, what is that if not deception?'

'– and everything he has written in that pamphlet is true.'

Ficino glanced over it again. 'It sounds true, but there is something missing. He says it is his work to bring the kingdom here on earth. This is a mistake because, as I have striven to demonstrate all these years, the kingdom is *already here*. Only a philosopher will know that in his own experience, yet Savonarola denies philosophy and would ban it. I assure you that faith without reason is a bird with one wing, a bird that cannot fly. Poets, diviners, philosophers – they experience the ineffable in the mundane. The religious do not. They believe heaven is in the future and not of this world. Now is the moment, here, now. *Now!* Wake up, Tommaso!'

In my mind I was back in the monastery and looking for signs of the antichrist in Savonarola. I came back to myself. 'I am here.'

'Good. Only in the present moment is joy, eternity, immortality. Past and future – delusion. This is what Savonarola does not teach, because he does not know it. He teaches awareness of sin, and that is separation from God. The first, original sin – separation from God. It is the creed of hopelessness. By all means, do not sin, but if you do, abandon all thought of repentance and grace: know what you have done and do it no more. What Plato and the Platonists teach is unity, the true identity of the

437

quintessence of all creatures with the One. What you think you are, the body, mind and nature, are sheaths which hide God. You *are* God. It is not a question of finding him, or uniting with him; it is a question of knowing who you are. The man who weaves down the street convinced he is the pope – what difference is there between him and you, who think you are Tommaso Maffei? It is all misidentification. Drop it. Be God. Savonarola would say this is heresy. I say it is the truth. Choose, Tommaso, choose now.'

I had never heard him speak so urgently and forcefully. In that moment, the choice seemed easy: I believed everything he said. More, I knew it to be true from my own experience. But a sneaking nervousness at condemning the Christ-like Savonarola kept me quiet. What if Ficino were wrong? He understood my hesitation.

'If all creatures are in essence divine, that includes Girolamo Savonarola, whether he be the antichrist or no. Serve the essence, not the man.'

'What do I do? Go back and denounce him?'

'Not if you want to live. I dined with Poliziano and Pico a week before Angelo was taken ill, sharing the harvest of their vineyards. The French were at the city gates but up on Fiesole we were laughing about it, happy and elevated. There was no shadow on that evening, no foreboding, no malign messages in the stars. Angelo and Pico were both anxious that I decide whose wine was best, and we got a little drunk in the contest. Any quarrel I'd had with Pico in the past was forgotten. There was work to be done, great work, and together we were going to synthesise Plato, Aristotle and Christianity into one great teaching. So, the French were coming and the French would go. We had nothing to fear, for we were children of God. That was how it felt, that lovely September night. A fortnight later, Angelo was dead; eight weeks later, so was Pico. Thirty-two years old! Let us speak of it, Tommaso. The death of these two friends, these two great, very great men: were they not suspicious?'

I hung my head. The death and burials of Poliziano and Pico

were facts so uncomfortable that I rarely dared think about them.

'Such untimely deaths, and so close to each other. At that dinner, Pico told us that it was his intention to divest himself of all worldly goods, but he said nothing about entering the Dominican Order. He was going to take to the road, he said, a pilgrim, a mendicant, to throw himself as a feather on the breath of God. You know what Pico was like: once he had an idea, no matter how insane it was, he was going to do it. I fully believed what he told me: he was going to take to the road. He had already given his titles and goods away.'

'Do you know who to?'

'Yes. He left everything to his brother, Antonmaria.'

'Not to Gianfrancesco?'

'No, nothing. He had no time for Gianfrancesco. You must have known that. "One of God's sycophants" he called him.'

'Why has Antonmaria not claimed his inheritance? The books are still in San Marco.'

'Too busy fighting wars and not very interested, I should think, other than in their monetary value.'

'Gianfrancesco has spent these past months editing the papers, making everything ready for publication. And he has been working closely with Savonarola to complete Pico's refutation of astrology.'

Ficino blanched. 'What are they doing? What ideas are they putting to his name? This must be stopped at once!'

'How could we possibly stop it?'

'You must write to Antonmaria.'

'And consign Pico's works to oblivion? Better they are published, surely, in whatever form.'

Ficino told me to copy everything I could from the original documents. 'The friars tell us that Pico and Poliziano died Dominicans,' he said, 'but is it true?'

'No, of course it is not true. If Angelo did convert, it was in delirium. I don't know. I was kept from him. But I was with Pico,

439

and he died a Cabalist. Both corpses were dressed in Dominican habits, which I myself removed in the night so as to clothe them in their own apparel. They lie together in their finery; that is the best that can be said.'

'What if they died, were killed to propagate the faith?'

I leapt from my chair, sprung by words being said out loud that I had only dared think in my darkest moments. Ficino rose and took my hands in his. 'I believe our friends were about to denounce the friar, and that is why they were killed.'

I shook my head, trying to clear it. 'How could that be possible? If a man has convinced himself that he is God's prophet, that makes him less, not more likely to commit murder.'

'But as you say, the men around him are strange, and might be moved to commit sin for what they believe to be the greater good.'

'The manuscripts Angelo was working on when he died have gone missing, stolen I think. Maria said a friar took them for safe-keeping, but they're not in the library. I've searched it thoroughly.'

'Manuscripts of what, Tommaso?'

'He was working on a revision of his Account of the Pazzi Conspiracy; there were some letters he was collating for publication; and the second miscellany, ending with an entry on pygmies.'

'Nothing else?'

'Yes,' I said, and then I began to tremble. 'There was something. I noticed a fresh work fastened to his desk but did not read it. It was about the antichrist!'

'As I thought. Autumn, 1494. The moment was precarious. The French were at our gates. Piero de' Medici, as I remember, had succeeded in his negotiations, but it was put abroad that he had failed and a second deputation was sent to the camp. When Savonarola returned, he was feted as a hero. If Pico and Poliziano had chosen *that* moment to speak out, we would still be ruled by the Medici.'

'Many would say that would be an evil.'

'They would be wrong. There was much left to be desired in

440

the days of the Medici, not least many of our republican freedoms, but what we did have was the freedom of thought, opinion and belief, and that is the greater freedom. The last time the Platonic Academy was closed it was by Justinian, a Christian emperor as straight in his religion as Savonarola is in his. If you look over history, you will see that philosophy flourishes in times of decadence and goes underground in times of strict, enforced theology. Strict theology, the interpretation of bigoted and arrogant men, is a tyrant deaf to anyone's truth but its own. That is the religion that puts non-believers to the stake. Theology and Philosophy are sisters. When they run freely hand-in-hand, no one is killed for his beliefs.' Ficino stood up and thanked me for helping him to see the matter clearly. 'I am now convinced,' he said, 'that Savonarola is the antichrist. Tommaso, you must leave San Marco.'

'How? I am in the Order. And the books – I cannot leave the books!' I tried to evade his gaze, my eyes moving now left, now right, but wherever they moved Ficino placed himself in the way of my sight. 'Leave,' he repeated, fixing my gaze with his.

'The books...'

'The books have their own fate, and you have yours.'

'Yes, indeed I have, if it is to be a runaway friar!'

'Go to the Pope and have your vows annulled.'

Pope Alexander? The Borgia pope? Here I laughed out loud at the enormity of the suggestion. 'Now he *is* the antichrist!'

'There can be more than one. Indeed, we all have the antichrist within us, as much as we have the Christ, but we do not all presume to stand up and speak on behalf of God. Listen to me. We may not see each other again. The Platonic Academy will not outlive me, at least not for long. Listen. Tommaso, concentrate. I want you to go north and take what you know of Plato to those who know nothing. Be an apostle of philosophy. Free yourself of these vows. Whatever authority you acted under, I am superseding it. Do as I say. Tommaso Maffei, for once in your life, do as I say, and leave.'

441

94 SARZI
1497

WHEN I RETURNED TO THE MONASTERY, I FOUND
Savonarola preaching to a group of women, telling them how to
be good wives and live the Christian life. I stared at him across the
cloisters: there was nothing on him, no mark of the antichrist at
all. And yet, if I were to go to him and tell him that the kingdom
of heaven is here, now, he would have risen in wrath and shouted
at me. I went to my cell, locked the door and fell into a torment
of thought as to what I should do. Succeeding in nothing but
giving myself a headache, I returned to my work collating the
papers of Poliziano ready for publication. After the steadiness of
work had calmed me down, it occurred to me that, once finished,
I could contrive to take the collection to Venice myself – and then
not return. Simple! I resolved to get the work done as quickly as
I could. It would take a fortnight perhaps, or a month – no
more – to finish. Then I would do as I had been told to do and
quit Florence.

A quiet knock on my door made me jump. 'Fra Tommaso?
It is me, Alessandro.'

'It is I, not me,' I thought going to the door and turning the
key. For one who called himself an editor, Alessandro Sarzi had a
weak grasp of grammar. Sarzi – a man so oily you could have made
an everlasting torch of him. I ushered him in.

He was a Bolognese who worked with a printer of Bologna who
had the gall to rename himself 'Platone'. Sarzi had first sought me
out not long after Poliziano's death, asking for any Italian work not
yet published. Although I disliked the man on sight, I gave him
several pieces for Platone to print. After that, he has been assiduous
in his help in finding copies of Poliziano's work around the city.

He sat down in my only chair and looked about my cell with
tremendous satisfaction. 'How is the work? Is it done yet?'

'Not quite.'

'I have had a letter from Aldo Manuzio. He is keen and willing to publish the complete works, the *Opera Omnia* of Angelo Poliziano. Wonderful news, eh?'

I was swallowing bile, a bitter, acrid lump of pride that would not quite go down. 'Why – why you?' I managed.

'Because I suggested it. There's no point in collecting everything together and then sitting on it. It must be published.'

'I know! I was about to... I was going to write to Aldo.'

'Well, I have done it for you. And I've offered to be its editor.'

I was the editor. By all that was holy and true, *I* had to be the editor. But I was a friar... 'Oh,' I said.

He picked up the stack of finished papers and began to look through it. 'Did you find the Account of the Pazzi conspiracy?'

'No, not yet.'

'The second *Miscellanea*?'

'No.'

'That is a tragedy, a tragedy.' He made a great intake of breath. 'Keep looking, Fra Tommaso, and send anything to me in Venice that you find.'

'When are you going?'

'Next week.'

'I need a fortnight.'

'You have a week.'

I had been making a copy of everything I had found. I carried on with the work until it was time for Sarzi to leave Florence but had to let a few things go without making a copy. I packed them in a chest with dread and prayed God they would arrive safely.

To watch the chests being carried away was to experience Angelo's death all over again. There was a great hole in my life, with nothing to do other than my given duties. Ficino's instruction sat on me like a hair shirt, but I steeled myself to ignore it. I had made a vow to Cardinal Giovanni to protect the Medici books and I must stay. Had God himself not sent a sign in Alessandro Sarzi? I was not meant to go to Venice.

443

I repaired my relations with Gianfrancesco and offered to help him in his collation of Pico's works, which he, somewhat overwhelmed by his chosen task, accepted. When I told him that Sarzi had taken Poliziano's works to Venice to be published by Aldo, he warned me to be careful of him. 'When I was in Bologna last, I came across a book of Poliziano's Italian verses printed by Platone.'

'Yes, I gave the manuscript to Sarzi myself.'

'Well, I knew them for Poliziano's verses, and perhaps other men will recognise them as such, but the name on the frontispiece was "Alessandro Sarzi".'

That should have served to release the arrow from the bow; that should have sent me out of the monastery and to Venice in pursuit of the thief, with or without permission. Why did it not? Because I convinced myself that a letter to Aldo would suffice, warning him not to allow Sarzi near Poliziano's *Opera Omnia* in any capacity, editorial or otherwise.

The reply, when it came, said that Sarzi was proof-reading, nothing more. But I heard other things over the following year from friends of Poliziano, who were being asked to rewrite the letters they had written to him, 'for the cause of the refinement of style'. Each of them said they had been contacted by Alessandro Sarzi, the editor of Poliziano's works.

Now I trusted no one. Working with Gianfrancesco, I found he was leaving out of his collation anything to do with magic and Cabala. My new work became the rescue of the full works of Giovanni Pico della Mirandola. I stored the copies in the library of San Marco for posterity.

The books of Poliziano and Pico were duly published in the following years. Neither deserved the name *Opera Omnia*. But most of the works that survived those two great scholars do still exist; copies have been made of my copies and are in circulation, amassing ready for future editions put together, I can only hope, by men more faithful to the authors.

95 SAVONAROLA IS ATTACKED
1497

GOING TO OGNISSANTI ONE EVENING TO COLLECT A BOOK from the Palazzo Vespucci, I called in at Botticelli's workshop. At the front were various images of the Madonna and saints and a smell of incense hung on the air. I crossed the shop, empty but for a dozing apprentice, thinking that Sandro must have succumbed to his brother's urgings and become a Piagnone. Hearing voices in the back room, I opened the door – and stopped dead. About twelve young men were variously draped on settles and benches, drinking Sandro's best wine. They looked as thunderstruck as I did, but recovered quicker.

'Get out, you dog!' shouted Doffo Spini, his face screwed with rage. The young man next to him, one of the Ridolfi, picked up a jar of yellow pigment and flung its contents at me. They all crowed with laughter and within moments I was daubed with every colour of Sandro's palette.

'Paint the dog! Paint the dog! Put some colour in his cheeks, Doffo!'

I was too weak from our continual fasting in the monastery to resist them and mewed like a kitten.

Botticelli shouted at them to stop and bundled me out of the room. 'I'm sorry, I'm so sorry,' he said, taking me to the well.

Only now did I find my voice. 'You, you who would rather draw images of paradise than earn a living, you of all men, to keep such evil company!'

'I'm so sorry.' He did what he could to wash me down but it was hopeless. 'I'll lend you my mantle. It will get you back to the monastery. And keep you warm. Tommaso, you are so cold and thin.'

'It's you I'm worried about, not me. Please tell me why you allow Doffo Spini near you.'

'I've known him since he was a child!'

'Then you know he is evil.'

Sandro looked at me severely. 'You are beginning to sound like a Dominican, but I know you for a Platonist who believes that goodness is the essence of all men. Yes, in Doffo it is overcome by evil, and he reacts to goodness with evil. When my brother lectures him, it makes him worse. Just the presence of the Friar in the city makes him worse. So how do you make him better? By giving him a drink and letting him prattle.'

I looked at him doubtfully.

'Very well, it may not work, but at least I know what he is planning, where you do not.'

Now I looked at him with interest. 'What is he planning?'

'There is a conspiracy to assassinate Savonarola.'

'By the Compagnacci?'

'No, by others, but Doffo knows all about it, the when and the where of it, and the Compagnacci are going to create the necessary turbulence. It is what they are good at, after all. Doffo does not care whether Savonarola lives or dies: what he wants is rid of him.'

'Who is behind all this, Sandro?'

'Rome.'

'*Rome?*'

'The Pope, The Duke of Milan – and the Florentines, raw with austerity, will shout for Barabbas when it comes to it. Doffo's only a puppet. Now, if you will allow it, I must return to my companions and somehow explain how it is that I have a friend among the Dominicans. Perhaps I shall tell them that you were planted in the monastery as a spy. What of that?'

I blinked rapidly.

'Painters have eyes,' he said, widening his own to stare into mine as he cleaned off my face with a wet rag. 'Do you think I am stupid? Those books on the bonfire: they had as much value as my Venus. True?'

He went back inside to fetch his mantle. I looked round the yard where once I had posed for the figure of Mercury. It all seemed so long ago, that age when the gods lived with us. Now

446

there was but one God. I looked up at the sky and ached with the sense of loss. Botticelli came out and threw his mantle around my shoulders.

'You don't understand me and I don't understand you. Where did my lovely young Mercury go?'

'He died, Sandro. He died twice. Once with his wife, then again with Lorenzo.'

Sandro kissed me on the cheek. 'Resurrect. Be your own man. What did Virgil say to Dante? *I crown and mitre thee lord of thyself.*' With that he pulled the hood over my head and slapped me on the back.

In the old days, the Signoria – elected every two months – had always comprised Medici men. Savonarola did not stoop to such corruption but wanted the people to be free to elect whom they chose. They chose Barabbas. When it came to the next election, enough of these outwardly pious Florentines dropped a bean in the bag of self-interest for the new Signoria to be composed of men of the old and powerful families – the Arrabbiati. These were not men to go to San Marco on their knees to kiss Savonarola on the hand. Instead, they banned him from preaching. Faced with the choice of disobeying the government or obeying God, Savonarola announced that he intended to preach at the Duomo on the eve of Ascension Day. I told Fra Silvestro what I had heard from Botticelli but he said I was not to allow fear into my heart. 'The hour of our passing is for the Lord to choose.' No one I spoke to was concerned about the Compagnacci; they were minor demons compared to the devil that was Pope Alexander. But when Savonarola went to the Duomo, he was accompanied by almost all the brethren of San Marco and those of us who were left behind were told we were to protect the monastery.

My growing tendency to tremble was, I believed, as much due to continual fasting as to cowardice; despite the gravity of the hour, as soon as the brethren had left I hurried to the larders beyond the refectory. I found there every other friar who had remained behind and together we sliced a ham, boiled some eggs and made a feast at the refectory table.

'Do you think they will try and assassinate the Frate?'

'Not with two hundred of the brethren around him.'

'If they are as weak as I am,' I said, 'they'll be of little use.'

'Some of them are armed,' said Fra Luca della Robbia through a mouth full of bread.

I was astonished. 'The friars? Is that true?'

Several heads nodded in agreement. 'More than we are, who have been left behind to defend the monastery.'

'How are we supposed to defend it?'

'By our prayers,' said Fra Zenobio, ripping meat off the ham bone.

'Every martyr in history is witness to the efficacy of those,' Fra Luca complained. 'Oh, God, this feels good. Pass the eggs. They won't assassinate him: it's just their tactics of fear.'

As I pushed the bowl towards him, I heard a noise. 'What was that?'

Zenobio limped to the door and looked out. 'A dead dog,' he said. 'Thrown over the wall.' None of us were interested, not with food still on the table, but Zenobio went out and came back with a bloodied piece of paper. 'Poor mutt. I don't think it was found dead. It was still warm. This was under its collar.' He put the paper on the table.

Death to the Hounds of the Lord.

Zenobio sat down with a sigh. 'I do not understand the Compagnacci. Born of good family, educated well, they offend every human and divine law.' Every day we found some obscenity painted on the outside walls, some piece of doggerel tacked to the church doors. 'What do they stand for? Do they cause trouble just for their pleasure?'

'There's more to it,' said Fra Luca. 'They want to change the age of eligibility for public office from twenty-nine to twenty.'

'They want to *govern* us? Mother Mary and all the Saints!'

'They are being used,' I said, but before I could continue there

448

was another noise, and something much more threatening than a dead dog. It was the sound of the gate opening and brethren returning, noisy and agitated, at least an hour before they were due. Burning with guilt we swept away the litter and crumbs and had just cleared the table when they came in. None amongst them was in a condition to wonder why we were all in the refectory; each of them had his own sin to worry about – the sin of desertion.

When they had got to the Cathedral they had found the pulpit defiled. The Compagnacci were everywhere in the streets and people had had to fight their way through them to get in to hear the sermon. Once the pulpit had been cleared of shit, piss and the reeking skin of an ass, Savonarola had mounted it and begun to speak. Not long afterwards the Compagnacci had forced their way in and started throwing things about. The confusion had been terrible and it was at that point that these wretches had made their escape.

'And Fra Girolamo?' we cried. 'You left him?'

Some amongst them wept at their weakness and we fellows with our bellies full walked away in disgust. More brethren returned with more to tell, and soon Fra Girolamo himself arrived. There had been a fight in the cathedral. When the Compagnacci began to disrupt the sermon, the congregation had stampeded in panic, but some went home and returned armed. In the melee, two members of the Signoria had detached and advanced on the pulpit with their swords drawn, evidently bent on killing Savonarola. Wearing a habit does not change a man's nature: as Savonarola called on God, a young friar punched one of the Signoria in the face, so hard that the man brought his companion down as he fell. Other friars bundled Savonarola out of the cathedral.

We were all compromised on that day, each and every one of us. Hypocrites.

Letters went back and forth to Rome. The Pope, we knew, planned to excommunicate Savonarola, but then a shocking thing happened in the Borgia family: the youngest son of the Pope, Cesare, murdered the eldest. The Pope was so grief-stricken that he resolved to reform both himself and the Church. This was like the old days – God using Savonarola as His agent – and the mood in the monastery lifted to the sky. But as the Pope's grief subsided, so old habits reasserted themselves and soon he was back to normal. He wrote, ordering the Frate to present himself in Rome. When Savonarola refused, a bull of excommunication was issued.

We were led in solemn procession to Santa Maria Novella and there, at the high altar, before that chapel decorated by Ghirlandaio, we, the friars and the Piagnoni, gathered in torchlight to be told the dread news by Fra Domenico. As he read from the papal bull, small bells tolled and the torches were extinguished one by one. A mortal sigh breathed from the crowd, to be living in such a world where evil triumphs over good.

As we processed back to our enclosure at San Marco, we were pelted with stones and dung, and Savonarola and his closest brethren were lashed by whips. The drunken Compagnacci were dressed up as if for Carnival, wearing the wigs and cosmetics that had never gone to the bonfire. Bacchus, it would seem, was mocking Christ. That was how it did seem, and many looked on what they took to be the Passion of Savonarola, wondering how long it was to be before the crucifixion.

In July of that year, plague came to the city, carrying off fifty or sixty a day. We assumed we would be safe in the monastery, that God would protect us, but friends of Savonarola pleaded with him to escape to the country. He refused to leave himself but did send away all the novices and nuns. I gasped with relief when I heard this, for I feared for Maria. We were not safe in San Marco: the plague had already taken two of our number.

Now I was thrown into the pastoral work Savonarola had promised me. Each day I went out in the streets with the brethren, bringing help where we could, not only to the dying but to the widows and orphans also. Yes, I feared death and could not help but cover my nose against its stench, but if I was going to die, I wanted to die doing good. To get to heaven? A cynic would say so; but the heart knows instinctively the right way to die – and to live. Nevertheless, ideas of holiness and its rewards had seeped into me: how could they not? But one day out in the streets behind the Duomo I saw members of the Misericordia running with stretchers towards the hospital of Santa Maria Nuova. I stared at them. The Misericordia, a company of merchants and notaries dedicated to charitable work. It was like a punch in the face, the realisation that not only the religious do religious work. And more. As I looked about, I saw Franciscans as busy as we were. I knew it then, forcefully: the arrogance of the Dominicans. We truly believed that we were the only ones who had any goodness in them, and it was not so.

'Your Vicar General is a saint,' one old woman told me as I fed her.

'The city never suffered like this under Lorenzo,' complained her husband.

'That's not true,' said the woman. 'We had plagues then, and war, and flood.'

'But not like this,' her husband insisted. 'This is continual: one thing following another. If this is the New Jerusalem, you can keep it.' His view was becoming the general one. Each week fewer people attended our services and the numbers of the Piagnoni were visibly shrinking.

When the plague had passed and the nuns had returned, Savonarola preached to them from the pulpit above the church door. I looked down from a window and studied every upturned face. Maria was not there. I made enquiries: did all the nuns return from the country? I was told no. Three had died: Benedicta, Immaculata and Chiara. No one I spoke to knew their birth names, but remembering that Maria had wanted to call herself Benedicta when she was in the convent at Montepulciano, I folded up over yet another knife wound in the heart.

96 GIANFRANCESCO REVEALED
1497

YES, THAT IS WHEN I GREW BITTER AND HARD. A CURIOUS sickness ate away at my innards and I fasted now by my own volition as if I could starve the sin out of me. I pushed at Death to provoke a response, but none came. I lived. I lived on the scent of books.

The air in the city was taut with menace. A new law had admitted younger men into the Great Council and the Compagnacci had not only taken up council seats but Doffo Spini was elected to be one of the ruling Eight. This encouraged those people who had only paid lip service to personal reform: sumptuous dress began once more to be paraded in the streets. Without any sermons to draw impressive crowds, the city reverted to old ways. But tract after tract came from Savonarola's pen and it was clear that it would take more than an order for silence to keep him quiet. The air in the city grew tauter.

When many of the younger friars began to smuggle arms into the monastery, I kept to the library, surreptitiously storing books in chests ready for easy transportation should the need arise and the way open up. I waited to hear from Cardinal Giovanni in Rome, but heard nothing.

There were rumours of a conspiracy to reinstate Piero de' Medici. Of course I heard them, since some of the men involved were old friends from the Platonic Academy and frequent visitors to the library. Florence was still under French jurisdiction: all that we suffered was being caused by a battle between France on one hand and Rome and Milan on the other. The ruling Arrabbiati worked for Rome. Savonarola's intention was that Florence be independent, that her only king should be Christ. The King of France thought differently, and wanted Piero back. But the people did not understand: they eddied like autumn leaves and never stopped to ask the name of the wind.

452

Out one night late in August, I had been delayed in returning to the monastery and it was dark. It did not do to be out at night in those times and I hurried through the empty streets of Ognissanti trying to make no noise.

I smelt them first, that woody, sweet, earthy scent of the wealthy that is ambergris; that smooth perfume that is a lodestone to any nose, that hangs in the air long after the wearer has gone – or before he has arrived. And there was something mixed with it, the animal scent of young males which even ambergris cannot disguise. I stood still, waiting, listening. I could hear the rustle of their silks and brocades, a stifled giggle, a hiss to be quiet. They were round the next corner, waiting for me to pass. Turning to go back the way I had come, I found Doffo Spini and two others behind me.

'Where are you going, dog?' one asked as the rest of the gang joined them. I felt vulnerable and doomed in my Dominican habit, wanted to rip it off and say, 'I'm a Maffei!' But they knew that, or at least, Doffo Spini did.

'This is no common dog,' he said. 'It's the very one we want to talk to.' He was taller than me and, with his chin raised, he looked at me down his nose. His ears poked through his hair like sharp toenails through hose.

'Fra Tommaso,' he drawled. 'The Medici spy in San Marco.'

I quailed. Who had told them? Botticelli?

'What do you know of this conspiracy to reinstate Piero?'

'Nothing! I swear it.'

They prowled about me, poking, pushing, the ritual of humiliation.

'There are going to be arrests made tomorrow. Your name is on the list.'

'But I know nothing! Piero de' Medici is the last person I want to see ruling Florence!'

'Oh? And who is the first?'

If I gave any name other than one of their own, I'd be condemning myself. My throat caked with fear.

453

'It's an impossible question, isn't it?' Doffo smiled. 'But I'm telling you I'd rather have Piero than your Savonarola. That can never happen – that miserable zealot in charge. So, if you would like your name removed from the list, as I'm sure you would, you will agree to stand as witness in any coming trial of the crimes of the Friar.'

At that moment I was a Christian and a Platonist all in one. Putting aside the question as to whether Savonarola was the antichrist or not (and it was difficult to believe that he was, in the face of this evil) I was driven to speak the truth. It was my only recourse.

'He has committed no crimes.'

'Would you say that on the strappado?'

I was caught by the wrists, had them tied behind my back and pulled up behind me to give me a taste of the torture to come. I screamed, my innards dissolving. Then an older man joining the group barked at them to let me go. I raised my head and gazed at Sandro Botticelli in horror. How could he be part of this?

'Untie him.'

'*Mio zio*! He is only being encouraged to help us.'

'I said untie him, Doffo!' Sandro spoke as if to a child, and Doffo Spini nodded sullenly at his companions. The gang dispersed, whistling and jeering, leaving that wonderful scent behind them. Sandro undid the rope binding my wrists.

'Why do they listen to you?' I asked. 'Are you one of them?'

'You know I am not. But Tommaso, get out of Florence tonight. There's been a confession to a conspiracy and anyone with Medici connections is in great danger. Many of our friends are already in flight.'

'I shall be safe in the monastery.'

'You will not! San Marco is not the haven of security it once was. Get out of the city!'

'How far will I get as a runaway friar?'

'Come to me for clothes. And a wig.'

'Sandro, did anything of yours go on the bonfire?'

'Nothing I'd miss.' Laughing, he escorted me back to the monastery, making me promise at the gates to do as he said.

Was the vow I had made to Cardinal Giovanni so strong that I would disobey this advice, both from Ficino and Botticelli? It seemed so. As the arrests began on the following day, I stayed in the library and became even more avid in my packing of books. Names of those arrested reached me: Giovanni Cambi, Gianozzo Pucci, Niccolò Ridolfi, Lorenzo Tornabuoni and the Gonfalonier himself, the seventy-five-year-old Bernardo del Nero. Men from Ghirlandaio's frescoes were being dragged through the streets on a public cart. All day I waited for the approach of officers in the library. What came, however, was a summons to see Fra Silvestro. He instructed me to go to the Palazzo del Podestà to visit one of the accused, 'since he is a friend of yours', and comfort him with words of faith. He gazed at me piercingly.

'Who is it?' I asked.

'Cristoforo Casale.'

'A conspirator? That cannot be true! None of those arrested are guilty, I am sure of it, or else they would have fled.'

'I do not know if Casale was part of the conspiracy. What we do know, since he has confessed it, is that he murdered his master, the Count of Concordia.'

That piercing gaze, looking to see if I could rise to the challenge of consoling the murderer of my friend. I gazed right back to let him know I could.

How different are our prisons to those of the King of France. I found Cristoforo barefooted, half naked and in chains, lying broken in a dank and tiny cell that he shared with a man dying of the sweating sickness. There was livid bruising round his wrists and his face had swollen so that he could hardly open his parched, cracked mouth. One shoulder was clearly dislocated.

I knelt down beside him. 'I have been sent to give you words of faith and consolation. Let me remind you instead of the immortal soul.'

'I didn't do it, Maso.'

'I know that.'

'The strappado will make a man say anything. I would have confessed to killing Jesus.'

'Retract your confession.'

'What, and go through that again? Never. I long for death. But Maso, you are in danger. When are they going to accuse you of murdering Angelo? It is so convenient, to close the case. Quit Florence at once. There are dark things here, so dark, dark. Pico – he raised a dark angel.'

'What do you mean?'

'His magic was stronger than he was. He didn't know what he was doing. Quit Florence.'

'Not before I get you out of here. You have the right of appeal.'

He went to smile but it made his lips split and he winced. 'No one leaves here alive, do they? I will go to the block with the rest. But Maso, gather the fragments. Save of Pico what you can. It was Gianfrancesco who had me arrested.'

'*What?*'

'I am certain of it. He wants rid of me, so that he can butcher and steal his uncle's work with impunity. I made too much fuss. Never poke a scorpion with a stick.'

I left, determined to invoke the new law somehow, no matter what the personal risk, but on the way out, passing a closed door, I heard a sound of winching and a man's scream rising to a roar which loosened my bowels. To have your hands tied behind your back and suspended by your wrists… Who was it? Venerable old Del Nero? Young, gentle Lorenzo Tornabuoni? By the time I got to the street, I was throwing up.

I did nothing. Neither did Savonarola. The Great Council, his creation, voted unanimously for the execution of the traitors and no appeal was granted. In the middle of one hot, August night, I walked backwards to the place of execution, holding an icon in front of Cristoforo so that he could gaze on the holy image in his last minutes. But what he chose to gaze at was me. I stared into the eyes of a man about to die.

'Have faith,' I whispered.

'Have you forgotten everything? Why should I fear death? You are the dying one, my friend. Remember. Remember.'

And for a moment I was in a high tower in France, floating in stillness and silence, deep, deep in the all and everything. The jeers of the crowd seemed far away. As the axe came down on Cristoforo's neck, as his head rolled, it was as if nothing was happening at all.

Back in the monastery, I had great difficulty looking anyone in the eye, lest they read my soul. I shrank from Gianfrancesco and was relieved when he departed for Bologna. He had, he said, finished his work on his uncle's papers and wanted to initiate their publication. Having made copies of everything, he left the originals behind.

When at last Antonmaria, the rightful heir, made arrangements for Pico's books and papers to be sold, I looked after the sale, but not before I had read everything and copied as much of it myself as I could. If I had not, even more would have been lost by Gianfrancesco's 'editing' than was; for in Giovanni Pico's *Opera Omnia* when it was published was anything but the complete works.

Gianfrancesco was to Giovanni Pico as Sarzi was to Poliziano: a leech, a weevil, seeking to make another man's greatness his own. Did I suspect him of anything worse than editorial tampering? Of course. How could I not? But let us not wildly accuse men who are still living. I am, after all, not only a hypocrite but a lily-livered coward. The sound of that scream in the gaol will live with me forever.

Lorenzo di Pierfrancesco had been among those fleeing the city when the conspiracy came to light. I presumed his brother had left with him, for certainly Giovanni di Pierfrancesco disappeared at that time. It seemed the Medici had gone forever. The

457

plague, too, had gone. What remained was a city ruled by a party advocating a return to the past (and all its rivalry between families) – and a monastery urging a new republic. The people were too hungry to care. The day that a train of wagons came over the mountains loaded with thousands of bushels of grain, a few called on the rest to see it as a miracle and to share it amongst themselves, putting the poor first. The state let it be known that this was no miracle but its own pragmatic act. The majority rushed at the wagons and took away as much as they could carry, kicking anyone who tried to stop them.

Giovanni di Pierfrancesco was too wily to become embroiled in any conspiracy, and too popular to be accused of it. It had been he, on behalf of the state, who had ridden to Imola to negotiate the purchase of grain with its Duchess. Cynical men said that it had been his looks that impressed the Duchess more than his money and that part of the deal had been that he share the bed of Caterina Sforza. Medea and Botticelli's angel – lovers! Even my imagination was inflamed by that. I thought of Maria and sighed. Had I known where she was buried, I would have gone to her grave and told her the story. And I would have gone again, the day I heard that Giovanni di Pierfrancesco had married Caterina Sforza.

97 FICINO TURNS HIS BACK
1497

IN THE DUOMO AT THE FEAST OF THE NATIVITY, I SAW among the canons the familiar figure of Marsilio Ficino. He was looking over his shoulder in my direction. As I approached, he looked me up and down as if not knowing me, his eyes blank and unseeing. Then he turned and walked away. I knew in that moment the state of my soul. I had not done what he had told me to do, and I was dismissed. More, in my staying in the monastery, I was arguing with him, for what man would stay knowingly in the presence of the antichrist? And it was true: I did not believe what Ficino had said. We were no longer disciple and master: I was independent, and had to take the consequences.

What have I lost? I tell you, John Colet, that in that moment it was as if the door to heaven finally closed on me. Ficino was the keeper of the gate, who always kept the portal open. Through his hymns, his remedies, through his Platonic teachings, I always had a route of escape from this world when it proved too much for me. Now the door was closed, and it had no handle.

98 THE SACK OF SAN MARCO
1498

THE FOLLOWING APRIL THE FRANCISCANS CHALLENGED Savonarola to prove his innocence by entering a walk of flames on the site where we had been holding the Carnival bonfires. If he was the voice of God, then God would preserve him. An ordeal by fire. The shame of it! We were being hurled back a hundred years into the age of superstition. While most of the friars went in the procession to the Piazza della Signoria, I remained behind to protect the library. I wanted none of this event.

It was a fine spring day and a silent one, except for a sudden and violent thunderstorm in the afternoon. I was using my solitude to pack more books. Under orders recently received from Cardinal Giovanni I had already been sending some chests out to safe houses and now, while everyone was distracted by what was happening in the piazza, I and others of the Company of the Library removed quite a few more. But I could not stop thinking about Fra Girolamo walking through flames. Was he burnt? Or was he walking on fire with the soles of his feet unharmed? Was he floating, as saints float in paintings? Had his faith saved him? Was he even now proving to everyone, incontrovertibly, that he could perform miracles? But the truth was that, in a long day of suspense and frustration, nothing dramatic happened other than the storm. Between the piazza and the Palazzo della Signoria there had been much coming and going and delay. Savonarola refused to take the challenge himself but Fra Domenico insisted on entering the fire in his place. All day the crowds waited for this spectacle, but delay followed delay and in the end no one entered the flames, which anyway were doused by the storm. Jeered at, accused of not being willing to burn his own vanity, Savonarola returned with his procession to San Marco at night and went to his cell.

There had been no ordeal, and no miracles. One would have thought that the storm counted as a miracle, but the Florentines had grown less gullible and had been more impressed by Savonarola's refusal to accept the ordeal. No one spoke, no one put their thoughts into words, but we, the brethren, glanced at each other, the eyes of some of us tinged with doubt. We kept to our rounds of duties and, once they were done, joined a vigil in the church. All night long the jeering continued with gangs of Compagnacci in the piazza San Marco stoning our walls and breaking our windows. Fra Domenico and Fra Silvestro walked amongst us, encouraging us to have faith. The Lord would protect us, they said.

In the cloisters several of the younger friars held a meeting. They invited me to join them, having heard that I could use the sword. They had, they said, a whole arsenal stashed in the cellars but needed men who could use the weapons. I threw up my arms and declared myself to be a man of peace.

The next day was Palm Sunday. The olive branches that we should have been carrying in procession lay in heaps. At last the Frate came from his cell and, walking in haste and in silence through the brethren, broke the rules of excommunication and went to preach in the church. His sermon was short. He offered his body as a sacrifice to God and declared his willingness to face death for the good of his flock. I knew for certain, my skin turning cold with the realisation, that I would never hear him speak from the pulpit again.

That evening those going to the Duomo for a sermon to be given by one of our friars were pelted with a hail of stones and insults on the way. At the doors they met the Compagnacci pushing and spitting at anyone trying to enter, telling them that there would be no sermon and that they might as well go home. Some of the more stubborn and courageous retorted that there certainly would be a sermon, at which point swords were drawn. It was the excuse the Compagnacci had been looking for, the spark to dry tinder, for almost at once fights broke out all over the city, the result of previously laid plans and not the explosion of anarchy that it seemed. The faithful rushed for arms through streets where the Compagnacci were gathered at the corners. Meanwhile hostile bands, including many disaffected citizens, marched armed towards the monastery with the chant, 'To San Marco! To San Marco!' Several innocent men were killed in passing, men either on their way to church or out trying to quieten the mob. To be singing a hymn on Palm Sunday was enough reason to be slaughtered on that day. Worked into a frenzy by this taste of blood, the mob poured into the piazza San Marco. There they met the people leaving the church after vespers and, hurling stones at them, sent them into flight.

I do not remember much of that night. My mind has blanked it out from shame. I remember being in one cloister when about a dozen of the younger friars came out of the door leading to the cellars. What a sight for painters! Like St Michael and St George these holy men were wearing helmets and breastplates over their robes. Halberds and crossbows, and that new instrument of death, the arquebus, with a barrel of powder and some lead bullets, were brought out and distributed. I shrank back into a doorway while a self-elected captain directed his little force to the weakest points of the monastery, giving them sharp instructions as if he were a seasoned soldier. Like warrior angels they shouted *Viva Cristo!* to call the brethren to arms.

I backed silently into the dark cell behind me and closed the door. Then I could hear breathing, the hard, raspy breathing of a creature in terror. My own breathing began to sound the same. I stood there, too long, trying to summon courage either to move or to speak. Each of us terrified by the other. I felt the air with my left hand, touched the wall, felt along it to the door, touched the handle and turned it. The door creaked open an inch. Wan dawn light filtered in through the crack and showed a friar huddled in the corner, a tall, lean man once noble, now gibbering. I could smell his urine, imagined it running warm around his buttocks and seeping into his habit.

'Fra Silvestro?'

'Don't tell them I am here. I beg you. I beg you.' He wept like a child.

I crouched beside him.

'You!' he said.

'Yes, it's Fra Tommaso.'

He drew back as far as he could, clutching his head, staring at me. His whimpering became words, strange words, uttered in a high, sing-song chant. Angel. Angel? *Angelo.* Angelo Poliziano. I was listening to a mad thing in confession. A wild confession of fragmented sentences, from which I gathered that Poliziano had not been poisoned. He had had a fever, and the friars left him untreated, wanting him to die, for only dead would he convert. Under Fra Silvestro's orders, they had killed him by neglect.

'What happened to the stolen papers?' I asked.

Fra Silvestro looked at me with the eyes of a child in whom innocence has been polluted by wrong-doing: hope, remorse, fright all mixed into a look that is a plea for forgiveness. I drew back from him in revulsion, breathing hard. 'It is for God to forgive, not me. Make your peace with Him.' Looking out of the door and, seeing the cloister empty, I came out and left Silvestro in his hiding place.

I returned to the library and was now feverishly packing books, despite the thought that I was only making it easier for looters to carry them away. I don't know what I was thinking. I worked for work's sake. Anything to remove myself from the conflict. I tell you, if ever I outdid St Peter in anything, it was in shame on that night and the following day. Many were escaping, climbing the walls to drop into the arms of friends calling to them from the outside, a few were in prayer in the chapel, most were fighting.

All day long stones were thrown at our walls, crossbow bolts and spears flew over and into the cloisters, gates were rammed. All day long militant friars hurled back at the attackers. I packed books. About an hour before sunset there was a lull in the noise and a booming voice from the gate.

'You are ordered to lay down your arms!'

And then I knew anger. Here we were, friars assailed by a vicious and armed mob, being told by the state to lay down our arms.

'The Frate is under sentence of exile,' the voice continued. 'He must quit Florence by the morning. Anyone who wishes to leave now will be given safe conduct.'

I dithered at the window, sore tempted. But a man below in the cloister was shouting back, 'A safe conduct, from this rabble? Aye, rabble, and I include the Signoria in it. What government lends its aid to a mob attacking a monastery?' The man, not one of the friars but a leading citizen and Piagnone, turned to address the brethren. 'Anyone who walks out of here by the main gate goes to his death. We need to get out in secret and make a fair fight of it in the streets.'

Now I was two men in one. Half of me was already over the wall and running for his life, but the other half stood rooted. I had given years to this library and I was not going to leave it in its hour of peril. Better to die doing one's duty than live as a coward. Men and their parties are shifting sands, but in books I could have faith, for books are knowledge, and this library had been built for the good of all mankind. If I wept then, it was not for my own safety but that of the books. What could I, this thin, fragile stick of a man do to save them? Only one answer came to mind, which was to pray, and, as if to confirm it, at that very moment the monastery bell began to ring the hour.

I went to the church, knelt down and threw myself on God's mercy, begging Him to protect the books gathered together in His honour. I apologised for them not all being scripture, but felt sure that God, my God, loved all good literature, for surely He was the source of it? God was the astuteness in Cicero, the anger in Euripides, the eroticism in Ovid, the wisdom in Plato, the mysticism in Hermes, the wonder in Aristotle. The stubborn wilfulness in myself. In full communion now with God, I laughed with Him at the magnificence of it all.

Then the doors splintered under the force of a ram and the rabble broke in. Still in that presence of divinity, I snatched a heavy crucifix and ran at our assailants. Others did the same, Fra Zenobio with a burning torch, Fra Luca della Robbia with a tall candlestick, friars picking up anything they could to use as a weapon. We lunged, swiped, fought and drove the mob out into the cloisters where they were met by our St Michaels, the armoured friars with swords, halberds and crossbows. Suddenly there was an explosion to make the ears bleed. My head whining with the noise, I turned to see a young German friar staggering from the shock of having fired the arquebus, and several men dead or dying from its shot. Others hurried to reload the terrible weapon, and one took a blow from a sword on his skull. He, a boy of about eighteen, died in my arms, his brains oozing on to my lap as Fra Domenico hastily, incoherently, gave him the last rites. As soon as the body was laid down, I ran from the church, pushed through scuffles, knocked aside anyone in my way so as to get to the library. Running across a cloister, I hurdled over the body of a noble youth lying dead near the well, his young face smashed by the bucket that lay beside him.

Reaching the upper corridor, where it was quiet, I stood there heaving for breath. Through an open window I saw friars up on the roof of the church, hurling tiles down on the mob below. Every minute there was another explosion from the arquebus, creating dense smoke within the church. Someone inside broke a window to let in air. A moment later, the church was on fire.

I heard someone coming, not the rush of attackers but a more careful, deliberate tread. Around the corner came Savonarola, carrying the Host, accompanied by those few brethren who had heeded his call to lay down their arms. He came to the library and I opened the door for him. Solmenly and carefully he set the Host down and turned to address us.

'My last exhortation is this: let faith, prayer and patience be your weapons. I leave you with anguish and grief, to give myself into my enemies' hands. I know not whether they will take my life, but I am certain that, once dead, I shall look after you in heaven far better than I have been able to here on earth. Take comfort, embrace the cross and by it find your salvation.'

With that, he went back out into the vestibule, followed by his faithful companions. There he turned and nodded, as if to tell me that I knew what I was to do, and to do it. I nodded in return and locked the doors of the library behind him. Then I stood there in the dark, holding the Host and listening. I heard Savonarola being arrested in the vestibule; I heard the protests of the friars, which became a lament, gradually fading away as they left the corridor, following Savonarola to prison. In the profound silence I heard my heart thudding in my chest, then footsteps approaching, the grate of a key turning in the lock, the click, the turn of the handle and the opening of the door. I breathed deeply, inhaling the odours of learning, the musty smell of ancient codices, the tang of new leather, the animal scent of parchment and vellum. I breathed them in. If it were to be my last breath, let it be of books. Let my soul absorb the library so that my next birth be a rebirth of learning. Let my blood drip into Hades as a libation to the poets. These were my thoughts as I clutched the Host to me.

The twin, oaken doors opened. The sinking sun blazed in through the corridor window, full into my eyes. Silhouetted in the doorway was no rabble but an orderly group of guards of the Signoria. The Company of the Library were wise owls; at least one had got himself elected into the Eight. He walked in at the head of the guards.

'*Salve*, Tommaso,' he said cheerfully.

'*Salve!*'

While Savonarola was in gaol, being tortured beyond endurance by the strappado, while Savonarola was on trial, with Doffo Spini amongst the judges, while Savonarola – along with Fra Domenico and Fra Silvestro – burned in the last bonfire of the vanities, the library went into safe-keeping and I was on my way to Venice, via Botticelli's costume box. This is not the story of a hero.

99 SEEDS AND CUTTINGS
1498

'CONTINUITY,' FICINO ONCE TOLD ME, 'DOES NOT REQUIRE transmission of knowledge from one physical body to another.' He picked up a humble terracotta dish in the loggia of his villa. 'No poet survived to continue the School of Poetry: it simply arose again in Florence, in the time of Lorenzo's father.' In the pot were houseleeks, one of which was striving skywards in a most ithyphallic manner. 'But it helps to plant seeds or take cuttings. When this has flowered, it will die. The Platonic Academy will die with me but it has seeded children. Now it could be that all those children will die – very dark times lie ahead of us. But it will come again, for it survives in its original Form. The Platonic Academy is a portal by which the soul can find its way home and stop winging through the ages, crying plaintively like a gull. The portal never closes, but it is not always in the same place.' He broke off one of the offshoots dangling over the edge of the dish and led the way to the outbuilding used by the gardener. There he filled a new pot with soil, tamped it down, dibbed a hole, put in the nubby stalk and pressed the soil to enclose it. Then he watered the new plant. 'All it needs to grow is water, light and air. Plants feed off the elements, as do men.'

I looked into the centre of the tiny house leek, saw the spirals and rhythms of its perfect geometry.

This was years earlier, before I was a Dominican friar. It was a prediction of things to come, and my instruction as to what to do when it happened.

In Venice I received a letter from him.

Marsilio Ficino to Tommaso de' Maffei, most devoted of Platonists.

Why did you not come to see me before you left Florence? I hear you are in Venice, working for Aldus Manutius in making divine work of the devil's invention. Please oversee the publication of my letters, which are with Matthias Capcassa in that city. I suspect there are many faults in the original since my eyesight is now failing badly and I am almost blind.

Have you abandoned your Marsilio, along with your mother city? I trust that, in casting away the husks you have kept the seeds. Take the Platonic teaching north, Tommaso. Sow the seeds in the north. Go to England, if you can. Plant Plato there and help John Colet cultivate that barbarous country.'

Ficino was nearly blind? I remembered and relived the moment in the Duomo when he'd turned his back on me. Of course, he had seen only a Dominican.

I thrived in Venice. Once my tonsure had grown over, I could take my cap off and convince even myself that I was a layman again. The serene city was like heaven after the hell of the New Jerusalem and, following Ficino's dictum, I cast off the past and rejoiced in the present. In the printing house under the sign of the Dolphin and Anchor, I worked with Aldo on the task of producing beauty by machine. I gave freely of my knowledge to his engravers and compositors and set out the proportions of harmony they should follow. I looked after the publication of Ficino's letters as requested, and corresponded with him several times. I wanted to return to see him, but the publication by the Aldine Press of the *Opera Omnia* of Poliziano kept me busy. Sarzi was there, acting as editor, and I had to hold both my temper and my tongue, pretend to co-operate and work at night to repair what I could. As proof-reader, I was the last to see a page before it was printed, and therefore he was oblivious to my restorations, but I did not catch all his outrageous additions and deletions. And then there was the mysterious and cryptic *Hypnerotomachia Polifoli,* that strange, erotic book written in cipher, with which I became insanely fascinated. It drew out of me such inspiration on the design of founts and placing of pictures in text that the inkers and compositors gave me a wide berth, saying I had sold my soul to the devil.

The inner voice, the voice of my soul, nagged at me but there was always such good reason why I could not put down my work long enough to visit Ficino in Florence. Then, a year later, a letter came to tell me that he had died. Born in 1433, he died in 1499 at the age of sixty-six. Only God can paint such patterns. I went up the great campanile and stood looking south-west, as at a stage that is empty after the actors have gone. Ficino had drawn the curtains across the old century and the Platonic Academy of Florence. The parent plant had died. Now it was for the offshoots to establish themselves in new ground.

But if I thought to do that in Venice, I failed. For one thing, it already had a flourishing academy set up Aldo himself, and patronised by two fine Platonists in Bernardo Bembo and his son Pietro. For another, keeping my temper with Sarzi proved to be a Herculean labour of which I was incapable. Two months after the death of Ficino I was on the run again, this time to England.

Turin, September 4th, 1506

As I could not say goodbye to Erasmus without speaking to him, we made peace of a kind for the sake of saying farewell. I tried to tempt him to come with me to Venice.

'You would love that fair city,' I said, 'a city of a hundred islands set in a lagoon, each linked by little bridges. The shops sell all that the heart could desire; long, crooked, narrow streets full of bright things: jewellery of gold and lapis lazuli, coral and topaz; fabrics – silks, damascene, brocade, shirts of the finest linen and capes of sable, gloves perfumed with ambergris and musk. Iron ware – the most marvellous lamps of oriental design. And glass of course, Venetian glass.'

'Let the earth retain its treasures undisturbed,' he said.

I changed tack. 'Sweets! Such sweets! Marzipan and pine kernels. Little cakes that are works of art. And then there is the fish, fish of every shape and size – flat and round, small and rainbow-coloured. Squid – you can have pasta blackened by its ink. Octopus. Tiny little octopuses, smaller than your hand. In Venice you can eat fish every day of the week. And then there are the *calli* to wander, just looking at the shops or the great palaces, each narrow alley leading to a canal, or a campo where the people gather. Churches – so many churches. San Marco's cathedral! Oh, you would love that. All a soft, subtle gold mosaic that shimmers – it seems the very door to heaven.'

'All looted from poor Constantinople,' he replied. 'Nothing of what you say attracts me.'

'Not even the sweets? It is not just a worldly city like any other. How can I describe it? It is founded on water. Water is everywhere, reflecting off everything in a thousand subtle colours, and it makes a difference. Everything is slower in Venice. You cannot cross a

469

street, you have to take a ferry. There is not so much bustle in the lanes, and everyone is so elegant, so very well dressed.'

'They can afford to be, given what they charge poor pilgrims on their way to Jerusalem. Tommaso, listen to me, the very name of Venice is the sound of money sliding into a purse of the finest, softest leather. Mention it no more. As soon as it is safe for me to travel south, I am for Bologna.'

'The bells...'

'Bologna has bells.'

'So have cows, but the bells of Venice sing songs. Oh, the sound of bells across water...'

'No more!'

'And then, of course, Venice is the city of printers, and the finest of them is Aldo Manuzio, or "Aldus Manutius" since he publishes under his Latin name.'

Erasmus gave a grunt as if I had winded him. 'Bologna has printers,' he said, but weakly.

'Rogues and knaves! Pirates! You would think that a book printed by a Bolognese had been written by him, for you will not find the name of its author.'

'I am sure that is not true of all of them.'

Although I had argued in vain with Erasmus I could almost taste the sardines and calimari, the cured hams, the wines of the Veneto. Waves lapped at my heart and called me there. Erasmus will not be persuaded to divert to Venice; therefore I took my leave of him.

'Our journey together ends here, my friend. As soon as you have done your duty to these boys, instructed them in Bologna and visited Rome, join me in Venice.'

'When Colet sent you home, I presumed he meant Florence.'

'I shall make a brief visit at some point to measure the hospital, but there is nothing left in that city. I want to spend my time with Aldo. You will find me at his printing house.'

'Manutius! I would not dare come near the man. He publishes real writers.'

I embraced him affectionately. Erasmus is pride floating in humility – the two liquids never mixing but forever separate, one held in suspension in the other. To my relief, he returned my affectionate embrace, saying with his arms what his face refused to admit.

'Make things right with God,' he muttered gruffly, walking away.

'I'll leave my book with you. I've come to its end.'

'I am too old to read fiction!'

'It is history,' I replied, stung.

'That is fiction. I must devote my time to holy books.'

'Liar!' I called to his back as he strode off.

I heard him chuckle.

Venice, September 7ᵗʰ, 1506.

One leaves all nature behind on the mainland, clothed in bright fruit, and goes to the water-bound city of stone where nothing grows but men's fortunes and their vanity. The last time I came here it was as a Florentine, up the Brenta canal and over the lagoon to enter the city between the twin pillars leading to the piazzetta San Marco. Now it is as an Englishman, one of a herd of pilgrims corralled on the mainland to be shipped efficiently and expensively across to the islands on a barge. And we entered not through the gate of the Doges but on a back route. I told the officer in charge that I was not on my way to Jerusalem but to San Polo and paid an extra fee for the barge to make a special stop and put me down near Campo Sant' Aponal.

As we approached the Rialto bridge I saw that the Fondaco dei Tedeschi, that great warehouse and commercial centre of the German colony, has burnt down and is being rebuilt. As we passed, however, the gangs of masons and builders were scurrying for shelter for the weather that has been grey now became suddenly black and rain was beginning to lash down. As the Venetians pulled oilskins over the barge to cover the pilgrims, I disembarked and was left to find a gondolier to take me into the narrow canals leading to Sant' Agostino. None were to be seen. I stood alone in the rain. At last an old ferryman hobbled from an inn to tell me that he was willing to travel in a rainstorm – at the right price. I had put on my best clothes to greet my adopted city but now they hung around me like something out of a dyer's vat. My hose had so stretched that they gathered in folds at my ankles.

'You go Jerusalem? Want to see the cathedral?' The old ferryman, unmooring his boat, spoke to me in broken English.

'No, I want the house of Aldo Manuzio,' I told him in his own dialect. I was surprised that the man did not beam with recognition at the name. Instead, he stood waiting for some more detailed direction.

'At the Campo Sant' Agostino – he has a printing house – you must know it.'

As we rowed through ever-narrowing rios, under bridges and round corners, we left the grandeur of the Grand Canal and entered a Venice as melancholy as I was. Shutters flapped on abandoned houses. A costly window hung from one hinge. Great slabs of stucco had fallen from walls, leaving gaping patches of bare brick and lath.

'What's happened here?' I asked the ferryman.

'Plague in '99. And now that they go to India by sea, where's the trade for us? It's all gone to Portugal. Lisbon – that's the place to be these days. Who's going to come through Venice? The merchants have gone, more or less. All we get is miserable pilgrims now, pleading poverty.'

'If they are not poor by the time they arrive, they are certainly poor by the time they leave.'

'They don't leave us boatmen any richer – there are too many of us.'

472

The rain by now was running down my neck, and my misery, I would have thought, was complete; but no, worse was to come. Having paid off the ferryman and struggled across the campo with my baggage, I discovered that the house of Aldo, a once pretty, gabled house and a very monument to industry, is dark and empty, the printer's sign missing from its hook. Aldo is famous for his mottoes, one of which is *studio!*, warning everyone 'I am working'. Some wit has daubed on the shuttered door, *non studiamo*, 'we are not working'. In despair I crossed to the church and found its priest, who remembers me. To my relief he could tell me that Aldo is not dead or out of business. He has simply removed to the Rialto island and the family house of his partner, Torresani. I had to squelch back to a main canal to find a boat.

Venice is a city of lacework, its tiny islands linked by formal bridges and informal planks. But today, my heart heavy with the loss of the company of Erasmus, it seems like lace gone dark with age and accumulated filth. The smell from a local fish market woke me out of my reveries and as we glided past on a canal bobbing with detritus I looked into the arcaded market to see nothing but the relics of a once-thriving trade.

At San Paternian by a canal dark and narrow, bordered by tenements seven storeys high, I found the old, familiar sign of the Dolphin and Anchor now swinging over an open-fronted shop and an empty stall bearing only puddles. The stock had been taken in, out of the rain. Now in his fifty-fourth year, Aldo welcomed me with delight. We were both embarrassed about our parting in 1499 and quickly apologised to each other.

'I was galled,' he said, 'that you had deceived me, that you were a Dominican, a runaway friar living and working in my house. And I was already upset by your accusations about my editor. One thing a publisher rarely has time for is to read his books once published, especially those he has already read in manuscript. After you left, I read the *Opera Omnia* of Poliziano and found that you were right. Sarzi had made changes which had not been authorised.'

'There was a letter in which Poliziano praised Pico's secretary, Cristoforo. I caught Sarzi deleting that line, scratching out the original before passing it to the compositor. Then I knew that Sarzi was working together with Gianfrancesco Pico.'

'But to accuse me of colluding with them!'

'I'm not going to say any more about it, Aldo. The truth will work its way out like a thorn one day. I apologise to you, but I shall never apologise to Sarzi. When I caught him in that act of barbarism, I could not restrain myself.'

'Some would say that attempting to strangle a man is an act of barbarism.'

I smiled. 'I was just trying to frighten him.'

'You succeeded.'

Aldo said that he wished he could print a revised edition of the *Opera Omnia* and hire me as the editor. 'But we can't afford to print anything these days. No one wants works of scholarship and there is no money in translations from the Greek.' He led me through the bookshop to the printing house. The great presses lie still, the cases where the compositors once laboured idle in dust, the drying lines hang empty. The quietness of the place – it was as strange as coming upon hell in a state of desuetude.

These were the presses that had printed the Aristotle, the *Hypnerotomachia Poliphili*, the *Opera Omnia* of Poliziano, Ficino's translations of the neoplatonists. On these presses Aldo had made the 'libri portatiles', little books or 'hand books' made from sheets of paper folded into eight, with a fount based on the flowing script of Bartolommeo Sanvito that brought authors such as Virgil, Dante and Petrarch to an eager public. My eyes misted over at what we have lost. Those were the great days, the heady days of success, but then came the new century and its terrible darkness: the ravages of Cesare Borgia, the war between France and Spain for the possession of Italy, the blockading of Venice, the death of trade. Aldo has been forced to leave the pretty house that saw the formation of his Greek Academy and move to these seedy premises. Now, pinched in the face and bowed in the back, he moves silently through the printing house, picking up a book on the way and handing it to me.

'Last thing of note that we printed: *Gli Asolani* by Pietro Bembo.'

To Aldo at the moment the book just represents debt, with the stock piled up in the warehouse moving too slowly. When I began to read it later, I saw what he would have seen when he initially agreed to publish it: a book to change Italy. It is a dialogue on Platonic love worthy of Ficino, and it is written in the Tuscan language of Petrarch. Bembo has revealed himself as a true son of the Platonic Academy. Here is a Venetian saying to his country that Tuscan is the language to unite the nation. It is like standing in a forest destroyed by fire and seeing the first unfurling stem of new life. The great work is not dead, not while Bembo lives. I was startled to discover that the book is dedicated to the Duchess of Ferrara. Lucrezia Borgia, daughter of Pope Alexander, is not a lady who springs readily to mind when speaking of Platonic love.

Aldo took me to the living quarters above that are inhabited by his large and sprawling family and staff. In the years since I left, he has married the young daughter of Torresani and has a son of his own. Both families live together. Although there is no work here, he has offered to accommodate me and I have agreed to the arrangement since I would rather save on the price of a hostelry than have its dubious comfort. Aldo showed me to the room I am to share with five others.

We met together alone after a supper which, as a result of Aldo's new asceticism combined with Torresani's miserliness, was not the most convivial affair. I told him I had heard that he had caught the plague and had recovered and that I thanked God for it. 'I also heard that you had promised God that, if you were spared death, you would retire to a monastery.'

'The Lord made it clear that I am to fulfil my purpose in printing.'

'How?' I asked. 'How did He make it clear?'

Aldo gazed at me queerly, as if having second thoughts at being happy to see me again. 'I had forgotten your questions, Tommaso, and how aggravating they can be, irritating, exasperating, a very provocation to the soul. I had quite forgotten. I was absolved from my vow by the Pope. There, does that satisfy?'

This interested me. 'How much did it cost?' I asked.

'God save me from Florentines!' he cried.

'I am not being cynical. I want to know.'

Aldo smiled suddenly. 'There was a price for everything with Pope Alexander.'

'Oh, you were absolved by Pope Alexander?' I wanted to know if Aldo thought he would have got absolution as easily from Pope Julius but Torresani interrupted.

'He's marching on Bologna,' he said, sucking on a bone. 'Heard it today.'

'*Bologna?*' I thought of Erasmus with alarm, even now travelling on his way south. Erasmus – how many dreams are going to be stripped from him on this journey? That Julius is a 'good' pope will be torn from him as skin from a living animal when he meets the papal army besieging Bologna.

'Yes, I heard it, too,' said Aldo. 'He will probably take the city without a fight, as he did Perugia. The sight of a pope leading an army is enough to send everyone to their knees.'

'I thought Julius was an old man.'

'Older than I am. Not everyone dies young, Tommaso. Look at me. Look at you, come to that. Do not let your body dictate to your soul what you are capable of.'

'I travelled to Italy with a man I want you to meet, a Dutch monk in love with the Greeks who is translating Euripides. He's on his way to Bologna.'

'Well, then, may fate preserve him. Euripides, you say?' Aldo's sad eyes glowed for a moment and then dulled, like the sun in an English winter. 'We're not printing any more. We're just selling what books we have left.'

'And then?'

'And then God take me. I shall be ready.' Aldo's spirit has been broken by Torresani's insistence that they only print books people will buy. Their last book was a translation of the Fables of Aesop.

'Don't let the spirit dictate to the body what it can and cannot do,' I said smartly.

'Look at these,' said Aldo, rising to fetch a portfolio of engravings. 'Do you remember Albrecht Dürer?'

'I never met him – he had left before I came – but, yes, I remember all the talk about him swaggering about, saying he had come to teach the Italians how to do woodcuts. "The stinking druid" you used to call him, even though the druids were Celts and not Germans.'

'They're all the same. Anyway, he's back. Staying at the Fugger house and working on an altarpiece.' Aldo brushed crumbs off the table and opened the portfolio. 'See what the stinking druid can do on wood now.'

The sheets were full size, each one bearing a print of a scene of the Apocalypse from *Revelation*.

'Images for our time, eh? But he still hasn't quite mastered perspective.'

In the face of these designs, that seemed a petty quibble.

'Who cares? Does it matter that much? I have been five years in England where native art is at such a low ebb that they have to import painters. Now I am home, where art is divine. In between, Germany and the Germans and their wood.'

On my way north in 1499 I saw figures carved from limewood which made the heart melt. Now I held prints that, I was told, had been made from single woodblocks, which every Italian engraver would say is not possible. The flowing lines of a horse's mane, the wings of an angel, the scales of demons, clouds, mountains, seas, little ships, a fantastic tapestry of detail carved by metal in wood.

'We prefer clean lines in our Italian prints,' I said.

'We certainly do.' We both chuckled.

'Admit it,' I said.

'No. You first.'

'The Germans are better than us in some things.'

'Go – wash your mouth out, you traitor!'

'What is he doing with these? Selling them as a set?'

'Binding them in a book with the relevant text.'

I laughed. 'What is it called? *The Woodcuts of Albrecht Dürer illustrated by the words of St John the Divine?* Oh, was there ever a man who knew his own worth so well? I want to meet him. Aldo, it's time to reconvene your academy.'

As if I were using a pair of bellows on a spent fire, I thought I detected a glowing ember in my old friend.

In my arrogance, when I came to Venice in 1498 I considered it to be the 'north' where I could plant my Platonic seeds. But I found here a flourishing garden of philosophy, established mainly by the Bembos. Bernardo was a lifelong friend of Ficino, and his son, Pietro, is of that rare and perfect kind that grow up to continue the work of the father. But Bernardo Bembo has fallen on hard times and is now living in Padua while Pietro seeks patronage in the Court of Urbino.

Aldo had an academy that met in the evenings at his printing house at Sant' Agostino. There with scholars and artists we discussed philosophy and the spacing of letters, Greek literature and the width of margins, Italian language and new printing founts. From Aldo's house poured works of beauty to which, alas, I contributed very little apart from my inventions on the *Hypnerotomachia Polifoli.* If I had left Florence with the Medici, I would have been in Venice in time to invent the portable handbook; it would have been me applying the secret laws of proportion to page design, me who carved letters based on the hand of Bartolommeo Sanvito, me who suggested to Aldo that he use the Greek comma and paragraphos to punctuate text and make it easier to read. I would have been hoisted on the shoulders of famous men and declared the Priest of Beauty, the one who, single-handedly, had elevated printing into an art. Hosannah!

Hmmm.

In the main I was the proof-reader on the *Opera Omnia* of Angelo Poliziano, of which Alessandro Sarzi was the editor. It has been put about, probably by Sarzi, that I left Venice in a hurry, accused of attempted murder. It is not true. All I did was squeeze him by the throat until his eyes popped, then I let him go. He forgave me, that oily carp, excusing me by saying that, while I was admirably in tune with the literary ethics of Poliziano, I had no understanding of the economics of book sales or of the needs of readers, for whom text must be simplified. And I grant him this, it was not Sarzi who betrayed me and told everyone I was an escaped friar. No, what made me leave in a hurry was the arrival of Gianfrancesco Pico.

One more chapter for Erasmo then.

100 THE HEART IN A BOX 1499

VENICE, AT THE END OF THE CENTURY. THERE WAS A meeting of the Greek Academy in the house of Aldo, and one new guest arrived late. Recognising Gianfrancesco as he entered, I shrank back until I was concealed by the painter, Giorgione, a giant of a man who often entertained us on the lute. Gianfrancesco Pico was carrying a small wooden casket as if he were one of the Three Magi. Of course, it was not long before someone asked what was in it.

'The heart of a saint,' he replied, and took off the lid to show his relic to the assembly. 'It is the heart of Fra Girolamo Savonarola, taken myself whilst his body burned on that irreligious fire. Miraculously my hands received no injury.'

I kept mute behind the titanic painter.

On this night, as it happened, our group had been discussing history and what constitutes a reliable witness. Putting the lid back on his box, Gianfrancesco arranged himself on a settle. I sat down behind Giorgione to keep out of his view. Pietro Bembo continued the discussion, standing in the tradition of Herodotus and claiming that the truest history comes from eyewitness accounts, but others disagreed. One thought that the best history is written by those able to see beyond the superficial details and understand the causes of events. I had to concur with this. Gianfrancesco Pico, who had become so gaunt since we'd last met that he looked like a heron, proposed that the best history is moral history, written by those who follow the faith most ardently. My throat burned with the urge to refute him; I was relieved when Bembo spoke out.

'Of all the stories abounding in this city,' he said, 'one of the most fabulous is that of the death of Lorenzo de' Medici.

According to this tale, derived from friars, Lorenzo died unshriven.' He was obviously unaware that this version of events had been published in Gianfrancesco's *Life of Savonarola*. 'I raise it this evening as an example of *im*-moral history, that is, facts freely bent and twisted so as to offer a cheap moral point. In this particular fable, dying unshriven is the fate of a tyrant.'

Gianfrancesco objected. 'Are you suggesting my account is not true? Who are you to say so?'

Bembo, sensitive as ever, was aware that I was hiding. 'I had it from a friend who had it from Poliziano, who was there when Lorenzo died.'

'A courtier, a Medicean. Why should he repeat the truth? It was not in his interest.'

I began to tremble with outrage. Giorgione's large hands reached out behind him, took hold of my wrists and squeezed, as if to say, 'Keep quiet. We know the truth. We are not stupid.'

Gianfrancesco stood up to address the guests. 'I will tell you the true version, as I heard it from Savonarola himself. It was in April, 1492, that Lorenzo de' Medici lay dying. Fearful for his soul's salvation, he called for Fra Girolamo Savonarola to come to his bedside. Fra Girolamo accordingly came to hear his confession and found the tyrant dying in agony and full of remorse. Before giving him absolution, however, Fra Girolamo asked him three questions. The first was: Do you repent having sacked Volterra? Because of his guilt, Lorenzo started violently at this, then he nodded and said that, verily, he did repent, and called on God to have mercy on his soul. Fra Girolamo then asked, do you repent stealing of monies from the fund for dowerless girls? Lorenzo cried out then, as if stabbed; writhing in torment he called on God to have mercy on his soul. Then, rising to his full stature, Fra Girolamo asked his third question. Would the tyrant restore liberty to Florence? At that, Lorenzo's face hardened and he turned his back on the friar. Accepting this as his answer, Savonarola denied Lorenzo the absolution he sought and, moments later,

Lorenzo died and went unshriven to suffer the eternal torment of hell.'

The company was quiet, then Pietro Bembo spoke gently. 'This is a very different version from that of the man who was there. You can read it for yourself in Poliziano's *Opera Omnia*.'

'He was lying. He was not there. How could anyone be at a man's deathbed confession other than the man and the confessor? I heard it from the confessor.'

'POLIZIANO WAS THERE!' I shouted, bursting free of Giorgione's restraining hands. 'And so was I! Lorenzo did not confess to Savonarola. He had already confessed. You, you stoat, you weasel, you rape truth to propagate the faith,' I cried, jabbing my finger at him – his face had slackened, I noticed with satisfaction. 'I have seen Giovanni Pico's *Opera Omnia*. You have butchered it. You left out anything relating to Cabala or magic. You left out his Concord of Plato and Aristotle and his nine hundred theses. As for the poems, you told me your uncle had burnt them. I tell you now, to your face, I do not believe you.' I was whipping round the room, gesticulating, booming, fulminating like Savonarola himself. 'With your book you have given the world a false Pico, or rather, another Pico. It is the book of a bigot, for whom scripture is the ultimate authority, not one iota of which may be questioned, for whom magic and Cabala are pagan heresies. It is a perversion. Misrepresentation, deletion, mendacity – how low will you stoop in your love of Christ? Your life of your uncle begins with three letters addressed to you. To you? When did he ever write to you? You were a nobody until your uncle died. You have stolen his glory for your own. You are nothing but a tomb-robber. Shame, shame, *shame* on you!'

Gianfrancesco's face had regained its firmness. 'Tommaso de' Maffei,' he said menacingly and with a sneer. 'A runaway friar. And you have the audacity to tell me to be ashamed? The authorities will be interested to learn of your whereabouts.'

He took up his rather smelly pig's heart in its casket and left us.

'And I know for a fact,' I shouted after him, 'that Savonarola was burned to ash that no relic may be had of him!'

'Ha!' said Giorgione appreciatively, once Gianfrancesco had gone. 'Now I know what the voice of Truth sounds like.'

'It is the voice of a man,' I said somewhat hoarsely, 'who, for a moment, values truth above his life. I wish it happened more often.'

'At least Tommaso didn't catch him by the throat and try and strangle him,' Aldo told the rest of the company, waving his hands about apologetically. 'It seems our proof-reader has a vendetta against all editors. Now, while Maffei makes his escape, shall we continue with our discussions? Is it true, by the way,' he asked, opening the door for me to leave. 'Are you a friar? When you arrived you did have short hair, but I presumed you'd had nits.'

'I was a brother of the Dominican Order.'

'And you have the nerve to accuse others of omissions and deletions? Ha! Hypocrite.'

Pietro Bembo left with me and took me back to his house. I asked him if he had a copy of Poliziano's book and he led me to his library. The book was large and neat, with all its edges carefully, mechanically cut. Backed by wooden boards covered in red morocco leather and bearing panels stamped 'ihs Maria', it was heavy and potent. This was the big book of a big man, a giant among poets, a titan among scholars. The *Omnia Opera Angeli Politiani*, 1498. I thumbed through the pages and, as I did, relived my years of service, remembering the man in the titles of his works. At last, amongst the Latin epistles, I found what I was looking for, his letter to Jacopo Antiquario describing the death of Lorenzo. As with so much else, it had been tampered with. All manner of little things had been inserted so as to queer history. For example, it states that the death of Pier Leone, the physician, by drowning in a well was suicide. That was certainly what Angelo said himself, but I am convinced that in the original letter he had more carefully said 'unnatural means', but I have no way of proving it, since the original is lost. Then, in this version, Angelo refers to Lazaro di Pavia, the physician from Milan, as 'most learned' when in fact he considered him a fool whom Lorenzo only suffered so as not to offend Ludovico Sforza.

'Meanwhile Lazaro, the doctor from Pavia, arrived, most learned as it seemed to me, but summoned too late to be of any use.'

He was not summoned – he arrived unexpectedly.

'Yet so as to do something, he ordered various precious stones to be pounded together in a mortar for I know not what kind of medicine. Lorenzo thereupon asked the servants what the doctor was doing in his room and what he was preparing, and when I answered that he was composing a remedy to comfort his intestines ...

'Angelo knew full well what kind of medicine it was,' I told Pietro Bembo. 'It was an *epithema*.'

'A poultice?'

'Yes, made of powdered gems and pearls, so noisy in preparation that Angelo went to the physician to ask him what he was doing. He was told it was an *epithema*. But I am certain that it was administered internally, powdered gems given to Lorenzo as a drink.'

'My God ...'

'I have no way of telling if Angelo wrote these words himself or if they have been altered by the editor, but he did know what kind of medicine it was. Perhaps he wrote this himself, as a signal of his disquiet. Of course he could not write the truth, not in a letter being circulated. Who did he fear?'

'Who do you suspect?'

'Oh, everyone in turn. I have churned this milk for years but it never becomes butter. Be certain of one thing, Pietro. What you heard from Gianfrancesco Pico tonight is not the truth. Nothing he says or writes is true. His uncle, Giovanni Pico della Mirandola, was not the saint he would have us believe. He was a philosopher who, for as long as he lived, suffered no conversion to a religion that his perverted nephew would recognise. Gianfrancesco is motivated, driven by jealousy of his uncle. Those who are so uncertain of the truth of their faith that they will commit any atrocity, literary or physical, in its cause are a poison in the veins of humanity. There, it is said.'

'My friend, it is not safe for you to remain in Venice. Gianfrancesco will surely report you.'

I woke up then and apologised. 'I have told you things you should not know, things which Poliziano himself refused to tell me, for my own good. I am a poor friend.'

In the middle of the night, Pietro hired a boat to take me to the mainland. 'Take the road to Treviso,' he said, 'and go on to Bolsena and the Brenner Pass and thence to Germany. I will tell the authorities that you are heading for France via Padua and Milan.' He took my face in his hands. 'Go to England, as Ficino told you to do. Brother in Plato, go well and go safely.'

Venice, September 9th, 1506

I am fascinated by Dürer's beard, which is ginger and silky and makes him look the very image of Christ. He has a long face, his auburn hair falls across his shoulders in tight ringlets and he stares at you with beautiful eyes, watchful and unsmiling. Everybody hates him.

Since his last visit to Venice in the 1490s he has become a member of a lay confraternity which seeks to imitate Christ. 'A little beard and I even look like Him, so it reminds me at all times to make my thoughts and actions the same. And here in Venice I have plenty of opportunity to practise humility and forgiveness.'

The Venetian painters give the stinking druid a wide berth and put about rumours of his night walks in the calle of brothels.

'Jealous,' says Dürer, apparently unaffected.

Men say that he is the jealous one, furious that the walls of the newly rebuilt Fondaco dei Tedeschi are to be decorated by Giorgione. 'It is a German building with a German architect and Dürer says it should have German frescoes. German frescoes! What are they?' The Venetian painters are laughing until their ribs ache.

Dürer is a man whose pride protects him and he seems to need no friends. He keeps to himself, working in a corner of Bellini's workshop on an altarpiece for the German church. For old Bellini is an exception to Venetian painters, as he is an exception to much of humanity: kind, generous, sweet-natured, he has befriended the stinking druid.

He arrived this evening, with Bellini, at the first convening of the reborn academy, while I was reciting Poliziano's vernacular verse from memory. To my surprise, Dürer named some of Angelo's

486

poems he wished to hear. It seems he knows them better than the Venetians, and I discovered afterwards that in fact he is using them to learn Tuscan.

'The Venetian dialect is barbaric,' he told me later. 'I will never learn it. A man who speaks Tuscan is understood throughout Italy. A man who speaks Venetian is understood nowhere but Venice. So I learn Tuscan, the Tuscan of Poliziano and Lorenzo de' Medici.'

Warming to the man, I told him that it had been Lorenzo's work to make Tuscan the basis of a unified language for all Italy. It seems in Albrecht Dürer that I have discovered a man to whom I can speak openly, even of the most secret things, a man I can trust.

'Why,' he asked me, 'do the Venetians hate me so much? Do you know?'

'They think you are angry not to have got the commission for the Fondaco.'

'Ach! Fresco? It is the medium of artisans. The burin is nobler than the brush, and the brush nobler than the plaster trowel. You must see my altarpiece.'

'They say it is your intention to conquer Italian art.'

'Is that what they are saying? No wonder they despise me. Conquer Italian art? I am more prone to fall to my knees weeping, as indeed I do before Bellini's Madonna, at least once a week. Have you seen it? You must see it! Tomorrow I will take you. His genius freezes mine. I have laboured all summer on my altarpiece and every time I pick up the brush I am fixed, crippled, paralysed by the belief that Bellini can only be imitated, never surpassed.' He looked crestfallen and from behind the dark clouds of arrogance came the lovely sun of his nature. With his hazel eyes, rosy lips and terracotta hair, Dürer is every inch a German, a heathen from the forest. If he is arrogant, that only serves to make his humility the more devastating.

Venice, September 10th, 1506

Late last night I went for a walk in the city, making my careful way beside dark canals and over little bridges, aware that I was sure to get lost but not minding. One never does mind in Venice. Caged nightingales hanging outside shops filled the calli with their plaintive songs of yearning. Torch-lit gondolas slipped along the canals, the serenades of the gondoliers echoing under arches, sometimes singing in a choir with other gondoliers close by or even with those distant and out of sight.

Out in the lagoon were water parties, their distant music and laughter floating back to the city over the water. Gondolas with cabins, moored at the quayside, bobbed out of time with the tide while the discreet gondoliers stood on the quay nonchalantly exchanging bets and arguments. Their hose, parti-coloured or striped, and wasp-waisted jackets make their shapely legs seem unnaturally long and tapering. With their artfully crimped hair topped by a jaunty red cap and floating plume, these peacocks belong to an exclusive club, an Academy of Manly Beauty, in which novices are trained to capture maximum attention while affecting indifference. A negro has stepped from slavery into this Guild of Adonis and while the rest mock him gently within their own company for his tight hair and black skin, in public they defend his honour as their own and do not mind that he commands the largest fee of them all. Everyone wants the Black Gondolier. On this evening he is leaning idly against a wall, watching others play dice while picking meat out of his teeth. He reminds me of the first negro I ever saw, in attendance on a young girl of the Pazzi family walking down the street of booksellers to the church, my Elena. Maximo, I think his name was. He had the same air of dignity as this fellow, and shared his indifference to the stares of the curious, such as me. Every man wishes he were a gondolier. I walked along the quayside watching these evanescent parties, feeling that ache in the soul so constant that mostly I am unaware of it, until nights such as this.

All beauty reminds me of one beauty, which is Elena. Though long ago I had the soul ripped from me, I have continued to live, looking through a window on a world inhabited by others. I look in as a leper looks at the altar through a squint in the church wall. I stood staring into the waters of Venice until, one by one, all the torches died, leaving the lagoon and the canals as black as Lethe.

Where am I to go? What am I to do? I should be with Erasmus. I was asked to accompany him to Italy and commissioned to measure the hospital. Why do I always step off the prescribed path, the straight and narrow way? Deflected, always deflected, by my own errant will. Is it possible that I could forget the past and start again, here, now? I only came to Venice to make my peace with Aldo, but he says I am renovating him and his academy. He is taken with the idea of printing Erasmus's translation of the plays of Euripides, whatever his partner might think about it. So, I shall stay then. We will write to Erasmus and draw him here, publish his book and then he and I shall return to England. Simple. I'll commission someone else to measure the hospital, for it is impossible to travel to Florence without meeting the Roman army on the way.

My eye falls on the letters of Cardinal Giovanni de' Medici, addressed to the Pope. You coward, Tommaso de' Maffei. Stay here? Was Odysseus able to row around Charybdis, gazing into the sucking centre of the whirlpool? No, you must go forward and hope for a tree to cling to, even as your boat is wrecked.

Venice, September 15ᵗʰ, 1506

Albrecht is very fond of the Tarocchi cards. This afternoon he made me choose one at random, having dealt out the deck face down. I turned up the card of Venus, showing her being born from the foamy waves.

'Ah, so, what do we have? Love, yes. You must be guided by Love. You must overcome your fears, my friend, to find love. So you will come south with me.'

'You are going south?'

'I want to go to Mantua to meet Bellini's brother-in-law, Andrea Mantegna. A great artist, a very great artist. I wish to learn the art of perspective from him.'

'Diviners divine what they wish to divine.'

'No, no! It is here in the cards, as clear as day. What are you frightened of?'

I turned the cards the right way up and arranged them in their five orders: the classes of men, the Muses, the liberal arts, the virtues, the heavenly spheres – a programme of the ascent of the soul in woodcuts. 'Now these are crudely drawn.'

'What are you frightened of?'

'Failure, Albrecht. Failure.'

'In what?'

'In the matter of my soul. I'm afraid I will get to Florence and find nothing. John Colet told me to come home to find what I have lost, but what I have lost is gone forever and cannot be found in this world.'

'Have you seen Bellini's Madonna yet?'

'No. You said you would take me.'

'Incredible. How long have you been in Venice?'

'A week.'

'A week! And you have not seen the Madonna yet? Incredible.'

Dürer took me to the church of San Zaccaria. Bellini's altarpiece is vast and so new that there was a crowd around it. The scene shows the Madonna on a marble throne in a vaulted chapel, the holy infant standing on her knees, with four attendant saints.

'They are calling it "The Sacred Conversation".'

'Why? Each figure has its mouth firmly sealed.'

Dürer glanced sideways at me and smiled.

'What is it?'

'No. You look. Just look.'

I gazed at the saints and the architecture and marvelled at their reality, at the suffusion of light, the exquisite harmony of colour and form.

'It is most beautiful,' I said.

'No. Look again. Just look. I will leave you. Perhaps an hour.'

An hour?

'Keep looking. And, when you have seen, then listen. It is magic my friend, believe me, pure magic. An hour, then.'

I looked again at the forms and colours. The whispering crowd about me moved, changed, came and went as I stood still before the altarpiece. I could see on two levels. I could see paint on panel creating the illusion of figures; I could enter the illusion and forget about the paint. Then a word punched my heart, and the word was *believe*. I gasped in shock. For now there was no painting and no illusion. I was alone with the Madonna.

Look on me.

I realised that my eye had been avoiding the Madonna. Why do I have to steel myself to look on purity? I took command of myself and gazed on Our Lady and the Child, and my breath slowed, quietened, stopped altogether. Or it seemed to. I was held in a hush. I was on my knees. And weeping? Yes, I was weeping.

The Madonna smiled, softly, indulgently. 'Do not fear,' she said. 'I shall look after you, you who would bring the truth to others and have not brought it to yourself. Your wounded heart allows no light. To find the truth you must return to Florence.'

'I cannot go to Florence!' I said, whether out loud or not I do not know.

'Tommaso, you are allowed to love.'

Allowed to love. That was what she said, the Mother, and then the weeping knew no bounds. Heedless of anyone around me, I cried out my soul on the floor of San Zaccaria.

Firm German arms came about me, drew me up, a broken doll brought to its feet. I wept into Dürer's shoulder.

'Magic, no?' he said.

Padua, October 10ᵗʰ, 1506

I have spent this evening with Pietro Bembo, who is here at his father's house in Padua. I am glad of the diversion since Albrecht is at the Scrovegni chapel, where he went this morning to see the paintings of Giotto and will not be drawn away. He intends to spend the night there, saying that he wishes to sleep with the greatest art in the world.

When I reminded him that only yesterday he considered Bellini's art to be the greatest in the world, he told me without the blink of an eyelid that Giotto and Bellini are the same. I laughed. How can that be? With over a hundred years and the discovery of the art of perspective between them, how can they be considered the same?

'Ach, scholars! When are you going to stop reading philosophy and begin to see? It is the *quality* that is the same. The Madonna by Giotto or by Bellini – the same Madonna.' I gazed on the nativity scene in the chapel and I did see what he meant. The purity was the same.

Dürer turned me round to look at the Last Judgement on the west wall. 'I have heard that Giotto's friend Dante used to visit him while he painted that. Imagine… Right here, where we stand!'

I gazed at the devils and the torments of hell, at the angels drawing the good to heaven. 'It is very out of fashion, the Last Judgement. We do not paint that scene any more.'

'We should. If we believed in hell, we might behave better. If the popes believed in it… imagine that.'

'Do you believe in hell?'

'Enough to want to spend the night here, for the good of my soul.'

At his father's house, Pietro Bembo paced up and down the sala, trying to tell me about the beautiful court of Urbino and its

492

people, the duchess who rules on behalf of her invalid husband, his friends Baldassare Castiglione, Bernardo Dovizi and Giuliano de' Medici. The youngest son of Lorenzo, who is now twenty-eight years old, is spending his time of exile as a courtier. But I could tell that Pietro's mind was not on Urbino.

'What is it, my friend?'

'This.' He sat down and handed me a letter from a 'well-wisher' informing him, with a callous disregard for his feelings, that Lucrezia Borgia is in love with Francesco Gonzaga, Marquis of Mantua.

'And why should she not be?' Pietro said hopelessly. 'She the Duchess of Ferrara; he, the handsome Marquis.' He got up again and resumed his pacing. 'What am I but a poor poet? What could I give her? Oh, Lucrezia, Lucrezia…' He sat down again. 'Have you ever seen her?'

'No, never, but I hear she is very beautiful.'

'Beauty! Beauty of form, beauty of nature, beauty of conduct, beauty of intellect. She is a ladder to God. You look doubtful. You have heard the gossip, that she has murdered husbands and lovers.'

'We heard that even in England.'

'Well, do not listen!' Pietro thumped a table with his fist. 'Her father murdered them, he or her brother, Cesare. Always wanting her to be free to marry someone else of their choice, the latest pawn in their game.' He sighed. 'Oh my poor Lucrezia. Do you know what it is that people hate about her? That she survives, that she recovers from each new tragedy. But not with me. With me she wept. She laid her head on my shoulder – those golden filaments of her hair in my hands! – and she wept. She said I was the only man she could love without fear. But now I am informed that she loves another.'

'When did you last see her?'

'A year ago. Tommaso, we are poor, but I cannot accept any Venetian office, cannot be an *administrator*,' (he said this with great distaste) 'a secretary of the Serene Republic. With no time for literary study I would die! So I went to Rome and Urbino to find my fortune and she... she could not wait.'

'Have you had other mistresses since?'

'Yes, but not pure love, not as I had with Lucrezia.'

'She is your Laura.'

'She is my Laura, and I her Petrarca.' So saying, he recited some verses he had composed. I sat back to listen, expecting to hear the usual verses that come from lovesick (and fickle) poets, but this was Pietro Bembo. Lucrezia Borgia's Petrarch, he sang like a nightingale. Pietro succeeds where I fail: for him human love is a divine matter. Lucrezia is his ideal of perfection to which his soul aspires. In the crucible of his heart, he transforms base love into pure love, and he does it through poetry, as Petrarch for Laura and Dante for Beatrice. Could I not do this, too? Turn pain into beauty? I have tried, tried to write poems about Elena, but they are the wooden conceits of incompetence.

As I listened to his songs of grief, I realised they were songs of pain and surrender. He was letting Lucrezia go. I began to grow agitated, remembering how, when I was first married, I would lie awake at night just to see Elena's profile in the moonlight, and sometimes... I confess, at last I confess... sometimes, once or twice, I wished her dead so that I could possess her utterly and forever. God in your mercy forgive me. But it was the kind of love that is a rapacious appetite that will not be satisfied, that can never be fulfilled. I suffocated her with my love.

The love you love is the wrong love.

Padua, October 11ᵗʰ, 1506

I have heard a story from Pietro Bembo that may not be generally known. Certainly we heard nothing of it in England. In 1500, the year of Jubilee, the one and a half time, God struck the antichrist, if, as I believe, the antichrist was Pope Alexander. He struck him twice. The first time was during a mass when he suddenly fell to the floor as if dead in some kind of seizure, the kind that is usually fatal, but he survived. The second time was with a thunderbolt hurled at the Vatican palace which sent the ceiling of the audience room down. The pope on his throne disappeared in a tremendous fall of rubble and a great cloud of dust. They dug him out with shovels, pulled away with their hands blocks of stone, plaster, fallen hangings, and came at last to the holy pontiff, still sitting on his throne, dazed. Alive.

It was three years later when the pope finally died, 'peacefully in his sleep' the official announcement had said.

'He was poisoned,' Pietro told me. 'No one knows who did it; in daring and aptitude whoever it was matched Pope Alexander Borgia himself. A servant perhaps, a human instrument of Divine Will.' Pietro sat back and stretched out his thin legs. 'That man, that man, he was a monster. Impossible to believe he was the father of my beloved.'

'Pope Julius, then, is an improvement.'

Pietro laughed acidly. 'I am going back to Urbino,' he said at last. 'Nothing will tempt me near Rome, not while Julius reigns. But in Urbino we have a court that is a sunny glade in a dark forest, where we entertain ourselves with music and discussion. Everyone has something to say, usually misguided. It is my function to inspire them with reason.'

He told me of a recent discussion on the subject of love, and recited his part of it, a speech on love as the ladder to God. It was Ficino's own Platonic teaching turned into poetry, and there was something in it that made my skin prickle, a modification of the divine theory. For Plato and Ficino both, the lover and the beloved are both male, for male love is chaste and unconfused by sensual desire. That is the pure love. Pietro Bembo has modified it. For him the beloved is a woman.

I quickened. 'Do you believe it?' I asked him. 'That it is possible for a man to love a woman platonically?'

'I am the living evidence,' said the lover of Lucrezia Borgia.

'But does that mean you have no desire?'

'No. It means that desire is curbed, is not carried into action.'

'Chivalrous love, then.'

'Yes, that is it: the love of the knight for his lady.' He sighed.

An inn near Mantua, October 17th, 1506

With the papal forces encamped outside the walls of Bologna, the way south to Mantua was clear. Dürer and I spent the tedious ride across the Lombard plain discussing many things: the best medium for painting, whether oil or tempera; the virtue of engraving; the quest for absolute beauty; the corruption of the church; Savonarola; reform; the nature of the world and the discovery of new lands; the mortality of bodies and the immortality of the soul; whether the cosmic model of Ptolemy is true, or whether the heresies being whispered in the universities could be possible. Above all, we discussed proportion, the secrets of which Albrecht desires to know and is travelling to Mantua to learn from its greatest living adept, Mantegna.

And we discussed melancholy, the humour which Dürer assumes to predominate in his own being. His bright eyes and healthy complexion contradict his own analysis, and yet he insists that he is melancholic. And as is common with those of that disposition, he cannot resist joking.

'I am not naturally melancholic, no. By nature I am a sanguine man. It is my wife. She makes me melancholic – irritable, spiteful and bad tempered. I thought I loved all humankind until I met my wife. She is my – what was the name of the wife of Socrates? – Xanthippe, my gadfly.'

'According to Ficino,' I told him, 'Melancholy arises from too much thinking, from the sterile quest of worldly knowledge to attain the divine. He said that the best cure for it is music.'

'Nonsense. Melancholy arises from nature, and in Germany the cure is flogging. But I like the ideas of your Ficino. Yes. I will adopt them. I will listen to the music of sweet lutes as I have my wife flogged. One must deal with causes and not symptoms, no?'

He told an unhappy story, of a woman who fills his house with the smell of boiled cabbage, whose beauty is only skin deep, who cannot understand why he would rather be an engraver than a goldsmith – but if he must be an engraver why must he do those dreadful images of the Apocalypse no one wants when he could be doing the Madonna? A wife who is uncooperative in bed and would rather sleep than suffer his attentions. 'And all the time she wants to talk about our neighbours, the very very dull details of their lives. I tell you, my friend, she is as superficial as – what do you call them? – do you have them? Water boatmen? Little beetles with long legs which walk over ponds. She is like them, walking tippy toes on the surface of life. She is scared, that it is my opinion, scared of anything which will make her *think*. She does not want to think. As when you are alone in a haunted house. You try not to think. The world, my friend, this great starry cosmos, is just a haunted house to women like my wife. And they would rather not think about it.'

'So she is not melancholic herself, then.'

'Choleric, pure and simple.'

Dürer asked more about Ficino and his Platonic philosophy, attracted by a man who could turn the dominance of the planet Saturn into a virtue. I told him all I could remember, of the villa at Careggi where, with his herbs and fragrances, his chants and prayers, Ficino could put a man's humours back into balance, alleviating the malign effects of one dominant planet by invoking the aid of another.

In turn, Dürer told me about the ideas of the philosopher Henry of Ghent, according to whom there are two kinds of thinkers. Firstly there are the philosophical kind who have no trouble with metaphysical abstractions, and then there are those whose imaginations are stronger than their reasoning powers,

497

who can accept a demonstration only to the extent that their imagination can keep step with it. Familiar! Such men, he said, cannot extend their thought beyond time and space but can only think in relation to objects. That is to say, some men can think without images, others cannot.

'Like geometers,' Dürer said, 'who must make shapes out of numbers. And these are the architects, artists and poets. It seems to me that this is the essence of melancholy: to such men, to us, the beloved is out of reach. However much we strive we cannot attain the divine because it is beyond any image.'

Suddenly I went so limp in the saddle that my mount came to a standstill.

'My friend! What is the matter?'

I struggled to speak but all I could say, and that with great effort, was 'Elena.'

Dürer dismounted quickly to catch me as I fell near senseless from my horse.

'She died,' I said, hiccoughing into the chest of the man embracing me. My grief at San Zaccaria, which I had considered profound, had been just a warning, the tremor before the quake.

'You were married? Had a wife? She died? Ah,' Dürer said, slapping me on the back heartily as if I were a baby with wind, 'that is a great tragedy which befalls many women. Unfortunately it has not befallen mine.'

'She did not die in childbirth,' I told him, offended by his breezy, Germanic responses. 'She fell from her horse, riding in the night.'

'Why was she riding in the night?'

'She was trying to reach the Medici and safety. I had deserted her. Left her alone. I thought… I thought…'

'Yes?'

'I thought if I did my duty… It was to be with Ficino, and he had left the city. And I thought… I believed, it was right to go with him, and God… God would protect her.' The truth was haemorrhaging now. 'They said I was uxurious, too fond of my wife. Not manly. I did my duty. And God didn't...'

My whole frame began to vibrate involuntarily. It was an admission of doubt, of loss of faith, coming in a deluge of grief, a dissolution of self. I fell to my knees on the dusty road to Mantua. Like the good Samaritan, Dürer lifted me up. Reduced by his own extremity to speaking in German, he called me back from Hades not with meaning but with sound, the sound of humanity in his voice. My soul harkened to it and turned around.

Ficino and Savonarola had both brought me to the edge of total surrender but it has taken a young German engraver to perform the necessary operation on my soul. Because of Dürer's simple command of the language, I had not been able to be subtle with him, had not hidden my emotions behind a hedge of ambiguous phrases. I had told him direct: in not following my intuition, I had murdered my beauty. Me. I was the sinner, not Ficino, not God.

'Please, please,' Dürer said, in Tuscan again, 'do not die on the road! I hear that Italians can die of broken hearts, but I do not believe it till now.' I lay in his arms like a dead thing but slowly became aware of the sky, the bright blue sky behind my friend's auburn head.

I remembered the mystic death that Lorenzo and Pico had discussed so often. *To see God you must die to this life.* Was this it? This corpse-like inability to move; this conviction that there is nothing in life that is true and worthwhile; the torpid acceptance of death. Was this it? Everything past and future had lost its savour; everyone past and future had turned into ghosts; all beings merely cicada skins clinging to trees, empty of essence. All effort was futile, and no goal was worth obtaining. Yes, this was it. This was the death of the spirit.

At that point the blackness came like a swirling night fog and sucked the colour out of the blue sky and the autumn hair.

I had a dream in which I was lost in a dark wood, dense with brambles and thickets. In the crackling dark full of wild beasts, I discerned a light in the distance which, when I came to it, was a candle burning in the cellar of a black castle, the barred window of which was at ground level. Kneeling down, I reached towards the hand thrust out from between the bars of the dungeon. I knew that hand so well. It was my wife who was the prisoner there, but when I asked her who had done this to her, when she spoke my name, I sprang awake.

I found myself in a bed in this inn. I lay listening to the faint voice of Elena, calling me to let her go, to let her return to God. Before I opened my eyes, and to the sound of prayers being recited by Dürer, I performed that sacrifice, begged her forgiveness and released my wife from my heart.

The sun was streaming in through the window. I propped myself up on my elbows. Albrecht was at prayer with his hair apparently aflame in a mystic fire. There was a small majolica dish on the windowsill containing fruit; Albrecht's sketches of it were on the table. The breeze that lightly moved the linen curtains played over my skin, and the air was fresh. Lovely. *You are allowed to love.* I blinked and looked about me: there was nothing that was not beautiful and full of life, as if the world has been reinvested with spirit.

Sancta Maria, Mater Dei, ora pro nobis peccatoribus, nunc et in hora mortis nostrae, Dürer intoned with that sweetness of a man at prayer.

'Amen,' I said. '*Grazie, Madonna, grazie Deo.*

'You are awake, my friend?'

'Fully.'

Modena, October 21ˢᵗ, 1506

That inn near Mantua had a walled enclosure containing stables and a garden. We were collecting our horses from where they were tethered by a trough set in a wall made of great blocks of stone as old as time, piled up in courses with dying ferns and grasses rooted in every crack and crevice. Ivy scrabbled over the place in that artless perfection of design that only nature can achieve. Dürer was looking at a snail crawling along a ledge, pale yellow and banded brown, the common snail, the kind which, when boiled, you can shell easily and pop in your mouth.

When Dürer says 'Look!' he gives you the eyes to see. I saw light, light in the form of a snail. The creature glistened like the rock with moisture and light, its feelers sensitive, touching the air. The air. The air that touched me touched the snail. The light shining in it and around it was the light by which I saw it. I traced the spiral of it back to the point where it began, the point where the light had entered, had become form, the form of a snail or, in my case, a man. The same light. The consciousness of the Creator.

'What do you see?' Albrecht asked me softly.

'I see love,' I replied.

'Then you are an artist.'

I laughed. The sound of a fountain in a desert.

'It is good to see you laugh, my friend,' said Dürer. 'It is good.'

You are allowed to love. I turned my gaze on him and found that the vision of love need not be confined to a snail, may include a fellow human being. How often can we look another in the eyes and find nothing between us? No idea, no thought, no sense of me and you. That Albrecht so resembles Jesus made the moment that much more profound and I lost all sense of my limits, of being in a body at all. I gazed on God and God gazed back at himself.

'Very good,' he said. 'I just draw this fellow and then we go.'

While Albrecht made his drawing, I stared into a clump of grass on the top of the wall, at eye height. The grass was home to life, little beetles for whom this clump was a vast city. The sense of wonder was not diminishing but increasing. I had had this sense of transcendence once before. Was this what I had lost? One glimpse of God, as the one I had had all those years ago in a bunch of grapes in Ficino's vineyard, and then you spend your life

501

thinking about it and never experiencing it again. The aridity that is theology or philosophy when it loses touch with its object! The veils of thought and opinion that cover our senses! The gloomy, monochromatic wash over life that is the view of the miserable, closed heart.

I had sought my wife everywhere while all the time I had her locked up within. I had sought God everywhere, only to find Him in a snail on a stone ledge. The temptation to keep the snail was enormous, but beauty captured is beauty lost.

'How does one keep contact with the ineffable moment?' I wondered out loud.

'Stop thinking about it,' Albrecht answered. 'Keep looking.'

The ostler approached us to receive his fee. 'Where are you bound?' he asked conversationally.

'Mantua, to see the greatest artist in the world,' said Dürer.

'Andrea Mantegna? He died yesterday.'

Dürer took it stoically. 'Ach, it is the will of God,' he said, 'and I always accept the will of God. It is so much more interesting than my own.'

'Where shall we go?'

'To Bologna. There is another man who can teach me the secrets of proportion: a mathematician called Luca Pacioli.'

I longed to tell him that I knew those secrets myself, but if he did not ask, I could not tell him. It isn't only the rest of us who are blind to what is under our noses. 'Albrecht, the city is under siege.'

'Those letters you carry will safeguard us.'

Now we are in Modena, the last stage before Bologna, and we pick up news as bees pick up pollen. Some say the pope celebrates mass in tents; others that, when he catches any spies, he has them roasted on spits. Milan is sending the pope reinforcements five times the size of the army he already has and the Modenese are frantic, knowing that the Milanese will cross their lands like locusts. Their barns will be stripped to the ribs this winter.

502

I look out at the Appenines, rising in the south, and am so drawn to them that I am sure I will walk there in my sleep tonight, south and into the mountains. For beyond those forests and crags lies Tuscany.

Modena, October 24ᵗʰ, 1506

I had another dream last night, as vivid and terrible as the other one. Many things were happening which I forget, but Albrecht was there, as too was Erasmus, both encouraging me although I could not move. Then the papal guard came and dragged me into the presence of the Pope and threw me on the ground before him. I lay down and could not rise when he commanded it. Rough hands took hold of me again and hauled me to my feet. Then I saw His Holiness, a gigantic knight in armour standing before ranks of spears and fluttering pennants bearing the crossed keys of St Peter. I realised that I was standing out in front of an opposing army and had been chosen to do single combat. Me, a David to this Goliath in his dazzling armour and lowered visor. I tried to move back into the ranks but I was pushed forward.

'Draw your sword!' I was told from behind.

Sure enough, I had one in the sheath on my belt and I drew it out, for if I could not go back I could only go forward, and die in the attempt if necessary.

My enemy's helm was in the form of the triple tiara. I stepped forward, both myself and not myself. I shook with fear and had courage. I was a man in his fifties and I was a youth. I was clothed and I was naked.

The Pope raised his sword with both hands, then, with a roar, lunged forward. I blocked his strike with my sword. The impact jarred every bone. He struck again, again I parried, our swords clashing. Clash after clash, blow and parry, blow and parry, he always having the advantage but never quite overcoming me. It seemed this match would last forever but then he doubled his effort, sent me down on my back and raised his sword for the death blow. I had one option. It was not lawful, but I took it. I thrust my sword upwards, under his iron skirt and between his thighs. The Pope stumbled, roaring in agony. In the rage of death, he drew himself up and, grasping his sword with both hands, drove it down into my unprotected heart. And then it was as if I were the giant. From a lofty perspective I saw a shower of roses falling gently on the ground, red and white. The roses became blood and semen flowing in clear rivers in a lovely land of green meadows, forested in the south and the north by the two armies which had become trees.

Now, what does all that mean?

Bologna, November 9th, 1506

Laying siege to the red and solid stone of Bologna are some wind-flapped tents, striped in the papal colours. The city of many towers huddles within its walls like a cat shrinking from a mouse. The crack of iron shot sounds now and then, a lazy sound, as if the troops are firing at the walls only to remind the inhabitants that they are there. They say the city is on the point of surrender.

My letters gave us easy passage through every control post on the road and soon, too soon, the papal pavilion bearing the arms of the delle Rovere was before us.

'This is a joke army and a toy battle,' Albrecht observed. 'Was it to this that Perugia surrendered without a fight?'

'This is the Pope,' I said, breathless, my skin crawling with the memory of my dream.

We presented ourselves to the guards and waited. The letters were growing waxy in my hands. I knew the contents of one

– what were the contents of the other? Could I trust Cardinal Giovanni?

'Do not be afraid,' Albrecht said. 'Forget all you have heard and speak to the Pope as the Vicar of Christ. Speak to the role, not to the man. If you can see God in a snail, you can see him in Pope Julius, can you not? All things are possible.'

A servant came for me. Life began to pound in my ears and my knees suddenly lost their power. Albrecht pushed me forward and I entered a tent filled with cardinals, a sea of red that parted to allow my approach to the throne. Yes, Julius did sit on a throne, but he was not in armour and held no sword. He was an old man sitting with his shoulders up round his ears and his gnarled hands resting on the arms of the ornate, gilded chair. His long, white beard mingled with the ermine border of his scarlet robes and his old eyes were watery. He did not smile nor did he speak but waited for me to state my business. I took a deep breath.

'Your Holiness,' I said, sweeping down in a bow and proffering the letters. 'I was asked to give you these in person.'

Someone took them from me, broke the seals and handed them to the Pope. He read them without hurry.

'Do you know their contents?'

'Only of one of them, Your Holiness.'

'Is it true, about the legitimacy of Giulio de' Medici?'

I grew hot but my skin went cold. 'It is true, Your Holiness.'

'Speak up, Maffei, I can't hear you.'

'It is true, Your Holiness. I was a friend as well as a servant of Giuliano de' Medici. He told me himself, in confidence, of his marriage to his mistress and the birth of his son. I was the only one to know. When Giuliano was… When he died –'

'When he was murdered.'

'When he was murdered, I myself gave the news to Lorenzo, that there was a son.'

'That assassination brought the papacy low. An execrable affair, execrable. So that is the letter of which you know the contents. Can you guess what is in the other?'

505

'I believe I can.' Now my throat was lined with sand.

'Cardinal Giovanni informs me that in 1494 the bearer of this letter entered the Dominican Order and took the vows, but four years later left the monastery of San Marco without permission and went into voluntary exile. True?'

Is that all that it said? Then I was betrayed! I could hardly keep my feet.

'It is true, Your Holiness,' I said in a scraping, hoarse voice.

'Look at me.'

I dared to look up at him and was fixed in the gaze of rheumy blue eyes in a face of tired, stretched skin.

'That was an abhorrent act, abhorrent. The act of a coward. You must return at once to the monastery. The punishment is at my discretion, but I am content to leave the matter to the Vicar General. You can be assured, however, that you will never again have pleasant duties but will scrub latrines until you learn to love it.'

'Your Holiness, I would be absolved from my vows.'

'Of course you would, but on what grounds?'

'I was deceived by Girolamo Savonarola.'

'Yes, many were. Nevertheless, you were not forced to become a friar. What was the reason?'

'I was in a low state and felt I had done with the world.'

'Was there no other reason?'

'No, Your Holiness.'

He leant forwards, the knuckles standing out on his hands grasping the arms of the chair. 'Tell me the truth. The truth, Maffei.'

Glancing about nervously, I suddenly recognised a man towards the back of the tent, his face in the shadow of the men in front of him: my second-row brother, Rafaello, staring at me, encouraging me with his eyes, willing me to speak.

'In this letter,' said the Pope, 'from one of my cardinals, it says that the salvation of the Medici Library is largely thanks to you. True?'

'No, not true,' I said, flooding with relief that the letter held more than a simple denunciation.

The Pope raised his bushy eyebrows.

'It is wholly due to Cardinal Giovanni himself, but it is true that I was a member of his Company of the Library.'

'He tells me that you entered the monastery at his express wish, surrendering your life and, he says, a prospect of marriage, in order to protect the books. True?'

'Yes, that is true.' I felt more than saw Rafaello's look of amazement.

'That was a great sacrifice. However, you made your vows to God, not to Girolamo Savonarola. Tell me what happened when you made those vows.'

My vision now excluded the watching cardinals and curia. The curious. I saw only the Pope, and in him I saw more than I had expected to see: one who takes his divine duty seriously. I could not lie now. I told him of that morning in Savonarola's cell, that when I came to repeat the vows after him I felt as if I were sinking to the bottom of the sea but not drowning. I remembered that moment of grace, the full surrender. 'In that moment, I meant everything I said,' I told him, he, my spiritual father. 'I gave my life to God.'

'But you took it back again.'

I smiled wryly. 'It was either that or lose it.'

Those rheumy old eyes twinkled for a moment, then the Pope inhaled and sat back, considering the matter. I glanced about at the audience, expecting to see them laughing at me, but all were following the exchange with interest. However much each man falls, we are united in this: the wish to be better than we are.

'I have a solution,' the Pope said at last. 'Keep your vows, make your peace with the Vicar General, then come to the Vatican. I would have you working in my library.'

I stood staring at him, unable to comprehend this alteration in my fortunes, my destiny. All I had to do was nod and say thank you and the course of my life would change. I would live in Italy, among books. All I had to do was nod. It was then that I remembered my dream.

'I cannot.'

He cupped his ear. 'What did you say?'

'Your Holiness, I thank you for your offer. Everything, almost everything within me strains to accept it, but I cannot.'

There is a place within that is beyond vows. It is so light it is dark. The unknowable light. My God within. Under direction of that light, in obedience to that light, not knowing what I was saying or why, I said again, 'I cannot.'

'You would prefer latrine scrubbing?'

I swallowed. 'I would be released from my vows.'

'For what reason? Do you wish to marry?'

'No, it is not that. I have lived eight years in deceit. I need to be right with myself.' In truth I did not know the reason and groped to express that which I did not know. 'I wish to be free, if only to make the choice again, except this time it would not be under the influence of anyone else.'

The Pope nodded, and seemed to be losing interest in me. 'Very well. You are absolved. I will have letters written to that effect. Go now. But Maffei, the offer of a position in the library remains.'

When I left the tent, I was still shaking but for different reasons.

'Librarian at the Vatican?' said Albrecht, amazed when I told him what had passed.

I looked to the north and to the south. 'I am back on the fence,' I said.

'You get a better view there.'

Dürer said that he intends to enter Bologna as soon as the city surrenders, to find his master of proportion. 'Will you come with me?'

I looked north. I looked south, to the mountains that only yesterday I was yearning for, but now... Now I am free to return to England, to go to John Colet and tell him I have found what I have lost: my integrity. That integrity, however, demands I fulfil my duty. 'The King of England has commissioned me to measure the hospital of Santa Maria Nuova. I am going to Florence.'

Florence, November 13ᵗʰ, 1506

As a free man I entered a city enjoying a new republic and a stable government under Piero Soderini, who has been elected Gonfalonier for life. Florence has become the city it always wanted to be: safe and prosperous. It has found a middle way between the Medici and Savonarola, a way that is much to be preferred to both, even if it is dull. And colourless. Everyone seems to wear undyed cloth or, if dyed, then dyed black.

Dürer seems destined to miss opportunities, for in not coming to Florence with me he has missed meeting Michelangelo. Not that I can imagine them meeting, let alone befriending each other. No, Tuscany has been spared an earthquake. As Dürer has his destiny, so have I mine, and it is to be accompanied throughout this journey by northerners. Erasmus passed me to Dürer; now Dürer has passed me back to Erasmus. I met him by chance in the Piazza della Signoria, staring up at the great marble giant made by Michelangelo and placed outside the palazzo.

'If this is David,' I said, 'how big is Goliath?'

Erasmus turned. When he recognised me, his face held none of the righteous anger that had dimmed it the last time we were together. 'You have found what you have lost,' he said affectionately.

'To know what you have lost is not the same as finding it.'

'So, what was it?'

'Something perhaps I never had. Purity.'

'We all began in purity,' he said. 'So you had it once. Can you remember a time?'

Yes, I can remember a time. It was when I put my hand into that of the Bishop of Volterra, that time when, as a small and frightened boy, I'd been hiding in the cathedral from the tumult. I found the new bishop in prayer. Here was not a lofty man or a clever or a patronising one. Here was a man who loved truth, though I could not have expressed it that way at the time. I took him by the hand and led him to his palazzo, where I lived as a servant. He taught me the New Learning. He arranged for my apprenticeship as a scribe. He taught me wonder. I was a naughty pupil and often punished, but in that moment when I took truth by the hand, in that moment I was pure.

There have been other such moments, I suppose, but that is the one I remembered when Erasmus asked. We get gnarled with age. One's bark thickens. I had forgotten what I loved – not books, not Greek, not even Plato, but what this literature contains: an invisible essence that calls to the soul. Love of goodness. Love of truth.

What have I lost? My love of God. When did I lose it? When Elena died. Perhaps it is enough to know the answer without finding it. I shall not take long at the hospital but soon begin the journey home.

In the company of Erasmus I look upon my city with the eyes of a stranger. He is disappointed with Florence, that it is not full of buildings designed on ancient principles. Instead of the triumphal arches and marble palaces of his imagination, he finds palazzi of stone the colour of honey, churches without façades, many soaring towers that have stood now for three hundred years.

I took him to Santa Maria Novella to show him the façade designed by Leon Battista Alberti according to Vitruvian geometry. Erasmus peered at the bands of green and cream marble, the pointed arches of the doors, and saw a style that was familiar throughout Tuscany, the barbarian style of the dark age.

'But that is its magic,' I protested. 'Alberti could not change the church itself, which was built in the twelfth century. He had to incorporate its features, such as the pointed arches. And then he used the old Tuscan style of banding, as you say. But then look what he did...' And standing in the piazza, I showed Erasmus the geometry of the façade, its three tiers, its squares and volutes, all in the proportion of 2:1, the relationship of Man to God, and how each detail, being in the same proportion as the whole, is joined in harmony. 'Alberti returned to the past to find his solutions but slavish imitation is not the way. Poliziano said that often enough with regard to poetry.'

Erasmus squinted, for the light was bouncing off the marble and giving him a headache. 'Can we go inside?'

'Indeed. There are two men I wish you to meet.' So saying, I took him inside the church and to the chancel behind the high altar, the Tornabuoni chapel painted by Ghirlandaio, where I formally introduced him to the portraits of Ficino and Poliziano that are so utterly life-like.

Despite his headache, Erasmus was impressed, even touched as he looked on the faces of men whose books have inspired him. 'Is this where you met Michelangelo?'

'Yes, right here, when Filippino and I were stealing a preview of the paintings.'

I took him to the next chapel to show him Filippino's frescoes, but their wild design and trompe l'oeil had a bad effect on my friend and he began to feel sick with his headache.

'I have seen enough wonders for the day.'

'We have hardly begun!'

'Nevertheless...' Erasmus thanked me for the tour and said he would meet me later. He needed to return to his inn to rest.

I remained in the church, going back to the chancel to gaze up at the portrait of the wetnurse, the portrait of Elena. I smiled at her, my wife, as she smiled at the child in her arms. I was aware of someone entering the chancel but took no notice until the man came close, peering at me. I turned, disturbed by quite a powerful smell. I expected to see a beggar but saw instead that strong, crushed face I once knew so well.

'Ah, thought it was you.'

'Michelangelo! I heard you were in Rome.'

'I escaped.'

'Escaped?'

'Julius held me prisoner! Did you know that? But I escaped when the devil went off to conquer Italy. Stop looking at this confectionery and come and see some real meat.'

Michelangelo has been commissioned by Piero Soderini to decorate the newly built Hall of the Grand Council in the Palazzo della Signoria. He had been working on the design before being called to Rome by Pope Julius. Now, back in Florence, he has completed the cartoon and is putting it on display in the upper cloister of Santa Maria Novella. 'I saw you from a window, staring at the façade. Giving a lecture on proportion, I think.'

I followed him upstairs into the rooms which had once been the papal apartments when the pope resided here in the time of Cosimo. There, pasted to a vast panel and set up against a wall – many men struggling to fix it so that it did not topple over – was a design writhing with the figures of naked men, hastily dressing and fastening on their armour: an heroic moment in the history of our republic, the Battle of Cescina, when the Florentine soldiers, bathing in the river, were surprised by a Pisan attack.

'Hey! Raise it on the right, up, up. Careful now! That's it.'

I gazed in particular at the figure of an old man wearing a wreath of ivy, struggling to draw his hose on over wet legs. The thrust of his muscles, the sinews, his grimace: I could feel his urgency and frustration as if it were my own. 'It is not possible to do this with lines on paper,' I said eventually.

'Not possible by anyone else, I agree,' said Michelangelo.

Once the cartoon was in place and the workmen finished, he offered to show me the wall where it is to be painted in fresco and we walked together through Florence to the Palazzo della Signoria, swathing ourselves in our mantles against the chill air.

His mantle was old and torn and he covered his head with it as well as his body. Peering out of it like a beaten-up vagrant, he told me the story of the tyrant who is Pope Julius II.

'I was working on the design for the battle two years ago. Leonardo was here in the city, having deigned to visit his motherland after riding with Cesare Borgia...'

'Leonardo rode with Cesare?'

'He will work for anyone who pays him enough.' Michelangelo spat on the pavement. 'A commission for an altarpiece at the Annunziata had just been granted to your Filippino Lippi, but then Leonardo arrives back here and tells the authorities that he is willing to paint an altarpiece, such as the altarpiece for the Annunziata.'

I smiled, imagining my friend's reaction.

'Filippino withdrew.'

'What?'

'He just withdrew, quietly and without fuss, saying "Let the better man have the work." But of course, Leonardo had not reformed, had not perfected himself as a man the way Filippino had. He took the money for the commission, made a start and then abandoned it as soon as Soderini asked him to decorate the wall of the Council. The commission for the altarpiece went back to Filippino, but he died, alas. A great soul, Filippino Lippi.' The sense of loss yawned like a pit in the bottom of my soul but Michelangelo rattled on, telling me how all the painters in Florence had closed their workshops the day Filippino was buried. 'A great soul,' he repeated.

'And Sandro Botticelli?' I asked. 'Is he still alive?'

'Yes, but losing his wits. He's just a mad old man living with his family in Ognissanti.' Then he went back to ranting about Leonardo, saying any talent he has he gets from the devil. 'I'm certain of it. You wait until you see the mess he has made on the wall of the Hall, this man made so rich by his inflated reputation that he strolls about like a prince, while I, I...' Michelangelo began to hee-haw with rage.

513

'Michelangelo, you are the most famous artist of our times and there is never a moment when you do not have work. Why is it that you are so poor, you who made the figure of the dead Christ in the lap of his Mother, a statue so famous that I have seen drawings of it in England. Why do you have no money?'

He stopped and faced me. 'The Pope demands so much of me. He fixes the price at the beginning but then keeps adding to the commission. Now he wants me to do his tomb – was there an Egyptian pharaoh more vain and arrogant? His own tomb, and before he is dead. A tomb of marble with many figures. I bought the stone with my own money. Now it lies wasting in Rome, for the Pope changed his mind.'

'I trust you remonstrated with him.'

'Of course I did! Either that or starve. It was a simple enough request: pay me for the stone. But he met this with such fury that I nearly wet myself. So I took off. Better that than finding a dagger in my ribs. Now I am home, ruined in everything except my talent.'

'But all these other great works you have done: you should be a rich man, like Leonardo.'

Michelangelo spun to face me. 'I'll tell you the difference between me and Leonardo da Vinci. I serve my art, not my vanity. I will suffer anything for my art. If it takes me twice as long to finish something as I've estimated, so be it. In my art is God, and I will give Him nothing less than everything I have.'

How I envy him, this bedraggled, proud, frightened man. Some artists serve their public, giving their commissioners exactly what they want. Some serve the Muse. 'If wealth is in integrity,' I said, 'then you are rich beyond measure.'

'I do not want money and what it buys. But I do want justice – why are these vain and empty men rewarded? What I want is time and peace. But the Pope is calling for me to come back. Even while he is besieging Bologna, he keeps writing to Soderini to send me to him, and Soderini replies saying I am too scared to return. "Michelangelo is scared?" cries His Holiness. "Of me? For what reason?" I told Soderini I'll go but only if he obtains a safe conduct in writing. He wrote to the Pope requesting it and got such an abusive reply that yesterday I was called in to see our Gonfalonier – he's a good man, I like him – and he told me that he will do everything he can for me, but he will not go to war with Rome on my behalf.'

I looked askance at my friend, wondering how much of all this could be believed. 'I have met the Pope. You have nothing to fear if you treat him with respect and tell the truth.' Well, some of the truth, I thought wryly.

'Then you have not met the Pope but some impostor.'

'I have met him. He absolved me of my vows and offered me a post in the Vatican library.' The addition of this last part was, of course, made in pride. If I must be a gnat walking beside an elephant, I could at least be a big gnat. A big, swaggering gnat. 'I turned it down.'

Michelangelo came to a halt. 'Now I know you saw an imposter. No one refuses Julius anything he wants.'

I shrugged. 'I did.'

'Does he know you are here? He will be coming for you as he will for me. I tell you, both of us will be dragged to Rome in chains.'

I laughed. 'Your fears are as exaggerated as your work.'

'What do you mean, "exaggerated"?' he cried, hurt.

'Larger than life, that is all.'

He growled, gesticulated, began spewing more stories of what he has suffered, telling me how Leonardo had humiliated him in the street. When we entered the Piazza della Signoria, he did not even glance at his David. I had to interrupt him to tell him how marvellous I consider it to be, this portrait of the Florentine Republic.

'But exaggerated.'

I begged his forgiveness for what I had said, and he nodded, appeased. He told me about the faults in the marble, all the difficulties he had had to overcome, the solutions he had found, and as he stood talking, people passing said, 'Bravo, Michelangelo, bravo!'

The leading artists of the day had met in council to decide where the David should be placed and there had been much argument. 'Most thought it should be here, near the Palazzo and not at the Duomo, but they could not agree where precisely it should be put. Some wanted it to replace the Judith...' here Michelangelo waved dismissively towards the statue by Donatello now set up in the Loggia de' Lanzi.

I looked at the statue of the maid raising a sword to behead a tyrant and grimaced. 'I have never liked it.'

'Some say it is a thing of evil omen, that we can date all our troubles to the day it was set up. It is unnatural, that the female kill the male.'

'It is rare, but not unheard of.'

'In the end our good Filippino prevailed. "Let Michelangelo decide for himself," he said. And so here it is. And there is the Donatello.' He flipped his hand dismissively at the Loggia de' Lanzi.

I gazed at the David, this naked giant who frowns, his eyes fixed on the south and Rome. Ah, my proud city, what a symbol you have set up. May it serve you well.

Michelangelo entered the Palazzo della Signoria without even acknowledging the guard at the gate, let alone explain his purpose. He is so famous throughout the city that he can go wherever he wants, this unkempt, unwashed artisan. He walked through the great palace of the government of Florence and led the way to the new hall which has been built to house the council of the republic.

'There!' he said. I looked up at the empty wall made ready for his painting. Had I been brought all this way to look at fresh plaster? Of course not. Michelangelo at once turned to the opposite wall and Leonardo's painting of the Battle of the Standard, a composition to celebrate another great moment of

516

the history of the old republic. I saw as if in double vision a masterpiece and a disaster.

'Look what he has done! Taken the money and left.'

In the subdued, misty colours of republicanism, Leonardo has designed a marvellous scene of a battle, set in a rocky landscape, but the colours have run into each other. Michelangelo explained about the technique of applying colour to hot wax, which Leonardo had read about in Vitruvius and tried here, in the Hall of the Great Council.

'It's stuck fast – to the wall and to us. We can't get rid of it. The studio is the place to experiment, not the site itself.' Michelangelo wore an expression exactly like that of his David, a frown of anger mixed with concern. 'Leonardo ought to be drummed out of Italy. Instead men queue up to commission him. He struts about in his fine clothes, daubs a little here and there, takes the money and scrams, while I, I put in more hours of labour than a workman would ever do, and all I get is commissions that ruin me and, when I complain about it, threats of death.'

He drew out of a wallet a sketch of one of his bathing soldiers. 'I still write poetry,' he said, handing it to me. On the back was a stinging verse about Pope Julius. 'You can keep it. When I am found dead in the river, produce it as evidence.'

Florence, November 14ᵗʰ, 1506

I have been looking forward to introducing Michelangelo to Erasmus, but I received a note this morning saying that Erasmus has left for Bologna. Now that the Pope is in possession of the city, he deems it safe to go there. 'When you have finished your work in Florence,' he wrote, 'join me.'

I went to the hospital of Santa Maria Nuova and discovered that the man in charge is an old friend, Antonio Benivieni, once physician at San Marco. He was too busy to talk long but, having greeted me affectionately and heard my purpose, he gave me permission to measure the place.

The hospital is vast. Cloister leads on to cloister, to chapels, cells and various infirmaries. 'Are there existing plans?' I asked him.

'Not that I know of. The Portinari may have them.'

'No, they do not. The king has already asked.'

'Then spend as long as it takes.' He smiled the smile of Eurystheus when he imposed the labours upon Hercules. 'It will not be done in a day.'

He gave me the use of a cell in a small cloister and here I have set up my equipment, nothing more elaborate than some rolls of paper, a measuring stick, compasses and dividers. Having done this much, I now sit staring at the blank sheet of paper. I am in the middle of a sprawling warren of buildings. The central part, the church-like hospital itself, is comparatively easy so I shall leave it until last. It is the rest which must surely defeat me, the various cloisters, the cells, the adjacent buildings which house the oblate nuns who serve the place, all added to the site over time. I remember seeing a map of Venice drawn by a friend of Aldo and regret not having asked the man how he did it. Surely the only way is to be hoisted into the sky by angels.

I sit here, and if I were not tormented by the immensity of my task, I would be at peace. Sparrows cheep in the quiet cloister. The great bell of the campanile calls the hour and I feel its reverberations in my heart. I close my eyes and lift my head, listening to Florence. I am home.

Florence, November 17ᵗʰ, 1506

I pace the hospital, trying to keep count of my steps but getting distracted at every turn. I have now at least an idea of its plan and how everything fits together, but the details tire me. The oblates are sweet. They do not go about wearing the heavy and solemn air of the professed nun. They are voluntaries and have not left the ability to laugh outside the hospital gates. When off duty, the younger ones play and no one reprimands them. I am in a sea of women. When I am about, pacing north or south, east or west, trying to keep count, they become shy. But sometimes I observe them unseen and then I can be distracted for an hour or more, not quite sure what it is I am looking at. A mystery closed to man. Such is its charm that only by an effort of will can I go back to my work of reducing three dimensions to two. Sometimes I think there is a fourth dimension and that it holds the secret that will unlock my work and make it easy. It eludes me. It lies in the mystery of women.

Florence, November 20ᵗʰ, 1506

Early this morning I was disturbed by a dreadful clamour on the streets, the Florentines baying and howling. I ran out of the hospital and, near the Duomo, saw a small company of soldiers riding through the city bearing the heraldic arms of the papacy. Their way was impeded by Florentines banging on pans to alarm the horses and unseat the riders. What was this? Some embassy from the Pope being met with hostility? But at the rear of the party I saw Michelangelo riding backwards on a horse, his arms bound behind him.

'They are taking me to my death!' he was shouting at the crowd. 'The Pope means to kill me!'

I ran as close to him as I could.

'Tommaso!' he shouted. 'I told you this would happen! It will be you next!'

Officers of the Signoria were moving into the crowd and forcing them back to let the soldiers through. The government will do nothing to save its famous son. The one is being sacrificed for the sake of the many. I do not think the Pope will kill him, nevertheless I am made nervous by the incident.

Florence, November 25ᵗʰ, 1506

I found 'the mad old man' in the family house a few steps beyond the San Frediano gate. His nephew took me to the room where he was working at a sloped desk, looking through a magnifying lens as he drew, an old man with long grey hair, hunched over his work, a pair of crutches propped against his chair.

'There is someone to see you, *zio mio*.'

'*Va via*, you mosquito!'

'It's true!'

Botticelli turned and looked up at me, wincing to refocus his eyes. 'Fra Tommaso?'

'I am no longer in the Order.'

'If that moves you beyond hypocrisy, I'm very glad of it.' He swatted his nephew. 'Out, you horsefly! Leave me with my visitor.'

I stooped to look at a picture in dry point of Dante and Beatrice in the river of light. 'So, you have attained Paradise, at last.'

'It feels more like hell.'

He gave me the lens so that I could see better the miniature figures.

'This is where Dante is finally lost for words. And it is where my art fails me. How can I draw light? Paradise has little in it but stars and angelic sparks. Drawing devils was so much easier...'

In tiny lines, he has caught Beatrice gazing on Dante with love, their arms touching. I squeezed his shoulder, rather lost for words myself. He did not seem mad to me, just in that blissful, if rather irritable, condition of the elderly when they are no longer concerned with what anybody thinks. 'You never married,' I observed. 'Never had so much as a mistress so far as I know, and yet you know love better than any of us. You were never a priest nor a friar, and yet you are the more religious.'

'More religious? I don't know about that,' he said. 'The Frate was innocent, you know, and we burned him. All of us culpable, the whole city. "Crucify him!" we cried.' Botticelli's head sank even lower between his shoulders.

'I think most people presume his innocence, given what was done to him to get a confession.'

'I know his innocence for a fact. Doffo Spini told me.'

'That pointy-eared imp! Why should he know the truth?'

'He was on the board of examiners.' Botticelli was amused by my expression of horror. 'Oh, yes, Doffo went far in government. A year after the burning, when he was in my workshop and filling up with my wine, I asked him if the Frate had been guilty or innocent. And he told me, laughing, that without doubt he had been innocent. Everything was cooked up: the accusations, the trials, the confession. "It was him or us," Doffo said. Besides, it was the wish of the Pope.' Botticelli spat on the floor.

Although I had not been offered a seat, I sat down. 'What does Doffo Spini know about the truth of men's hearts? I hesitate to accuse Savonarola himself, who seemed to be without stain, but he unleashed evil. The fruit of his actions was rotten. Things are never as they seem. While the time of the Medici appeared to many to be a time of decadence, yet it was a time when wisdom was prized and beauty venerated. Beauty, Sandro. Your goddess. Savonarola burnt her. Labelled "vanity", she was sacrificed on a pyre.'

He wept then. 'It's true,' he said. 'I have no one to discuss these things with. I get confused… Dante is my only solace. So…' he said, blowing his nose hard on his apron, 'where have you been? I thought you were dead. Everyone else is. I wish I were dead myself. They are cruel to me here. They neglect me and keep me prisoner.'

'That is not true,' said his niece, walking through the room. 'Why do you tell these lies, old man? It is enough we have to look after you without suffering your accusations and insults.'

'Tommaso, take me out for the afternoon,' said Botticelli. 'I'd like to go and visit the past. They've moved my paintings from the Casa Vecchia to the Villa Castello. Lorenzo di Pierfrancesco is dead, you know, like everyone else. No one here will take me out – they're all too busy.' He threw a chalk hard at his niece.

'Too busy looking after you, you crazy old beggar!' she cried, throwing it back.

It is a fair journey, out beyond Careggi, and I hired a donkey and cart to carry my friend. We made our way out to the hills with Botticelli shouting directions to Il Vivaio, for I could not quite remember the way. But then, neither could he. Although he shouted with much conviction, he sent us up paths that led nowhere. In the end I had to ask directions from people we met on the road.

'Who lives at the Villa Castello now?' I asked Botticelli as we approached and I could see the villa in the distance.

'It's alright. She's not at home.'

I presumed he was speaking of the widow of Lorenzino.

'She lives alone? That is most unusual.'

'She is a most unusual lady. Who would want her in their house?'

'We are speaking of the widow of Lorenzo Popolano?'

'No. No. The widow of his brother, Giovanni. Caterina, the black spider. How long have you been away and how far?'

I brought the donkey to an abrupt halt. 'Caterina Sforza? Is that who we are going to see?'

522

'I told you, she's away. She's fighting Cesare Borgia. Hand to hand in single combat.'

I stared at him. Perhaps he was losing his wits after all, swinging between lucidity and confusion. 'That was years ago, at the turn of the century. She lost and was brutally raped by Cesare. Last I heard, she was in prison.'

'No, she got out and came here to claim her inheritance, Giovanni's widow. An alchemist, they say. And a poisoner.'

I set the donkey off again. 'Now what nonsense are you talking?'

'She knows her simples and her compounds.'

'That doesn't make her a poisoner.'

'No, but poisoning people does.'

'Who has she poisoned?'

'Pope Alexander for one.'

'Caterina Sforza killed Alexander? I have never heard that. I was told it was a servant.'

'She tried to poison Alexander but did not succeed.'

'How? How did she try to poison him?'

'From a distance. That is her way, poisoning from a distance. She had a document impregnated with some evil tincture, rolled it up in red velvet and sent it to the Vatican. It was designed to kill on contact.'

'Like the tunic of Hercules.'

'That's right, soaked in snake poison, but Alexander was a bit more astute than Hercules and had someone else open the package, saying nothing good comes wrapped in red velvet, not from Caterina Sforza. She poisoned from a distance. Who knows who she poisoned?'

Seeing the gates of the villa ahead, I trembled and, despite my rapacious curiosity, hoped that Caterina was indeed not at home. The villa lay long and low amidst its gardens, the plants of summer reduced to dank, rotting stalks. The gatekeeper was dozing by the fire in his lodge. We tried to gain entry by citing Botticelli's name but it did no good. Money succeeded, however, where fame failed and on receipt of a few soldi the gatekeeper sent to the house to see if we might enter. At last a servant returned to say that we could. 'Everyone is resting so you are to be quiet and not stay long.'

'Is the Duchess at home, then?' I asked fearfully.

'She is, but resting. Take care not to disturb her.'

I led the donkey cart up the long gravel drive to the house with blank windows. In the courtyard I paid out more money for my friend to be lifted up the stairs to the sala above the grand entrance of the house. Once there, Botticelli regained his crutches and creaked his way across the tiled floor.

'Here they are, here they are,' he cried out, too excited to remember to keep his voice low. I was arrested by what was ahead. On the long wall opposite the fireplace and set in a row in the wooden panelling were three paintings, two large ones flanking a smaller one, all more or less of equal height but the central one much narrower than the other two.

'Didn't intend them to be a matching set,' said Botticelli. 'But they look well together, they look well.'

On the left was *The Realm of Venus* with its serpentine row of figures, a zephyr, Chloris fleeing, Flora stepping, Venus standing still, and then the Graces dancing and Mercury pointing to heaven. It had been so long since I last saw it that it had become somewhat blurred in my memory. I stood in front of it for some time, becoming familiar with the figures again. How wrong Filippino had been to say that Botticelli could not paint the smile. It's in the eyes, not the mouth.

In the middle of the three, *Pallas and the Centaur*, which I had only glimpsed in Lorenzino's chamber. Now I gazed at leisure on the figure of Minerva, or Pallas, drenched in Medici symbols, pulling up a centaur by the hair. I read its meaning as easily as if it were a book, but Botticelli raised a crutch and jabbed at the scene beyond the figures to draw my attention to the bay. 'I told Lorenzo Popolano that it was metaphor, the sea of the soul, but for me that is the bay of Naples and the little galley is the one carrying Lorenzo il Magnifico to his triumph at the court of King Ferrante. That is what it means to me, but Lorenzo Popolano was never too keen on his elder cousin.'

On the right was that painting of Venus which I had seen unveiled in Botticelli's workshop twenty-five years previously. I recalled the workshop crowded with so many familiar faces as if it were a scene painted by Ghirlandaio: Lorenzo de' Medici, Angelo Poliziano, Marsilio Ficino, the Benivieni brothers, Lorenzo Tornabuoni, Lorenzo and Giovanni Pierfranceschi. So long ago.

I gazed upon Venus, wafting to shore in her shell. Symbol upon symbol, working on my soul like heat on an alembic. Meaning arising. Transformation underway. My soul began to tremble with the significance.

Botticelli was similarly transported by his own work. As he stood staring up at the paintings, his eyes grew watery, and when he went to speak, he could not.

'What is it, my friend?' I asked.

'I gave up painting myths – my brother made me – it was dangerous – there weren't any patrons, anyway. I started painting God. Painting my idea of God. The God that once possessed me when I painted these. Don't ask me what these paintings are about: I barely understand them myself. Did I paint them? I can see my hand in them, but where did these images come from? I listened to the ideas of others as to Orphic hymns and my imagination brought forth figures. Savonarola was wrong. He never understood. He never understood the soul...'

'Hush!'

There was the sound of swishing silk, the sound of footsteps made in velvet slippers, a sibilant sound, the approach of a snake. The hair on my skin stood on end.

'Who are you and what do you want?' She stood in the doorway, the virago, the woman-warrior. She is in her mid-forties but if Caterina Sforza has lost her youthful beauty, it has been replaced by that of maturity, of majesty. She was admirably if starkly dressed, her hair loose and hanging over her bare shoulders and down her back as straight as a veil. In a large, silk gown with puffed sleeves, she emanated greatness, offended greatness, and I felt as if I had just been caught in the act of theft. Botticelli was too old to worry about such things.

'Just looking at my paintings, Madonna.'

'*Your* paintings?'

'They came from my hand.'

'You are Alessandro Botticelli? Oh, forgive me! Why did you not announce yourself?'

'I did. They had never heard of me at the gate.'

The Duchess sent at once for refreshments and while we waited she asked for an explanation of the enigma of *The Realm of Venus*. 'No one has been able to tell me what it means.'

Botticelli said nothing but seemed to be waiting for me to speak. Believing that Caterina Sforza had been brilliantly educated, I launched into a profound and complicated explanation involving the myths of Ovid and neoplatonic mysteries, showing how the composition depicted the birth of the soul and its return to God. Within a minute she looked dumbfounded; a few seconds later, bored. 'Please, stop! I never learnt my lessons in literature and philosophy,' she confessed. 'I have always been happier in a pharmacy. When it comes to the properties of plants, I have no equal. All these flowers painted so exquisitely in the meadow here – these I understand and can read. But when it comes to metaphysics, well, Messer Alessandro, please explain as if to a simpleton.'

'It is as my friend says, and it is more.' Botticelli smiled at his painting as if sharing a secret with it. 'They call it *The Realm of Venus*. I call it *La Primavera*.'

'Yes, I can see why you would. This figure here – Flora, did you say? – she is the spring. Dancing in the realm of Venus, this lovely orange grove.'

'It is the Earthly Paradise, Madonna. While Ficino and Poliziano were giving me so many lectures and notes about what the picture should contain, I was referring to a book no one seems to understand properly. Do you know your Dante, Madonna?'

'Well, of course I do.'

'Reading it does not equate to knowing it. I have it within me, heart and soul. I painted the picture they wanted, but behind it is a picture of my own. This lady in the middle is not Venus: it is Beatrice, the one men do not notice. "Flora" is Matilda who, you will remember, first appears in canto twenty-eight of *Il Purgatorio*. *Prima verra* – she who comes first. Her earthly model was Giovanna, Beatrice's friend, so beautiful that she was called *Primavera*. When Dante met her in the street, it was a prelude to his seeing Beatrice. Beauty leads to love, as Plato teaches us, but it is a Christian painting, Madonna, for those with the eyes to see.' Glancing at me and my expression, he chuckled. 'One thing on top of another.'

I gazed now in awe. The painting is a fusion, a harmonisation of Christianity and Platonism. A painter has succeeded where the philosophers continue to struggle. One thing on top of another. The Platonic mysteries shining through the Christian faith. It reminded me, suddenly, of John Colet, he who fuses both within himself, as Sandro Botticelli has done.

Now that it had been pointed out, it was hard not to see Beatrice and Matilda, Adam and Eve, the three Virtues – Faith, Hope and Charity.

'It is the story,' Botticelli said, 'of our redemption after the Fall. Our way back to paradise is through Love. Ah, Matilda...' he stared adoringly at that fine-stepping, flower-bedecked figure of Spring. '*O thou dost put me to remembering of who and what were lost...*'

'Did no one suspect?' I asked.

'Lorenzo il Magnifico, of course, recognised it at once, the subject behind the subject. Lorenzo knew Dante as I know Dante, as a living guide and teacher.'

Caterina Sforza quickened at the sound of Lorenzo's name; her bright, cruel eyes watching it form on Botticelli's lips, but her attention was distracted by a boy of about seven or eight years running in to join her.

'Ah, Giovanni,' she said, looking on him devotedly. 'Come and meet the man who painted these funny paintings!'

The son of Giovanni di Pierfrancesco has inherited his father's beauty. It was like seeing Giovanni himself, all those years ago, running about in the Palazzo de' Medici. While Botticelli was giving his explanations all over again, I was drawn to a pile of books that had come out of an open chest, presumably also recently delivered from the Casa Vecchia. Lorenzino had amassed a fine collection, among them a familiar, battered old book that made me catch my breath: Ficino's original copy of Plato's *Dialogues*. Beneath it was the copy of the works of Hermes Trismegistus in my own hand. The death of my art, just one death amidst so many. I heard Botticelli telling the boy that the dream of the Golden Age is that longing within us for the paradise of innocence.

'That is a handsome book,' said Donna Caterina beside me, 'unlike that old thing.' She waved dismissively at the *Dialogues*.

'It may not seem so, Madonna, but this is your greatest treasure. It must have been bequeathed to Lorenzino by Marsilio Ficino.'

She looked surprised. 'It has value?'

'Indeed it does – it is the book that brought Plato to the West.'

'But I prefer this one.' She opened the Hermes and turned its glowing pages.

When I told her it was my own work, she wanted to know my name.'Maffei?' A fleeting gleam came into her eyes. 'Ah, yes, I remember: you worked for Poliziano. And you have a brother in the Curia.'

It was disconcerting that she knew such things.

'A man of Lorenzo's circle. A rare survivor of the Golden Age.' She laughed. 'So, you read Greek?'

'I read and write in it, Madonna, and teach it.'

She gazed at me and laid her hand on my arm. 'I have been looking for someone to teach Greek to my son, to read to him from these books which are closed to me. It is very hard to find a good man...'

I understood what she was suggesting and it was tempting. A full-bodied, warm woman who is ageing like fine wine. I felt inexplicably drawn to this Circe. A life of leisure in a villa, reading Greek and making love... It could delay my journey to Ithaca for years.

'He died in such agony,' she said softly, as if to the book in her hands.

'Who?'

'Lorenzo...' And she turned her head away as she said this, to hide her smile. Her smile... She was enjoying the thought of Lorenzo's death. Lorenzo himself used to smile like that, trying to hide it, whenever anyone mentioned the death of Caterina's first husband, Girolamo Riario. And why? Because it was the smile of satisfaction in an act of vengeance well-conceived and executed. Lorenzo had assassinated Riario by proxy, had paid someone to throw the wretch out of a window in his castle at Forlì. I knew that much. Riario was such a devil in my eyes that it had never occurred to me that someone may have loved him, but what if his wife had? Suddenly all those adventures of Caterina Sforza I'd heard about were the desperate acts of a very faithful wife. Even as I realised this, I realised it all. One moment I was in ignorance, in the next, I knew. I just knew. It was so obvious. It has always been obvious, except to the blind.

For a long time I suspected Lorenzo di Pierfrancesco but then I had begun to suspect and with better reason his brother, Giovanni. He of the blameless features had had a restless spirit and a dark heart. When Giovanni had gone to Caterina's court, like had gone to like. No wonder they had become lovers. I saw them now, lying together at night, plotting Lorenzo's death and the overthrow of Florence, perhaps even hatching the conspiracy that had taken good men to their deaths. Who knows? But of this much I was certain: this woman who poisoned from a distance was the one who had murdered a dying man.

It had been the Milanese physician who had given Lorenzo powdered gems as a drink rather than a poultice, and because of that I had suspected Ludovico Sforza. Now I was facing Sforza's niece, realising the truth even as she gazed at me. In that moment I excelled myself in hypocrisy, hiding my thoughts, smiling, accepting the position she was offering.

'Return to me next week,' she said. 'You will be well rewarded.'

I bowed. 'I will, Madonna, and I thank you.'

Back at the hospital, I spoke to Antonio Benivieni. It seemed that my suspicions were no revelation to him: he had worked out the mystery of Lorenzo's death for himself years ago.

'Does she realise you suspect her?' he asked.

'I think not.'

'Then you are safe enough, especially here.'

I shook my head. 'Thirty years ago Girolamo Riario tried to assassinate the Medici. He was, as you know, behind the Pazzi conspiracy. The plan to murder the brothers only partly succeeded, and we lost our Giuliano. But Lorenzo was saved...'

Benivieni's eyes widened. 'Thanks to you, as I remember.'

'Yes, and she knows that. I saw it in her eyes when I told her my name. As soon as that sorceress realises that I am not taking her position she will make arrangements for my dispatch.'

'Nonsense. Does she know you are here? No. And how would she find out?'

'She will find out. If I would continue to be a rare survivor of the Golden Age I must go, quit Florence and fly back to England. Could you find someone to finish my plans? I've done everything apart from the central building.'

He looked surprised. 'All work begins at the centre, surely.'

I admitted to him that I had not liked to go into the wards, amongst the sick, not because I am afraid of disease, but because... I shrugged. 'I don't know why. It just seemed the easy part and best left to last.'

'Tommaso, stay one more day.'

530

But that force was alive within me, that Mercurial impulse to fly that has sent me hither and thither my life long. 'I cannot.'

Benivieni seemed in two minds, as if there were something he wanted to say. Then he shook his head sadly. 'Very well.'

Tomorrow, therefore, I shall say goodbye to Florence.

Florence, December 5ᵗʰ, 1506

Ten days have passed, and I am still in Santa Maria Nuova. Ten days as a patient, spent in a bed in the main ward. According to Benivieni, God was moved to drastic action to make me stay. I have this morning been given a private cell with a desk, for Benivieni insists I write everything down.

'A servant of Caterina Sforza came yesterday,' he told me, 'making enquiries.'

'What did you say?'

'That you had had a terrible accident and died ten days ago.'

'I think that's true enough.'

'No need to mention that you came back to life.'

'No, none.'

He handed me my journal. 'Set it down, Tommaso, as you told it to me – the best story I've heard from a living man.'

'You said I wasn't to strain my eyes.'

'Set it down, but in daylight. No writing at night.'

So, ten days ago I went round the city to pay homage to the past before I left Florence forever. I went to the cathedral and said prayers on the spot where Giuliano died all those years ago, directly under the great cupola of the mighty dome. The sound of people talking and walking through that vast space echoed with indifference, the sound of people mindless to history, concerned with their own affairs and their own little lives, Florentines of the sixteenth century.

I passed the Palazzo de' Medici on the Via Larga and heard no bustle of the bank, no sweet airs of a lutenist or singer. San Marco, too, was quiet, a Dominican monastery trying to forget its tumultuous past and continue with the simple business of preaching sermons to the few. I recognised hardly anyone in the monastery and was recognised by none apart from the librarian. It was as if the old century had swept all those fervent friars away. The scholars who study in the library now are broadly distributed and not all crowded together in the theology section. I walked the aisles and saw men reading books I had catalogued, books I had copied, books I had helped save. The sense of excitement has gone from the place, but it will come back in due course and, when it does, the books will be there, ready to give up their treasures of knowledge, wisdom and inspiration. On the way out I saw above the door an escutcheon of the Medici arms with the Cardinal's hat above. If ever an escutcheon was rightfully placed, this was it.

In the secular cloister I prayed by the simple tomb shared by Pico and Poliziano set in the wall. Someone had laid a posy of evergreens at its foot. A friar came along with a vase filled with water and, picking up the holly, ivy and twigs of olive, arranged them in it. I looked askance at him.

He shrugged. 'We never know who leaves them, but we find something here at least once a month, once a week in the time of the lilies and the cornflowers.'

'They should have proper tombs, these two great men.'

'Friars do not have tombs.'

'Were they friars?'

'Both took the habit in the days before they died. I was not here myself at the time, but I have heard the story from those who were.'

When he had gone, I completed my prayers, folding my hands over my heart and the memory of my friends. Inwardly I spoke to them and said my farewells, telling them that I must go back to England and this time leave the past behind me, but that I would carry their memory with me for as long as I live and spread their fame abroad. Outside the monastery, in the bright piazza of San Marco, I looked across to the sculpture garden where the gate was closed and from whence came no sound of chisels on marble. The garden seemed empty; indeed, the city seemed empty without Lorenzo.

I went to the Camaldolese monastery of Santa Maria degli Angeli with its little dome by Brunelleschi. Here it had begun, the Platonic Academy, in the person of Ambrogio Traversari, the spiritual mentor of old Cosimo, who made the first translations of Plato and recognised in the ancient Greek the great truth exemplified by Christ – the divinity of the soul, the kingdom that is within. Here those wise men met who knew the influence of Plato on the Greek Fathers and desert hermits, who knew that the original Platonic Academy was the seed of monasticism, who knew that the only way forward for our troubled Christian religion is a united Church founded as much on reason as on faith. Here they planned the Great Council seeking to reconcile East and West, a vision which failed in its intent but which nonetheless gave rise to the new Platonic Academy of Marsilio Ficino. Here Ficino gave lectures himself as a young man. Close by was the house where Ficino once lived and I recalled going there as a boy with my beloved guardian, Bishop Antonio degli Agli, and how I had been frightened to meet a Platonist in a house lit by a thousand candles.

'Tommaso! Stop dreaming!' The voice of Ficino resounded so clearly and forcefully it seemed I heard it with my ears. I flinched like a boy caught by his teacher in the act of doing nothing useful.

'You have always dreamt of philosophy but never practised it.' The voice was as loving as it was stern, and the truth of what it said went home painfully. 'What have you forgotten?'

'I do not know! What have I forgotten?'

'Why did you come back?'

'To find that which I have lost.'

'And have you found it?'

'Yes, perhaps. I don't know. I have found peace of a kind.'

'Where are you going now?'

'I am on my way to the Via del Proconsolo and the Palazzo dei Pazzi, there to say goodbye to my memories of a little girl called Elena.'

'More nostalgia! Follow me.'

I went through the city on the heels of a diminutive shade in a scarlet cap who led me to the piazza Santa Croce. It was almost noontide and cold and the piazza was empty apart from pigeons. I stood, held enchanted by memories coming from so long ago, of the aftermath of a joust when all the crowds had departed except for small boys, collecting shards of lances and charging at each other with them, their shouts bouncing off the walls of the surrounding houses. That day I had had a vision of the joust as if I myself were a god. I had been in the stands when suddenly I found myself looking down on it all from the sky above. I wondered how it is that I could see things aright in my raw youth when, after a lifetime's study, I can see only this drab world we call reality.

'It's because you are asleep,' said Ficino. 'Time to wake up, Tommaso.'

He led me to the cloisters next to the church of Santa Croce in which is a chapel that had been built by Brunelleschi as a commission from the Pazzi family. So long ago. I had only visited it once before, when I was an apprentice scribe and had come to Florence with my master, Piero Strozzi. He had taken me there to introduce me to the new wonders of the city. The chapel, almost twice as wide as it is deep, is a strange, uncomfortable space for those who are ignorant of the new architecture. The interior is overwhelmingly white and grey, the circles and lines of its geometry visible in grooved pietra serena, the only colour being in the glazed terracotta roundels by Donatello and della Robbia. The main cupola over the chapel is the dome of the cathedral in miniature, illuminated by a circle of small round windows. It is decorated with a picture of the night sky and its constellations in the form of animals. Such is the Pazzi chapel seen through the eyes.

A stone mason and his assistant were up a scaffold, struggling to fix a stone escutcheon to the wall, a scrolled shield showing three dolphins and daggers, the emblem of the Pazzi family being returned to its rightful place after being hacked down in the 1470s. I regretted their presence, for I wanted to do as I had done as a boy and sing: that is the better way to appreciate architecture – through the ears and not the eyes. But that part of me who would be a dignified, sober man, had no wish to appear the fool. 'Keep quiet and leave now,' I told myself.

'Wake up, Tommaso,' whispered Ficino.

The bell of Santa Croce began to ring the angelus, its great booms reverberating and answered by the angelus bells of the other churches of the city. Then something bubbled up within me, some boyish energy long suppressed. I knew I should never come here again. Be bold, I thought. Be reckless. Just this once.

The sound I made was a dry, husky squawk. That part of me wishing to retain dignity rose up in protest, ordering me to leave *now*. But I cleared my throat and tried again. Then came a good, clear sound on a single note, and as it continued it purified. It was answered, as I had hoped and expected, by a harmonic note resounding in the cupola. *The voice of angels,* the Bishop used to say of harmonics, when he taught me the principles of music in my boyhood. Running out of breath, I inhaled and let the sound come again. Again it was answered. Harmonics? This was no echo of my own voice. Tears welled in my eyes, but I concentrated on the sound, and the answering sound, which was the voice of a lady.

I sounded the note again and then began to sing the sol-fa scale.

Up on the scaffolding, the mason and his apprentice were standing with their hands clasped and eyes closed in the angelus prayer, but the apprentice couldn't concentrate and moved to look over the edge to see what kind of idiot was singing scales during prayers. Did I see the hammer falling? Not that I can remember. I was sounding *ti* when suddenly the cupola was no longer there. In its place was the great, starry, limitless sky. I found myself rising, with wings unfolding, up through the stars to paradise. Holding my hand and leading me upwards, my lady.

I rose to meet her, and we rose together, embracing, into the starfields of heaven. Who was she? She was Elena, but she was also Beatrice, Venus, the Madonna. She was all of them, and the one.

I did not find heaven as I expected. Yes, there were the Elysian fields, the heavenly Arcadia. 'Lower paradise,' my lady told me, as we passed it by, rising ever upwards until we came to a great cathedral, so great that each step leading to its doorway was half my height. And yet we mounted them with ease, for always we were rising. The great door was partly ajar and we went in as if floating. The whole length of the vast nave, which disappeared into the far distance, was filled with desks; the walls of the aisles were lined with books.

'Wise souls spend the afterlife in study,' my lady told me.

'The whole of eternity?'

'Until the Judgement.'

I looked about in wonder, knowing the identity of those I saw without being told. I saw Homer and Hesiod, Virgil and Ovid, each of them writing, and I saw their words leave their pages to fall spinning to earth like aerial seeds. Searching the crowds, I knew all of them to be poets, and in one aisle I found the Tuscans side-by-side with the troubadours of Provence listening to Moorish singing girls who sang of love in a way to make your soul faint. There was song everywhere, layers of song, each layer in harmony with the rest. Dante was lecturing in song and in the audience were Petrarch and Boccaccio. Beside them, Poliziano and Lorenzo.

Angelo rose, left the group and came to me, his arms open, his face luminous as it had been on those rare occasions when he was without care.

'What are you doing here? Are you not in the Piazza Santa Croce?'

'I was a few moments ago.'

'We do not have the plural form of the word *moment* here. Haven't you noticed? No space. No time. Is it not wonderful?'

I looked about and for sure everything seemed to be happening at once, the air billowing with souls. There was certainly space, and much of it, but things did have a curious way of superimposing.

Angelo looked at me doubtfully. 'You are not dead! What, would you be the soldier of Er who will awake on his pyre and tell of what he has seen?'

'What shall I tell them?'

'Tell them not to fear death. Oh, how much time and thought I wasted in that occupation! There is nothing to fear, except the Judgement.'

I was puzzled since we seemed to be in paradise, which must mean the judgement had already happened.

'No, no. This is eternity. Heaven, hell and purgatory? Is that what you believe? I thought you were a good Pythagorean!'

'Then…?'

'After the Judgement, the Rebirth. Back to the prison of the flesh! But the soul may choose its prison, under guidance of the Three.'

Angelo beckoned to one of the companions of Boccaccio, a man with fair hair and pointed beard, and introduced me to Geoffrey Chaucer of England. 'This is my erstwhile pupil, Geoffrey, a man signally incapable of seeing the obvious or putting his knowledge into practice. You tell him what he needs,' Angelo said. 'He never would listen to me.'

Chaucer took four books from a shelf nearby and handed them to me: Homer and Plutarch in Greek, Ovid and Virgil in Latin. 'The tradition of poetry that I revived in England has been broken again,' he said.

I have been teaching the wrong thing. You cannot force philosophy upon a young and unwilling mind; you cannot teach the theory of love if you do not know its practice. 'Give the children poetry,' said Chaucer. 'Give them myths and stories, and they will be tomorrow's philosophers.'

Even as I turned to Angelo to ask him where Pico was, I found myself in a cloister, sweet and serene. There were two main groups, one to the left, the other to the right. Each group was divided into many separate groups, each gathered round its own teacher; but the whole was governed by Plato on one side and Aristotle on the other. Here was no sound of disputation or debate, but a chanting as of monks. Aristotle's group looked down towards the earth below and studied the laws of creation. Plato's group looked up to the starry sky and from that group a staircase ascended, with a few souls rising to a place beyond view.

Ficino sat at Plato's right hand. Pico, with his own group, sat in the centre of the cloister, and some of his students looked up and some of them down.

'Both,' Pico said, in answer to a question I had not yet asked. 'Let your heart encompass both the worldly and the divine, for *all* is One. There is no division in truth.'

At this, Plato and Aristotle both turned and smiled at him.

That was what I learnt in paradise: there is no either/or. The answer is both. The identity of the One is *All,* of the All, *One*.

As I stood listening, enchanted by this dawn chorus of souls, I became aware that all the songs and sounds had one source, one voice. Angels were dancing in a circle of light, in the centre of which stood a lady with stars in her hair. She was singing a song full of semitones and harmonics, a song of simplicity, purity and loss, the song of the soul for God, in a voice that could dissolve hearts as it dissolved cupolas.

She was beauty. She was love. Was she Elena? No. It was who Elena had reminded me of. Someone I knew so well and had yet lost. She was what I had loved in all I had loved. And as I gazed on her, she filled with ineffable light, transfiguring. As I gazed on her, I filled with the same light, transfiguring. And then, just for a moment, a single, limitless moment, I fully understood Pico's *All*. All this, this heaven, was not outside of me but within me, and this lady, this song, was my own soul. And with this realisation, spiralling stairs opened up before me, so that I might rise to a greater knowledge and a greater beauty still. As I stepped towards them, however, I found myself at the place of judgement, standing before a terrible figure, blackened by fire and thrown into shadow by the orange flames belching all around him. Although I could not see his face for the cowl pulled over it, I knew it was Savonarola.

'It was the wrong love,' I said, and knew then that I was the Judge, he a soul ready to return. 'You preached love but your heart was closed to beauty. You taught love and created misery. How dare you presume to speak on behalf of Wisdom? Bare your head for the judgement!'

But when the soul threw back its cowl, I met my own beseeching eyes in my own haggard and miserable face. 'Who will you become?' I thundered.

'He who I was born to be!' I cried. 'And not the antichrist!'

Suddenly I was being drawn backwards at a sickening rate, all the time becoming heavier and more gross, physical. With a thud to the brain, I rejoined my body where it lay on a stretcher, being shaken and jolted as it was carried at a run by two men through the streets of Florence. My eyes opened to a dizzying view of towers and tall houses, of overhanging eaves and balconies, of someone throwing out some slops that just missed my head, through winding lanes, under the vaulted arches that turned streets into tunnels. Shrines on the corner of houses. Striped black and white banding of stone windows. A dog running alongside, wanting my legs if they should be of no further use to me. Dull shapes of a grey reality, seen like ghosts.

I was so surprised by the stupidity of a beggar who tried to ask alms of me that I raised my head. She smiled at me, she with that strange goat's beard, her eyes in her ravaged, grinning face penetrating, all-knowing. 'Who are you?' I demanded.

'We are men of the Misericordia,' said one of the stretcher bearers. 'We're nearly there.'

'That beggar – who was she?'

'You've been hit on the head by a falling hammer. You have been crowned, lord and master of yourself.'

'What did you say?'

'Take no notice of him,' said the other bearer. 'Always quoting Dante. Lie back and rest. We thought we'd picked up a dead man. Nearly there. Nearly at Santa Maria Nuova.'

At that, the darkness returned. But within the darkness there was a light, the brightly shining flame of a candle in the centre of myself.

When I awoke again, Benivieni was examining my head. 'A sharp blow,' he said, 'at the very place where you once wore a tonsure. I never did ask…'

'My vows have been absolved by the Pope,' I said, screwing my eyes shut again, feeling sick.

'By the Pope, perhaps, but obviously not by God. You must rest,' he said, 'and not move. Can you see alright?'

'The light hurts most painfully.'

Benivieni had one of his assistants bandage my eyes.

'Where am I?'

'At the hospital.'

'Which hospital?'

'Santa Maria Nuova.'

'Oh, I'm to measure this place for the King of England.'

Benivieni laughed. 'You have been, for the past three weeks.'

'Oh? Yes, I remember now.'

'Do you really remember?'

'Yes.'

'You left this morning.'

'Yes, I went to paradise.'

Benivieni instructed a nurse to stay with me, to keep my head cool and to give me certain herbs to drink. 'You must rest here for at least a week,' he told me, 'until we are certain there is no serious damage to the brain.'

And so I lay there like a corpse for many days, seeing nothing but hearing the place. Oh, what makes Santa Maria Nuova special cannot be measured. The sounds echo mysteriously in a place as

540

big as a cathedral, vaulted and arcaded. Prayers are said frequently, incense burns in censers, a priest keeps the hours at an altar and sustains an atmosphere of holiness that heals. All would have been well but for my nurse. She was rough and heavy-handed with me, and never spoke other than the occasional *tssh!*

'The oblates here are famed for their kindness,' I told her as she slapped a freezing poultice on my head.

'*Tssh!*'

She washed me as if I were a dead fish and straightened the sheets with a brutal efficiency.

'Have I offended you in any way?'

'*TSSH!*'

She gave me a compound to drink that tasted of vegetation rotting on the coast of the salty sea. I struggled to resist. 'Who are you?' I demanded. 'Has Caterina Sforza sent you?'

'*Tssh!*'

'You are poisoning me!' I cried, at which she pinched my nose until my mouth opened and then she poured the medicine in and left me gagging and choking.

I complained to Benivieni that the nurse he had assigned to me was an angry, cruel woman who would be better employed elsewhere, such as scrubbing latrines. Benivieni laughed until he wheezed like a donkey and told me that she was his finest assistant, a physician in her own right.

'She does not seem to have the spirit of the place.'

'Perhaps you annoy her,' he said, and went away, still laughing.

This went on until two days ago. Hearing her familiar tread, I flinched.

'Good morning, goddess,' I said bravely.

Without a word she soaped my face and stropped a razor. 'Oh, God…' I whimpered. But for once she was quite gentle and I listened to her breathing as she shaved my chin. 'Now,' she said, as she towelled me dry. The next thing I knew, she was kissing me. It was not the kiss of eros, but neither was it a mere peck of affection. It was a long, concentrated kiss that infused my soul with a memory of itself. These oblates, I thought, will do anything to get a man well!

'*Vita osculi*,' she murmured as she withdrew.

I struggled with my bandage but, by the time I had it free, she had gone. I rang the handbell beside my bed frantically until an oblate came. 'I want my nurse. Where is my nurse?'

'She is off duty.'

I told her to get the doctor. 'Antonio!' I said, when Benivieni came, 'what is the name of my nurse?'

'How are your eyes? Still seeing double?'

My breathing was so shallow and rapid it must surely give him concern. 'Tell me her name, man!'

'You know it well enough: Maria Poliziana.'

She was still off duty the following morning when, with the help of two assistants, I stood up and took my first, staggering steps. Antonio had told me the story, how Maria had never left the convent of San Marco but had worked in the pharmacy and infirmary, even during the plague. But at the time of the sack, when she had gone to draw water from a well, she had been attacked by one of the Compagnacci: presumably that young man I had seen with his face smashed in by the well bucket. After that she had fled the monastery and sheltered in the house of the Benivieni family.

When I asked Antonio why she was so angry with me, he was surprised I had to ask. When she had seen me measuring the hospital, she had begged Antonio not to tell me of her presence. 'She is happy,' he said, 'and does not wish to be reminded of the past.'

'But why is she so angry?'

'Because the ardent young friar who ordered her into the convent is now a layman, who has not thought to enquire about her.'

'I thought she was dead! Why are women so irrational?'

'Usually it's a case of unrequited love,' the doctor said.

In love? With me? I wanted to search the hospital until I found her, but my legs buckled after a few steps and I was taken back to bed. I lay there, waiting for her. A beam of winter light from an upper window lit the nave. I listened to the cadences of plainchant being sung at the altar and inhaled the cool air purified with incense while I rearranged the past into a new pattern. He who was blind can now see. The light absorbed me. I dissolved in that light, became that light. I am the Light. That light is love. I was born in that love and became that love. I am Love. Love: the fourth dimension. That which cannot be drawn, or painted, or sculpted, or written: that which draws, paints, sculpts, writes. Love. And now I understood that which Savonarola never understood: to love is enough. It is all that God asks of us. *That ye love one another.*

Then she was there, the woman clothed in the sun. To a worldly eye she was a round woman of forty or so, but years sit easily on nuns and her face was just as I remembered it, only with a radiance that shimmered, particles of light in a dance of divinity that no artist can capture. We call it a smile.

'*Salve,*' she said.

'*Salve,* Maria.'

We meet as two great rivers in confluence, our speech tumbling to tell each other what we have done in the intervening years. In her cell, which is next to the one where they have put me while I finish my work, she has a little shrine that would not be considered holy by anyone but myself. Beneath a niche, in which there is a fine majolica vase containing a spray of evergreens, she keeps two medals wrapped in velvet, one bearing the emblem of Pico della Mirandola, the other the image of her brother, Angelo, both with her own portrait on the obverse. This is the shrine of her heart. 'I had no image of you,' she said, wistfully, then with a measure of spite, 'not that I wanted one.'

I have been considering, of course, our future, and thought I would consider it for about a month, but last night, while she was telling me about the medicinal properties of common vegetables, I suddenly fell to my knees.

'Maria, there is something I must say, but I fear if I do you will die.'

'What do you mean?' she cried.

'I realise I am second best, that Pico was your love…' I began hesitantly.

She laughed. 'Pico was a radiant light and I a moth. I burnt myself in his light over and over again, loving him as Plato enjoins us to, as my educator, my guide to truth, but not as a maid loves a man. No, Tommaso, you are and always have been completely wrong in that presumption.'

To hear Benivieni's diagnosis of her irrationality confirmed, I blushed like a boy.

'Remember Dante?' she asked. 'How he convinced everyone that he loved another woman so as to keep Beatrice secret? Pico hid from everyone, even myself, the name in my heart. Now what do you mean, I am going to die?'

And I told her about the gipsy who, so long ago, told me that everyone I love will die before me.

'If that's the price I must pay,' she said, 'so be it.'

As a tertiary at San Marco and an oblate at Santa Maria Nuova, Maria has taken no vows. We are to marry tomorrow in the hospital's chapel. And that is the story which Benivieni considers the best he's heard from a living man, and not my trip to paradise, which he says was merely delirium consequent to a blow on the head. For myself, I think it is all part of the same story.

Palimpsest

A word from the Greek meaning to rub smooth again. Stone-masons know about it, as do brass engravers. And scribes. Vellum is an expensive material and sometimes, for want of it, a scribe will scratch out the words of an old book and make the vellum smooth again for the writing of a new one. In this way Roman codices were lost to Christian monks while, in my time, inferior works of faith have been scratched out and replaced by renewed works of antiquity. One thing on top of another.

When I was an apprentice scribe in the early 1470s, I was taught the tricks of *trompe l'oeil* by the man who decorated my master's pages. It is the art of making things seem real so that you would try and brush away the bee that seems to have alighted on the vines of the border.

In a book I have seen of Aristotle printed by Nicholas Jenson, one page is decorated in such a fashion that it seems as if the paper is tearing into holes and curling back at the edges to reveal a temple in a landscape with fauns and putti. Such is the realism that it confounds the brain to touch a printed page, whole and complete, which the eye believes to be a torn fragment.

Throughout my life I have sought the divine world in books, in the words of books, but this picture, seen so many years ago but never forgotten, is the nearest a book has come to showing me the truth. Where is the divine world? At the end of a ladder of ascent from the material to the spiritual? No. Is it a heaven to be attained after death by the pure? No. It is here, now. One thing on top of another. The world we see that beguiles us and frightens us in equal measure, the world of the senses and daily concerns, has been written over the divine world. You can look at your wife as another being, someone who shares your space and with whom you must

545

learn not to collide, and your marriage will depend on one thing only: your ability to co-habit in harmony. Love? It is stored away with the important documents of your life, your legal contracts, always operating but never referred to. Stand back and look again and the wife will reveal herself in her glory as the Aphrodite of your soul. Love? It will tingle in your pores.

The divine world is here, now, but we clothe it in temporality, in desire, in misery and know it not.

For those with the eyes to see, see.

Volterra, May, 1507

I have heard from Erasmus in Bologna that he is being driven mad with tedium. He wants to go to Venice and have his book published by Aldo. I have agreed to go with him, but first I have come to my native city to clear up family matters and put my affairs in order. Rafaello has a fine house in this high city. From the loggia on the roof you can look out on one of the most beautiful views in the world, a green sea of rolling hills capped with a castle, a monastery or a little village made out of rock. A mineral land of mines and sulphur baths. A land of great wealth and poor people. My land. Home.

'Of course, there is no need for you to return to England,' Rafaello said at dinner last evening. 'This is too large a house for me, and besides I am rarely here.'

Now I look out on the Volterrana and my heart is squeezed with longing. Home at last with my beloved hills and my wife: why should I travel any further? As the sun rises and kisses the fields and vineyards, resurrecting the land for another day, dark, musty, ignorant England seems a place of dreams.

Rafaello told us something remarkable last night. A year or so ago he went to a lecture given by a young Polish astronomer called Nicholaus Copernicus who spent his youth in service to a disciple of Pomponio Leto. Although the speaker was careful of what he said at the lectern, Rafaello had private conversation with him afterwards – 'very private conversation' – and was told by Copernicus that he believes he can prove that the Sun is not only the symbolic centre of the universe but the literal one. I watch the sun setting and rising and must doubt this by the evidence of my eyes. Sun rises, sun sets, and there's an end to it. Rafaello says that this is an illusion caused by the earth turning. I look at the land

and it is still. But the theory resonates wonderfully with the symbol; I think back to Lorenzo's Triumph of the Seven Planets and his re-ordering of them with the glittering, gilded Sun coming first. Sometimes – always? – the imagination knows things which are only proved later by scholars.

Rafaello is as excited by new discoveries in the earth as in the heavens. Quarrying in the Baths of Titus, they have found a statue of Laocoön; Rafaello tried to describe to us the wonder of this great sculpture, carved in ancient Greece from a single block of marble, in which Laocoön, the son of Priam of Troy, is shown with his own two sons in a group of agony, being squeezed to death by serpents. 'Now Michelangelo really does have a contest with the past,' Rafaello said, laughing. 'Nothing he may do will ever surpass this.'

'Are the achievements of the past always greater than those of the present?' I wondered.

'Everything we discover about the ancients rather gives credence to the concept of the Golden Age.'

'But clearly Homer believed that the Golden Age was somewhere in what he called "antiquity", that whatever age he was in it was not the golden one,' said Maria. 'So somewhere, perhaps lost to us forever, is there a statue that would make the sculptor of the Laocoön faint with admiration?'

This tipped us into a long discussion of Plato and the theory of *ideals*. I told Rafaello that Ficino had once said that the Golden Age was not somewhere in the past; it could be here, now, and required only men of golden minds.

'The notion that truth and beauty are out of reach, either in the remote past or the highest heaven, is a strong habit of mind I seem unable to rid myself of,' he said. 'How long have we spent this evening talking about antiquity?'

'About two hours.'

'Two hours spent in oblivion. What was happening here and now?'

'The sun was going down, throwing long shadows over the Volterrana and its hills, all at peace,' said Maria. 'And yet I do

548

believe that such discussions are the very mark of men of golden minds.'

Rafaello looked fondly at my wife. 'Tell me,' he said, 'how did he propose?' Maria gave her version, of how in the middle of one of our many long conversations I suddenly dropped to my knees and asked her if she would marry me even if it meant her certain death.

She and my brother laughed heartily.

I looked down on the main square of Volterra below us. 'It was there, right there on those steps, that I met that gipsy from Constantinople who cursed my life with his prophecy. He predicted our brother's death, and told me that all who I love shall die before me.'

'I told him,' Maria said to Rafaello, 'that I am forty-six years old and have had double the span of most women. Death is always certain. It's our only certainty.'

'I had been trying not to ask her,' I explained. 'But then, as we were discussing something or other –'

'Carrots.'

'Carrots?'

'Whether they are best cooked or raw.'

'Oh, yes. As we discussed the medicinal properties of the carrot, the dam broke and I found myself on my knees and offering Maria her doom.'

Rafaello was mopping at his eyes. 'Not quite Romeo and Giulietta, is it?'

'A comedy, not a tragedy,' said Maria. 'I accepted at once.'

'The gipsy's prophecy does not frighten you?' Rafaello asked her.

'I would rather have one day with my husband than all my days without him, especially,' and here she looked at me darkly, 'if I have to spend those days in a convent.'

I gazed on her, this woman who has loved me all her life and I knew it not. *All* her life? That is what she claims. She says that when she first met me, when Filippino and I discovered her in

Poliziano's flooded house in 1478, she recognised me. 'That's what love is,' she says, 'recognition.'

Rafaello asked me if I remembered the Greek mercenary, Michele Marullus.

'Of course. He was in Florence for a year or two. Married Alessandra Scala. Now drowned, I believe.'

'In the Cecina.'

'Really? Close to here?'

'He was my guest – slept in the very bed you are using. The day he left, eager to go to war against Cesare Borgia, the rain was torrential. I begged him not to go, to delay a day or two more, but he was on a crusade against the Borgias and dedicated to ridding the world of Cesare. It was just before Easter. The Cecina, swollen with rain and the melting snows from the mountains, was almost bursting its banks as it rushed along. Peasants standing near the river cried out to him not to be a fool, saying that it was madness to try and cross, but Michele told them he was not frightened. When he was a boy, a gipsy had told him that it was Mars, not Neptune, he should fear. So he spurred his horse into the river. For a little while the horse withstood the force of the current but then it lost its footing. Michele was carried away on the surging water, cursing the gods as he went. They found his body downstream the next day.'

'He was your friend, Rafaello, but do not ask me to mourn him. He was very cruel to Angelo.'

'His poor, abandoned wife, Alessandra Scala, entered the convent of San Piero Maggiore,' Maria told us with a sigh.

I grew reflective. 'I wonder if it was the same gipsy?'

'I think it must have been,' said Maria, 'for he was just as wrong about Marullus's future as he was about yours.'

A letter has come from Cardinal Giovanni. He wants me to go to Florence and oversee the transportation of his father's library from San Marco to his house in Rome, where he is now residing. He says the position of custodian will be a permanent one, should I desire it.

A house in Volterra, work in Rome, a wife. I am offered all that I have ever wanted, more than I ever dared hope for. The sun is rising – or, rather, the earth is turning – and the city is flooding with warmth. I hear my language being shouted in the streets below and look down on colourful awnings and the flags of our *contrada*. England seems like Hades, a misty place of shades and shadows. *Stay then,* I think. *You are bound by no contract to return.* And then it came, the scent of roses. No physical perfume, but the memory of it, all combined in one moment of ethereal scent, Elena, Ficino, Botticelli – and a street in London called Bucklersbury.

When Dante met him in hell, Odysseus told him how, after arriving home at Ithaca, he had only stayed awhile before moving on and leaving his faithful wife, Penelope, once again to continue his restless wanderings, even beyond the pillars of Hercules. Terrible, isn't it? I have never liked that version. It is unresolved – poor Penelope! Still, this is my story, not that of Odysseus. Maria will be coming with me.

I look out on the Volterrana and see a hawk stationary in the sky, high above its prey. I stand back and look again and see my land for what it is: Beauty. It shimmers with that iridescent radiance that is in and around all things, if you see them aright. I am free. I can move on, for I have found that which I had lost, and it is a portable thing: the courage to love.

The test, of course, will be a class of children in a London school.

Those who immerse themselves in their work become confined to a narrow space. As Pythagoras said, 'Take care not to get boxed-in so that there is no more sky for you.' O, my friends, live happily and do not be boxed-in. Live happy. You were created by the happiness of heaven; you were declared by heaven with laughter. Live every day happy in the present moment. If you spend the present in worry, you will lose the present and the future, too. I implore you, again and again, live happily!

The fates allow this, so long as you live without care.

To live without care, do not allow one single care.

Never worry about anything.

Live in the present.

Live now.

Be happy.

MARSILIO FICINO.

HISTORICAL NOTES

In writing historical fiction, one uses facts to create a story. Story is the novelist's prime consideration, and it is usual to let fiction have dominance over fact. I have not gone that way, however. Early on in the project, which began in 1974, I decided to stick to the facts. Sometimes they were awkward and annoying, but I found that, when I stuck to them, even though it meant much re-writing, the story grew richer and deeper. But, of course, the imagination was constantly in play, either to plug holes in the documentary evidence (which is particularly thin with regard to the women), or to interpret the facts in such a way that a plausible story was created.

Many of the so-called 'facts' are a bit dubious: so much is received opinion, transmitted over the ages. Current ideas about the character of Poliziano, for example, stem from slanders put about by those probably responsible for his death. Using the story-teller's instinct for what is true and what is not, I have picked my way through nearly five hundred books and learned papers, trying to reconstruct a world and its characters to the best of my ability.

As a novelist, you must consistently imagine yourself as a particular character in a particular place and time. You have to *be there*. This use of the imagination nearly always has surprising results, reconciling apparent contradictions, providing solutions to nagging questions. 'Facts' may be true in an empirical manner, but the imagination – and storytelling – often lead to a psychological truth which the facts alone cannot supply. It is the imagination which can make the facts 'add up'.

Almost everything about Maria is pure fiction, as it had to be. All we know is that she lived with her brother and features on the obverse on two medals of Poliziano and one of Pico della Mirandola. Not an ordinary sister, then, but one valued and esteemed by two of the greatest minds of the time, unless, of course, she had the medals struck herself.

To look in the catalogues of the great libraries and see all Poliziano's works neatly listed, it is natural to suppose that their fate has been orderly, that publication was arranged during his lifetime, since when the books have passed unchanged through various editions. In fact, when Poliziano died his only surviving work was his boyhood notebook which included his Greek epigrams (including some which have blighted his moral reputation ever since – proof that all poets should burn their early work). For the *Opera Omnia* everything was collected together by friends. Aldus states his regret in the preface that he could not include works which he heard were hidden in Florence, one of which would have been the *Account of the Pazzi Conspiracy*. The *Second Miscellanea* was for centuries believed to be irretrievably lost. In fact it was passing through private hands and it was only on the death of its last owner, when it went to a library in Venice, that it 'came to light'. Acquired in 1961 as a battered old book containing pages neatly written in Poliziano's own hand, it was first published in 1972. We do not know what happened to it on Poliziano's death, who acquired it and how, but its re-emergence gives us hope that more works will appear in the future.

The shared tomb of Pico and Poliziano was last opened in 1940 and the contents viewed by H. C. Bodman.[1] The body of Poliziano was reduced to a few fragments of bone, but Pico's was well preserved 'in as perfect condition as an Egyptian mummy'. That he was dressed in brocade contradicts absolutely the Dominican claim that the Count of Concordia took the habit in his final hours. It seemed so odd that Pico wasn't buried in a habit, whether he had converted or not, that I created the scenes of Tommaso re-clothing the corpses of both Pico and Poliziano. No doubt more will be revealed by the scientific tests currently being done in the latest exhumation by a team from the University of Bologna, led by Professor Giorgio Gruppioni, which was announced as I was making this book ready for publication. Modern forensic techniques may finally establish the cause of their deaths.

1 Juliana Hill Cotton, 'Death and Politian', Durham University Journal, vol. xlvi no. 3, 1954, appendix iii.

The general view up to now has been that Pico was murdered by his secretary, Poliziano died of some affliction of love (either syphilis or falling downstairs in rapture) and Lorenzo of gout. It was Juliana Hill Cotton in her seminal paper *Death and Politian* (1954) who drew attention to the large number of deaths of friends of Lorenzo in 1494. She did not, however, question Lorenzo's own death. And yet the storyteller intuitively felt that Lorenzo died in mysterious circumstances.

What the 'gout' was, was solved with the exhumation of four generations of the Medici in 1955. Lorenzo's grandfather, Cosimo, and father, Piero, both showed evidence of ankylosing spondylitis, an hereditary and crippling form of arthritis. Lorenzo, however, did not. What skeletal abnormalities there were in his body indicated another form of arthritis.[2] It is unlikely to have been a cause of death – much more lethal were the remedies he was prescribed.

Although the material rather suggested I should write a murder mystery, I was shy of accusing the dead and in the end stayed more realistic; while pointing fingers at suspects, I allowed Tommaso to be as I am: ignorant of the truth. But then certain things came to my attention in the last year of writing, all rather in the nature of a revelation, which caused a great deal of revision to the end of the story.

I was told several years ago that the three great paintings of Botticelli which have inspired each volume of this trilogy were hung together at the Villa Castello. When I looked into it, I found to my amazement that it was true: *La Primavera, Pallas and the Centaur* and *The Birth of Venus* were hung together, but not until 1506, which made it seem irrelevant to my plot. Tommaso would not have seen them there, not unless he visited Castello in 1506 – but why would he do that? Then, in 2006, I read Carol Kidwell's biography of Marullus, which told me much more than I had previously known about certain characters, not only Marullus

---

2 A. Costa and G. Weber, 'Le alterazioni morbose del sistema scleritico in Cosimo dei Medici il vecchio, in Piero il gottoso, in Lorenzo il magnifico, in Guiliano duca di Nemours', Archo De Vecchi, 1955, 23: 1-69. (I understand that the exhumation of 49 members of the Medici family in 2004 did not include the body of Lorenzo.)

himself, but also the Pierfranceschi and Caterina Sforza. Suddenly I had a suspect for at least one of the deaths who I was not shy of accusing, and this feeling was somewhat heightened when I discovered, after five minutes browsing the internet, that in 1506 the Villa Castello came into Caterina's possession and it was she who hung the three paintings together. So now I had both a suspect and an excuse for Tommaso's visit to Castello. It all fitted together so plausibly that I really wouldn't be surprised if it proved to be true, that if Lorenzo *was* murdered, then Caterina is the prime suspect.

It was in the same book on Marullus that I discovered that one of the first accounts mentioning Copernicus was written by none other than Rafaello Maffei. It was this that inspired the return of Tommaso to Volterra at the end of the trilogy, back to where he had begun.

All the words of Pico della Mirandola have been drawn from his works, most notably *Heptaplus* and the *Oration On the Dignity of Man*,[3] where he does indeed refer to the sacred sentence of Eastern mysticism, 'That Thou Art', as well as say that the western tradition derives from the east. These supremely important works did not appear in the *Opera Omnia* compiled and edited by Gianfrancesco. Pico is often referred to as the man who destroyed astrology, but his refutation of astrology needs to be analysed, given that the manuscript remained with Savonarola after Pico's death and seems to have been reworked.[4]

Cardinal Giovanni de' Medici became Pope Leo X in 1513, before he was thirty; his cousin Giulio, who reigned as Clement VII from 1523, was the pope who refused to sanction the divorce

---

3 'The Oration on the Dignity of Man' has been translated by Elizabeth Forbes (E. Cassirer, P.O. Kristeller, *The Renaissance Philosophy of Man*, Phoenix, Chicago, 1948) and C.G. Wallis, P.J.W. Miller, D. Carmichael, New York/Indianapolis 1965. The latter includes 'Heptaplus'.
4 See Stephen Farmer, *Syncretism in the West: Pico's 900 Theses (1486),* pub. Arizona, 1998. Although there is now work being done to absolve Gianfrancesco of the crimes which many, particularly Farmer, have suggested, it remains that Pico's life does not make a coherent whole unless his works were doctored after his death and the picture confused. Gianfrancesco's portrait of his uncle as a pious Christian gives a distorted impression without the Cabalism. See Frances Yates, *The Occult Philosophy in Elizabethan England.*

of Henry VIII. Giovanni, the son of Caterina Sforza, grew up to be Giovanni delle Bande Nere, the sire of the Grand Dukes of Tuscany, and laid out the grounds of Castello as one of the first and finest of the great Italian gardens.

Of the Pierfranceschi there are surprisingly few surviving records. Lorenzo di Pierfrancesco is a good example of known facts not adding up to a coherent portrait. He was tetchy, litigious and traitorous; he was also the patron of Botticelli and Ficino. Perhaps the most revealing fact as to his true character is that Ficino bequeathed to him his original copy of Plato's *Dialogues*. I have done my best with these clashing ingredients, understanding full well that a love of philosophy does not, in itself, make a philosopher. I think that Lorenzo di Pierfrancesco had to struggle against his own nature and that Ficino, his tutor, was aware of it and tried to help.

Cristoforo di Casale (or da Casalmaggiore) was arrested at the same time as the conspirators aiming to reinstate Piero de' Medici. Under torture he confessed to poisoning Pico but, since confessions gained by the strappado are so unreliable, I have chosen to believe that Cristoforo was innocent.

Lorenzo's brother-in-law, Bernardo Rucellai, became the head of the Platonic Academy after the death of Ficino, but he also appears in the records as a shadowy figure behind the Compagnacci. This apparent contradiction of character was not something I was able to pursue and needs to be looked at. It would seem that my comments about Lorenzo di Pierfrancesco may also apply to Rucellai.

Piero de' Medici is another complex character and historians tend to treat him simply as a wretch. Certainly he was disliked in his own time and called 'Piero the Fatuous' by Florentines, in the sense, I presume, of 'foolish'. But a fool can have good intentions and I believe Piero did have them. My own reading of the documentary evidence threw up something which, so far as I know, has struck no one else as odd: since Piero's humiliating surrender to Charles VIII resulted in success, there appears to have been no need for the second deputation, other than to oust Piero. Charles VIII was sufficiently impressed with the young man to support his efforts in the following years to return to Florence. Piero's decline into conspicuous decadence in the time he spent in exile was, I think, the consequence of self-loathing. Although the story led me in a different direction, I still think Piero is suspect in relation to some of the deaths, that of Pier Leoni and Poliziano among them.

The Company of the Library is a plausible supposition: some association like it must surely have existed.[5] The part that Tommaso played in the rescue of the books conflates with what was quite possibly the true story of Fra Zenobio Acciaiuoli. When in 1508 Cardinal Giovanni moved the Medici Library (preserved at San Marco) to Rome and enlarged the collection, Fra Zenobio became his librarian. Clement VII subsequently arranged for the library to return to Florence and, by a bull dated 15th December 1532, provided for its future security. He engaged Michelangelo to design the rooms in San Lorenzo where the library, the Biblioteca Laurenziana, remains today.

John Colet gave his entire estate – while he was still alive – to the foundation and maintenance of St Paul's School. Having dismissed Linacre's Latin grammer as 'too abstruse', he set about writing one himself, calling on the help of William Lily. This became known as 'Lily's Grammar' and formed the basis of classical teaching for more than three centuries. It is not known whether John Colet's visit to Italy in 1496 included Florence. I have presumed that it did. There exist a few letters between Colet and Ficino, a correspondence in 1498 apparently inspired by Colet's reading of Ficino's works. What is clear from the letters is that each man recognised himself in the other, and expressed that recognition in ecstatic words of love, whether or not they had ever met in the flesh: a good instance of a meeting in angelic mind, which I have suggested with regard to Ficino and Pomponio Leto. The age was graced with master teachers in the wisdom tradition who, drawing on the same inner resource, were subtly and profoundly in touch with each other.

5 That the library's preservation was due to Medici supporters is suggested in Berthold L. Ullman and Philip A. Stadter, *The Public Library of Renaissance Florence* (Padua 1972).

As is now well-known, Shakespeare's philosophy was largely founded on the Platonism of Marsilio Ficino. One book which had direct influence on him was an Italian work translated into English: *The Book of the Courtier* by Baldassare Castiglione, in which the concluding speech, made by Pietro Bembo, extols platonic love – the first time, I believe, between man and woman. The source for *Romeo and Juliet* was *Giulietta e Romeo* by Luigi da Porto, a story edited and published by Bembo.

In 1508 Erasmus spent three months in the workshop of Aldus Manutius in Venice, overseeing the publication of his translation of Euripides and a new, enlarged edition of his *Adages*. In his colloquy *Opulentia Sordida*, we get a bitter portrait of his time spent with Aldus. Erasmus was clearly used to a more comfortable, less austere life. On the return journey to England he composed *In Praise of Folly* which he dedicated to More. The time he spent in Italy, during the papacy of Julius II, evidently taught him to appreciate the foibles of men and look on them with humour in the vein of 'you have to laugh or else you would cry.'

Venetian art of the period shows that an era ended in 1506 with a great, bravura display of old values. While Bellini was heralding the high Renaissance, while Titian worked as an apprentice to Giorgione, Carpaccio was painting a terrific series of panels depicting daily life in the city in a style belonging wholly to the previous century. 1506 – the year of Tommaso's journey with Erasmus – was more than 1500 the year when one age became another. (The mention of 'millennium' in the text is taken from contemporary references: 1500 was the one-and-a-half millennium, the one-and-a-half time.)

It may seem that I have contrived to bring famous men together, but I have been very careful with chronology and location. If, without contrivance, Tommaso happened to be in the same place as a famous sculptor, printer, painter or a German engraver, then I considered it my duty as a novelist to let them meet. One of the aims of the trilogy was to put history back together again, to plait the thread of lives that have been separated by historians, and to give the reader a context for so many famous characters too often viewed in isolation. In so doing, I have laid myself open to accusations of name-droppery but thankfully, according to at least one reviewer, have been found innocent of the charge. Nevertheless I was conscious of it particularly with the character of Dürer – was I being self-indulgent? Apart from anything else, one should never introduce new characters at the end of a work. However, every effort to cut him out failed: Dürer, and his practical Christianity, were fundamental to Tommaso's 'rebirth'. So he stayed and I am glad of it. Much more work needs to be done on this enigmatic man who stands in the line of transmission of 'occult philosophy' between Ficino and Cornelius Agrippa. I have been told that the 'master of proportion' he sought in Bologna was Luca Pacioli, and that the young, red-haired man in the famous portrait of Pacioli is Dürer. This is unsubstantiated.

The essence of Renaissance philosophy is an understanding or recognition of the fundamental harmony of creation and the unity of Man and God. When I began this work, this philosophy in our own age was occult in that it was studied by few, not in secret but beyond the notice of the many. In the following three decades, I have seen it come out into the light, almost into general accept- ance. Our arts may not reflect it (if only because contemporary sacred art is occulted by popular decadence) but many of today's visionaries would have been entirely at home in the Platonic Academy. As history shows, renaissances are brief and tend to occur when organised religion is weak. While I have been watching philosophy come out into the light, I have also watched the rise of fundamentalism, not only in Islam but also, and perhaps more worryingly, in Christianity. One can only hope that, when it comes to false prophets, we don't have to wait for their fruit in order to know them for what they are. Our culture is in desperate need of Beauty: let her not be burnt, in some mistaken sense of piety, just as she is reborn.

ACKNOWLEDGMENTS

Over the years I have been helped and encouraged by a great many people, all of them kind and generous. I would like to give particular thanks to Angela Voss, Pamela Tudor Craig, Tim Pears, Valery Rees, Clement and Juliet Salaman, Adrian Bertoluzzi, Jeremy Naydler, Noel Cobb, Arthur Farndell, Michael Shepherd and my dea-ex-machina Dr Carol Kidwell. It was Andy Green who pointed out to me that the three great paintings of Botticelli were hung together at the Villa Castello.

Being a novelist is the least financially rewarding occupation there is, short of charitable work, but, like the Gangines mentioned by Pliny, I live off the scent of apples: many readers of the first two volumes have taken the trouble to write to me and those aromatic letters have been more sustaining than anything else, greater than gold in fact. So I would like to thank my appreciative readers wholeheartedly – you have sustained me throughout.

Despite the size of my bibliography, there have been some works that I've consulted again and again for this last novel in the series. Stephen Farmer's *Syncretism in the West: Pico's 900 Theses (1486)*, pub. Arizona, 1998, not only gives a translation of the theses but voices suspicion about the editorial work and motives of Gianfrancesco Pico, following in the vein of the seminal paper on the mystery of the multiple deaths of 1494 by Juliana Hill Cotton (*Death and Politian*, Durham University Journal vol. xlvi no. 3, 1954, especially Appendix II). The most expensive paperback I ever bought was Stanley Meltzoff's *Botticelli, Signorelli and Savonarola*, Theologia Poetica *and painting from Boccaccio to Poliziano*, Florence, 1987. It was worth every penny and is the only modern book I know of that not only deals justly with Poliziano but amplifies his reputation.

As ever I am indebted to the Language Department of the School of Economic Science, their devoted translations of the letters of Marsilio Ficino, and their loving support in the duration of this project.

Quotations from Dante have been taken from the Dorothy L. Sayers translations (Penguin). Quotations from the bible in the London sections (1 Cor 3 – 4 lines) come from *The New Testament in Modern English* by J.B. Phillips as, in my opinion, that work has the power and simplicity I would imagine Colet's own translations to have had, given that he made his sermons in English. The lines from Poliziano's epic *Giuliano's Joust* come from *The Stanze of Angelo Poliziano*, translated by David Quint, Massachusetts, 1979. Quotations from Savonarola's sermons and texts come from Pasquale Villari's *Life and Times of Girolamo Savonarola*. Late on the scene have come Charles Fantazzi's translation of Poliziano's Silvae (Harvard, 2004) and Shane Butler's translation of Poliziano's letters (Harvard, 2006). Thankfully they confirmed rather than contradicted anything I'd already written, although the correspondence between Poliziano and Pico reveal a sweetness and humour in their relationship that I fear I have not done justice to. I believe that conversations in their circle would have been so funny that you would have cried with laughter, but it was beyond my powers to convey their erudite wit.

That Botticelli's *Primavera* could be an illustration of Dante's *Il Purgatorio* I owe to Kathryn Lindskoog's fascinating website (for the account of the moment of insight, see www.lindentree.org/discovery.html).

Lastly my thanks to my husband, David, always encouraging and supportive, even when I covered the walls of our landing with chronological charts and sat on the stairs tearing my hair out. He has not seemed to mind about sharing my heart with my characters, and is very forgiving of my more ditzy behaviour in the kitchen when writing is in full flow. Now he has his wife all to himself, at least until the next project comes along.

GODSTOW PRESS

Because philosophy arises from awe, a philosopher is bound in his way to be a lover of myths and poetic fables. Poets and philosophers are alike in being big with wonder.   ST THOMAS AQUINAS

THE SONG OF ORPHEUS, the music that charms stones, wild animals and even the King of Hades, is the song of poets who have a sense of the divine at heart. For the forces of greed and evil to succeed, that song must be drowned out by noise.

What is today if not noisy? Not only in our society but within ourselves there is the clamour of many distractions. Just living life we forget ourselves and the song that we heard as children is heard but rarely if at all.

The aim of Godstow Press is to sing the Orphic song, through books of fiction, poetry and non-fiction, as well as through CDs. Besides publishing first editions we shall include on our list works which have been privately produced by writers and musicians who have thought, perhaps, that they sing alone.

Together, artist and audience, we shall form a choir.

We have no plans at the moment to make our books available through the trade and we depend entirely on personal contact with readers. For more information and inclusion in our database, please get in touch with us.

Godstow Press
60 Godstow Road
Wolvercote
Oxford
OX2 8NY
UK

www.godstowpress.co.uk
info@godstowpress.co.uk
tel +44 (0)1865 556215
fax +44 (0)1865 552900